PRAISE FOR TERR

VALI

I thought you'd like to know I have distributed copies of your book, "Valiant Volunteers" to the previous Secretaries of the Air Force, former Chief's of Staffs, current Secretary and Under Secretary of the Air Force, as well as the current 4-star generals and numbered Air Force Commanders. Bottom line...this is a great book and I'd like to share it with the Air Force's top leadership. T. **Michael Moseley, General, USAF, Chief of Staff**

A great war-time read!

Filled with real characters both honest and treacherous, the confusion of trench fighting, realistic flying episodes, war-time politics and even a bit of romance. Couldn't put it down. I can't wait for Johnson's next volume. What happens to Charlie? **John H. Moran "Jack Moran", Colonel, USAF (Retired)** Poquoson, VA. February 22, 2006

What a great read and "cliffhanger" ending!

As a military aviation history enthusiast since I was a boy I've read a lot of books—*Valiant Volunteers* ranks among the best. **Rick Goldblatt** (VA)

I have really enjoyed your book.

I only read one book a year so this year it was yours. **Mike Becker, Colonel, USAF (Retired)** (VA)

Excellent Historical Fiction!

This is a great book that interweaves the lives of actual historical characters with 2 fictional heroes. The author really ties together the lives of Americans helping fight WWI before the US entered the war. It is well researched. **A Shilkitus** (TX). June 3, 2006

Valiant Volunteers

A Novel

Based on The Passion and the Glory of the Lafayette Escadrille

Terry L. Johnson

Bloomington, IN

authorHOUSE®

Milton Keynes, UK

AuthorHouse™
1663 Liberty Drive, Suite 200
Bloomington, IN 47403
www.authorhouse.com
Phone: 1-800-839-8640

AuthorHouse™ UK Ltd.
500 Avebury Boulevard
Central Milton Keynes, MK9 2BE
www.authorhouse.co.uk
Phone: 08001974150

First published by AuthorHouse 3/21/2007

ISBN: 978-1-4259-9911-7 (hc)
ISBN: 1-4208-5587-5 (sc)

Printed in the United States of America
Bloomington, Indiana

This book is printed on acid-free paper.

To My Wife, Ginny

Contents

When men who have no obligation to fight, who could not possibly be criticized if they did not fight—yet nevertheless decide upon their own individual initiative to risk their lives in defense of a cause they hold dear—then we are in the presence of true heroes. The young Americans who entered the Légion Etrangère and the Escadrille Américaine are in every sense heroes, and France owes them all the homage that word implies.

French General Henri Gourard
One-armed, one-legged hero of the Dardenelles

Prologue

Charlie tasted dirt in his mouth. His head throbbed though he couldn't hear anything but a faint howling. Spitting and choking, he tried to get up, brushing the wet warm gunk from his eyes. *Blue sky above, have to move*, his mind shouted, but something heavy held him in place. He pushed frantically struggling to move his limbs. Once he snorted his nostrils clear, the stench gagged him. Wriggling his head and shoulders free he saw a heavy timber across his chest. It was embedded in the ground grotesquely impaling the lower half of a torso. Charlie retched. *Could that be me? Am I dead, dying?*

Gulping the foul air, Charlie heaved at the timber. The revolting sight curiously fascinated him. Thick wood stuck up obscenely from the crotch. Still confused, Charlie focused on the source of the smell, shredded entrails, likely his own.

Spitting and thrashing he tried to clear his eyes. *Why didn't it hurt*, he wondered? Hands clawed at his face. Figures appeared. Deep within him something demanded action. Dead or alive, mutilated or whole, he had to fight for the light. He saw the timber rise trailing a pair of legs still wrapped in puttees and wearing boots. *God the stink*, Charlie thought. *Is this what we are reduced to?*

Staring back at him, an incongruous blue sky glaring pure and unstained. *Death?* Was he caught between life and death? Each labored breath stung of bile and that horrible smell. *Lord, have mercy on me!*

He began to wonder how he could live without half his body. Someone was digging, tossing chunks of material and dirt off him. Charlie slipped momentarily into self-pity. This wasn't new. He'd seen enough of it happening to others. *Time to make peace with God. Not too late, never too late.*

Time slowed. Waves of despair rolled over him. He couldn't quit, but seeing his torn body and smelling his own entrails made him long to sleep, to escape somehow. Why it didn't hurt baffled him. He squeezed his eyes shut, concentrating, trying to feel the pain that had to be there.

Nothing.

He forced his eyes open. Across the robin's egg blue moved a single object with bright circles of color on its extremities. *A flying machine*, his brain registered.

As his rescuers dug, his thoughts shifted to soaring above the muck. He imagined being astride an airborne mount moving freely in all dimensions unrestrained by walls of dirt.

"*Allez-y*," someone commanded, the voice coming as if through a cloth.

"*Affreuse*!"

"*Allez cochons*," a voice of authority urged, "*il n'y a pas du temps*!"

Time for what? Charlie thought. The feint trace of the single aircraft, now out of sight, pushed him past imagination until he was flying high in the sky birdlike—angelic. *Yes! Like an angel.*

"Water, you fool! Clean him off. Mother of God! What in heaven's name have we wrought?"

"Get out of the way, *Aumonier!* This one's not ready for you."

"Goddamn chaplains!" someone shouted. "Always in the way, but never there when you need them."

"Watch your tongue soldier," the priest said. "Even here in the trenches the Lord hears your wickedness."

"Blast the Lord!"

"Jesus, have mercy on this blasphemer," the chaplain muttered, helping lift Charlie free from the muck

"He's in one piece unlike poor Baudin. Lucky soul. Such a blast! Sheared the top off the bunker and cut Baudin…."

"Shut up and help me get him up! He's choking on something."

"Baudin, no doubt," another soldier noted with typical Legion coarseness.

"Don't you pigs ever show respect for the dead," the priest lamented? "When your time comes I hope one of us is there to commend your soul to the Lord."

"To the devil, you say! Get away, *pretre*! Take your oils and water somewhere else. This *mec* is more important to us than to your God right now. The *boches* don't give a piss for your prayers. Quick! Splash some water in his face and put a Lebel in his hand. *Ils arrivent!"*

Charlie grasped the rifle thrust into his hands dumbfounded. Someone pulled on his harness jerking him upright and thrusting him forward to the collapsed edge of the trench. Somehow he found legs beneath him. Raising the rifle, he began to fire blindly, automatically at the blurry field gray forms moving towards him. *Shoot, shoot, reload, shoot*...his training took over.

Though exhausted and stunned by the artillery barrage, Charlie's platoon easily repelled the feeble German counterattack. When the threat subsided Charlie sank to the ground and tried unsuccessfully to sort out his fortune. The process was severely hampered by his powerful impression of already being mortally wounded.

Charlie Keeler shuddered as he brushed at the pieces of flesh and bone still clinging to his uniform. *What a fragile thing the human form*, he thought. *What a fragile hold on life we have!*

This was his fourth sortie into the front line trenches and the first since Rejik's treachery the night before. Tomorrow he would go to another regiment. *Tomorrow*, he thought. *Minutes ago I was mourning my mutilation and pending death. Tomorrow. Oh sweet Jesus! What am I doing here? Why didn't I accept the chance to fly?* Even as he thought it, he felt remorse. He'd come to fight, hadn't he? He'd proven himself well enough, but maybe it was time to make a change.

Nearby, the same day, after the German counterattack.

Jack Buck watched a poilu with a huge hole in his thigh being lifted on his stretcher into the back of his Ford ambulance. The man, clearly in great pain, kept reaching down and pointing, saying, "*n'oubliez pas ma Rosalie*!" Thinking he was trying to get the *brancardiers* to get a message to his wife or girlfriend, Jack smiled empathetically. When he began to close up the back, though, the man became agitated and yelled even louder for his Rosalie. Finally, one of the French stretcher-bearers handed Jack the poilu's bayonet, saying: "*Voilà Rosalie*!" The man relaxed as soon as Jack placed the bayonet on his stretcher. Funny just what they cling to, he thought.

During another run that same day; Jack's ambulance stalled just a short distance from the *poste de secours*. He got out and began to work on the engine when the loud crack and thump of incoming artillery sent him scurrying for the nearest ditch. Landing on something soft, he rolled over to find he was on top of a little girl! She had braided hair with red ribbons and a sweet look on her face. He hadn't seen her when he had pulled up. She shouldn't have been there in the first place!

Her fixed expression disturbed him. Hoping he hadn't hurt her, he touched her cheek and shook her shoulder. She didn't respond, her eyes staring straight ahead as if she couldn't see him. When he shook her again he saw she lay in a puddle of blood. Turning her as gently as he could, he nearly gagged when he saw the gaping hole in her back. She must have been picking flowers at the roadside when the shell carried away most of her spine. Jack cried unashamedly as he leaned over her, thinking of his little sisters back in Minnesota, thanking God they were not in this hell.

Impossibly, the motor fired immediately when he cranked the handle. He lifted the child's broken body, laying it carefully on one of the stretchers, his eyes still filled with tears as he turned around to return to the nearby village.

Someone found her mother, an attractive young woman. On seeing her daughter bleeding and lifeless on the stretcher, the woman began to wail. Jack felt immense pity. A man standing nearby took his arm and pulled him aside telling him that the girl's father had been killed early in the war. The child had gone out to pick flowers to dry and send to her papa every day, refusing to believe he was gone.

A growing rage welled up in him. His anger could be directed at no one in particular, not even the Germans. French artillery killed equally indiscriminately. Still, the French hadn't invaded Germany. Seeing such suffering shamed him deeply. He had carefully built a shell of indifference to fend off such feelings. Now he was embarrassed to have acted so detached. Jack had changed in two months driving ambulances. He felt impelled to do more.

Soon after the incident McConnell asked, "Why the long face, Jack?"

"Jim, it's bad enough seeing soldiers suffer and die, but, the girl and her mother?

"Tough finding her like that," Jim said.

"She was the same age as my sister. Jim, either my nerves are getting frayed or I'm losing my senses. I'm starting to think like you. I've got to do more to help these people."

"I've said it before. I can't stand playing the non combatant much longer myself," Jim observed, smiling at his younger friend.

"Did I tell you that my motor started right up after the shelling? It was eerie, Jim. Like God stopped it there for a reason. Am I getting mystic or something?"

"You and the rest of the section. You wouldn't believe George. The other day he had to huddle in a dugout with a bunch of French soldiers during a barrage. Several of the poilus were wounded, waiting to go out on George's car. One, seriously wounded in the chest, struggled to breathe and shouted he was about to die.

"George says another *brancardier* came in a few minutes later and knelt down with what George thought was a hypodermic. Instead, he opened a little bottle and a booklet, heard the soldier's confession, and gave him *Extreme Unction*—isn't that what you Catholics call the last rites?"

Jack nodded, forgetting about himself as he listened. "So the guy wasn't a stretcher-bearer after all?"

"Not unless you papists have just anyone doling out your precious sacraments," McConnell said. "Anyway, the man calmed down instantly according to George. Can you beat that?"

Jack just shook his head.

"Now as if that wasn't enough," McConnell continued, "our George—you know the same guy that never said a word for hours on end—said that the dirty little dugout with the dirty stinking poilus suddenly became—what were his words? Oh yeah, '*big and awesome, and filled with a breath of something more than mere life or death, or war, or human meddlings.*' Now, tell me, Jack, can you picture George saying anything like that?"

Buck just sat there. Masters was quite content to tend to the wounded. He had something mystical about him, yet there was something hidden in the man, something related to the story Mac just told. Jack couldn't put a finger on it, but it made him think even more about getting off the sidelines.

He and McConnell had talked about flying before. Doctor Gros was after all the American drivers to give it a shot.

"Let's do it Jim," Jack said voicing the thought they both had.

"Enlist? Leave this mercy mission to the likes of Masters? You haven't even seen a flying machine up close, Jack."

"So what if I haven't?"

"I told you I've had a couple of lessons," McConnell said, smiling. "If your driving is any indication, you shouldn't need more than that, but you know what happens if we wash out? It's the trenches for sure and I'm not too keen on mud if you know what I mean."

Jack knew precisely what big Jim McConnell meant. Enlisting in the Legion meant not being able to go back to driving or "unvolunteer" from the war like they could now. It was a big step. It was hard to picture Jim as a simple soldier. There was something of the knight about him. "Jim. You behave like a Christian but you don't go to church. How do you feel about dying?"

"Getting philosophical like George, are you?" Jim said lighting up a cigarette. He paused like he had to think about it before continuing. "It's pretty much all the same to me. I mean, I really don't have any specific religion. Oh they filled me full of the Sunday school stuff, and I know what the inside of the Bible looks like—got a good shot of that in college philosophy. I can't see myself being comforted by a priest or anyone else praying over me when I go let alone *after* I'm gone. More power to those who need it," he said before adding quickly, "No offense to you, Jack."

"So you don't believe in life after death?"

"It isn't that I don't. It's just that I don't know and pretty much don't care. I mean, if I do my part and have to face Saint Peter or God in the end I figure I have as much right to heaven as those bastards who thump the Bible and then go out and commit every sort of sin you can imagine."

"I hope you're right, Mac. I hope you're right," Jack said looking closely into McConnell's blue eyes. What Jim said didn't track with what Jack knew from catechism, but it made more sense now than it would have back in the comfort of home. Driving ambulances or soldiering, their chances of dying were high. The dead girl drove that point home. He couldn't shake the image of her sweet expression. *Well, she knows,* he decided.

Flying would make him a combatant, but it didn't seem to matter anymore. He felt committed. He and Mac agreed they'd enlist on their next rotation back to Paris. What had started as a noble adventure for Jack had turned into a personal crusade.

Part One

Getting There

La Traversée

No person within the territory and jurisdiction of the United States shall take part, directly or indirectly, in the war, but shall maintain strict and impartial neutrality.

Woodrow Wilson
August 3, 1914

Chapter 1
Painful Decision

The Keeler Residence, Saint Louis, Missouri, December, 9 1914

"Dad, I'm enlisting in the Foreign Legion," Charles Andrew Keeler announced with more confidence than he felt. He lowered the *Saint Louis Herald,* thinking about Kiffin and Paul Rockwell, North Carolina brothers who volunteered in August along with forty-one other Americans. The article praised the volunteers, explaining that by joining the Foreign Legion they could do their part for liberty without sacrificing their citizenship.

Charlie worried about President Wilson's strict proscription against violating United States neutrality in the now four month old European war. He'd toyed with the idea all fall. When the news of Germany's attack on the French reached them it stirred up deep passions in the heavily ethnic neighborhoods of Saint Louis. Charlie knew he was going to join, but dreaded his father's reaction.

It was his twentieth birthday. Maybe that would help him break the news.

"Charlie," his father said through a puff of fragrant pipe smoke, "it's only one more year until you graduate. What the devil are you thinking? Been listening to the LaClède crowd again?"

He waved his free hand dismissively and stated with a note of finality, "Not our war. Old Wilson swore to keep us out of this mess. Where's your common sense, anyway? The Legion? That's a hard bunch, kid! Criminals and ne'er-do-wells. They'd chew you up the first day."

Charlie, tired of college, tired of working to pay for books and tuition, and even more tired of increasing criticism at home, yearned to escape. Nothing he did pleased his father since beginning his junior year at Washington University. The LaClède comment made him wonder if his father was leaning with the many immigrants working for the Busch family.

The war riled both French and German factions in Saint Louis. Brewery boss Adolphus Busch, Charlie's part-time employer, kept a low profile, though he left his wife in Germany when the hostilities began. Within days of the news of war, German and French sympathizers began parading the streets. In a city ironically established by the French, German flags, German music, and German food were everywhere evident. The police force—heavily German and Irish—maintained an unsteady peace with French agitators. Charlie knew that many locals on both sides had answered their native countries' mobilization calls, often sailing on the same ship. In the Keeler household his father espoused neutrality, while his mother quietly supported her native France.

"So, Charlie," John Keeler said jabbing with the pipe, "you'll stay, finish college, get a decent job, and forget about sticking your nose in somebody else's business."

Angry and frustrated, Charlie muttered, "I already quit school, dad."

"You what?" his father said, his face reddening. "You quit!" he growled menacingly, evidently drunk, something that had begun to spiral out of control since August.

"I leave tomorrow."

"We'll see about that, *dummkopf*!" Charlie would have welcomed a slap rather than the tongue-lashings, not that it would have mattered now.

Angelique Keeler understood why John couldn't sleep, why he drank to escape unpleasant memories and his gnawing conscience, but he'd forbade her telling the children the story of his flight from Germany.

Prussia, 1884

A piercing scream woke him with a shock. His brothers were away at the academy, leaving him alone in the room. Hearing his mother wailing downstairs, he grabbed a poker from the fireplace and crept barefoot down the stairs prepared to do battle.

His mother, her head on her arms, wept at the table. An officer—a general he had seen before—stood on the other side of the table holding one of those spiked helmets that had seemed so thrilling last summer.

He crept up to his mother touching her shoulder tentatively. She lifted her head slowly, her eyes red and swollen.

"Johann, your father's gone, she moaned, wrapping her arms around his neck."

It was a terrible night, but the funeral a week later was worse. His uncles wore their dress tunics bedecked with medals that clanked when they moved. His brothers looked stoically sharp in their cadet uniforms. It all should have made young Johann proud, but he felt empty and frightened by the changes in his mother.

She begged him to run away before they forced him into uniform. He didn't dare mention it to his brothers or uncles. Service in the Prussian Army was a noble Keller family tradition. He remembered the thrill of seeing rank upon rank of men in spiked helmets swaying with Prussian precision, every impossibly glossy boot striking the cobblestones in unison. The shiny swords, bright buttons, and flashing bayoneted rifles had dazzled his youthful eyes. He and his friends ran alongside, idolizing the troops, longing for the day they could join them. Why would his mother deny him such glory?

Ingrid, forty-five, was six months pregnant. A week after burying her husband she went into premature labor. His brothers tried to tell him later when they were called home on emergency leave what had happened. "Stillborn," they said. "Our sister never took a breath." After they went back to school, he moved in with his aunt to wait for his mother to recover. She never did.

Ignoring his mother's plea, Johann entered the military academy. His brothers before him had excelled at riding, fencing, and tactics, and were well remembered by the faculty. Johann won academic honors but showed little aptitude in martial arts.

His aunt and a professor of mathematics urged him to enter the university at seventeen rather than accept a commission. By then, the luster of service had dulled and Johann, remembering his mother's entreaty, decided to break family tradition. His brothers wouldn't hear of it.

"You will do your duty, university or not, or you are no brother to us! Father's estate is in our names as is the land owned by mother. You will get your share the day you are commissioned or not at all...."

Johann simply could not embrace his older brothers' enthusiasm for things military. After earning a degree in mathematics and foreign languages, he decided his inheritance, however substantial, was not reason enough to waste his life in uniform, but there was no easy way to escape the familial bonds and Prussian duty ethic.

A courageous circuitous trip landed him penniless in New Orleans in 1894 where he became John Keeler. His prestigious diploma meant little in the swirling excitement of the Louisiana port. Working his way north, John refined his English. When he arrived in Saint Louis, he found work tutoring for a number of wealthy German families. He soon met Angelique who taught piano to one of his pupils.

Their romance, fueled by their common flight from unsympathetic families, grew quickly. Both felt a need to integrate as rapidly as possible in America. Hard work and never looking back helped their marriage to flourish, but when the guns began to roar, so did the past in John's troubled mind.

For all he knew, Charlie's father sprang full-grown from the fairytale Black Forest before landing in America. He knew his father had a degree from the old country, but everything else before the immigration was shrouded in secrecy.

Charlie and Jennifer knew more about their mother. She still corresponded with relatives in France. All of her male cousins and uncles were already in uniform. An aunt had recently written of Uncle Bertrand Toussaint's terrible wound in the Marne battle. The children had heard stories about how Bertrand and his mother grew up together in Provence—more fairytale in the colorful telling than their father's imagined origins.

The tone of her father's conversation with Charlie disturbed Jennifer. She whispered, hoping not to aggravate the situation, "Charlie, how on earth do you expect to get to France? You don't have two coins to rub together."

Charlie could not get over the fact that this pudgy little baby had bloomed into a beauty. Though two years separated them, they were like twins in sentiment if not physique. Whereas Charlie was burly, Jennifer was slender, almost coltish. Her hair was fine, straight, and the color of pale straw while Charlie's was darker and unruly. The Keeler children had their father's penetrating blue eyes and an electric sense of empathy from their mother.

"I'll hop a freight train to New Orleans and hitch a ride on a merchantman," he replied a little weakly.

John Keeler said little at dinner. He gulped his wine, refilling his glass frequently. While Jennifer cleared away the dinner plates and went to fetch the birthday cake, Charlie turned to his mother and said, "Mom, I have something to tell you." His father glared smugly, as unprepared for his wife's reaction as he was for Charlie's earlier announcement.

Angelique saw the exchanges between her husband and children, wondering if it had something to do with the girls Charlie seemed to have to fight off. Guessing, she asked, "Who is it this time, Betsy or Julie?"

"Never mind them, mom," Charlie, answered, quickly blurting out, "I'm leaving tomorrow for the Foreign Legion." He flinched at her gasp and the squeal of her chair scraping the floor.

She threw back her shoulders saying: *"Mon Dieu c'est un Toussaint!"*

Charlie watched his mother breathe deeply, her bosom rising, a flush reddening her face. Mindful of his father's reaction, he braced for an angry outburst.

Angelique made an effort to compose herself before rising majestically. Charlie got up automatically. She came to him and placed her arms on his shoulders. What she did next surprised them all. She rose on her toes and moved her right cheek to Charlie's left kissing him lightly before swinging gently to the other side to kiss him there. She held her son at arm's length looking up to the boy who towered over her.

"You make me so *fiere! Je suis fiere de toi!* You understand? Of course you do. I am so proud!"

The tense moment lingered until tears filled her eyes. "You must finish college, *bien sûr,* but there will be time later. Oh, but I should be ashamed to want you to go! No! You mustn't leave, but *la France*, my poor France...."

Charlie ventured a look over her shoulder at his father who remained sitting watching them incredulously, shaking his head.

The next day Charlie set off with a little money from his mother, a knitted scarf from Jennifer, and a small bag packed with changes of clothes and every pair of socks his mother could find. "You'll need these," she'd insisted. "You must write! I'm sorry you cannot ask my family for help, but if you really need it, remember the name *Toussaint.* They are good people."

His father didn't even say goodbye.

Chapter 2
Buck's Farewell

Buck Residence, Minneapolis, Minnesota, Thursday, November 26, 1914

Snow covered the walkway and lay lightly on the hood of the Pierce Arrow. Jack fussed with the levers and switches, wondering how it would handle in the snow. It was a fine machine, painted forest green with black trim. There were only two in the city, and this one belonged to the company where he worked.

Jack fingered the ticket in his jacket pocket, playing his half-baked idea over again in his mind. Get to Chicago on the *Milwaukee Line* the day after Thanksgiving. It was as far as he'd gotten—the first leg of a trek that he hoped would lead him to a job as a volunteer ambulance driver in France. Just the thought of leaving made him sick at heart, but he'd show her.

Three years of on-again, off-again romance. He'd tried everything to make it work, but he never really had a chance.

"Jack," she had said avoiding his eyes, "it isn't just my parents this time. I can't fight them *and* my church...."

"Listen Sandy, we've been through all this a thousand times," he'd tried to reply.

"Stop! She shouted, clenching her fists and shaking her head. Her short blond curls vibrated. Her mouth twisted unattractively, the lips he loved to kiss pinched white. "What do I have to do to make you listen? It won't work! It could never work. It's not you...but it is too. What do I have to do? Say I'm in love with someone else?"

"Cut it out! Don't even joke about that. Sandy, that's not you! We're in love, or I thought we were. I know I am. What more do we need?"

"Jack, you are so damned pig-headed!"

He smiled, cutting her off by putting his hand to her lips before she could finish. "Why keep harping on it not working? We can make it work, religion or not!" She touched his cheek tenderly, shaking her head. Then she turned and rushed to catch the streetcar, anxious to escape hurting him.

Early in high school, circumstances threw Jack and Sandy together. He found her impossibly attractive with her long legs, blond curly hair, and pixyish smile. She was the most vivacious girl in their class. She encouraged him and flirted openly with him, but they never went on a real date. She was Baptist. He was Roman Catholic. Her parents loved Jack as long as he was no more than a good friend.

Working together on the class play, in choir, and in classes their senior year increased Jack's passion, and she did little to discourage him until the Prom. Jack was crushed when he learned she was going with Dennis Burns. Dennis had the lead in the play. Dennis played trumpet. Dennis was Baptist.

Jack almost gave up until the senior class trip right before graduation. Sandy sat with him on the train, not with Dennis. They began with their usual interplay, joking, laughing, touching each other in that flirtatious game that sends such a thrill through the players. Soon they were kissing tentatively in the darkened railcar. By the end of the trip Jack was in a state of besotted euphoria, convinced Sandy loved him as much as he did her.

He had spent hours in the library reading everything about other religions he could find. After graduation, he approached her parents politely to talk about dating Sandy. Infused with an innocent sense of ecumenical enthusiasm, Jack pleaded with them. They were very fond of Jack and unwilling to hurt him. Nevertheless, they left no doubt that they would oppose any romantic relationship with all their parental influence. Sandy's mother had a hard time letting him down, but she tried to make their point by relating a family scandal caused by a mixed religion marriage.

"But, this is different ma'am!" He protested futilely, leaving later in the uncomfortable knowledge that the only way to Sandy would be over her parents' objections.

Only slightly daunted, Jack pursued Sandy throughout the summer, discreetly arranging to be together in public places. "Jack, I can't believe you talked to my parents like that! They can't stop talking about what a nice and sincere guy you are."

"Great! Then they shouldn't mind me taking you out," he smiled with that crooked smirk that all the girls loved.

"Jack, they made it pretty clear that if we keep it friendly things would be fine."

"What does that mean to you, Sandy? Is our kissing *friendly*?"

At the University the next two years Jack did everything he could to see Sandy. He hung around the Student Union hoping to catch a glimpse of her. He went to the department store where she worked every chance he got to say hello and ask her to go out for an ice cream or coffee. Sandy seemed to welcome his pursuit, but she assiduously avoided anything that would alarm her folks.

His work at the Cartage Company down below the Lowry Bridge kept him busy and paid for his tuition and books. He had shown a penchant for driving horse-drawn wagons and Ford trucks, and they loved him at the company. Nights he hauled newsprint delivered from mills up north while attending classes at the University of Minnesota during the day. It gave him precious little time to woo Sandy.

Jack loved hanging around the *Tribune* offices after delivering a load at their docks. One day he saw a poster soliciting volunteers to drive ambulances in France. The ad said all comers would be welcome. Healthy men from nineteen to thirty had only to report to the Cunard Lines office in New York City for guaranteed passage. He didn't think much about it at the time.

Jack wanted to write for the Tribune after graduating, but Rowan, the city editor, told him he was too unsophisticated. "No life's experiences, sonny," he said. "Come back and see me when you have a degree, or get some traveling under your belt. See the world."

Jack had worked his way through almost three years at the university. He wrote small pieces for *The Gopher Gazette*, but he wanted more. He figured Sandy's parents might soften their stance if he could make a name for himself. Sandy seemed to agree, giving him hope.

Then the blow fell. He'd just come home from work and was sitting down to the dinner his mom had re-warmed for him. "Jack, have you read the paper?" his mother asked gently.

"No. Something new on the war in Europe?" he asked, savoring the stuffed cabbage. His mother's face was incredibly sad. He thought someone important must have died. "What is it, mom?"

"Sorry, Jack. I'm sure you didn't know. This is a terrible way to find out."

"Find out what, mom? For crying out loud, what's the fuss?"

She reached behind her to the counter and handed him the paper folded open to the page in question, not saying anything. He set his fork down and quickly noted that it was the society page. There at the bottom was a short announcement reading "Noslen-Burns to Marry." His eyes flew to the words in disbelief hoping against hope that there could be another Noslen and another Burns in Minneapolis.

New York City, December 18, 1914

After the incessant click-clack of the wheels, the conductor's shout of "Grand Central, end of the line," woke Jack. He stepped off the train into the cavernous maw of the station, and gawked at the pigeons flying about the vaulted ceilings. Steam and the press of bodies created a heavy atmosphere redolent of cigar smoke and roasting chestnuts. He looked around trying to get oriented.

Standing there, he reflected on how quickly the past three weeks had gone. The image of snow-covered woods in Wisconsin racing by the window remained etched in his memory. Chicago did not seem very different from Minneapolis, just bigger and dirtier, and now he was dead center in New York City. He should have been excited but the thought of Sandy's engagement still ate at his heart.

Chicago had been a great diversion. Aunt Bernice and Uncle Jerry put him up at their lakeside home. Jerry Brunnell ran a very successful distribution business in Chicago dealing mostly in pies and cakes. When they learned of his intent to drive ambulances, the Brunnells, dedicated Lutheran pacifists, promised to buy his ticket to New York, solving that problem for Jack.

His older cousin, Annette, took him on the elevated train into the city. She had babysat him when her parents lived in Minneapolis, but now she wrote for the *Chicago Tribune.* He went on assignment with her to cover a fatal apartment fire. They arrived at the General Hospital behind the ambulance taking the woman to the morgue. Not much of a story there, Annette explained, but it was close to Christmas and there were some parentless children involved.

"Hey, Buck, aren't you after going to drive a meat wagon?" their Irish driver asked him.

"Yeah, Rory, why do you ask?"

"Dunno, though you might be interested to hear this was the first hospital in the country to use motorized ambulances."

Jack, surprised at the driver's knowledge, took the bait, "You don't say!"

"Jack me boy, you'll be a-wanting the likes of a gombeen man like me where you're headed." Jack smiled when Rory stepped aside uncovering a large plaque testifying to the initiation of motor ambulance service at Morgan General Hospital in 1899!

When it came time to board the train for New York, Jack felt a powerful reluctance to leave at all. He was already homesick. His heart ached over Sandy, and Annette told him she could get him a job on her paper if he decided to stay. It had been a strong temptation, but he needed to do something big to show Sandy what a mistake she'd made.

Now Jack found himself on Madison Avenue. His reminiscing evaporated in the face of his current reality. He slipped back into the station to check his suitcase, figuring on some exploring before heading to the piers.

Compared to the sub-freezing temperatures he had left in Minneapolis and Chicago, New York seemed balmy. He opened his heavy coat and took off his hat as he strolled down Madison Avenue away from the station. Craning his neck, the closely packed tall buildings reaching for the sky like the straight pines back home made him feel dizzy. It occurred to him to check with someone on the whereabouts of the Cunard office before wandering too far. A policeman suggested taking a hack or the subway, as it was a long walk. He gave Jack an address on the Lower West Side of Manhattan at Pier 52.

Suddenly the enormity of what he was doing crashed in on him. He felt very lonely, and not nearly as adventurous as he had at the outset. Exploring no longer seemed like such a good idea. Every blond woman he saw reawakened a sinking feeling in the pit of his stomach. After retrieving his grip, he hailed a horse-drawn taxi, worried he'd lose his nerve if he didn't get to the docks immediately.

"How much to take me to the Cunard Lines, sir?"

"That'll be a buck sonny and two bits fer yer bag. Hop in, ain't got all day y'know," replied the cabby, a dark-skinned man with a huge mustache and a strong accent Jack couldn't decipher.

Moving marginally slower than the gaggle of automobiles on the streets, they arrived at the pier in twenty minutes. After Jack produced $1.25 in correct change at the Cunard curbside, the cabby held out his hand gesturing for more. Hesitating in confusion, Jack rummaged in his pocket, drew out a few pennies, a nickel, and a fishing hook that was stuck in the lining. Leaving all but the hook in the outreached hand, he quickly turned away and ran smack into the largest woman he had ever seen in his life.

"Is this here hack spoken for Mac?" she bellowed, catching Jack by the front of his shirt as he bounced off her. The driver, probably afraid the woman who weighed every bit of 300 maybe 400 pounds would break his axle, decided to settle for the meager tip and skedaddle. The woman shrieked, grabbed the rear post of the cab, stopping it dead. Jack almost fell over laughing when the nag pulling the hack, in clear defiance of tugging any more at the harness, raised her tail, peed a huge stream, and then dropped a load.

Jack backed away from the curb chuckling. He made his way inside the elaborate Cunard building and approached the nearest counter to ask about the volunteer program.

The uniformed attendant looked at Jack as if he had leprosy. "'Ave you got no sense, sir?' 'Tis bloody 'ell on the continent! Gaw 'ome is wha' aye say."

Jack understood the part about going home, but he pressed on. After much head shaking and finger wagging, Jack found himself in front of a pair of desks, one covered with a British Union Jack and the other with the French tri-color. Propped up on a stand behind the desks was a colorful poster announcing:

BRAVE VOLUNTEERS WELCOME!
THEIR MAJESTIES, THE KING AND QUEEN OF ENGLAND
OFFER THEIR COMPLIMENTS AND GRATEFULLY ACCEPT
YOUR SERVICE.

The absence of any reference to ambulance drivers alarmed Jack.

Mingling with a handful of other would-be volunteers, Jack heard that some had been there for weeks, and that the last ship that had taken any volunteers had left days ago. On top of his earlier sense of homesickness and near panic, this was not good news. He wasn't prepared to stay in the city for any length of time.

Just then a familiar well-dressed man walked up. Haviland had boarded the train in Chicago. College stickers on each other's suitcases marked them as fellow Minnesotans. They'd only exchanged names before getting on different cars.

"Buck isn't it?" Haviland reached out to take Jack's hand. "What a joy to see a fellow Minnesotan in this Sodom and Gomorrah of a city. Hey! How did you get here?"

Jack sheepishly described his aborted attempt at tourism, and related the curbside episode colorfully enough to get Haviland to laughing uproariously.

Willis Haviland looked every bit the world traveler in his neat wool suit and bowler hat. He was a very handsome man, even by Jack's limited understanding of what that meant.

"Aren't you a bit young for this?" Haviland asked softly, sizing up Jack. In spite of his broad shoulders and height, Jack's baby face made him appear younger than his twenty years.

"To drive ambulances?" Jack responded, not feeling obligated to prove his age. "I saw an advertisement in Minneapolis. It said Cunard was offering free passage for ambulance volunteers. Is that why you're here?"

"No. I thought about it, but in order to fly I understand the Legion is the way to go."

"Fly? Wow! You do that?"

"Well, I haven't even ridden in an aeroplane, but I hear it is possible to get trained and qualified right there in France. Read it in 'Heroes of the Air.' Anyway, I don't think these folks give a crap as long as it's to help the cause. What's the latest on the ship?" Willis looked around acting as if he knew something Jack didn't.

"Ship? Last I heard there hasn't been one taking volunteers for days. They say that bunch over there has been here for weeks."

"Odd. A man at Grand Central gave me this." He handed Jack a handbill with the Cunard Lines distinctive insignia. It announced the boarding of *H.M.S. Reliant*, a warship with berthing for twenty able-bodied volunteers at 2:00 P.M. that very day!

Jack and his new friend Willis joined a group of men for a cursory physical examination to insure they were not bringing infectious diseases onboard. The paperwork to get them admitted to England or France was a simple visa prepared on the spot. Two hours later Haviland, Jack, and eighteen other volunteers mounted the gangplank of the *Reliant.*

Once settled in the cramped bow of the cruiser, Jack suffered another bout of despair. He drifted off to sleep in his assigned hammock remembering how the Brits impressed American merchant sailors during the War of 1812.

Chapter 3
Heroic Rescue

New Orleans, Louisiana, early December 1914

Charlie hitched a ride on a tug pushing a coal barge down the Mississippi rather than ride the rails. The price of passage was to look out for snags during the day.

His scheme of hopping a freighter to Europe hit a different snag almost as soon as he found his way to the harbormaster's office in the old port of New Orleans.

"Think about it, young man," the man behind the counter said. "Where are we and where do you suppose the ships go that dock here?"

The man was patient with Charlie, taking the time to explain how some ships went to the Pacific through the Panama Canal, but only a handful headed east. "Best bet would be to try to get to Cuba or another Caribbean island port," the schedule clerk told him.

On his second full day in the city, Charlie overheard a conversation in French emanating from two men and a striking redheaded woman in *Madame Begué's* café where he went between trips to the port authority. Charlie strained to understand what they were saying, disappointed that his mother had never reinforced his college French.

The older well-dressed man was short. The other, his hair slicked back and shiny, appeared to be with the young woman. Charlie had just caught her eye in the big mirror behind the bar when a rough-looking man with a kerchief wound around his head blocked his view. Suddenly this man bumped into the woman, upending a drink. He leaned over the younger man at the table as if he was trying to catch his balance, and deftly slid a hand into the man's coat lifting his wallet. Simultaneously a boy about twelve dashed by snatching the lady's handbag.

Galvanized into instant action, Charlie leapt over a table, beat the fleeing pair to the door, and blocked their exit. The boy kicked at Charlie's shin only to have his leg grasped in mid-air in an iron grip. Charlie upended the scrawny youth forcing him to release the handbag as he toppled. The older thief, brandishing a Bowie knife, growled, "Let 'im go and step aside!"

Charlie twisted the boy's leg forcing the kid onto his face in a practiced wrestling move. When the man lunged with the knife, Charlie turned sideways to the thrust, chopped down with his right hand, and thrust his left knee sharply into his assailant's crotch. By then other hands subdued the squirming boy, and the short, fat, comic-looking proprietor of the café waddled up waving a nasty-looking club. A police officer burst through the door with pistol drawn, assuming he had caught Charlie in the act.

"Hands up buckaroo!"

Writhing in pain on the floor, the thief tried to scurry between the officer's legs and Charlie's to gain freedom at the open door. In the ensuing confusion, the boy broke free; scrambling out the door and down the street before anyone could react. By the time the customers and proprietor convinced the police officer of Charlie's innocence, the three victims had also slipped out the back of the café.

"You all right, young man?" the owner asked as the policeman led the older thief off in handcuffs.

"Yeah, I guess so," Charlie answered, trying to get his breathing and heartbeat to slow down. He couldn't believe the audacity of the thieves or his own reaction to the armed man. When he realized the people he'd helped had left, he was disappointed.

"Come, sit down, have a drink. It's on the house! Why I've never seen such a display of skill, and in such a young buck at that!"

"Did they get their things back?" Charlie asked. A pretty waitress delivered a brandy with a flirtatious wink. Mr. Tujague, the owner, nodded. "Any idea who those people were?" Charlie asked.

"The thieves or the foreigners?" Tujague chuckled, his face beet red from the excitement. "The smaller man was Monsieur Alexandre Fleury, a businessman from *Renault* in France. I think the woman and the other man are traveling with him, but I never pry. Tips lavishly. Nice to chat in French when he's here."

Curiosity drove Charlie back to the French Quarter that evening. Some gaudily made-up ladies crooked their fingers in invitation from doorways as Charlie passed. At home, the streetwalkers did not seem to be nearly as pretty or plentiful—nor as bountiful. These "ladies" made him very uncomfortable. Attracted and repulsed, Charlie fought the desire to go back for another look. Even were he able to overcome his moral repugnance, his few remaining dollars would not support such dalliance.

While he struggled with images of Ulysses fighting the lure of the Sirens, he nearly knocked over the little Frenchman from the café.

"Meester Keeler, *c'est vous*!" Alexandre Fleury exclaimed. "Michelle, it's Charles Keeler!"

Hearing his name caught Charlie by surprise. Seeing the young woman up close only added to his shock. She was more beautiful than Charlie remembered.

Noting his discomfiture, Fleury said, "Meester Keeler, permit me to introduce myself. I am Alexandre Fleury and this is my traveling companion, Michelle de Vincent."

Charlie decided to try his French, "*Bonjour Madame, je suis enchanté de faire votre connaissance*."

Michelle smiled, holding out her hand. "*Mademoiselle* would be more correct Mister Keeler, but bravo on the French! I'm afraid we were a bit rude at *Madame Begué's*, leaving as we did without thanking you." The clipped British accent threw him again.

She was nearly a full head taller than the minuscule Fleury, even in his straw boater. A large broad-brimmed hat covered her curly red hair. She wore a dark dress that made her waist seem impossibly small. The green sheen of the satin seemed to be reflected in eyes that never left Charlie as she spoke. He felt like he could melt into their greenish depths. He couldn't help thinking how much she contrasted with the brassy ladies that had so recently stirred his interest.

"So, you know my name?" Charlie said trying not to stare.

"The harbormaster, Tujague, a couple of ship's captains, and a curious policeman all seem to know you fairly well," Michelle answered. "It didn't take much detective work to find out that you are trying to get to France."

Under the yellowish glow of a gaslight, Fleury studied Charlie's reaction to this information. He asked Charlie what his business in France could be.

Charlie told them his plan.

"The *Légion Etrangère*, indeed! Why would one so young and so far from Europe want to get into our bloody little fight?" Fleury said rhetorically. "Perhaps I can be of assistance Mister Keeler?"

"Not unless you can conjure up a ship going to Europe, sir. Please call me Charlie. This 'mister' stuff makes me nervous."

"Charlie, then. Join us for a drink? We will try some conjuring." Fleury took one arm and Mademoiselle de Vincent the other as they steered him into the nearest restaurant.

When they were settled, Fleury continued, "You are in luck my boy. *Le Rochambeau*, a French steamer, is due in this week. She sails for New York Wednesday."

"How can that be?" Charlie spouted. "I've checked everything for the last two days!"

"Of course! I'm sure you are puzzled. You have made quite a pest of yourself at the docks. The *Rochambeau's* schedule is a closely held secret in order to protect her from German sympathizers. That charming fellow, the harbormaster, practically insisted that I take money for getting you out of his hair, and now that I know your plans, I have ample reason to do just that."

"You mean there's a chance I can get on board?" Charlie asked full of skepticism.

"As my guest," Fleury smiled. "It is the least I can do to repay your gallantry."

"But Monsieur Fleury, this is too much!" Charlie's skin tingled as he absorbed the unbelievable news.

Fleury, sensing Charlie's continued disbelief, explained, "Your country is far from the guns and far from the slaughter. One day the United States will have to—how do you say?—*reckon* with the war over there.

"I just hope you get on our side, because if it comes to it, I think the outcome may well depend on America. Fellows like you volunteering to help my country—and young Michelle's Britain—are like money in the bank. When the time comes to pick sides, I hope there are enough like you already in place to make the decision an easy choice."

"Perhaps, sir, you don't understand," Charlie began again in what he hoped was a conciliatory tone. "I really cannot pay."

Fleury's eyes seemed to twinkle as he said: "*Mais, ce n'est pas un problem*—I said you will be my guest!"

Charlie looked at Fleury and then at Michelle, thinking about their fine clothes and cosmopolitan demeanor. "You see me for what I am. I'm afraid I am not a good candidate for polite shipboard company."

Michelle said in an admonishing tone, "Nonsense! Just yesterday we lunched with a couple of longshoremen who would have made my dear mum blanch at their language." She wrinkled her brow as if she had smelled something unpleasant.

Charlie listened closely, absorbing the fact that she was British while trying to figure out if her polite gorgeous exterior hid a bit of a snob.

Fleury chuckled and said more seriously, "Please don't give it another thought. Money and position have no meaning where you are going. Courage and commitment are the currency in combat."

Charlie tore his eyes from Michelle and repeated Fleury's last sentence aloud, slowly, as if memorizing it.

"Yes! You have it, my boy. *Bien, alors*, I must leave." Fleury announced. "Please order dinner for the two of you, Michelle." Turning his attention back to Charlie he said, "Would you be so good as to walk Michelle to the *Monteléone* after dinner, Charles? After the incident at the café, I don't feel right leaving her alone. She'll show you the way and you can meet us there tomorrow for breakfast if you are *really* interested in getting to France."

Charlie could not believe his luck. Only yesterday, he had been thinking of going home and calling it quits. He shuddered involuntarily as it dawned on him that boarding the ship would put him beyond the point of no return. Where had he heard the sage warning to be careful what you wished for lest you get it?

"Mr. Keeler. Are you all right?" Michelle asked, breaking his reverie. "Is something wrong, or are you always so quiet when left alone with a lady?"

"No, I'm sorry," Charlie temporized, genuinely pleased that Fleury had left them alone. "It's just...well a little hard to believe, you know. You have me at considerable disadvantage. You know my name and what I'm about, and I know nothing about you."

"I'm famished. Can I enlighten you over dinner? You don't mind staying to eat, or do you have another engagement?"

Charlie shifted uncomfortably in his seat wondering how he could possibly pay for a dinner in the elegant restaurant.

"Oh, don't worry, Mr. Keeler. Alexandre arranged everything when we came in. You needn't worry about paying."

Charlie continued to stare at her, very much at a loss for words at how 'arranged' things seemed to be that night.

At the table Michelle began to talk. "Mother is British. Father is French. He is an associate of Fleury's, Renault's representative in England. After I finished school two years ago, my parents sent me to Paris to be a governess for the Fleury children. Now the children are in *maternelle*—French nursery schools—and Monsieur Fleury asked me to stay on as an assistant. I teach little Henri and David English in the evenings."

She ordered for both of them before continuing. *De Vincent*, she explained was an old noble family in France while her mother's origins in England were less pretentious. Michelle fell between two brothers, one an officer in the Royal Fusiliers on duty somewhere in Belgium, and the other, only fifteen, finishing school south of London.

Uninterrupted by Charlie, she plowed on.

"I went to the right schools and know how the game is played—how to keep up the side, as the public schoolboys say—but I've seen what a leveler poverty is in London's slums." She placed her hand on Charlie's arm. "I'm sorry. I've been running off at the mouth. You must think me a terrible bore."

Charlie felt electrified by her touch. He didn't want her to stop, but the waitress arrived with their meals. Charlie barely tasted the roasted chicken in tarragon Michelle had picked for them. As hungry as he was, he couldn't get over the turn of events and the tantalizing presence of such a beautiful woman.

After the waitress cleared their plates and brought coffee, Charlie asked, "Why would Fleury spot me passage? I am a complete stranger, after all."

"These are strange times, my American friend." She stopped to collect her thoughts and looked off into the distance before beginning again. "I've been to visit the American Hospital in Neuilly just west of Paris with Madame Fleury. Your countrymen are helping to bring in the wounded by the hundreds and your doctors work side-by-side with the French surgeons trying to repair the horrible damage done at the front.

"That little display in *Madame Begué's* counts, you know. Believe me, Fleury does not give his hospitality lightly. He has already told me to make sure you get *whatever* you need." She hesitated, a faint red blossoming on her creamy white cheeks.

For the second time Charlie began to wonder at how pat this meeting with Fleury and Michelle had been. He felt a little like a trapped rat. What did that say about the charming Michelle? Was she part of the bait? Was the good French gentleman on a recruiting mission? It didn't matter in the end if he got what he was after. In the meantime, why not indulge in his fantasies with Michelle?

Charlie studied her exquisite face as it flashed through moods much like a kaleidoscope twisting through colors. Every emotion brought a new cast to her eyes, a slight twist to her full lips, accented by an even slighter rise to one of her long elegant eyebrows. Every mobile facet fascinated Charlie making him want to freeze her like a portrait that he could contemplate at his leisure. He was so mesmerized that he didn't notice that she had set her cup down and stopped talking.

"Where do you come from Mr. Keeler?" She said, breaking their staring match. "Are you a cowboy?" she asked, perhaps remembering the policeman's use of the term *buckaroo*, or his rough and tumble behavior.

"*Please* call me Charlie." He felt like laughing. "No, Michelle, I come from Saint Louis, Missouri, about 500 miles north of here. Maybe you have heard of it? My father teaches high school, and I am—or at least used to be—a college student."

"Why that's wonderful! Education frees the bonds of mind and soul. And what did you study?"

"I originally wanted to become a medical doctor, but the classes didn't interest me enough. I'm doing architecture—I like to sketch things. I do well in philosophy, literature and, believe it or not, French."

"Then you will love Paris. It is an architect's dream, full of beautiful monuments, marvelous buildings, and plenty of subjects for you to sketch. It has spawned some of the world's best philosophers and writers—and they do speak French there, so I am told."

Charlie smiled. He wondered how far Fleury's *anything he needed* might go. Imagining holding her or kissing sent a surge through him that made his knees weaken.

"Will you join us for breakfast here?" she asked at the hotel entrance only a short distance from the restaurant.

He assented and watched her go to the desk for a key without so much as turning around to look at him. Charlie made his way back to the docks feeling light-headed.

Chapter 4
Safety in Numbers

Off the Atlantic coast, December, 1914

H.M.S. *Reliant* took up its position in the formation, about midway among twenty allied ships of all types. The British began convoying after the first sighting of a U-boat off the coast of Ireland in August. The British fleet had all but bottled up the German surface navy from the outset of the war, but the new submarine threat posed a major threat to Allied ships. No policy required merchant ships or passenger liners to submit to the time-consuming protection of convoys, but open agreements between the British and French governments allowed vessels flying friendly colors to avail themselves of whatever protection the convoys could offer. With large numbers of Canadian soldiers filling troopships to Europe, a convoy formed just about every week.

Getting underway greatly relieved Willis, Jack, and the other Americans. The tars—what the Brits called their sailors or "bluejackets"—kept up a routine of watches and chores. The Americans were mostly in the way, but once aboard, they could not disembark. A seaman escorted them everywhere to keep them out of trouble.

Jack took in everything, admiring the way the sailors meshed with their machinery. The passengers played cards and dice side by side with the sailors, and crabbed about the bland seaman's fare dished out from the galley.

Jack was surprised to find out how many of his fellow passengers had some college education. Less surprising was their abundant sense of adventure. Jack was probably the youngest. Willis Haviland at twenty-eight was one of the oldest, though one fellow claimed to be thirty-nine and looked every bit of it.

The shipboard routine fascinated Jack. He befriended a junior officer who proudly explained that *Reliant's* five-inch guns and the new load of torpedoes were insurance against unseen torpedo-wielding U-boats. By positioning her on the southern flank of the convoy's spread out formation, the admiral hoped to buy some early warning. With *Reliant* and others like her serving as trip wires, he could alert the motley flock of merchantmen and warships of impending attack. At a minimum, it would allow the captains to execute abandon ship drills.

"HH doesn't relish herding a bunch of unarmed ships across the Atlantic, but he is confident we can handle anything the German Navy throws our way," the ensign explained.

"HH?" Jack asked.

"Vice-Admiral Howard Hewitt, old Navy."

Since forming the convoy off the coast of New Jersey, Hewitt had maneuvered the ships in protection drills within range of coastal batteries. America might remain neutral, but he was assured of support if attacked in territorial waters. After two days of zigzagging in formation, he had ordered the convoy to begin the trek that would have only taken five to eight days in peacetime.

Life on *Reliant* took a turn for the worse for the Americans when a bluejacket reported seeing two Americans hanging around his duty station after his pocket watch disappeared. The ship's executive officer conducted a search of the American's gear that turned up nothing. Trying to force the culprit to come forward, the British officer ordered the Americans to begin pulling cleaning details under the supervision of petty officers.

Jack didn't mind the work. It gave him a chance to learn more and see more of how the cruiser operated.

"See that big liner on the horizon, Jack?" Willis Haviland asked during one of the times they were allowed on deck. "I hear it's The *Rochambeau,* a French passenger ship. There's one more like it in the convoy, a British liner, the *Southampton*, loaded with Canadian troops. 'Tis a grand affair we've launched ourselves into my friend."

"Willis, you've done this before, haven't you? I mean you know so much."

"Two years in the U.S. Navy, Jack, if you must know."

"No kidding? I'll be damned! Wait! Why?"

"Am I sailing on a British ship to fly with the French in a war with Germany that the United States isn't even in?"

"Well, yeah."

"Not that it's any of your business, Jack, but I was discharged honorably. Got out to finish college. Money problems and some trouble at home set me on this glorious path."

Haviland pointed out the *Carpathia,* the ship that had picked up *Titanic* survivors. "She's why we're going so slowly," he explained. "I heard she's carrying a load of horses for the British Army," he said, adding that its skipper reported sporadic engine problems that had Admiral Hewitt fit to be tied. Everyone wanted to finish the crossing before the Christmas holidays, but the *Carpathia* was the convoy's lowest common denominator. Rumor on the *Reliant* had it that a bunch of American deckhands on the *Carpathia* were in open mutiny against its master.

"Haviland, thinking about flying?" Amory Ferguson, a blowhard who claimed to have graduated from Yale, asked sarcastically. Haviland, Jack and Ferguson were swinging mops on the forecastle during the dawn watch. Amory was a short guy with a shock of curly red hair. He made it clear to all within hearing that anything less than a combat billet with the British Army would be shameful shirking. He scorned the French as perfumed pansies. His boasting and needling others did little to endear him to anyone.

"*Thinking* is about all I dare do now, Fergy," Willis began without slowing his mopping. "You see its *intelligence* they're seeking for the flying services, so I am exercising my brain rather than jacking my jaw." Jack smiled at Haviland's aggressive response.

Ferguson raised his mop and aimed it at Haviland's head. Willis moved so fast that Jack couldn't see how it happened, but there was Ferguson sprawled on his back, soaking wet. Without breaking stride, Haviland resumed swabbing the deck just as the duty mate rounded the corner.

Seeing Ferguson with an upended bucket in his lap, the mate muttered something about *bloody Yanks* and disappeared. As soon as the British petty officer moved off, Ferguson beat a hasty retreat, mop and bucket in hand, leaving a wet trail.

"Jack, that's a bad one. I don't think we've heard the last of him," Haviland observed.

Several days out of Southampton the older hands warned that the last part of the voyage could be rough. They were entering the greatest submarine danger zone.

"When we make it through, all I want is to drive an ambulance," claimed Cyrus Teeter, an ex-glassworker from Syracuse. Teeter looked as if he could slide through the cracks in the floor. His angular features, bony frame, and pockmarked face made him singularly unattractive. But Teeter was everyone's favorite. He regaled the bunch with preposterous tales of female conquests that were both comic and titillating.

"Driving ambulances would be doing some poor broken blokes a service without killing anybody," Teeter announced.

"Or jeopardizing their citizenship," someone added.

Hearing this reinforced Jack's resolve. His father and uncles had fled Norway to avoid mandatory military service. While not pacifists—descendants of Viking warriors after all—they saw no value in spilling their blood in the useless and continuous battles in Europe.

The Bucks were a combative bunch when it came to personal honor or their families. Many of Jack's uncles had won money boxing in the northern Minnesota lumber camps. Jack had learned some from his father and could handle himself pretty well with his fists.

Citizenship was a constant topic. Ferguson's noise about joining the Brits had some worried more than the lurking U-Boats. One could join the Foreign Legion, they heard, because it consisted of soldiers from many countries whose only sworn allegiance was to the Legion. Driving ambulances was technically non-combatant, unlike joining the British Army.

Let the saber-rattlers like Ferguson go to their destiny, Jack thought. *Ferguson*! *Probably stole the pocket watch just for amusement.*

The warships would put in for replenishment and short shore leaves for the crews when they docked in Southampton. The volunteers would disembark too. British and French officers were waiting there to determine their eventual postings. Jack was too excited to notice. He was in England, his first step in the fabled British Isles.

Chapter 5
All's Well That Ends Well

Aboard the Rochambeau near Newfoundland, December, 1914

"Michelle, how can I possibly sit at the Captain's table? You've seen my clothes. This is all I have. I watch the dandies stroll the deck before dinner with their fancy coats and stiff collars and I know I just don't fit. Even if I didn't embarrass you and Alexandre, I would probably make a fool of myself as soon as I opened my mouth. I am perfectly comfortable eating in steerage."

Michelle stared at the nearest ship from the rail. She wore a warm overcoat with woolen mittens and a scarf pulled over her head to protect her ears from the biting sea breeze. Her cheeks were bright red in the cold. Charlie could not get over how close they had become in the few days they had known each other. They had spent hours talking and walking together.

Charlie dropped his guard about Fleury's motives after leaving Hampton Roads. The Frenchman had had plenty of time to recruit other Americans there and earlier in Charleston, but hadn't. The remaining friction between Michelle and Charlie revolved around his discomfort mingling with the paying first class passengers.

Michelle tried to get him to see past what she called 'quaint provincial prejudices.' She hoped to convince him that no one cared about his origins or his attire.

"You are so stubborn! All the time I've spent trying to convince you that class and money are unimportant you've been brooding about how you looked and what you might say. Can't you see that you are looking down your nose at us? You drive me to distraction, Mister Keeler!

"Captain Richard is looking forward to meeting you tonight, and I will brook no more of your Missouri self-pity."

Charlie felt wronged and unjustly attacked. "You won't *brook* my what? When did I become your vassal?" Almost as soon as the words left his mouth, he regretted his rudeness.

She seemed to recoil. "You can be the most ungracious boor! Suit yourself. Go back to your little corner and sulk." She turned from the rail and marched away.

Charlie couldn't understand why sitting at the Captain's table was so important to her. How could he compete with all those fellows, their airs of superiority?

"Ah, monsieur l'américain, comment-allez vous?" The *Rochambeau's* captain startled him. It was the first time Charlie had met Captain Richard.

"Bonjour Capitaine." Charlie replied. *"Je vais très bien,"* though he felt anything but very good.

"Come up to the bridge and let me show you around?" The captain asked politely in excellent English.

Forgetting for the moment the angry Michelle, Charlie followed Richard through the passageways and up the *escaliers,* French for stairs or *ladders* in Navy lingo. When they arrived in the magnificent teak, chrome and glass enclosure of the bridge, Charlie felt as excited as a child climbing on a locomotive.

A sailor announced, *"Le Commandant sur le pont!"* Everybody snapped to attention slapping their sides with a loud clap. It was Charlie's first exposure to uniformed Frenchmen, albeit merchant seamen. Richard put them at ease and took him around to the officers, introducing Charlie as *"le voluntaire américain."*

Charlie could hardly believe the way these experienced seamen earnestly shook his hand. Some of the younger officers, wearing only one or two stripes on their sleeves, spoke a word or two of English, but nothing to compare with Captain Richard's Oxford accent.

As a sailor poured coffee, the captain asked Charlie what made him decide to enlist in the *Légion Etrangère.*

"*Mon commandant,*" Charlie replied hesitantly as he took the small cup. "How do I address you, sir?"

"*Captain* is fine Mister Keeler, and so is English. I can use the practice. Please go on."

"Well sir, in a word, *adventure*. Your cause is just and right," he replied, making no mention of trouble at home.

Richard asked, "Do you know anybody in France?"

Charlie, remembering what his mother had said, replied, "We are related to the Toussaint family from Provence, but I have never met any of my French relatives." A mustachioed officer turned from the chart table and nearly dropped his heavy instrument. The whole bridge went silent as everyone's eyes turned to the startled officer.

"Mister Keeler," the captain began with a broad smile. "May I present my navigator, *Lieutenant de Vaisseau* Claude Toussaint, lately of *Saint Raphaël en Provence*."

Charlie faced the dark-haired French officer, unfamiliar with the rank, suspecting the name was no more than a coincidence. A series of quick questions and the name *Bertrand*, removed that doubt. Claude was Charlie's mother's brother's oldest son, making him a first cousin.

Neither could conceal their surprise. They agreed to meet again after Toussaint came off his watch, and Richard insisted that they join him for dinner. Charlie didn't give it a second thought.

Claude Toussaint was about the same size as Charlie though clearly several years his senior judging from his weathered complexion and the crow's-feet etched at the corners of his eyes. Claude's English was rudimentary. When they met in his quarters Charlie didn't know what to expect.

Claude showed him photos of himself during naval cadet training at Toulon and made Charlie understand that he'd earned a commission and had sailed with the French Navy for three years before the war. He'd transferred to the merchant fleet early in 1914. Richard had turned down his application to return to active service, but Claude would rejoin the navy after this voyage. After an uncomfortable moment of silence, Claude offered to lend Charlie a suit for dinner.

Charlie arrived at Richard's table looking uncomfortable in the formal clothes. Michelle almost didn't recognize him. Her momentary confusion quickly turned into anger. What kind of fool had he taken her and Fleury for?

Charlie didn't notice Michelle's reaction. He assumed she was still angry with him for his comment about being her vassal. As close as they had gotten, Charlie harbored no illusions. The young man from the New Orleans restaurant with the slick hair seemed to be with her all the time. What chance did he have? They didn't speak at dinner.

The next day Claude shepherded Charlie about the ship mixing French with English as he explained that the *Rochambeau* had been built in 1905 and was the fastest trans-Atlantic passenger liner until the launching of the British *Titanic.* The struggle for words actually sharpened Charlie's growing vocabulary. He heard the latest about the Toussaint side of the family though he couldn't relate to the tumble of names and places.

Fleury cornered him on the morning of Christmas Eve, asking what he had done to make Michelle so upset.

"She wanted me to come to the Captain's table. I must have offended her."

Fleury looked quite vexed as he worked out the reason Michelle was angry. "You deceived her Keeler," he said seriously "Don't hurt her, Charlie, and don't try to fool me either."

"But Monsieur Fleury," Charlie protested, "I would do nothing to hurt you or Michelle. I could never be so ungrateful. I was only trying to avoid embarrassing her."

Fleury got a pained and confused look on his face looking squarely at Keeler's starched dress shirt. "Charlie, please don't patronize me. I am a good judge of character, and it disappoints me to learn that your simple style and poor trappings were nothing more than a ruse. We know about your rich French relatives. What else are you hiding?"

"Sir," Charlie began, eager to protest his innocence. "I am but a distant cousin of *Monsieur le navigateur* Toussaint...."

Fleury cut him off with a wave, stepping away muttering something. He marched off head down. It finally dawned on Charlie why Fleury and Michelle thought he was a phony. He went looking for Claude. Maybe his cousin could set things straight.

"Not on deck," the sailor informed him at the bridge. "Try his cabin," the man suggested.

Claude answered, reacting visibly to his cousin's dejected manner: "Why the sour look, *cousin*?"

Charlie tried to explain the mess with Fleury and his fracture with Michelle.

Claude laughed and exclaimed, "But she must be in love with you *mon fou*!" He went on to say that Charlie was one lucky man considering that every man in the crew was burning with desire for the English lass, and half the eligible bachelor passengers had asked her to dinner every night since New Orleans. "*Allez,* go to dinner. Think nothing of it! I'll see you there."

Charlie entered the ballroom, wondering if the ship had supplemental tanks for sparkling pale golden fluid they dispensed like water. Charlie found champagne more palatable than the beer he had grown up with, but too intoxicating to quench his thirst.

Prominent passengers, many of whom Charlie now recognized, surrounded Richard. Many expatriate Frenchmen were rushing to answer the call to arms. It was no wonder this ship was a floating party.

Richard broke away from his entourage at Charlie's arrival. Taking the American by the elbow, he guided him to a corner. "Now Charlie, whatever is the crisis? Toussaint told me I should talk to you."

"Sir," Charlie began, unsure of how to start, "Monsieur Fleury booked my passage simply because I was volunteering to serve for France. Now he and Mademoiselle de Vincent think I'm a rich French heir that has taken advantage of them."

"Hmm. What could I have told old Fleury? I only told him you were a Toussaint. The Toussaint family is well-connected and very well to-do. Your cousin Claude is one of the many seafaring Toussaints."

"But I only borrowed Claude's clothes! I talked about his family, of course, but I'm a Keeler with no connections whatsoever. Charlie racked his brain to see what he had done wrong.

"Ah, I begin to see the source of this unfortunate misunderstanding," Richard said. "With your permission I will speak with Fleury tonight. Don't trouble yourself about this anymore."

While the two men mulled over their individual thoughts, Michelle entered the dining room on the arm of Claude Toussaint, laughing and leaning into each other like young lovers. *Oh kind cousin, how you have wronged me,* Charlie thought, imagining the worst. He hastened from the room and headed to the railing for air. *First he taunts me with that baloney about her loving me and then he moves in on her himself!*

The cold wind braced Charlie and dulled the sting of seeing Michelle with his two-faced cousin. Hadn't Claude said that the whole crew was "burning with desire" for the fair lass? A*n officer on a sailing ship, and dashing with his uniform and mustache, I shouldn't be surprised that Michelle would find him attractive. But how could he take such blatant advantage of me?*

Charlie began to feel the bite of the wind, but was not about to go back in the dining room, Christmas Eve or not. He started to shuffle away from the rail to head for his small berth when Fleury approached from the dining room door.

"Charlie, Charlie, Charlie! I knew I was right about you from the start! Richard has explained me about you. Please my apologies accept. I have had some unpleasantness with your mother's relatives in France. Ah, to think you might be mixed up with the Toussaint tarnish. Come Charlie. *Maintenant c'est clair!* It is a great relief to me. Come in. Let's get out of this cold."

Charlie's mind raced. Just what have the Toussaints done to gain such instant disapproval? All Claude's hospitality and generosity made sense now. He'd been used to get to Michelle. The hell with him and with her too! He was ready for some of that champagne, a lot of it in fact.

As Alexandre and Charlie entered the dining room, everyone stopped in place and someone clinked on a glass to signal for attention. Another clinking started, and another. Soon the whole room was reverberating with the tinkling of wineglasses. Captain Richard stood at the head of his table with Michelle on his arm. He called for attention and proposed that all raise their glasses in a toast to America and to her volunteers. Charlie understood the French words, but was thoroughly oblivious to the fact that they were toasting *him*.

He looked for Toussaint, still wanting to throttle the two-faced bastard. People began to press forward in a queue in front of him and Fleury. When they began to shake his hand and thank him, he realized that this outpouring was truly directed at him. The few Americans on board made their way up to offer their congratulations and make it clear that Charlie was quite the hero.

Charlie finally spotted Toussaint arm-in-arm with a young French lady. Then Charlie remembered being introduced to her as his *petite amie*. Was one woman not enough for his cousin? Going through the motions with the passengers, Charlie's mind seethed in anger. The line was down to a handful of smiling beaming happy people. Charlie resented their happiness, but kept up the show.

At last Richard arrived, still shepherding Michelle. The captain bowed slightly, shook Charlie's hand and then placed that hand in Michelle's. Charlie looked even more befuddled. Richard said: *"Vous savez mes jeunes que je possede l'autorité necessaire pour executer les mariages?"* Michelle's eyes went wide.

"Merci Capitaine, mais évidemment notre ami est… " Michelle stopped, seeing the look on Charlie's face. "Maybe we should speak English Captain. Mr. Keeler looks very distraught."

"I'm sorry, Charlie. We French are so rude sometimes thinking everyone can understand our precious language. I was only pointing out that I have the authority to perform marriages should you two decide to crown this trip with such a gala event." Michelle's joy turned to apprehension as she watched Charlie and felt him squeeze her hand roughly.

"Marriage?" Charlie exclaimed incredulously. "But what of *mon cousin*, Michelle?" He asked, hissing the French words.

Now it was Michelle's turn for confusion. What did Toussaint have to do with this? She completely misread Charlie again when she brightly asked: "Oh you mean a double wedding—Claude and Marie—and us? Wouldn't that be rich?"

Charlie was now more confused than ever. Could he be hearing this right? Was she actually joking about marrying him? Was their recent estrangement nothing at all? Charlie relaxed his grip and looked again into Michelle's green eyes. She wore an expression of deep concern—almost fear. She seemed to be pleading, caressing his wounded pride. Tears formed making her eyes glisten. Charlie's anger slowly dissipated, softening his features. He was mesmerized again, forgetting the captain, Toussaint, the rest of the passengers, seeing only her. His knees felt wobbly. An involuntary shiver made his skin prickle with a sensual thrill as the magic of her evident concern sunk into his muddled mind.

This exchange took only seconds, but seemed to them to last for hours. Everybody was still watching the American. Captain Richard had moved away, leaving the couple alone, entranced with each other, oblivious to the people around them. "Speech, *discours*!" Shouted some of the guests and Fleury stepped forward to nudge Charlie saying: "*Un mot* my boy, tell them what you told me about how you want to repay Lafayette."

Chapter 6
England at Last

Southampton, England, December 29, 1914

Jack watched the ships from the rail of *Reliant* as the convoy maneuvered off the southern end of the British Isles. The warships executed synchronized turns as they departed. Most of the merchantmen and the two passenger ships were continuing on to Le Havre with smaller gunboat escorts for the Channel crossing.

The threat to shipping in the Channel was minimal. U-boats operated in the North Sea but dared not run the pickets put up by the British at the Channel entrances. Nevertheless, news of the sinking of the French battleship *Jean Bart* in the Strait of Otranto on Christmas day gave rise to increased vigilance.

As the civilian ships began to move out of sight, the warships approached the port of Southampton and jockeyed into berths like horses into stables. Jack and Willis lined up at the rail with the other volunteers and sailors.

None of the Americans lingered once the gangplank was down and permission granted to debark. All they could think of was getting away from the cramped quarters, getting a hot meal, and maybe a British girl to keep them warm for the night.

As promised, a greeting party awaited the Americans. A distinguished gentleman with a bowler hat and a cane introduced himself as Mr. Frazier from the American Embassy. In turn, he introduced Sergeant Major

Bowles from the British Army staff and Colonel Gervais de Lafourcade, the French Attaché.

Frazier quickly explained that the government of the United States was in no way encouraging her citizens to take part in the current conflict. These gentlemen would give information for which he, Frazier, could not take any responsibility, and they would direct any of the debarking passengers to the right place should they decide to engage their services in either country's armed forces. Frazier warned that enlistment would jeopardize their American citizenship, but that he would not stand in their way. Almost as an afterthought, Frazier said he could endorse ambulance services. Jack's ears perked up and he made note of a Mr. Andrew in Paris who Frazier said had just begun to organize the American Field Service.

Frazier ended by telling them to think this over carefully, noting that ferries to the mainland would be departing from Southampton and Dover daily. He issued chits to all twenty, complements of Her Majesty's Government, good for passage one way any day from any port. With that, he sat and ordered his driver to depart. Evidently, answering their many questions would be a violation of America's fragile neutrality.

"Let's talk to the colonel, Jack," Willis said tugging gently on Jack's arm. "Even if you only want to drive an ambulance, he is our best bet for getting to France and finding our way to Paris."

Some of the "volunteers" wandered away down the pier. They saw their friend Ferguson with that bunch. "See that, Willis?" He asked, pointing to Ferguson.

"Sure. Hot air and curly hair. Better to see him sneak off now before one of us gets a rifle in our hands." Willis pushed to the front near Colonel de Lafourcade.

The French officer wore a blue tunic with five narrow gold bands on the sleeves. His red trousers ended in highly polished riding boots. A cylindrical hat, impeccably white with a black visor turned up slightly, crowned his over six-foot height. Jack had seen these hats in magazine articles on the fierce looking Foreign Legionnaires. *Kepis*, they called them. The colonel did not look fierce, but very gentlemanly. His magnificent full mustache curled up with wax at the ends. Red, blue and green ribbons with impressive medallions hung from his left pocket.

His left sleeve; folded over his forearm riveted their attention. They assumed it was the first tangible evidence of a war in progress they had seen. A huge saber hung at his side. Jack thought he had never seen a more impressive-looking man.

"Bonjour mes amis et bienvenue en Angleterre." Jack didn't understand a word. Willis started to translate for him, but the colonel switched abruptly

to British-accented English. He spoke in an unexpectedly soft voice that made them lean forward to hear him.

"La France and Great Britain, Italy, Belgium, and Russia are united in the greatest struggle for survival man has ever known. The Huns and their henchmen have once again invaded our peaceful homelands, destroying our villages, killing our citizens, and threatening Paris. Père Joffre has held the attack on the Marne, but at terrible cost. In the first months, our French forces have suffered over two hundred thousand casualties, and the British are paying dearly as well. You must know all this or you would not be here. We welcome you and ask you to join your countrymen in the ranks of the Foreign Legion. We will defeat the Boches, of that I am sure. I am sorry that I cannot join you now, but I will be back in the fight soon enough. *Vive La France, vive la compagnie!"*

The little group gave a hearty cheer, and many started asking at once where to sign up. The colonel's speech moved Jack, but not enough make him want to join the two hundred thousand casualties. Willis seemed transformed. This was what he had come over to do, and here was a wounded hero to show him the way. There was no need to listen to the Sergeant Major's pitch. They were France-bound one way or another.

Jack watched Willis and the other Americans, wondering how many of them would survive and thinking about remembering this moment. He intended to continue to record his observations in the diary he had started the on the train from Minneapolis right up until he went home—an event whose inevitability Jack Buck never doubted.

On the Rochambeau in Le Havre, France, December 31, 1914.

Crossing the Channel, *La Manche*, normally took about three to six hours depending on the departure and arrival ports. The convoy, however, zigged and zagged, guided by the smaller gunboats in what Claude told Charlie was defense against balloon bombs. "The Boches have already dropped incendiary devices on Dover," Claude explained. "We believe they are a threat to shipping in the channel, so we maneuver haphazardly, to make ourselves difficult targets."

Charlie's reconciliation with his cousin had been shaky. Before Michelle could tell him that Claude had all but arranged the toast himself, Charlie had growled a challenge to Toussaint. The French officer proved as volatile as his American cousin. Unable to believe the ingratitude and pettiness, he demanded an apology. Fleury's arrival prevented a more violent encounter. Once Charlie got the story straight, he sank down onto a folding chair burying his head in his hands.

"Oh Claude, god I'm sorry. It's just that when I saw you with Michelle I thought you two were..."

"*Assez!* Enough. You are more Toussaint than you even know!" Claude lingered a moment to make sure his cousin had recovered his composure, and then announced that he had an important rendezvous with a certain blonde.

Fleury remained standing as Charlie slowly got up from his seat saying: "How many chances does one get Monsieur Fleury? I'm afraid I am using mine up foolishly."

"Alexandre, Charlie, *Alexandre.* We are all guilty of misjudgment here. You are inexperienced in the ways of the world. Go back to Michelle. She's distraught. Make her smile again."

Michelle was more confused than distraught. They had gone back to her cabin to get away from everyone for a minute. When the door was closed, she stepped up to him to take his coat. The two of them came together in an embrace and kiss that left both uncomfortably aroused, throwing their return to dinner into question.

In the ensuing two days of endless zigzagging, they spent nearly every minute together. Neither dared discuss plans beyond their arrival in France.

Charlie had never held a woman, kissed a woman, or wanted a woman as much as he wanted her. When they were alone and she pulled the pins out of her red tresses, he thought he could taste his desire. They kissed until her cheeks and chin were rubbed red by his beard. It was a new plateau of intimacy for both of them making their language and actions tentative, exploratory, and a bit awkward.

Charlie had never been truly in love before. His introduction to feminine mysteries had been limited to fully clothed wrestling matches with a girl name Josephine. Neither of them would go to communion at Mass the Sunday's after being together. Yet, both looked forward to their next tryst.

Michelle and Charlie were twenty, at sea in a world at war and far from the influence of Father O'Brien in Charlie's case and McGuire in Michelle's. What or who was to stop them?

"I love you, Michelle," Charlie managed to say almost involuntarily. Her "I love you Charlie Keeler" seemed to originate somewhere down around her waist. He slid his lips to her bare neck, producing a response strong enough to make them sag onto the settee in Michelle's cabin.

Charlie opened his eyes to see her face inches from his. She had those dangerous tears in her green eyes. "Charlie, I have never done this. I have never been touched like this. I have never had such joy...."

Talking about it was not easy for either of them. Charlie's mind bounded crazily between love, lust, guilt, and tenderness.

"Charlie, what are you thinking? If it is any of that Catholic guilt at what we are doing, I may never forgive you! This can only be something bad if we think of it that way. We could finish what we've started," she said somewhat wistfully. "But we won't, will we?"

"I love you too much to hurt you," Charlie stated.

"I was just thinking that we generate so much energy. There is so much more of that to share. I am just putting into words what I'm sure you are thinking in that prudish mid-American mind of yours."

"Midwestern, my dear. Reading my mind now?"

"Get up and straighten yourself out," Michelle smiled coyly. "We are going to walk out of here and go to dinner as soon as I change my dress. Mum used to tell me that anything good is worth waiting for. She said the same words when she told me about men. I think you are worth waiting for. Will you last long enough to find out?"

"Michelle, I… I…," he stammered. "Someday, if we can still stand each other, I hope to finish what we started here tonight," he sputtered, immediately regretting the corny words.

"Come what may, Charlie Keeler, I expect you to do the same or I'll tell that handsome cousin of yours you disgraced the family name and took advantage of me."

ON NEW YEAR'S EVE they enjoyed the last and most sumptuous dinner of the entire voyage. Normally, passenger ships put in to port in daylight, the process of maneuvering a huge ship being tricky enough when one can see clearly. Since the war, many of the port calls on the French coast had been put off until night. Spies in the ports reported the comings and goings of ships to the Germans. More than one attack had been attributed to espionage.

This last dinner, Michelle told him, would be a *fête à la Française*—Champagne before dinner accompanied by hors d'oeuvres of caviar on tiny toasts. Silver trays laden with canapés of all sorts of shapes and colors—thin slivers of smoked salmon, white asparagus tips on hard cooked egg slices topping small crackers, and delightful delicacies Charlie couldn't even name. Michelle's appetite obviously benefited from their earlier passion. They took turns giving each other tidbits of savory crab-filled puff pastries, looking lovingly in each other's eyes, and sliding around the tables greeting everybody. Elderly couples beamed at the young pair.

Alexandre was deep in conversation with Captain Richard. Fleury's dealings with the British were at a sensitive head. Renault was now manufacturing aeroplane engines, and the output of motor transport had doubled in November. December 1914, saw the factory operating twenty-four hours a day with a vehicle coming off the line every thirty minutes—nearly three times the rate of the past August.

War demands already taxed French shipping to the limit, and factories needed raw materials, especially steel and rubber, to keep functioning. Supplies were plentiful in the French colonies, especially of rubber. Fleury was querying Richard on the capacity of passenger ships like the *Rochambeau* to handle more cargo. The festive air on the ship gave way in small steps to the realities of the war, but the dinner went on.

"A last waltz before we debark?" Charlie asked Michelle, with a smirk. He had told her about his horror of dancing and she had assured him she would never force him onto a dance floor. They had gorged themselves on the poached salmon and *boeuf en gelée*. The wines were like nectars. The atmosphere heightened every sense. Michelle's perfume sent Charlie back to their second meeting in New Orleans. How they had changed in that short time. The violins and cellos seemed to vibrate in resonance with their hearts. Intoxicated by the whole experience, neither could even think about going ashore and parting company. At 10 P.M. the last of the crew left the ballroom for their posts in preparation for the docking. They would begin debarkation at 11:00 P.M.

The orchestra played the last song, a French Christmas carol: *Il est Naît la Divin Enfant*, at 10:30 with the whole contingent of passengers singing along tearfully. A few linked arms and swayed to the familiar refrain. Charlie would never forget this experience. To be on a noble mission in the midst of celebrating the Christmas season, seemed so terribly incongruous. For the moment he was in love. The war would get his attention soon enough.

Part Two

To Arms

Aux armes

...to serve with faithfulness and honor and to follow the corps or any fraction of the corps wherever the government wishes to send it.

Foreign Legion Oath

Chapter 7
Ah Paree

Aboard MV Cantor on the English Channel, December 31, 1914

Jack gazed into the green churning water trying to dig up his memory of the Spanish Armada. He recalled 1588 and Francis Drake, but no more. Movement on the *Reliant* had seemed subdued. After his initial discomfort as they left New York, Jack found the ocean voyage relatively uninspiring. This was different. A nudge broke his reverie.

"Not the same as Lake Minnetonka, is it Jack?"

"Willis! Jeez! Don't sneak up on me like that!

"More like Mille Lacs," Jack replied remembering how he became slightly nauseous at not being able to see the opposite shore the first time he saw the huge lake. It seemed laughable now.

"That's Calais on the horizon, Jack." Buck looked where Haviland was pointing. "We'll be there before you know it. France. Are you ready?"

Jack didn't need to answer. Once ashore it went very quickly. With their passports stamped by the *douanier*, they climbed in a taxi for the five-minute trip to the *Gare de Calais* to catch the train.

"Why first class, Willis?" Jack asked seeing the big one on the tickets Haviland picked up for them.

"The whole train's booked by the British Army. It was the only way I could get us seats. Come on. We have to hustle."

They made their way up the line of cars through rank after rank of brown-clad soldiers.

"Good Lord, Jack, these guys look pretty young."

"To you maybe. Here it is!"

They wrestled their bags up the aisle and deposited them on a rack at the end of the car. Just before the train began to move, a man with two women settled in the seats across from Jack and Willis. Jack's continued to stare out the window while Willis addressed the man politely in French.

"Américains? Vous êtes américain!" Jack heard. Willis responded in French, startling Jack as he made the introductions.

Pierre Étienne Flandin and his wife, Berangère, looked to be about his parents' age. Willis explained that they were returning to Paris with their daughter, Isabelle, from a visit in England.

Isabelle held back almost in the shadows, perhaps intimidated by the strangely dressed Americans. Jack strained to catch her eye, but he failed to get even a mild response.

Flandin refused to believe that Minneapolis had streetcars and electric lighting.

While Haviland's French was limited and Flandin seemed reluctant to try English, Jack perked up when Flandin showed interest in their streetcars.

"He says the *Métropolitain* in Paris opened in 1900 and is the most modern underground transport system in the world," Haviland explained. "He's talking about riding the 'tube' in London on his latest trip."

According to Flandin, London's underground dated from 1886 making it oldest in the world. He said it was already the dirtiest and smokiest due to the long use of coal-fired steam locomotives. It took Willis several tries to get Flandin's proud explanation that Paris powered their *Métro* with cleaner electricity.

In the meantime, Madame Flandin knitted, concentrating on every stitch. She looked up only to nod occasionally in agreement with her husband's comments about the glories of Paris. The girl, Isabelle, kept her nose in the *Compleat Works of Shakespeare*. Both women stole frequent quick glances at Haviland for some reason.

When a conductor announced the *Gare du Nord,* Flandin leaned over to whisper something to his wife who nodded in obvious assent. Isabelle brightened up at once, closing her book with the mark not two pages from where Jack thought he saw it at the start of the trip.

The bustle in the Gare du Nord astounded Jack. Men of all ages in uniforms of every description and color were coming and going. He found it hard not to stare at the gurneys and wheelchairs grimly reminding them of the war. An enormous number of vendors hawked fruits, jewelry, scarves, paintings, and flowers. Coal smoke mixed with the smells of cooking, coffee, and strong perfumes to create a distinctive, almost pleasant odor.

Willis and Jack expected to be on their own once they arrived, but Flandin insisted that they accompany him. He offered to put them up while they sought their eventual postings.

"C'est le moindre chose que je puisse faire au nom du patriotisme," Flandin said.

After convincing the Americans that further arguments would be futile, Flandin hailed two taxis. Madame Flandin and Willis climbed in the first and Jack got in the second with Isabelle and her father. Jack was uncomfortable not being able to speak a word of French. Isabelle remained silent, mysterious.

Paris had a sense of permanence and age that Jack could not help comparing to Minneapolis. He concluded that the American cities were more modern, less imposing, and decidedly less *historic.*

Despite the number of men in uniform, it struck him that people on the streets seemed oblivious to the war. He had read that things had gone badly for the Allies. The Germans had penetrated to within 75 miles of Paris before being stopped by Joffre's "Miracle of the Marne," the costly defense in mid-September. The casualty figures staggered his imagination—over 200,000 on the French side alone. The so-called "Race to the Sea" ended with the massive armies spread on either side of a jagged line stretching from Switzerland to the English Channel. This city was entirely too normal.

Isabelle, noticing his slack-jawed staring, surprised him by speaking in slightly accented but perfect English. "Mister Buck seems to be overwhelmed by our city of light Papa. Perhaps we should take him on a tour?" Flandin looked amused at Jack's expression.

"Good English, no, Monsieur?"

"Very good." Jack answered looking more closely at Mademoiselle Flandin who returned his gaze unabashedly. High cheekbones nicely set off her warm brown eyes. The brisk air reddened her cheeks. Her mouth was small, almost pouting, but when she smiled, her lips parted uncovering even white teeth. A cap-like hat struggled to keep her chestnut curls from emerging here and there. Her coat and long skirt hid everything else other than a hint that she was tall.

Jack got out of the taxi, offering Isabelle his hand as she stepped down. "Wasn't that Notre Dame we just passed?" he ventured. Pierre Flandin looked confused by Jack's question, but Isabelle gave a light laugh at his pronunciation and honest mistake. She gently explained that the old church at one end of the massive intersection of five avenues was Saint Augustin. "I will be happy to show you 'noter dayme' later," she said, smiling. Jack blushed, feeling mocked.

The Flandin's ushered them into the apartment on the second floor of a large building facing the Place de Saint Augustin. A double door opened into an enormous room dominated by a grand piano and brightened by light from windows set in doors that led to a balcony. Mirrors and paintings covered the walls. The beautiful furniture, carefully placed around the room, made Jack think of photographs he'd seen of elegant hotels. Plants flourished in containers at every window. Isabelle showed Jack and Willis to guestrooms in the back of the apartment where they deposited their luggage.

Soon after they arrived Monsieur Flandin assured them he would call the Préfecture the next business day to find out what Willis needed to do to join the Legion, but that there was not much they could do until after the holidays. He told them the American Embassy was within a fifteen-minute walk, but most offices would be closed. "I must introduce you a long-time friend and Paris resident, Dr. Frederick Gros."

"An American as well papa," Isabelle noted.

That evening—New Year's Eve—Madame Flandin presided over dinner. Before moving to the table, they entered a brightly lit room warmed by a fragrant fire in an elaborately carved white and gold marble fireplace. Flandin poured chilled champagne into tall thin glasses and passed little finger-like cookies that he dipped to excite the bubbles. While trying the champagne, Jack couldn't help staring at the Flandin women. Freed of their travel garb the ladies were dazzling, mother no less than daughter.

Madame Flandin led them to the adjoining dining room illuminated with small electric bulbs set in a magnificent crystal chandelier. Flandin seated Haviland at his right and Jack at Madame's right, opposite them. Isabelle moved to her father's left across from Jack, allowing him to steal looks at her eyes, her hair, and her inviting cleavage. Willis had an equally charming view of Berangère Flandin's richly displayed and only slightly more mature beauty.

Dinner began with slices of velvety foie gras on little toasts followed by roast squab with a puffed potato accompaniment. A gratin of thin green beans tasted so good that Jack wanted to ask for seconds. Jack and Willis traded glances across the table from time to time, reflecting disbelief at their good fortune.

Madame Flandin spoke no English, but she kept up a constant conversation, dutifully translated by Isabelle. The two women would address first one, than the other, asking about their families and why they wanted to fight. Jack hesitated to correct them about that.

After dinner, Flandin took the guests into a room with walls lined with books. He offered cigars and vintage cognac in huge balloon glasses of heavy crystal. Willis took the cigar with practiced ease, but Jack declined. The cognac burned all the way down his throat, reminding Jack of the nauseating taste of siphoned gasoline. The immediate flush of warmth wasn't unpleasant, but he set the glass down for good.

They spoke of what it would take to get America to wake up. Without Isabelle to translate, Willis rapidly reached the limits of his two-year's college French. The conversation began to flag until Flandin told them about the exploits of the growing air service. He himself was on the board of the *Société Provisoire des Aéroplanes Déperdussin.* These words all flowed together until Flandin wrote out the letters one at a time: S-P-A-D. Haltingly, French and English competing in every sentence, he described this aircraft factory as one of the pioneers in France. It took Willis several tries to sort out the word *pioneers* that sounded amusingly like "pee on ears" to Jack.

When Willis reminded Flandin of his flying aspirations, Flandin reacted with concern. "But you wish to join the *Légion, n'est-ce pas*?" He said shaking his head. He hummed a few notes from some remembered event bringing tears to his eyes. Flandin picked up a framed photo of a magnificently uniformed young officer in a white hat.

As he passed the picture to Willis and Jack, he said it was Isabelle's older brother, their only son, Jacques-Antoine. Hesitating and visibly fighting to maintain his self-control, Flandin told them he had been killed in October in a place called Craone.

"He was leading an attack of Legionnaires…" Flandin offered, his voice trailing off. Jack and Willis stood respectfully holding the photograph like a treasured icon, both remembering Colonel de Lafourcade wearing a very similar uniform. After several moments of awkward silence, Flandin shook his head, smiled sadly, and said: "*Mais, c'est la guerre*!"

Without wanting to prod, Willis managed to get Flandin to explain that Jacques-Antoine graduated from Saint Cyr the previous spring. He had jumped at the chance to command soldiers. In May 1914, war clouds seemed too distant for one eager to get combat experience. The *Légion Etrangère,* on the other hand, promised travel and action. Jacques-Antoine reported to a training camp in Tours where he got his first exposure to the hardened soldiers and vagabonds of the famed Legion.

Flandin said his letters were full of tales of North African soldiers and their strange eating habits, of Annamite orderlies from the French colonies in Indo-China or *Tonkin.*

"He wrote of his German section sergeant—the toughest, meanest and most competent non-commissioned officer at Tours. Jacques-Antoine said the sergeant carried a pack twice the weight of his own on the long training marches.

"When the war broke out in early August and German advances threatened Paris, the Army ordered Jacques-Antoine's regiment to move to Toulouse to get them away from danger. They received an influx of foreign recruits in late August including some American volunteers," Flandin hesitated unsure if they fully understood. Seeing their rapt attentive faces, he continued.

"A month later, Jacques-Antoine wrote that they were on their way to the front. His section of Americans and Arabs was an unruly lot, spoiling for a fight with someone other than themselves."

His son's Regiment arrived near Chalôns-sur-Marne in late September. Writing the Flandins after the battle, the new regimental commanding officer told how Jacques-Antoine's company made a 50-kilometer march to a large Chateau near Craonnelle.

Here Flandin's voice dropped in both tone and volume as he recited the details from the letter. "Almost all the officers were killed or wounded on October 3, including my son's company and regimental commanders." Flandin's eyes grew moist but his chest rose as he described how his son had carried a wounded sergeant to an aid station.

"It must have been instantaneous," he muttered, confusing Buck and Haviland with the unfinished thought.

"He was so young!" Flandin gasped. "Shells hit the aid station. They were all killed—Jacques-Antoine and all the wounded."

Flandin composed himself, continuing in increasingly fluent English. He pulled out a red leather box and showed them his son's *Croix de Guerre,* a cross in bronze traversed by two sabers suspended from a ribbon in alternating green and red stripes. He said his son's last letter told about how proud he was to be leading the Americans.

Noticing another older photograph of a uniformed officer, Willis gently asked, "Is that you Monsieur?" pointing to the old frame.

Flandin nodded, but quickly changed the subject. "When you joined us on the train, we saw Jacques-Antoine in you, Willis." Jack looked again at the picture and then to his friend. The resemblance was incredible. Haviland's square jaw and sparkling eyes matched those of the lieutenant peering out from under the visor of the kepi.

Willis smiled kindly at the older man and said something in French that Jack couldn't understand. Flandin smiled back and said: "Perhaps our hospitality makes more sense to you now." Jack felt a tingling sensation well up inside him.

Flandin took a deep breath and slowly brought his cognac to his mouth as he looked thoughtfully at Willis. "I think you must consider the Ambulance rather than the Legion."

Rejoining the women for coffee, Willis drew Isabelle apart while Jack stayed with Flandin. Madame Flandin sat demurely, saying nothing, but nodding as her husband translated Jack's condolences into French. It was nearly midnight. In the space of a day, the young men had made a larger contribution to their hosts than either of them could imagine.

Jack noticed that Haviland had Isabelle's full attention. Willis was slightly shorter than her, but he was so handsome that Jack didn't think he could compete. Remembering how Willis had leveled Ferguson made for quite a contrast to his polite and gentle demeanor in this Paris apartment.

As the clocks chimed the arrival of 1915 there were few manifestations of celebration in or out of the Flandin household. Nineteen-fourteen had brought the French suffering and loss. The New Year could promise little but more of the same.

Chapter 8
A Growing Passion

Le Havre, January 1, 1915

The *Rochambeau* emptied rapidly. A black Renault, its chauffeur dressed in an equally black suit, awaited Fleury. Charlie's thoughts of Paris were mixed with his need to remain at Michelle's side every possible minute.
Charlie managed to notice that the French countryside was very much like the farmlands back in Missouri except for the trees that lined the roads in Spartan-like rows. They were bare of leaves now with their branches cut back severely so that every tree looked to be exactly the same size. The absence of signs of the war prompted Charlie to query Fleury about it.

"Well, Charles, the front lines are well to the north and east of Paris. You'll be seeing more as we get closer to the city."

It amazed Charlie that the war could leave so much of the countryside untouched. After passing through several towns and villages, he began to notice the absence of young men. He saw many old men, women, and children. Uncannily anticipating his question, Michelle said: "Just about every man over the age of eighteen is now in uniform. That's why you see so few. Those you do see are likely invalided—rejected for physical reasons."

They covered the 128-mile trip to Paris in just over four hours with two fuel stops. Gasoline, a commodity only recently available in many of the villages, was becoming scarcer every day. The Renault had two supplementary tanks strapped to the running boards, but the chauffeur, Stephane, had learned to fill up wherever he could. The gasoline—*essence* in French—flowed from hoses attached to large tanks raised high on wooden stands. Charlie saw hand pumps on steel barrels evidently used to fill the larger reservoirs.

During the second fuel stop near Compiègne, Charlie heard and then saw three aircraft flying several hundred feet overhead—*aéronefs*, Fleury called them. Stephane stared just as hard as Charlie at the passing machines, saying almost inaudibly, "*Quelles machines magnifiques*!" The biplanes bore the red white and blue French cockade on their wings, tails, and sides. "Caudrons," said Stephane. They were awkward looking birds from the ground.

Michelle held his hand while he mused about the flying machines, remembering the trio of barnstorming pilots thrilling the crowd in their Morane monoplanes at the Missouri State Fair just last August. Most watching were hoping for a spectacular crash, but fortunately—at least for the intrepid aviators—the bloodthirsty crowd left disappointed.

Since huge supply convoys blocked the western access to the city, they approached Paris from the north. Even there Charlie saw hundreds of wagons drawn by teams of horses, trucks—lorries Michelle called them, and the first large groups of soldiers he'd seen since Le Havre.

Fleury kept up a running commentary about the passing scenes. Keeler heard that the large church at Saint-Denis was the resting-place for France's monarchs. He also learned to identify the various motorcars and trucks, especially those that bore the distinctive diamond Renault trademark.

Entering the city at the Porte de Clichy, Charlie's excitement mounted when he saw the top of the Eiffel Tower in the distance. Eventually, they came to a broad boulevard Fleury called the Champs d'Elysées. Michelle said it meant the Elysian Fields, words Charlie vaguely recalled from his classic literature class meant the place of the blessed dead. The boulevard was the widest street he had ever seen. As they circled *l'Arc de Triomphe*, Fleury told him it had been commissioned by Napoleon in 1806 to honor French soldiers.

Stephane deposited them in front of *l'Hôtel Crillon* facing the Place de la Concorde. Michelle told Charlie it was Fleury's residence in Paris and one of the classiest hotels in all Paris. Michelle's room was part of a suite that housed the whole Fleury family one floor up from the room she said he would have.

On entering his room, the fresh flowers on the dresser and a small candy with a note from the maid on the pillow attested to her claim. Charlie lounged on the bed resting his head on the unusual cylindrical pillows while staring out at the busy Place de la Concorde. He noticed the obelisk dominating the huge square where, according to the hotel guide in the room, Marie Antoinette's head fell along with more than a thousand others during the Revolution. The 3300 year-old pink granite obelisk, he read, came from Luxor, the Valley of the Kings, in Egypt. Charlie wanted to go out and explore, but he dozed off for what seemed like only minutes before a knock at the door jarred him awake.

Michelle, freshly bathed and dressed for dinner, stood demurely at the door, her eyes asking if he was going to invite her in. She looked so lovely that he swept her into his arms, kicked the door closed, and kissed her full on the lips before she could utter a word. Michelle said, "Easy, you savage American. Don't mess up my careful preparations, or we'll never be on time."

Time had become a terrible muddle for him. They'd slowly adjusted the clocks on the *Rochambeau* so the shipboard routine would correspond with daylight as they progressed eastward. Charlie knew that it was dark outside, but the precise hour meant nothing as long as he was with Michelle.

He released Michelle reluctantly. She told him that at dinner she would introduce him to Madame Fleury and some influential men that might be able to help him with his plans. She agreed to meet him in the dining room after he got dressed.

Charlie donned one of the suits his generous cousin had given him. Claude had been excited when they had docked because he'd just learned he was returning to active service with the Navy. He told Charlie he would have little need for civilian clothes.

The gleaming wood, brass and etched glass of the Crillon's dining room reminded Charlie of the *Rochambeau*. The first person Michelle introduced was Madame Fleury. Béatrice Fleury bore an incredible resemblance to his cousin, Claude, and looked a little like his mother. Michelle introduced him to the other diners in the anteroom where they all mingled awaiting the call to dinner.

His head swirled with the names and titles, but one man made a lasting impression on him, Captain Frank Parker from the Embassy. Parker was the first West Pointer Charlie had ever met. During their brief introduction, Charlie learned that Parker had also attended the French Cavalry School at Saumur and now served as an observer and assistant Attaché at the nearby

American Embassy. Parker and his charming wife went out of their way to make Charlie feel comfortable.

He learned that the American expatriate community numbered several influential financiers in its ranks. Some names seemed familiar to Charlie, but the man most eager to meet him and offer his help was Doctor Frederick Gros of the American Hospital and Ambulance Service. Gros handed him a card with his address.

Dinner turned out to be an elaborate four course meal with two wines, followed by a delicate dessert of *mille feuilles* which Michelle told him meant a thousand leaves, a very clever way to name the crème-filled flaky layers of pastry. Charlie devoured every course with great relish, following Michelle in selecting the proper utensil. He was beginning to like this style of life, though he'd get fat and slow eating like that every day. At the same time it nagged him that such luxury seemed incongruous, almost shameful in war. Given the opportunity he would have marveled at his current state in the light of sleeping on cotton bales back in New Orleans.

During the meal, Michelle listened with growing interest to the doctor's description of the fledgling Ambulance Service. She knew of Charlie's aspirations, but hoped this "chance" meeting with Doctor Gros would change his mind.

Doctor Gros asked, "So, Mister Keeler, you intend to enlist in the French Army?"

"*Charlie* please, Doctor. Yes sir, I do. I'm sure your volunteer drivers are doing a swell job, but I came to fight."

"Have you thought about flying, Charlie?" Gros asked.

"Well, we saw some warplanes on our trip here. Monsieur Fleury's driver seems determined to enlist in aviation, but I had never given it much thought." Charlie's notion of the Legion was full of images of manly pursuits, overcoming impossible odds, and supreme glory. Flying didn't quite strike him that way.

Doctor Gros made it his business to find out about every American living in or passing through France, particularly Paris. He served prominently on the Franco-American Friendship Committee, an assemblage of American expatriates. Since the outbreak of the war, Gros or another member of his committee had contacted nearly every American volunteer soon after they arrived in the capital. The outgoing American Ambassador, Mr. Myron T. Herrick, quietly supported Gros and his efforts. The new Ambassador, William Sharp, appeared to be following the same path, though the Embassy had to maintain the appearance of strict neutrality.

Around them, everybody seemed to be talking about the war. Fleury described the horrors of the Prussian occupation in 1870. Though 45 years separated the two conflicts, survivors kept memories of the siege alive. Fleury remembered little as he was only four-years-old at the time, but his parents never let him forget. An infant brother had died of malnutrition when his mother could produce no more milk. Fleury delicately described the way some resorted to rats for food. He pointed to the fire in the large hearth and told them how Parisians had denuded the Bois de Boulogne for firewood.

"Your point, my friend, being that the Germans were savage then and are no less so now, right?" Doctor Gros asked.

Fleury picked up the signal from his wife to change the subject, but not before replying, "Not at all Doctor. It was the Parisians that became savage. The Prussians merely left them no option. After they left, the Commune nearly ended civilization here. War brings no good and often ends in the status quo ante bellum…." He stopped in response to Béatrice's tug on his arm. They got up to adjourn to the ballroom.

"Well, my friend, you are not alone in your quest," Doctor Gros said, stopping Michelle and Charlie before they left the dining room. "A good number of Americans are now on the front with Legion regiments. Some of them want to fly but had to join the Legion first. Bill Thaw from Pittsburgh, for example, is already a trained pilot. He and Bert Hall are just starting military pilot schools this month after their stints in the Legion. A fellow named Cowdin just arrived and is trying to get into flying. That's why I asked you about flying earlier. We may be able to form an American unit."

Charlie unfolded the article on the Rockwells he'd brought from home and showed it to Gros.

"But, of course!" the Doctor exclaimed. His apartment at *23 Avenue du Bois de Boulogne* was a favorite hostel. "Kiffin and Paul Rockwell made a big splash with the ladies during their short stay in Paris. There's also a Charles Johnson from your city driving ambulances up around Dunkirk."

"Chouteau, I think, sir—a founding family."

"The same! See, you are in good company. Near as I know, Charlie, we have about seventy-five Americans in French service and over thirty in our Ambulance organization alone. The Norton-Harjes Ambulance has another twenty-eight. Have you heard about them?"

"No sir." Charlie simply was not interested in the ambulance effort. He had no conception of the path he would have to follow to join the Legion. "Can you tell me more about the way these men got started and how I can follow them?"

"Absolutely," Gros said his eyes twinkling at the thought of increasing the number of Americans involved in the war. "I am meeting a friend Tuesday who has two other young Americans staying with him. I think one is looking to enlist in the *Légion*. Perhaps the two of you can go over together? Les Invalides is where you need to go. I'll even meet you there if you like, but, pardon my suggesting it, why don't you take time to see this city before going off to the fight? Get Michelle to show you around, relax, and enjoy Paris first."

"Thank you kindly, Doctor, for both the advice and assistance," Charlie hesitated to stretch his good fortune any further. First Fleury, then Toussaint, and now Gros. He wondered if there was a limit on patrons—and friends.

Tuesday, then at Les Invalides?" Gros asked with a kind smile.

"Yes sir," Charlie responded tentatively.

"Very well," Gros said bowing slightly to Michelle before leaving them.

After dinner, the guests danced to a full orchestra in the third floor ballroom. Charlie felt painfully out of place even in his cousin's clothes. Were it not for Michelle he would have slipped out quietly. Michelle wore a mauve evening gown cut enticingly low, baring her shoulders and drawing his eyes to the broach perched inches above her bosom. Her beauty drew admiring looks from several beribboned officers at the dance.

The Fleury's rose to dance, leaving the young couple alone. Michelle looked into Charlie's face inquiringly, her eyes twinkling in a teasing invitation to take the floor. He ignored the hint, shrinking a little in his seat, ashamed of his inability to dance.

When the Fleury's returned, the orchestra began again. Madame Fleury, eager to help Charlie relax, asked him to lead her to the floor for the next waltz. Charlie could not think of a reasonable excuse, trapped as he felt in a web of *politesse.*

Madame Fleury laid her hand on his arm and gently steered him to the floor in fluid motions timed to the Bizerte waltz. Charlie wiped the thin line of sweat from his brow and manfully faced his demise. Madame stepped up offering her right hand to his left and he placed his right hand on her corseted waist following the example of the other dancers. His breath came in shallow pants reminiscent of the barely controlled panic he felt before a wrestling match.

Charlie immediately stepped on Madame Fleury's delicate shoe causing her to recoil and almost fall over but for his supporting hand on her waist. She and Charlie swept in clumsy circles with the crowd. Charlie stumbled and faltered stiffly, but gave it his best. Somewhere in him, he thought, lurked a lithe athlete, but that fellow seemed to be on holiday. Turning his head, he caught sight of Michelle gracefully swinging on the arm of a French officer.

Three circuits of the dance floor proved two too many for Madame Fleury. She ushered Charlie to the side and exclaimed: "*Mon Dieu, c'est un Toussaint!*"

Already red from his neck up, hearing the exact same words his mother had said a month earlier knocked Charlie for a loop. He stared at Madame Fleury apologetically and curious at the same time.

Laughing lightly, she said, "Steeck to the driving *mon ami américain*."

Despite this minor disaster, the evening ended well enough. Charlie escorted Michelle to her room forgetting the incredible coincidence of Madame Fleury choosing the same words as his mother. They collapsed on the bed facing the ceiling.

In all the time she had lived with the Fleury's, Michelle had never brought a man to her room. Charlie chuckled to break the tension. "What's so funny, Charlie?"

"Me dancing for one thing, and then feeling jealous all over again seeing you with that officer. I have a lot of nerve just being here let alone thinking I can have you to myself."

Michelle put a finger to his lips changing the subject, "Must you join the Legion? It will break my heart to lose you. Why not consider Doctor Gros' offer to put you in the Ambulance Service?"

He remembered Madame Fleury's comment about sticking to driving, beginning to suspect an elaborate plot to try to persuade him not to go into the Legion.

"You really do care for me that much?"

"Oh Charlie, you fool! Can't you see that I am in love with you?"

He sat up abruptly and leaned over her so their faces were inches apart. "And I with you, but that changes nothing. I can do more to help the cause in the Infantry than I could ever do with the Ambulance people. It is hard to explain, but I mean, *look* at me. What do I have to offer but brute strength? I feel a *calling* to soldier. I didn't know it before coming, but I do now."

He kissed her eyebrows one after the other making her flutter her eyelids and smile. After a few moments he observed, "It's something you said, you know."

"Something I said makes you want to throw your life away in the trenches? Oh, Charlie! I'd sooner cut my tongue out!"

"No, I mean, when you told me about the hospital and the sacrifices people are making I felt ashamed that my country isn't doing more."

"Oh dear, please don't say that! I of all people don't want to be the one responsible for sending you off to be killed." She actually sobbed, pulling him over on top of her.

"Killed?" He said a little too brightly. "I have too much to look forward to in coming back to you."

They kissed long and hard; tasting each other's tongues. Her fingers twined in his curly hair holding his head still while she twisted and turned gently exploring his mouth. Her hair came undone and his cravat somehow disappeared. Charlie's hand closed over the top of a breast that seemed to be struggling to free itself from the fabric covering it. She moaned and kissed him even more passionately. A loud knock at the door startled them.

"*Oui, qui est-ce?*" Michelle mumbled in a breathless small voice.

Chapter 9
Revelations

Paris, January 4, 1915

New Year's Eve with the Flandins left a warm glow in Jack. He was amazed how Willis' resemblance to Jacques-Antoine somehow made their relationship almost familial. On this first ever separation from his family during the holidays, Jack savored the experience. He found Isabelle so tantalizing that he didn't have time to feel homesick or even brood about Sandy.

Isabelle proved a superior tour guide as well. They visited Montmartre, Lafayette's grave, and the statue of Washington behind the impressive Trocadéro. Knowing Haviland had some experience of Paris, she took them off the beaten path ending up at the celebrated *Folies Bergères* in the evening. Jack kept glancing at Isabelle to see her reaction to the bared flesh of the dancers. He did have to admit that the girls were very good at what they did. Isabelle didn't seem fazed by it at all.

The show stirred Jack up and Isabelle seemed to tease him on purpose with glances and frequent little touches, but she did the same with Willis. Back at their apartment he dropped off to sleep toying with an image of Isabelle kicking a shapely leg in the air.

As Flandin promised, he arranged a meeting with Doctor Gros the first Monday of the year. Carefully planning their excursion to make the most out of the trip, Flandin hired a landauette, an open carriage with a folding cover. Horse-drawn conveyances were still popular in Paris in spite of the shortage of horses. Pierre explained his disdain for the noise and noxious gases of motors.

He took them on a circuit of the Jardin d'Acclimatation at the edge of the Bois de Boulogne. Even in the midst of winter, the garden was worth seeing. They passed the racetrack at Longchamps on the way to their meeting. Flandin told them they were meeting the doctor at *Les Cascades*, a restaurant in the park, at half past noon.

Neither Jack nor Willis had the slightest idea what to expect, but they looked forward to meeting other Americans. Their circuit of the park, gardens, and racetrack ended at the restaurant.

"Look at that Willis," Jack said as they approached the elegant building nestled in the trees and flanked by two natural-looking waterfalls. The sight of flowing water and greenery in January impressed Jack.

"Be frozen solid back home, wouldn't it?" Haviland replied, now used to Jack's almost refreshing naiveté.

Flandin made the introductions once they settled in the saloon room. Gros immediately made both Jack and Willis feel as if they were the first and only American volunteers he had ever welcomed (though they knew from Flandin that he had sponsored dozens). Another American joined them, a man both Jack and Willis knew by reputation, William K. Vanderbilt, scion of the Vanderbilt family of New York.

The Americans conversed in rapid English leaving Flandin somewhat flummoxed until Willis valiantly tried to translate. Gros and Vanderbilt smiled at each other as if at a private joke. Finally, Gros said: "Flandin, you sly fox, two years at Oxford and you can't handle English?"

"English, indeed!" Flandin ejaculated. "Even three days with these two fine young men isn't enough to tune my ear to your dialect. You may as well be speaking Bohemian."

"Please excuse our host, boys," Vanderbilt rocked back chuckling. "We've been bad, hey Pierre? Speaking not only English but fast *American* English."

"*Ce n'est pas Anglais*," Pierre Flandin mumbled. "Perhaps you could try to throw a bit of the King's English into your gibberish just to humor me?"

Lunch at *Les Cascades,* is never a quick affair. The conversation loosened markedly after the third round of wine. Flandin only sipped, but the older Americans quaffed their *Chateau Grand Cru de l'Hermitage '98* in deep swallows.

Doctor Gros proved to be an ebullient man. The doctor pumped them with questions about the States, and filled Jack and Willis in on the not yet sanctioned American Ambulance Service, headquartered at the American Hospital at Neuilly, one of the western suburbs of the city.

"The little hospital where I work has grown rapidly to accommodate the overflow from all the other Paris hospitals. Yet, we are barely able to keep up with all the new volunteers," Gros began. "French authorities tell us that they can't meet the demand for ambulances and drivers, so it seemed logical to put some of the men looking to help to work as drivers. Then, what do you suppose happens?" Without waiting for an answer, Gros told them how the French squashed the proposal, citing security considerations. This happened in September after a rash of foreign spies turned up posing as volunteers for the *Légion*. "Frustrated with the system, our group outfitted a number of donated cars as ambulances and quietly dispatched them up north near Dunkirk.

"Now, a man named A. Piatt Andrew, a former assistant Secretary of State in Theodore Roosevelt's administration, is working on expanding the effort. Almost all of the drivers are college students or graduates. Mr. Andrew thinks in grand terms, envisioning hundreds of ambulances and drivers, even thousands, sponsored and manned by Americans."

"We heard about this Andrew in England," Haviland pointed out.

"A godsend if you ask me. There are never enough drivers. The job had its hazards," Gros explained. Accidents and German fire had already claimed several ambulances.

After lunch, Gros asked if they wanted to cable messages to their families. He offered to forward any return messages. When they asked how much it would cost, he waved his hand pointing to Vanderbilt. A waiter produced two French telegraph forms that they completed immediately.

Willis wrote his mother, who lived alone in Saint Paul since the death of his father ten years earlier.

"Haviland, you appear to be a man of some experience," Vanderbilt observed. "You will be an asset here, I'm sure. What's your background, son?"

Haviland said he had learned the trade of electrician's apprentice in the Navy before going back to college. "I would have re-enlisted to become an officer if America was in this show, but, alas, here I am. I want to give flying a go. There's a future in aviation unless I miss my guess."

Gros brightened up at this. "Like I've been telling you Vandy, we need a bigger voice in the headquarters to make it easier for our boys to get into flying."

"Freddie, I already agreed to help, but sticking our noses in riles up the Germans and embarrasses the ambassador. It's well enough we're pushing volunteer drivers. Until Wilson gets a declaration of war we have to watch ourselves."

Jack only heard a few words of this conversation while he tried to compose his message. He'd already posted at least ten letters home since their arrival. He was happy to send Gros's address so he could at least start getting some mail himself.

Leaving the restaurant at close to 2:30, Jack wondered how the French could stay so thin with sumptuous two-plus-hour feasts at midday. Though he and Willis were ready to take a long nap on the trip back to the Flandin's, "Old Pierre" had other ideas. Guiding the gelding in the carriage's harness, he headed south to the Seine and continued back into the city along the right bank. At the Pont d'Iéna he crossed to the left bank. Seeing the Eiffel Tower again, Jack thought they were going back there.

Flandin kept up a running commentary, never mentioning his ultimate destination. He spoke of the *arrondissements* arranged snailshell-like from one to twenty starting at *L'Ile de la Cité* in the center and winding clockwise inside the trace of the old walls of Paris. Soon they were in the court of the gold-domed *Les Invalides*. At the grand gate Flandin explained the origin of the building as a hospital and home for veterans of the Napoleonic wars. It also provided offices for the Minister of Defense and the Army, as well as a repository of artifacts from France's long and glorious history of combat. Flandin's English, reinforced by their repast, continued to improve. He showed them the cannon surrounding the center court and the captured German staff car and artillery piece displayed at one end.

His reason for stopping there remained a mystery until he ushered Jack and Willis into the building that dominated the grounds. Inside, a hushed air of solemnity contrasted starkly with the bustle on the city streets. There in the middle directly under the dome stood a giant monument in reddish wood polished to a high luster—a sort of box or arc with elaborately formed curved carvings at the corners. Flandin whispered "*Napoléon reste ici.*" It took a few seconds for that to sink in. Willis looked at Jack to see if he understood. Jack just shook his head. He thought Napoleon died at Saint Helena in exile. How could he be here? How could the French, so fond of their sense of liberty, honor an Emperor, an absolute monarch?

"*Gloire*," said Flandin, seeing the confusion in the American's faces. "It is for the Glory of France more than for the man himself." It would take a long time for them to understand this paradox. Wasn't the revolution fought and heads rolled to end dictatorships of the few and the privileged?

Flandin led them to an office located in one wing of the U-shaped building where he introduced Commandant La Garde, Chief of the Foreign Legion recruiting office. La Garde explained the relatively simple process of enlisting, all the while managing not to look at Willis and Jack like a hungry vulture. The line of persons stretching down the corridor was part of the two hundred or so recruits signing up every day since October, according to La Garde. Roughly half of them passed the physical screening. Missing fingers, teeth, toes, hearing, sight, or other debilitations accounted for the remainder.

The French *Commandant*, a rank equivalent to major, asked if they were ready to enlist. Willis nodded without hesitating. Jack shook his head nervously. Flandin convinced Willis, fortuitously as it turned out, that he could come back later in the week without missing any of the war. Jack was sure Haviland would have happily signed up on the spot. As for himself, he couldn't wait to get out of harm's way.

Jack watched the way his friend handled the affection showered on him by the Flandins. Haviland seemed a saint to him. Jack appreciated his self-effacement. Only Isabelle's attraction to Willis marred the picture for Jack. When Willis asserted that he had no interest in romance, Jack felt a rush of excitement.

Haviland received an answer to his wire the next day. It obviously disturbed him, but he kept the details to himself until later when he announced that he would have to return to the United States as soon as he could. Jack wasn't able to wring the slightest detail from him. Haviland assured him he would return as soon as he could. Jack wanted to believe him, but couldn't imagine making two more crossings. Where would he get the money?

The Flandin's were disappointed by Haviland's news, Isabelle more than anyone else save Willis himself. Jack wondered if she was feeling the loss of her brother all over again. With Haviland's concurrence, they decided to continue with their plans for a cocktail party to wish him *bon voyage*.

With Isabelle on his arm, ostensibly to translate, Jack related the events of their reception in England, describing the strange greeting by the American, the impeccable Sergeant Major, and the impressive French colonel. When he described the latter, mentioning the name *de Lafourcade*, three jaws dropped in unison.

"*Mais, c'est pas vrai*!" exclaimed Berangère Flandin.

"*Impossible*!" added Pierre.

Confused, Jack looked to Willis for support, but Haviland looked equally confused.

"De Lafourcade was Jacques-Antoine's regimental commander at Craonnelle." Isabelle finally said, shedding some light on their reaction to hearing the name. "He was slain in the same battle. Surely we would have known if he had survived. Why, we were in England at the same time as you! How could this be?"

Willis, temporizing, said: "Jack didn't mention the colonel's missing arm. Perhaps he survived the battle after all?"

A lieutenant colonel from the French Army staff overheard the conversation. He whispered something to Pierre Flandin who slowly smiled as the mystery of the resurrected colonel unraveled. *"Mais bien sûr*!" he exclaimed, "*Incroyable, deux comme ça en service ensemble*!"

Jack couldn't keep up until Willis asked: "There was a second Colonel de Lafourcade?"

The staff officer nodded, perceiving the Americans' surprise though he only caught a word or two of their English. "*Jumeaux*, how do you say eet? *Tweens*, *c'est ça*?"

He went on to explain in rapid French, translated now by the recovered Isabelle. The two cavalry officers had both volunteered for the Legion at the beginning of the war. Both were senior lieutenant colonels and graduates of the Ecole de Guerre, the prestigious French War College. Gervais had already commanded his cavalry regiment for six months, but the mobilization caught his brother, Didier, between assignments. Gervais led his regiment in three attacks on the Marne before having his arm blown off by a machine gun bullet in September 1914. He refused to be invalided and obtained posting to England as Attaché after two months in the hospital.

Didier, the one known to the Flandins, had replaced their son's original commander, a Breton whose health failed during the first month of the war. Didier, like his brother, had entered combat with his regiment just before the attacks that were all part of the Marne defense. He led his regiment in the terrible assault on the heavily defended Chemin des Dames. Only two officers of the regiment escaped wounding or death; Didier not among them. The lieutenant colonel from the staff held the listeners in rapt attention, his pauses for Isabelle's translation increasing the tension. He told them the story, now circulating in the offices of the General Staff. The general commanding the Moroccan Division had to nearly physically restrain the surviving twin in his hospital bed after telling him of Didier's death. Both Jack and Willis listened incredulously.

Jack felt Isabelle's arm grip his and had to reach to support her as the officer described the battle that eventually cost her brother's life. Nevertheless, the general effect on the Flandins and those around them was palliative. Pride and honor seemed to lift their spirits as they imagined the one-armed Gervais struggling to get up to go to his dead twin brother's side.

The time to take Haviland to the Gare de Saint Lazare for his trip to Le Havre arrived too soon, provoking farewells far more emotional than warranted. Haviland's uncanny resemblance to Jacques-Antoine undoubtedly triggered the scene made by the women. Madame Flandin cried and dabbed at her cheeks with a handkerchief while a woman guest comforted her. Isabelle nearly broke down completely, turning to her father saying "*pas encore, Papa,* not again."

Relieved to get outside in the cool air, Buck and Haviland followed Flandin to a waiting Peugeot, his sole concession to modern transport. Jack offered to take the wheel. Flandin, drained by the emotional scene inside, willingly ceded. "It is very close. We'll be back before dinner. I'll show you the way. You do know how to drive these damned things?"

Jack chuckled. "Yessir. You just navigate and keep speaking English and we'll be fine."

Haviland would board the *Rochambeau* on January 7. Flandin told Jack that Dr. Gros and Mr. Vanderbilt had tried to pay for Haviland's transportation to Le Havre. Willis refused, producing a check and purchasing passage on the French steamer at the same time. When Jack heard this, he wondered why Haviland hadn't bought a ticket to come to France rather than ride the British destroyer like the rest of the penniless lot. Another mystery he would keep to himself.

After returning to find the Flandin women recovered and busy placing guests at the table, Pierre and Jack took their seats as Flandin called for a toast to Buck's impeccable driving. "You have a job with me any time you want my young friend."

An hour later Jack and Isabelle resumed their *pas de deux* as the dinner party stretched into the evening. Isabelle seemed to have recovered. Jack couldn't know that she suffered similar bouts of uncontrollable tears almost daily since her brother's funeral.

"We have a tradition Monsieur Jack," she said steering him away from the knot of people in the dining room.

"A tradition?"

"You have a—how do you say *petite amie*—a special girl back home?"

"No," he answered a little too quickly.

"Well, then there will be no harm. I will be your *marraine*."

He smiled, thrilled that she wanted to be anything to him. His smile faded when she explained that a *marraine* was a sort of godmother.

She tried to explain, "We send you, our godsons—*filleuls*—socks and other necessities. You write us. We write you back. You come to visit us when you are back. Like a sister, no?"

Jack's disappointed expression escaped her notice. He let his chin drop before slowly responding, "sister…" letting the word trail away.

"But Monsieur Jack," she began again, "have I said something wrong?" He was *Monsieur Jack* and the Flandin's all called Haviland *Weellice.*

"No, Isabelle. You have said nothing wrong. It's just that I…well…I have two little sisters at home. When I think of them and you I don't think I could ever treat you as a sister."

Her cheeks reddened. She put her hand on his and whispered "Not my brother, my *filleul,* not your sister, your *marraine.*" Her emphasis on these words implied something he could not guess, but her touch was more than sisterly.

"*Mais, certainement, Mademoiselle*!" Jack ventured in words he tried for the first time. "I would be honored to have you as my friend—*marraine* if you prefer." Jack, an optimist by birth, thought nothing would keep him from a long life, wife, children, and grandchildren. It didn't cross his mind that these knowing French women offered whatever *comforts* they could—many different degrees of that telling word, chaste and un—in the knowledge that their "godchildren" were likely never to return.

With Willis gone, Jack felt a little out of his element. Grateful for Isabelle's friendship and for her parents' hospitality, he nonetheless knew he had to get out on his own. He figured it best to wait until the morning to announce his departure. The Flandins were still nursing the loss of their surrogate son. Although Jack didn't think they would be as pained by his departure, he didn't want to chance it by prolonging his stay. Isabelle excited him. He wondered what kissing her would be like. There was something exotic about the thought of kissing a beautiful Frenchwoman.

Chapter 10
More Revelations and an Assault

Paris, The Hôtel Crillon, January 1915

An urgent feminine response to Michelle's "who's there?" caused her to bound from the bed and race to the door. Without pausing to straighten herself out she turned and waved Charlie into the other room. She opened the door to find Madame Fleury in her nightgown, obviously upset about something. Mindful of the ruffled bedclothes and the man's cravat lying on the floor beside the bed, Michelle wondered if it was because of them. They conversed in French far too rapid for Charlie to understand, though he did catch the name *David* and something about *malade*.

Madame soon left the room and Michelle rushed to get Charlie. "That was close! The first time I have a man here and I thought we were caught, but no, thank God. It's David. They've sent for the doctor. I must go at once. Oh my dear Charlie, look at you!" she said smiling, relieved and disappointed at the same time. "We will have to continue this another time. Madame Fleury is beside herself for leaving the boy alone in his room while we partied. I just hope it is nothing serious. Go to bed, sleep well and think of me." She pinned her hair and rushed from the room.

Later in the morning, he woke from a dream in which he and Michelle were gliding smoothly to the sounds of an orchestra. He sat up puzzled, wondering how he could have learned to dance overnight. As full consciousness returned, he remembered where he was and where he'd been before he stumbled back to his room the night before. He realized it was Sunday.

The crisis with young David turned out to be nothing more than a cold with a slightly elevated temperature. Michelle had stayed with him throughout the night and was sleeping soundly when Charlie gingerly tapped at her door. When she didn't respond, he guessed at what happened and headed down to the café for breakfast.

Charlie could not get used to the French idea of *petit déjeuner*, a meal in name only. The bread and croissant were truly excellent, but he would dearly love to have a couple of eggs and a rasher of bacon. He buttered some bread and spooned some *confiture*, a thick jam of some sort of berry, on top. Stephane, the chauffeur, came up to his table, and asked if he might join him.

It wouldn't occur to the American that servants didn't eat with their employers. He motioned Stephane to sit down, hoping to practice some French. Stephane looked to be a year or two older than Charlie. Keeler wondered how to ask the man why he wasn't in the service. His attempt to form the question politely flopped.

Stephane smiled. "*Mais, c'est simple*!" he explained. Certain soldier-aged men employed in essential industries or positions were not called to service. Doctors, some factory workers, and members of the government could also be exempted. He himself worked at Renault as a mechanic installing motors. He said he was temporarily on loan to Fleury whose original chauffeur was with a regiment of infantry. Stephane loved his current job that included being a bodyguard for the Fleury family. Most executives and government members had engaged security agents since the scare of August when a rash of German saboteurs seemed to be storming the gates of Paris.

"I know what you are thinking. You are here offering your life for my country and here I am in Paris. How can I live with myself you are wondering?"

Charlie replied: "Yes, I guess I do wonder about that, but you said you were a bodyguard too. Do you carry a gun?"

"*Alors*," Stephane nodded, "I too am troubled not to be *aux armes* with my countrymen. Monsieur Fleury has promised to let me go in March so that I may join the aviation either as a *mécanicien* or *aviateur*."

Charlie stopped him and asked: "I understand the *aviateur*, pilot, right? But what is *mécanicien*?"

Stephane told Charlie about the soldiers they were training at the plant on the Renault aeroplane motors. They were *mécanos, mécaniciens*. After a little more discussion, they arrived at the English word *mechanic* as the equivalent. Charlie could now see why Stephane had shown so much interest in the aircraft they had seen on the trip to Paris. He asked a few more questions as they finished their coffee.

Fleury entered the dining room looking around and catching Stephane's eye. Getting up to join his boss, Stephane told Charlie that he was a very lucky man to have Michelle so devoted to him.

Charlie asked after David and Michelle. Fleury said his boy seemed to be fine enough, considering the cold, but that Michelle, on the other hand, was not herself.

"She fairly floats as she moves these past several days. There was a time when I could not get her to take a break from my boys or my paperwork. Now she can't seem to focus on anything. She must be very tired after the trip. No doubt you have a great deal of responsibility for her state of mind, my young friend."

If Alexandre had not been smiling knowingly, this statement would have alarmed Charlie. He sat there stirring his coffee before saying, "I'm not sure how much I have to do with Michelle's state of mind, sir, but I can tell you that I am very taken with her. I am also very impressed with Madame Fleury. She must be a very strong lady to deal so gracefully with all my clumsiness last night."

Still smiling, Fleury leaned closer to Charlie and began: "You will take the car and Stephane for the next three days. I want you to see as much of Paris as you can before you leave. Michelle will undoubtedly insist on going with you, and I've decided I can get along without her for a couple of days. Meanwhile, would you care to join me for *la messe* at the Madeleine? It is just up the street. I'm afraid the ladies will have to go to a later service. Oh, forgive me, it is Catholic."

"As am I sir."

They found their way to the front of the imposing Madeleine. The pews were packed. An older priest celebrated the Mass. Charlie found the Latin familiar enough, but the sermon baffled him. He found it difficult to follow both because of the French and because of the echo in the cavernous church.

They began a whirlwind tour of the City of Light that afternoon. Michelle planned to show Charlie places she hadn't even visited herself. Montmartre, the Louvre, the Chateau de Vincennes, and Versailles were on her list.

The ominous presence of war seemed distant and unreal. Charlie had never been happier in his life. Their embraces became more intimate, though by some tacit agreement, they held back from completing their union. When they pried themselves apart and returned to their respective rooms, both felt physically and emotionally frustrated, dreading his imminent departure.

The day before Charlie was to enlist dawned sunny and unseasonably warm. Michelle suggested a trip to the Bois de Boulogne where they could ride in a carriage, stroll around the pond, and drop in on Doctor Gros. She placed a call to the American Hospital at Neuilly after their breakfast in the hotel. Gros agreed to meet them at his apartment for lunch.

"Let's leave Stephane behind and take the Métro," Charlie suggested. "I would like to go up the Eiffel Tower with you this morning for a last look at the whole city. After lunch we can tour the Bois if it is still nice out."

"Stephane would like that. I'm sure he is tired of seeing us snuggling like a couple of teenagers. You know I have never been atop the Eiffel myself? If we leave now, we may even have time to go up on *l'Arc de Triomphe*. I like the idea of embracing you from dizzying heights." She chuckled at something humorous she thought of when considering the two monuments.

"What's so amusing Michelle?" Charlie prodded until her face reddened. She steadfastly refused to tell him how she saw the Eiffel Tower as a giant phallic symbol and the Arch as a fitting female counterpart. She might be a progressive and liberal woman, but such thoughts were better left unexpressed.

"Please Charlie, allow a woman some secrets." Remembering their struggle over the Captain's table, he decided not to push the issue.

Charlie learned a few new words and phrases under her tutelage. She spoke French to him when they were alone and English when there were others within earshot. He did his best, wishing his mother had taught him French as a child. At the top of the Eiffel Tower she started with the gold dome of Les Invalides as a point of departure. She then grilled him on the sites they had visited as they walked around the observation deck. She made him repeat the name of each place in French.

Starting from the Southeast and going counter-clockwise he pointed and said: "Le Quai d'Orsay, l'Ile de la Cité, la Cathédrale Notre Dame, le Louvre, la Bastille, l'Opéra, Montmartre—how am I doing?"

"You've been an apt pupil, my dear Charles. How is it that you were failing anything at university?"

He was always attuned to her English mannerisms. She said *at* university and *at* hospital, where he would have used *the*. Her question made him pause before he cleverly replied: "I never had so charming a teacher, Mademoiselle, nor have I been distracted by other young ladies in your classroom."

"And a good thing that!"

"Yes, and keeping the la's and le's straight is so simple." Charlie felt like a performing seal as he turned around the observation deck announcing the names, arriving finally full circle at "L'Ecole Militaire," the last major landmark before Les Invalides. He surprised himself at how well he remembered each place and their names in French. He had always learned best by association. Every one of these famous places stood out in his mind for the dress or scent Michelle wore, the meaningful, soulful glances they had shared, the kisses they had stolen. She filled every place with her warmth and beauty.

The Métro took them in minutes to the station nearest the Arch. They had saved this monument for last. Michelle explained its significance and its history as they climbed the stairs to the top. Though less than half the height of the Eiffel Tower, the Arch gave them a commanding view of another part of the city.

Charlie could see the length of the Champs Elysées to the Place de La Concorde and Les Tuilleries beyond. Each road radiating away from the massive monument to Napoleon's victories was lined with stone and brick buildings filled with shops, restaurants, and apartments. Taxis, omnibuses, carriages, and pedestrians crowded nearly every street that January morning. Michelle pointed to the northwest towards the suburb of Neuilly where they were meeting Doctor Gros, asking him if he wanted to go to the hospital early to see some of the patients.

Suspecting her of trying to shake his resolve to join the Legion by the sight of mutilated soldiers, Charlie nevertheless agreed. He was willing to see the effects of the war up close, believing it would help steel him to the horrors he might face.

He recalled Fleming in Crane's *Red Badge of Courage* and the young man's struggle with his fears of cowardice and running from the enemy. Charlie had always thought the feeling must be very much like the butterflies he felt before a wrestling match. He'd been able to overcome his apprehensions in individual physical combat on the mats. Would he be able to master himself in the lethal ring of modern war?

Fleming's description of the dead soldier's fish-like eyes and of ants crawling on his gray skin had always fascinated Charlie in a macabre sort of way. He hoped he could handle the carnage, though he had yet to see a dead person.

"We can go if you like, though I suspect I'll be seeing enough blood in due time. Is there somebody in particular you want to see?"

"No, but I was hoping to meet some of the drivers from the Ambulance. According to our Doctor Gros, there are some aspiring pilots in that bunch. I would be a whole lot more at ease with you taking up flying." She reasoned that the life expectancy of pilots must be longer than that of the ground-bound soldiers. From what she heard and read, most aeroplanes were not even armed.

The Métro extended to the edge of the city, discharging them several blocks from the hospital. They decided to walk since they still had an hour before meeting Gros. Coming up the steps they found themselves surrounded by a group of six ruffians. Charlie, sensing danger, pulled Michelle closer. The men stopped climbing, allowing other pedestrians to pass while blocking Charlie and Michelle and nudging them off the stairs into a maintenance alcove off to the side. Charlie didn't dare separate himself from Michelle. They had to be after her. Kidnapped, she might bring a handsome ransom from the Renault executive.

In the close confines of the alcove Charlie was confident he could disable one or two of the assailants long enough to make a break for it. He backed Michelle into the nearest wall putting himself between them and her. Two of the men guarded the opening while the others circled the couple, wary of the strong-looking American.

"*Nous sommes armés! Résistez pas!*" one growled. Charlie understood well enough, but he chose that moment to cold cock the speaker with a boilermaker punch he had never learned on the wrestling mat. The man dropped and the other three attacked as one. Charlie locked one man's head under his left arm, simultaneously toppling another with a sideswipe kick. The third backed away, hailing the other two. Meanwhile, the man in Charlie's grip went limp, his brain starved for air. Down to four to one, Charlie charged the nearest ruffian with his head down, knocking the man's breath out and slamming him hard against a stanchion. It began to look as though he would disable them one at a time, but Michelle's screaming galvanized the remaining kidnappers. Two lunged at Michelle, distracting Charlie enough for the third to bring a weighted leather blackjack down on the back of Charlie's head, stunning him and driving him slowly to his knees. Covering Michelle's mouth, the remaining three began to hustle her out of the alcove and down the stairs before Charlie could rise from his knees.

Shaking his head in a vain attempt to clear the cobwebs, Charlie struggled to his feet, feeling both nauseous and distressed at the thought of Michelle's abduction. He staggered to the stairs, stepping over one of the men. Just as he reached the steps, he saw Michelle, rushing to him! She'd escaped. *Need to get out of here,* he thought, still having trouble focusing his eyes. Michelle stopped him as he tried to pull her up the stairs.

"Wait!" she shouted. "I'm fine. Relax. Let me look at your head."

"But, the men!" Charlie said.

"Under guard," he heard a familiar voice say in French. Out stepped Stephane, brandishing an American M 1911, .45 caliber automatic, one of the few weapons Charlie recognized.

Two gendarmes followed close behind, quickly cuffing the remaining assailants before they revived enough to cause any more trouble. Charlie realized that Stephane was not only armed, but also under orders to guard them even when not driving them around.

"Oh Charlie, you seem to be always having to rescue me." Michelle said as she checked his scalp to make sure he wasn't bleeding. She found only a nasty lump. "I didn't know Stephane was following us, but thank God!"

She told how Stephane had fallen behind them in the crowd leaving l'Arc de Triomphe, barely getting on the same train as them in the Métro. He'd been trapped several cars back and hampered at the Neuilly station by the press of bodies. Consequently, he didn't catch up with them until he came upon the ambush.

"Ambush?" Charlie asked. "You mean this was *planned*. They were waiting for us?"

"Not now," Michelle said, concern for him showing on her face. "Come, let's go. We can have you checked at the hospital."

As they approached the high-fenced, cream-colored building, they saw a steady stream of ambulances coming and going. They were lined up at the entrance marked "Urgences" in big red letters.

Though other signs in French and English indicated this was the American Hospital, Michelle pointed out that the sick and wounded were a mix of French, Belgian, and British soldiers. The staff was composed of many French nationals though most of the doctors were Americans. She had learned much on her visits here with Madame Fleury.

Charlie began to understand why she wanted to show him this place. It was an international effort at life-saving and alleviating pain. With all the evil of war hanging like a pall over them, here was a place of refuge, and of great suffering. Here caring hands tried to undo or repair the damage of warfare. He was glad she had brought him to see the hospital.

In the small lobby at the entryway to the hospital, several men in the uniform of the Ambulance, a khaki ensemble with a large red cross on the right sleeve and an American flag sewn to the left breast pocket, lounged in visitor's chairs. Charlie approached one of the men who showed much more interest in Michelle than in Charlie. The man introduced himself as Elliot Cowdin from New York, one of the men Gros had mentioned.

Cowdin had been driving only a few days. When Michelle asked him if he had thought about flying, Cowdin broke into a very bright smile.

"I have indeed miss. I have indeed. In fact, I am in contact with a couple of other Americans over here who are thinking about trying to form an American-only squadron. Some of my fellows have already flown as civilians. I just might enlist in the aviation myself."

Elliot, at least five years older than Charlie, listened to Charlie's plan to enlist in the Foreign Legion with a knowing look on his face. He'd carried some of those boys.

"Are there any others here who are planning on joining aviation?" Michelle asked.

"Not as I know miss. There are four of us in my section, Balsley, Johnson, Hill, and Rumsey, who have been mulling it over. You might ask Doctor Gros about it since he seems to be encouraging the drivers to give it a go. Kinda curious isn't it? Here they need more and more drivers and he is pushing us to join aviation."

It was paradoxical, Charlie thought. He filed it with other questions to ask at lunch. The good doctor was beginning to look like more than he at first appeared. They would not have long to wait to pose their questions.

"You know Chouteau Johnson?" Charlie asked.

"You know we signed up at about the same time? Chouteau spent a good month rooting around in Paris looking up his family and trying to get some of their affairs in order. Did you know that his grandfather fought with the French in the Franco-Prussian War? Boy can he parlez, that Chouteau. I wish I had his tongue. Pity he isn't here. Half the section is based up by Dunkirk. I'm on my way back tomorrow. Fancy another Saint Louis fellow. Write your name here," Cowdin said, producing a slip of paper, "and I'll tell Chouteau to look for you."

"I don't really know him. He's just from my town."

This would not be the last time that Charlie would marvel at how small the world could be. He wondered why Johnson had chosen the ambulance over the Legion.

Doctor Gros met them in the lobby at precisely noon. Michelle quickly related the details of the attack and asked him to look at Charlie. Gros turned to Charlie and held a little light up in front of his face. Looking into first one pupil and then the other, he then asked Charlie to follow the light with his eyes. Next, he looked at the bump, noticing the thick muscles joining the neck to the base of Charlie's head.

"It looks like you won't be getting out of enlisting for this, I'm sorry to say," Gros announced, his examination completed. He led them to his own motorcar parked in the front of the hospital and off they drove to his apartment some three miles away in the midst of the Bois de Boulogne. He listened to their account of the attack, carefully concealing his growing anger. "So Stephane is the one following us?"

Both turned around to look. Sure enough, the chauffeur was in a car behind them, a gendarme at his side at the wheel! *Was the threat to Michelle that great*, Charlie wondered?

"Bloody nuisance, this mess. Between the legitimate spies and hired hoods, we all have to watch ourselves. Fleury sure has you well protected, Michelle." After a moment he asked, "Do you know Monsieur Flandin?"

"Yes, a friend of Fleury's. Isn't he in the government now?" Michelle replied.

"Well, he is back in country with a couple of Americans in tow, Minnesotans, I hear. Somehow, he picked them up off the ferry. Looks like we might get one of them as a driver. Anyway, Flandin has hired a team of Pinkerton guards, of all things, not to protect him, but his wife and daughter. As if we don't have enough to worry about with the war!"

"If you are still intent on it, all is set for us tomorrow, Charles," Doctor Gros went on, changing the subject once again. "I will try to meet you at 9:00 A.M. There will be a medical examination that I might be able to waiver for you. After that, they will have you sign the enlistment papers. There is no oath of allegiance other than to agree to obey the orders of the Legion officers and go where they send you. A new group is leaving for Valbonne for training tomorrow afternoon."

Michelle sat next to Charlie in the back seat of Gros's Citröen, tightly gripping his hand, shivering slightly after the narrow escape. "Do you suppose those men have been following us, waiting for an opportunity to attack?" she asked, unable to forget her recent terror. No one tried to answer. They were at the doctor's door.

A woman in maid's clothing greeted them, taking their coats and hats. Doctor Gros then introduced his wife, Honora, a Pennsylvanian he'd transplanted to France. Honora struck them as no match for the hyperactive doctor. A slender blond, she didn't look like she could handle the sight of blood let alone be the wife of a surgeon. It was a very mistaken impression.

"Let me introduce Mrs. Weeks, one of the linchpins of the American community here. Some call her *Maman Légion*—her son is in the legion." Gros said as he presented his other guests. "And this is Monsieur Jarousse de Sillac, a friend of mine and of all Americans.... Alice, Jarousse, this is Charles Keeler, and I think you already know Miss de Vincent. Come in everybody."

They had arrived at around 12:20 and weren't finishing until very close to 3:00 P.M. Every detail of the meal had been orchestrated, from the seating arrangement to the centerpieces of crossed French and American flags surrounded by flowers. Mrs. Gros' hand became increasingly evident as she quietly guided the servants and kept the conversation flowing. Charlie learned that de Sillac was an influential French official and that the other American woman, Mrs. Ovington, was a widow with a son driving an ambulance.

After listening to the account of the failed attack on the young couple, the listeners nodded and shook their heads, some relating similar incidents. Soon, however, the general drift of the conversation revolved not around Charlie or Michelle, but on attitudes in the United States toward the war and what could be done to get the Americans to join the Allied cause.

"It is so clear to me!" Gros said looking from one to the other at the table. "We have to do something to get our country to wake up."

"After the Marne, Père Joffre has made no progress. I think we need the United States on our side," Jarousse de Sillac observed.

"Before Russia falters," Alice Weeks added, revealing a concern shared by many of them.

"Yes, and look at Turkey. I read that the Turks are siding with Germany," Mrs. Ovington said.

"And Italy isn't stable even with old Garibaldi at the helm, Honora Gros commented, adding yet another female voice to the conversation.

Charlie came away very impressed. Everyone at the table had an opinion supported by knowledge of the current situation. The women had something to say and the men listened. He hadn't paid much attention to the house itself, but he felt rather than observed its orderliness and elegance. The meal must have been very good, but he didn't have much appetite with his head still throbbing from the blows. The passion these people felt was remarkable.

Charlie sensed he was putting together what he had been searching for ever since his bold announcement to his father about joining the Legion. Real people facing real problems woke him to the fact that this war was more than a little game or adventure for Charlie Keeler. He caught a glimpse of his personal insignificance compared to the talk of nations and alliances. He also sensed his personal commitment growing from something intangible into a powerful purpose or goal. Between falling in love and discovering this new mission in life, Charlie was being transformed. He thought about his father for the first time in days and how differently he'd been treated here than at home. Home. Would he go back any time soon?

Chapter 11
Ambulances

January 7, 1915, American Hospital, Neuilly, France

The day after Willis left for Le Havre Jack donned the khaki uniform of the fledgling American Ambulance Service. They would receive a meager two francs per day from the French, supplemented by an allowance of ten francs from the Ambulance Service. Fortunately, they didn't have to pay for food or Jack would have run out of money in less than a month. He knew he couldn't ask for money from home, though his uncle had promised a stipend of $50 monthly if he needed it.

Jack joined a dozen other volunteers in the training section. The section leader was a Spaniard named Félix Alejandro, a most friendly and amiable chief. Self-taught in French and English, Félix exuded energy. Jack, always alert for someone to emulate, decided on the spot to study Alejandro's every move.

After the administrative preliminaries, Alejandro ushered the recruits to the hospital motor park adjacent to the Hippodrome in the Bois de Boulogne for driving trials. Jack's professed driving skills led Alejandro to give him the first shot at proving his mettle. After some preliminary instructions on the controls of the converted Renault taxi, Jack got in and easily negotiated the serpentine course. Some other volunteers fared less successfully. Jack received his brevet as driver after the first training session. Most of the rest had to stay for the *stage de conducteurs*, driver's training.

Over the next week, the volunteers alternated driving instruction with classes in the hospital on emergency first aid. Their mission was not to treat the wounded but to transport them. They would pick them up from clearing and aid stations, normally after the casualties had received immediate care by medics or battalion surgeons. The most seriously wounded would remain in field hospitals near the front until they could be stabilized. Many would not survive long enough to require further transport. Those who did often suffered from serious wounds that could need attention en route. This was the purpose of the rudimentary instruction Jack and the others received.

A four-hour stretcher drill taxed all of them. In teams of three, the recruits had to carry one of their numbers on a hilly course through the woods for up to a quarter of a mile against the clock. The losing team had to repeat the course. Jack's team consisted of a huge New Yorker about 35 years old, and a former shoe salesman from Connecticut who had never lifted anything heavier than a size 12 boot. When Jack and George, the New Yorker, carried David, who weighed about 140, they flew through the course. David and George made good time with the 175-pound Jack, but when George got on the stretcher, it was another story altogether.

Jack tried taking the front position reasoning that he could pull the load better than the weaker David could. On the command *lift*, Jack jerked up his end. David gave a hearty tug, losing grip of one side, dumping the hapless George on the ground. Switching ends, they tried it again more slowly, managing to just clear the ground with their 240 pound load. A few stumbling steps confirmed that they would never make it through the course in time. George tried to dangle his legs to help, only to unbalance his bearers enough to find his butt on the ground again. After a futile 45 minutes of sweating and swearing, Alejandro came to them with a smile on his face. He took the left handle in front with David on the right and the three of them set off making reasonable time through the course. As the last team, however, they would have to do it again.

"Mein Gott nein!" shouted David setting the whole section to laughing. In the spirit of the competition, the second to last team volunteered to make it a four-man carry with the hefty George as patient to see if they could beat the best two-man time. David took the right front with one of the other recruits on his left. Some discussion ensued when Alejandro tried to pair up with Jack in the back. The recruits shouted him down until a fellow named McConnell took up the other handle.

Jack, still dripping sweat from the last carry, looked at McConnell and sighed in relief. James was a big fellow who looked as if he could carry George all by himself. They set off on the course awkwardly at first as they tried to adjust to the four-man canter like an eight-legged horse. George, battered and bruised from the first trip kept up a stream of invectives and curses the likes of which Jack had never heard. When the team crossed the finish line a full minute under the best two-man time, the onlookers raised a great ruckus made all the more boisterous by the intentional dumping of the cantankerous George Masters in the muddy pool beside the course. *What a merry band of fellows,* Jack thought to himself.

The volunteers learned that French Army officers from the *Service des Automobiles* would be their commanders. The authorities were extremely reluctant to issue free passage authorization to foreign non-combatants whose allegiance they could not verify. Mr. A. Piatt Andrew, who preferred *Piatt,* told them that he spent most of his time fighting French red tape. As foolish as this seemed, he explained, the threat of espionage and sabotage warranted caution. Before releasing any of them to the combat zone, the volunteers had to produce letters of good standing from prominent members of their home communities. This was no problem for the men already in France, but Jack knew any letters from home would take weeks. David Abramowicz, the former shoe salesman, discouraged by this requirement, soon left to join the Foreign Legion.

Piatt Andrew informed them that all the drivers would stay in the dormitory at the American Hospital. They would practice driving, and help the orderlies in the hospital. He explained that he would dispatch one of their teams when he could obtain authority. The French Army, in spite of governmental precautions, wanted to get all the help it could.

Mr. Andrew turned the class over to Alejandro each morning after his opening information session. Jack listened closely to both men, grateful that his crazy adventure had gotten him this far rather than out in the trenches. Yet, after three days of this routine, the men were getting bored. Alejandro eased that feeling with the news that they would do something more meaningful for the next several days. French authorities had relaxed their restrictions enough to allow the volunteer ambulance men to transport wounded from the train stations to Paris hospitals. Until security considerations had been met, the Americans would have to work in three or four man teams.

Alejandro disagreed with the French Army Captain on the minimum size of the crew. He believed there should be at least two in spite of the cost in manpower. The captain, more sanguine with the knowledge of his years in the service, knew that one driver sufficed. In January that year it didn't make much difference since the number of volunteers outnumbered the available vehicles by more than two to one.

Consequently, Jack joined McConnell and the oafish Masters to form a three-man crew. McConnell spoke French fluently. Jack became the primary driver for their team. All three had to be able to take the wheel. Eventually, Alejandro explained, they would reduce the teams to two or even one as more ambulances became available.

The Army Automobile Service—not associated in any way with the *Service de Santé*, the French Medical Service—was responsible for all evacuation. France's extensive rail system enabled relatively rapid evacuation from the forward hospitals to larger facilities far from the zone of combat. The Army sent many to Paris where some of the best hospitals in the world operated around the clock. The little American Hospital at Neuilly grew quickly in the fall of 1914 both in size and reputation.

Learning all this and more in the volunteer orientation, Jack felt a sense of despair at their inability to do more. Jack's group went into action in the wake of a group of men who had preceded them by about a month. This group, a partial section of the recently organized *Section Sanitaire Unitaire Numero 1,* had left for the Dunkirk region about the time Jack's group began its orientation. SSU 1 had just 12 ambulances, still without official French clearance. For that reason, sending it north to where the British, French and Belgians shared a sector, allowed the Army hierarchy a little more time to persuade the politicians to release the growing numbers of volunteers.

Meanwhile, George, Jim, and Jack learned the routes from the various *Gares de Paris* to Neuilly. Most of their trips took them to the Gare du Nord or its nearby Gare de l'Est, the north and east railway terminals serving Paris. The trip from station to hospital took less than an hour. They would leave the American hospital at eight in the morning and post their Renault outside the assigned station awaiting the arrival of trains from the north and east. When a large load of patients came in, twenty or thirty ambulances, each capable of taking three or four stretcher cases, could make three or more turns just to clear a single trainload.

Between trains or runs, the drivers and crews would read, play cards, write letters, or make diary entries. McConnell, Jack noticed, wrote many letters, and kept a diary.

"I keep one too, Jim." Jack said as they sat drinking coffee inside the Gare du Nord. "I want to write for a newspaper back home when this is over, so keeping track of what I see seems to be a good idea."

"I've been keeping a journal since I started college at the University of Virginia." Jim told him, motioning Jack to look at the sleeping George whose head bobbed and dropped. "Wake up, you lummox, we have work to do," he said, good-naturedly. The hissing sound and distinctive huff huff of the steam locomotive announced the arrival of another train.

A French Army sergeant directed them to a line of other vehicles with a sense of urgency. He blurted out a quick flurry of words that McConnell picked up with no trouble. "There's been a big attack," McConnell explained. "Casualties are overwhelming the field doctors. They are routing some of the wounded right to the trains. We are to get our vehicle into the line and dismount with our stretchers right away."

Jack maneuvered the ambulance into position as George hopped out of the back and pulled out two of the stretchers with him. Big as he was, George moved quickly and surely. A line of bearers was already loading up the front-most ambulances. Soon they loaded their first load of wounded—three stretcher cases, *couchés*, and two sitting, *assis*. It would only get worse as the day wore on, foreshadowing their coming work in the field.

Chapter 12
Enlistment

Les Invalides, January 8, 1915

Following a routine repeated by nearly a hundred of his American predecessors since last fall, Charlie went through the Légion recruit mill at the magnificent building housing Napoleon's tomb. After his visit there with Michelle, the place now seemed to have an ominous air about it. He was in a line with at least thirty other foreign volunteers awaiting their chance to be poked and prodded by the French military doctor.

Charlie studied the other volunteers with a critical eye sharpened by Michelle's efforts. She had opened his eyes to notice the seemingly insignificant. Buildings fell into periods of architecture and style. Even trees became a challenge to catalog. People, Michelle had shown him, defined themselves by their posture, clothes, and a myriad of gestures and expressions.

He found his fellow legionnaires-to-be a motley mix of young and old, short and tall, fit and fat. European men seemed to dress in monotonous blacks and charcoals, distinguished only by the difference in headgear and cut of cloth. It was easy to distinguish the well off by their pressed trousers, and shined shoes or boots. Most of the men in line looked more or less the same. Some bore the downtrodden look of the men he remembered from the docks in Saint Louis—hungry, dejected, resigned to some terrible unspoken fate. Charlie fantasized about them, imagining beaten wives, starving children, or horrible crimes. Some looked eager, anxious, chafing for action. These were often the youngest and the least foreign-looking. He tried to identify the Americans in this batch. Two or three of the men looked like possible candidates simply by the loose way in which they held themselves. He wondered how many Russians, Poles, Algerians, or other exotic nationalities were represented.

When he stepped in front of the desk, Doctor Gros appeared. It would not do for the Doctor to try to exert pressure for special treatment in this so-called egalitarian society—especially in the microcosm of the Légion Etrangère, the most egalitarian arm of the French Army. Gros was only there to attest to Charlie's health, something he had done for many of the other Americans.

Frederick Gros bade farewell and reminded Charlie to look him up on every return trip to Paris. Gros ended by saying: "And don't give up the idea of flying. We will be putting an American Squadron together if I have anything to say about it. I want you to keep that in mind once you have satisfied your soldierly aspirations."

"Thank you, sir. I appreciate your coming here and all your help. I might be interested in flying after I get a taste of the infantry, but for right now, I'm where I want to be. Thanks again, doctor. I'll try to keep in touch."

"Me too. Look me up whenever you get back here, Charlie. Oh, and by the way, you must be one special fellow. None of the many others that have approached Michelle got anywhere at all. Congratulations!"

Uniformed Non Commissioned Officers hustled the recruits to the Gare de Lyon and to railcars for the military Camp de Valbonne, near Lyon, France's second largest city. War still seemed unreal to Charlie, but the foul air in the *huit chevaux ou quarante hommes* boxcars was real enough. Eight horses might have fared well enough in the airless confines of the car, but forty men were hard pressed to survive. The sixty in Charlie's car began to suffer in less than an hour as the train crept along at a snail's pace.

They had *boites de singe*—literally translated as monkey meat—a type of canned beef intended to feed four men for three meals. The Russians, who kept to themselves, ate their ration of the meat all at one time. Since there was no water available in the car, they began to wail from thirst within an hour. One of them appeared very sick, but all the banging the men in the car did served no purpose. By the time they stopped at Auxerre, about five hours out of Paris, the unfortunate Russian was comatose from dehydration. It just didn't seem possible in the time they had been in the confined car. It was not even hot, though the air was stale and still with no circulation possible unless they cracked the doors. This solution brought blasts of cold air into the car that set those nearest to the door to loud vile complaining.

At Auxerre the cars had barely stopped when the recruits burst from the doors hitting the siding running in search of water and a place to relieve themselves. It reminded Charlie of cattle in a pen crushed by the mindless rush. It appalled him to think that men could be reduced so quickly to this elemental level. What, he wondered, would happen when they faced the enemy? What would keep them from similar panic? He also thought of the soft life he had so recently enjoyed at Michelle's side. Could it only have been hours since they last embraced?

In about forty minutes the sergeants herded the recruits back into the cars. The sick Russian disappeared and rumors whispered in the car said he had died! Dead before they even got close to the fighting. What a tragedy. Charlie huddled with a burly Slovak who spoke a little English and near-fluent French. They couldn't sit in the car since every man had only enough room to stand. If someone fell asleep, he slumped but stayed erect by the pressure of his neighbor's bodies. Actually, the kicks and knees a sleeper earned kept even the most tired awake.

"Why have you left your country?" Charlie finally asked.

"I could ask the same of you American, but I don't."

"I'm sorry. I don't mean to pry," Charlie said as they jostled each other on a curve.

"Listen, Mr. Keeler," the Slovak began. "It doesn't do to ask questions in this outfit. We are most of us here to escape something. No history, no past. Nothing to tie us to whatever we want to leave behind." The big Slav turned a severe eye to Charlie and willed him to silence with a withering look. He whispered, "Not here, not now!"

Charlie looked at him more bewildered than chastised. What did he have to hide? He clammed up for the next several hours. They picked up speed once out of Auxerre and raced down the tracks passing the towns of Beaune and Mâcon without stopping. It was early evening when the train finally stopped.

The doors burst open at Valbonne and the recruits poured out again falling over each other. Legion noncoms quickly brought order with shouts and blows. The commotion looked more like a circus than an effort at military decorum. As the men formed into a semblance of columns and moved off onto the nearby street a rumble of angry voices alarmed Charlie and his compatriots. The villagers were booing them! Rocks and garbage pelted the group.

"*Sales Boches*!" they screamed. Dirty Germans!

They thought the recruits were German prisoners! How could it be? They weren't even in uniforms. Some blue-coated gendarmes joined with the Legion officers in subduing the crowd and correcting their mistaken impression. Charlie could feel the hate. He felt guilty as if he was himself at fault for their mistaken perception. These raw mob emotions were truly new to him. As the passion faded and he was able to calm himself, he began to reflect on what had provoked such animal hatred in the crowd.

Rejik, the Slovak, sidled up to Charlie as they continued their march to the Legion barracks. "Dat is what I run from. Dis is why I join Legion." Charlie couldn't imagine what had happened in Rejik's Slovakia to make him leave, but no analogy was necessary. If he had fled from such craziness, he had even more reason than Charlie did.

The camp, a waypoint on their way to war, served as a Legion training and rest area. Covering a sprawling wooded area northeast of Lyon; the camp also served as a prisoner of war compound for the expanding number of Germans captured in the fighting. This news explained their reception, though it did nothing to lessen the negative impression on Charlie and the other recruits.

As they mustered into squads with veteran corporals as leaders, Charlie was happy to find Rejik would be his bunkmate. He wanted to find out more about this enigmatic man. As the day ended, the exhausted volunteers laid their heads on hard legion pillows of rolled straw in scratchy rough ticking cloth. The next day they would receive the rest of their issue and begin their training. Charlie's last thoughts as he slipped into blissful sleep were of Michelle on his bed in the Crillon, the night before he had left.

Part Three

A Bloody Spring

Le Printemps Sanglant

As when a flower feels the sun
And opens to the sky,
Knowing their dream has just begun
They hasten forth to die.
John Jay Chapman

Chapter 13
Bloody Baptism

Near Dunkirk, France, early February 1915.

Section One departed Neuilly with ten ambulances, a two-ton truck full of tents, stoves and supplies, and a kitchen trailer. Jack drove the second ambulance behind their French Army lieutenant, Dombasle, and his French NCO. Jim McConnell sat shotgun while George stretched out in the back. He'd be fine there as long as they stayed on the roads. The roads had to be smoother than their preparations.

Dombasle, a stickler for detail, personally checked the oil levels on every vehicle, checking underneath for leaks, and verifying they had requisite spare tire, tools, water cans, and *bidons d'essence*, their emergency gas cans. The Americans bitched good-naturedly behind his back. Not Jack. He'd been stuck in too many snowstorms back home—this wasn't Minnesota winter, but just as threatening.

The independent-minded civilians frustrated *Maréchal de Logis* Cartier, their senior NCO. With much hand waving, cursing, and head shaking, Cartier moved from crew to crew muttering, "*O là, O là là, quels enfants*!" Used to soldiers outfitted to the man with the same gear, clothes, and personal items, the hodgepodge collected by the volunteers nearly drove him over the edge.

After a night spent in their cars in Saint Omer, Section Sanitaire Une arrived at the French Naval Base near Dunkirk. The Americans wanted to hit the town, but Dombasle and Cartier drove the crews hard into the night before allowing them to turn in. Exhausted and frustrated by the relentless pressure, some of the crews were mutinous.

"Son of a bitch," Jack heard a man moan several cots away. "That bastard Cartier made me pull my wheels three times before he was satisfied I'd greased the damned hubs enough."

"Made me flush the radiator twice just to prove I knew how," grumbled another.

"Shut up and get some sleep boys," McConnell said. "The lieutenant has us on the dawn watch shadowing a French unit. Be thankful at least that we got fed, thanks to Cartier."

"And not laid, thanks to Cartier..." another voice mumbled down the row.

Jack admired Jim McConnell's calming leadership. George, on the other hand, was so quiet and unexpressive that they sometimes forgot he was there. Jim managed to get Masters to mutter a few sentences about his family in Brooklyn, but George kept to himself most of the time, meditating like some Hindu, his eyes open, fixed, unseeing.

They went to work with the Army ambulance crews hauling mostly British wounded. It perturbed Mac that the French made them have three men on each ambulance while the French got by with one or two at the most. Knowing the Americans felt insulted by the slight, Dombasle blamed it on high command's concern about security, shrugging it away Gallic style—*"c'est la vie."*

It didn't take long for the drivers and stretcher-bearers to feel like they had seen enough blood and suffering to last a lifetime. Compared to their relatively routine runs to and from the train stations in Paris, the front-line carnage was overwhelming. Close to one in three patients died en route. The mutilations and massive wounds defied modern medicine. Yet, Masters proved uncannily capable of knowing who would make it and who wouldn't.

"Jim, did you see how George treated that man, the one with the chest wound? If I didn't know better I'd guess he had some medical training," Buck said during one of their refueling breaks.

"There's more to George than meets the eye, if you ask me," McConnell observed.

McConnell was a driven man. Fortunately, his charges responded to the challenge, seldom complaining. Jack wondered what pushed Jim so hard. Granted, he thought, they were just one of dozens of ambulance crews doing the same job, and their work might save a few limbs or lives, but there was a limit to how much they could do in the end.

Cries of "this is too much, too much!" gave way to grim acceptance. Jack remembered working in the slaughterhouse on his uncle's farm and hauling the warm haunches of beef to the coolhouse. He had to remind himself that these were humans.

Cartier told them that some of the Army Ambulance crews had had wholesale mental and emotional breakdowns earlier in the war. Those that carried on grew callous, resigned, even macabre.

"George, don't you feel helpless? I mean, the blood, the screams! Makes me sick—no mad! It doesn't make sense. I don't hate the Germans. Why do I want to hurt them back?"

After several minutes of silence, George looked up from his cot, fixed Jack with a steady gaze, and said: "You are close to the Kingdom of God…."

George had never seemed religious before, but Jack suspected that the horrors they saw could provoke even the hardest cases to contemplate their spiritual well being. He remembered Jesus saying this to someone in the Bible. Leaving George, Jack found McConnell outside smoking a cigarette.

"My family is Scottish," McConnell said, like he'd been thinking about them. "I think some of my forebears fought with Robert the Bruce. Some intermarried with the Irish volunteers. Not much difference in the long run." Jim said without being asked. "Look at you: Swedish, Norwegian, and half Slovak. I've a touch of Seminole Indian from my mother. If they get the two of us, the stew of our mixed nationalities would season this ground richly."

Jack laughed at the macabre metaphor. This man used words like tools.

Jack knew that James Rogers McConnell had graduated from the University of Virginia, the school Jefferson established. Jim was enrolled at the Beaux-Arts School in Paris before the war started. He had traveled extensively in Europe and knew his way around, an asset immeasurably valuable in their current situation. Jim said he was born in Chicago, had lived for a time in New York, and had spent several years as a youth in France with his mother. Because of that experience, Jim spoke fluent French. Jack didn't doubt McConnell came from a wealthy background, but Jim acted like a regular joe, modest about himself to a fault.

"I once drove all the way from Chicago to New York," McConnell said snuffing out the cigarette. "A record-breaking trip, the first ever."

It was yet another revelation to Jack. He wondered what Jim was telling him that for now.

"Records like that used to matter, Jack. Do you think anyone will remember who made that trip ten years from now? But they will be writing about this fifty, a hundred, heck hundreds of years from now. You're part of history, Buck, my friend. Pay attention, write things down. You'll have lots to tell your children and grandchildren."

THE MAJOR ALLIED OFFENSIVE OF 1915 kicked off in February with an enormous thundering artillery preparation. German counter-preparations were deadly. Jack's section was one of several sent to work on the boundary between the French Armies and the British Expeditionary Force.

Shuttling wounded day in and day out hardened the ambulance crews both physically and mentally. *Dead is dead*, the ambulance crews began repeating as they tried to cope with what they saw, touched, and smelled. It didn't matter whether it was a little hole in the head or the whole head blown off—*mort est mort*.

Artillery terrified them. Nothing tore, shredded, or pulverized flesh more thoroughly than the shrapnel flung by high explosive shells. Pieces ranging from pea-sized to wicked, jagged-edged scythes more than a foot long whistled through the air, denuding large sections of wooded areas in the battle zone. The devastation overwhelmed the eye. A six-ounce chunk of razor sharp metal ripped like paper from the shell casing by the explosion of thirty pounds of high energy TNT, propelled at immeasurable speeds, could shear off a twelve-inch solid oak tree at its base. No wonder the most common life threatening injury on the battlefield was traumatic amputation of a limb.

Surprisingly, Jack had observed, the worst injuries seemed to produce almost no immediate pain. Many victims reported feeling heat and violent shock followed by surprise and the terrible sight of an arm, foot, hand or leg, or more than just one, missing or hanging by a shred of skin. Jack saw a man trying to hold his severed forearm in place after the medics had applied a tourniquet, fascinated by the fact that he could pull the arm away and push it back together.

One day, Jack held the hand of a French lieutenant whose left leg had been severed six inches below his hip. The young officer had dragged himself nearly a half mile on the ground before being picked up by the *brancardiers*. He said he could still feel his missing leg while he crawled. Every time he tried to get up on his knees, his brain sensed he could do it but the absent leg bewildered and frustrated his attempts. Mud and the searing action of the shrapnel had staunched the flow of blood, saving his life.

The drivers soon learned that blood loss led the list of causes of death from otherwise survivable wounds, followed closely by infections—chiefly gas gangrene. If the bleeding could be stopped, most wounds could be overcome. The damage done might not be so easily repaired. Some questioned the quality of such a life, but Jack decided that he would rather live maimed than die. They had to talk about it, often at night after a grueling day.

"Soup or stew?" Masters asked when Jack set the hot Army-issued cans of food on the table.

"Neither. Something like *le pan*," Jack said reaching down with a ladle to pull up chunks of meat. McConnell chuckled.

"*Le panne?* My word! That means broken, Jack. Oh, it's rabbit!" McConnell exclaimed. *"Lapin.* I've had it before. Not bad either."

"So, George, it's bunnies for dinner. Dig in," Jack said, knowing Masters didn't hesitate to eat anything.

When Jack asked McConnell what he thought about the work they were doing, Jim didn't take long to respond. Drawing on his art-trained eye, Jim often contrasted Nature's beauty and the raw horror of the battlefield.

"Try this on for size," he began to read from his ever-present notebook. "France and England are turning the flower of their fighting men into withered warriors hobbled by hellish wounds."

"Alliteration, right?" Jack said, wiping some of the gravy from his chin. "This is pretty good, isn't it George?"

"The rabbit or the words? 'Hobbled by hellish wounds'…that's very good Jim. Is this for some magazine or paper back home?" Masters said, chewing loudly.

"The point, my friends, is simply that *war is hell.*

"Mankind stands at the mouth of hell teetering on the edge with all the forces of evil trying to pull him in. Whatever is good, noble, and godlike, keeps him from falling. It doesn't matter whose side you are on. What's happening to the poor fellows we carry is certainly happening on the other side. We need something to hang onto to keep from falling. The minute we give up trying and become jaded or cynical about death and suffering we slip a little further into the pit."

He told them he was sending it to *Harpers*, asking if they thought it would get anyone's attention. The editors told Mac they thought it was noble and might even energize some of the folks back home.

"Fat chance of that," Jack said, trying to imagine the folks back home worrying about anything but making ends meet.

"You know, indifference is a tendency common to coroners, embalmers, and graveyard diggers," Masters observed.

"Yeah, but there has to be something that makes all this worth it. I mean, this suffering can't be for naught, can it?" Jack observed, not really expecting an answer.

George looked like he wanted to say something, but when he didn't, Jack answered his own question.

"The *cause*—France, England, Belgium, Russia—united against aggression. Old Fritz thinks he's fighting for the fatherland, but who attacked first?"

They finished their meal lamenting America's apparent indifference. Masters went off as he did every night. Jack fell asleep as soon as he lay down on the cot. McConnell sat up smoking a cigarette while jotting in his notebook.

When missions were slack, Jack prodded Jim. He asked if he had met or knew of the Brunnells in Chicago. Jim reminded him that he had left Chicago as a young child. "The last time I was there was for that big drive."

"How did you end up at Virginia?"

"The University? Well, dad wanted me to become a lawyer, and Virginia has a great law school. We were living in Carthage, North Carolina, at the time.

"I had a kilt from the family and an old set of bagpipes. Never mastered the dusty sacks, but I'd go out and screech in the commons at night," he smiled, remembering. "They'd boo and throw things to get me to quit.

"Nearly got kicked out for climbing on Jefferson's statue and crowning the founding father with a chamber pot."

Jack cracked up at the image, remembering that McConnell graduated with a law degree in 1910.

The ambulance crews shuttled from regiment to regiment, following the tide of alternating attacks and counterattacks. At mid-month Jack's squad set up in a small complex of farm buildings. They housed their nearly worn out French ambulances in the stables. The crews found refuge in outbuildings and sheds on the farm or simply slept in their ambulances. Mac reminded Masters and Buck that they were still much better off than the men in the trenches, but the bitter wet cold accentuated by the biting wind off the Channel made them long for the relative comforts of the barracks.

George respected Jim's maturity and leadership ability. Young Jack reminded Masters of himself at 20—full of zest for life, innocent of any grievous wrongs, and idealistic to the point of naiveté. George wished he could turn back the clock and re-experience that time of excitement and the feeling that all was well with the world.

"There's a certain splendor in what these poilus do, isn't there?" He said to McConnell while Jack worked on the motor. "To be willing to sacrifice one's very life for one's country or for a friend. *No greater sacrifice hath a man than to lay down one's life for another.*"

"Scripture George? You read the Bible? I don't have much faith in organized religion myself, but there's wisdom in the Bible. Wouldn't have thought you would go in for that."

Masters winced at McConnell's comment. *Alas, he thought, looking back led nowhere. Hiding behind his chosen façade had served him well enough. Maybe he would open up with McConnell. Confession, he well knew, is good for the soul, but he didn't relish troubling young Buck with his past.*

Jack found himself largely on his own in keeping the Renault running. At least at Dunkirk there were qualified mechanics and a machine shop. The engines and drive trains on the Renault touring cars could take an enormous beating, but when they quit, they defied simple repair. He made up a small toolbox assembled from spares in the garage. He had spent hours assisting the trained mechanics in order to learn basic repair techniques. It had been good for his language training as well, for he picked up useful terms like *bougie* for spark plug, and *freins* for brakes. Before long he could fix just about anything he could reach.

On one trip, with three *couchés,* and two *assis*, the vehicle sank to its axles in the mud. They labored carefully to remove the stretchers and place the injured off the road to lighten the ambulance. A poilu swathed in bandages covering his head and eyes, asked for a cigarette as soon as they sat him on a fallen tree. Jack slid one between his lips while one of the other wounded men lit it with his one good hand. Jack noticed a bloody rag on this fellow's other hand.

One of the stretcher cases stunk to high heavens.

"Intestines, Jack," Masters explained as they set the man down. "He's been gut shot. He's in a bad way. We've got to hurry."

George actually lifted the rear of the now-emptied Renault high enough for them to throw sticks and roadside debris under the driving wheels. Using a long telephone pole, McConnell and Masters were able to lever first one side up and then the other while Jack rushed to stuff straw and sticks under the front wheels.

After all this effort, the three stood sweating beside the ambulance and almost laughed at the folly of trying to drive out of the mud. They had raised the vehicle onto four little islands. Clearly, as soon as Jack tried to drive in any direction the wheels would spin off their perches. The moans of the man on the stretcher kept it from being funny. They had to find a solution soon.

George ran back to the French artillery battery where they had picked up the wounded. He returned with four horses, a wagon full of hay and small logs, and a detail of fifteen poilus. In less than a half an hour, the men laid a twenty-foot long road of logs in a bed of straw. They called it a 'corduroy road'—a technique well known to the artillerymen for getting their heavily laden ammunition vehicles back to battery positions.

They harnessed the horses to the front axle while the soldiers got behind and beside the vehicle teetering on its pathetic little islands. On the command *allez!*, the men and horses moved as one pulling and pushing the ambulance onto the log road, a raft afloat on the river of mud. With shouts and cheers, the men slogged out of the mud.

Jack was to get the motor going and drive the ambulance off the corduroy road onto the more solid shoulder, balancing the roadside wheels on the center hump of the road while keeping the other wheels on the shoulder. If they could make it another thousand meters doing this double tightrope act, they would hit the macadam *Route National.*

Unfortunately, the delay proved deadly to the man with the stomach wound.

"God was merciful to him," Masters commented, brushing tears from his eyes as he covered the man's face. "He bled to death, but he will feel no more pain. I don't think he would have made it to the hospital anyway."

Jack had performed the straddling maneuver in the winter in Minnesota. Doing it on the mud was little different from in the snow. The trick was to keep the vehicle moving. If the driver hesitated or failed to keep the gears engaged, the wheels would slide off to one side or the other.

Once reloaded and on the way east, the three Americans remained silent, thinking about the soldier they'd left to be buried by the artillery section.

"God, I wish we could have done more," McConnell lamented, a feeling shared profoundly by his fellows.

They slept in the ambulance, often on the stretchers recently occupied by wounded poilus. When away from their own little kitchen trailer they ate at field kitchens in the rear areas of the regiments and divisions where they were working, taking care of personal hygiene as soldiers had for ages, using slit trenches and whatever paper they were able to hoard, often the coarse wrappings from used bandages.

Fresh water was a precious commodity. The ambulance had two large cans they kept filled for the wounded and for washing the blood off the stretchers. Their *bidons*, the French Army canteens, filled as often as not with *pinard*, the coarse red wine issued to the French poilus, slaked their personal thirst. Jack found it useful for brushing his teeth, a technique he had observed some soldiers using. Washing was all but impossible except during the short turn-around at the rail clearing points or hospitals where they delivered their wounded.

At the end of February Dombasle sent the entire section to Paris to pick up new ambulances and take a hard earned 48-hour leave.

"I'm more excited going back to Paris than if I was going home," Jack said, guiltily. The days he had spent with Willis in Paris and the thought of seeing Isabelle spurred his excitement. He wasn't sure that Isabelle had even gotten his letters. He knew she could read them, but did she even think about him? He hadn't received any mail from anyone.

Jim McConnell was anxious to see his girl, Marcelle Guérin, a beautiful French woman he'd met during his months at the Ecole des Beaux-Arts before the war. She had corresponded with him nearly every day. He had a photograph of her that he kept in a small satchel along with his important papers. "I just hope her parents let me see her," Jim said. "They claim to like Americans, but they don't want their daughter hooked up with one."

"Don't want her living thousands of miles away. I'd say." Masters observed.

"That or not wanting her shattered by losing you," Jack observed. He thought about Sandy for the first time in days with the usual pang only slightly diminished.

"Well, Jack," McConnell said, "When am I going to meet this Flandin Mademoiselle?"

"You've got to be kidding Mac," Jack said, looking over Jim's shoulder at the picture of a stunning young blond. "What could tear you away from Marcelle? Besides, I'm not sure I can trust you with that puppy dog face of yours."

George laughed at their banter. "Hey, it's me you two should not trust. When your ladies get a look at a real man they won't be sticking with the likes of you for long."

Taken aback by George's uncharacteristic comment, both Buck and McConnell regarded his homely features, looked at each other, and broke out laughing harder than they had in weeks. The incongruity of it all just tickled them. It was hard to imagine George on the arm of one of the delicate Parisian Mademoiselles. After days in the field, Mac and Jack thought of George as more beast than man. Only his tender and skillful ministrations to the patients in the back of the ambulance challenged this impression.

George got a hurt look on his face as the two continued to laugh. He walked away shaking his head. McConnell muttered loud enough for George to hear, “I for one am not going to let my girl near that woman-killer, how about you Jack?”

Picking up the cue, Jack said even louder: “I’m not going to allow Isabelle to even hear about either of you two wolves!” He said it in the light spirit of the exchange, but he couldn’t help remembering how he’d lost Sandy to a friend.

George slowed down, turned, and smiled slightly.

Chapter 14
La France est nôtre mère!

Camp de Valbonne, early February 1915

"*Allez! Vous êtes tous des têtes de mules*," the Adjudant shouted as he trooped the firing line. *Mule heads?* Charlie was picking up French quickly, though he knew he couldn't use much of what he had learned in polite company. Profanity took the place of normal conversation. Between coarse language, boots, and fists, the non-commissioned officers communicated their general displeasure with the trainees in an oddly affectionate manner.

Bassic or Recruit Training, normally an eight week course, had been compressed to a scant six. Charlie's company had struggled through the first two weeks learning to give instant obedience or face a beating. After the rude reception by the townspeople, the harshness of the NCOs added to the sour taste in Charlie's mouth. He hated *la vie de caserne,* the French term for the barracks routine or garrison life.

Charlie picked up his heavy blue overcoat, white duck fatigue trousers and blouse, a red kepi, laced field shoes made of iron, wool shirts, a nine foot long blue sash, two blankets and a suit of long underwear. All this fit into one canvas bag. He also received a rifle with a twelve-inch bayonet, a scabbard for the bayonet, a harness to hold the scabbard and two large leather cartridge boxes along with a small musette bag. In the bag went a tin-plated bowl with a canvas cover, a knife, and a fork. The issue items stacked up into a pile three feet high, weighing about a hundred pounds.

Charlie was dismayed that they received no socks. Instead, they were issued muslin squares that they were supposed to lay on their feet in patchwork patterns before pulling on the uncomfortable boots.

The French drilled and drove the ragged troops until they could move as one, responding to the strange commands instantly. Conditioning marches made the purpose of the muslin squares become clear. Since they adhered to each other only by friction, the squares slid relatively easily against the inside of the boot while staying in place on the foot from the moisture of sweating. Instead of the skin sliding against the boot, the squares absorbed the rubbing and helped to prevent blisters. Keeler enjoyed the marches because they got him out of the hated barracks, and he liked the physical activity. The songs they quickly learned mesmerized them as the squads swayed in double file on the country paths.

Charlie found the food as coarse as the language. It wasn't the *Crillon* or the *Rochambeau*. They ate at 11 A.M. and again at five. The first meal consisted of a substantial soup, coffee, and an issue of *pinard*—the hearty red wine that Charlie grew to like. Supper included a goulash filled with hunks of meat and vegetables, coffee, more pinard, and a half loaf of coarse peasant bread.

They lined up to fill their bowls in the *ordinaire*, their mess hall. The men sat together jabbering in at least six different languages during the meal breaks. Simple and boring as the food might be, Charlie and the other recruits couldn't wait for mealtime. They got more time than necessary while the sergeants and officers ate meals served on china by recruits.

Between drills and long conditioning marches, the squads learned trench construction, how to set booby traps and signaling devices for warning of approaching enemy, and the care and handling of various weapons. Most instructors impressed Charlie, while others reinforced his father's comment about the Legion being a refuge for the dregs of the Earth. One in particular, a crude man named Pasqualli, suspected of homosexual tendencies, took sadistic pleasure in beating up the weaker of the volunteers.

Pasqualli routinely commandeered the men's ration of tobacco, the *Scaferlati des Troupes*, issued every three days. Charlie never touched the stuff, giving it away as soon as he got it. Others used it as trading material. One day, Pasqualli demanded Charlie's ration. When he told the short, smelly man with the pockmarked face that he no longer had it, Pasqualli reached up to slap Charlie. Charlie caught Pasqualli's wrist in mid-air, twisting and squeezing hard enough to force the corporal to his knees. Charlie knew he was in for it. The worst infraction a recruit could commit was to raise a hand against a cadre member. He expected the whole company's worth of NCOs to descend on him as soon as he released the greasy little pervert. Luckily, they had to rush off to the bayonet course.

Antonelli, a stout Corsican with swarthy skin and no noticeable neck, awaited them at the bayonet pits. The sergeant stood the hundred-man company around the sawdust-filled pits and ordered them to raise their nine pound 1868 Lebel rifles over their heads. Facing them to the right, he started them marching around the pits.

Walking like children at a cakewalk amused Charlie until Antonelli picked up the pace. Soon they were trotting. After three or four minutes, their arms began to burn. As soon as a man lowered his rifle even a little, a non-com was on him in a flash with blows and kicks. In five minutes there were more men faltering than there were NCOs to discipline them. Soon only a handful remained in the circle with their rifles overhead.

Pasqualli singled out the smaller men for abuse. Charlie was tempted to boot the man out of the circle. Charlie's arms were thick and strong from wrestling and loading boats. He, Antonelli, and three other strong fellows were the last remaining at the end of ten minutes. The excruciating agony didn't seem to faze Antonelli. When he finally commanded *reposez armes,* the recruits hoped for a long break, but Antonelli was just getting started.

He ordered the men to fix bayonets on the fifty-one inch rifle, adding two pounds. Next, he instructed them to raise the rifle overhead in one hand and begin to march. After thirty seconds arms started to droop, and in two minutes some of the men were throwing up at the side of the pit. The NCOs shouted threats, but stopped the kicking. The falterers would be on the worst details that evening.

Antonelli stopped when only two recruits remained, Charlie and one of his squad mates. Antonelli had them hold their rifles out in front of them at arm's length. He mirrored them with his own Lebel, one with very shiny frogs on the sling. After less than a minute, the husky Italian recruit began trembling. Antonelli held rock steady with a smirk on his face.

Once the Italian faltered, the ring of recruits began to chant *Charlie! Charlie! Charlie!* Antonelli's grin turned serious. The NCOs roared *Tony, Tony!* Charlie's face was tense and red and his shoulders shook gently as he tried to keep the blood flowing into his aching arms. He knew he couldn't keep this up, but he thought he might be able to beat the Corsican. Seeing the serious glint in Antonelli's eyes, Charlie sensed that winning here would only embarrass the sergeant and add to his misery. He'd just decided to let his arms drop when a Captain stepped into the pit and seized Charlie's rifle with a snap. *Assez! Enough!* He shouted.

Putting his arm over Charlie's shoulder, he motioned Antonelli over to his other side. Captain de Lattre spoke loud enough for all to hear, "Never has a recruit lasted so long in competition with *Sergent* Antonelli. What is your name soldier?"

"Keeler, mon capitaine, Charles Keeler."

"Bon, monsieur Keeler, you have just earned a promotion. You are now *acting Corporal* Keeler. I expect great things from you, from all of you," he said, addressing the company as a whole. "Antonelli here is today promoted to Adjudant [sergeant major]. You have two weeks until we move to the front, the most important weeks of your training.

"You will learn to shoot your weapons and to kill the dirty Boches with this!" He whipped a gleaming bayonet from his scabbard and held it high over his head. "And I will be your commander!" A sergeant started singing the Legion marching song and soon the whole company joined in:

Nous sommes soldats de la Légion
La Légion Etrangère.
N'ayant pas de Patrie,
La France est nôtre mère!

Charlie felt caught up in the excitement and sense of brotherhood. *France isn't my mother,* Charlie thought, *but she does have my heart.* He had proven his manhood to a body of the toughest fighters in the world. All that remained was to put that strength to the test in the cauldron of battle. Undoubtedly, there were other hurdles ahead, one of which would soon trouble him more than Pasqualli.

On the firing range, they learned how to operate the old bolt-action Lebel. It held eight 8-millimeter rounds, and could get all eight off in about a minute. The instructors on the firing line weren't interested in rapid fire. They insisted on careful marksmanship, though the Lebel was ill suited for accuracy.

Charlie had no experience with firearms. His father wouldn't allow them in the house, and his friends who hunted didn't dare invite Charlie to join them at the risk of incurring his father's wrath.

While the company was organized in garrison into three sections of three squads each, sized according to height, at the firing range they ranked the men by skill. Charlie, already in the ninth squad, the tallest, and last in line of march, found himself again in the ninth. These were the bolo firers, those so hopeless with rifles they would be better armed with spears. When the rest of the company took a break, the bolos got additional training.

Charlie's left shoulder was bruised by the constant firing. He had improved, but he still had trouble keeping a steady aim. At the end of the firing week, he faced a qualification round that would decide his immediate future. If he couldn't qualify as a rifleman, he would be assigned to the machine gun section as an ammunition bearer, a prospect Charlie didn't relish.

The course consisted of targets at 25, 50, 100, 200, and 300 meters. He would have to score 35 out of 50 shots in order to qualify. So far, his best was 25. He completely missed the targets at 200 and 300 meters. He fired at the 25-meter target hitting it all five times, and did the same at 50 meters. Taking aim at the 100-meter target, he felt the presence and warm breath of someone lying beside him.

"*Vous êtes gaucher*?" Antonelli exclaimed, acting surprised at Charlie's left-handedness. "*Mais oui! C'est la raison*!"

Charlie hadn't had much to do with the newly minted Adjudant since the contest in the bayonet pits. Antonelli, on the other hand, had watched over the American's performance. He had high hopes for Keeler. He assigned the best marksman on the cadre to personally tutor Charlie, but it hadn't worked. He decided to see what could be done in person.

"*Voyons*," Antonelli began, explaining that firing the Lebel from the left shoulder placed the firer's left cheek on the same side as the bolt action, causing the shooter to twist the stock to the right to hold it comfortably. This canted the weapon just enough to change the bullet drop over range. Instead of the sights compensating in a vertical plane by causing the firer to raise the aim point to achieve more range, a lefty tended to move the front sight up and to the left at an angle. This caused the bullet to fall short and to the right of targets beyond 150 meters.

Watching Charlie shoot his first round at 200-meters, Antonelli spotted the bullet's impact with binoculars. As he expected, it hit just short and to the right of the target. The second round produced a puff of dust in the exact same spot as the first. The American was at least consistent.

"*Alors*, let's try this, corporal." He pulled out a small hammer and tapped the front sight about three times. It didn't seem to move, but when he handed it back to Charlie, it looked like it had been bent a little to the right.

Charlie's next shot hit the 200-meter target, as did the next. At three hundred meters Antonelli told him to aim just to the right and above the target. Charlie's next four shots hit the target. Keeler had mastered the trigger squeeze and breathing techniques as well as the best shots in the company. It just took someone who knew left-handers. Antonelli shot left-handed.

After qualifying on the Lebel, Keeler would have walked on coals for Antonelli. "Rejik, I tell you the man's fantastic. He isn't like the others. I'm lucky he showed up on the range."

"Yeah. Lucky. You do have a lot of that," Rejik said with unguarded envy.

WORD REACHED VALBONNE that the company was to make haste for the Pont à Mousson area for an upcoming offensive. There would be no *congé*, no *permission*, French terms for leave or passes.

This disappointed Charlie more than he cared to admit. He missed Michelle with an almost physical pain. She had sent him socks, candies, a scarf, and a photograph taken especially for him. He wrote something everyday, mailing his missives every other day. He wrote about what he was doing and about his fellow recruits. Since the incident in the bayonet pits, no one, not even Pasqualli, messed with Keeler. Charlie suspected that the Corsican had protected him from Pasqualli.

Michelle wrote every day and sent at least one package a week. Her letters told of Fleury's business and of her volunteer work at the American Hospital. She wrote that Stephane had left Fleury's service to answer an urgent nation-wide call for mechanics to join French aviation, implying that it would please her if Charlie would take the same step. She said she missed him and always signed the letters with 'All my Love.' Charlie worried that her feelings for him had cooled. He wanted to see her, touch her, and reassure both of them that their relationship was more than a shipboard fling.

Moving to the front lines didn't concern him. It was the reason he was there, but observing the growing excitement of his fellow legionnaires, he wondered how many would still be standing after their first week.

Even Rejik, his cynical bunkmate, was fired up for action. Rejik bitched and moaned about everything. When Charlie became an acting corporal, Rejik didn't compliment him, insisting that the American was no better than the rest of them. He carried a well-thumbed copy of Karl Marx's *Das Kapital,* exclaiming to anyone who would listen that there should be no elite, no privileged leaders to suppress the men. Charlie knew what *anarchy* meant, but he couldn't take Rejik seriously.

Rejik, a fugitive from his native Slovakia, was a zealot, and possibly a dangerous man, but Charlie was attracted by his deep and sincere commitment to what he believed. The politics bothered Charlie, but he expected them to dissolve when the lead started flying. He could not have been more wrong.

Chapter 15
An Amorous Interlude

Boulevard Haussmann, Paris, March 1, 1915

Isabelle greeted Jack at the door of their building just as he was about to ring for entrance. She had stood all morning at the window watching for his approach, fighting the urge to go down to the street to wait. Jack's message, relayed from the American Ambulance switchboard at Neuilly, indicated he would arrive before noon. Why couldn't he be more precise? The tension was excruciating. Had it only been six weeks since the American had left?

She saw ambulances going in both directions on the Boulevard Haussmann. At half past 11, a vehicle with large Red Crosses stopped below their window. The uniformed driver stepped out of the right door, looked up, and waved. Isabelle flew down the stairs, not trusting the slow elevator, unable to contain her growing excitement.

The young couple stopped just short of each other touching hands and chastely exchanging kisses to each cheek in the French manner. Checked by the two other smiling men, Isabelle resisted the urge to throw herself into Jack's arms. Jack wasn't sure what to do. He held onto her hands and stared mutely into her deep brown eyes.

McConnell broke their spell with a polite introduction of George and himself. Isabelle smiled charmingly to each, and quickly invited all three to come in for a coffee. George started moving towards the door when Jim caught his arm. "*Désolé*, Mademoiselle, we have to get this machine back to the hospital. I'm sure Jack will be happy to let us take it there for him. We can meet up later this weekend. Come on George. Let's go!"

Jack was still tongue-tied. He knew Jim was anxious to see Marcelle. They hadn't planned to drop him off first, but the ambulance seemed to drive itself directly to Flandin's door. Mac took the wheel and waved as they pulled away, leaving Jack and Isabelle on the sidewalk.

"Come inside *filleul*," she said with a twinkle in her eye. "I have a little surprise for you."

Recovering his tongue, Jack showed off his improving French saying, "*Mais oui, ma petite marraine, à ton service*."

She smiled and took his arm. Once inside Jack noticed that the place was quiet. He looked around the plush apartment wondering if he had really spent four glorious days there with Willis and Isabelle.

Your parents?" Jack asked, anxious to show off his French to them as well.

"That my American friend is my surprise! Maman and Papa are in Bordeaux on official business. Papa now works for the government on the development of our aviation. They are coming back tomorrow," she said, her eyes twinkling with suggestion.

"You will stay tonight, no?" she said softly, her face flushing.

Jack took a moment to respond, slowly absorbing the facts. "Stay?" He touched her shoulder provoking a slight jump. "Isabelle, you catch me by surprise!"

"I have let the help go for the day. I prepared a meal for you myself. I hope you have hunger."

Used by now to the peculiar French sentence construction, Jack said simply, "You betcha!"

Isabelle looked momentarily confused, but she went on. "Come and take an *apéritif*. You must tell me about your work."

She took his hand and gently guided him into the same room where he and Willis had spoken to her father. The picture of her brother brought that evening back in a flood. "Oh Isabelle," he half-groaned, "the things I have seen."

She poured a small measure of whisky in a tumbler, handed it to him, and stroked his cheek gently. "Say nothing. I was wrong. Of course, you do not want to talk about it. How foolish of me. You must want to forget...." she trailed off as he took her hand.

"No! I do not want to forget—can't forget. The bravery and suffering. The horrible wounds. No, it is unforgettable!" Jack paused, unsurprised by his passion, but relieved to be able to share it with someone other than his ambulance mates.

"I am so frustrated that I can do no more. You know, your soldiers are sublime, so extraordinary. We feel helpless and awed in the face of their sacrifices. It is hard to stand by while others give so much for the cause. It makes me sick that my country is on the sidelines," Jack said, hearing echoes of Jim McConnell in his words.

Isabelle watched his face and felt his words more than hearing them. *How he has changed*, she thought. *How he has grown. He is the same man, but different. He needs nourishment in body and soul*—nourishment she wanted to provide now more than ever.

Jack actually gulped half his glass of whisky, thinking of the cognac he had tried in that room a short month and a half ago. The scotch tasted harsh at first, making his mouth burn. Then the smoky liquor seemed to course through his bloodstream, warming and filling him with a pleasurable sensation. He felt his cheeks flush.

Isabelle took the glass from him and set it down. Then she took his face in her hands. She moved close to him, raising her face, pulling his closer to hers until their lips touched. It was a heady embrace far more warming than the drink. Jack felt her stays through the fabric of the back of her dress with one hand, and cradled her head with his other. His knees trembled. His arousal became noticeable, embarrassing, and uncomfortable.

Isabelle broke the spell. "We will eat. Then I will embrace you more. We have the whole afternoon and evening." Her cheeks were also flushed. She stood up too fast and almost fell but for his steadying hand. Jack realized that he wasn't the only one aroused.

What was he getting into? *They were alone! What was to stop them from doing anything they liked? What would it be like? Could he do it? Wasn't it wrong?* These thoughts tumbled around in his head as she pulled away and left for the kitchen. He had to support himself on the back of a chair as the powerful surge of erotic energy slowly dissipated.

Jack remembered the wonderful meals he had enjoyed at the Flandins' during his first stay. Isabelle now served a simple roast of pork cooked with prunes and served sliced thinly on a bed of rice. They lingered over the meal, sipping rich Bordeaux between forkfuls. After the soldier's fare Jack had tolerated, every bite seemed a luxury, while the nearly palpable sexual tension hung in the air.

Just to break the tension, Jack asked about Pierre Flandin's involvement in aviation. Many of the men driving ambulances were talking about joining French Aviation. Doctor Gros encouraged all the drivers to apply. Jack knew McConnell was giving it serious thought. It would be a big move, but he agreed with McConnell that they needed to do more.

Isabelle knew little about her father's affairs. She focused on Jack. She wanted to hear about his work, his friends, and his family. She laughed loudly at the story about getting the ambulance unstuck near the artillery battery. He left out the poilu's death, painting George as a giant that could have carried the vehicle out by himself had they let him.

Jack had absorbed a good deal of French while driving the *blessées*. Often he was alone in the ambulance while Mac and Masters loaded stretchers. He listened to the injured men. Some moaned and uttered words he learned to recognize. He improved his vocabulary at the canteens and messes where they got their meals. Jim did most of the talking for them, but Jack picked up a lot of slang, *argot,* as the French called it.

One of his stories captivated Isabelle.

"I came up on a column of poilus moving forward, singing, looking determined. My ambulance fell in their line of march until I was able to maneuver away in the square of a village. I heard the music of the division band, playing the *Sambre et Meuse*, I believe. Stopping to watch them pass, I was caught up in the excitement. The column stopped and the men fell out on both sides of the road for a break. Going up to a small group, I saw that they had broken out a pack of dirty, well-worn playing cards. Others played with a puppy, telling jokes and smoking. I said in my best French, 'You find an opportunity to enjoy life even here?' A grizzled vet looked up at me and smiled saying*, 'Mais il le faut, on est si vite tué.*' Can you imagine that? *One has to, one is killed so quickly*, n'est-ce pas?" Jack looked inquiringly at Isabelle, who nodded thoughtfully.

As the clock chimed two o'clock, Isabelle poured the last of the wine and stood up to clear the plates. Jack stood as if to help, but she insisted that he stay seated. In moments she returned with a desert she called *sorbet*, a smooth fruit-flavored ice that Jack had never tasted before. Next came coffee. Not the harsh brown thick fluid he had gotten used to near Dunkirk, but a rich wonderfully flavorful strong brew.

Jack could no more have taken the initiative in seducing Isabelle than he could have lifted the ambulance. It was not in his character or experience to do such a thing, but he was torn by his desires and the possibility of realizing them. *What kind of woman is she, and what was he to her? Could he make her pregnant? What would his parents think? What would the old stern Father Musch at Our Lady of Victory say? Fornicator, undoubtedly.*

As Jack wrestled with these thoughts, Isabelle tangled with her own. She had played this scene in her mind for weeks, long before she even knew her parents would leave her alone. The main problem to solve had been to find a place and time. Now that they were alone she trembled inside at what she was about to do, getting more and more excited.

Jack appealed to her even more than she had imagined. *Why was she feeling so scared?* She knew that intimacy should be ecstasy though she had yet to experience a man fully. She knew she was risking her future. Jacques-Antoine's death made time compress for her. She felt pressed to experience life and love before it was too late. She hoped Jack was as gentle as he seemed. She knew God would forgive her, even if the strait-laced old curé at Saint Augustin would not. With the moment at hand, she wasn't sure she had the courage to seduce Jack. The fear and anticipation sent a thrill through her heart.

She led Jack to the sitting room in the back of the apartment where her mother had arranged a small jungle of houseplants to take advantage of the many windows. The room smelled fresh and earthy. They sat on a divan with a floral pattern and stared out at the twin steeples of Saint Augustin. Jack stroked the back of her hand with his roughened fingers.

She turned her head to him. Looking into his eyes her lips began to tremble. Jack realized with great relief that she was just as scared as he was! Before he could speak, she kissed him tentatively. He returned the kiss, shifting to put his arms around her. Awkwardly at first, they kissed, rekindling their earlier passion. Soon Isabelle lay back on a pillow, drawing Jack partially on top of her. Still in his wool Ambulance uniform, Jack worried the buttons would scratch her.

Feeling Isabelle's generous curves against his chest and smelling her perfumed hair gave him a sense of possession and protectiveness. Their kisses became bolder. Jack found her tongue teasing his lips and penetrating his mouth. It was exquisite. He returned the kiss, exploring her tender mouth. She unbuttoned his jacket and pushed it off his shoulders without breaking their kiss. Things were moving so fast that Jack felt like an observer watching his own seduction. *How far would she go? How far would she let him go?* He heard a voice in his head urging restraint, while his body fought to proceed.

Isabelle struggled with her carefully laid plans. Feeling Jack's evident excitement brought home the reality of what she was about to do. As his hand found her breast, her skin tingled. She flushed deeply from within, feeling warmth between her legs and a falling sensation. She stopped thinking. She worked at the buttons on his shirt anxious to touch and kiss his chest. She didn't stop him when he began fumbling with the buttons at her bodice. Her chest heaved. She heard herself moan as he kissed her neck.

Jack shuddered when his hand cupped her full breast. She reached up, not to take his hand away, but to clasp it, moving in a circular motion that made her nipple harden in his palm. He heard, felt, tasted, and smelled everything. Her skin was so soft and smooth. Touching wasn't enough. He had to see her.

She'd gotten his shirt off one arm and was helping Jack release her catches. They said nothing, grasping, stroking, and tasting each newly exposed patch of skin. When he reached the spot between her full breasts she moaned even deeper.

Isabelle thought she was hearing alarms going off in her head, drowned out by the strange animal sound she herself seemed to be making. *How much she wanted this!* Her second thoughts faded in a sense of abandon that coursed through her in a flood of desire. But, the ringing bell pulsed in pairs of jangling tones. She sat up abruptly, startling Jack. The telephone! It seldom rang, but now it did, insistent, scolding, demanding attention.

Isabelle raced from the room to the entryway where the instrument stood on a small table. Jack rose more slowly, feeling the passion sapped by the interruption. He heard Isabelle down the hall speaking in rapid French. Could something be amiss? Going to her, he looked at her face for clues. She was smiling at him, her breathing controlled, and her eyes twinkling!

"C'est papa," she whispered, holding the mouthpiece against her chest where Jack's lips had been moments earlier. She listened several more minutes before replying to her father's questions. Jack understood her response had something to do with him, but she spoke too quickly for him to comprehend exactly what she said. He watched her face work as she spoke into the phone.

"*Oui, papa, il est là. Oui, nous serions biens occupé...au revoir cher papa et adieu à maman.*" She replaced the earpiece on the hook. "Papa was only seeing that you had arrived. He was concerned about leaving me alone and wanted to make sure you were here to protect me! How droll! If only he knew, he would send someone to protect you from me!" Isabelle looked down at the floor demurely, moving closer to him.

"Your father is not worried about leaving you alone with me?" Jack asked, pulling her close. "Can we betray such trust?"

Isabelle looked up sweetly. "I guess it is as it should be. Fathers protect the virtue of their daughters even from a distance, *n'est-ce pas*?"

"We have to stop? I mean, do you want to stop?" Jack asked, feeling the moment had passed. She pulled the cloth of her dress top up to cover her breasts.

"What do you think, Mr. Buck?" She said with a pouting look that made him melt.

"Don't ask," he encircled her, stroking her hair. His breathing slowed to almost normal and his loins relaxed a little.

After several long minutes of standing like that in the hallway, Isabelle pulled away slightly and spoke very carefully. "The trust we must not betray is that which we have for each other," Isabelle touched his lips with her finger and looked deep into Jack's eyes before continuing. "I was ready to make you love me, you know."

Jack gasped very slightly at the realization of how close they were and how easy it would be to continue. "And now?" he asked.

"And now I find that I love you instead. Do you see? In loving you I cannot let you make love to me. Oh it is so confusing!"

Somehow, Pierre Flandin's call had checked them. The weekend became a thing of beauty and warmth rather than a slide into premature intimacy. Neither could articulate this phenomenon, but both felt relieved, and excited about the next time when stopping might not be as easy.

Chapter 16
The Devil's Own Playground

Pont à Mousson, March 3, 1915

Charlie ached everywhere. The straps of his pack rubbed his shoulders raw. While the boots no longer hurt his toughened skin—the blisters now hardened calluses—the long hours under the load of his seventy-pound pack made every muscle from toe to neck protest in dull pulsing agony.

His regiment moved into the communication trenches to relieve a unit now straggling back, each soldier vacant-eyed. After the forced march from the detraining point at Thiaucourt, twenty kilometers to the west, this glazed look distinguished the relieved from the relievers. Charlie's fellows, though exhausted and bedraggled, still possessed a measure of eagerness gone from the men they were relieving.

Captain de Lattre de Tassigny proved true to his word. Not only were there no leaves for the trainees, but they sacrificed even Sundays to accelerate the company's availability for combat. Charlie's six-week camp was longer by a whole week than projections for the next companies in the pipeline. Something had the French training command shaving everything superfluous. All grumbled, but few regretted getting out of Valbonne early.

Antonelli and the other non-coms seemed to change personalities overnight once the regiment entrained at Lyon for the trip north. Most of the squad leaders became solicitous of their men, checking their packs and sharing cigarettes. Only the most callous continued the abusive tone used in training. Out of the camp and out from under Antonelli's constant scrutiny, Sergeant Gueulard, the ninth squad leader, stopped hiding his seething anger.

Gueulard had been a naval ensign with the French fleet. Cashiered for hitting a superior, the pugnacious Gueulard joined the Legion and received his current rank based on his previous military training. His sadistic streak ran only inches below the surface. Charlie's favored position and acting corporal rank didn't sit well with Gueulard, not surprisingly a friend of Pasqualli. Now he had a chance to take the cocky American down a notch or two.

Gueulard ordered Charlie to lead a detail to pick up the extra equipment and ammunition for the section. Instead of drawing a few men from the other squads, Gueulard insisted that Charlie do it with three members of the ninth squad. The other men hefted their own heavy packs and deposited them on the railway siding before plopping down and dropping off to sleep while waiting for the train.

Charlie' detail started off-loading the supplies from a truck and placing them on the siding near where Gueulard said their rail car would be stationed. It took the men an hour to transfer the load. Just as they finished and were about to snatch some sleep, Gueulard returned, shouting that they had put the load in the wrong place.

Charlie was sure he had positioned the load exactly where Gueulard had told him. Assuming the sergeant had made an honest mistake, Charlie wanted to get the whole section to help. Instead, Gueulard berated him and told him to do it with his detail or do it himself. Knowing he would also have to load the stuff into the train, Charlie decided not to move it at all, reasoning: *Why move it twice? Besides, the train would be there before they could get it all moved. Why not just wait and put it directly into the car?*

Gueulard began to rave and kick at the men in Charlie's detail, shouting obscenities at Charlie when he saw they hadn't moved the load. Charlie didn't want any trouble, but he couldn't let the sergeant kick his men for something he had done. Charlie suspected that Gueulard knew the load was in the right place in the first place just to make him look stupid. If so, Charlie's failure to respond caused the former sailor's ploy to backfire. Now Gueulard would be the stupid one. Keeler expected him to get even later.

Detraining at Thiaucourt-Regniéville, the regiment still had a long march to the forward trenches. Charlie wasn't sure about Gueulard's little game. Rejik and the other members of the squad tried to warn him. No one liked the sergeant. Since leaving Valbonne, Gueulard hadn't missed a chance to abuse his people. As the rest of the company moved off, Gueulard kept Charlie's squad at the rail car, ostensibly for a final inspection. Consequently, the company got a ten-minute head start that forced the ninth to have to catch up.

At the traditional break after an hour's march, the ninth squad arrived just as the company moved out, Gueulard signaled no break. *More of this*, Charlie thought, *and the men would be wasted before they arrived in the first-line trenches.*

After marching since dawn, the company broke for breakfast at mid-morning. Gueulard sent Charlie to get the squad's rations near the head of the company column. That meant a trip of nearly twenty minutes while the rest of the squad rested. Charlie, still avoiding confrontation, grabbed two men and rushed off to get the rations. They returned with lukewarm coffee and soup, but now had less than five minutes before the column moved out again. Charlie saw Pasqualli standing behind Gueulard, smirking with undisguised pleasure.

Around noon, the ninth squad passed the second line trenches and descended into the labyrinth of communication trenches leading to the front. The constant flow of men moving to the rear made it difficult to keep together. As they neared the front-line, signs of recent activity and death assaulted their eyes. Discarded uniform items from both sides littered the tortured ground. A body facedown in a puddle at the bottom of a shell hole stunk to high heavens, swollen to the point of bursting. Charlie and his fellow legionnaires couldn't tear their eyes from it as they passed.

Arriving in the front trenches, the company spread out left and right with guides from the relieved regiment taking each section to its sector. Section lieutenants called their squad leaders together for the handover briefing by the guides. Gueulard sent Charlie in his place while he scouted out the best dugout for his own use.

Listening with the lieutenant and the other squad leaders to the other regiment's officer, Charlie found he could follow this guy's French pretty easily. The accent was different, more like his way of saying things. After describing fields of fire, artillery aim points, barrage sites, and known enemy positions, the man asked in plain English, "Any questions boys?"

Charlie's ears perked up. This was no officer, after all. Just a tall boyish-looking poilu covered with dirt. Waiting until his lieutenant had asked a question, Charlie ventured, "American?" The man stepped down off the dirt ledge and came over smiling.

"Chapman, Victor Chapman," his face breaking into a grin as he extended his hand. "I'd heard there were some other Yanks here!"

"Charlie Keeler, Saint Louis. Gosh it's great to see a fellow American!"

"Same here," Chapman said, beaming in spite of his haggard look. "I'm rotating back with what's left of my company. Listen, Keeler, it's the devil's own playground here. Every one of our officers went down in our first attack. That's why I'm here. My squad leader is now the company commander, not that there's much of a company to command. Never seen anything like it before." He heard a command in the distance and said, "I gotta go. Good luck! Make it through this week; I'll look you up in the reserve line."

Chapman saluted the lieutenant, shook Charlie's hand again, and shouldered his Lebel rifle. As he left the observation post and headed away, Charlie thought, *my God, he's not much older than me.*

Back with the ninth squad, Charlie surveyed his new surroundings. The trenches here were relatively newly dug. Every twenty feet or so there was a small loop cut as firing posts. They would serve as refuge should a Boche drop into their trench and try firing down the length of the line.

About every fifty feet, the poilus had carved a dugout in the backside of the trench wall. These were relatively shallow here since the other regiment had only been there a couple of days. Still, some of the dugouts were veritable rooms with meters-thick roofs reinforced with logs capable of taking all but a direct hit from artillery. Charlie decided being holed up in the ground ran counter to his fledgling sense of soldiering.

As he pondered this, a whistling sound followed by a deafening explosion, slammed Charlie down. More rounds began landing all along the company's front. "*Wilkommen!*" the Boches seemed to be saying. Dirt sprayed everywhere and men pressed themselves against the trench sides or dove into partially dug shelters ducking the rain of steel. Charlie's ears rang. The fall forced the air out of his lungs. As he struggled to refill them, he moved his arms and legs. With the shelling still going on, he resisted the urge to get up.

As suddenly as it started, the artillery barrage stopped. Officers shouted warnings up and down the line of the inevitable attack that would follow the preparation. Charlie got to his knees surprised to find he hadn't been scratched. Moving his right hand to brace himself on the side of the trench, he felt something wet and warm. He jerked his hand back from the gaping hole that had been the side of one of his squad mates.

The man's body was plastered to the trench wall erect and disturbingly normal looking. Blood and flesh spattered the soil around him. It looked as if a giant animal had chomped a bite out of his side. Charlie recoiled in horror. The soldier looked at Charlie through lifeless eyes with an expression of mild shock on his face. Dead! They hadn't been there an hour. It was the big Italian, the one with a wife and kids. Charlie wiped his hand in the dirt, expecting the Germans to jump into the trench at any second.

His lieutenant raced up and down the length of the section's line urging the squad leaders to keep alert. When the officer came to Charlie's position and saw the dead soldier, he reached over to close the man's eyes, telling Charlie to pull the man's body away from the parapet. "*Ou est votre chef, Keeler*?" the lieutenant asked.

"*J'ai pas, mon lieutenant*," Charlie replied, shaken by the concussion and the discovery of his dead comrade. The officer was anxious to find the regular NCO instead of this green acting corporal. They searched the line. Shrugs and looks of sheer terror offered no help until they poked their head into a partially collapsed dugout. Hearing a weak groan set Charlie to digging furiously. Soon he had uncovered a boot still attached to a moving limb. Fearing the worst, Charlie dug more carefully, calling for help. Two other soldiers came off the line to lend a hand, using their tin hats as scoops. Soon they uncovered the head of their cantankerous squad leader, Gueulard. More digging freed the sergeant enough for the men to pull him out spitting and choking on the dirt he'd swallowed. Gueulard seemed no worse for the wear.

"*Ils arrivent*!" A burst of machine gun fire seemed to growl and mount in volume marking the arrival of the expected Boche attack. A legionnaire poked his head over the edge of the trench only to fall back into the trench with a hole in his forehead. The lieutenant shouted to keep down and fix bayonets. Ignoring the groggy Gueulard, he grabbed Charlie by the shoulder and ordered him to gather his squad together for an immediate counterattack. Charlie couldn't believe his ears.

Seconds later the few German soldiers who survived the withering French machine gun final protective fires, leapt into the trenches only to be mowed down by the legionnaires. Instead of waves of attackers as expected, only a trickle made it to the trenches.

"*Maintenant*! Keeler. *Attaque*!" the lieutenant shouted, waving his saber as he climbed out of the trench. Charlie had no choice but to follow. His squad mates rallied to his side and the small party of eight legionnaires set off across the shell-torn ground towards the German line.

Dead and wounded Germans lay everywhere. The lieutenant began to run, his saber flashing, his white gloves standing out like beacons. All along the company's front the legionnaires rose to join in the counterattack. De Lattre himself led from the front of the first section far down the line. There was no question of coordinating the mad exhilarating headlong rush until the pre-registered German artillery and mortar fire slowed their momentum.

Surprisingly, Charlie's section made it to the German trenches unscathed. The lieutenant jumped in beside Keeler and was about to say something when a bullet tore half his lower jaw away. Shouting for the stretcher-bearers, Charlie felt sick to his stomach. Maybe the brave handsome lieutenant would survive. Keeler wished for Gueulard or anyone to take away the awful responsibility now facing him.

Squatting in the bottom of the German trench, Charlie pondered what to do next. His squad mates looked to him expectantly. He had no training or preparation for this! Charlie called Rejik over and sent him in search of the adjacent squad. Maybe one of the other NCOs could take charge.

Charlie was about to order the men to continue the attack when Rejik jumped into the hole with Antonelli on his heels. Captain de Lattre had placed the adjudant on the right flank of the company. The lieutenant in the second section in the middle had fought in the Marne battles with distinction, so he was fine. Antonelli, de Lattre knew, was as good as any officer. He cared about the men. He fought like a tiger and thought like a general.

De Lattre insisted that his section leaders launch immediate counterattacks when attacked. Charlie's lieutenant had done that, as had the other company sections. Following a long Legion tradition, prudent commanders developed their NCOs to take over when their officers fell.

Antonelli sized up the situation while the stretcher-bearers hustled the officer to rear. "Where's Gueulard?" he asked, not surprised that the troublesome former ensign wasn't where he was supposed to be. Keeler's brief account of the attack and Gueulard's burial would have been funny in another situation. Antonelli took charge of the section leaving Charlie in command of the ninth squad with orders to hold in position and expect an immediate German counterattack.

The counterattack turned out to be nothing more than some harassing artillery fire. Evidently, the Boches were worn thin in this sector after the two-week long series of attacks and counterattacks.

De Lattre's losses were minimal; though a sister company in the regiment had been decimated. Charlie's section had two killed and ten wounded, including the lieutenant. Charlie expected Gueulard back at any moment. After all, the man hadn't been wounded. Swallowing a little dirt wouldn't kill him, though the dirt he dealt his squad ought to make him worry about being shot by his own men.

Antonelli informed him that Gueulard now had Pasqualli's squad, and that Charlie was now the permanent—whatever that meant—ninth squad leader. Pasqualli had gone out with his squad and didn't come back. The men murmured about the hole in his back wondering if it had been his own men or the Germans when he had turned and ran.

The legionnaires settled into the trench routine. They had more than the Boches to contend with. Pont à Mousson, located on the Moselle River south of the German city of Metz, was cold and wet, the bane of all soldiers. At night the temperatures dropped below freezing, hardening the mud into ridges and valleys and layering a crust of ice on puddles of water in the trenches. During the day it warmed enough to turn the ground into a viscous muck that could suck the boots off a man.

In the trenches recently occupied by the Germans, the Legionnaires discovered another enemy—*Monsieur Toto.*

Lice, or "cooties" resided everywhere, often embedded in old blankets or straw so that the unsuspecting poilu using these convenient bedding items often became home to *Monsieur Toto* and his family. The cold drove the vermin to the warm human hosts. With the lack of hygiene in the forward trenches, the presence of these parasites added to the misery of the soldiers. Between the itching, crawling feeling, and the ever-present dirt, it became difficult to conceive of a more miserable existence—until one considered the food.

Prepared in field kitchens in the reserve lines of trenches, each squad and section had to send a pair of men back to get hot meals twice a day. The fare was simple and nourishing enough, if monotonous. The long trip to the rear usually meant that the stew or soup arrived at the front trenches no warmer than the frigid air with a layer of unappetizing congealed fat on the top. *Well,* thought Charlie, like many another poilu in the French Army, *there's no shortage of pinard.*

In the space of a day and a half, men already weakened by exertion and exposure, began to suffer from respiratory illnesses and foot problems. Standing in freezing water for hours on end didn't help. They named a new ailment *trench foot,* a condition that became increasingly painful as the skin sloughed off in the wet boots.

To add to the misery, machine gunners on both sides regularly raked the opposite trenches with devastating fire. Sharpshooters sat poised to plug any unsuspecting soldiers careless enough to expose themselves.

Even with that, in two days of holding the same line of trenches, Charlie and his fellow legionnaires had fallen into a sort of lethargic pattern punctuated by flashes of stark raving terror. Long periods of idleness gnawed at the soldiers. Some whittled pieces of wood, turned shell casings into *briquets*—homemade cigarette lighters—or scratched letters by the light of shielded candles in the dugouts. Cards appeared, dice were found, soldier's *sous* wagered.

Monotony reined but briefly between the *arrivées*—the incoming shells, and the *départs*—the shells fired by the French batteries several hundred meters to their rear. Charlie learned to distinguish the type and size of the artillery by the sounds alone. The German 77-millimeter shells had a distinctive high-pitched whistle as they began their murderous descent. Hearing it, the poilus had about three seconds to get to the *abri*—shelter of whatever type. The larger 120 and 155-millimeter rounds came in with a throaty whine. Most of them seemed to be targeted on the second line of trenches. When they impacted, the ground shook hundreds of feet away. A barrage fired by a German battery, or worse a regiment of three batteries, could cover an entire kilometer of the front. Men in the immediate zone of impact, if not shredded by the rounds, often emerged from their holes with blood pouring from burst eardrums.

By the end of the fourth day, Charlie welcomed the order to form a patrol to try to find the flank of the opposing German company that night. Everyone seemed to be itching for action.

They had a supper of surprisingly hot stew and fresh bread, before blackening their faces with burnt corks. They would take nothing but their trench knives, the rifle and trusty bayonet. Their mission was not to fight but to crawl close enough to the German line to try to determine the location of the gap that normally indicated the boundary between adjacent units.

Largely blind except for the reports from *les saucisses*—the line of tethered observation balloons used for adjusting artillery—the French command relied on patrols and captured enemy soldiers for intelligence. The Germans had studied the American use of cavalry during the Civil War, especially by the South. It had become a centerpiece of instruction in their military schools. The French, with a long tradition of cavalry, had begun the war by squandering thousands of splendid horses with their magnificent riders charging into the scything hail of machine gun bullets. Both sides quickly learned that traditional mounted cavalry, though not yet dead, was at best moribund. The thinkers at the great French school of cavalry at Saumur were reluctant to part with their classic mission. Information about the enemy was critical to breaking the stalemate, and, if dashing horsemen were out of the question, eyes on the ground, very close to the ground, were always available.

At 2 A.M. Charlie's patrol would leave the trenches. Crawling diagonally across the 400-meter space between the lines; the patrol would seek to arrive near the German trenches by 3 A.M., the time in the morning when sentries seemed least vigilant. They would advance in pairs a meter apart, just close enough to be able to communicate in whispers. When they reached the German lines they were to look for the large twin scopes of a spotting sight that would mark a company or regimental command post. That location would be combined with other information at the regimental command post to estimate the location of a seam between units, the best place to launch an attack.

If the patrol encountered any German patrols, they were to try to get back to friendly lines without firing. Captain de Lattre told Charlie not to risk the loss of his men, but that a Boche prisoner would certainly earn the patrol members the *Croix de Guerre*.

Charlie could barely recognize the men's faces. The Algerian, Hamed, already dark-skinned, was the most difficult to distinguish. He would be in the lead pair with Rejik. Charlie would follow with the Dutchman, Johann Hedjil, and his inseparable companion, a Corsican named Martini. These latter two, paired up during training, were tight as ticks in spite of language differences.

Antonelli and de Lattre were both at the parapet to see the patrol off. It was only the third patrol the company had launched, and the last before their relief by another regiment the next morning. The first met with disaster when a flare lit up the three-man team, inviting a withering spray of bullets that tore the men to pieces. The second patrol was a vengeance mission doomed from the start. This team of five set off to capture a German and ran dead on into a reinforced German patrol. Not daring to call on artillery or other fires to break the stalemate, the opponents resorted to vicious hand-to-hand combat. Two of the Legionnaires made it back, beaten and bleeding badly from knife and bayonet wounds. The Germans left at least seven of their own dead from this fracas.

Charlie was too excited to be afraid. De Lattre's insistence that this was a critical patrol weighed heavily on his mind. He'd built it up in his mind as the mission that could mean the end of the war. He, Charles Keeler, a nobody from Saint Louis, was going to lead it to glory. Though Charlie wasn't usually prone to such fantasies, allowing them to run their course had helped him pump up his men. His complete faith in them, unfortunately, would soon be shattered.

Chapter 17
Tous et tout pour la France

Paris, March, 1915

After their interrupted lovemaking, Jack and Isabelle found their passion somewhat cooled. Isabelle felt a combination of regret and relief. She couldn't believe how methodically she had plotted her deflowering. She recognized that her feelings for the young American were heavily colored by the excitement of their first encounter, of Haviland's resemblance to her brother, and by the aura of abandon fostered by the war.

For his part, Jack wasn't sure what was right. He couldn't ignore the strong urge that lingered from how close they had gotten. He was half proud of their restraint, feeling extreme tenderness toward Isabelle. Being so far from home, in a foreign culture with a foreign woman under wartime circumstances would tempt anyone. His brushes with blood and death and the *give a damn* attitude of many of his fellows challenged his scruples. Yet, the physical need had not diminished, and he doubted he would be strong enough to stop should they find themselves alone again.

The Flandins returned Sunday evening before the dinner hour, ushering in a visitor. "I believe you are already acquainted," Pierre said to Jack and Isabelle as the big man behind him stepped forward, bowing slightly.

"George!" Jack exclaimed. "What brings you here? I thought we had until noon tomorrow before we had to report?"

"Relax Jack. I am here with even better news. I thought it best to deliver it in person so that you could relax."

"Do come in," Isabelle said taking George's hat. "You can stay for dinner, can you not? *Papa, Maman, c'est bon?"*

"*Certainement*, come in, Monsieur Masters. *Un apéritif, Benoit*," Flandin ordered as he removed his coat.

Having Masters stay might be a little awkward, Jack thought, considering the man's usual reticence. He wondered what news warranted delivering in person.

"You are too kind Monsieur. I came only to pass a message to Mr. Buck."

Madame Flandin, as ever baffled by English, picked up enough of conversation to respond in her own manner. "*Bon. C'est décidé. Vous allez diner avec nous*." She swept away the big awkward man's feeble objections and took his arm, leading him into the living room.

"Looks like you are staying George. Now what is this news?" Jack asked.

"The whole Ambulance is in turmoil. The French are going to approve organizing our service into an official part of the French Army. Mr. Andrew told us himself that he wants to form a new section from the crews that went up to Dunkirk and flesh them out with new volunteers. We are to begin tomorrow. I don't know the details, but Mac says to anticipate being here at least a couple of weeks. Isn't that grand?" George stopped, looking a bit sheepish, not knowing how his news would be received.

"But, Jack, that is wonderful! We can see more of the city," Isabelle reacted before Jack could absorb the news.

"Hey! That is great! I'll bet Jim's tickled," Jack said, thinking about the formidable Marcelle.

Jack had a sense of *déja vu* as they sat down to dinner. They continued talking, eating and drinking into the evening until George left at midnight. Jack marveled at his friend's previously hidden social skills. Masters spoke French somewhat better than Jack, though not quite as well as McConnell. Jack could only guess at where the man had achieved his propensity for languages. George also seemed very much at ease in the presence of the women, reminding Jack of their exchange before returning to Paris. His table manners and conversation were impeccable. He had said more in that single evening than he had in the entire six weeks in the field.

The next day, Jack bade good-bye to the Flandins, promising to drop in as soon as he could. Isabelle kissed him chastely on both cheeks at the door. George's late stay kept Jack from private time with her. He felt faint pangs of jealousy when he noticed George's undisguised admiration of Isabelle, though he immediately dismissed this ludicrous thought.

MCCONNELL AND THE OTHER VOLUNTEERS gathered in the courtyard outside the small out building that served as the Ambulance Service headquarters at the American Hospital. Piatt Andrew, wearing the khaki uniform he had designed for the new American Ambulance Service, stood talking with two distinguished looking men.

Andrew addressed the rest of them, "Well, sports, it's finally coming together! We are going to be 'official' with all that implies. And, we are getting a new fleet of cars! I don't suppose anyone will object?" He said, with the men raising a cheer.

"Not just any cars either. Fords. American Ford Model T's!" he announced, producing another rash of cheers.

Mr. Andrew and his staff had feverishly sorted out the details for the new organization as soon as the government announced its change of heart. Several colleges and universities from the States had pledged to purchase and sponsor ambulances for the volunteers. Rather than send them by ship, they decided to buy the vehicles from the French-owned Ford factory at Lavallois outside Paris. Henry Ford would allow no discount or wholesale purchases of his cars for any sort of war service, even as ambulances. Ford's curious anti-war sentiments provoked anger in the volunteer organizations, but protests would be futile.

Andrew told them that they would pick up new equipment in the next two weeks. They would assist the French crews in constructing the box-like shelters that would go on the back of the Model T's to carry and protect the wounded. They would need to train a batch of volunteer drivers expected off ships arriving in the coming weeks.

Section Sanitaire Unitaire Une (Américaine) would be made up of the first group of experienced volunteers, still working in the Dunkirk region. Section Two, Andrew informed them, would be formed from the new arrivals with a core of experienced drivers from the old sections. French concerns about security and the threat of spies had been relaxed to allow single drivers. Andrew ended with his usual inspirational statement, the motto of the fledgling American Ambulance Service *"Tous et tout pour la France."*

The thirty or so men broke up into little knots around their leaders. Andrew gave each of them a written plan with specific section responsibilities. Dombasle would command Section Two, much to the delight of Jack and the others who had grown to respect the French officer. Dombasle's English hadn't improved, but his caring leadership and competence more than made up for it. *Sergent* Cartier was also staying. He too possessed little in language skills other than the ability to curse in at least three dialects of French. The Americans liked Cartier because he treated them as equals and knew more about motors and medicine than any of them.

McConnell translated for Dombasle as he read their instructions. Jim's near literal renderings of Dombasle's words produced some snickering. Like Jack, these men had picked up sufficient French to understand most of what the lieutenant was saying. McConnell's translation of *aller recupérer les chassis* came out 'going to pick up the bodies,' macabre humor at best.

Dombasle explained they would be organized like French Army Ambulance Sections and incorporated into the Automobile Service. Dombasle named McConnell as his second in command—a junior lieutenant's position in a normal section. *Section Sanitaire Unitaire Deux (Américaine)* would consist of thirty men including Dombasle, Cartier, a French driver, and a French cook.

Jack was terribly disappointed to learn that Félix Alejandro had stayed in Dunkirk as second in command of SSU 1. McConnell, on the other hand was pleased when his old friend and former business partner, Charles Chouteau Johnson, showed up. Johnson had been driving in the Dunkirk sector with a partial squad made up of American Ambulance men.

"Chute, you son of a gun, we meet again!" McConnell said slapping the smaller man on the back. "How the hell did you manage to hook up with the Ambulance without my knowing it?"

Johnson's compact five-foot seven frame and simple features were unremarkable—until he spoke. Chouteau's eyes danced to his words. His trimmed mustache kept time while his hands gesticulated between trips to rake through thinning hair.

"You guys left before I could join you! I asked about you and tried to get sent up to work with you, but I got involved in another section. Seems I can't shake you, Mac!"

"You know Jack Buck? No, I suppose you wouldn't. Let me introduce you to our own Swedish Norwegian Slovak. This guy drives like you wouldn't believe. A real lady killer too."

"Not another like you? I don't suppose he's a Hot Foot too?"

"What's a Hot Foot?" Jack asked, studying the man with the thin mustache and twinkling eyes.

Johnson said. "Mac here was president of the Society back a couple of years at Virginia. Guess you didn't go there?"

Jack looked to Mac to see if he was going to shed any light on this. McConnell just smirked. They wandered out the gate of the hospital and headed south. Jack divined that Chute also had a law degree, that he came from a prominent Saint Louis family, and that he hoped to fly.

Of the twenty-six American volunteers, about half were new men who Jack didn't recognize. Dombasle gave Jack the task of training the new drivers.

The next day, Mr. Andrew and Dr. Gros showed up at their morning formation. Andrew called for McConnell, Masters, and Buck to step forward. Dr. Gros then presented all three certificates of recognition signed by the commander of the British Expeditionary Forces, General Sir John French. Gros explained that the certificates arrived with a letter from the general apologizing for not being able to award military decorations to civilian volunteers.

The ceremony caught the three men by surprise. They looked at each other thinking there must be a mistake. Seeing their consternation, Piatt Andrew raised his hand to say a few words.

"The team of McConnell, Masters, and Buck is my personal choice to receive this distinction. Think of it as an award given not to individuals but to the whole volunteer ambulance effort by General French. Why did I pick these three, you might ask?" Murmurs in the ranks gave credence to this statement.

"The answer is this. They cannot see that they did anything more than any of the rest of you near Dunkirk. Their very modesty and selflessness is what I wanted to acknowledge before you all. It is the spirit of this Ambulance Service that is embodied in our motto, All for France, all to France. Remember that!"

Dombasle, McConnell, and Cartier found it ironic that the Americans should have to learn about an American car from French mechanics. The wisdom of that decision became startlingly apparent to Jack and the others when they discovered that each of their teachers had been trained at Ford's assembly plant in Dearborn, Michigan.

Jack took the men in groups to pick up Model T's at Lavallois. Back at Neuilly, Jack recruited Chouteau Johnson. Between lessons they picked up stripped Model T's for spares, a Ford staff car for Dombasle, another Ford light repair car, a couple of two-ton trucks, a trailer, and support equipment from a French Army caserne located west of Paris.

If the drivers wondered how the plain Model T with its open bed was going to serve as an ambulance, the answer came in the form of on-the-job training. As soon as a driver was assigned to a vehicle and certified by Jack as competent behind the wheel, he headed out to the *Quartiers Général du Commandant des Services Automobiles* in Versailles. Here French soldiers slapped a coat of battleship gray paint on the car and affixed numbers to the chassis. While the paint dried, a Paris police officer personally verified drivers as competent by having them drive a serpentine course in the park behind the splendid Chateau de Versailles. Only after passing this "test" would he issue the drivers their *livret matricule,* a combination of driver's license, registration booklet, and authorization to obtain fuel, oil, and tires anywhere in France. The drivers usually spent the night at the caserne, taking advantage of their free time to tour the nearby Chateau.

The next stop for the now militarized flivvers was at Kellner's factory in Sevres, not far from Versailles, across the Seine River from the famous porcelain factory. Here men and women assembled the bodies of wood and iron brackets that were then mated to the cars. The unwieldy looking body overhung the back wheels by at least three feet. Inside the box the space was cleverly arranged to hold three stretcher cases and up to two seated. The third stretcher was suspended on brackets in the middle while the other two were mounted over the wheels. A canvas cover completed the body, separating it from the driver.

As the work of collecting and preparing the section's equipment progressed, Dombasle and McConnell assembled and trained their remaining personnel. One day while sitting in the small office of their makeshift headquarters, Mr. Andrew interrupted Dombasle and McConnell to introduce them to a rather special volunteer.

"Allow me to introduce the Honorable Robert Bacon, lately a driver in a sister squad of yours, and before that our Ambassador to France."

Dombasle popped to attention and saluted sharply, saying, "*Mes respects, Excellence.*"

"Relax, lieutenant," the middle-aged man said in perfect French. McConnell couldn't believe that a former ambassador would stoop to the job of ambulance driver, but there he was, and his reputation had preceded him. All had heard about Bacon's sponsorship of the American Field Service effort and of his wife's chairmanship of the *American Committee of the American Hospital.* Bacon had also been Theodore Roosevelt's Secretary of State, McConnell recalled.

"How do you do McConnell? Andrew tells me you and your crew are famous already. Good show! Your friend Johnson was with me last month. I'll bet you're glad to be reunited."

"Pleased to meet you sir," McConnell said, at a loss for other words for once in his life.

Bacon looked to be in his mid to late forties. He dressed simply and had an unassuming demeanor that reminded McConnell of his father. Jim smiled at image of his father driving one of the ambulances, remembering the *brancardiers* they had worked with up north. Those dedicated French

Army stretcher-bearers were often too old to serve in the trenches. Jim saw that Bacon's service was no more than living out what he believed in, all the more remarkable considering Bacon's reputed wealth.

Jack and George walked into the little building, making it a bit crowded even for introductions. Bacon, who had been appointed ambassador by President Taft in 1909, awed both of the newcomers. He went out of his way to let them all know how much their volunteer efforts meant to the overall cause. He was extremely enthusiastic about the formal acceptance of the service by the French, a decision he had heartily endorsed. He asked them if they knew how extensive the effort in the United States was becoming to support the Ambulance Service.

"Well sir," Jack began. "I have been here only a couple of months. I didn't see much encouraging volunteers back in Minnesota other than a single poster." Masters and McConnell claimed ignorance, both having been in France since before the beginning of the war.

"Let me tell you—this is really exciting you know—there is an organization forming called the *Friends of France* with offices on several key college and university campuses in the states. You know about the Yale support for the Fords for Section Two? I foresee this really taking off. That man in the White House may take a long time to wake up, but nothing can stop true red-blooded Americans from seeing a good cause and finding a way to get into it." Bacon stopped, realizing he was starting to sound like a politician.

Clever idea bringing him around, McConnell thought.

JACK HAD NOT SEEN ISABELLE during the entire week. He worked long into the night trying to get their vehicles and equipment in shape, going over procedures with Dombasle and Cartier, and doing orderly work in the hospital whenever a large intake of wounded occurred. He hoped to get away Sunday to see her. Jim McConnell was planning an outing with Marcelle and had suggested they make it a double date. He had tickets to the opera *Mikado*. Jack agreed to ask Isabelle.

New volunteers trickled in a few at a time until late Saturday when a group of six from Yale arrived all at once. Their assignment to Section Two filled the manning chart. Dombasle asked Jack to see to getting them settled in the small attic dormitory of the hospital and to begin their driving instruction immediately. Jack forgot about the opera and Isabelle, and took charge of the group with growing enthusiasm.

Consequently, McConnell found himself with two extra tickets. Chouteau had a dinner engagement at an aunt's, so Jim asked George if he would go, thinking the man would have little interest in such a delicate production. George surprised him and offered to take both tickets and bring a date.

The matinee performance of *Mikado* was packed with opera lovers, soldiers on *permission*, half the diplomatic corps in Paris, and any number of Parisians seeking to escape the war. McConnell arrived early with Marcelle and waited in the elaborately decorated foyer for Masters, anxious to see who his friend would bring.

"Hello Mac." George said softly coming up from behind. McConnell turned around and did a quiet double take when he saw the lady on George's arm.

"Isabelle?" McConnell searched George's eyes for a clue as to how this could be; remembering the way Buck had pined for the French girl during their sojourn up north. Recovering his composure, Jim said, "*Je vous présent Mademoiselle Marcelle Guérin.*" Marcelle had met George during a visit to the hospital. The two French women exchanged polite, if cool, greetings. "*Alors, nous avons notre boîte à chercher, allons y,*" McConnell said leading them to their box in the beautiful Opéra Garnier worried that he might be the agent of a major falling out between George and Jack.

Chapter 18
Treachery Between the Trenches

Pont à Mousson, 0155 hours, March 7, 1915

Captain de Lattre slid in next to Charlie a few minutes before they were to begin their patrol. "*Mon ami américain*," the French officer said in a whisper. "It is I who should lead this patrol. I wish it were so, but I cannot disobey orders. Do you have any questions?"

Charlie wondered why de Lattre would share such information with him. He already knew that the captain wouldn't ask his men to do anything he himself would not do. His courage was legendary. If this was such an important patrol, Charlie thought, then why didn't they send a more experienced non-commissioned officer or one of the remaining lieutenants? It didn't occur to him that he and his men might be considered expendable. Charlie answered the question negatively and nodded his men up over the lip of the trench one at a time.

Not a star shined through the thick cloud cover. Mercifully, the rain had let up the day before. Joussef Hamed quietly slithered under the tanglefoot barbed wire in front of the squad's position with Havel Rejik close behind. Charlie started next, hoping no German observer chose that moment to launch a flare. Johann Hedjil and André Martini followed a few seconds after Charlie. Their plan was to crawl in two parallel lines with Charlie in the middle. They could still communicate while being spread out enough not to be taken out by one grenade or burst of machine gun fire.

Hamed's legendary night vision, developed in the darkness of the Algerian mountains and deserts, had already proven better than a cat's.

The man seemed to be able to see as well at night as many could during the day. The ground undulated haphazardly, churned by countless shells. After they cleared the belt of defensive wire the only obstacles they faced were more deep shell holes. They had been warned not to try to use them for shelter. Many were filled with water deep enough to cover a man's head. Charlie shuddered to think of drowning in the cold murky water.

In an hour of slow crawling, the patrol covered the 200 meters between the two sets of defensive obstacles. Now they had to negotiate the German network of barbed wire strung tightly between iron stakes six to eight inches off the ground. Ingeniously diabolical, this obstacle defied easy breaching. If a man tried to crawl on his belly underneath the wire, the barbs caught at his belt and harness and on any equipment sticking up. As he continued to move, pulling on the wire, cans and other noise-making devices would alert sentries to his presence. If the soldier tried to get up, the wire grabbed his legs casting him to a painful fall on the barbs.

Hamed led the way on his back wriggling and holding the wire up as he moved, looking out for the telltale noisemakers. The Germans favored cowbells that made a lot of racket. Poilus liked to take potshots at them when things were getting dull.

Progress through this next belt of wire was slow, but not as slow as it had been going out through the French wire. The Germans hadn't had as much time to develop their defenses in the short time since they had been driven back by Charlie's regiment.

Hamed cleared the wire and crawled parallel to the German side to make room for Rejik and the others to get through before they continued. Charlie had to make a decision whether to go to the right or left. Choosing the wrong way could mean exposing themselves twice as long. He checked his watch, the new one Michelle had sent with the luminous numbers he could read at night. They had been out nearly an hour and a half. In order to start back before first light, they had only about thirty more minutes.

He decided to split the patrol, something no one had suggested or warned him not to do. Hamed and Rejik would scout to the right for no more than fifteen minutes or until they found the observation post, whichever came first. He would go with Hedjil and Martini for the same amount of time to the left.

Charlie's group crept along the wire, venturing a little closer to the trench line every two or three meters to get a better view. Nothing! The quarter-hour went so fast that Charlie had to be reminded it was time to turn back. Martini got in front of him to begin the trek back on his stomach. After a few minutes he stopped.

"Something's queer here." He whispered to Charlie. "There are lights up ahead, faint ones, moving our way."

Charlie reached for Johann's shoulder, tugging on his harness to hurry him along. He led them a headlong belly race to get back to their rally point. If Rejik and Hamed had been discovered, their only chance was to scurry back to the French lines directly. When Charlie reached the place where they had come through the wire, he thought he saw Hamed, the whites of the man's eyes stood out prominently in his darkened face. Not daring to utter a sound, he inched forward to the unmoving figure, hoping it wasn't a Boche on patrol. He saw the lights Martini had mentioned. Definitely some action up ahead.

Reaching the still figure, Charlie whispered, "Hamed? Rejik?" He was greeted by a gurgling sound. Crawling closer, he verified it was Hamed, his head lolling unnaturally. Examining the Algerian closer, he found a trench knife sticking in the side of his neck, blood pulsing from the severed carotid artery.

"What happened?" Charlie whispered, fearing the worse for Rejik too. Hamed would bleed to death in minutes. The Algerian was trying to talk but nothing but a liquid rasp came from his mouth. Martini closed up on them and tried to see what Hamed was holding in his hand. It was too dark. Charlie knew he couldn't linger there much longer, but he'd be damned if he would leave without at least looking for Rejik.

"Come on, we'll retrace Rejik's path before we get out of here. There must be a German patrol out here." As soon as he said Rejik's name, Hamed jerked. He pounded his fist on the ground trying to say something in great agitation. He was close to breathing his last when Martini succeeded in wrenching the object from his hand. It was a grenade! One with the pin out! The bastards had put it there so that if it didn't go off when he died, it would if anyone tried to move him.

Martini flung the grenade as far as he could towards the lights. They heard it clatter, explode, and initiate a cacophony of gunfire that started in random shots and grew to a roar. Whatever the lights they had seen earlier had been, they were no longer visible. It was time to get the hell out of there.

Hedjil made one final attempt to help Hamed, saying something in Arabic. Hamed gave one final effort to speak and gurgled out what sounded like "Rejik, traitor!"

Charlie wasted no more time getting them on their way back. They dragged the lifeless body of their squad mate back with them. Hamed, who had so effortlessly negotiated the wire on the way through, became hopelessly entangled as his friends tried to drag his body back to their lines. They had no choice. They left him and scooted on their backs through the rest of the wire, coming out in a different place from where they had entered.

Just meters away at the point of their original entry, a German patrol lay in wait for them, unaware of the trio clambering out so close by, their movement masked by the continuing fires. Charlie couldn't make out much more than the outlines of the enemy patrol. A flare momentarily exposed the enemy. Their faces weren't blacked, except for one! Rejik! Still armed, and looking cozy with the Germans. Charlie's rage overcame his common sense at his friend's treachery.

"Rejik, you bastard! Burn in hell!" Charlie shouted, freeing his safety and firing all eight shots of his Lebel into the clump of men waiting to ambush them. Evidently, Rejik guided the Germans to their rendezvous point. If Hamed hadn't muttered "Rejik, traitor," Charlie might have thought him a prisoner.

Charlie's rounds nailed the six-man German patrol. He hoped he had hit Rejik in the process. No time to find out. He set off with the other two in a crouch, covering the distance to their own line of wire—what had taken them over an hour to negotiate on their stomachs—in several minutes. Charlie shouted the recognition word given his patrol exclusively for that night, "Brooklyn!" They were back in their own company's sector. They heard "*Allez, toute de suite, avancez*!"

Stepping over the wires, the three Legionnaires were inches from the trenches when more flares lit up no man's land like daylight. Murderous gunfire sluiced across the field catching Hedjil in the hip and knocking Martini from his feet. Caring hands reached out from the trenches to pull the men to safety.

"Where's Keeler?" Martini asked, holding his useless arm to his side. He started back up over the side only to be pulled back. Hedjil too had to be held down in spite of his terrible wound. He held the trench knife pulled from Hamed's neck and asked to talk to an officer. Antonelli, now an acting lieutenant, appeared as if on cue.

"Tony," Hedjil moaned before losing consciousness. "We were betrayed! Check this knife to see if it is not Rejik's."

"Where is Keeler?" The Corsican asked his countryman, Martini.

"He was behind me when I was hit," Martini replied. "Get him back, Tony!"

"Tais-toi André, je t-assure que je le trouve." Antonelli reassured the wounded man.

In seconds, Antonelli had a party of six soldiers moving out under the revealing light of new German flares, braving fire for one of their own.

They didn't have far to go. Keeler was facedown and unconscious with his ankle wrapped in a strand of barbed wire. They freed his foot and rushed him to the trench just as German mortars began to fall around them.

Antonelli had the three injured men moved immediately to the shelter of the nearest dugout. The French medic who had already bandaged Hedjil and Martini stood ready to bind Charlie's wounds. At first they couldn't find any. Back in the dugout under the light of the lantern, they could just distinguish a line of red on Charlie's scalp. He had been lightly grazed—not enough to knock him out from the looks of it. Apparently, the fall had taken care of that. He had a large lump on his forehead where he had hit the ground hard. Aside from a headache, the medic told Antonelli, the American should be fine when he regained consciousness.

Martini, the only coherent survivor of the patrol, was distraught that his buddy Hedjil was so seriously wounded. He was still confused about what had happened on the patrol, having been in the process of throwing the grenade when Hamed had uttered his damning "Rejik, traitor." He'd heard Charlie's shout and saw him firing, but he didn't understand anything but Rejik's name in the burst of English. Maybe Charlie was firing to avenge his friend? Martini wondered what Johann had meant when he told Antonelli to check the trench knife.

Charlie seemed to be coming around. Antonelli knelt beside him, looking up as Captain de Lattre entered the dugout. He told the captain he thought they had a major problem here.

"What is it?" De Lattre asked.

"*J'ai peur qu'on a un espion, ou un saboteur dans nos rangs, mon capitaine.*" Antonelli replied, telling de Lattre about Johann Hedjil's last words. Quickly piecing together what had happened from Martini, Antonelli realized that his fellow Corsican still didn't suspect Rejik of betraying the patrol. The key was the knife that Martini agreed had been used to kill Hamed. A German might use a soldier's *own* knife to kill him in a tight hand-to-hand fight, but how would he get *another* soldier's weapon? The trench knife had the initials "HR" clearly scratched in the handle in accordance with company policy. It wasn't much to go on. They would have to wait to hear from Charlie. If there was a spy in their ranks, it was a damned good thing they were leaving for the second line that day.

Chapter 19
A Different Betrayal

Paris and Northeastern France, late March to April 1915

The day of the opera Jack Buck had gotten his group of Yalies settled only long enough for them to ask when they would be free to do some exploring. He told them they would begin training immediately, provoking shouts of derision and catcalls.

"Hey, isn't it Sunday, the day of the Lord? You know, the Sabbath, no work and all that," one shouted.

Another claimed they'd all learned to drive before shipping over. They were indeed the first batch of volunteers who had received some preliminary instruction on campus. Jack listened sympathetically, learning that each of them had paid their own passage to France. They were told they would have to buy their own uniforms. All came with the requisite bundle of letters attesting to their character. *Heck,* Jack thought, *these guys are more ready than I was. What's the harm in letting them have a little fun?*

As the only one having any idea how to get around, Jack found himself pressed into service. The Yale men, all but one from the Class of 1916, deferred to Jack as though he were an old soldier, a treatment that amused Jack.

He took them on a tour of the more famous sights, using the Métro or walking to avoid being separated in taxis, though these boys seemed to have no end of money. By the time he thought to call on Isabelle, it was too late in the afternoon. Going to a couple of bars and helping them decide where they were going to buy him dinner seemed infinitely better than some screeching old opera.

At Chatham's Bar on Rue Daunou, they met Elliot Cowdin, one of the veteran drivers who had just enlisted in French Aviation. Cowdin introduced them to Norman Prince, another recently arrived American. Prince, an older, somewhat reserved Harvard man, was cool to the Yale boys, but he did take interest in Jack, the only one in uniform.

"Buck, you know I am working with some influential businessmen and French authorities trying to get an all-American flying squadron organized. Elliot here is interested. Some other fellows are already flying in French uniform. Why don't you give it some thought?"

"I like the sound of that, Mr. Prince, but I'm in the middle of organizing a section of the new American Field Service. Can't switch horses in mid-stream, you know." The thought of flying seemed out of reach, if intriguing.

"Well, keep it in mind. I was just telling Elliot about Pau, where he is headed for flight training. I spent many a summer there with my family. Do you know the place?"

"Somewhere in the south, isn't it?" Jack guessed, a little ashamed he didn't know French geography better. He looked around for his group, finding all five at a table busy trying out three or four different concoctions from the bar.

"Pompous sot, your Prince," one of them commented.

"That's Harvard for you," another added.

"Mr. Buck, come tip one with us! Wash the conceit away, good fellow."

Jack ended up having to pour the boys into a car, all thoughts of dinner abandoned. Remembering Isabelle with the phone pressed between her breasts the last time he was there, pushed him to call. Maybe she would still want to see him.

Her father answered, surprised that Jack didn't know she had left earlier with Mr. Masters for the Opera. Jack hung up quietly and scratched his head in total confusion. *Isabelle with Masters?* He climbed the stairs to the open ward where they slept, miffed, feeling the effects of the drinks he'd had, but mercifully dropping off in minutes.

Without time to dwell on Isabelle, Jack threw himself into the work of training the newcomers. Suspecting George of moving in like that irritated him, but the big man was older and more experienced. It wasn't anything like being thrown over by Sandy for a high school classmate. *Sandy,* he wondered for the first time in days. *Hope you are happy.*

"Jack, let's talk," George said in a very solicitous tone. "I know what it looks like, but let me explain."

"Explain what? You took Isabelle to the opera because I couldn't. I should thank you, right?" Jack said unable to hide a trace of sarcasm.

"Well, she's a nice girl, but I am almost old enough to be her father." Jack looked at Masters skeptically. The man was such a mystery.

"Okay, *dad.* Hope you enjoyed the opera. See you around, George."

When he saw them together at the hospital entrance after work one night, he quickly turned back into the building hoping to avoid them. Jack didn't know that Isabelle was trying to avoid him as well, suffering guilt and embarrassment from throwing herself at him.

Jack retreated even deeper into his work. He cursed himself for thinking he had a chance with the daughter of a rich businessman, forgetting Flandin's kindness and genuine affection.

One day Jack found Jim McConnell lounging, smoking a cigarette in the shade of a plantain tree. "Jim, how are you? Got another one of those? I'm fresh out."

McConnell passed the pack and patted the ground beside him. "Take a load off. You've been working so hard that you make the rest of us look like slackers. What's going on, Jack?"

He listened with interest to Jack's description of Norman Prince and of the Massachusetts man's scheme for forming an American Squadron. Many of the drivers were buzzing about getting a chance to join the glamorous, exciting, and enormously popular pilots of the French Aviation. If they didn't already have such a demanding and challenging mission, Jack observed, he thought about half of the drivers would run down to enlist in aviation.

"Yeah, I've heard the scuttlebutt, but that's not what's driving you so hard. George is acting strange too. Clue me in."

"George is seeing Isabelle."

"Yeah, but there's nothing there. He's like an older brother to her."

"I suppose so…. Ah, forget it," Jack sighed.

"Hey Jim, weren't you President of the Aero Club in school?" Jack asked, anxious to change the subject. Chouteau Johnson squatted down in front of them catching Jack's question and adding that Jim practically organized the club.

"Nothing but a bunch of model makers and dreamers, Chute. We did go to the field at Charlottesville and try to bum rides on their Wright Flyer, but nary a one of us got up on my watch."

"No end to surprises with you, are there, Mac?" Jack said, getting up and brushing off his pants.

"Not as many as old Masters, though. Come on. We can talk about it later."

THE NEWLY OUTFITTED *SSU 2, SECTION SANITAIRE UNITAIRE 2,* left Paris the day the Battle of Woëvre began, March 30, 1915, two days before the American Field Service charter was signed. Lieutenant Dombasle was proud of his team. Getting to their assigned station behind the lines should be a breeze with guys like McConnell, Buck, Johnson, and Masters interspersed in the column.

At Dieulouard the mayor led a contingent of young girls, laden with flowers, parading to greet them. Word of their arrival had obviously preceded them. The town, nestled in a bend of the Moselle River, consisted of clusters of neat buildings lining cobble-stoned streets. At the southern end a French Army caserne belonging to the Automobile Service became their headquarters.

The men moved into long open wooden barracks recently vacated by an infantry company. The infantry was barely twenty miles away on the Woëvre River, just north of Pont à Mousson. SSU 2 was there to support them.

Dombasle and McConnell disappeared the first day, leaving the others with instructions to prepare for immediate action. The Fords, covered with dust inside and out, needed cleaning and servicing.

Dombasle reported to the division headquarters. He and McConnell gathered information on the battle situation, the condition of local routes to the front, and the locations of the *postes de secours* or aide stations. SSU 2 would slide in beside a French Army *Section Sanitaire* and take over evacuations for two of the division's four regiments. Their sector would be in a place called *Bois le Prêtre*, or "Priest's Woods."

Jack and the other drivers made trial runs to the various postes de secours and back to the clearing stations, taking advantage of the lull in action. Things were calm until April 15.

The major offensives planned by the French that spring included attacks in the Champagne region with supporting attacks further east on the Woëvre north of Pont à Mousson. The French lobbied heavily to get the expanding BEF to launch an offensive in the Ypres region of Belgium in the hopes of spreading the German effort so thin that a breakthrough might be accomplished elsewhere.

The slight lull in action in February and early March allowed both sides to hunker down in their static positions. German engineers, often using the great French engineer Vauban's designs, hardened as many of their positions as possible. French attacks into the teeth of these defenses produced staggering casualties.

At Bois le Prêtre, SSU 2 built a reputation that became the envy of every section of the American Ambulance thereafter. After two weeks behind the French First Division, wounded French poilus actually began asking to be carried away on an American Ambulance.

Jack enjoyed being on his own. He had leaned heavily on McConnell. He even copied some of Jim's gestures and style while training the newcomers. He was thankful for the mentorship. His confidence increased when he realized he had a knack for being in charge.

Being alone gave him time to think. He wondered if Willis Haviland would make it back. He tried not to think about Isabelle. He probably should be irritated with George, but for some reason he wasn't. They saw each other infrequently in the frenzy of their work. Jack wasn't lonely, but he did miss Mac and Masters and the banter they'd kept up during the work in Dunkirk.

Even though Isabelle had stopped writing, Pierre and Berangère Flandin sent him a package every week. Pierre wrote at least a page of English, doing much better than Jack could in French. Flandin's letters told of the growing importance of fighting aeroplanes and of men to fly them. Jack looked forward to the letters and the candies Madame Flandin packed along with jars of jam and tins of crackers.

He received his first packages from home at Dieulouard. They were full of notes and drawings from his sisters, more candy and chewing gum, and copies of the Minneapolis newspapers. The packages made him homesick, but the weeks old papers frustrated Jack because they carried so little news of the war. He resolved to write some articles. He certainly had some interesting stories to tell, though he was realistic enough to doubt anyone would publish them.

One morning McConnell found Jack sitting in his ambulance with tears in his eyes. Buck told him about bringing a child back to her mother in Dieulouard. "I keep seeing one of my sisters lying dead on that stretcher, Jim. I don't know how much more of this I can take."

"We're due for a break," McConnell said, sliding in beside Buck. "Dombasle tells me the French are trying to get one of their sections up here to spell us. When we get back to Paris I'm looking into flying. I can't stand watching all this and doing so little to bring it to an end."

"Getting to *you* too, Jim? And here I thought you were trying to ease *my* mind."

"Yeah," McConnell continued. "You aren't afraid to cry at the terrible things you've seen. You think it's weakness, but I admire it. Being *sous-*

chef means I have to keep the proverbial stiff upper lip with all the rest of the drivers. Dombaşle expects me to keep us Americans happy."

"But, Jim, you've been driving as much as the rest of us."

McConnell shook his big head, and turned to Jack with subdued fury in his eyes. "We have to get into this war! What is wrong with our country? I can't stand by and watch this marvelous nation bleed to death like the poor poilus we carry."

Mac had something Jack had yet to feel—*commitment.* Jim was ready to take up arms for the French cause. The little girl's lifeless eyes kept swimming before him pleading, begging him to do something. *What can one man do?*

Spring was now fully upon the Vosges, the blossoms defying the squalor of winter and war. Trees in full bloom filled the air with sweet fragrance. Yellow and lavender fields defied the dust raised by countless hooves, boots and tires. Hints of optimism crept into the hearts of the men of SSU 2 as their relief approached. Some of the men even broke out the baseball gear brought by the Yale group and began limbering up for some intra-section competition.

As April gave way to May, their six-week stint ended. The men spoke excitedly about their plans while in Paris. Many planned excursions into the Saint-Denis area where the ladies of the night kept shop. Some talked of quitting and going back to school in America. All wondered where SSU 2 would go next. Some talked about joining the Legion or going into flying.

Jack looked forward to the break, but he dreaded going back and seeing George with Isabelle. He had made his mind up to stay with the Ambulance and try to find out something about his friend Haviland. If the opportunity to look into flying arose, he wouldn't turn his back on it. Maybe he could get into something where he wouldn't have to shoot or bomb anyone.

Chapter 20
New Friends, More Action

Bethonsart, late April, 1915

Charlie still wondered why he had been transferred to the *Premier Régiment d'Infanterie* after the crazy fracas with Rejik. He'd awakened with a huge headache and a lump the size of an apricot on his forehead. Captain de Lattre and Antonelli hovered over him with great concern. All he could remember was the mad dash across no man's land, yelling out *Brooklyn!,* and then everything going black.

Trying to clear his aching head, he sat up, almost passing out again. Antonelli gave him a cup filled with cognac. It worked almost instantly. Keeler wanted to go back to sleep, but de Lattre and the others insisted on answers. Then he remembered Hamed.

"The bastard! All that bull about equality. I thought he was my friend. Oh *merde,* Martini, Hedjil? Were they…are they here?"

"*Doucement,* Keeler. Both will live," Antonelli told him. "Hedjil has been evacuated with a serious wound to his leg. Martini is still here, wounded in the arm, but he won't let them take him until he talks to you. What happened to Rejik?"

Charlie had been unconscious for about an hour, long enough for them to question Martini. De Lattre wasn't taking any chances. If there was one spy, there could be others. Charlie's explanation fit Martini's up to the point of Hamed's accusing Rejik. Martini hadn't heard that. Charlie insisted he had no doubt what Hamed said or meant. Rejik had been a plant. He must have spoken German, he reasoned, like many Czechs and Slovaks. He had no idea how Rejik did it, but he told them about seeing Rejik with the Boche ambush in the flashes of light from the firing. Clearly, Rejik, who still had his rifle and held it at the ready, was not a prisoner. Moreover, Jack remembered, the Germans wore their distinctive coal bucket helmets, while Rejik was bareheaded like the rest of Charlie's patrol.

"*Quel dommage! Quel trahison*!" de Lattre hissed, his anger mixed with the frustration that he didn't know who else to trust in his company. He told Charlie he would do everything he could to get him not only a *Croix de Guerre*, but the *Médaille Militaire*, an award not given often to foreigners, at least not to those still living.

The French command wasted no time. In the next twenty-four hours de Lattre's company was dispersed into other regiments in far-separated divisions in the hopes of preventing any collaboration between potential conspirators. Charlie would go to the First Regiment of Infantry.

"I go too, Keeler," Antonelli said, assuring Charlie that he was under absolutely no suspicion. "I get a company, Charlie. I'll be sorry not to have you in it, *mais c'est la guerre*." The tough Corsican actually had tears in his eyes as he embraced the American, bidding adieu.

Charlie hated leaving. Antonelli, had been his first real mentor and guardian angel, like the older brother he never had. Hedjil and Martini were both recuperating in a hospital near Nancy. There was no time to visit them. At least his orders read *Caporal Keeler*. Captain de Lattre gave him a packet, addressed to his new regimental commander, including the citation for the *Croix de Guerre* and a very strong recommendation to give the American a leadership position.

Charlie arrived just in time to join the regiment on its march to Arras, near Bethonsart, a different sector entirely from the one he had just left. The best thing about the transfer was his assignment to the section that had some Americans. Company 2, Battalion B seemed every bit as colorful as his first unit. Charlie went, naturally, to the so-called *American* squad, at least in name. It didn't bother him that another corporal led the squad; a giant Moor named Didier. Charlie had had enough of leadership, in spite of de Lattre's strong endorsement.

The other Americans in his squad were Paul "Skipper" Pavelka, a fellow named Kelly from Virginia, and Larry Scanlon. According to Kelly, there were about fifteen other Americans in the regiment. Keeler fell right in with them and the other interesting characters of the squad. Neanmoin, an Indian from Delhi, was an Oxford graduate. Zannis, the Greek, came from Constantinople. Two others, veteran legionnaires named Jury and Godin, were Belgians.

His countrymen quickly took him under their wings. Some had been in the Legion since August of 1914. Their stories fascinated him. They were equally impressed to hear of his experience at Pont à Mousson. He wearied of telling how Rejik had befriended him until that terrible and fateful night of betrayal. "Judas!" they would holler whenever he finished the story, everyone's blood boiling at Rejik's horrendous perfidy.

Russell Kelly told him about going to the Virginia Military Institute, and leaving before graduation in order to join the Legion. Charlie hadn't heard many genuine Southern accents. Russ's dripped with magnolias, rang in Confederate calls, and evoked a time and place Charlie knew only from reading.

"Ah was a raht, somethin' yaw'll kin thank yer Lawd ya'll ne'er be." Kelly would begin, telling about sleeping on the springs of a military cot as a first-year "brother rat." Charlie discovered that Kelly came over in the same convoy with the *Rochambeau*, having sailed on the *Carpathia*, the tramp steamer with its load of 650 horses. Kelly told him he lost fifteen pounds on the trip due to the lousy food and being sick most of the time. Few could rival Russ as storytellers, Charlie realized, especially after Pavelka told him Kelly came from New York, not Virginia!

"Wasn't it the *Carpathia* that picked up *Titanic's* survivors?" Pavelka asked.

"Heard that tale a thousand times," drawled Kelly. "Damnation it had been a fine ship at that time. Rotten luck for us that it had seen better days."

Kelly's faked accent and reputation as a raconteur notwithstanding, Paul Pavelka's tale was even more incredible. Pavelka was a short stocky man with a ready smile. He'd left home at sixteen.

"Sheared sheep from 1908 to 1912 in Vermont and New Hampshire then hired on as a cook in a lumber camp in Canada." So far believable, Charlie thought.

"Got shot by mistake by a police officer in San Francisco. I was an assistant nurse in the hospital. They brought in a tough in shackles who decided to use me as a shield. Lord it hurt! Right here in the side," he pulled up his shirt to show them the scar.

"Did they get the guy?" someone asked.

"Fainted dead away at the sight of my blood," Pavelka laughed.

Charlie began to doubt Pavelka after hearing him claim he had then sailed on every ocean, *and* walked all the way across South America! Even more incredible, Pavelka said he spent two years in the U.S. Navy before finding his way to England and eventually France and enlisting in the Foreign Legion.

"Makes you about fifty to have fit it all in," joshed Scanlon.

Larry "Red" Scanlon seemed a little out of place. A Cedarhurst, Long Island native, Red had arrived in France about the same time as Kelly and Charlie, but he had no great exploits to relate. As modest as he was, Red looked strong and solid. He enjoyed Charlie's story about the day in the bayonet pits with Antonelli. Scanlon's story didn't have a happy conclusion.

"We went to Toulouse for our basic where we were placed under an American named Morlae, a real son of a bitch if ever one existed." Others in earshot when Red told this story nodded vigorously in agreement.

"Morlae had joined up before the war and completed training before we got there. The French must not have liked him much either since they decided not to send him out with a regiment, keeping him there instead. Morlae kissed more ass than any person I have ever seen. They made the bastard a corporal and gave him the American squad in my company. He went out of his way to make us miserable."

"Reminds me of one of my sergeants," Charlie commented.

"Anyway, Morlae kept putting guys under arrest for piddly things, costing them what little free time they had. Some of the guys hoped he would be sent to the front with us. They even drew straws to see who would shoot the crumb. We got our wish back in February, going into action near Craonnelle. Would you believe a shell buried Morlae before one of us could do him any harm?"

"No! You've got to be kidding," Charlie exclaimed. "That's what happened to my squad leader! We dug him out."

"Morlae survived too, but the little shit did stop harassing us after we dug him out. He was all smiles and buddy-buddy until he split." Red smiled when he said this, obviously relishing the fact that Morlae wouldn't bother them any more.

Charlie decided he was going to like his new unit. The men were certainly friendly. The Greek, Zannis, could cook a piece of wood and make it taste like steak. Listening to the Indian's Oxford accent when he recited poetry from the *Oxford Book of English Verse* made the time pass almost pleasantly, though rumors of a big push planned at Arras had them on edge.

Kiffin Rockwell, one of the brothers Charlie had read about back home, came to the regiment a few days after Keeler. Rockwell looked about his age. He was dark-haired and good-looking. His energy was contagious. Charlie took to him immediately.

Kiffin had spent the past seven months with two different Legion Regiments beginning with the first one to take on volunteers in August

1914. He came loaded with information about all the Americans in the Legion. His brother, Paul, had been wounded in December and invalided out of the Legion. Paul now worked in Paris as a combat correspondent with the *Section d'Information* of the French Army, writing Kiffin long newsy letters.

Charlie pumped Kiffin about the first months of the war, finding out that the Rockwells and the twenty-eight other Americans had undergone almost exactly the same experiences as he had.

"Back in March, or maybe it was earlier—I can't keep track any more—we had our first American casualty. We were back behind the lines at Cuiry-les-Chaudardes at the time. A bunch of us were in a courtyard drinking coffee when a couple of tough bronzed vets came up taunting us and claiming they could lick any or all of us. I think they were Algerians—Arabs, it doesn't matter.

"René Phélizot, a tough little guy born in France but raised in the Bronx, decided to defend our honor. He knocked one of the braggarts on his ass and started in on the other when a big Alsatian came up and conked poor René on the head with a two liter bidon full of wine. Phélizot went down like a log and all of us jumped the bums. It was a helluva brawl.

"Your friend must have had a heck of a headache," Charlie said. Kiffin shook his head.

"The regimental doctor, a real hard case, thought René was shamming and refused him treatment. A couple of days later they found Phélizot sitting beside the road near Fismes, dead from a fractured skull and tetanus. It made all of us sick. We got into another brawl with the instigators. The damned Alsatian, well, he got his. They kicked him to death."

"What about the doctor?" Charlie asked.

"Oh, they sent his sorry ass back to Paris where he treats hangnails in a prison sickbay."

On May 5, the regiment moved up to the front-line trenches, supposedly for 48 hours. At first, everything was calm though the German trenches were as close as eighty meters away. Snipers kept everybody's heads down, so moving out to the listening posts was a dicey and chilling proposition.

That night the adjacent squad got some action. A Légionnaire corporal took two Spaniards and three Russians from the squad out to the listening post. They'd been there several hours when they heard someone saying in a loud whisper: "kamerad, kamerad." They listened more closely. One of the Russians who spoke German told the corporal he heard the same voice saying, "I have information, kamerad!" The Russian answered in German "You are close! Come this way." Soon the voice became a body which the men in the listening post saw was a Légionnaire! They'd lured him in the wrong direction! The offender received swift Legion justice from six bayonets right there on the spot.

The First Regiment's leaders reasoned that the upcoming attack would take care of any other would-be traitors. Hearing about it the next morning, Charlie worried that they might be wrong.

The men dug tunnels leading forward. Instead of being relieved, they were told they would lead the attack at midnight. They spent the day making trips to the rear for ammunition and food and building embankments right up to the German wire. At eight that night, they settled down to wait for the order to attack. At ten, their leaders announced the attack had been postponed.

Charlie sensed the relief felt by all of them at this reprieve, but almost everyone bitched like they were disappointed. The next morning another regiment relieved them. They marched twelve kilometers to the rear, an incredible four of them in trenches. They didn't get to lie down to sleep until nearly seven that night.

At one in the morning, they were awakened and told to pack. All the grumbling was ignored. By daybreak, they moved back to the second line of trenches. The attack was on! The bombardment started at dawn. The men shaved off their beards. Their officers dressed in their cleanest uniforms with all their medals shining, and donned fresh white gloves.

"Is it a ball we're going to?" Kiffin snarled.

"Damned exciting, isn't it?" Charlie replied, remembering his first exhilarating charge.

"Into the valley of death rode the six hundred," Kiffin quipped, hoisting his pack onto one shoulder.

At ten, the First Regiment attacked. Seven minutes later, Charlie's company went over the top. Charlie felt like he was floating, carried on a wave of furor, his pack like nothing at all on his back. He ran in between Skipper Pavelka and Kiffin. Their company commander, Captain Boutin, was only a yard ahead of them. In only a minute or two the Captain's face turned red with blood, hit by a shell fragment.

"*Cochons*!" he shouted, not losing a stride in his advance. Charlie thought about his lieutenant at Bois le Prêtre. *These officers are incredible! Where do they get their courage?*

They advanced in dashes of ten to twenty-five meters, jumping into holes in between. By three that afternoon, they had gained three or four kilometers. The colonel and two of the battalion commanders were down. Whistling shards of bursting shells whizzed through the air. The racket of hundreds of machine guns, rifles and explosions drowned out the shouts of the wounded, making passing orders almost impossible.

Charlie jumped into a hole with Kiffin and Skipper Pavelka, both of whom were lying next to the sous-lieutenant. All four were surprised to be untouched so far.

A messenger jumped in to tell the lieutenant that both the captain and the senior lieutenant were hit, meaning the sous-lieutenant was now company commander. The lieutenant gave them the direction to advance, rose from the hole and started running toward the enemy. Charlie heard Kiffin yell "we might as well get it over with!"

Charlie jumped up first, running close on the heels of the lieutenant. He dared not look back so he didn't see Pavelka coming up behind him or notice him stop and go back. He pressed on mesmerized by the movement of the back of the officer in front of him.

By dark, the company closed in on La Targette, a village ten kilometers deep in the German lines. Pavelka told him that Rockwell had been shot in the thigh and was working his way to the rear. Their corporal, Didier, the big Moor had been nearly cut in half by machine gun fire. The rest of Charlie's squad survived the attack. The lieutenant ordered a head count and called all the NCOs together. A pathetic little assembly showed up to report only fifty-five effectives of the original 250 in the company. The lieutenant made Charlie squad leader of his eight survivors and gave him two more from another squad. He ordered them to prepare for the inevitable counterattack, knowing the depleted regiment could do no more than fight a delaying retreat.

Charlie got Skipper Pavelka, Russell Kelly, Red Scanlon, and the rest of his squad to go back and police up as much ammunition as they could carry. He asked the lieutenant where he wanted the American squad and got a strong "*Avec moi, caporal, avec moi*!"

They had a respite of about three hours during which the Germans poured artillery into their old positions. Messengers came from the regiment, now down from 4,000 to a mere 1,700 men, saying no reinforcements were possible, but they were to hold their positions.

Charlie started thinking about fields of fire and withdrawal lanes. It would be difficult fighting a rearward holding action without firing at each other at night. He decided to pair his men up and space the pairs no more than a couple of yards apart. He would stay in the middle with the lieutenant who would let them know when they could pull back.

The first counterattack came at midnight, followed closely by a second wave. The sky became bright with all the fires, exposing the defenders and attackers alike. The legionnaires made the Germans pay dearly for the regained ground, but, before first light, had to give up nearly six kilometers of the ten they'd gained.

At about six the morning of the tenth, Charlie could barely keep his eyes open, his adrenaline reserves depleted. Pavelka and Kelly tried to shake him awake, succeeding in making him just a little angry. "I'm all right dammit! Leave me alone. Where's Kiffin?"

"Charlie, I already told you he was wounded in the thigh yesterday." Pavelka said, looking at Kelly.

"Come on Charlie," Russ pleaded, trying to hide his concern. "Let's go!" They grabbed Charlie under the arms hoping to get him on his feet for the next jump to the rear. Charlie yelped when they touched him. Their hands were wet with blood. Somehow, in the heat of the retreat, Charlie had been hit without letting on, or maybe without even knowing it himself.

They opened his blood sodden shirt. He had a hole no bigger than a little finger in his left armpit and a nasty crease under his right arm. Charlie must have been hit at some point with his arms in the air giving signals. How long had he gone without telling anyone?

They were far enough back to be able to call for brancardiers. Caring arms carried the Missourian back to the nearest *poste de secours*. Pavelka and Kelly wondered how long it would be before their turn came. Neither had long to wait.

Chapter 21
Revelations

Mid May, near Arras

Instead of being sent back to Paris as they'd been told, SSU 2 received instructions to proceed with all haste to Arras on the 5th of May. Dombasle was as disappointed as the drivers. While the poilus served four to six days in the first line trenches, they at least rotated to the second line for about the same number of days for some rest, and then to the rear for another week or so. The ambulance drivers went six or more weeks straight without break.

Having been essentially in one place for the whole six weeks, the men of SSU 2 had acquired so much junk that they were pressed for places to put it. Dombasle insisted on keeping ambulance space free, so the drivers had to resort to strapping things on the outside or getting rid of them somehow.

When the section pulled out that morning, it was quite a spectacle. Children and young women gathered whatever the men discarded.

Dombasle set up a control point outside of the town to check the vehicles as they left. A growing pile of contraband—lots of it items of feminine apparel—sat on the side of the road.

Jack became tearful seeing the waving townspeople. He recognized the young widow whose daughter had died. He would not forget this town. *Dieulouard*, they told him, meant *God is Lord* in Old French. Considering their experiences there and in the 'Priest's Woods,' Jack prayed that faith would help these people and France get through this terrible war.

SSU 2 arrived at their temporary campsite in time to learn that the coming battle had been postponed a day or two. The section would have no fixed facility to base from near Arras. They set up tents and waited for orders.

Several false starts resulted in ambulances departing on wild goose chases. The attack was to go on the sixth, then the seventh, and then—and everyone insisted this was the final word—at midnight on the eighth of May. By then at least the drivers knew the lay of the land from all the running about trying to find their assigned pick up points.

The rumble of artillery at dawn on the ninth woke Jack from a sound sleep. He rolled up his blankets, folded the stretcher he used for a bed, and raced for his Ford. An orderly came around shortly with assignments. Jack headed to the *poste de secours* serving the First Regiment of Infantry of the Foreign Legion. He got some breakfast at the poste, located more than twenty kilometers behind the first line of trenches. The men there told him that the trenchworks in that region were so extensive that the wounded might have to be carried as much as fifteen kilometers before they could be put in an ambulance.

Within an hour of the start of the preparation, casualties arrived. Jack made his first run with five patients at 9:30 that morning. When the attack kicked off at ten o'clock, the casualties mounted astronomically. Jack had just returned after his first load when a batch of twelve more wounded came in needing transport. George Masters showed up with another ambulance. Soon Chouteau Johnson also fell into the relay team.

Another American Jack barely knew rolled through in a flivver so full of holes that it would have to be junked. He tried to get another ambulance and join in the evacuation effort, but none were to be had. Harold Willis, an architect from Boston, had no choice but to catch a ride back with his wounded ambulance in tow.

Their trips continued unabated throughout the rest of the day with stops only long enough to refill the gasoline tanks. At each drop off, Jack sent word to Dombasle that he needed more drivers. No reinforcements appeared. By midnight, they calculated they had carried an incredible three hundred wounded between the three of them. Considering their ambulances couldn't hold more than five that meant that each of them had made at least twenty turn-around trips in a period of about fifteen hours.

Chouteau's ambulance developed motor trouble forcing him to leave Masters and Buck to finish whatever work needed to be done that night.

They'd been too busy to do more than utter essential phrases. Twenty-four hours after the original attack began; three French Army ambulances came to relieve the exhausted Americans. Both agreed it wasn't worth the effort to go back to their headquarters just to sleep in a tent. It was a warm May morning. They would stretch out in their ambulances after swabbing them out.

George crawled in the back of Jack's ambulance. He fell sound asleep. Jack couldn't leave the blood to dry in Masters's vehicle so he hastily rinsed it down, using the long-handled broom to scrub the bed and pull the reddened water out the back. Then he crawled in beside George, lying on one of his dry blankets, thinking about the work that they'd just done before sleep came.

An enormous explosion and loud screams woke them rudely. Both jumped out seeing from the long shadows that it was early evening. Racing in the direction of the noise, they came upon a horrifying scene of carnage worse than anything either had seen before. A German artillery round or a bomb had hit the *poste de secours* destroying the earth shelter and scattering the remains of the unfortunate occupants over a radius of close to fifty meters. At least twenty wounded men had been in the shelter along with about half that number of attendants. An ambulance, one of the French Peugeots, burned at the former entryway, its driver incinerated at the wheel, and four *couchés* cooked on their stretchers. Jack and George looked for someone to help, something to do, all to no avail.

George knelt beside a brancardier they had come to know earlier in the day. The man was at least fifty-five. He had a gaping wound in the belly, his insides spread all over his legs and the ground. Still breathing, Jack watched as George made the sign of the cross and muttered something in barely audible Latin. The man opened his eyes and said, "*Amen, merci,*" and breathed his last. Jack saw it, heard it, and thought he understood what it implied, but refused to believe it.

McConnell and Dombasle showed up in the staff car; took in the scene with great compassion, and directed Buck and Masters to leave the cleanup to the French. A French section, part of a larger battalion of ambulances, had arrived in Arras. SSU 2 would go into reserve for a couple of days and then be released to Paris with a load of wounded for the hospitals.

Jack's mind still reeled from the double shock of the destroyed *poste* and of Masters' behavior, but his Ford wouldn't hold up for the trip to Paris without a lot of attention. He would focus on that and confront George later. The story about the poilu calming down after receiving the last sacrament came back to Jack. Maybe the *brancardier* in Masters' story was Masters himself!

When news of the Moroccan Division's fifteen-kilometer penetration and subsequent six-kilometer retreat arrived at SSU 2, Dombasle had already reorganized his crews for the next several days. Casualties kept pouring into the rear faster than the various ambulance sections could carry them out. Dombasle obtained permission to release his crews two at a time over the next six days, with each ambulance taking a full load of patients to intervening hospitals or all the way to Paris.

Dombasle insisted that McConnell lead the first pair back to Paris. Jim objected that he was the sous chef, the second in command, and that he was needed in the field. Dombasle told him he needed someone in the rear to secure their gear and vehicles. Reluctantly, Jim headed off with one of the Yalies and ten patients. Four more drivers left the next day, and six the following. Buck told Dombasle that he would stay until all the rest had left. Masters asked to stay with Jack. Johnson left on the 12th with another of the new drivers. By the 13th, the battle was clearly over and the last of the ambulances were ready to depart. Wounded legionnaires still trickled in to the postes, but many of these were walking wounded, cases that could be treated close to the front.

During a break the day before they were scheduled to return to Paris, Masters asked Jack if they could talk.

"I don't know how to say what I want to say, Jack, but I have to say it anyway. I know you feel wronged by me and by Isabelle. Maybe you hate me, and maybe I deserve it." Jack's negative nod didn't slow the big man down.

"I went after Isabelle to prove something to you and Jim and to myself. Everyone thinks I'm one thing and no one knows anything about me. I almost told Jim a couple of weeks ago, but I chickened out. I'm going to tell you now just so you'll understand who I am and what I have done." Masters looked pleadingly into Jack's eyes. Jack felt extremely uncomfortable, but his curiosity was piqued.

"Go ahead, George," he said. "But, I have to tell you that I don't hate you or Isabelle. I'm kinda over all that. I sensed that she was out of my league even before I tried to fall in love with her. These last weeks have dampened my pain, if you know what I mean."

"She is not out of your league by any account."

"What's the big mystery, George? You aren't going to tell me you're a priest." Jack said, only half joking.

George gasped. His voice sounded hollow and raspy. "I'm not a priest, at least not anymore."

"Then you were a priest! I *thought* there was something about you!"

George slowly told Jack of his downfall after fathering a child with one of his unmarried parishioners back in Queens. He had tried to resign, marry the woman, and go on with a normal life, but the community excommunicated him even if his church did not. The shamed woman took the child and moved to the west coast, leaving no trace. George went into a nearby monastery to try to sort out his spiritual confusion.

He sailed to Europe before the war for a supposed sabbatical, but found that he couldn't return to the vows he'd broken. As a result, the church defrocked him, removing his right to perform the sacraments, and leaving him distraught in the process. He went wild for a couple of weeks, boozing it up and enjoying the company of loose women. With that out of his system, he repented and sought confession. Frustrated by unsympathetic priest-confessors, he gave it up to become a driver.

Jack listened mutely, totally dumbfounded. The guy he and the others originally thought of as dull-witted was more complex than any of them could have imagined. Many of the incongruous things George had said and done now began to make some sense to Jack.

George told Jack how much he hated himself for his failures, but how much more he regretted losing his child and its mother. Bitter and feeling worthless, he contemplated suicide, but his training as a priest kept him from total despair. Going after Isabelle was like a safety net for him. "For the first time," Jack, "I had a woman's attention as a man, not the pastor or a paying customer."

"And, what's to keep you from making Isabelle pregnant?" Jack wondered out loud, regretting saying it as soon as he had.

"I couldn't hurt that woman any more than you could," George replied with a pained look on his face. "She told me how she threw herself at you and how you didn't take advantage of her vulnerability."

"Did you, I mean, have you?" Jack's voice failed.

"I'll answer the question you might be asking in a minute—just *listen*!" he said when Jack acted like he was going to interrupt. "I told her everything. Isabelle is a sophisticated young woman. She took my past much better than my fellow priests did. I think it intrigued her to see a former priest and find out what makes the breed tick. She isn't too fond of her French *Curé* and others of his ilk," he paused realizing he sounded evasive. "She is still the maiden you spared as far as I know. I'm not that kind of predator."

Jack, a victim of his own Catholic upbringing, couldn't stop thinking of how he'd always thought of priests as sort of living saints. Like all Catholic boys, he had been encouraged by nuns and his mother to listen for his "calling," a voice he expected to come from heaven. He'd thought seriously about giving the seminary a shot. His raging hormones and passion for women—an exercise more in theory than in practice—cooled his religious fervor. He had a view of the clergy, Catholic priests in particular, that discounted their humanity.

They'd been sitting under a tree, their ambulances parked nearby. It was almost getting dark when George finished. Jack felt relieved and somehow ennobled by George's revelation. He also felt better about Isabelle. He could see George relax, visibly unburdened. They agreed to keep George's past between them before rolling over in their blankets to sleep.

Minutes later a French soldier came running up shouting, "*Venez, venez vite*!"

In no time they cranked both motors. The poilu hopped from one to the other trying to speed them up. He jumped in with Jack as he sped off toward the lines. Masters followed.

The mystery of the man's agitation unfolded in the lengthening shadows near a makeshift clearing station in an abandoned stone barn. Thirteen wounded men had holed up there, unable to continue to the rear. French ambulance crews had carried off as many as they could, leaving the less serious cases to fend for themselves.

German troops could be seen working their way across a field not five hundred meters away. Buck and Masters were all that remained between rescue and capture.

Four of the wounded propped themselves at openings prepared to fight. Two more struggled to get up to join them. They were all legionnaires except for one with a bleeding heart insignia on his helmet, the man who had summoned them. Chaplains, almost all Catholic priests, wore the same uniform as the troops they served. This fellow, whoever he was, had to be one brave man to return with the enemy so close.

Rounds chipped at the stones of the barn as the Germans closed within range. Nothing seemed to be slowing their advance. Jack helped George rapidly load the stretcher cases, filling all six slots in their two ambulances. Normally they could squeeze two more wounded sitting in the back and one up front. There was room for all but two! There was no way to wedge one more into either vehicle without hurting someone. The two legionnaires still in the barn firing at the advancing Germans would have to stay.

"George, take your load and get the hell out of here! I'll try to get these two heroes in if I have to put one on my lap."

"I can't go, Jack. The man who came for us, where is he?"

"Dammit, George, go!" Jack yelled, but the big man ran back into the barn to look for the French priest. Jack followed, tapping the two defenders on the shoulder and motioning them to follow him. One had a serious leg wound and could barely walk. The other was pale from the loss of blood, but he tried to help his buddy anyway. Jack got between them and tried to rush, only to send the man with the leg wound sprawling. The man yelled

"Damned Yankees!" as he fell to his good knee. Jack kept dragging the pale one out the door.

The pale poilu grabbed Jack's tunic saying: "Get Kiffin!" *Two American voices?* Racing back to the barn, Jack found the one called Kiffin already on his feet, leaning on his rifle.

"It's about time," Kiffin hissed, smiling through the pain.

"No time to talk. Can you hang onto the side? Your friend is too weak. I'll try to hold you, but you'll have to support yourself until we can get some distance between us and the Boches."

"Go!" Rockwell shouted. "If I fall off, you can come back for the body later, just take care of Keeler there."

Jack looked over to George's ambulance. Still no sign of George! He ran back a third time to the barn to find his friend with a neat hole in his forehead. The French priest cradled the big American ex-priest in his arms, probably not knowing that another man of God had given his life for him. With no time to even think, Jack grabbed the French chaplain and dragged him out of the barn. "I sure hope you can drive padre!" Jack shouted over the growing racket of the nearby firing. Masters' car was running. Jack pushed the little man behind the wheel and ordered: "*Conduisez! C'est leurs seule chance*!"

The *aumonier* looked baffled by the levers and wheel. "*Allez, prêtre*!" The wounded man beside him said. "*Je vous guide*." Jack raced to his ambulance, ducking involuntarily at the sound of ricochets.

Buck tried to start off slowly so as not to jar the one called Kiffin off the running board. Kiffin had cleverly undone the strap from his rifle and wrapped it around his waist, securing it through the doorpost. Jack looked back relieved to see the other ambulance moving. They had to hightail it down the rutted trail at least another mile before they would get to the road. From there, Jack hoped he could hail some help. No telling how long the aumonier would be able to keep the cranky Ford on the road.

"You son of a bitch!" Kiffin shouted through the open window. "Am I ever glad you came along, but I owe you for letting me fall back there!" He grimaced and managed another pain-twisted smile.

The man beside him in the car—Keeler, he thought he'd heard—had fallen asleep or passed out. Jack was too absorbed in the immediate escape to dwell on George. Now, the image of his friend lying dead in the French priest's arms came back to him. Jack wished George lived long enough to confess, but decided it didn't matter. God would surely forgive someone who had laid down his life for another. The French chaplain, realizing they didn't have enough room in the two ambulances, must have secreted himself in the barn. Ironically, another priest had made the supreme sacrifice in his place.

God, he hated this war!

Chapter 22
Crossed Paths

Paris, late June 1915

Hell could not be any hotter than the storage room of the American Field Service on the Neuilly grounds, Jack decided in less than five minutes. He was pulling out moldy sheets and blankets left there since March. The shed leaked. The linen, marked with the donor's emblem, the *Hotel Imperial*, wherever that was, might be salvaged, but the smell was noxious.

George's funeral in late May, a week after his death, drew the whole American community together. The Ambassador even showed up to make a short speech after Jack's heartfelt eulogy. McConnell, devastated like the rest of the men by Masters' death, still didn't know about the New Yorker's secret. No family members were listed on George's emergency card, though a child by the name of Victor Jones in California was the sole heir. The Americans couldn't let the *Légion d'Honneur*, the *Croix de Guerr*e with star, and the *Médaille Militaire* from the French government go unawarded, even posthumously.

Jack frequently replayed their last hours together in his mind. He and the survivors had provided the material for George's citations. Once the two ambulances had reached a point of relative safety, Jack stopped and rushed back to see how the harried cleric was doing. He approached the Ford full of trepidation. The racket from the front of the vehicle made no sense to his American ears. "*Cochon! Vous vous appelez un homme de Dieu? Dieu misère, vous êtes l'âne de Dieu!*"*

The legionnaire in the passenger's seat was less than reverent subsequent to their short jangling journey. Nonetheless, the little chaplain had brought them back alive. One of the wounded in Jack's ambulance couldn't walk due to a bullet lodged in his calf, but he could drive. The chaplain didn't want to give up the wheel after his first taste of driving. The ruckus his passengers raised put a stop to that.

Jack dropped the lightly wounded men at a hospital at Senlis, a small town north of Paris. The *médecins* there kept seven of them including the American Kiffin called *Keeler*. Jack found out that Kiffin was named Rockwell and had a through the thigh bullet wound he'd tourniquetted himself. The image of the two wounded Americans preparing to fight to the death and of George's sacrifice was burned into Jack's mind. It became his watershed, the clear point at which he knew he had to join the fight.

Rockwell, before being sent off to a recuperation hospital at Romilly, told Jack about Charlie Keeler. Keeler loomed large in the telling. At least Rockwell thought his friend to be a hero without equal. Keeler had two debilitating wounds and an enormous loss of blood. How he'd been able to stand at the barn window firing his rifle was beyond understanding. Keeler got a special room at the American Hospital in Neuilly at the request of a French family named Fleury.

Jack and Jim McConnell visited Charlie Keeler once the man had recovered some of his strength. Both came away impressed by Keeler's genuine modesty. He had done amazingly heroic deeds, but he thought nothing of them. Charlie made both Jim and Jack feel like *they* had done the extraordinary in their ambulance work. Something resonated in Jack about Keeler. He made a point to visit every chance he got. Since Keeler was a superbly conditioned athlete, his recovery went amazingly fast. Without further complications, Charlie would be ready for release by the end of June.

The doctors at Romilly released Kiffin Rockwell, sending him back to Paris for his next stage of recuperation. After a stop to see his brother, Paul, Kiffin came directly to the hospital at Neuilly. He found Buck rummaging in the steamy storage shed.

"All right, you son of a bitch! I'm here to kick your Yankee ass to beejesus!" Rockwell sounded off in mock challenge.

---

* [*Translation: "Dirty pig! You call yourself a man of God? God have mercy, you are God's jackass!"*]

Jack came out of the shed beaming. "Kiffin, you whore of a southern slave! How good to see you standing on your ass-kicking leg!" The two stood looking at each other for an interminable moment before stepping forward and throwing their arms around each other.

"Where's that big guy? I want to thank him too."

"You mean Masters? I thought you knew. Heck, you even went to his funeral, Kiffin."

"No not Masters, God rest his soul, the Harvard guy with the mustache. He was the one that got us as far as that barn before his ambulance gave up the ghost. Had to leave Keeler and me there, and roll the damned thing downhill with three *couchés* in the back. What's his name?"

"That's got to be Harold Willis. I didn't know he'd hauled your sorry tail. How he managed to keep that car going without getting hit himself is a miracle. He's back at our old headquarters picking up one of the ambulances we had to leave there.

Rockwell and Buck then hurried up to see Keeler, who Jack swore was as cantankerous as a Missouri mule. They came into the room full of flowers from innumerable admirers, to find Charlie grasping a gorgeous redhead with his useable arm.

When Jack first met Michelle, he inevitably compared her to Isabelle who was now deep in mourning for George. The Englishwoman emanated lightness and joy like the subtle fumes of her perfume. She had a temper according to the nurses on Charlie's ward, but only when it involved a slight to Charlie. Where Isabelle was morose and moody, Michelle exuded enthusiasm and hope. Jack couldn't help envying Charlie.

In the weeks since he'd returned to Paris, Jack stopped at the Flandins' at least five times. He went first to tell them of George's death. It had become one of the most painful events of his short life. Isabelle carried on so demonstratively that her parents had to ask him to leave. He came back the next day to more of the same histrionics. Now, Pierre Flandin told him, it was because Isabelle thought she was going to lose Jack next. Jack realized his feelings for Isabelle had turned brotherly. If she was worrying about losing him, how would she react to this?

On his subsequent visits, her parents explained that Isabelle was not well emotionally or mentally. It had started when they learned about her brother. Masters' death pushed her over the edge. She alternated between bouts of euphoria and acute melancholy. Pierre feared that he would have to send her to the asylum in Malmaison. Jack stopped coming after Isabelle tore open her blouse, baring her bosom and begged him to take her. The Flandins kept sending him letters. He'd become a distant surrogate son to them. *Ironic,* he realized, considering the way he now felt about Isabelle.

As June ended, SSU 2, refitted and reinforced with new drivers, prepared for its next assignment. While many of the veteran drivers would return to ambulance duty, a number chose other paths. Jack chose to stick with the section at least through the next rotation to the front. Dombasle practically begged both McConnell and Buck to stay.

"*Alors,*" he said, "aviation can wait, but we cannot. What is better? For you to go to learn to fly for months before you can make a contribution to the war, or to go back and save more lives now? Give me one more mission, my friends. Your experience I cannot replace. You can leave with my blessings *after* this rotation. *Je vous prie messieurs.*"

Part Four

Winning Wings

Gagner les Ailes

*Les Etat-Unis d'Amérique n'ont pas oublié que la première page de l'histoire de leur indépendance a été écrite avec un peu de sang francais.**

Maréchal Joffre, 1916

---

* *The United States of America has not forgotten that the first page of the history of their independence was written with a little French blood.*

Chapter 23
Courage and Competence

Paris, July 4, 1915

Stars and Stripes flourished everywhere around the immense square of the Place de la Concorde. For days the French, aided by the *Franco-American Association;* representatives of the *Friends of France*, the main sponsor of the American Field Service; and other groups partial to the United States; had prepared for this celebration of the 139th anniversary of the American Declaration of Independence. Getting help from the American Embassy had to be done on the sly, President Wilson's orders hanging resentfully over would-be French supporters.

However, the growing visibility of the American volunteers in the *Légion Etrangère* and the ambulance services, gave the savvy French ample cause to recognize these American heroes. The American Hospital provided a nearby source. Other candidates worked in the flying squadrons protecting Paris. The French issued a 72-hour pass to all Americans serving in French units, encouraging these men to spend the pass in Paris to celebrate the occasion.

"Damnation, Paul, I refuse to be paraded like an animal," Kiffin Rockwell said. The doctors released the younger Rockwell from the hospital in mid-June and transferred him to the Patient Holding Detachment in a convalescent status. He chose to stay with Paul, but he had to check in at Neuilly every three days.

"Look at it this way, Kif. You and the others will make a great show for the folks back home. The papers want as many pictures as I can get.

This soirée could swing some weight. Don't you still want to see America in the picture?"

"Yeah, Kiffin," Charlie Keeler chimed in, "and don't forget the hoards of mademoiselles just waiting to swoon for a Southern gentleman."

"I'm too ugly to worry about that," Paul Pavelka observed, shifting uncomfortably in his wheelchair.

"You won't get any argument from us on that, Skipper," Kiffin laughed. "At least you can count on getting kissed by Monsieur Poincaré, if not by a pretty girl!" They'd heard the President of the Republic himself would be there to pin on their *Croix de Guerre*.

"Don't make me laugh," Charlie groaned, the expansion of his chest stretching his stitches painfully.

"Sorry, chum," Kiffin said, looking chastised.

Pavelka had taken a bayonet in his calf on June 16. His evacuation lacked the drama of that of his friends; though he brought the heavy news that Russell Kelly had died trying to protect him. Pavelka managed to shoot their assailants, but not before one had run Russ through with his bayonet.

Kelly's death hit Kiffin hard. The Regiment buried Kelly in a French military cemetery, presenting him with the *Médaille Militaire* posthumously. The four of them: Kelly, Keeler, Pavelka, and Rockwell; had become a tight group. Russell's death sounded a deep knell. Kiffin dreaded writing Kelly's folks. He'd send them their son's citation and medal.

McConnell stuck his head into the alcove. "Time to load up the circus wagon, boys." McConnell and Buck, among the Americans to be honored that day, were bringing the other three from the hospital to the Place de la Concorde in a spiffed up ambulance. Mr. Andrew thought a Model T with *American Field Service* painted on the side would be a fitting symbol of the United States.

They arrived at nine that morning. The ambulance smelled of wax and soap instead of blood and guts. Buck tended Pavelka in his wheelchair. Rockwell could get by with a cane, while Keeler stood awkwardly, his left arm immobilized in a thick plaster cast. Chouteau Johnson walked up with Norman Prince and Elliot Cowdin, the latter two clad in French Aviation colors with pilot wings adorning their right breasts.

Charlie, meeting Charles Chouteau Johnson for the first time, wondered if he would be snobby. After all, he came from the founding stock of Saint Louis. Instead, Chouteau approached him beaming, "Mr. Keeler, what an honor!" He gently shook Charlie's right hand and congratulated his fellow Saint Louisianan on his prowess in combat.

Fleury's words in New Orleans seemed to echo in Charlie's head. *"Courage and competence are the currency of the battlefield."* Wise council, but such a price, he thought.

"Nimmie, lookee here!" Cowdin said to Prince. "Remember Jack Buck, the Swede from Min-ah-Soh-tah?"

"Hello, Mr. Buck! I see you are in good company," Prince said, shaking his hand and looking over the wounded Americans.

Prince, twenty-eight, had something of the patrician about him. His sharp features, neatly trimmed mustache and impeccably tailored uniform signified wealth to Jack. He caught a whiff of cologne, remembering that some French officers used scents. A little out of place in their current situation, Jack thought.

A young captain led them to a reviewing stand adorned with French and American flags. He explained the ceremony and told them where to stand, and when to salute. The Americans' casual indifference caused him to shift nervously from one leg to the other.

Jack saw Prince fall in with the rest of them, thinking, *maybe he's okay.* He was close enough to Cowdin to ask about flight training. Prince overheard his question and said he attended the Curtiss School at Marblehead in Massachusetts, learning on modified Wright Flyers.

"Had to use an alias there lest my father got wind of what I was doing."

Cowdin had somehow managed to leave the Ambulance Service after less than two months and get into an accelerated flight course. Both were flying Voisin bombers in an escadrille designated VB. 108 in Nancy.

A curious crowd continued to gather. Herald trumpets sounded a fanfare. Charlie strained his neck trying to see Michelle in the crowd. As close as they were to the Crillon, he knew she had only to walk out the door to the gilded wrought iron gates of Les Tuileries. He could barely turn his head because of the cast, and his shoulder itched.

Jack saw a brigadier general usher the Flandins to the distinguished visitors' area. He saw Isabelle on the arm of another senior officer. She craned to see him, waving and trying to get his attention.

McConnell seemed to be mentally recording the proceedings for one of the articles he had been sending off to the *Atlantic Monthly.* Marcelle was tending to an ill grandmother and wouldn't be able to come. Jim McConnell continued to intrigue Jack. In spite of his education and wealth, Mac knew how to be one of the guys.

Kiffin Rockwell shifted his weight uncomfortably. His wound had mended very well, but he would have a slight limp. Spotting his brother

Paul reassured Kiffin that at least one observer would record this circus accurately.

At precisely 10:55, an open touring car entered the Place de la Concorde from the Rue de Rivoli carrying Raymond Poincaré. Beside the war-beleaguered President of France sat General Joffre, the immense man who headed the armed forces. The crowd quieted down once the President and Joffre arrived at their positions.

A new flourish of trumpets, horns, and drums caused the Americans to stop talking and fidgeting. Someone called them to attention.

Appearing as if from thin air, the magnificent Republican Guards trotted before the reviewing stand, hooves clipping rhythmically on the cobblestones. The men were truly breathtaking astride their splendid steeds in their dark blue jackets, red riding breeches, shiny leather boots and gleaming silver helmets topped with plumes of horsehair. A glance confirmed Jack's suspicions that even the cynical Kiffin was caught up in the pomp.

The ceremony consisted of a bewildering series of orders followed by short fanfares. They must have heard the commands *Ouvrez le ban* and *Fermez le ban* a dozen times. Each time, one of their numbers stepped forward. Poincaré picked up the green and red ribbon of the *Croix de Guerre* from the case carried by a sharp looking soldier. The president then pinned the award on the left pocket of the recipient.

Keeler stood last in the line, and now they discovered why. After awarding Charlie's *Croix de Guerre*, Poincaré stepped back and picked up another medal, this one with a yellow ribbon bordered by green stripes. "*Au nom de la République, je vous présente la Médaille Militaire, pour actes d'héroïsme extraordinaire....*" the president intoned. Poincaré placed his arms on Charlie's shoulders, his right arm resting lightly on the cast. He then kissed Charlie on the right, then the left and again the right cheek.

Afterwards the French held a reception and luncheon at the *Rotonde* of the *Ecole Militaire* in honor of the Americans. The same nervous captain lined up the awardees to receive the guests. After they shook at least a hundred hands each, the captain directed them to different tables for the luncheon. Poincaré made a few remarks about the warm friendship between France and America before departing. That left General Joffre to preside. He waited until the president's party had cleared the room before saying something about French blood being poured for American independence.

Charlie didn't look forward to eating. He was thankful to have Michelle and her father at his table with Joffre and the other senior officers. She discreetly cut his food.

Jack found himself with Chouteau Johnson and some French officers and NCO pilots from Escadrille Voisin 97, the squadron protecting Paris. Another American from the Ambulance Service, Clyde Balsley, also sat with them. While Balsley had joined the Ambulance at the same time as Jack, their paths crossed infrequently.

Johnson dazzled his countrymen with his French. He translated and embellished whatever the flyers said. Before the exquisite luncheon ended, he had all three Americans ready to sign up for aviation.

Prince held court at a table with two other American *ambulanciers*, Lawrence Rumsey and Dudley Hill. Their tablemates were prominent financiers and businessmen, some of whom knew Prince from before the war. Prince was counting on them to back an all-American flying squadron. Hill said little, thinking about how many of the drivers were abuzz about flying since Cowdin's enlistment. Rumsey seemed more interested in the wine.

"I would like to do more than drive ambulances," McConnell commented in French. He was the only American at his table. Louis Dumesnil and Jarousse de Sillac, prominent businessmen who already endorsed forming an American Escadrille, nodded when Mac said, "It would be wonderful to have an American unit, wouldn't it?"

"Your French is excellent Monsieur McConnell, and your passion evident," de Sillac observed. "You plan to start flight training, do you not?"

"I'm not sure how to go about it, sir, but, yes, as soon as I can."

Jack enjoyed talking to the flyers, but after the delightful meal, he went looking for Jim McConnell. The two of them dragged Balsley and Johnson over to Charlie's table as Joffre's party began to exit.

Joffre looked very tired. His jowls hung loosely under white whiskers. His cheeks were flushed. His uniform, replete with gold embroidery and a rainbow of ribbons, stretched tightly over a massive frame. Yet, the man carried himself with dignity. Those around him acted respectful to the degree of being obsequious. Seeing so many important people in one day dazzled Jack.

An officer detached himself from the crowd surrounding Charlie and Michelle, stepped over to Jack's little group, and introduced himself as General Hirschauer, Director of Military Aeronautics. Hirschauer recognized Prince and greeted him like a friend in spite of the corporal stripes on Prince's arm.

"Didn't I see Isabelle with that officer, Jack?" McConnell asked.

"Come to think of it, I think he *was* the one," Jack said, relieved in a sense that Isabelle wasn't there.

"I guess she's doing better now. Have you talked to her or her parents lately?"

"She reacted so strongly the last time I was there that her mother thought it best I should stay away. George's death really got to her."

Hirschauer smiled broadly when Alexandre Fleury joined them. Fleury, dwarfed by all but Chouteau Johnson, welcomed the opportunity to say hello to all the Americans. Turning his attention away from Hirschauer, he focused on Jack.

"So you are the one that rescued Charlie and Rockwell?" he asked, drawing attention to Buck.

"Rescued us?" Kiffin Rockwell said *sotto voce*, leaning on his cane. "Hell, sir, he nearly finished the job the Boches started. Ask him about dragging me alongside his ambulance and forcing a helpless French priest to drive another in our wake."

"*Ah oui*," Fleury said, "let me see if I got this right. If Monsieur Buck had been a little cleverer, he might have been able to figure out how to drive two ambulances at once, and fit a few more passengers on top of those nearly dying in both of them. Pity, isn't it?"

"I guess you have me there. Monsieur," Kiffin chuckled, hoping his kidding hadn't been misunderstood.

Jack pitched back. "Think nothing of it, Kiffin. If I had the presence of mind I was born with, I would have simply left you there to hold off the Kaiser's kamarads, and we'd be celebrating your *Légion of Merit* today instead of the measly *Croix de Guerre*."

"*Médal Militaire*," McConnell noted, "anything but measly."

Chouteau was talking to Charlie when Jack came up.

"Sorry Charlie, the Toussaints I know aren't in Saint Louis. Involved in some kind of financial scandal, I hear. Good show on the awards. I can't wait to write home about this. Ought to be good for a column in the *Post Dispatch*, don't you think?"

"You know, Chout, that's how I first heard about you. In fact, you could say it's partly your fault that I'm here at all." Charlie sat down rather heavily. Michelle quickly gave him a glass of water.

Norman Prince chose that moment to suggest getting something more substantial to drink than wine. "I know the barkeep at the *Continental* mixes a mean French Seventy-five and decent whiskey sours. What say we move this show over there?" He politely invited Fleury to join them as well.

"*Mais non, non.* It would be infinitely jollier to drink to your health, but," Fleury observed with a hint of concern in his eyes, "perhaps Mr. Keeler needs to return to the hospital?"

Charlie did indeed look pale. While his wounds were healing well, he had contracted a touch of the flu. Michelle wouldn't hear of him heading off on a drinking spree. Over Charlie's protests, Fleury agreed to drop him and Michelle at the hospital.

The remaining eight Americans piled into and onto the ambulance in an unplanned re-enactment of Jack's hairy rescue. Two hung on the running boards while the others wedged themselves in around Pavelka in his wheelchair on the stretcher-less bed of the vehicle. Jack was thankful that the trip was quite short.

At the Continental, the American *Légionnaires*, *aviateurs*, and *ambulanciers* took over the bar; regaling each other with tall tales for the rest of the American holiday, while cooking up plans for their sketchy futures.

Chapter 24
Marie-Louise

Pont à Mousson Region, July and August, 1915

Although the major fighting on the Woëvre tapered off in late April, shortly before SSU 2 made its move to Arras, French casualties in the region continued to mount. For that reason, SSU 2 returned to Dieulouard arriving in time for the town's quiet celebration of Bastille Day. Jack Buck felt strange reentering the town and going back to the same barracks they had vacated so recently.

Lieutenant Dombasle remained in command, though he had been selected for promotion and would leave for another job in August. Americans now commanded their own sections so McConnell was in line to replace the lieutenant. This suited Mac fine though he planned to leave as soon as his orders for flight training came through.

Balsley, Rumsey, and Dudley Hill joined them in Paris. Balsley seemed greener than most, probably because he looked so young. He and Hill had become pals. Balsley wouldn't tell anyone what the "H" in *H. Clyde* stood for, insisting on being called Clyde. Everyone took to this good-natured native of San Antonio, Texas.

"Dud," Jack said to Hill, "what in the hell are you doing this for? I heard your family has a great business in New York. Clyde tells me you are supposed to take it over. Why come over here?"

Hill looked at Jack for a moment before replying in his typical monotone. "Ever make a stove, Jack? Ever been to Peek-scumming-skill, New York?"

"No to both," Jack answered, turning his mattress over and beating it repeatedly to try to drive out any lingering vermin.

"I love being *here*, doing something good for others, not grubbing for bucks—no pun intended—or acting important at the country club. Dad might want me to take over the business, but for now, I just want to do my part here in spite of my infirmities." Hill couldn't see with one eye and could only hear with one ear. He told Jack that a hockey puck on the frozen Hudson River accounted for the eye, and he'd a burst eardrum from a too deep dive in Long Island Sound.

Larry "Red" Rumsey struck Jack as a jolly sort. He too came from New York, not Peekskill, but Buffalo. The more men Jack got to know, the more convinced he became that they were all basically the same. War was a great leveler.

To Jack, Dieulouard's celebration of *Bastille Day* was a pale imitation of the Independence Day celebration in Paris. There were no parades, no speeches, only a few tricolors in evidence, and nothing of the festive air they'd enjoyed in Paris. Perhaps, Jack surmised, proximity to the front had something to do with it. He could discern two Frances: Paris, and the rest of the country.

Dombasle only reinforced this impression when asked why things were so subdued.

"*Ecoute*, Jack. Some people in France think July 14 should be a day not of celebration, but of mourning." Seeing Jack's confusion, Dombasle explained that the revolution actually made things worse for the French in nearly every strata of society outside of Paris. In the capital where the blood flowed and mobs ruled for weeks, the sudden collapse of the royal government created chaos. All institutions, good and bad, came under attack. Fiery orators promised bread for all with their liberty, fraternity, and equality rhetoric.

"With so many officers coming from noble families, the anarchy inspired soldiers to turn on their leaders, forcing many to swear oaths against their relations." In the provinces, Dombasle explained, no one heard about storming the Bastille until months later. A few hotheads attacked clergymen and other figures of authority, but most *liked* the status quo. Peasants and simple folk in the countryside, strongly influenced by the church, accepted their lots almost cheerfully.

Dombasle, a graduate of Saint Cyr, studied history at the Sorbonne before entering the French military academy. What made Dieulouard unique, according to Dombasle, was the enormous power of several wealthy families who had managed to retain their lands or regain them after the revolution. This explained in part why the French were making such an effort to hold the line at Pont à Mousson, ten miles to the north. Dieulouard had been evacuated twice during the fighting in April. Now the inhabitants struggled to maintain a semblance of normality.

Soon after they settled, the phones began ringing. "*Monsieur Américain, un blessé urgent à Champey....*" Jack took the call. He jumped in his ambulance and raced over the roads. The man was in terrible condition. He'd been hit at least twice, but there was so much blood that one couldn't be sure. Jack took him back to the hospital at Blénod.

When he got there it was already dark. He rushed into the building calling for stretcher-bearers. Inside the scene was chaotic. Fifty-two men had been brought in over the afternoon and evening. He found two *brancardiers* lounging on a bench smoking cigarettes.

"*Allez, messieurs. J'ai un blessée grave!*" he shouted. They just sat there not moving, not reacting at all to his call. "Come on guys. I have someone who will bleed to death if we don't get him in here now," Jack urged. They just sat there.

"You goddamned bunch of *embusqués,*" he shouted. "You sit around here all day and raise hell when a wounded man is the cause of some work, just as if you blamed him for it. I hope to heavens you all get sent up and get a taste of it yourself."

Finally, they got up. Going out to his ambulance they carried the man into the hospital and deposited his stretcher on the floor outside the emergency ward. "*Il est fini,*" one of them said. Jack couldn't believe it. They weren't even going to take him into the doctors. He burst through the door into the ward and demanded attention.

One of the surgeons asked what he was doing there. "*J'ai un blessée grave,*" he stated. "You have to tend to him!"

The surgeon looked harassed. He stepped out with Jack and looked at the wounded man. "Take him in and put him on the side," he told the waiting *brancardiers.*

Jack was astonished. They weren't even going to look at the man! "*Monsieur,*" he said in a controlled voice, "I have driven this man back at great risk. You must treat him."

"I am sorry," the doctor said in English. "We have too many wounded already. This man is going to die anyway. I can do nothing."

Jack's face reflected his frustration. He was powerless to influence them. He went to the wounded man and took his hand. "I tried *monsieur.* Please forgive me. God will take care of you even if these bastards won't." He made the sign of the cross on the man's forehead and left disgusted.

THE WORKLOAD FOR SSU 2 TAPERED OFF at the end of July. It seemed as if the Germans turned to the harvest at the same time as the French, calling an unofficial pause in the hostilities. With more free time on their hands, the ambulance drivers took off on short excursions to tour the beautiful countryside in the nearby Vosges Mountains.

One morning, Jack stopped for coffee in Dieulouard at a café he had passed many times. Behind the counter stood none other than the young mother whose daughter's body he had picked up back in April!

"*Mon Dieu, c'est vous*!" she exclaimed. She came out from behind the counter and took his hands, practically bowing before kissing him three times on the cheeks. Several old men, the only others in the dark narrow café, smoking and having their bowls of coffee and baguettes, stopped talking and looked up with smiles on their wizened faces. Jack, taken aback by the greeting, didn't know what to say.

"*Venez*," she said, pulling him by his hand to the back of the café. There in the kitchen, her arms dusted with flour, stood a middle-aged woman, kneading dough with hands gnarled by years of labor. "*Maman, c'est l'américain qui a récuperé notre Chérie*." The woman stopped her kneading, reaching out for Jack before remembering the flour and stopping to wipe her hands on a damp towel. She too embraced him, her cheeks smelling of flour and yeast.

All thoughts of his excursion went on hold as mother and daughter vied for ways to repay him for his compassion. Remembering how he'd cried over the girl's body, he realized he hadn't heard her name, *Chérie*, until that morning.

"*Je m'appelle Jack*," he proffered to break the uncomfortable silence while they looked him over. "*J'étais très touché par l'histoire de la petite fille. Mes sincères condoléances, Mesdames.*

"*Ah, Marie-Louise, il parle le francais*!" the mother said smiling. "*Allez! Je prends le comptoir. Vous deux, asseyez-vous dans la chambre*."

Jack found himself in a sort of drawing room adjoining the kitchen. He took a moment to look at the woman called Marie-Louise as if seeing her for the first time. In fact, he was seeing her for the first time without tears. She wore a simple dress with a spotless white apron. Like so many of the people in the region she wore *sabots,* wooden clogs. They reminded him of the decorative pair of hand-carved shoes from Sweden on a bookshelf at home.

Marie-Louise had a pixyish turned up nose. Her light brown hair was pulled back under a white kerchief that framed her face almost like a nun's. Her cobalt blue eyes were so arresting that he couldn't break his stare. She had to be older than him, but she just didn't look like the mother of a seven-year-old girl.

Marie-Louise returned his gaze just as boldly. As he sat sipping coffee he learned her story. Married at fourteen, pregnant with Chérie at fifteen, and widowed at 22, she had borne more than her share of life's blows. Losing her daughter nearly drove her mad. The child had been a living reminder of her beloved Guillaume. It had only been three months since they'd buried the girl. The bereaved mother sought solace in the village church, and had been persuaded to begin the process of taking vows to enter a Carmelite order of nuns.

Jack couldn't visualize this vivacious woman in a nun's habit. Her eyes alone could make a man consider selling his soul. She was too animated in her conversation, too passionate, too full of life.

At noon he reluctantly told her he would have to go. He didn't want to keep her from her work as people started to trickle into the café for lunch. He smelled a stew cooking in the kitchen that made him feel a gnawing sense of hunger. Marie looked disappointed and asked him if his duties were so pressing.

"*Non, pas du tout*," Jack answered honestly. "I was actually going to try my luck fishing in the stream and have a little picnic."

Marie's eyes darted back and forth rapidly. "Can you take me with you?" she blurted out, fixing her gaze on him. "Maman can handle the café. We only get two or three for lunch these days. I need to get out for some fresh air. A *pique-nique* would be perfect."

It began so innocently that idyllic afternoon. Arriving near the stream, they carried a basket laden with Jack's meager sausage and baguette and hard cooked eggs, fruits, cheeses, wine and mineral water added by Marie.

Jack did manage to get his line in the water, but the two of them splashing in the cool current assured an empty creel. Without her apron and bonnet, Marie looked even lovelier to Jack. When she raised her skirt to wade in the stream after kicking off her clogs, he felt a stirring of desire not at all appropriate with a nun-to-be.

Marie behaved like a young girl, splashing water on Jack, running barefoot along a sandbar and darting back into the water to splash more water on him. She giggled, laughed uproariously, and generally let herself go like the child she wanted to be, or perhaps like the one she had lost. Jack found her laughter infectious. He hadn't played like this in years.

They sat in the grass with their bare feet in the clear cool flowing water. Minnows and fry darted in the eddies. The sun sparkled on the surface, penetrating to the smooth pebbles and sand in the shimmering water.

After eating a little bread and cheese and drinking some of the rosé wine, Jack screwed up the courage to ask her why she decided to become a nun. The sparkle faded from her eyes, but only momentarily.

"*Je suis de la Croix de Valois*," she began, causing Jack no end of confusion since he recognized neither the name nor its significance. Thankfully, she began to elaborate.

"Guillaume, my poor departed husband, comes from one of the noblest families of France. Perhaps you have not noticed this in our republican France, but believe me, there are many who long for the monarchy.

"The de la Croix de Valois family owned great tracts of land in this region before the Revolution. They have never accepted the egalitarian stripping that resulted in 1792 and its aftermath." Jack could hardly believe his ears. Not only was she repeating Dombasle's lesson, but her articulateness revealed more education than he would have expected in a village girl. She explained that Guillaume's great-great grandfather rode with Napoleon's cavalry, continuing a tradition that dated back to Henri IV.

"Every first-born son since has been a cavalryman. At least one daughter has been given to the church and often a son as well. Marriages are arranged almost at birth. Ours was an anomaly, of course, a love match that would never have been allowed had we not eloped.

"When we were little children Guillaume came to the town every morning with his mother to go to Mass in the church. We got to play near the fountain while his mother gossiped after the service." Her face lit up as she remembered this, then she paused and went on somberly.

"There are six boys left, four in service. Guillaume was the first to die, and his brother Philippe was killed during the offensive last March, when you were here before. After Guillaume's death his family allowed Chérie and me to continue to live in their chateau, the one you can see above the town on the hill to the west. This pleased me since I could continue my lessons with Professor Brecht who had tutored Guillaume and his brothers as well as our Chérie.

"I never felt truly accepted. We had been married in Switzerland. Since I was only fourteen, Guillaume had to pay the priest and tell a white lie before he would marry us. Guillaume was seventeen. We had read *Romeo and Juliet* together as children. My family could not have objected to Guillaume, but his would never accept a penniless, titleless, under-aged girl.

"We returned from Switzerland on my fifteenth birthday after six months traveling the capitals of Europe on money Guillaume got directly from his paternal grandfather. Apparently, his father and grandfather didn't see eye-to-eye. Anyway, when we got back I was four months pregnant with Chérie and the de Valois were faced with a *fait accompli.* At first they tried to get our marriage annulled, but the child and the official Swiss documents thwarted them. Eventually, Guillaume's parents relented and accepted us back. If it hadn't been for *grandpère* Valois, I don't know what would have happened.

"The news of Guillaume's death nearly killed me. I wasn't there to see how his parents reacted, but a servant told me that they actually smiled at the news. I think they allowed me to stay at the chateau to maintain appearances, but when Chérie was killed, Guillaume's parents turned cold. She was the only grandchild, you see. I felt like an outsider.

"Madame de Valois told me about their tradition of sending at least one daughter to become a 'bride of Christ,' suggesting, since she had no other daughters, that I might become a *real* daughter to her if I took the vows and habit of a nun." Marie-Louise said all this without a trace of bitterness or rancor, much to Jack's surprise.

"I returned to my parents, but I felt it was my duty to Guillaume's memory to try to enter an order. I had been crying all the time. The nuns from our church were ever so supportive. I found great solace in praying with them. I could lose myself; lose my fears, in praying to the Blessed Mother. I fought a great desire to kill myself in order to be with Guillaume and Chérie, staying my hand in greater fear of eternal damnation.

"It is five weeks since I began the process of the novitiate. I do not go to live at the convent until I take my first vows in three more weeks. Then I will remain a novice until I have passed a full year and proven myself worthy. It is not hard. The only thing I don't like is the somberness. No one seems to be able to smile or laugh. True enough, there is little for us to laugh at, but does God want us to have long faces?"

Jack had not listened to so much French from one person at one time in his eight months in France. Isabelle spoke English. The wounded uttered pained snippets. Most of his conversations were short, choppy, *get the point across* affairs. He wasn't sure he understood every word Marie had said, but he definitely got the gist. The de la Croix de Valois family seemed too cruel and heartless to have produced Guillaume.

"But Marie, you are so young and so beautiful! You can have any man you choose. Start a new family. Perhaps Guillaume's folks are too grief-stricken at the loss of two sons to see how they are hurting you?"

"Oh no, Jack, you are wrong! It is me who hurts them. Every time they see me they see Chérie and Guillaume. I must become a cloistered nun. You cannot understand how it is."

Jack's equilibrium reeled. Maybe it was the wine. He couldn't believe what he was about to do. Taking her hand and bringing it to his mouth he said, "I understand this, Madame de la Croix de Valois, you are a beautiful young woman full of life." He kissed the back of her hand and then leaned close enough to look directly in her face. Marie shuddered but didn't pull back. Before he knew it they were locked in each other's arms.

Impulsively, he kissed her full on the mouth, tasting the sweetness of the wine and the fresh berries they'd just eaten. She went limp as if she had swooned but recovered abruptly, stiffening against him. She began to return the kiss with a passion he had never experienced, not even with Isabelle. They lay back on the grass.

When he got up some time later, exquisite joy permeated his every pore. Had he really just made love to a woman about to become a nun? His conscience remained curiously silent about losing his own chastity, but the thought that her husband had been dead less than a year gnawed at him briefly.

What the hell, he thought*; I could be killed tomorrow like George. Yeah, like George, the priest who not only did what I have done but also had a child. Jesus, Mary, Joseph! Marie could get pregnant!*

Marie-Louise took her time rearranging herself. She looked up at Jack seeing his look of consternation pass like a dark cloud over his face. "It was your first time, wasn't it?" She mouthed the words in slow soft French not looking at him but into the water.

He nodded, unsure whether to apologize or thank her. They sat on the bank not saying anything for several moments before Marie began again.

"You are my second lover. I have not felt such hunger for so long. You cannot imagine what it is like, I suppose. You were so gentle, so loving. I can only thank you and hope you don't think too badly of me."

Though it wasn't a question, Jack felt compelled to speak, his breath still not quite back to normal. "Of you? It is I who should be ashamed...."

"Nonsense! If there is anything my faith has taught me, it is to follow your conscience. I feel no guilt, and you should not feel any either. You have brought me back to life! I had beaten down my needs as a woman since Guillaume left last August," she swirled the water with a stick and turned to look at Jack.

"Do you want to know what my first thought was when I heard he'd been wounded? I hoped he had not lost his capacity to make me feel the joy you just gave me. Perhaps that sounds selfish, but I didn't know he would die two days later. You are what, twenty-one? I am only a little older. I am not numb. I still have needs."

Jack wanted to ask more, to press her about the nunnery and about getting with child.

"It is the wrong time for me to conceive, my sweet innocent American." She said to his unasked question. "I have not thought about it much lately, but now I realize how much I would like to be a mother again." She curled her finger in Jack's hair, kissing him lightly. The sun trickled through the leaves, warming them as it danced over their faces. There was wine cooling in the stream. They had the rest of the afternoon, and the glade she had selected near the stream gave them complete privacy. Marie's tender tutelage brought Jack to ecstasies he had never imagined while her commitment to the novitiate dissolved in his arms.

When they returned to the town that evening, neither was the same person that had sortied for the picnic. The glow in Marie's cheeks could be attributed to the sun, but her new internal glow would be less easily disguised.

Jack glowed in his own way. Part of him wanted to crow like a rooster. Another part tangled with guilt. The warm summer sun and the taste and feel of Marie lingered deliciously. He wanted to savor the excitement. He couldn't be blamed for not seeing the storm clouds gathering on the horizon.

Chapter 25
Tempted to Fly

Paris, summer, 1915

After Fleury dropped Charlie and Michelle at the hospital that July 4th, she almost panicked when Keeler drooped and nearly passed out in the lobby. Orderlies and nurses rushed to support him and bring him to a chair. He protested that he was all right, just a little nauseous from the ride. A stern nurse, a renowned disciplinarian with the name *Wilson* embroidered on her starched uniform front, would not hear of it. She ordered him directly to the Emergency Room.

Charlie woke some hours later, wondering what had happened and where the cumbersome cast had gone. Michelle's face hovered over him. She kissed him as his eyes regained their focus and told him how he had been bleeding into his cast. Fortunately, the doctors decided he no longer needed the cast. Charlie noticed that he was hooked up to a bottle of blood again. Had he really lost that much? At least his arm didn't itch, and the familiar antiseptic smell of the hospital had replaced the lingering stench of the unclean cast.

During the rest of the summer, he fell into a regular routine of hospital treatment, physical therapy, and frequent short outings. Michelle came nearly every day. Both longed for privacy, but his setback caused the doctors to fear infection. For several days he was not allowed to leave the hospital grounds for more than a couple of hours, even after his temperature had returned to normal.

Paul Rockwell and Kiffin visited frequently, bringing him letters from home and other news. Paul had begun corresponding with Jack Buck. Buck's interest in journalism provided Paul a good excuse to keep up with the exploits of SSU 2.

"Young Buck is in love," Paul reported. "Seems he snatched a young widow named Marie-Louise from the doors of a convent. Doesn't that beat all? Now he is in big trouble with in-laws; bluebloods, apparently."

"I thought they dropped that nobility business with Marie-Antoinette's head," Pavelka said, scratching his bandage. "Damn, this thing itches!"

Charlie, thinking about the Toussaints, said, "Skipper, I'm no expert, but my gut tells me that *liberté, éqalité, et fraternité* aren't necessarily universal bywords over here."

"Yeah. Some folks are more equal than others," Pavelka agreed.

Many lively debates between them began like that, fueled by the brandy or bourbon Paul Rockwell often brought. Were it not for his wounds and burning desire to get out of the hospital, Charlie might have found their little sessions more pleasurable.

The subject of aviation came up frequently. Doctor Gros never failed to put in a plug during his visits. "Listen, Kiffin, and you too, Pavelka," the good doctor began. "In my professional opinion neither of you is fit for the infantry no matter how well you recover from your injuries. The muscle damage will make it extremely painful for both of you on long marches. There is nothing for it." Gros paused, letting this unpleasant news sink in before saying: "On the other hand, one doesn't need to walk a lot in aviation . . . ."

"Doc, begging your pardon," Pavelka interrupted, "I *am* going back to the infantry. I can almost walk unaided now. I sure hope you won't stand in my way."

"I'm not the final word here, Skipper," Gros replied. "Bully for you, boy! But, you *would* be a great addition to the American Squadron we are trying to organize."

Gros had already gotten Charlie to look into flying. Charlie's wounds would not keep him out of the infantry, but if Michelle had anything to say about it, he would not go back to the trenches.

Charlie got a full day's pass in early August, but Michelle could not be torn away from Fleury's office. Stephane, their onetime chauffeur, showed up to visit the hospital and Keeler in particular. Kiffin and Pavelka were happy to accept his invitation to take them to his field at Villacoublay to see the work he was doing and watch some test flights.

Villacoublay consisted of a cluster of buildings and Bessaneau canvas hangars arranged alongside a field just south and west of the city. Stephane drove them there in a staff car. As a *mécanicien-chef* he rated special privileges. Stephane knew motors better than some of the engineers Fleury employed at his Renault plant. His skill and knowledge earned him his posting to the escadrille at Villacoublay, one of several testing and acceptance fields around the city.

Stephane took great pride in pointing out his own handiwork on a *Bébé Nieuport*. The sleek little machine stood apart from a cluster of others of mixed varieties. He explained the workings of the big rotary engine now sitting on a stand beside the machine, trying to avoid using too many technical terms.

"You mean this whole group of cylinders turns *with* the hélice?" Skipper asked.

"What the hell is a *hélice*?" Kiffin said, asking the question on the tip of Charlie's tongue.

"*Propeller*, that slick piece of wood behind you, Charlie," Pavelka answered.

Stephane had to shout to be heard over other machines on the field. A heady combination of blown up dust, petrol fumes and the distinctive odor of burning castor oil wafted over them. The three Americans watched with awe, each imagining themselves in flight. Stephane pointed out a Morane Parasol, a descendant of the Blériot that made the first Channel crossing.

"Roland Garros, the tennis player made the first crossing of the Mediterranean in one of those in 1913." Garros, he told them, had also developed a system for firing a machine gun through the propeller by attaching steel wedges to deflect the every sixth or seventh bullet that hit one of the blades.

"Worked pretty well, I hear, until he got shot down and became a permanent guest of the Germans."

Stephane took them to the NCO mess where the three Americans caused quite a stir. Charlie's *sergent* stripes and *Médaille Militaire* were rare in one so young. French mechanics and NCO pilots flocked around them, offering beers, wine, or pastis. The three Légionnaires noticed a difference in the atmosphere from what they knew in the Legion. The men here were open and relaxed instead of wary. They seemed to enjoy each other and what they did.

By the time they left that afternoon, Kiffin and Charlie were sold on flying. Pavelka was no less impressed with what they had seen, but he couldn't give up his quest to prove he could soldier as well as before.

Charlie couldn't wait to inform Michelle of his decision. He telephoned her at Fleury's office, promising he had something important to tell her that he couldn't discuss on the phone.

He didn't realize how she might have understood what "something important" might be.

Chapter 26
Outrage

Dieulouard, August, 1915

Monsieur de la Croix de Valois, Guillaume's father, scowled at the group gathered in the *Mairie*, the Mayor's office. Tall, thin, and aristocratic, De Valois cut an imposing figure. His official complaint against Buck had passed through Army channels arriving with Dombasle for action.

"It is inconceivable that this animal, this low creature, this *adulterer....*" de la Croix de Valois sputtered; mouthing the words in French with such venom that Marie-Louise and the others recoiled. Jack didn't have to understand the adjectives to realize he'd been insulted. Because of his lingering remorse, he remained silent, embarrassed more for Marie than for himself.

"*Arrête, monsieur, je vous prie,*" Dombasle interjected. He told the mayor how Monsieur Buck was a decorated veteran of the ambulance service and an American with impeccable references. Whatever had happened between Buck and the widow de Valois was between the two adults.

The session ended inconclusively. The mayor refused to intervene in what he considered an affair of the heart. He could not force them to marry as de la Croix de Valois insisted. De Valois announced that he would see about that, stating that he had friends in the government who would not tolerate such an outrage.

Marie-Louise fought tears not of shame but of anger at the injustice of it all. Was she no more than the chattel of the Valois family? She knew Guillaume's father possessed enormous influence. He could make things intolerable not only for her, but for her struggling parents. Since she knew nothing of the law or of her rights as Guillaume's widow, she assumed she was no worse off than she'd been before they'd married. She didn't question why they backed off so easily on wanting her to enter the convent. Undoubtedly they considered her unworthy. But, why would her father-in-law try to force her to marry Buck?

The mayor had registered Guillaume's will in which Marie-Louise and her children were guaranteed his portion of the de Valois estate. It stipulated that if she remarried less than eighteen months after Guillaume's death she would lose control of the large parcel of land ceded to Guillaume by his grandfather. This year and one half, the mayor understood, was Guillaume's way of protecting her.

Dombasle, soon leaving to take his own command, hoped to avoid a scandal. He saw through the ruse perpetrated against Marie-Louise by her in-laws. In getting her to enter the convent or marry before eighteen months, the family would retain control of one of the most lucrative portions of their land holdings.

After the scene in the Mairie, Dombasle pulled the distraught couple aside and told them of his suspicions. Jack's guilt slowly turned into anger. He was so outraged and protective of Marie that he wanted to throttle the arrogant old man. He would do nothing to hurt Marie, hoping Dombasle had something in mind to resolve the situation.

Marie-Louise resented being branded an adulterer and being shamed publicly by the de Valois family. Their intimacy had been one of loving and tenderness. Calling it adultery sullied the beauty of her rescue from despair. Besides, de Valois was only speculating on what they'd actually done. Marie found herself thinking of Jack and how unjust it would be for him to suffer from de Valois' greed. She too looked to the French officer for help.

Dombasle contrived a scheme that he thought would work. He convinced Jack to go back to Paris and seek temporary release from the Ambulance Service to get out of Valois' immediate reach. He could reenter the service or another part of the Army in a couple of weeks.

Dombasle urged Marie-Louise to return to her parents as if nothing had happened. De la Croix de Valois was on shaky legal grounds. She had every right to claim Guillaume's inheritance as long as she remained single six more months. Once in possession of the estate, he assured her, she would be free to remarry or do as she pleased.

The mayor confirmed Dombasle's information. The dominating Valois had been his continuous nemesis. The family was in enormous debt. Only with Guillaume's land could they hope to regain dominance over Dieulouard. He secretly hoped for the young widow to use her inheritance to unseat the haughty family on the hill.

Stunned by this information, Jack was nearly overcome with an urge to ask her to marry him. A voice in his head warned him to wait, but their parting was charged with passion. The fierce strength that had carried Marie-Louise through the loss of husband and daughter rose to the surface. "I will not forget the man who gave me back my life. Come back for me! *J'insist!*"

Getting away was the moral escape he needed. He knew she faced a fight with her in-laws that he would only complicate. Jack also smarted from the public excoriation visited on them by de Valois. Until then, his entire service overseas had been crowned with praise and glory. He was justly proud of his work. Having it all trashed along with his reputation made him feel like a punished child, wanting only to hide and escape.

Jack would never forget how Marie-Louise had transformed him. Her courage contrasted starkly with de Valois' cravenness. Yet, he felt ashamed to sense relief in being compelled to leave. With Sandy it had been constant pursuit, anticipation and ultimate frustration. Isabelle drove him to the point of frustration. Satisfaction shouldn't bring pain, should it? Love or lust, his conscience asked? Love *and* lust, his intellect told him.

Marie fought tears at the train. Tenderness competed with his urge to run. He felt cruel, dirty, somehow defiled by the hand of de la Croix de Valois. He would not soon forget that man.

Jack needed friends now. As the train pulled away from Dieulouard, he began to feel relief compounded by loneliness. Jim McConnell had stood by him and encouraged Dombasle to protect the Minnesotan, but McConnell, was staying in Dieulouard.

THE CONTRAST BETWEEN RURAL DIEULOUARD and cosmopolitan Paris struck Jack even more than his last visit. The noise of traffic the high-pitched voices of hawkers in the open market were unsettlingly normal. Were these people ignorant of the carnage of Verdun? Of course, in Paris one seldom heard the thunder of artillery.

Even before going to the hospital, he looked up Paul Rockwell. Rockwell was surprised to see him. Paul asked immediately what had torn Buck from his section.

"It's complicated, Paul. Remember the widow I wrote you about? Well, it got out of hand."

"The noble family scorning a plebian American, right?" Paul asked, knowing a bit of the story from Jack's letters.

"Worse than that. It's also a legal matter now, something between her and her husband's family. I keep getting into messes with French women, Paul."

"So what will you do now?" Paul asked without judgment. "Your commitment with the Field Service is up this month, isn't it? I could use some help here, but you *can* go home! I'll bet your folks would be delighted to get you back."

"Undoubtedly. I miss them terribly. But, Paul, how can I leave? There's something here that I really care about. Oh, I don't suppose one person can make much difference in this war, but I can't leave knowing that others like Kiffin are still doing their part." He paused, reflecting, trying to compose his thoughts. "I'm going to try to fly."

"Damned if you are! Damned if you are," Rockwell said, a smile suffusing his mustached face. "And don't you know that Kiffin, Charles Keeler, and maybe even Pavelka, are about to do the same thing? I even tried to get Gros to clear me to start flying, but my astigmatism and respiratory record are disqualifying. Damn!" he said again. "Bully! Hey, Kif's doing therapy at the hospital. Let's go tell him."

They took the Métro to Neuilly, arriving just as dinner was being served in the hospital. The ambulatory patients were gathered in the dining hall.

"Go, Charlie!" Kiffin, shouted. "You can beat Skipper!" Keeler's wounds had cost him much of his renowned strength. He lifted weights daily at therapy trying to regain range of motion and strength. His left arm remained in a sling. He could have whipped most any man in arm wrestling before his injuries. Now he had all he could to hold Pavelka off from pinning his mending right arm.

Taking advantage of their visitor's interruption, Skipper tried to jerk Keeler's arm to the table. Charlie grimaced in pain, his face red from exertion, the veins bulging noticeably in his neck. His arm stopped inches from the table and began to rise. Pavelka grunted, fighting to maintain his advantage. Several other patients gathered around the table to watch the contest. Skipper's short powerful forearm trembled as Charlie regained the vertical and began to push his opponent's arm to the table. Bets flew among the onlookers.

"Don't let him win, Skipper," Jack said. "He's already intolerably conceited."

"You can do it Charlie!" Kiffin cheered, greeting Buck and his brother with a wave.

Pavelka was now in the same position he'd placed Keeler in minutes earlier. The two had a running wager on these contests. Charlie had to let Pavelka kiss Michelle every time he lost. Skipper loved the little pecks he claimed from Michelle after each victory. This time Charlie wanted to collect. If he won, Skipper would have to kiss old Nurse Wilson in front of the whole dining room.

The noise they were making brought this estimable lady over to the table just as Charlie slammed Pavelka's arm to the surface.

"Pay up time, Skipper!" Kiffin yelled gleefully, nudging Nurse Wilson over to the sweating former cowboy and onetime male *nurse*. The big bosomed woman tried to look stern but played along, secretly knowing of their bet. She pursed her lips and closed her eyes.

"*Allez, allez y, allez*!" chanted some French patients.

"Pay up, Pavelka," Charlie chuckled.

Kiffin and his brother grabbed Pavelka under the arms and pulled him up to Nurse Wilson, the shouting and banging on glasses becoming even louder. Pavelka screwed up his face in feigned disgust and stood on his tiptoes in order to avoid the lady's protruding chest. He looked left and right like a trapped rat, smirked broadly, and kissed Nurse Wilson on her lips, holding the kiss for a full thirty seconds. Wilson opened her eyes and grabbed the short man pulling him against her bosom, raising even more commotion. Before order returned, the men, bandaged, on crutches, some missing one or more arms or legs, shook with paroxysms of healing laughter.

It was a defining moment for Jack Buck. Looking around at the unfortunates, a few former passengers of his among them, Buck realized the de Valois incident was petty compared to the suffering of these laughing men. It was time to bid farewell to Sandy, Isabelle, and even Marie-Louise. He'd had enough of being a bystander. Marie-Louise would always hold a special place in his heart, but it was time to move on.

Chapter 27
Bigger Than Life

Paris, late August, 1915

"You are still under doctor's orders, all three of you." Dr. Gros said as he signed the final discharge papers for Keeler. "I want to see you in two weeks. If you go back to the States, and you already know you have that right, I want you to see your doctor at home."

Charlie and Kiffin decided to forego their thirty-day leaves in order not to jeopardize their chances of beginning flight training. Surprisingly enough, their injuries wouldn't keep them from flying, according to Gros. He told them about Nungesser, a French aviator who had already been severely wounded and injured in two crashes. The lieutenant, Gros said, had returned to flying each time.

While the opportunity to go home sorely tempted Charlie, Michelle's reaction to his decision to enlist in aviation baffled him. He expected her to be enthusiastic when he shared the news, but she seemed profoundly disappointed. He simply didn't understand.

They had talked about becoming engaged, but Charlie believed she wanted to wait until after the war. Upon reflection he realized he must have misread her. Instead of his decision to try flying, she had anticipated a proposal! No wonder she looked hurt. How had he missed that? Going back to the states just didn't have the appeal it should have had. Michelle had a lot to do with that, but so did having to face his father.

Michelle, recovering from her initial disappointment, suggested a trip to England to meet her parents. Before they could arrange it, her father cabled that he had business in Paris, and would be arriving with her mother in two days.

Michelle had begun to exchange letters with Jennifer even before Charlie's injuries. Charlie's sister wanted to come over to work in the American Hospital. Charlie asked Michelle to send the requisite papers. She had, and it began a relationship anchored by the man they both loved.

PAUL PAVELKA TOOK HIS *PERMISSION*, heading not back to the states but to the Riviera. He intended to relax on the beaches and do some legwork to get his injured calf back in shape before reporting to the 170th Infantry Regiment in September. Kiffin and Jack considered going with him for a short vacation, but decided to standby in Paris in case a seat became available in the flight schools at Buc or Avord.

All through August a group of men avidly worked to create an all American *escadrille*. On the periphery of this effort, Pierre Flandin quietly planted word in government circles to drum up enthusiasm for the idea. Flandin, now in the office of the Under-Secretary of State for Military Aeronautics, kept in contact with the loosely-organized Franco-American Committee and the other organizations interested in getting the United States involved in the war, if not militarily, then economically. He had approached Hirschauer in the spring, gaining his support.

An American named Frasier Curtis, a friend of Norman Prince, showed up to throw his support behind the idea. Curtis linked up with Harold Willis, convincing Willis to take him to the hospital at Neuilly to recruit drivers for the proposed American squadron.

Willis had missed the July 4th ceremony, narrowly escaping in his Ford ambulance during the battle at Bois le Prêtre. Going in several times under fire, Willis earned a citation for bravery. He brought his damaged ambulance back for repairs and several free days in Paris. Curtis, like Willis, was a Harvard alum and friend of Prince.

Kiffin Rockwell remembered Harold Willis from his ride in Willis' bullet-ridden ambulance back in May near Artois. After crawling and dragging himself nearly a mile from where he'd been wounded, Kiffin had lain in a makeshift clearing station for two days with about a hundred other wounded men before Willis came along to evacuate him. Several brancardier teams with their curious two-wheeled carts had passed him up as not seriously enough wounded to warrant immediate evacuation.

Willis had a loaded ambulance when he passed by the shell of a building where the remaining wounded soldiers were gathered. He had driven through a hail of fire that had punched holes in his vehicle, puncturing the radiator. He put Rockwell up front and nursed the Ford to the *poste de secours* where the drama with Masters would play out later.

Willis was forced to leave his passengers after filling his radiator with pinard, the only liquid available at the poste. The wine began to boil away almost immediately, but Harold made it to the road where a passing truck took him under tow. He didn't find out about Masters until later and felt miserable about not being able to help more.

Willis, a tall affable man, always went out of his way to help his fellow Americans. Prince glommed onto him because of his Harvard ties. The two of them found plenty of receptive ears among the drivers at Neuilly.

Piatt Andrew ribbed Doctor Gros about the way they were losing drivers to aviation. Unrepentant, Gros reminded Andrew there were already more volunteers than ambulances to drive. Volunteers were pouring in, challenging the AFS resources. Five *Sections Sanitaires* now served three French Armies. A sixth in training would soon be sent to the Balkans.

Meanwhile, Pierre Flandin encouraged the French Army staff to form a bombing force of 750 airplanes. As a manufacturer and businessman, Flandin knew the damage such a fleet of German bombers could do to French industry. His idea was to bomb the German city of Essen out of existence. Essen produced almost forty percent of the war materiel for the German Army. Though the government passed on this idea, Flandin managed to stir up enough interest to get the authorities to widen the door for pilot training.

At that time, seven Americans were either already flying or in flight training. Frasier Curtis washed out of French flight training, but remained to push the idea of an American squadron. Victor Chapman left the Foreign Legion at the end of July in quest of flight training. Instead, the French sent him to serve as a machine-gunner in Norman Prince's squadron. Prince urged Willis and Curtis to help get Chapman into flight school.

"We've got two issues going here, fellows," Kiffin Rockwell said to the group at Chatham's. "Prince, Gros and that crowd can push all they want for an all-American squadron, but if we can't get into flight training, the whole scheme's shot." He suggested making a trip to Escadrille C. 42, the Caudron Squadron then located near Compiègne, about fifty miles north of Paris. His friend Bill Thaw, who had joined the Legion with him in August 1914, had written from C. 42 inquiring after Kiffin's health.

Thaw, Kiffin recalled, was already a pilot but had had to pull some strings to get into aviation.

Charlie Keeler offered to borrow a car from Fleury. Buck would drive. Willis, newly arrived from Dieulouard, didn't seem too enthused about the trip. They were debating over drinks when none other than Bill Thaw himself walked in with a pretty girl on his arm!

"They told me I'd find you here, Kiffin!" Thaw said, quickly introducing the young lady. "You don't look too much worse for the wear, a little thinner maybe."

"Damned if we weren't just talking about going up to see you!" Kiffin said, getting up a little awkwardly. "You look great too, Bill, and maybe a little thicker?"

"Good thing you didn't come up, at least not to where C 42 was last week." Thaw responded, patting his small paunch. "The Boches knocked on our doors with their big guns and mounted a ground attack. You never saw me move faster! Hey, have you heard that Bertie Hall is with Morane Saulnier 38?"

"That reprobate? Did he actually know how to fly like he always boasted?" Paul Rockwell asked.

"Not at all," Thaw laughed. "You know Bert. It took them three smashed machines before they realized he was bluffing. Can you believe they kept him on and eventually gave him his wings?"

"Considering how much trouble we're having getting in ourselves, you have to admire Bert." Kiffin said, stopping to introduce Thaw to Charlie, Jack, and Willis. Thaw stood about five eleven. He had dark hair and a full mustache that masked his youthful age of twenty-three.

"Keeler? Why, you are a living legend in my outfit!" Thaw said, looking Charlie over more closely. According to our captain, you ought to be a couple of feet taller. I kind of expected a Hercules."

"That wouldn't be Antonelli, would it?" Charlie asked incredulously.

"The same. Tony tells a tale about a day in Valbonne that I'm sure couldn't have happened that way, now that I see you." Thaw turned to Kiffin. "Antonelli thinks this guy walks on water."

"Don't tell me he doesn't," Buck said, chuckling. "I already wrote the papers back home about this guy. I'd have to print a retraction."

"How in the hell did Antonelli end up a captain in an aviation squadron?" Charlie asked.

"Not in aviation, Charlie. He's 'our' captain because his company protected our asses during the Boche attack I just mentioned. One helluva tiger too. If you were able to impress Tony, there must be more to you than meets the eye."

"Anybody thirsty?" Chatham's bartender, Santos, asked, always happy to serve Americans. They ordered a mixture of beverages that ranged from a *demi pression*—a quarter liter of beer on tap, to *porto*—port wine, to whiskey or *whisky* as the English insisted it should be spelled. Chatham's even managed to stock name brand bourbons, and Monsieur Santos, the multi-lingual barkeep, prided himself on being able to memorize each customer's preferences.

The long session of stories and catching up kept Jack fascinated for hours. Keeler didn't say much about himself. Thaw's embellished rendering of the bayonet story had Keeler taking on one after another of the instructors, whipping them one, and then two at a time until only the trainees themselves were left standing. When Thaw came to the part about the French Captain stopping the contest, he said they'd offered Charlie command of the company there on the spot. Keeler just sat sipping on a beer, rolling his eyes and shaking his head.

"And you guys say this fellow Hall knows how to fling the bull? Can't hold a candle to Thaw here," Charlie interjected.

Thaw offered a possible explanation of the French reluctance to enlist foreigners to fly.

"I ran into Bert Hall down at Buc just before I got my brevet. Bertie told me that while he was at Pau the French put a couple of ringers in his barracks to keep an eye on him. He couldn't figure out why these guys weren't out on the flight line with him and yet always showed up at night to sleep in the cots on either side of him. One day he followed one of them and overheard him reporting to an officer that this American didn't seem to be a spy!

"Turns out an American guy named Hild enlisted back in the fall. Hild claimed to be a pilot, but like Bert, he couldn't keep a plane on a straight line on the ground let alone get one into the air. He'd cracked up one machine, but went on with his training. Right after getting his brevet, Hild skedaddled. He turned up in the States where he started spreading it thick about how lousy the French were and how incompetent their flying training was. This got back to the French, of course, making them think Hild was a German spy. It also made them leery of letting other foreigners into aviation. Hell, even Bert managed to wreck three costly airplanes. Can't blame the French. Imagine what a real saboteur could do?"

At some point in the evening Elliot Cowdin showed up to claim the young lady Thaw had brought in. Buck and some of the others knew Cowdin. Elliot said he had just been released from VB. 108, a Voisin Bomber squadron. He was on his way to *chasse* training at Pau. Naturally, everyone wanted to know how he'd managed to get selected for the coveted pursuit or *fighter* planes the French cleverly labeled *chasse*, their word for hunt.

Cowdin began his tale with his hands weaving in the air in what had become the trademark gesture in Chatham's. One followed the other as Elliot described his last combat. Jack's ears perked up when he heard the objective of Cowdin's last raid, the Imperial Palace of Trèves. Flandin had talked a lot about a great bombing raid, mentioning the name "Trèves" disdainfully. Pierre told Jack he wanted to hit the German's where it would hurt their war effort, not try to knock off a crown prince in a palace.

"Nimmie's squadron was there, and Victor Chapman—any of you guys know him from the Legion?" Thaw and Rockwell nodded, listening more closely. Charlie's ears perked up at the name.

"Chapman gets to the squadron one day and makes two training flights as a machine-gunner, right? Next day he's the gunner for our lieutenant! So here's the scene: Picture sixty bombers from seven different squadrons all taking to the air and marrying up over Toul. Never seen so many airplanes in the sky at once. We crossed Commercy and Saint Mihiel before going over the trenches north of Verdun. The major in the lead ship had to dodge the clouds while keeping his whole flock together. What a sight! I thought we were going to get all mixed up in the clouds. The visibility kept getting worse. Trèves wasn't that far, but before we got there a white shell, the signal to abort the mission for bad weather, burst just over our lines."

"You all turned back?" someone asked.

"Yeah, but it wasn't pretty. Five of our ten in VB. 108 ended up on other airfields. I just stayed close to the major's plane. Luckily we weren't bounced by the Boches, but the Germans evidently had better sense than to fly in weather like that. Anyway, we get back and I go looking for Chapman, just to see how he liked his first mission, you know. I find Vic beaming from ear to ear, practically bursting to get back in the air.

"'Why did we quit?' he asks, saying he was just beginning to enjoy himself when we turned around. Then he starts asking me if I remembered some lines from *Alice in Wonderland*, of all things. Something about flying in the clouds reminded him of having to run very fast just to stay in one place." Cowdin stopped, looking around expecting a bunch of blank stares. Literature, it turned out, wasn't one of Elliot's strong suits. The Rockwells really appreciated Chapman's analogy though neither of them had been up in an airplane. Charlie thought about the young man in the trenches hoping he could get to see him again soon.

By two in the morning the Americans were still going strong. Cowdin's girlfriend, clearly fascinated, though she couldn't speak a word of English, enjoyed the attention. She made Jack remember Marie, his appetite for sexual union even more pressing than before.

With the trip to Compiègne off, they had another day to pass in Paris. Thaw agreed to go with them to the recruiting office to see what he could do. He suggested going over to Les Invalides in small groups of no more than three, in order not to overwhelm the bureaucrats. His plan worked better than any of them would have imagined that night—at least to those who could remember that night.

Chapter 28
Time to Tackle the Air, but Penguins Can't Fly

Avord, September, 1915

"You would think they would have this down to a system by now, wouldn't you, Kif?" Charlie asked, still puzzled at how he and Rockwell had been enrolled in flight training while Buck and the others were made to wait. All of them went to Les Invalides as Thaw suggested. Some of the ambulance guys got held at Dijon for initial military instruction of all things. Keeler and Rockwell only passed through the Aviation Headquarters long enough to draw a flying outfit and sign some papers

"I'm pissed with a capital P, Herc," Kiffin said, fuming. "Why the hell aren't Balsley, Buck, Johnson and Rumsey here? We would have made such a great team!"

"We'll get to see them soon enough, I suspect," Charlie replied, his mind full of Michelle rather than their left behind friends.

Michelle's parents had taken to him like one of their own sons. Georges de Vincent was a voluble Frenchman very well schooled in English ways. Michelle's mother, Janet, latched onto Keeler, determined to size him up. Charlie saw where Michelle had gotten her beauty and her feistiness.

Two days before they were to leave for Dijon, Georges de Vincent pulled him away for *une virée en ville*, a man's night out. He took Charlie to some of the back street cabarets. At one small brasserie a girl not more than twenty danced totally nude with a big snake draped over her vital parts. Charlie discovered a side of Paris he'd not experienced, wondering why de Vincent chose those particular places.

Apparently it was a test. By the time the de Vincents declared their visit over, Charlie felt like a specimen on a microscope slide. He hoped he'd passed muster. When they accompanied him to the Gare de Montparnasse, Georges gave Charlie a small medal on a chain.

"Saint Christopher," he said. "Some believe he protects travelers. I don't know if it works for flying, but we want you to wear it." Charlie interpreted the gift as his graduation present. Michelle whispered that they liked him almost as much as she loved him. It made Charlie feel relieved and even more reluctant to depart. Kiffin had to pull him away from Michelle to board the train.

AFTER THEIR ALL NIGHT STOP AND GO TRAIN RIDE, they reported to the *Poste de Sécurité* at the gate of the caserne on the outskirts of Avord, orders in hand. The officer on duty was sleeping on a cot and the soldier at the desk refused to wake him before eight o'clock. *Most curious*, the former legionnaires thought. At least the guard was able to point the way to the *ordinaire* where they could get a coffee and wait. After rising before the sun in the Legion, Charlie and Kiffin couldn't help feeling a bit scornful.

The Americans learned that the French Army had put the brakes on the flying schools after a costly summer of accidents, injuries, and deaths. Even with added precautions, training casualties remained horrendous. Nobody told the arriving students this, but it didn't take long for them to hear about the latest *coucou cassées*, French argot for crack-up.

Rockwell and Keeler went up in a dual control Maurice Farman that very day. During Charlie's twenty-minute orientation flight, he felt an almost erotic thrill when the instructor let him touch the controls. Kiffin, too, gushed later that there was nothing like it.

Lousy weather precluded flying for the rest of their first week. To fill the time the *éleves* performed *corvées*—work details run by the cadre. At Avord, these centered on the *aérodrome*, the catchall term for everything on and around a flying field. The main landing area was called a *piste*, which could equally stand for a football field, a pasture, or the middle of a racetrack.

Charlie and Kiffin detested the pick up detail the most. They stretched out across the *piste* picking up any debris or junk that might be sucked into a motor or strike some vulnerable part of the flying machines. Even in the rain they invariably found the most unlikely of projectiles, including some used *french letters* which might have gummed up something. In the end, as demeaning as this task seemed, they saw its ultimate utility, especially when it became their turn to *utiliser la piste*.

Avord, a relatively small town on the rail lines between Bourges and Nevers, lay almost at the geographical center of France. The town itself was about a mile and a half from the *Camp d'Avord*, the official designation of the military installation. The camp was an old artillery base. A *champ de tir*, or firing range, covering nearly a thousand acres south of the town, was off limits to everyone. Though no longer in use, the impact area was *polluée*, meaning full of unexploded shells. A grisly photograph of an unfortunate gutted cow that had set off a dud 75-millimeter shell was sufficient warning to most.

Except for their uniforms, newly tailored at Le Bourget before they left, Keeler and Rockwell relied on their legion issue. Their battered musette bags were marks of honor, as were their combat ribbons, tucked away except for ceremonies.

They found their accommodations, shared with eighteen other pilot candidates, austere in the worse sense of the word. The barracks were clapboard buildings thrown together to house itinerant artillery units passing through for firing practice. Never intended for permanent use, the walls were not insulated inside or out. In the mild September weather, this presented little problem, except for the leaky roofs and the water that came in between the boards of the walls when the wind howled, driving the rain vertically. An iron stove with a pipe routed through the wall stood at one end of the building. Windows allowed light in during the day and ventilation, wanted or not, around the clock. A single electric bulb hung from the open rafters in the middle of the building. No plumbing graced their home-to-be. A nearby washroom and shower building served four similar barracks. At least the French were thoughtful enough to install regular toilets as opposed to the squat holes they'd found in many other places.

The twenty occupants of the building vied for the cots closest to the stove in anticipation of cold nights. As late arrivals, Kiffin and Charlie had to settle for bunks near the door at the other end of the building, not suspecting that this apparent misfortune would later prove fortuitous.

After several classes on motors, carburetors, and the basic reasons why a wing tried to fly, Charlie felt bored. His old reticence at sitting in classes returned with a vengeance. Kiffin, on the other hand, seemed to thrive on these classes, though both wanted to get through this phase as quickly as possible.

"Better pay attention," Kiffin chided Charlie during a break. "Even though someone feeds and stables a knight's horse for him, he still needs to know when its shoes need changing."

"Guess you're right, Kif," Charlie observed, stroking his chin. "Never know when you'll have to get out and shoe one of these mounts."

"Laugh all you want, wiseass. Just keep goofing off. If you fail this phase you get to do it all over again."

The cadre at the school could turn a student out for any number of reasons, chief among them disciplinary. Right behind that fell the category of "untrainable," a subjective call the *moniteurs*—ground and flight instructors—could make at any given moment. Motivation seldom became a factor since most volunteers had come from the infantry or artillery and were in no hurry to go back to the trenches.

Kiffin couldn't wait to get his hands on the controls of an airplane. Charlie had similar feelings, though he couldn't get Michelle off his mind. *What was she doing? What was she thinking?* He found being away from her an almost intolerable challenge.

Finally the weather broke. Kiffin and Charlie were up at four o'clock. The Annamite orderly, Thieu, came in quiet as a mouse and woke only those men who needed to be up. He gently shook Charlie's shoulder and then waved the hot coffee bowl under Charlie's nose. Thieu memorized each student's preferences for their morning libation. He lit the oil lamp between Rockwell's and Keeler's cots before moving on to the next student, pushing his little rolling cart laden with pitchers of hot coffee, chocolate and tea.

At 4:30 the bleary-eyed students climbed into the Renault bus for the ride to the Blériot field, one of about eleven different training fields at Avord. Arriving fifteen minutes later, they piled out into dark and gravitated to the edge of the field where a small fire in a brazier caught their attention. The knot of students rushed over to the light and lined up. Charlie and Kiffin held back a bit, moving to see what had attracted their French classmates.

"So much for banker's hours," Charlie grumbled.

They could just make out the shape of a stand of sorts. He smelled the charcoal fire and coffee. They saw their French classmates, lined up rubbing their hands together in that peculiar gesture they used to ward off the slightest chill. A little old woman, her wrinkled face eerily lit by the coals of the fire, dispensed coffee and fresh baguettes. Rockwell and Keeler got in line with the rest of the men.

Dawn had yet to brighten the sky when an NCO ushered them into a small building. A five foot, four inch adjudant introduced himself as

Monsieur Vierau, *le chef de piste et Roi des Pingouins*. Charlie understood the chef de piste part, but wondered what the man was king of. Vierau shifted to broken English to explain. *Pingouin*, they learned, meant penguin, the name given to the clipped wing Blériot trainer they would be using. Vierau had crowned himself king of the penguins, though with his red hair and beard he looked more like a leprechaun.

Vierau went on in slow clear French in deference to the foreigners in the class. He told them that before the beginning of 1915, all flight training in the French military followed the same program. When observation balloons and airplanes began to have an impact on ground operations, both sides raced to develop counter measures. Shooting balloons down proved too difficult for conventional artillery.

They heard again about Rolland Garros' experiment with steel deflectors on the propeller and the race to find a solution to firing a machine-gun on the axis of the airplane without damaging the propeller. The Germans coerced a Dutch engineer, Anthony Fokker, to develop an interrupter gear. Fokker soon became one of their chief aircraft builders. It didn't take long for the French and British to make similar interrupters for their fighters.

Vierau said that aerial bombing and weapons effectiveness had increased rapidly. Both sides experimented with ground-to-air weapons with mixed results. Conventional artillery with its long arching trajectory and impact fusing proved totally inadequate to attacking aerial targets—here the French assistant instructor pointed to a diagram on a paper chart depicting trajectories. By modifying the fusing, explosives, and aiming systems, the belligerents began to improve the likelihood of knocking down an airplane.

In less than twenty minutes Vierau confused the somnolent group with an excess of information. He slapped a table with a riding crop snapping many heads to the upright.

"You, my friends are about to see what I am talking about." He led them to the edge of the field where they could just make out a line of machines that looked like airplanes without wings. A pinkish glow in the east promised good weather. Vierau stopped and turned to face the group. "You are here to learn how to become a *Chasseur*, a hunter of enemy prey. Some of you will not be able to master flying by yourself. We will determine which of you are capable of becoming *chasseurs*. We cannot say this officially, but the *chasseur* is the *crème de la crème* of pilots."

Just as Vierau finished, two sleek-looking monoplanes roared over their heads, startling them enough for some of the students to duck. The two flew wing-to-wing only feet apart. Suddenly the one with bright red white and blue cocardes zoomed almost straight up climbing hundreds of feet before executing a loop and coming back on the tail of the other unmarked aircraft. They heard the rat-a-tat-tat of a machine gun. Some of the students looked anxiously at Vierau. Smoke began to pour from the lead airplane that disappeared over the trees at the end of the field. The *chasseur* roared skyward, flipping on its back, and rolling snappily right over their heads before landing and taxiing over to the group.

"It's a Morane Parasol," Charlie said. "Saw one like it at Villacoublay."

A slender man descended from the machine. *"Navarre,"* someone whispered. "It's *Jean Navarre*, the ace!" Charlie and Kiffin had heard the name. It appeared regularly in most of the French papers.

Finally, Vierau reacted. He snapped to attention shouting, "*section à vos rangs fixe*!" The students responded instantly, coming to rigid attention. "*Mes respects, mon Lieutenant*," Vierau said to the approaching aviator, saluting smartly. The dashingly handsome officer returned the salute casually, removing his leather headgear and goggles in the same motion. "*Messieurs*," Vierau said, turning to the class. "Let me present Lieutenant Navarre."

For the next thirty minutes the students badgered the cocky young lieutenant who basked comfortably in their admiration. Already credited with shooting down six Boche aircraft, Navarre looked the part of a rugged knight of the air. His flight that morning, he explained, was a reenactment of his last combat. The "enemy" plane, flown today by a French pilot, was the very Fokker Eindekker he had forced down inside French lines.

The rounds they heard were *les blancs*, literally 'white' rounds, meaning the bullet had been replaced in the cartridges with waxed wads of harmless paper. Well before the famous lieutenant took off to return to his unit, he had transformed Vierau's class from a bunch of sleepy, bored men into an energized body of enthusiasts eager to join the ranks of aces.

ROCKWELL'S INITIATION INTO THE *SYSTÈME BLÉRIOT* nearly ended in disaster. After their fundamental instruction, Vierau chose four of the students, Kiffin and Charlie among them, to try the Penguins. Charlie climbed into the three-cylinder Blériot trainer and felt a surge of adrenaline when the mechanic pulled the shortened propeller through, igniting the roar of the modified Le Rhône rotary. He waited until the ground crew pulled the chocks holding the wheels.

Pulling the throttle smoothly and slowly as instructed, the funny-looking machine began to move. Until forward motion produced sufficient airflow, Charlie remembered, the rudder wouldn't be effective. In other words, the machine would roll in whatever direction it was pointed until it had about twenty miles per hour airflow.

As he picked up speed, he pulled the throttle even further while tentatively trying the rudder bar to see if the penguin would respond to his touch. *So far so good,* Charlie thought, fancying himself a natural pilot. Just then a gust of air lifted the short right wing, pushing the nose a little to the left. Charlie applied pressure with his right foot to try to compensate. The nose swung violently to the right. Charlie tried counter pressure with his left foot causing the machine to spin in a tight left-hand circle. He retarded the throttle, hoping to stop the ground loop. The Le Rhône burped and banged twice before going silent. An embarrassed "natural" pilot crawled out to join one of his equally flustered classmates whose machine had turned Ostrich.

They had to laugh. It looked like a traveling circus. Two penguins circled wildly providing the center ring act. The French called it *chevaux de bois*, or *merry-go-round.*

Kiffin's spinning machine made him a little nauseous after the third or fourth circuit. He frantically pulled and pushed on every lever and handle he could find in an effort to stop the motor, but he pulled when he should have been pushing and pushed where he should have pulled. It would have been comical had not another student's machine joined the party. Charlie heard the loud crack when the two penguins meshed propellers sending splinters flying everywhere. Everyone flocked to the scene. Rockwell lifted his goggles, grinning sheepishly.

Four small brown-skinned men in blue coveralls rushed to the smashed machines, helping the students out and then dragging the wounded penguins off the field. These Annamites from *Indo-Chine* were part of the so-called *Oriental Wrecking Crew.* Charlie had seen them working all over Avord, talking in their high singsong language. Some, unlike Thieu, spoke a few words of English. Many had teeth blackened intentionally with some sort of shellac.

Kiffin's grin faded when one of the Annamites pointed to the long inch-thick splinter embedded in the fuselage just behind Rockwell's head. "*Beaucoup de chance, monsieur*!"

Lucky indeed! The varnished laminated wood fragment from one of the propellers pierced a poplar spar, itself an inch thick. Rockwell felt sick when he realized how close the splinter had come to impaling him. Death and injury were bad enough companions when you were mentally and physically prepared to face them. Flirting with them blindly was not Rockwell's style. He told Charlie later that only a fool squanders his life haphazardly, and that he felt very much the fool.

Keeler needed no convincing of the dangers of the flying. Only days before they'd arrived at Avord, a French student pilot cartwheeled his clipped wing Blériot, breaking his neck. The unfortunate student didn't die in the crash but expired slowly in the ambulance, unable to breathe due to a severed spinal cord.

Crashes were common enough in the Blériot System. Following the early pattern of pioneer flyers, the French opted for training most students to fly in single seat aircraft. Early machines were not usually capable of carrying more than one person. Though multi-place aircraft played an important part in the French Army from the beginning of the war, the French considered dual instruction for all but the poorest pilots to be uneconomical and—though never officially admitted—somehow unmanly.

Le Système Blériot, Vierau explained, served to weed out those whose dexterity, adaptability, or nerve made them unsuitable for single seat, highly maneuverable aircraft. Failures deemed otherwise apt could be sent to train in Voisin or Caudron machines equipped with dual controls. Rockwell and Keeler were determined to make it through the *Blériot* program.

Mastering *les pingouins* took a frustrating week. The limited number of machines—aircraft recovered from the front and modified for training—allowed each student about an hour in the cockpit each day. They needed six successful straight "flights" before they could go on to the next phase. They made straight-line runs until 8:30 when classes ended. Back at the camp they shaved, and went for the first mess at 10:15. The bread was fresh, but the coffee or chocolate was usually only lukewarm.

At 11:15 they lined up for roll call. Someone read the orders of the day. Then they had to do fifteen minutes of drill, a series of turning movements ridiculous to the veterans in the class. They were off until 3 P.M. Some made the two and a half mile trek to *Farges'* Cafe just north of the camp. Others went to the *Café des Aviateurs,* a half mile away. For a few sous, about six bits, one could get a decent omelet, bread, cheese, veal, potatoes, peas or beans, salad and good coffee at either cafe. *Farges* made the trip even more worthwhile by hiring pretty waitresses to attract the students.

Charlie and Kiffin usually stayed back to write letters, play cards, or nap. At 4:45 P.M. the mess opened, serving a hearty stew along with the usual bread and cheese. At 5:30 they got on the bus for their second training session with Vierau, staying at the field until dark. Charlie got in three successful straight lines in three days. Kiffin, after his first disaster, mastered the penguin easily. Charlie hoped to catch up.

Of the twenty who started with their class, fifteen remained by the middle of the third week. A couple of new guys joined the class to take the washouts' places. Much to Keeler's and Rockwell's delight, one of them was Victor Chapman. Chapman, no stranger to flying after his time in a line squadron as a machine-gunner, caught on quickly. Both Keeler and Rockwell liked Victor immediately. He stood about an inch taller than the two six footers, and, like them, was very athletic. After their brief encounter at the front, Victor fell in with Charlie like he'd known him all his life.

Chapman, a sensitive and artistic type, said he'd been a student in Paris at the Ecole des Beaux-Arts at the time the war broke out. His father and stepmother were visiting at the time. They convinced him to go to England with them where he lasted a week before racing back to enlist in the Foreign Legion.

Charlie asked if he knew Jim McConnell.

"Mac and I go back a bit. He never forgives me for my Harvard background, swearing that the only school worth a hill of beans is his University of Virginia."

"You a Harvard man?" Charlie asked, impressed.

"Class of '13, Charlie, but only because my family insisted." Chapman answered. "I wanted to be an architect, not an academician."

"Hey, me too!" Charlie said.

Rockwell told them about his truncated college education; how he had been accepted at Annapolis, decided to go to Virginia Military Institute instead, and ended up with his brother at Washington and Lee, next door to VMI. Charlie knew Kiffin was 23, and figured Chapman to be 24 or 25.

Kiffin was one of the first selected to try the *rouleur*, a Blériot with full wings, and a six-cylinder, 31 horsepower motor. This machine could actually leave the ground, but only achieve a yard or two of height. Rockwell listened as the instructor repeated through an interpreter, "Keep it straight, no turns, land straight ahead, shut it down, get out and help turn it around. Then do the same thing coming back."

Charlie watched Kiffin's trainer leave the ground and wobble slightly just feet above the grass. He thought it moved slower than he could run. It looked so easy. Then he remembered their first attempts in the penguins. Kiffin's was aloft less than a minute before he had to let the machine down. From the start point to the turn-around looked like about a half a mile. The return flight took even less time. Charlie overheard the *moniteur* say something about *le vent*, the wind. He looked at the red tubular sock like indicator to see which way the wind blew. Sure enough, the wind slowed the upwind leg and speeded up the downwind. No wonder Kiffin had trouble getting it off the ground.

Kiffin couldn't wait for his second shot at the *rouleur.* "I tell you, Charlie," he exclaimed when he got down, "there's nothing like it! You float." Charlie remembered Kiffin saying almost the same thing about the charge at Artois, thinking, *this man thrives on thrills.*

"Is it hard to control? I mean, once you get off the ground?"

"I, I, hell Charlie, I don't know! It was over so quick and I was so excited about being off the ground that I didn't even think about the controls. I just did the same thing as in the penguins, you know, the little dance on the rudder bar? I almost forgot to pull back on the *balai* on the return trip. These things seem to do it all by themselves."

Manche à balai, Charlie thought, an extraordinarily appropriate term for the control that stuck up between one's legs. It did resemble a broomstick. The rouleurs with their open tailboom, single wing reinforced top and bottom by a pyramid of wires, and their flat oval-shaped rudder were more like a service airplane than the stub-winged penguins.

When Charlie's turn came, he hoped he could keep it straight and level. He climbed up on the left wingroot, swung his right leg into the open cockpit, and lowered his frame into the wicker basket seat. The controls were the same as in the penguins, but the three additional cylinders more than doubled the noise and vibrations. Signaling *ready* with his left thumb up, he opened the throttle, feeling the *rouleur* strain powerfully against the chocks. Seconds later he felt the machine pick up speed quickly into the wind. Keeping the stick neutral, he controlled the roll on the ground with his feet. When he passed the liftoff pennant, Charlie pulled back gently, careful not to overcontrol. The uneven ground shook the airframe uncomfortably. *Why wasn't he leaving the ground?*

Pulling a little harder to the rear, Charlie was alarmed to see the letdown pennant coming up. There was no choice but to slow down and stop. What had gone wrong? What had he forgotten? He cut the throttle, feeling foolish for making nothing more than a penguin-type maneuver.

"*Ah! C'est vous*!" Adjudant Michon, the downfield *moniteur*, said, a knowing smile on his face, as if to say 'one of the stupid Americans.' Charlie cut the magneto switch and climbed out on the right wing. Michon looked in the cockpit and grasped the stick to check its range of motion. It would move left and right, but neither forward nor back. Charlie saw why he couldn't take off, but what had frozen the control?

Michon leaned over the edge of the cockpit and rummaged around. "*Eh voila*!" he said, emerging with an even broader smile. He held up a silver cigarette case engraved "KYR." Charlie looked at it uncomprehendingly for a second until he remembered Kiffin had been in the same trainer before him. Apparently, the case had fallen and lodged itself between the floor opening and the control stick!

I'll kill him! Charlie thought, relieved to find that at least he wasn't entirely responsible for the foul-up. "So, *mon adjudant*, what could have happened here?" he asked.

"*Ici? Pas grand chose*," Michon, one of the best liked of the instructors, replied. Then he got a stern look on his face. "Never, never get in a cockpit without checking thoroughly for foreign objects; and never, ever start your motor until you verify the controls are free."

As that sunk in, Charlie stopped feeling so smug. He took his friend's case and slipped it into his chest pocket. On his downwind run, he achieved a near perfect straight flight, experiencing some of the thrill Kiffin had mentioned, but feeling chastised for not checking the control movement the first time.

Just as in the penguin phase, each student had to complete six straight flights in the rouleurs before he could go on to the next phase. One of the French students found that the *huile de rincin* fumes made him violently sick. Castor oil lubricated the rotary engines. In the penguins the smaller motor and fewer cylinders produced fewer fumes than those of the rouleurs. The student was sent to the *médecin*, the flight doctor at Avord, rated *inapte* for flight, and returned to his parent infantry unit.

Chapman moved through the penguins in two days and was able to join Keeler and Rockwell as they completed their rouleur tests. He took the place of the departed French student in their *promotion*, the French word for the group of students in a given class. Victor moved into their barracks, taking a cot next to the pot-bellied stove. A cold snap prompted their French classmates to fire up the old stove just before bedtime. It glowed red halfway up the side when the lights went out. Those closest to the stove were toasty warm—almost too hot. At Charlie's end of the building little of the heat took the edge off the cold.

Sometime during the night, Charlie woke with a start, thinking he'd been dreaming of Michelle in the bright sun. He saw a flickering glow reflecting off the glass of the window. When he sat up on his cot he sucked in a full breath of thick smoke! Fire! "*Au feu*! Fire!" he shouted, rolling off the cot and crawling over to waken Rockwell. The other end of the building was engulfed in flames.

Victor! Charlie grabbed a bucket and rushed toward the fire. The smoke was thick and the heat searing. He tossed the bucket, dropped to all fours, and tried to get to the cots where Chapman and the others slept.

Something grabbed his ankle and began pulling him back. He struggled, yelling "Victor! Wake up!"

"Charlie, you fool, get out of here!" He heard Rockwell's voice pleading.

"Vic's down there. We have to get him out!"

The flames lashed at the bare wood, consuming the very floor planks they were crawling on. Kiffin was no match for Charlie's strength. He screamed again and tugged at Charlie's pajama leg, ripping the cloth. Just then another pair of hands got hold of Charlie's other leg. Renewing their efforts, Kiffin and the newcomer were able to drag Keeler backwards. Charlie's strength began to ebb from all the smoke he'd inhaled. He was sobbing "Victor, Victor…" as they pulled him from the building.

Outside it was sheer pandemonium. Firefighters doused the flames while students dashed about looking for friends. Three men had to nearly sit on Keeler to keep him from getting up to go back into the building. Rockwell sat beside Charlie, coughing despondently.

Someone set up lights and mustered the building occupants for roll call while the firemen worked. At least two of the students had already been carted off to the infirmary with burns. Seventeen men slept in the building. Thirteen stood for the roll call. That left two unaccounted for after the two that had already been evacuated. Charlie kept moaning *Victor, Victor.* Kiffin stood beside him feeling helpless.

"Charlie, Kiffin!" a clearly American voice shouted as a figure rushed up to the line of coughing men. "Thank God you're all right!" Chapman shouted, standing there in his pajamas and slippers, a roll of paper in his hand.

Dazed, Keeler let out a big throaty sound somewhere between a shout and a sob. He picked Victor up in a bear hug, smearing soot on Chapman's clean face. Rockwell threw his arms around both of them. Their relief and joy turned to sadness when they saw the charred remains of the last missing man pulled out on a stretcher.

It took the *pompiers*, the crash-rescue and fire fighting team, an hour to put out the barracks fire. No one would sleep the rest of the night. Gathered in the mess, the survivors received a new issue of clothing while a doctor examined them. Kiffin and Charlie had slight burns on their faces and hands, but nothing to keep them from flying.

"How did you guys get burned if the fire started at my end of the building?" Chapman asked, ignorant of the dramatic rescue attempt.

Kiffin filled him in slowly, pausing to look at Charlie with renewed respect. When he got to the part where Charlie had to be dragged from the building and then restrained from going back in, Chapman had tears flowing down his cheeks.

"My younger brother, Jay, would be about your age Charlie. We played together every day as kids trying to outdo each other in feats of prowess. We climbed the highest trees, ran races, crawled into the darkest of tunnels, and scared the daylights out of our stepmother, Alce.

"When I was twelve and Jay ten, we were playing in the woods beside a fast-moving river near Gratz in Austria. Racing along the bank, Jay suddenly lost his balance and fell in the torrent of churning water. We couldn't swim. Jay's head bobbed up and down while I ran alongside the river screaming for help. I grabbed a long branch and ran ahead to try to fish him out, but the current pulled Jay farther out into the river. Men lowered a flatboat into the water and worked for an hour trying to save him."

"He drowned?" Kiffin asked gently.

Chapman's eyes filled again with tears. He said he had never been able to forgive himself for failing to rescue Jay. He got up awkwardly and put an arm on Charlie's shoulder.

"You remind me of Jay, Charlie. He would have tried just as hard as you did—harder than I tried to save him..." he broke off, unable to continue.

Kiffin, fighting the urge to cry with all his Southern gentleman strength, broke the somber mood.

"Thank God you are so full of crap, Victor. If you hadn't needed to go to the can, we'd have a reason to be sitting here crying like little girls." Smiles fought their way onto their faces.

"So, its back to school, brothers," Charlie said, rising and throwing his arms over their shoulders. "Time to tackle the air."

DURING THE NEXT PHASE THEY LEARNED to make level turns and fly around a serpentine course at 50 to 100 feet off the ground. The machines were still power limited—fifty horsepower compared to the 80 to 100 horsepower motors that powered service Blériots—but the student got the full feeling of flying and controlling his motion through the air.

This phase began with a *tour de piste*, a supervised flight in which the student took off, climbed to five hundred feet above the ground, circled the field at about a half-mile distance and returned to land into the wind. The only tricky part was cutting the motor for the glide to landing. If one did it too soon they risked coming down in the trees surrounding the field. Waiting too long could lead to driving the machine into the ground to avoid overflying the field which often resulted in a pile up—testified to by the half dozen smashed Blériots in the hangar at the end of the field. Judging height and rate of closure took practice.

When they took the Blériots up for the turns and banks, Charlie quickly learned to coordinate the turn with the rudder while keeping the nose up. Though the instructors explained all this on the ground, it just didn't set in until the student felt it himself. A moniteur demonstrated each new maneuver before any of the students were allowed to attempt it. They progressed from simple turns to climbing and descending turns in both directions. The torque created by the whirling cylinders of the motor made the Blériots *want* to turn to the right. After the serpentine courses, the students were ready for the altitude test.

Despite the early start and the late end of the training day, the students had ample free time. They were subject to any number of work details and petty little disciplinary infractions. Chapman characterized this as "guilty of something until proven otherwise." Even when they weren't found wanting, the French cadre seemed to be saying: "Okay, we didn't catch you this time, but we'll get you next."

The French students courted this attention almost joyfully. Every day one of them was placed under arrest or sent to sleep in the guardhouse at the gate for some sort of prank. One favorite pastime was to place a lighted cigarette in the hand of a sleeping classmate and wait until it burned down to his fingers. The victims invariably woke falling out of their beds, often setting their blankets on fire, or tipping over nightstands to the amusement of the prankster. The fatal barracks fire put an end to this stupid practice.

Rockwell and Keeler with their wound stripes and corporal rank were off limits. Along with Chapman, they eschewed the horseplay, preferring to read and write letters.

Charlie wrote his mother about Michelle. She had replied with some reservation. She always told Charlie that when the right girl came along he would know. Her lukewarm congratulations were deflating. She wrote about Jennifer's plan to work as a volunteer nurse in the American Hospital. Keeler dashed off a long reassuring letter saying he would not do anything without letting them know. He tried to discourage Jennifer from coming, secretly hoping she would ignore him.

Paul Pavelka wrote from the 170th Infantry Regiment where most of the Americans had been reassigned. *Les Hirondelles de la Mort* was a tough bunch, but it just wasn't the same. Too many of the old hands had left. He reluctantly admitted that he was having problems keeping up on marches. Flying looked better to him every day. He would regret leaving the Death Swallows, but he planned to enlist in aviation anyway.

"Kiffin, you rogue! Did you tell Skipper about your smashup and about trying to kill me with your cigarette case?" Charlie commented as he read the letter from Pavelka.

"I just told him how much I am enjoying this. No sense in painting a bleak picture, especially for Skipper. I really think he will be better off, don't you?"

Charlie agreed.

Paul Rockwell kept them informed about the American Squadron effort. Though everything seemed to be in place, something in the French bureaucracy had held up the decision.

"What else is new?" Charlie asked with a touch of sarcasm.

"Paul says Buck went directly to Pau after convincing the French recruiters that he didn't need the full course of instruction. Red Rumsey rode Jack's coattails and ended up at Pau, and Jim McConnell enlisted in aviation October first.

"What do you make of this, Charlie?" Kiffin asked, tapping the page. "Here we are going through all this crap and old Swede and Red both jump right into the brevet course."

"More power to Buck, but I don't know about Rumsey. Wasn't he the one that got drunk on the Fourth of July? That must have been one hell of a blast you guys had."

"He wasn't the only one in his cups. It was a good thing that Buck didn't drink or we'd have ended up in the Seine."

Thieu, their orderly, showed up one morning with a bigger than normal smile on his face. He stiffened in the French soldier manner, tipping his head back slightly and saluting Charlie and Victor perfectly saying, "Fuck you very much, sir!"

Taken aback by the words, the Americans saw Thieu smiling expectantly as if awaiting a compliment. Chapman deduced that his greeting was his first attempt at English. Laughing, he and Charlie returned the salute saying "And you, Thieu!" Thieu never suspected the inappropriateness of his words. He proudly began greeting all Americans the same way every day.

Early October brought fresh cool mornings and warm breezy afternoons. The region produced a significant crop of grapes that were made locally into very good wines. The local vintners began the harvest in September and continued it well into October. With war clouds hanging over France in 1914 and the great mobilization denuding the countryside of young able-bodied workers, a large part of last fall's crop had never been harvested.

Now the region teemed with women and children and men too old for military service. This was the first time Charlie had seen such activity. He thought it would be interesting to go out in the fields to help. Some of the French students took advantage of the long breaks to work for Puteux, one of the nearby vintners who paid them by the number of ten-kilogram baskets they were able to fill. Assured that the cadre would not object and that he would not be reported absent, Charlie joined one of the work details on a bad weather day just to see how it was done.

Just as the sun began to lighten the overcast sky Puteux issued the grape-stained wicker baskets in stacks of ten. It had rained all night turning the fields soft with mud. Everyone wore high rubber boots. The polyglot crew of off-duty soldiers, flight students, women, little children, and old men set off behind a cart drawn by one of the scrawniest donkeys Charlie had ever seen. The field they would work that day lay close to the western side of the military camp.

Puteux paired up newcomers with veteran pickers. Charlie's assigned partner could have been sixty or a hundred. His skin was deeply furrowed and browned by the sun. Only a few teeth remained in his tobacco-stained mouth. White strands of hair poked out from under a straw hat, and equally white whiskers covered the lower half of his face. Upon learning that Charlie was an American, the old man straightened his back and set about picking the full ripe grapes, leaving the still greenish bunches to ripen further. Charlie followed the old man's example, thinking this was going to be a breeze.

The old vines were a good six inches in diameter at their bases. Over the years they had been pruned and trained to grow in a tee-like manner so the vines bearing the grapes twined around a heavy wire staked the length of each row at a height of about one meter. Charlie's companion had filled his first basket before Charlie had caught on to the trick of using a small knife to cut the heavy bunches away from the vine. Even after he had mastered the technique, he fell even further behind the man working on the other side of the row.

By nine the old man had filled ten baskets to Charlie's two. Puteux patrolled the rows making sure no one pilfered too many of the luscious grapes while offering generous swigs from a large leather wine bag suspended from his shoulder.

At noon Charlie's partner had finished his side of the row and had started down Charlie's. Puteux had made four trips with his cart and donkey back to the barn at Terrieux where the grapes were stored in huge bins before being crushed. He had a big smile on his rosy cheeks when he gathered the dozen or so workers to pay those who were leaving, and to distribute bread, sausage, and cheese to those who were staying. The flying students, who received the equivalent of eight cents a day military pay, stayed.

Charlie could barely stand. He slumped down under the makeshift canvas shelter Puteux had erected. Charlie watched his partner drink a half-bottle of red wine in nearly one swallow, gum a hunk of bread soaked in wine, and suck on a piece of sausage. The man showed no sign of fatigue. In fact, he was the first on his feet to resume for the afternoon, looking over his shoulder to see if the big strong young American was going to quit.

Charlie got up slowly, feeling aches in various muscles he hadn't used for a long time. Since his release from the hospital, he had recuperated almost fully, but his muscle tone came back all too slowly. Now he was embarrassed to be upstaged by a little old man. They still hadn't spoken to each other.

As the afternoon wore on, the rain stopped. The constant bending and straightening to reach the lower vines and lift the bunches into the baskets took a toll on Charlie and the other students. He knew he would be miserable the next day, but he refused to quit. He'd seen the pickers working in the fields right up to sunset. He doubted if he could make it that long.

Fortunately for him, Puteux called them together at four. His vats were full and could handle no more grapes until they'd been emptied that night. He had to stop the harvest that afternoon as soon as his cart was topped off with the remaining baskets.

Charlie looked at the old man who was shaking his head and mumbling something he couldn't understand. Puteux addressed the man very respectfully saying, "*Mon père*, it cannot be helped. Don't worry papa, we will finish tomorrow." Could it be that this old wizard of a grape-picker was the elder Puteux? Charlie looked at the man who had literally whipped him at a physical feat of stamina and skill with even more respect.

Charlie refused to take his earnings. The old man asked if the American had had enough of French labor. Charlie smiled, admitting he had been soundly beaten. The old man reeled off a long speech. When he got back to the barracks that night Charlie wrote down as much as he could remember:

You have joined us today to pick grapes, and I showed you that it is not easy for you, and that I could out pick you all day long even at my age of eighty-five. You have joined us today to harvest something much more important than grapes, the dirty Boches who violate our land and our homes. You are strong and young like your country, but you couldn't keep up with someone older and more experienced—like my country. Remember this, my American friend.

Charlie wouldn't forget, but he didn't plan to pick grapes again. Antonelli had taught him that the French were not much different from men anywhere, but he still had to fight the urge to look down on them. He, like many Americans before him and even more to come, tended to see Europeans as an archaic people living in the past. Charlie saw the arrogance of that point of view. Some of the French he knew held an equally low opinion of Americans, thinking of them as little better than barbarians. It was dumb. When he lay down that night aching, he appreciated the wisdom of the old man's words.

WITH *ROULEURS* BEHIND THEM, the class began the *brevet* phase. There would be more training for combat, but they would receive their wings and pilot certificates if they could complete this challenging phase.

The Maurice Farman field was one of the eleven specialized fields surrounding Avord. The machine they'd made their orientation flight in the first day had a pusher propeller attached to the motor that took up most of the fuselage behind the *habitacle*, the cockpit. The cockpit reminded Charlie of a bathtub. In active service as a reconnaissance and light bombing machine, the Maurice Farman could carry two crew members. The pilot sat in the rear seat while an observer occupied the front, manning the machine-gun. At Avord, the front position was sandbagged with enough weight to compensate for the missing crewmember. Powered by a Renault 8 cylinder, air-cooled, in-line V that produced 100 horsepower, it could reach over 12,000 feet and fly at up to 66 miles per hour.

In the brevet phase there were two major tasks called *épreuves*. The first consisted of flights. to 1,000 meters, about 3,000 feet, and then to 3,000 meters An altitude recorder mounted in the front position out of the pilot's reach noted the maximum altitude the aircraft achieved. The second *épreuve* involved challenging cross-country navigation.

Some men could not overcome the physiological disorientation altitude produced. For every 100 feet they climbed the temperature dropped one degree. On the ground it might be a balmy room-like temperature, but by 3,000 meters the air could drop below freezing. Close to the ground one received visual cues from the horizon and other terrain features. The perspective changed at altitude. This aspect of flight stymied many of the early aviators.

Two French students in their group made the first ascents. The instructors sat in canvas chairs that allowed them to lay back to watch the climbing machines and make their critiques. The other students watched as the Maurice Farmans circled laboriously to the prescribed height. The instructors warned them not to let the nose rise too high or lose forward speed lest they stall prematurely.

At the apogee the student had to deliberately enter a stall, begin the *vrille* or spin, and—ideally—recover before hitting the ground. Stalls occurred when the wings stopped providing lift due to insufficient airflow. The corrective action was to allow the stick to come to neutral and ride out the inevitable spin. More accidents occurred in this phase than in any other.

Charlie's first turn came on a clear day with almost no wind. He'd found flying the lumbering Maurice Farman much easier than the sensitive Blériots. Once the instructor had set the recording stylus over the slow-moving roll of paper on the barograph, he cleared Charlie to take off. He circled the field, wagging his wings over the instructor's station to indicate no mechanical problems. Then he began the climb. The instructors recommended right hand turns, a throwback to the Blériots and a precursor to the Nieuport's rotary torque effects to the right.

Charlie remembered that the cockpit altimeter was unreliable. He planned to go at least fifty meters higher than the indicated altitude to assure the recording barograph achieved the required thousand meters.

The ascent seemed to take forever. After fifteen minutes, he'd achieved only 300 meters. With the throttle at full, he could do no more than ride the slow-moving elevator. He became a little bored staring at the meager instruments. In addition to the altimeter, there was a small dial for the magneto, and a clock. Between the pilot's knees, just behind the stick, sat a brass compass.

At 750 meters the air became noticeably colder. His engine continued to hum comfortably. It was his longest flight to date. The countryside diminishing under his wings fascinated him. Charlie tried to make out the field where he'd picked grapes, imagining the old man down there showing up another young buck.

Charlie noticed that the controls responded more slowly as he climbed. He'd been making a slow climbing right turn without having to adjust much of anything up to 900 meters. He had to make a significant correction to keep from losing speed. Even a slight drop of the nose produced a corresponding reduction in his rate of climb. The last hundred meters seemed to take forever.

At 1,050 meters of indicated altitude, Charlie allowed the nose to rise intentionally, anticipating the stall and resultant spin. The machine just continued to fly. Frustrated, he pulled the stick back almost to his stomach.

Nothing happened! He had achieved that fleeting state of flight where the machine was going too slow to respond to the controls but continued to fly because of its lightness, buoyancy, and favorable winds. He knew turning sharply to the right would accelerate the stall, but he hesitated, feeling uncomfortable and apprehensive.

When the machine began to shudder, he held on, waiting to see what would happen. After hanging in the air nearly motionless, the abrupt drop startled Charlie and made his stomach rise uncomfortably. The nose fell. Soon he was falling like a leaf. The spin thrust him against one side of the cockpit in a most unnatural posture that terrified Charlie. His instinct was to whip the stick around to stop the spin—just the opposite of what he needed to do. He looked at the spiraling needle on the altimeter astonished to see that all those hard-earned meters of height were peeling off in mere seconds.

He reluctantly let go of the control and centered the rudder bar. The horizon spun dizzily. Sure he would crash, Charlie said a quick *Hail Mary*. At three hundred meters, the Farman began to catch the air. In two more turns the aircraft settled into controlled flight, again responding to the controls. Charlie was completely disoriented. He looked down to see he had drifted well to the west of the field. He was over the vineyard! Below him he could just make out small figures in the field waving to him. He thought he saw the old man in the straw hat.

Charlie adjusted his course, descending smoothly onto the Farman Field, the terror forgotten in his relief at safely landing. After the instructor checked his recorded height and signed off the test, Charlie felt like an accomplished pilot. He almost looked forward to the 3000-meter flight, though he couldn't imagine how the Farman could make it to such a height.

Rockwell's altitude flights went flawlessly. Kiffin wasn't fazed by the *vrille*. He waxed eloquent in telling Chapman how thrilling it was. Victor listened, smiling. During his month in VB 108 he had been up to the maximum altitude a Voisin could achieve—about 5000 meters. The helpless machine-gunner was at the mercy of his pilot. Victor had been in spins, violent maneuvers in combat, and several near-crashes. He found his friend's naïve enthusiasm amusing.

The final test for the brevet involved making two navigational flights. The first consisted of relatively short legs of between thirty and forty kilometers. Charlie paid attention in the navigation classes. The geometry and map work appealed to his artistic talents. Translating three-dimensional objects into pictures, after all, was the business of an architect. Navigation with a compass as a squad leader made this familiar ground.

"So, are you ready for your first triangle?" Charlie asked Rockwell, Thursday morning, the 14th of October. Kiffin found the navigation classes a bit more difficult than he'd expected. Every time the instructor talked about drift and the effects of winds aloft, he found *himself* drifting. It just didn't make sense to him to deliberately aim several degrees off course in order to stay on a given line over the ground. Charlie's attempts to explain the mathematics using billiards only confused Rockwell more. While Kiffin shot a great game of eight ball, he'd never thought about the geometry. In fact, geometry contributed to his leaving VMI.

"I hope to make it without a *panne de chateau*." The infamous castle breakdowns experienced by so many of the students were a big headache to the Avord cadre. The more they proscribed unauthorized landings for anything less than a real emergency, the more the students seemed to get the idea that an unscheduled stop was a great idea. Tales from the class ahead of them painted tantalizing pictures of being fêted by local demoiselles along with other fantastic adventures as the result of setting down in the right place.

Since this phase involved the first long excursions from the instruction field, a number of the students became genuinely disoriented. Failing to find one of the designated turn points, some flew on until their fuel ran out. Others landed to ask directions, often crashing during the attempt due to selecting poor terrain or bad technique or a combination of the two.

The Maurice Farmans were very forgiving airplanes. They could take a good deal of abuse. Being relatively light for the expanse of canvas covering the two wings, the airplane tended to float to the ground with any kind of headwind. The landing gear, two pairs of wheels equipped with multiple Sandow bands, bounced rather than breaking during most hard landings. Sandow cords, strong elastic bands named for the famous strongman, were wrapped around the articulated axles in an ingenious manner borrowed from bicycle and carriage mechanics. The bands held the axles in place near the wheels. During landing they would flex to absorb some of the shock. Nothing, however, could make up for some of the clumsier students' heavy-handed smashups.

Charlie's flight was postponed three times for weather. He and the rest of the grounded aviators fretted and fumed while watching the skies, hoping for a break in the overcast and fog. Kiffin made it under the wire, completing his first triangle without a hitch.

The French used artillery weather balloons to determine cloud heights and wind speeds at altitude. A meteorological section at each major airfield made hourly observations. They used the same techniques utilized in calculating artillery trajectories. Most of the students at Avord could care less that the winds aloft at 500 meters were coming from one direction while those at 250 meters came from an entirely different quadrant. Since these winds affected projectiles passing through them, artillerymen devised ways to determine their direction and velocities by tracking balloons, a difficult task with the limited instruments available.

Determining the ceiling, the height of the bottom of the clouds that constituted an overcast layer, depended on knowing the rate of ascent of the balloon. A simple calculation of time and distance gave a reasonable approximation, though the balloons seldom ascended vertically.

Aviation pioneers quickly realized it could be unhealthy to intentionally fly in the clouds. Ducking in and out of cloudbanks was already a favorite tactic, but more than one dauntless pilot came out of those clouds inverted. The danger of hitting a peak or high terrain generally pushed pilots into climbing to avoid the so-called 'granite' cloud. As long as their barometric altimeters kept indicating increasing altitude, a pilot could be reasonably sure he was upright and climbing.

On October 22, the weather broke early. Charlie took off on his navigation problem at about the same time as Kiffin began his final *épreuve,* the flight with legs as long as fifty miles. Successful completion would make Rockwell the first in the class to win the coveted brevet.

Charlie was anxious to complete the short course and catch up with Kiffin. He shouted *coup!* The motor sputtered, caught, and roared into full revolutions. His mechanic pulled the chocks. Reaching the end of the strip, Keeler turned into the wind and looked at the instructor's platform where his latest *moniteur*, Jacquot, waved the green flag as the signal to take off. Once in the air, Charlie savored the wind in his face, the familiar smell of castor oil wafting over the cockpit. He glanced behind to see Avord moving away.

He passed Farges, noting the time as he turned north and east to about sixty-five degrees. He had calculated eighteen minutes to reach La Charité, his first turn point, thirty-two kilometers from Avord. Jacquot made a big point out of plotting major landmarks and setting barriers beyond which the students would not fly. Even if Charlie missed La Charité, his barrier was the Loire River. Planning the flight reminded him of looking for the observation post on the patrol with Rejik. The Loire could be the enemy lines when they emerged from the wire. If he hit the river without finding his objective, he could turn north or south for a short distance until he found a known point.

As it happened, Charlie passed over a major road he assumed to be National Route 151. He saw a small town that had to be Sancerques. He could make out the buildings of La Charité behind which the rising sun peeked. He located the field southwest of the town and landed. A moniteur signed his logbook and Charlie took off for the second leg.

He headed south keeping the sun to his left on a heading of 200 degrees. This leg was almost forty kilometers long, or nearly thirty minutes at his calculated speed of 110 kilometers per hour. Charlie had adapted to the metric system used by the French more easily than Rockwell had. Kiffin converted everything to miles. Forty kilometers Charlie knew to be about 25 miles. When he reached the prescribed 300-meter cruising altitude and looked for his first landmark Charlie drank in the beauty of the countryside. The silver ribbon of the Loire glimmered off to his left. The sun had just begun to burn off the wisps of ground fog in the valleys and depressions. A golden glow in the early morning sky enveloped him.

Eight minutes into this leg, Charlie saw the big mountains of sand and gravel that marked the cement factory at Bettes. He should have passed directly over Bettes, but he'd inched east toward the Loire. Picking up the railroad spur that joined Bettes to his next landmark, La Guerche, he relaxed, confident he couldn't get lost now. He had time to try short climbs and descents, but he didn't dare turn too far off course for fear of messing up his time calculations. Eighteen minutes into the second leg, he clearly identified La Guerche, a medium-sized town on a major highway. It was at the end of the railroad spur that teed with the line going east from Avord. *Child's play!* Charlie began to think, not even feeling the cold.

The turn point at the village of Sancoins came up almost right on the thirty-minute mark. Charlie glided onto the field northeast of the village anxious to get his log signed and get off again. At the field a moniteur he hadn't met gave him a hard time for landing with the wind. Charlie argued that there was no wind, but the instructor crouched down, pulled some of the dried grass, and dropped it from eye level. It slowly drifted to the ground landing no more than a foot from where it had been dropped. There couldn't be more than a breath of a breeze, but the instructor would hear nothing of it, placing a negative grade in the log. Charlie could still pass the flight, but he would have to repeat the whole problem if he got one more bad mark. Fuming at the pettiness of the instructor, he took off on the last leg.

The final leg of thirty-four kilometers would make the whole flight just over one hundred kilometers, about sixty miles. Charlie turned to 320 degrees, noted the time, and looked for his first landmark, the town of Ourourer les Bourdelins, the tongue twister. This leg would be one of the easiest since it ran between two major roads, with the tracks coming east out of Avord running parallel to them. Charlie marked the passing minutes of this twenty-minute leg, cooling off slowly over the bad mark as he approached Avord.

All indications looked good. His motor fired flawlessly. He kept his head turning, looking for other aircraft. The closer he got to Avord, the more planes would be in the air. He had left with the rising sun. It was 7:45 A.M. when he left Sancoins. He might be able to do the brevet navigation that afternoon if he finished this test satisfactorily.

At a little past eight he began to make out the shapes of other machines buzzing around. The French had wisely spread out the aerial activity at Avord by locating the various fields well away from each other. Charlie's field was the one closest to the camp, between the town of Avord and the camp itself. Wending one's way onto the field without hitting someone else challenged the best of pilots. Charlie knew students had priority, but he searched the sky as he approached the field. Assured he was the only one in traffic, he cut his motor and glided to the field, careful to aim into the barely discernable breeze.

Charlie walked over to the instructor's station where Jacquot stood, scowling at him, holding his watch. *Now what?* Charlie worried.

"*Mon cher Keeler,*" Jacquot began, his scowl softening into a concerned look. "Did you see another Farman between here and Sancoins?"

Charlie had not seen anything until he got close to Avord. Jacquot told him that a student had taken off ten minutes after Charlie on a reverse course with his first landing point being Sancoins. He had not shown up there, and they were seeking the missing student's whereabouts. They would not launch a search until three hours after the student had departed. The Farman could stay aloft three hours and forty-five minutes before turning to the last ten minute reserve fuel.

"Who is it?" Charlie asked.

"Chapman," Jacquot replied.

"Victor? Hell, he is probably drinking coffee at one of the chateaux," Charlie quipped, not feeling quite as glib as he sounded. Maybe Vic had engine trouble. This was the easiest phase for Chapman. He already possessed something the other students would develop only with time—air sense. Victor's time as a machine gunner in a Voisin gave him a leg up on the novices.

Jacquot signed Charlie off, snickering lightly at the note about landing downwind. He shook his head, looking disappointed. He asked Charlie if he hadn't been taught better. Charlie found the criticism hard to take, especially from Jacquot.

Jacquot was non-committal when Keeler asked about doing the final flight that afternoon. Rockwell had taken off that morning for his brevet flight. Putting up another American that same day with one American currently missing didn't seem like such a great idea.

Nevertheless, Charlie proceeded with his planning. The flight to Châteauroux, Romorantin, and back to Avord lay to the west of the school. It was an area unfamiliar to the students for obvious reasons. The map showed ample landmarks. Charlie knew better than to become overconfident, but he didn't see this test as any more difficult than the morning flight.

Charlie craved success. His Legion time bolstered his self-esteem, but physical feats weren't necessarily marks of intelligence. Charlie considered the coming brevet flight as a rite of passage. It would be something he could proudly hold up to his father.

Rockwell and Chapman stood out like icons to him. Their enthusiasm was infectious. He fantasized about them as Knights of the Round Table conversing in lofty terms of self-sacrifice, nobility, courage, and commitment. Fleury's use of those last two words on the *Rochambeau* never left him. The *currency* of the battlefield, Fleury had said.

Becoming a combat pilot would place him in the ranks of men like Jean Navarre. He needed to prove himself to Michelle, his family, and himself.

While they waited anxiously for word on Chapman, Jacquot gave Charlie permission to proceed on his navigation flight. Jacquot had singled Keeler out as one to watch. Instructors developed a sixth sense from the way a student handled himself on the ground and in the air. Not flying with them made this hunch an imprecise science at best, but since the beginning of the war, those who had succeeded in aviation shared certain characteristics.

Jacquot knew from first hand experience the value of keeping one's *sang froid.* He became a moniteur as the result of wounds sustained in aerial combat. He'd been flying an artillery *réglage* mission near Arras. His observer, a popular artillery lieutenant, spotted the German formations, plotted them on his map, and stuffed the coordinates in a weighted metal tube. Jacquot flew over the artillery observation post so the observer could drop his message. They'd worked for months with the same artillery regiment. Whenever Jacquot's Breguet appeared over the lines, the Germans caught hell.

On May 8, the same day Charlie and Kiffin were wounded, the Germans launched a flight of five Fokker Eindekkers with the sole mission of getting rid of the troublesome Breguet. Two of the monoplanes came up from below, well out of his observer's line of view and fire. Jacquot felt rather than heard their bullets stitching the underside of his lower wing. He quickly reversed course, turning to bring the lieutenant's machine-gun to bear on the attacking pair. One Eindekker continued to climb, passing on their right, but the other burst into flames—their fifth victory as a crew.

Whipping around, the lieutenant got a string of rounds off in the direction of the other Boche when all hell broke loose from above and behind. Blinded by the sun, the lieutenant could not see to aim at this new menace. The three remaining Eindekkers had lain in ambush, keeping between the sun and their quarry. By attacking in a line of three out of the sun, one after the other, they hoped to bring down the troublesome Breguet.

Jacquot instantly appreciated his predicament. He pulled back sharply on the stick hoping to throw off the attacker's aim. Just when the Breguet could climb no more, he kicked the rudder hard to the left, dumping the nose and sending the machine into a violent *vrille*. Glancing over his shoulder, much to his shocked surprise, he could not see the lieutenant! Still hoping to shake their pursuers, Jacquot didn't have time to mourn his officer.

The spin took him down over the battlefield on the Artois Plain. He hoped to recover soon enough to head back into friendly territory where the Eindekkers were unlikely to follow. Neutralizing the stick and the rudder caused the Breguet to stop spinning, but something seemed seriously wrong. Jacquot couldn't keep the nose down. He looked back to see if his elevator had been shot off only to receive the shock of his life. There clinging to the tail, his feet draped over the back, interfering with the movement of the elevator, was his lieutenant! Jacquot wondered how in the hell the man had been able to stay with the machine during the spin.

He glanced overhead to see the Eindekkers had broken off. The Boches didn't have the stomach to pursue their prey over the lines. The Breguet flew on always on the verge of a stall, losing altitude the whole time. Jacquot didn't dare try to turn for fear of entering another spin at such a low height. The lieutenant had to be reaching the end of his strength. There was nothing for it but to allow the machine to descend straight ahead and hope for the best.

Seeing a road and an open field, Jacquot made small adjustments to sustain the flight. He couldn't cut the motor for fear they would pancake to the ground. The machine could not glide with the center of gravity moved so far back by the lieutenant's precarious position. Certain they would be killed, Jacquot had time to think about his mother just before they settled to the ground. When the ground came up to greet them, Jacquot raised his left arm to protect his face. Nothing happened! He felt no pain, but his arm wasn't there!

The Breguet bounced once before flipping the lieutenant over the top like a whale flinging an unwanted passenger off its tail. Jacquot saw the body going by just before he lost consciousness, hanging upside down in his cockpit. When Jacquot came to, the lieutenant was tying a tourniquet around the stump of Jacquot's left upper arm. Except for a gash on his forehead, the lieutenant seemed no worse for the wear. They were alive! They were aces! Soon the pain came, erasing the thrill of their victory and survival.

Jacquot refused to be invalided, asking instead to become a *moniteur*. He thought he could still fly with one arm, but even if he couldn't, he could teach others. Every time he started feeling sorry for himself, he thought about the lieutenant whose tale he never tired of telling.

When the trio of Eindekkers began their murderous attack, the lieutenant sprayed bullets in a circular pattern, hoping to get at least one of the enemy. He reached up to change the drum on the Lewis gun, a maneuver that necessitated standing up in the cockpit, loosening the restraining lap belt. Jacquot's abrupt climb threw him out, the old drum still in his gloved hands, stubbornly sticking to the machine-gun, his last link to the Breguet.

When the spin started, his feet whipped in the wind like the ends of an old tattered flag. He tried to pull himself back into the cockpit, but centrifugal force made it impossible. If the drum or the gun broke loose, he knew he would be a goner. All the times he'd cursed the Lewis machine-gun and its cantankerous ammunition drum for not coming loose flashed through his mind.

One of the gyrations plastered him against the side of the fuselage, knocking one hand loose from the ammunition drum. He couldn't hang on and he couldn't find another handhold. Just as he was about to give up, he saw Jacquot's severed forearm still clad in its glove, flapping in the wire rigging as if it was pointing a finger at him. He couldn't see the pilot, but the moving control wires suggested that Jacquot was still flying!

The lieutenant saw that his only chance was to slide back onto the tail to get a better hold. He couldn't get his weight off the elevator though he felt Jacquot's efforts to move it. He decided to let go when they got close enough to the ground to survive the fall, expecting to break something and get some cuts and bruises. The machine settled slowly so he hung on until he somersaulted over the top, landing in the soft dirt of the plowed field. Picking himself up, he couldn't believe he wasn't hurt other than the headache from a bump on his forehead.

Rushing to the Voisin, he carefully lowered his savior to the ground and bound the stump of his arm with his belt. When Jacquot opened his eyes and smiled, saying they were aces, the lieutenant cried tears of pride and gratitude.

The lieutenant proclaimed Jacquot's actions as *sang-froid* at its most sublime. Jacquot insisted the lieutenant's tenacity outdid his own actions. Both received the *Légion d'Honneur* for their actions that day. The lieutenant, now a captain commanding an artillery battery, would not entertain entering flight training despite Jacquot's repeated urging. He never let Jacquot know that the blow to his head had blinded him in one eye.

Jacquot's rendition of this story transfixed each class as they began the brevet phase. Jacquot numbered Keeler among the men he thought would make the best pilots. He thought Keeler would finish first, but Rockwell garnered the honor that morning.

Jacquot liked the Americans. He found Rockwell high-strung—an admirable trait to a degree in a *chasse* pilot. Chapman, he thought impulsive, a thrill-seeker. Both flew as well as any—better than most—but Jacquot preferred Charlie's self-effacing style. When he chided Keeler for not knowing better than to land downwind, the young American's reaction confirmed his opinion of the man.

Charlie took off for Châteauroux at precisely *trieze heures,* October 22. He climbed to the prescribed 1,000 meters. This added time to each leg, but Keeler thought he could recover that time during the descent for landing. Châteauroux lay almost fifty miles west and south of Avord. His course would be 265 degrees for forty minutes. Kiffin told him that the red castle that gave the town its name was visible from nearly ten miles at that altitude. Though Romorantin, the second landing point, sat in the middle of several built-up areas, Kiffin reported little trouble finding it.

Charlie reached the town with its red castle right on the schedule. The moniteur smiled as he signed Charlie's carnet.

"You Americans," he said. "Two doing the brevet flight in one day. Bravo!"

Charlie wanted to know if they had any word about Victor. The French sergeant just shook his head. He asked to see Charlie's *Ordre de Service.* If this piece of paper wasn't available at the point of take off or at any scheduled landing point, it meant immediate grounding. Charlie pulled his from the folding leather map case Michelle had given him. The moniteur quickly glanced at the order that read:

> *It is commanded that the bearer of this Order report himself at the cities of Châteauroux and Romorantin, by the route of the air, flying an avion Farman, and leaving the Ecole Militaire d'Avord on the 22d day of October 1915, without passenger on board.*
>
> *Capitaine Beauchamp.*

After leaving Châteauroux, Charlie took up a heading of six degrees, close to due north. Wind from the east picked up off the distant Alps. He turned to compensate. This leg covered almost sixty kilometers and would take about thirty-one minutes. This test included fuel management. They had enough fuel to make the first two legs with a thirty-minute reserve. Any diversions could cause them to exceed the planned one hour and twenty minute flight. Tapping the *nourrice,* the small reserve that held about ten minutes of fuel, meant failure. Charlie left no room for error. He arrived at Romorantin within two minutes of his calculated time.

The leg from Romorantin to Avord would take the most time in the air even though it was exactly the same distance as the first leg, 78 kilometers. Winds from the east at twenty kilometers per hour were almost directly on the nose for this leg. His heading of 110 degrees, twenty degrees off due east, would cause Charlie's flight to take at least ten more than his calculated forty-one minutes. The real danger here, Charlie figured, would be to edge too far to the north and miss Avord.

He saw towering clouds, a disturbing sight that indicated possible thunderstorms. He estimated that he had close to five hundred meters separation from the base of the clouds, a comfortable margin, though he wished the sky was clear.

The strip map he'd prepared showed the next landmark he needed to find. He'd gotten cocky after the morning flight, allowing his attention to wander dangerously. Thinking about Michelle, caused him to drift a couple of miles in her direction. Alarmed, he searched for something familiar that correlated with his map. He was over a great forest that seemed to stretch to the horizon in every direction. Charlie suffered several minutes of extreme anxiety waiting for the main highway coming out of Bourges. He knew he was past Vierzon, the midway point on his route. He couldn't be sure how far to the north he'd gone. He worried that he'd go all the way to the Loire, overshooting Avord completely.

After forty minutes in the air, Charlie began to panic. How much longer dare he continue? The headwinds slowed him, but he felt confident that ten minutes more would be safe. He began to doubt how far he'd drifted north. The left quartering headwind would tend to push him to the south. His disorientation made him almost physically sick.

He descended two hundred feet for better clearance. The map seemed useless. He couldn't make out anything familiar. Panic rose like bile. Fuel wasn't yet a problem. He wouldn't have to use the reserve in the *nourrice* for at least an hour. Despite that small comfort, he began to resign himself to failing this test.

Huge banks of clouds on the horizon seemed to touch the ground in his path. Terrified of becoming engulfed, he toyed with the idea of turning around. Unsure of his direction, he turned right for a couple of minutes. Surely, he reasoned, he would run into a road, an intersection, a town or something identifiable.

After two minutes of seeing nothing but empty fields, he could hardly bear the tension. Crashing, running out of fuel, ending up miles from his destination raced through his mind. "*Why in the hell did I get into this business?"*

A glint of light caught his eye. The river! *Let it be the Loire,* he prayed. He strained to see *Route Nationale 151.* All he had to do was cross it going south and keep the river to his left.

Familiar buildings in the distance! Avord! He set up to enter traffic feeling cold from the sweat in his clammy flying suit.

"*Ça va*?" Jacquot asked, noting the time as Charlie stepped down. "We were a little concerned that you might have had a *panne.*"

"No, no. It was great!" Charlie exclaimed shakily. He knew how close a run it had been. *Funny,* he thought, *how the terror and anxiety disappear so quickly.* Now he would get his brevet with Kiffin.

Jacquot divined that something had not gone exactly right. *Good,* he thought. *Overconfidence could kill this young man.*

"Keeler," he said, "you have the makings of a fine pilot as long as you respect the machines, the weather, your limits, and the enemy. Take any of them for granted and you are dead.

"Your friend, Chapman had a *panne de moteur* short of Sancoins. I'm surprised you didn't see his machine this morning. And, I almost forgot, you have a visitor waiting at the commandant's quarters. Better get over there right away."

Chapter 29
Success and Seduction

Pau, October, 1915

Jack Buck and Red Rumsey slept for much of the train ride from Paris to Bordeaux and then through several smaller towns to Pau. Lawrence Rumsey liked his liquor and knew it well in its many manifestations. Jack had to work a little at acquiring a taste for some of the concoctions Rumsey persuaded Santos to whip up, but after his first strong cocktail, the others began to taste better and better. When he woke some hours later with his mouth dry as a bone and tasting terrible, he found they were well on their way to Pau.

Jack had a touch of a headache, but seemed better off than Rumsey. After several glasses of water, Jack began to feel a little better. He looked out at the countryside in the early morning hours, remembering their train was scheduled to leave Paris at nine the night before. Someone must have poured them onto the train. He couldn't remember leaving Chatham's. In fact, the last thing he remembered was raising the glass of his second French Seventy-Five. He felt guilty and stupid, but it had been a good party, hadn't it?

To pass the time he picked up a colorful travelogue. *In a valley whose plain spread widely in all directions, lay the provincial historic city of Pau. Situated in the southwestern sector of France, Pau and its environs attracted human occupation from prehistoric times. Well before the Romans occupied camps near present-day Pau, ancient man lodged in the limestone caves along the region's riverbanks. Some scientists contend that modern man originated somewhere near Pau. The number of tools and other primitive implements suggest a thriving community of humans somewhere around 4,000 or more years ago. During the Hundred Years War, Pau sat in the middle of the duchy ringed at ever increasing distances by castles and strongholds of the warring nobility.*

Jack's mild interest increased as he continued to read.

In addition to an incredibly beautiful setting in a fertile valley in sight of the towering Pyrenees, Pau offers more than esthetic and archeological appeal. The mild, relatively constant climate favored agriculture. Grazing animals thrived in the area year-round. The rich alluvial soil, deposited over tens of thousands of years by glaciers and rivers, supported the long growing season. Additionally, at this latitude, ample sunlight bathes and caresses the crops.

A sportsman's paradise, Pau appeals equally to wealthy and lowly. Game in the region, largely deer and wild boars, serve to fill both local tables and a growing outside demand.

Borrowing from their nearby neighbors to the north in the Perigord region, he read that the people of Pau cultivated ducks and geese for their treasured livers—the famous foie gras.

Jack, not too fond of liver, read on.

Local residents are renowned for harvesting the elusive black truffle, A rounded fungus frequently found at the base of oak trees, the black truffle, a cousin to mushrooms, possessed a pungent fragrance and flavor very much appreciated and craved by a large and growing number of connoisseurs, including chefs from big and famous restaurants.

Truffles? Jack thought. *Only the French would treasure fungus.* Then he remembered lutefisk, the gelatinous fish his father favored. He didn't mind it, but nobody on his mother's side of the family could understand why the Scandinavians would like such a slimy mess. *A chacun son gout.*

Jack was pleased that he could understand the French text and only had to refer to the English version occasionally. Rumsey still hadn't stirred when they arrived at Pau.

The aspects of the region that attracted early humans and favored agriculture, Jack continued to read in the brochure, made Pau and its environs an ideal area for flying. The French Army first established a flying field in the area in 1909 to provide the Wright brothers a place to assemble and maintain their Wright Flyer for their flying school.

A French captain, passing through Jack's car, stopped when he saw what Jack was reading. "The Wright barn," he said in accented English, "is a red wooden building used by Orville and Wilbur during their stay. It sits on a corner on the main landing field of the Ecole d'Aviation de Pau.

I assume you know that's about eight kilometers northwest of the center of Pau, no?"

"Merci messieur, non, je ne le savais pas, mais, merci," Jack replied, looking up to see a short, kind looking man with a mustache and the three stripes of a captain. He had an insignia on his right breast. It looked like a set of wings flexed up, surrounded by a wreath in a circle, all done in silver. Jack was about to ask about them when the captain moved on.

Chouteau Johnson met them at the station. He'd enrolled in the class before them and had already started his training. Elliot Cowdin had just finished a short course the French called *Stage de Chasse*, or fighter qualification. Cowdin had come to learn the acrobatic maneuvers typical of aerial combat in a Nieuport. He had left about a week before Buck and Rumsey to go to Cazeaux on the Atlantic coast for gunnery training. This left Johnson as the only American at the school until their arrival.

During the next three weeks, Buck and Rumsey followed an accelerated version of the instruction Charlie, Rockwell, and Chapman were taking at Avord. The French had dispersed their flight training early in the war in the face of the rapidly advancing German attack. As late as mid-1915 they still provided primary instruction at four different schools located at Buc, Avord, Chartres, and Pau. Increased specialization led them to open a school at Cazeaux, already a ground firing center, for aerial gunnery. Plans to consolidate initial instruction in order to free up more instructors for combat duty languished in Paris. The demand for pilots climbed at too fast a rate to shut down or consolidate any of the training. Consequently, some Americans started at Avord, others at Buc, still others at Chartres, and a handful at Pau.

Pau had the newly established School of Acrobacy. Ostensibly, students sent to Pau were earmarked *chasse* or fighter candidates, though many of the pursuit pilots came out of the brevet phase of one of the other schools or directly from a line squadron like Cowdin had.

Jack mastered penguins, *rouleurs*, and service Blériots as fast as the instructors could get him advanced. Rumsey made good progress as well. Kept from hard liquor, Red could be a great conversationalist and a very competent and attentive student. Jack liked the man from Buffalo.

He had one letter from Marie-Louise full of news about the new tone in Dieulouard and de Valois's comeuppance. He'd thought about her frequently, but couldn't bring himself to answer her letter. Somehow, he reasoned, she would be better off unencumbered by him. He knew Dombasle would look after her as he'd promised.

UNLIKE AVORD, PAU WAS A GENTLEMAN'S SCHOOL. No humiliating chores or drills. Many came wearing their wings. The cadre treated everyone alike. The attitude was relaxed with more liberty for the students than at other schools. This nearly led to Rumsey's undoing.

After completing their turns, banks and spirals, the class held a little celebration. Brevet flights would follow in the next several days, but the spirited French students considered the milestone one worthy of toasting on a sunny Saturday afternoon. The class gathered at the edge of Le Pave River with a borrowed staff car laden with wines, whisky, pastis and food.

Jack helped his French classmates carry baskets brimming with baguettes, cheeses, sliced hams, sausages, the little pickles the French called *cornichons*, along with glasses and plates borrowed from the *ordinaire.* The class leader, a very proper sous lieutenant named *de Maison Rouge*, opened the feast with a clever toast that poked fun at most of the cadre—none of whom were invited to the impromptu riverside party to *arroser les aigles.*

After the first drink, the French set to the food with great refinement and grace. Certain students served the Americans almost as guests. As the youngest Jack felt very out of place being served. When he tried to take over the task, his fellow student, de Maison Rouge, stopped him.

"*Non, non, mon ami Américain. C'est à nous de vous servir.*" Jack listened to him continue to explain. "After all," de Maison Rouge went on, "you are here as volunteers. We don't have that choice. If you die, you die for us. If we die, we die for our country, our families. You can let us serve you today. You have already served us, and you will tomorrow. *Vive l'Amérique, vive la France*!"

This little speech brought on another round of drinks. The food soon disappeared.

Later Jack understood why they were at the river's edge. Almost as one they lined up on the bank. Someone announced, "*c'est l'heure*!" Thirteen flies came unbuttoned.

Red, catching on quicker than Jack teetered to the bank fumbling with his buttons, shouting, "one for each stripe, Jack!"

Jack joined the group as they urinated ceremoniously in the river at precisely noon. *Arroser les aigles*—water the eagles, or sprinkle the wings—Jack wondered? It was almost as if these young male animals were marking their territory.

Some headed back to the barracks smoking cigarettes or pipes. The diehards would stay until the bottles were gone. Jack wanted to go, but he didn't feel he should leave Rumsey weaving on the bank. A loud splash followed by a gurgling shout caused Jack to turn around in time to see a carrot-topped head bob under the surface much like the red and white bobbers he'd fished with back home. Rumsey!

Without thinking or hesitating, Jack leapt into the current of the Pave, struggled to the surface, and looked around for Rumsey. Some of the remaining French students ran along the shoreline looking and trying to direct Jack. Red popped up face down about twenty-five meters downstream. Jack swam strongly, thankful he'd had only one glass of wine. He reached Rumsey, turned him over, and paddled him the short distance to the overhanging bank where two men helped him get the half-drowned American out of the water. One of them pounded twice on Red's back while the other lifted his arms. Rumsey rewarded them with a gag followed by a mouthful of water, closely followed by the contents of his stomach.

Sitting up, Rumsey, looking dazed, asked, "Hey, what's all the fuss?" The dunk had sobered him up a little, but he didn't remember falling in the water. "Who pushed me in?" he asked, still gasping for air.

"You fell, Red," Jack told him quietly, not wanting to call any more attention to them than necessary. Soaked to the skin, he felt more than a little embarrassed.

"So, tell me Jack. If I fell in, how did you get all wet?"

"I went in after you, you dope," Jack answered, allowing his annoyance to show. Rumsey said nothing to that and would later avoid the subject as if it never happened. Jack found this irritating, but not worth fussing about.

By the end of October Jack's class had completed most of their brevet work. Their routine had not varied. Awakened at 5:30 A.M. and out for roll call by six, the class got on trucks to go to the field for breakfast. Flying started at seven o'clock. On a good day each student got to make six fifteen minute runs in the morning before the trucks took them back to the caserne at 10:30 A.M. After lunch they hopped the trucks at one o'clock for six more flights. Supper at 6:30 P.M. marked the end of the duty day. Lights out came early at 8 P.M.

New students arrived. There were breveted pilots fresh from other schools as well as some experienced aviators coming for acrobatic instruction. Jack's original class was now spread out in different parts of the brevet phase so that only a handful of the starters remained. De Maison Rouge, two former artillery observers, and Buck, reported to the field along with the new batch of men. Red Rumsey had landed in the infirmary for three weeks after his accidental dip in the Pau River. Completely missing the brevet phase, Red would not get another chance until after Christmas.

Jack searched the new group for familiar faces. The tightness and camaraderie of being in a class simply didn't exist in this highly individualized advanced phase of training. After breakfast at the field, Jack felt a tap on his shoulder, turned, and could hardly believe his eyes. There stood Charlie Keeler and Kiffin Rockwell, both wearing the wreath-circled wings of French pilots!

It had been a long two months since the three had been together. Coincidentally, their aviation training had been parallel in almost every detail. Jack had not had to put up with the Avord regimentation, and had done most of his flying in Blériots. Unlike Kiffin and Charlie, he had not had any passes or leave except for the free weekends in Pau.

Heavy rain that day gave them time to catch up. It was *All Saints Day*, November first, a fact not lost on Charlie since it was a holy day the French called *Toussaint*, his mother's maiden name.

Buck told them that Johnson, Balsley, and Rumsey were there. Chouteau breezed through initial training and then bogged down during the spins and altitude tests. Jack laughingly told them that Chouteau could fly circles around most of them, but when it came to flying in circles, Johnson couldn't.

Balsley had started about the same time as the others. Clyde got hung up in rouleurs, and then jammed his hand during a hard landing, losing a week. Balsley, Rumsey and Johnson could complete their brevets before Christmas if the French kept the school open, but the rumor among the students was that all training would stop for three weeks for the holidays. Jack said he hoped to finish before that.

Kiffin brought Jack a stack of letters Paul had picked up at the American Ambulance. Jack quickly looked at each to see who had written, and set all but one aside to savor later. He opened the letter postmarked two months earlier in Minneapolis from Willis Haviland.

While Keeler and Rockwell waited patiently, Jack raced over the lines written by his long-absent friend. Willis wrote that he had settled his family affairs. He said he would be back in France by the end of October. In fact, Kiffin told him, Haviland had been in Paris and had met with Paul and Kiffin at the Flandin's to discuss the issue of an American flying squadron.

Charlie thought Haviland wanted to join the Foreign Legion. They had talked about it after Willis related the story about Jacques-Antoine Flandin. Kiffin said Willis may have wanted to go into the Legion, but now wanted to fly. Willis decided to go to the American Ambulance first, and Kiffin thought he was with the 2nd Section with Jimmy McConnell.

"That can't be!" Buck interjected. "Mac is here!"

"Well, that's what I heard anyway." Rockwell said.

McConnell enlisted in aviation on October 1. He'd gone to Dijon for a week and then to Pau.

"Jim got here about three weeks ago. He's in the rouleur class now. Their crazy schedule keeps us from getting together much."

"Herc's engaged!" Kiffin said, draping his arm over Charlie's shoulder. "Popped the question the day we got these," Rockwell gestured at the wings on his right pocket.

"Congratulations, Charlie! Good grief! Engaged! Hey, when are you getting married?"

"I can hardly believe it myself, Swede. Michelle surprised the dickens out of me showing up at Avord the very day Kiffin and I got our brevets. We got 48-hour passes before having to come here. Kiffin got a suite of rooms in the *Bordérieux* and we got a little carried away."

"*We*?" Kiffin laughed. "Paul came down with Michelle and his intended. The two women took one of the rooms and we shared the other. Keeping old Herc here away from his sweetheart proved a little too much, even for the Rockwell brothers."

"Yeah, and Mademoiselle Bougeassie," Charlie interrupted. "Tell Swede about Auguste's sister since you're going to make me look like a fool."

Jack's head was spinning. The two friends argued the finer points, but Jack ascertained that Bougeassie—the single lady—was the sister of a student of the same name in their class at Avord. She had taken a shine to Kiffin soon after she arrived in the town. Her brother was injured in a crash of two *rouleurs*. She had come to look after him in the hospital. Taking up residence in the *Hôtel Bordérieux*, the fair damsel laid siege on the handsome American.

When Paul and the ladies arrived unannounced the day before Charlie and Kiffin were scheduled to do their brevet flights they checked into the hotel where Bougeassie quickly joined them. Near as Jack could determine, the three couples spent little time together as a group. Sometime during the two days and nights, Charlie emerged long enough to announce his engagement. Paul took the opportunity to make the same announcement. Kiffin feeling the squeeze, grasped the tiny waist of his companion, lifted her off the ground, and shouted a rebel yell at the top of his voice. This brought the concierge running with a local gendarme in tow. The ensuing confusion provided just the diversion Kiffin needed to avoid getting swept up in the engagement frenzy.

They enjoyed a hearty laugh and ordered champagne to properly toast both the engagements and the brevets, consoling Buck that he too would soon have his wings.

JEEZ!" JACK GASPED, HIS HEART POUNDING LIKE A DRUM. He'd been cruising along in wide circles at 6000 feet for close to the required hour when a big tear appeared in the upper wing of the Caudron. He watched it grow, its ragged edges flapping wildly as the tear worked its way back from the leading edge to the middle of the wing. He looked at the clock. Fifty-seven minutes! He had to stay up a full sixty to qualify. His horror grew with every inch the tear grew. He ran through his options, not liking any of them.

If he began the descent now, the damned recording barograph would do him in. If he stayed up any longer the tear would only get worse until the left upper wing lost all lift. Then his chances of getting down at all were in peril. *How should I descend?* Jack wondered, anxiously watching the gash grow in the wind. They were supposed to initiate a *vrille* at the end of the altitude flight, recover at 1000 feet, cut the motor, and glide to land. The violence of the maneuver could be catastrophic to the damaged wing. He would have to keep it slow and smooth, nursing the machine down gently.

Fifty-eight minutes! *Damn!* Jack thought. *Only a minute and look at that tear!* He decided in a flash to take the chance and ride it out. He gently pulled back on the stick to slow the Caudron even more. Maybe he could keep it just above stall speed. The reduced forward motion might slow the tearing forces of the wind. He looked south toward the Pyrenees in search of a clue on the winds. It seemed that the wispy clouds were drifting slowly toward him out of the south. Far below, Jack saw smoke from a fire. It too was moving north. He would do slow turns speeding up on the northerly leg and slowing down on the southern heading. That way he could keep the relative wind at its lowest.

Fifty-nine minutes. A reinforced seam had stopped the tear's progress toward the trailing edge of the wing. Small comfort in that, he noticed, since the wind lapped under the fabric turning up flaps in both directions following the seam. *God, forgive me for my sins. I will go to confession and never ever sin again if You get me out of this.*

Watching the second hand creep ever so slowly around the dial, Jack recited one of his father's Lutheran prayers for good measure. He had a death hold on the stick. In fifteen seconds, the rip progressed another six inches. Jack could see the wooden ribs and stringers. He thought he could hear the cloth ripping. Thirty seconds to go. Time for the rosary he thought.

If he let the nose come up even fractionally, he could feel the shuddering of the Caudron on the edge of stalling. Maybe he could slip some. He pushed in a smidgen of left rudder, bringing the nose to the left, which changed the angle at which the winds struck the left wing. He craned his head to see that the tear now stretched a full foot in both directions along the seam. It seemed to be moving away more than coming closer to the wing root. *Of course!* Jack realized almost too late. The slip had made the hole in the wing become like the mouth of a funnel.

Tomorrow and tomorrow and tomorrow creeps in its petty pace from day to day and all my yesterdays have lighted fools the way to dusty death, popped into his head as he watched the second hand sweep off the last ten seconds of his obligatory hour aloft—seconds that seemed like hours. Shakespeare would be of no help.

A loud report and twang caused him to jump in the cockpit. He noted the time. Sixty minutes plus! With the roar of the engine and whistle of the wind, hearing anything at all always grabbed his attention. Looking at the wing Jack's terror increased when he saw the guy wire that had snapped. Whipping between the wings, the loose wire would tear both of them to shreds in minutes. He had to do something!

Unfastening his belt, Jack steadied the stick between his knees and slowly straightened up in the cockpit until he was standing up. He grasped the stick with his right hand and reached as far to the left as he could to grab the wire. He couldn't reach it! Already great gaping holes in both top and bottom wings threatened to denude the whole lifting surface of his left wings.

All he needed now would be for the motor to quit. Jack renewed his effort to reach the flailing cable. It was of no use. He would have to let go of the stick. *What the hell*, he thought, *it can't get much worse.* He took his hand off the stick, keeping it inches away to see what it would do. Since he was descending straight ahead, the stick stayed centered. He stretched, bending at his waist over the edge of the cockpit, keeping his feet down. The cable lashed back catching his hand and cutting right through the leather of his glove. *Damn!* Jack swore again, lurching for the offending whipping wire with renewed effort and anger. It snapped malevolently at his hand almost with a mind of its own, licking the bottom of the upper wing at the end of one swing and the top of the bottom wing at the other. Jack's lunge had brought his feet up to the seat bottom. He was now hanging over the edge of the fuselage with almost no more purchase than his heavily booted feet.

His weight threw the machine out of balance enough for the left wing to drop, beginning an uncoordinated banked turn to the left. In seconds

Jack was hanging nearly upside down by his toes. He flailed about for the damned cable, caught it, and tried to squat back into the cockpit futilely. The turn became a dive. Jack grabbed a strut with his free hand, and muscled his frame back until he was standing on the dashboard with his butt on the back edge of the cockpit rim. His only chance now would be to drop back down and try to regain control.

The dive accelerated the tearing of the fabric on both of the left wings. Fully a third of the underside of the top left wing was now bare of cloth. Jack shimmied down until he could lip his toes under the dash. With a giant effort, he scrunched his body, all the time hanging on to the snakelike cable that had done so much damage. Leaving the belt underneath him, he got his feet on the rudder bar, pulled back slowly on the stick, beginning to arrest the diving descent. The strain on the wing had now shorn great patches of fabric. What kept him up he couldn't tell.

He had already lost three thousand feet. Blipping the switch on the stick momentarily cut the motor. At least something worked right.

Jack took a moment to size up his situation. His left hand throbbed and blood oozed through the rip in the glove. He secured the wire around the strut over his left shoulder. Doing this with one injured hand while trying to fly with the other, proved almost as hard as his earlier gymnastics. The progress of the tears and shedding of great hunks of fabric no longer seemed to matter. The only noticeable effect on the way the Caudron flew was that he had to hold in a little right stick and right rudder to compensate for the greater lift on the right side of the machine. Now he had to worry about where he was and where he could set it down.

Passing through two thousand feet in a lazy left-hand turn, Jack began to feel almost fatalistic. Living or dying was out of his control. It gave him a strange sense of peace. He would struggle with all his might, but if he crashed, he crashed. If he was seriously injured, so be it. The fear drained from him. He stopped the frantic prayers, nodding his head as if to say, "Okay God, I'm at your mercy. Let it be done to me not as I wish, but as You would have it."

He had gone some distance closer to the mountains. He stopped the circling on the next turn and pointed the nose to the north. If he could keep the wings from collapsing, he could land just about anywhere.

The Pau River stood out better than any other feature in the valley. Navigation in the Pau Valley had come naturally during his required cross-country flights.

The Caudron now rocked to the left and tried to dive every time Jack let the motor run. He toyed with cutting it completely and gliding the rest of the way to whatever terrain might be under him. Spotting the spire of the cathedral of Pau to his northwest, he decided to go for home. He thought about the smile on Chérie's dead face and flowers in her hand. What did he have to worry about?

At five hundred feet and less than a mile from the aérodrome at Pau, Jack felt the fuselage twist violently to the left. He blipped the motor off and jerked the stick to the right, which arrested some of the rotation, but the Caudron had had it. The lower left wing fabric had come off completely on the topside, and he could see through the holes of what remained on the bottom. Why the upper wing hadn't followed suit Jack couldn't guess. He knew if he let the motor come back on it would probably flip him over completely. He still had some directional control. He saw the auxiliary field, nothing more than a strip of grass off to his left. Could he make it there?

Weaving back and forth and up and down, Jack pointed the Caudron at the strip. His emergency must have already gotten someone's attention. The red flag was up indicating danger, aircraft in distress. He lined up as best he could letting the machine down incrementally while trying to dampen the gyrations.

Fifty feet up and just short of the grassy strip the right wings finally succumbed to the excessive load. Jack watched first the lower and then the upper wing fold slowly upward. The ground seemed to swallow the stricken Caudron. No longer flying and lacking much in the way of forward airspeed, the whole broken birdcage simply settled to the ground, bounced once, and stopped.

Silence. Absolute deafening silence! No wind in the wires. No Gnome rotary growling, no shrieking tearing cloth. Nothing. For a moment Jack thought he must have died and gone to limbo or purgatory, heaven being out of the question. *Why didn't it hurt to die*, he wondered?

Jack saw that he was on the ground in the middle of a heap of broken wood, spars, wires, and shredded doped fabric. He could smell gasoline now. Time to get the hell out! He climbed out of the wicker seat, about the only thing that seemed intact. As he leaned on his left hand, the sharp pain reminded him of the lashing he had taken, but nothing seemed to be broken.

Realizing that the hot engine parts could ignite the leaking gasoline, Jack started to put distance between him and the wreckage when he remembered the barograph. Damn the thing! Running back to see if it had survived the crash, he was about to jerk it out when a voice yelled: "*Arrête! Ne bougez pas le truc*!"

Turning to the sound, Jack saw someone running toward the wreckage. *Why didn't he want me to touch it,* Jack mused somewhat angrily? This was the officer on the train, the one who commanded the brevet section. *Hell! All that and I am going to have to do this all again!* The captain looked quickly at Jack and then at the barograph. He quickly grabbed the American's arm and dragged him a safe distance from the machine, looking anxiously over his shoulder at the now smoldering wreck.

"*Mon Dieu, Mon Dieu! Incroyable*!" The French instructor said, staring at Jack as if he was an apparition. Jack didn't understand. Captain Thénault was far more agitated than Jack. He started slapping Jack on the back and shaking his hand, all the time muttering unbelievable, *incroyable*.

Thénault, it turned out, had been aloft observing students doing the altitude test. He saw Jack's Caudron starting to come apart. Jack was too busy to notice the other aircraft above him. Thénault would have given him credit for the hour at six thousand feet even if the barograph indicated several minutes short. As soon as he saw the holes developing in Jack's wings, Thénault moved in as close as possible, feeling helpless. Watching the American hang on until the last minute made Thénault proud of the courage of the doomed pilot.

Throughout Jack's descent, Thénault couldn't imagine what he would do in the same circumstances. When he saw Buck hanging from the cockpit, Thénault began to scream, "*Non! Non! Non*!" at the top of his voice, knowing the American couldn't hear him. Sure Buck was jumping out, Thénault maneuvered over to the left and underneath the Caudron, hoping to perform the impossible feat of catching the falling student. When he saw what Jack was doing, he couldn't believe his eyes. Fascinated, he flew a loose formation on the gyrating Caudron. When Buck slowed, Thénault in the much faster Nieuport Bébé couldn't keep his position. He simply circled at a safe distance, shaking his head in disbelief that the Caudron flew at all.

Jack's abrupt dive made Thénault wince. Thinking the wings would fold at any instant, he could do no more than follow the stricken machine to its final impact area. When Jack leveled out and pointed in the direction of Pau, Thénault S-turned to stay behind the Caudron. Buck's meandering settled into a pattern. The American had his machine on a definite, if shaky, heading for Auxiliary Field 4!

Thénault was incredulous that the machine could stay airborne at all. By rights, the airplane should have fallen off on the left side and spun to the ground. Some of the cloth on the upper wing remained, but not nearly enough to sustain flight. The strain on the right side bank of wings must have been incredible. That they had not buckled added to the miracle Thénault expected to end tragically. He had already decided to recommend the pilot for at least a Croix de Guerre for his sheer intrepidity. It would be some small compensation to his grieving family.

As the field came into sight and their altitude dropped below fifty meters, Thénault's opinion of Buck's fate changed from despair to cheering encouragement. He yelled, "*Allez, allez, allez*!" zooming his Nieuport right over the top of the Caudron at the very moment the right wings folded. Buck had slowed the Caudron enough so that his forward speed was negligible. As the remains of the Caudron plopped down at the approach end of the strip in a cloud of dust, Thénault landed straight ahead. He jumped from his Nieuport almost before it stopped and raced back in time to see Buck reaching in the wreckage for something. Fearing fire, but completely mesmerized by the apparently uninjured student, Thénault's shout in French didn't make much sense. He wanted to shout *run*, but all that came out was *don't touch it!*

They stood at the wood line looking at each other for a long silent moment. The Caudron did not catch fire. A vehicle approached them. Thénault waved, beckoning it over. Two brancardiers climbed slowly from the automobile and walked in no particular hurry to the wreck prepared to police up the remains of the pilot. Another officer, de Maison Rouge, got out with them and started for the wreck with his head hanging.

"*De Maison Rouge*!" Jack shouted. "What the hell are you doing here?"

Startled to hear his name in the mid-western twang he recognized as that of Jack Buck, de Maison Rouge sputtered, "Jack! I... I... I. Mother of God! You're alive!"

"*Mon capitaine*." One of the brancardiers came up saluting and looking very bewildered. "*Ou est le corps*?"

Thénault smiled and turned to Buck, pointing. "*Ici, messieurs, ici!*" Reaching into his leather map case, still hanging from his shoulder, he fished out what he wanted. Next he called the driver, the two stretcher-bearers, de Maison Rouge and Buck to attention. The men responded a little slowly, not comprehending the captain's intentions. Thénault then marched smartly in front of Buck. He saluted crisply, holding the salute until a very confused Jack realized that he should return the salute.

Dropping his hand, Thénault waited until Jack had lowered his before stepping toward the American. He then took out the silver badge of a military pilot and fastened it to Jack's right breast pocket. Thénault stepped back, saluted again and then vigorously shook Jack's hand.

Thénault said: "Having met the requirements for the awarding of the designation of military aviator, in the name of the President of France, I present you with this brevet." Thénault paused before continuing. He told the small assemblage that he had been witness to the most extraordinary display of courage and airmanship that he had ever seen. Looking at the smoldering heap, the four others listened in amazement.

Jack stood dumbfounded through Thénault's short speech. While he had just narrowly avoided death, he was more concerned about passing the brevet test. His hand hurt like hell, but there on his chest were the wings of a pilot! His head spun and the light slowly dimmed as his field of vision narrowed. He didn't feel himself fall.

BREVET CEREMONIES CALLED FOR CELEBRATION. Only a small handful of Jack's class had received the coveted wings in their three months at Pau. Arnoux de Maison Rouge completed his last requirement two days after Jack. The lieutenant had joined aviation from the cavalry. While he believed in tradition and distinct separation of enlisted men and officers, de Maison Rouge had relaxed his standards for the little riverside picnic, but he ended up regretting it. While he meant what he'd told Buck there, he didn't mix well with the enlisted students, and Rumsey's drunken dunk in the river soured him for life on Americans, Jack Buck excepted.

Buck had beaten him in the race to be the first breveted in the class. Thénault's field award impressed the cavalry lieutenant. Georges Thénault was cavalry, three years his senior at Saint Cyr. Thénault was at Pau to finish his *chasse* training while still technically commanding Caudron Escadrille 42. Given the additional duty of overseeing the brevet phase, Thénault was well within his rights in his action on Auxiliary Field 4.

Buck's recovery had been swift. His injured hand would take about a week to heal well enough for him to continue flying. It didn't keep him from joining de Maison Rouge and two other recently breveted students to plan the party. He couldn't get used to the word *pot* pronounced like the town Pau. He realized its origin came from the same word in English meaning 'pot' or 'tankard.' De Maison Rouge insisted on doing their celebration properly. The lieutenant graciously offered to pay for two thirds of the cost, suspecting Buck and the two other corporals couldn't afford much of anything. His insistence on no more than five guests each led to the first confrontation between de Maison Rouge and Jack Buck.

"*Mes respects, mon lieutenant.*" Jack said politely. "*Est-ce que je peu parler ouvertement*?" He wanted all the Americans at Pau to attend. Counting McConnell, Rockwell, Keeler, Balsley, Johnson, Rumsey, and a new arrival, Carroll Winslow, Jack insisted that he be allowed seven guests

"It is that important to you?" de Maison Rouge asked. "It is only a little pot. Winslow hasn't even started training, so he probably won't be able to attend."

"Okay, I will pay one third of the cost." Jack said, reasoning that Arnoux's objection might stem from some sense of monetary equality.

"Out of the question. I understand you are barely able to pay your mess bills."

"With respect, sir," Jack said, steaming slowly and not feeling much respect, "my finances are none of your business. Either all of my countrymen get invited or count me out." Jack never felt good in any kind of angry debate, not trusting his temper and touchiness. Doing it in French made him all the more uneasy. What was making Arnoux so stubborn?

"Perhaps we can compromise here, Monsieur Buck," de Maison Rouge said, looking genuinely concerned. "You may bring an additional guest, but…" the Frenchman paused, trying to find a way to say more delicately what he really meant, "I suggest Winslow instead of Rumsey."

Jack saw instantly the lieutenant's thinking. The officer didn't want another scene to mar their celebration. Jack felt a little angry at the suggestion that they couldn't count on Red to behave, but at the same time, he understood. Abandoning all pretenses of speaking French, Jack said, "De Maison Rouge, you have treated me fairly and I think you are a good officer and certainly a great pilot, but don't get between my countrymen and me. This is, after all, a social affair and not a military formation. If you insist on pulling rank on me, I will simply have my own pot." It was the first time he had stood up to any person in a position of authority or of superior rank. The lieutenant's reaction totally surprised him.

"*Mais, non*! This will never do. You are right, of course. I just, well…" he trailed off, saying something about God, fools, and drunkards that sounded vaguely familiar to Jack.

Saturdays at the school at Pau were like any other day of the week. Jack and de Maison Rouge joined their two other breveted classmates at the field for their *chasse* orientation at dawn. Already at the field were the eight students from Avord, including Rockwell and Keeler. They joined in the backslapping, hand-shaking gathering centered on Buck. The story of his amazing survival and ability to coax a crippled machine to the ground raced through Pau even faster than the news of a fatal accident. Jack had become a minor celebrity.

Each training day began with a class on maneuvers drawn on a board and demonstrated with a whole series of hand and arm gestures. The maneuvers were essentially new to all of them. Those who had been in line *escadrilles*, had a clear advantage in flight time and air sense, while those like Jack, relatively new to flying, hadn't developed any flying habits they would have to unlearn.

Following the chalk talk, the class proceeded to the field. That Saturday, the instructors introduced them to the Nieuport Bébé. Officially designated the Nieuport 11, the Bébé entered service earlier that year as a fighter or *chasse* airplane. Charlie reminded Kiffin of the one they had seen at Villacoublay with Stephane. The instructor was obviously fond of the Nieuport.

"This is the finest fighting machine on the front," he said, explaining that it evolved from a racing biplane built by Gustave Delage in 1914 for the Gordon Bennett Cup.

Rockwell whispered to Buck and Keeler that Thaw had come over to compete in a similar competition before the war. Everyone seemed to know about the international air circuit that had grown to be the favorite game of rich sportsmen from 1909 until the war started.

The Nieuport 11 sported an 80 horsepower Gnome rotary engine, similar to those on the Blériots and Caudrons many had already flown. It had a wingspan of almost 25 feet, was just over 19 feet long, and stood a little over eight feet at its highest point when on the ground. It weighed nearly twice as much as the little Blériots at 774 pounds when it was empty. Loaded, it went more than a half-ton. Even with that, it could make an amazing 97 miles per hour and climb to 15,000 feet. At the school the Bébés were unarmed, but the instructor showed them the Lewis gun mounted on the top wing of the demonstration model. Jack felt a thrill of excitement at the thought of firing anything. Kiffin and Charlie were thinking of what they could do to a German trench line with one of these fighters.

The Nieuport standing before the class had a number of patches on its enclosed fuselage. A French student asked if they were indeed bullet holes. The instructor smiled. "They are. Notice the line going up the tail toward the pilot?" They all looked closely enough to see patches every inch or so stitching a line that ended right behind the place they imagined the pilot's head would be.

"This was a lucky pilot. He had ducked into the cockpit just enough to rob his assailant of an easy victory. The Aviatik crew thought they had gotten this guy when they didn't see his head, and turned carelessly away. It was all *I* needed," the instructor said, changing to a personal point of view. "I brought him down with a single burst, my third victory in fifteen combats."

The French Army made excellent use of its veterans. When the group realized that *this* instructor had been in combat in *this* airplane, it riveted their attention on the otherwise normal-looking sergeant-instructor. They spent the rest of the morning examining the Nieuport up close. *Mécaniciens* stood by to explain the rigging, the points to look for before and after flight, and to describe the starting procedure.

The afternoon training session began with a demonstration of all the maneuvers they would learn at Pau, given by the same instructor who had introduced them to his own Bébé that morning. Another instructor acted as announcer.

"I tell you Jack, I can't wait to try these out. I feel it in my bones," Charlie exclaimed.

"Me too," Kiffin said. "Imagine hanging upside down at the top of that loop."

"After my last flight, it's hard to imagine deliberately whipping a machine around like that," Jack observed. He knew fear would not overcome him, no matter what the danger. Nursing the disintegrating Caudron to the ground had changed his perspective on death forever. Little Chérie's smiling face had flashed before him promising peace. Jack had not conquered fear. Fear, he reasoned, served a good purpose. It had motivated him to capture the broken wires and fight for life all the way to the ground. How much prayer had to do with it he wasn't sure.

BREVET POTS FOLLOWED NO SET PRECEDENT. Arnoux de Maison Rouge's reason for limiting the number each could invite had nothing at all to do with money or fairness. He just wanted to keep the affair low key.

They requisitioned a corner of one of the Bessaneau hangars at the main field. Jack and the two corporals set it up, while de Maison Rouge arranged the refreshments. It would start Saturday afternoon after classes and flights ended for the weekend. All Jack had to do was mention it to the chief mechanic who assured him his people would take care of it. Jack had yet to catch on to his celebrity status. He could have asked for the moon with largely satisfactory results.

Since he finished earlier than the rest of the class that day, Jack decided to make a final check of the hangar. It warmed his heart to see things in place. A horseshoe of white-covered tables stood near the entrance of the hangar. On each table, a dazzling array of crystal glasses of several different types stood in neat lines on either side of silver ice buckets. The only thing missing as far as Jack could see were the refreshments. Arnoux had mentioned champagne and hors d'oeuvres. It was still early. Jack headed for his barracks to clean up. As he walked back to the barracks, it dawned on him that there were more glasses than the fifty guests they had invited.

Just before five o'clock Jack arrived at the hangar. He noticed a few mechanics and other service personnel smoking outside. Taking no notice of Buck, they ambled slowly away. Thinking he heard some music, he stuck his head in the side entrance. There wasn't a soul in the hangar! He checked his pocket watch. Had he gotten the time wrong? What was going on here?

There *was* music coming from in front of the hangar. He was about to go to check it out when the big canvas doors parted. Jack moved in that direction. The music grew louder. Perhaps the school had something else scheduled. That would explain why no one was inside. He noticed the tables hadn't been touched. He cursed de Maison Rouge for not checking the schedule with the cadre.

The doors were halfway open. On a trailer in front of the hanger stood the wreckage of his Caudron. What was it doing there? He stepped out a little further only to see the whole school assembled in formation with a military band playing a ragtime tune. He must have missed an announcement. Hoping to avoid being reported absent, he tried to slip back into the hangar, hoping to sneak around to the back and find his way into the ranks.

No such luck! The colonel with all his medals on and a drawn saber came right at him. *God*, Jack thought, *he's going to make an example out of me in front of the whole school!*

"*Monsieur Buck*!" Colonel Lefebrve boomed.

Jack froze. He turned around sheepishly to face his fate. *Oh fleeting glory! And, wasn't I telling myself I wasn't going to be afraid of anything? Why are my knees shaking?*

"*On vous attend, sergent.*"

Great, Jack thought, *they're waiting for me, and the colonel doesn't even know my rank. How embarrassing. Why couldn't he just let me fade away? They can come and put me under arrest later. Maybe Thénault will stand up for me. All I did was miss a formation.*

"*Venez, si'l vous plait.*" Lefebrve said.

At least he's pleasant enough, and is that a smile on his face?

"*On va vous saluer ce soir.*"

Wait a minute! Did I understand that? They are going to salute me tonight?

The colonel stepped to Jack's right and asked him to follow. They passed the wreck and moved to the front of the formation. Over two hundred and fifty cadre, students, and support personnel stood in formation as for a *prise d'armes.* Trumpets and bugles blew a fanfare. An officer sounded attention. Leaders barked commands, bringing the troops to attention.

Jack soon found himself getting his second Croix de Guerre pinned to his tunic. He heard the citation, understanding every word. Silently he thanked God. Two citations in only one year! Jack was embarrassed to have been singled-out, but he couldn't wait to write home about it.

After the short ceremony, all were invited to come drink the health of *Sergent* Jack Buck, and the other three brevet winners. Jack, now beyond surprise, assumed another mistake until the colonel presented him with the *galons* of a French sergeant.

The pot turned out to be an extravagant affair in honor of Jack and the others. Jack saw Lieutenant de Maison Rouge standing beside the Colonel, smiling. Had all that about numbers been part of the charade?

The frequency of funerals with all their solemnity made the opportunity to celebrate a welcome contrast at Pau. Getting a Croix de Guerre for an action not involving combat was an extraordinary event.

Along with champagne, the tables were loaded with scotch, bottles of American bourbon, soda water, juices, and countless different types of little snack-sized foods. Jack helped himself to champagne and several small toasts covered with salty black tiny balls.

"Good caviar, huh, Jack?" Jim McConnell said as he came up to add his congratulations.

"Caviar? You mean fish eggs?" Jack asked. "Yeah, really good."

"First time?"

"For a lot of things, Mac, a lot of things..." Jack's mind drifted back over the past year. Thanksgiving was just around the corner. He felt a sharp pang of homesickness. He saw Charlie Keeler, remembering he'd been away from his family for about the same amount of time, but Charlie had Michelle. Before Jack could become nostalgic and maudlin, Charlie came up with Kiffin to offer his congratulations.

"Bucko, my boy, once again we get to sing your praises. You make me proud to be an American!"

"Damn, Charlie, I have something for you from Flandin!"

"It was gift enough for me to hear about your adventure."

"Well, nevertheless, he got something I think you'll like. It's just a book, a collection of photographs of Paris taken around 1900. I figured the sights and scenes would remind you of your idyllic days with Michelle. Maybe someday you will design some buildings like the ones in these pictures after the war."

"After the war...." Charlie looked off in the distance. He didn't say anything for a long moment. "Gee, Jack. I'm sorry. I was just trying to imagine what you said. Have you ever wondered? I mean, we've both had close calls now. Do you think we can make it through this?"

"I think about it. In the ambulance, death surrounded us. It seemed distant, detached. Masters' death brought it home for me. Remember my story about the girl with the flowers?"

Charlie nodded, taking a sip of his champagne.

"I thought I saw her Monday when the Caudron started coming apart. Her smile made me think that death can't be that bad. She had such a peaceful look. I'd been frantically running off every prayer I could remember..."

"You too?" Charlie interrupted. "I find myself doing that all the time. A Catholic trait, but you aren't...?"

"Yes I am. Dad's a Lutheran, but my mother made sure we were brought up Catholic. I even went to parochial school. It seems like my mind starts reeling off Hail Marys every time I brush danger."

Laughing lightly, Charlie realized he had found a new soul mate. As much as he liked Rockwell and Chapman, they were older. He hadn't connected with Kiffin on a spiritual level. Victor Chapman, on the other hand, was almost a fanatic Catholic. "Hey, come to Mass tomorrow in town. I haven't been to the cathedral. I feel a need for some spiritual refreshment."

"Sure," Jack said, ashamed that he hadn't gone to church in a while.

"Let's put a dent in this bodily refreshment. Can't have old Hercules waste away into a shadow of his old self."

ACROBATIC TRAINING STARTED IN EARNEST THAT MONDAY. They had to master the Nieuport first. The swift little Bébé took a lot of adjustment after Blériots and Caudrons. It seemed to leap into the air and respond to every movement of the stick and rudder like a touchy cat. It zoomed in climbs, nothing like the laborious struggle for altitude in the earlier trainers. Their first flights involved circuits of the field and several touch and go landings. Next, they took it to altitude for stalls and spins. The instructors warned them not to over-dive the Bébé. It had a tendency to shed the skin of the upper wings. Buck could identify with that terrifying possibility.

Charlie's first *vrille* made a believer out of him. He ascended to 1000 meters, pulled the nose up, and let the machine fall off to the right. Unlike the lumbering Caudron that seemed to want to fly no matter what you did to it, the Nieuport whipped around, skidding and plummeting uncomfortably. Once in the unclean air of a spin it took a long several seconds and hundreds of feet of altitude to recover. Charlie came so close to the ground that he was sure he would crash. When he regained control, he was at treetop level, his heart pounding hard.

Kiffin went up for his first loop on their second day full of excitement. He rose to 2,000 meters, dove the machine gently until his forward speed approached the limit, pulled back on the stick, and rode the buzzing Nieuport skyward. The nose passed rapidly through the horizon and in a flash he was upside down. Centering the stick, it only took seconds before the Nieuport tucked into a screaming dive. Thrilled by the speed and motion, Kiffin almost forgot to pull out of the dive to complete the maneuver.

Jack skated through the basic maneuvers. They flew twice each day for nearly two hours, once in the morning and once in the late afternoon. The weather remained magnificent. Just before Thanksgiving some received orders to proceed to Cazeaux for gunnery training. Jack, Kiffin, and Charlie had to stay to build up their hours before they could go on to Cazeaux.

There was a small community of American expatriates living in and around the city. Several were spouses of French men or women, and many had been there for years. At Thanksgiving, a group of them invited the American students to a huge feast in honor of the American holiday.

The school commandant whose brother was married to the former Amber Dickerson, socialite daughter of a San Francisco shipping magnate, readily approved permission for the Americans to attend the dinner. Their hosts reserved a great hall in the center of Pau, built sometime in the fifteenth century. The local Americans showed up at the school with a small flotilla of cars to pick up the students. At the hall, a gathering of the local authorities, the commandant of the flying school, and all the Americans living within about one hundred miles of Pau milled about awaiting the arrival of the honored guests.

"Remember Thanksgiving last year?" Kiffin asked after they had gotten to the hall.

"Do I ever!" Jack said, licking his lips. "My grandmother put on a feast to see me off that I'll never forget."

Charlie remembered fighting with his father and leaving days before the holiday.

Kiffin told of eating cold stew in the trenches.

Before they could finish their reminiscing, the mayor of Pau invited them to form a reception line.

Not finding anybody from either Saint Louis or Minneapolis disappointed Jack and Charlie. Kiffin met a middle-aged woman from North Carolina who claimed to know his family. The others discovered a few expatriates from their home states. The young Americans were treated like heroes. Everyone wanted to know when the United States would get into the war.

Keeler was astonished to find out that Lieutenant René Simon, the chief acrobatics instructor, had an American wife. He kept looking in their direction where they stood sipping champagne and nibbling on crudités.

"Jack, did you know that the lieutenant is married to an American?"

"René? No kidding? Isn't that rich? I'll wager she has some tales to tell."

"I'll bet they had something to do with the decorations."

A cornucopia with harvest vegetables and autumn flowers adorned each table. American flags were scattered throughout the big hall as well.

Dinner started at six o'clock, an ungodly early hour for the French who normally didn't eat until after eight. Much like the luncheon on the Fourth of July, the organizers seated the students at different tables in the hall. Jack sat with friends of Norman Prince's family, a Boston couple named O'Hara. Harold O'Hara owned an import-export firm that sold French wines and cheeses to American distributors in exchange for tools made in the USA. His wife, Judith, was a strait-laced, unsmiling Irish woman who looked entirely displeased. They had three sons and one daughter attending schools in New England. Judith fidgeted and fussed with her dress. Her large figure stretched the garment enough to cause Jack to conclude her sour disposition was due to its tightness.

Kiffin sat with the woman from North Carolina who had married a retired French diplomat. Her husband appeared to be about eighty, and she only trailed by several years. She reminded him of his Grandma Ayres, a woman Madame Poussière incredibly professed to know.

Charlie was with a much younger couple, Mister James Walker and his French wife, Claudine. They owned an estate in the foothills of the Pyrenees. Walker had been traveling in France on some sort of business when he met and married Claudine. She came from a very wealthy family which probably accounted for his staying in France and giving up his business. He said he spent his time hunting and riding. He guessed they were in their mid-thirties, though Claudine looked younger.

Charlie couldn't help wondering what she saw in her husband. James was paunchy, almost doughy. He had to be hard on their horses. He spoke coarsely, thinking it would loosen up the former legionnaire. Charlie wished he was at a different table, but Claudine made it her mission to make him feel wanted—too wanted.

A fleet of waiters delivered course after course of delicious American-style dishes ranging from roast turkey, ham, and beef, to mashed potatoes, gravy, and all the trimmings. Bottles of fine vintage wines added a French touch to the feast. After the main course, cheeses appeared in deference to French tradition. Waiters poured more wine. By the time dessert arrived, most of the students were almost too full to take the apple, minced meat, and pumpkin pies prepared by some of the American women themselves.

Jack thoroughly enjoyed the O'Hara's who treated him like a grandson. He kept an eye on the table where Rumsey was sitting with the Simon couple, hoping Red wouldn't embarrass himself. Jack had to fight tears when Mrs. O'Hara gave him a hug, inviting him to come to visit before he left Pau.

Kiffin too received an invitation to visit Monsieur and Madame Poussière. It turned out that the lady had indeed grown up and attended schools with his Grandmother Ayres. He couldn't wait to write home to tell about meeting her. He hoped Paul could come down before they left Pau so that he too could meet the Poussières.

Charlie was very uncomfortable. Walker drank too much too fast. His head bobbed and lolled off to one side as he drifted off to sleep at the table. Claudine ignored him, flirting openly with Keeler. The attractive blond woman boldly invited Charlie to accompany her home, using her husband's discomfiture as an excuse. She said they had come in a touring car she couldn't drive, and, since poor James was in no shape to drive, Charlie would be a dear to give her a hand.

"Perhaps we can get one of your neighbors?" Charlie asked, not wanting to be stranded at the Walker estate with Claudine in such an obvious state of lonely lust. "I have to be back at the school by taps."

"That won't be a problem, Charlie," she said, her eyes twinkling. "I will speak to Commandant LeFarge. I'm sure he can make an exception for you. Our man can drive you back."

Claudine would be a delightful diversion for a man with fewer scruples. He unwillingly compared her to Michelle. Claudine was older, but artfully maintained, and possessed of a figure slightly less voluptuous than Michelle's. She made men's heads turn for second and third looks. Her blue eyes sparkled and her lips danced a flirtatious caper as she spoke. Michelle would never be so brazen. He would have been tempted to see how far Claudine would go but for his love for Michelle.

"*Mon commandant, j'aurais besoin de l'aide d'un de vos étudiants,*" Claudine said when LeFarge approached their table. LeFarge, eager to please, readily agreed to lend her a driver.

"Madame Walker, please don't think me rude, but I really must get back to the school. I have an early flight tomorrow," Charlie protested.

Not used to being flummoxed, Claudine dug in her heels. She insisted on an American escort, a demand LeFarge was wont to deny. Just then, Jack Buck came up to summon Charlie. Cars were waiting to take the students back to the school.

"*Eh, voila, un autre Américain.*" LeFarge said, remembering that Buck had been an ambulance driver. "*Il est libre, madame*," he said, knowing that Buck had finished his acrobatic course and only needed about five more flight hours before going on to gunnery training.

Jack had been watching Charlie's body language, seeing his friend's discomfort in his shuffling feet and shrugging shoulders. The woman sure was pretty. Jack had only to report to the field two more times to make his last flights. He felt somewhat noble in relieving Charlie from the unwanted attention.

Madame Walker acquiesced readily in the choice, turning her measureless charm on the unsuspecting Minnesotan. Charlie accepted a ride with the Simons back to the school. At nine fifteen, the other American students departed with their sponsors.

A waiter helped Jack carry the somnolent Walker to the waiting Peugeot. They deposited his leaden form in the back seat. Jack saw her pull her dress up to step into the car, exposing her slender dark-stockinged calves.

"It is only about twenty minutes to our place, Mr. Buck, or should I call you sergeant?" Claudine asked, patting him on his thigh as he started the Peugeot, the first car he had driven that had an electric starter. He followed the directions without question or comment, wondering just where this was leading. James Walker snored loudly in the back seat.

The lamps of the Peugeot lit the driveway path to the grand porticoed entrance of their villa. A servant emerged to help them remove the sleeping hulk—a task he apparently had performed before. Jack began to worry that he might have trouble extricating himself from the clutches of Claudine.

"You must come in and have a brandy before you leave. It is only ten o'clock. Commandant LeFarge has already given you permission. Do come in," she urged.

Jack hesitated. He had gotten increasingly uncomfortable during the drive when she touched his leg with each new direction she gave him. She had unpinned her blond hair; shaking it loose and letting it fall to her shoulders. Jack thought she was pretty in a different way from Marie, more mature, more sensuous.

After depositing James Walker upstairs on the single bed in the room he evidently used separately from Claudine, Jack took a moment to look around before descending the stairs to rejoin Walker's waiting wife.

Walker's room was filled with hunting implements, guns, tall boots, and pictures of him on horses. The servant lit an oil lamp rather than turning on the electric lights. He murmured that Monsieur Walker preferred the softer light and would sleep until noon or later if not disturbed. The man disappeared almost instantly.

"Come here by the fire, Mr. Buck," Claudine purred in her most seductive voice. "Here, take this. It is Armagnac, a fine liquor I think you will find very pleasant." She had taken off her shawl, baring her white shoulders. Her breasts swelled above the bodice of her evening gown. Jack felt his loins stirring involuntarily. He had never been seduced, but he sensed her intentions.

"Why don't you take off that tunic, Jack? I'm sure that collar is very irritating. Here, let me help you." Claudine slid up to him, placing her hands at the fastening and gently touching his neck in the process. He smelled the scent of her hair. His excitement began to overcome his reason. He tried to back away, but she only moved closer. Her eyes beckoned. It was flee or succumb. Floods of coursing hormones diminished his resolve. She was too enticing, too luscious looking.

The fire crackled, adding to the warm, scintillating atmosphere. Jack stopped resisting her advances. She lowered herself onto the divan, pulling her dress to the side exposing her lovely legs up to the knee. She invited Jack to sit beside her and sip his Armagnac. He swirled the liquid in the balloon glass thinking, *what the hay? I am a man, after all.*

Claudine purred gently telling him he looked like a lion with his light brown hair. She touched his cheek and asked if he ever had to shave. Jack recoiled at the comment, thinking she took him for a child. She pulled his hand to her chest.

"It would make me so happy to have you be nice to me tonight," she said throatily.

"I really must go. Is it possible to get your man to bring me back to the school?" Jack said half-heartedly.

"I'm afraid he has left for the night. Didn't the commandant give you permission to be absent?"

"Listen, Madame Walker..."

"Claudine, Jack."

"Okay, Claudine. You are a very attractive woman, but I just can't take advantage of your husband's indisposition. I can't, I mean, I don't want to..."

"To what, Jack? Am I so repulsive?" Claudine asked, giving him her most enticing smile.

"No. Not at all, Mrs. Walker, ah *Claudine*. I just can't let myself..." Jack said standing up abruptly. He knew he should bolt for the door.

"Sit down," she commanded. "I am an honorable woman, whatever you may think of my intentions. James has not been able to love me for almost all of our three years of so-called wedded bliss. He drops off every night in drunken bliss, and spends all his days fooling around with the animals. Can you imagine what it is like for me? I have needs. I know about you young men. You must want me as much as I want you to take me.

"Listen, James won't wake until at least nine tomorrow. Who is to know? I promise you I will not say a word. I just want to be loved. It will be a passing thing, of course. Please?" She said in a pleading voice that aroused Jack's lust.

He still hesitated, turning to the fire, staring into the glowing embers. It was Thanksgiving. He was so far from home. He had no one and he felt such loneliness. But her husband? How could he cuckold a man he had just met? These questions raged in his head while she lounged, pulling her dress even further up her thigh.

Claudine, sensing his hesitation, tried another tack. "Listen, Jack Buck, I have been a loyal wife for these three years. I am going to give you a choice. You can spend the night here on the couch and my man will take you to the school at dawn, or you can take me now." Claudine pulled the strap of her dress off a shoulder exposing her breast, pulling her dress all the way up to her waist.

Jack lost all control at the sight of her underwear and exposed flesh. He dropped to his knees and kissed her breast with a passion that shuddered through his lips into her soft flesh. She moaned and grasped his head, pulling his face up to her lips. Mashing her mouth against his, she pushed her tongue into his mouth teasingly. Jack remembered kissing Marie and other girls, but none had done this to him. He put his arms around her and let himself go, thoughts of guilt and restraint forgotten.

They slipped onto the large bearskin rug before the fire shedding garments on the way down. Jack lingered at a swollen nipple before sliding up to her neck kissing her skin. She wriggled and trembled when he did that, lying back and spreading her legs, her hips moving almost of their own accord.

Jack pressed against her. Claudine peeled off the remaining layers of her clothing and fumbled at his waist trying to unbutton his tight trousers. She gasped at his hardness.

Jack could hardly stand her ministrations. Pulling the dress over her head and dropping her undergarments, Claudine lowered herself onto Jack.

As they rose to each other's passions, Jack already thought about the next time, hoping it would be soon. Remembering her sleeping husband, Jack felt a tremor of danger. Claudine's simpering grew to furious panting. He didn't have to move. She did it all for both of them. He wanted to have this blond vixen forever.

When it was over, her demeanor changed abruptly.

"You must go now," she said composing herself. "I will ring for Antoine. He is only minutes away in the servant's quarters."

"But, you said I would have to stay until tomorrow!" Jack sputtered, his breath only beginning to return to normal.

"No, you have to leave. James wakes up after a binge in an evil temper. He will shoot you and me too if he finds us together. Was it not wonderful? I needed that so much! I'm sorry, Jack. I have used you, but, quickly now, dress yourself, and leave before James rouses!"

Dumbfounded and frustrated, Jack jumped to his feet and pulled up his trousers. So this was adultery? He couldn't believe he had given in so easily. Claudine was so eager to get him out of the house after giving him all those assurances that they were alone and safe from detection. He smarted from the realization that he had indeed been used. Worrying whether she would keep their intimacy secret, Jack cursed his male passion.

CLOUDS AND A SERIES OF RAINSTORMS settled in the Pau valley during the last days of November, stopping all flying. The cadre conducted classes and discussions on tactics, and told tales about the emerging aces, but the flyers remained grounded.

A fellow named Max Immelman was one of the rising stars of the German jastas. Pictures of Immelman and a handsome blond pilot named Boelcke appeared in the *New York Herald.* In spite of the efforts at secrecy on both sides, French and German authorities almost encouraged worship of the new aerial heroes. *As*, the French word for ace, was the approbation hung on those credited with five or more victories in aerial combat. Victories earned rewards ranging from monetary bonuses to medals or citations in orders of the day. German standards topped the French and British at ten, a Teutonic form of one-upmanship. Immelman and Boelcke were their only confirmed aces in late 1915.

After three days of bad weather the cadre flagged. Knowing the *chasse* pilots would receive their gunnery instruction at Cazeaux, classes at Pau became dry and theoretical. Only so much could be taught in the classroom.

When the weather didn't improve at the beginning of December, the cadre temporarily halted formal instruction granting short passes for up to 48 hours.

Charlie and Kiffin obtained a 72-hour pass to Paris. Kiffin wanted to see Paul, and Charlie's longing for Michelle had become a small torture to him. The two left on a morning train that would get them to Paris that night.

Jack would have liked to go to Paris if for no more than to speak with Paul Rockwell. Seeing Willis Haviland, if he could, would really make the trip worthwhile, but Le Farge's summons checked his plans. He'd assigned Jack to lead a ceremonial party for the funeral of two aviators who had been Pau residents. Jack would be in charge of the salute firing team made up of fellow students. Going to Paris was out of the question.

Relieved that the Walker incident hadn't been the reason he'd been called to the commandant's office, Jack assembled his firing party immediately. Arnoux de Maison Rouge was the presiding officer with the role of escorting and assisting the families.

At ten in the morning on December 3, a cortege of vehicles carrying the family and friends arrived at the school. Jack knew the pilot and observer were members of Caudron Squadron 42, Thénault's command. Georges Thénault was there in full uniform, looking very sad. The observer, Malraux, was well known in the region. Thénault had recruited Malraux from his old cavalry unit. Brescau was a young sergeant pilot with a wife and two children, but no other relatives in the area. He had attended flight training with Thénault.

After a funeral Mass in the school chapel packed to overflowing with students, family mourners, and other sympathizers, the crowd processed to the gate on foot, escorting horse-drawn artillery caissons bearing the two coffins. A line of vehicles stood waiting outside the gate. They would bury the men in the Saints Pierre and Paul cemetery two miles outside Pau. Jack's detail rode ahead in a truck. He lined the men up at graveside and waited.

Nearly two hundred people gathered at the graveside. Jack recognized some of the civilians from the Thanksgiving feast. The ceremony started when the two coffins were transferred from their caissons to the biers over the gaping holes, newly dug in the soil.

Brescau's widow and her two toddler sons moved to folding chairs beside his tomb. Malraux's parents also took seats. Malraux's brother, in the uniform of a *Chasseur Alpin*, one of the renowned mountain troops, stood quietly behind them.

Le Farge said a few words before asking Thénault to do the eulogies. The captain dutifully recited the careers of the two aviators before announcing their Croix de Guerre. La Farge presented the medals to Brescau's widow and Malraux's parents. All three sobbed quietly. Jack looked at the two bewildered boys who probably couldn't understand why their father was in the box before them.

Four priests attended the funeral. Jack recognized the *aumonier* from the school. The chaplain wore his cassock and stole just like the other three priests. One of them led the prayers. He had the purple beading of a monsignor on his vestments. At the end of the prayers, Le Farge nodded to Lieutenant de Maison Rouge who quietly ordered Jack to fire the salute.

Jack saluted and turned to his squad of seven firers. He issued the commands that brought their rifles to their shoulders. The students snapped crisply, more militarily than they had in practice. *"En feu, Feu! Feu!"* Jack commanded in short succession. All seven rifles spouted in perfect unison at each command, the men rhythmically re-cocking between shots. The visitors filed by the gravesides dropping flowers on the coffins. Rain added to the melancholic atmosphere of the funeral. Jack marched his detail away, glad to have it over with, sadness and sorrow dampening his pride in performing his first mission as an NCO. Jack saw Lieutenant de Maison Rouge present the carefully folded tricolor flags first to Madame Malraux and then to Madame Brescau as he marched off to the trucks.

Sitting down to record it, he dashed off an account to Paul Rockwell who promptly forwarded it to *Atlantic Monthly*, attaching the title: *American Buries French Heroes*

Later, Jack itched to do something more after the emotionally draining funeral. He and three of the firing team quickly shed their gear and headed for the bar at the school to drink to the fallen aviators. Jack never felt so close to the French. He was an American wearing a French sergeant's uniform, flying their aircraft, and aiding in burying their dead. Though he didn't know the men they'd buried, he felt a kinship with them.

He still loathed war that so cruelly robbed children of their parents and parents of their children. It made him burn with desire to help put it to an end.

Part Five

A Gathering of Eagles

Sound the trumpets
Light the lamps
For heroes unbidden
Flock to our camps

Valiant young men volunteer
Naught but their lives to offer
But who could demand more
From eagles who gather to our shore?

Chapter 30
Near Misses, Naked Mrs.

Paris and Pau, December 1915

If the country wouldn't join the allies, the Franco-American Committee reasoned, they would give the process a boost by sending some seasoned veteran volunteer Americans to sell the cause.

Buck and Keeler would be in their last days of their training before going to Cazeaux for gunnery training. They could finish on their return. Their inclusion had been Flandin's idea. The others, Elliot Cowdin, Norman Prince, and Bill Thaw came from influential families, but Flandin argued that Keeler and Buck would appeal to the heartland.

Before this news Charlie had gone with Kiffin and Paul to talk to Doctor Gros about getting Paul into aviation, and to check on the progress of the all-American squadron. Gros sadly told Paul his disqualification could not be waived. Then he smiled, "You will be a great help here with the new American squadron."

"So it's happening?" Kiffin asked excitedly.

"On paper, at least," Gros replied, showing them the authorization signed by the head of French Aviation. "It is far from a fact, you see, but I'm hoping you can help with the effort, Paul."

"Not much I can do if I can't fly, can't fight," Paul said dejectedly.

"Not so, my friend. You will be a wonderful asset as a correspondent."

Charlie and Michelle took early morning walks in the cold damp Paris air debating whether to wait until after the war to get married or to do it when he finished flight training. Michelle didn't want to wait. Charlie didn't want to leave her a widow and refused to formally propose.

"We may have only days together," she confronted him before his return to Pau. "But it doesn't matter! If we have only weeks, it doesn't matter. Even if our time together is less than a year, *it doesn't matter!* I want you *now*. I want to have you for as long as God wills. Don't you see that waiting only robs us? What if you *are* killed tomorrow? For that matter, *I* could be killed here in a bombing or a stupid motor accident."

That morning Charlie found out that the Franco-American Committee had selected him and Jack Buck to join Elliot Cowdin, Norman Prince, and Bill Thaw for a promotional trip to the United States over the Christmas holidays. He'd made a decision.

"Michelle!" he shouted, startling the guests in the Crillon lobby. "We must talk. Now!" She nearly fell over as he dragged her by the wrist to the sitting area before the roaring fire. She was even more unbalanced when he dropped to a knee.

"Marry me, chérie. Come back to Saint Louis with me and marry me," Charlie said breathlessly.

This completed Michelle's disorientation. She looked at him in total bafflement. What could he be thinking of? Desertion? She was about to question him when the crestfallen look on his face convinced her he was serious.

"Yes, Charlie. I'll marry you! Of course I will. Why was there ever any question, but, how can this be?" As Charlie explained they embraced, shaking in tears of joy.

Quickly, Fleury arranged passage for Michelle and her parents to coincide with the Americans' tour.

Georges de Vincent had gone to Quebec in 1912 to assist in opening the first Renault factory in that hemisphere. The war had placed an enormous demand on the company for raw materials, and the wedding would be a good opportunity for de Vincent to shop for American commercial goods. Though Renault did not build airplanes, their factories fabricated engines and other sub-assemblies. Ash and poplar made the best propellers and the strongest spars for wings. Fleury wanted de Vincent to negotiate a contract with the Americans for a supply of both.

Charlie asked Jack to stand up for him, Jack readily assented. They'd become very close since meeting; not as close as Charlie was with Kiffin, but Rockwell had turned down the opportunity to leave, preferring to remain in France with his brother.

WINTER NEARLY IMMOBILIZED EUROPE AS 1915 ENDED. At Pau rains gave way to unusually cold temperatures and high winds. Charlie thought about his legion friends. This place was not that bad.

December afternoons at Pau were the best for flying. Morning fog hung in the valleys and often didn't burn off until late morning. Winds usually picked up later in the day. Jack genuinely looked forward to getting up in a Nieuport on a clear afternoon. He felt such a sense of freedom cruising at close to a hundred miles an hour at more than 10,000 feet. He savored the sharp bite of the wind in his face. It reminded him of skating back home with a scarf protecting his nose from the sub-zero temperatures.

The snow-capped peaks of the nearby Pyrenees stood out clearly, taking Jack's breath away, drawing him closer and closer to get a better view. He had to be careful though. Any pilot caught flying over the mountains or, worse, crossing the Spanish border, faced a heavy fine and several days arrest. Even as a certified "hero," and somewhat of a *personalité connue*, Jack couldn't claim ignorance. Nor could he risk arrest with the sailing date approaching.

Charlie drew a Morane-Saulnier monoplane for his last flight on a gray Wednesday afternoon, December 8, 1915. A *moniteur* went over the aircraft with Charlie. The Morane-Saulnier didn't belong to the school. The French shipped it to Marseilles from Salonika where it saw combat during the Gallipoli fiasco the previous summer. In Marseilles, Army mechanics put the aircraft back into flying condition. A pilot from the Navy agreed to fly the machine to Pau and then up to Cazeaux. There they would fit it with the experimental interrupter system that would allow firing forward through the propeller. The Navy lieutenant ended up in the hospital in Pau with a case of flu. In the interim, some of the more experienced students got to take a turn in the swift monoplane.

The instructor warned Keeler not to perform any vrilles or other violent maneuvers. He was simply to take the Morane up for one fuel load. He could land it and take off several times for the practice, but no acrobatics! Charlie, not feeling bold and adventurous with his wedding now on the near horizon, needed no warning.

To Charlie the Morane-Saulnier handled like the Nieuport. It was strange not having an upper wing blocking his vision above—a factor that would save his life later that day. He decided to fly to the Voisin field northeast of Pau to see if he could find Kiffin. Their instructors encouraged them to practice flying with another machine in preparation for the patrols they would fly in their first units. "Formation" in this case meant two aircraft following essentially the same flight path at about the same altitude.

Charlie landed, shut the Le Rhône down, and walked over to the shed that served as the field operations center. Just as he approached the door, Rockwell emerged from the building.

"Charlie! I thought you were flying a Morane-Saulnier today. What are you doing here?"

"I am, and it's parked over there," Charlie pointed. "I hoped to catch you. Want to do a little work together? I'm not supposed to do anything exciting with the precious monoplane. It's getting a little annoying doing nothing but boring holes in the sky. I have less than an hour to fly before I finish here."

"Sounds great, but won't it be tough keeping up with my speedy Voisin?" Kiffin laughed.

"Yeah, I'd better follow you first just to make sure I don't stall trying to keep from running you over."

They met over the Walker chateau. Charlie quickly overtook Kiffin, wagged his wings, and began to slow down to see if they could indeed fly together. Kiffin headed east at the Voisin's top speed of about eighty miles per hour. Charlie slid above and slightly to the left behind his friend. He had to be careful not to overrun the Voisin. Kiffin looked back and gave him a thumb's up signal. Charlie wished he had a camera.

Ten minutes of following Kiffin's slower Voisin was hard work. He had to concentrate and make multiple adjustments to hold his position. Every once in a while the Voisin would hit a pocket of air and rocket up or plummet down a good fifty feet. Charlie learned not to respond since he would be caught in the same up or down draft seconds later. Funny how you didn't notice them as much until flying with another airplane.

Tiring of the chore, Charlie broke off, circled back, and then shot out in front. By blipping the Le Rhône off for a few seconds, he could reduce his forward speed while nosing up to hold his altitude. He saw Kiffin inching the Voisin forward slowly. Charlie decided to make a left turn back toward the field. Kiffin held his position on the inside of the turn. Charlie started a slow descent. Kiffin was having problems keeping up, so Charlie began making little S turns to the left and right to both slow his forward motion and to clear himself below.

Kiffin also discovered that keeping position on another moving aircraft really took a lot of energy. He concentrated on following Charlie's moves once he'd closed the gap to about fifty meters. So focused were the two Americans that they failed to see a Voisin approaching from about three miles distance three hundred feet above them, blissfully bound for the same field.

About two minutes out Charlie looked back to see Kiffin comfortably tucked up slightly above and to the left. It was time for him to break off and let Rockwell continue on to land. He released the cutoff switch on the stick allowing the engine to roar back into action, grasping the air and pulling the Morane-Saulnier quickly up and away. Giving Kiffin one last look, Charlie turned his head back around just in time to see the underside of another Voisin filling his field of view! Its wheels were close to brushing his head when he plunged the monoplane into a screaming power dive a mere two hundred feet above the ground. The Voisin continued its descent obliviously. Charlie pulled up over the rooftops cursing the pilot of the Voisin and thanking God in the same breath.

After landing, Charlie was hot. He raced to the operations shack to call the Voisin field and find out what fool had nearly killed him. Near misses were reportable incidents.

"*Allô, allô, qui est à l'appareil*?" Charlie asked angrily wanting to know whom he was talking to.

"Keeler, is that you?" The disembodied voice asked, in very good English.

"Who's this? Are you the crazy idiot that tried to kill me?"

"Charlie, it's me, Chouteau. Calm down will you? I never saw either of you. Kiffin saw it all. He told me how close I came to smashing into you. Gosh, I'm sorry! I almost wet my pants when he told me what I had done. Imagine two Saint Louis boys expiring like that! I'm really sorry." He listened for several long seconds before Keeler replied.

"Jesus jumping Jehoshaphat! Chout Johnson! You owe me a drink, chum!"

At the bar that evening, after Chouteau made a very public apology for trying to land on Keeler, Charlie announced his marriage plans, bidding farewell to the others who were staying behind, and telling them he would see them in January at Cazeaux.

Jack had gotten a note from Claudine Walker asking if he could meet her that night. He guiltily wondered what she could want, tempted to have another shot at the lusty lady. With their trip so close and his conscience kicking back in, he didn't need to complicate his life with Mrs. Walker's charms. What would she do if he just didn't show up? The note asked him to be at the gate at nine. He was still struggling with temptation when Charlie made his engagement announcement.

"What's eating you, Jack? You look like you lost your best friend," Rockwell asked, refilling Jack's glass with champagne.

"Oh, hi, Kiffin."

"Are you going to tell me what's on your mind? I've never seen you looking so pensive. Aren't you excited about finishing up here and going home?"

"Sure am. It's just...," he hesitated. "Remember that Walker woman I drove home last month?" Jack asked, giving Kiffin an edited version of that night. Rockwell listened, trying to suppress his amusement at Jack's innocence and predicament. He didn't want to hurt the younger man's feelings, but he found it refreshing. He and Chapman had talked about how crass some of their compatriots were when it came to the fairer sex. They'd found it disgusting how few scruples these men possessed.

"I'll tell you what. I'll go to the gate for you and handle Mrs. Walker. If she just wants to take advantage of you, seeing someone else in your place might tempt her to take the bird in hand if you know what I mean."

"And you would go with her?" Jack asked, more than a little surprised. He'd thought of Rockwell as a paragon of virtue. The man had his choice of women, but was very discreet.

Kiffin got a twinkle in his eye, but decided to play it straight rather than aggravate the vulnerable younger man. "Don't be ridiculous. I'll just see if she goes for me. If she is smitten by you, she will insist on seeing you or finding out why you are sending me. If that is the case, do you want me to come and get you?"

"She's married, Kiffin! I should have never let her twist me around her finger. She told me her husband would shoot us both if he saw us together. As beautiful as she is, I didn't appreciate being used. No. Tell her I'm indisposed; tell her I've left.... No, don't lie. Just tell her the truth. I don't want to see her. Wish her well. Send her back to her husband."

"That's the spirit Jack! Your folks would be proud of you. Maybe that papist upbringing isn't so bad after all. Leave the fair Walker to me. One way or another, she will go away empty-handed."

"Jeez, thanks, Kiffin. I feel better already. How about if I wait here? These guys aren't going to go to bed for a couple of hours. You can come back here after she leaves."

Kiffin slipped out the door. Jack thought about following and trying to hear what Claudine said, but he didn't want to even see the woman lest he lose his resolve. He joined some fellows playing pool to wait for Kiffin.

At nine-fifteen, Jack began to worry. He flubbed his shot, allowing Clyde Balsley to run the table. Chouteau called for the winner so Jack gladly surrendered the cue. *Maybe Kiffin had gone straight to the barracks? Maybe Rockwell misunderstood him?* He found Kiffin just outside the bar, smoking a cigarette.

"Hi ya, kid," Rockwell said, his face lit by the gaslight outside the building.

"She didn't show up?" Jack asked.

"No, she showed up all right. Boy did she show up! I'm just trying to cool off out here. I thought you said she couldn't drive."

"Yeah, that's why she demanded a driver...," Jack stopped, realizing what Kiffin was suggesting. Claudine had driven down by herself.

"I waited at the gate. It's dark enough there so that anyone in uniform looks pretty much the same. I counted on that, hoping she would think I was you. I was afraid she might bolt if she saw anyone else. Anyway, I see this big Peugeot pull up outside the gate. The lights flashed and a lady's arm reached out beckoning me. I kept my hat down over my face and hair. Getting into the car, I tried to introduce myself when she climbed all over me. She didn't seem to notice it wasn't you. It was really dark in the car. I said "Whoa! Wait a minute!" She backed away and asked who I was. I told her, explaining that you didn't want to see her. She looked disappointed at first, but, sorry Jack, it didn't stop her from resuming her attack.

"Jack, she didn't have a thread on under her coat! I had to grab her wrists and hold her away from me just to be able to talk. I told her she'd better go and leave you alone. Her husband would hear of her nocturnal outing if she tried to give you any trouble. I'm afraid I was a little rough on her, but I could smell gin on her breath. She must have gotten her nerve up with a few drinks. I got out just as she slammed the car into gear, tearing down the street. I sure hope she makes it back safely. Let me tell you, I have never tangled with such a tigress."

Jack listened, amused at how rattled Kiffin sounded. Had the *older, wiser Southern gentleman* been more than a little tempted?

"I don't know what's wrong with Mr. Walker, but I wouldn't let that woman out of the house if I were him," Kiffin went on. "Such a lioness. I mean she must devour a man."

If he didn't know better, Jack would have thought Rockwell was toying with the thought of a rematch. "So which one is she, tigress or lioness?" Jack asked, harmlessly egging Kiffin on.

"Huh? What do you mean?"

"You called her both. She called me a lion. I don't see any claw marks on you, but you act lucky to escape yourself—or maybe a little disappointed?"

"Tigress then, you can be the lion. I remembered what she looked like at Thanksgiving fully dressed. I couldn't avoid touching her skin in the car. She was hot to the touch and so aggressive, like an animal in heat.

Okay, the thought did cross my mind, since you bring it up, but how could I face you after all my preaching?"

"Thanks anyway, Kiffin. I probably would not have been able to resist. Who knows, we might have ended up naked in a ditch locked in each other's arms. If we weren't already dead, James Walker would come up on a horse with a pack of hounds to finish the job, delivering the coup de grace with his hunting rifle." Jack chuckled at the image. Kiffin laughed too, slapping Jack on the back before taking him back in the bar for a nightcap. Kiffin still had some hours to fly before going on to Cazeaux.

Charlie and Jack left the next morning by train for Bordeaux.

Chapter 31
Excellency, war is hell

New York City, December 17, 1915

Coming into the harbor, passing the Statue of Liberty and sailing by the impressive skyline mesmerized Jack and Charlie. Georges de Vincent exclaimed that the pictures he'd seen could never do the city justice.

During the crossing Buck and Keeler absorbed an education in lifestyles, economics, and social graces just by listening and observing. Bill Thaw told them about his uncle, Harry K. Thaw, whose notorious affair with a woman in New York had led to his trial for the murdering of Sanford White, a Thaw family architect. Most of them had read about the scandal. Bill's family in Pittsburgh owned great holdings in the railroad and steel industry. His self-effacing and modest manner struck Jack and Charlie as anything but what they would expect of a wealthy globetrotter.

Cowdin, on the other hand, fit the mold of a man of the world. His father played world-class polo and ran a ribbon manufacturing business in New York. Elliot was an expert on New York City. He promised to show any of them around while they were in the city. The de Vincents readily agreed to Elliot's offer. Georges de Vincent planned to stay in the city for at least two days to meet with a large lumber company from Washington State.

Norman Prince wasn't overbearing, but he was self-possessed—a man with a mission. He talked often and constantly about his idea of forming an American flying unit. Listening to him, Jack wondered if Doctor Gros had borrowed the idea from Prince. Charlie thought Prince was pretty full of himself.

The *Rotterdam* had an international crew. While outfitted for the comfort of the wealthy passengers much like the *Rochambeau*, Charlie thought it lacked flair and ambiance. He realized how much he had changed. He wasn't the same bumpkin who had come over to Europe a year earlier.

Michelle's parents often engaged in long conversations with the flyers. All the Americans spoke some degree of French. Thaw and Prince had lived in France, and had studied French in college. The others had picked it up in daily discourse, a process that often led to embarrassing gaffs in the presence of the ladies.

Jack Buck spoke credible French, but, upon discovering that a professor who taught French to diplomats was aboard, Jack sought some help. The professor welcomed the chance to pass the time. After his lessons, Jack tried his skills on Michelle during the rare moments when he could pull her away from Charlie. All in all, the passage went fast.

A flock of reporters waited at the dockside that December 23. A royal couple and entourage from Siam were among the first to descend the gangway, attracting a fair number of photographers. When Jack and his fellows stepped on the ramp, the loud cheer surprised them. The newsmen rushed the party. The Americans sported civilian clothes on board but donned their French uniforms for the arrival. None of them suspected the uproar their arrival would create. Some angry shouts mixed with the cheers. *What was going on there?*

Representatives of the French-American Committee's small New York chapter rapidly gathered them and hustled them into waiting cars. Charlie refused to part with Michelle and her parents, so they too climbed into the vehicles. They inched away from the crowd and began the ride to the New York Athletic Club.

Thaw, like the rest of them, wanted to know what all the fuss had been about. Mr. Jackson, their guide, explained that pro-German demonstrators protested America's shipping of supplies to France and England. Word had gotten out that there were some Americans in French service on the *Rotterdam*. Jackson was afraid they would have to watch where they wore their uniforms during their stay.

The grand ballroom at the Athletic Club with its elaborate decor and plush furnishings impressed Jack and Charlie. Prince explained that the club had some of the best athletic facilities, including a large pool. Modeled somewhat after an English gentleman's club, the NYAC also had several lounges, accommodations for overnight stays, bars and restaurants that catered to the upper crust society businessmen who worked in Manhattan. In operation at its South Central Park location for nearly fifty years, the club sponsored numerous teams and athletic competitions. Some members interested in competitive aviation had made the place available for the visit, assigning Jackson, a club officer, to oversee the details.

To permit the men as much free time as possible, Jackson agreed to leave the promotional side of their trip to chance. Each of them received railway tickets to their hometowns or a place of their choice.

Prince would set off for Marblehead to show the boys at the Curtiss Flying School some of his new skills before going home to Pride's Crossing in Massachusetts.

Cowdin's parents lived in a brownstone on 82d Street. He would guide the de Vincents, and also agreed to talk to several prominent groups during his stay in the city.

As soon as he could break away, Bill Thaw headed to his favorite barber for a real shave and haircut. His family had major business ties on Wall Street. His uncle had taken him to this barber since he was 12. Bill didn't mind being treated like the well-dressed brokers and financiers who frequented Luigi's shop in the Ritz-Carlton Hotel.

He entered the shop and hung his cap on a rack. At first Luigi and his three barbers didn't recognize Thaw. He had been gone more than a year. His hair and mustache hid the boyish face they remembered, and Thaw's months in French service left him trimmer. After he hugged the 65-year-old Luigi, he sat in his chair for a shave. While Luigi toweled him off, Bill heard a familiar accented voice.

"Why, it is Bill Thaw!" boomed Count von Bernstorff, the German Ambassador to the United States. Thaw sat up a little saying nothing.

Luigi, continuing to trim Bill's hair, already short from the French barber, said, "Bill, those frog butchers really messed up your hair." Thaw caught his hand and squeezed it lightly.

"Please don't call them frogs, Luigi," he said calmly but loudly enough for von Bernstorff to hear.

"You know, Herr Thaw, it is clearly a violation of American neutrality for you and your friends to be serving in the French Army. You should intern yourselves here. I have known you and your family for many years. I hope you will come to your senses."

Thaw remained silent until Luigi finished his repair job. He rose from the chair, leaving a large bill on the counter, retrieved his cap and coat, and headed for the door.

"This is an outrage!" von Bernstorff roared, seeing for the first time Thaw's uniform and Croix de Guerre.

Turning to the German Ambassador, Thaw looked him in the eye and said, "Excellency, *war is hell*."

JACK STAYED OVERNIGHT AT THE ATHLETIC CLUB AS DID CHARLIE, Michelle and her parents. They couldn't pay for anything at the club, even had they wanted to. In the meantime, they mapped out their plans.

Monsieur de Vincent, after his business with representatives of the big lumber concerns that maintained offices in the city, planned to join Charlie and Michelle in Saint Louis before the wedding. Jack would take the train from Minneapolis to Saint Louis, and, after the wedding, they would all return to New York by January 6 to board the *Rotterdam*.

The New York Times reported increased fighting in the British sector near Ypres. Charlie, Michelle, and Jack scanned the pages over coffee, eggs, bacon, and toast. It was a pleasure to eat a real breakfast for a change.

"Hey, look at this," Charlie said, pointing to an article on the third page, and then reading out loud, "*The German Ambassador has formally requested the internment of the five Americans recently arrived from France. He claims their service in French uniform is an insult to Germany, a violation of American neutrality, and a threat to German-American diplomacy*. Can you beat that? They even list Bill Thaw's name."

"Can they actually stop us from going back?" Jack asked.

"I would not be surprised," Michelle said, thinking quickly. "You will have to go through customs to get out of the country. Your government may decide to stop you." She dreaded seeing Charlie go back into combat. He had given enough already. Though he loved flying and really wanted to fight for France, she thought being interned might be a godsend. Once married, she could stay as long as she wanted. After the war they would go back to Europe.

Mr. Jackson showed up looking grave and a little unsettled. Seeing they were discussing the article, he told them that he was confident the State Department would not act on von Bernstorff's demand. Unrestricted German U-boat attacks on civilian shipping had American dander up. "Just the same," he warned them, "it might be better to tone down public appearances and be prepared to leave on a moment's notice."

"But we are getting married on New Year's Eve!" Charlie exclaimed, trying to keep the panic out of his voice.

"I know, I know. It was going to be a real bonus. 'American Hero Marries French-English Governess,' Believe you me we were going to make the most out of your happy situation."

"*Was, were?* What are you suggesting, Mr. Jackson? Is the trip to Saint Louis in jeopardy?" Michelle asked, desperately.

"If German sympathizers mobilize it will be difficult for the government not to act," he observed, not wanting to dash their plans.

"Let's move the wedding up," Charlie said, thinking rapidly. "We could sneak back to New York, and get on a boat by the end of the month."

Jack would have to leave Minneapolis the day after Christmas, but he agreed with the plan.

Mr. Jackson said. "It just might work. Most government offices will be closed. We'd publicized your schedule somewhat foolishly without anticipating the clamor. People expect you to go back on the *Rotterdam* January 6th." He paused, "If you can make it back here by the 31st, I think we can throw anyone off your trail. The *SS St. Paul* sails New Year's Eve. I'll see about booking you."

AT THE CHICAGO TERMINAL DURING HIS SHORT LAYOVER, Jack gave Annette a bottle of French perfume and a bottle of champagne to his aunt and uncle. Annette asked him to send first-hand accounts of his activities after his return. She would try to get them published for him.

When he arrived at the Milwaukee Railroad Station in Minneapolis, he was unprepared for the reception. His family waited for him in front of a large crowd. Rowan himself stood before a phalanx of photographers.

After hugging his mother and sisters, Jack shook his father's hand and then Larry's. Men just didn't hug in Minnesota. It would have been embarrassing.

Jack greeted Rowan, "Sir, I never would have expected to see you here. You do me great honor, but…" he whispered Jackson's warnings about avoiding publicity.

"Right you are, Buck," Rowan said. "We're hearing some of the same cautions from the bureau in Chicago. I can't keep this out of our paper, but I won't publish anything about your plans. Don't tell me when you are leaving. Enjoy your time with your family. I like what you've written. Keep sending me your observations. You know you have a job here whenever you come back."

Jack saw a few of the boys from the Cartage Company hanging back behind the crowd. He worked his way over to them to say hello and ask how things were at his old job. "Toby! Toby Franzak. Why, I almost didn't recognize you! When did you lose all that weight?"

"Been kinda sick," Toby said, turning his head and coughing. Franzak looked older than his forty years.

"Toby had a bout with TB, Jack. He hasn't been able to work for quite a while, but he insisted we bring him down to see you," Jarvis Jenkins, one of his two black high school classmates, said. "He hasn't got much energy, but the docs think he'll pull through." Jack thanked them for coming, remembering how generous and thoughtful Toby had always been.

Jack couldn't wait to get home. It was snowing and well below freezing. He wanted to strap on his skates and hit a few shots into the goal at the hockey rink up at Fowell Park, but not before eating one of his mom's big meals.

Jack enjoyed his stay at home so much that he didn't want to leave. Of course, Christmas Eve and Christmas Day had to be celebrated in the traditional manner. Grandma and Grandpa Christian put on a royal feast Christmas Eve. Christmas Day fell to the Buck family to host. Jack delighted in helping prepare the dishes. He, Larry, and the girls decorated a special tree that Jack had bought and set up in a corner of the basement. Their accumulated gifts stood watch while the four siblings danced and sang Christmas carols as they decorated the small tree.

He and Larry walked to the park every day he was home. They put on their skates in the wooden shack with its pot-bellied coal stove, and went out to skate with all the abandon of youth. Though Jack still skated stronger and faster, Larry had become an accomplished hockey player. When they came home after several hours at the rink, they were exhausted and as hungry as wolves.

The day after Christmas, Jack packed his things. He hated to have to leave so soon, but he also looked forward to the wedding and to seeing Saint Louis. His parents agreed to let Larry come with him and stay until Jack had to leave for New York. The brothers had never been closer. Larry, now eighteen, wanted to go to France himself, but their father put a stop to that idea for the moment.

"If the United States decides to enter this damned vor," Ockie told them after Jeannie's birthday candles went out, "I'll let my sons fight for this country. I didn't leave Norway for nothin', doncha know? Europeans never stop fighting. Proud as I am of you Jackie, I von't let both my boys stick their neck into Europe's mess unless Vilson decides it's our country's fight as vell."

CHARLIE AND MICHELLE ARRIVED AT THE SAINT LOUIS TERMINAL not expecting anybody but his parents and Jennifer to greet them, but the crowd of friends and well wishers turned out to be very large. Chouteau Johnson's folks came up and introduced themselves. Jennifer took Michelle's arm, becoming an instant friend. Charlie noticed that

Jennifer no longer looked like a teen-ager. She looked ravishing, even for a kid sister. His father seemed subdued. He hoped he hadn't been drinking.

The Keelers hurried the young couple home. They stayed up until almost three in the morning getting to know Michelle and hearing all about her family. Angelique was glad she hadn't had invitations printed. The earlier date was going to call for some major adjustments.

At Charlie's request, John and Angelique Keeler kept the wedding out of the papers. Only family and close friends would attend. They had gotten threatening mail from some of the Busch crowd. It had the effect of galvanizing Charlie's father behind his son's actions. Charlie couldn't have been more surprised.

The de Vincents arrived Christmas day and were staying in the Hotel Regis, the place the Keelers arranged for both the rehearsal dinner and the reception. The management promised a spectacular French-style dinner and a reception flowing with French champagne. Georges de Vincent coordinated the final details, insisting that no expense be spared and that every bill be given to him personally.

Jack and Larry showed up in time to attend the rehearsal. Charlie, Michelle, and Jennifer met Jack and Larry at the station. After introducing Jennifer to Jack and meeting Larry, Charlie led them to the nearby Saint Benedict's Catholic Church. Jennifer agreed to be Michelle's maid of honor, and Charlie asked Larry if he would be an usher. They went through the ceremony three times until they satisfied Father O'Leary, their new pastor, that everyone knew their roles.

Jack escorted Jennifer up the aisle during the rehearsal. He felt a jolt of electricity run up to his shoulder and stab at his heart when she took his arm. He couldn't stop stealing glimpses at her throughout the night. She wore a simple dress. Something in her visage weakened his knees. Jennifer's golden tresses hung in gentle ringlets to her shoulders. His eyes traveled quickly from her sweet-looking lips to her bright blue eyes. Even the way she stood and walked unnerved him.

December 28, 1915, dawned clear and crisp in Saint Louis. Jack and Larry joined the de Vincent family for breakfast in the restaurant of the Saint Regis. Michelle wasn't with her parents. Jack asked if she had gone ahead.

"No, Jack," Mrs. de Vincent said, smiling slightly. "She has no appetite. She feels a little sick. Nothing serious. I remember feeling very much the same on our wedding day, remember Georges?"

"I thought she would not come to the church," he explained. "She locked herself in her room and would not see anyone. Even her mother couldn't get her to open the door. We were getting married at Notre Dame, and I think she was afraid the Pope would be there to steal her soul," Georges remarked in his acquired British accent.

"Rubbish, Georges! You know better than that. I converted to Catholicism freely, and you better not tell these young men otherwise," Michelle's mother rebuked in mock severity, smiling.

"All the same," Georges continued, "Michelle's mother only unlocked the door to her room with minutes to spare. I was sweating at the altar rail in the June heat wondering if she would show. Don't worry about Michelle. I think she just wants to look perfect today."

Larry looked uncomfortable in dress clothes. He wore denims and wool shirts back home. Fishing, hunting and sports were his only interests before Jack infected him with the flying bug. He did his best to fit in with the people his older brother introduced him to, but he just smiled and said little, absorbing it all.

The nuptial Mass took almost ninety minutes. Later, the bridal party led off the dancing that followed the luncheon. Their train for New York would board at five-thirty for a six departure, a fact that dampened the reception only slightly. Angelique Keeler proudly danced with her son. He had allowed Michelle to teach him to dance on the *Rotterdam.* In the end, he forced himself to see parallels to wrestling moves that helped him decide he liked dancing. Holding a pretty woman was so much better than grappling with a sweaty man.

Georges de Vincent took Michelle to the floor and John Keeler cut in to finish the dance. Though he seemed very proud and happy at the wedding, Charlie's father also acted as if he had something else on his mind. He didn't drink and was scrupulously polite. Charlie still wasn't comfortable talking to his father. He hoped it had nothing to do with Michelle.

Jack left Jennifer's side only twice to dance with Mrs. Keeler and Michelle. Larry talked to Jennifer during these dances, but didn't have the nerve to step on the floor. She was only about a year older than he was, but he could see something brewing between Jennifer and his brother. He might have asked one of the other young women to dance, but he felt too self-conscious.

Jennifer told Jack that she would be coming to France in a couple of weeks to work as a volunteer nurse at the American Hospital. She was just finishing a two-year nursing program.

"Maybe we can see each other then? I am sure to pass through Paris. Would you write me?" Jack asked, more excited than he dared show.

"I'd like that. I mean, I'd like to see you in Paris, and I can write, though I don't have much to say."

"You know, it doesn't make any difference what you say. Soldiers love to get mail. It is a reminder that life continues with some degree of normalcy somewhere else in the world."

"If you promise to write me back, I will write you the first letter."

CHARLIE DIDN'T CARE HOW THEY PASSED THEIR HONEYMOON even if it was in a sleeper compartment on a moving train. They had nothing but a curtain to protect them from prying eyes, but Georges de Vincent paid for two berths just to be sure they would not have to share one with anyone else. It was nearly nine when they were able to pull themselves away from the others in the dining car and head to their honeymoon "suite."

"I love you, Mrs. Keeler," Charlie said when they entered their compartment.

"Now love me, Mr. Keeler." Michelle said with a throaty purr, putting her arms around his neck and pulling his face to hers. "I want this to be all that we have been dreaming about in our private little dreams, you and me. We just might make a baby tonight. Would you like that?"

"Is it possible? I mean, on our first time?" Charlie asked, a little stupidly. After all their previous restraint, their lovemaking achieved incredible passion. They had eighteen hours before reaching New York, counting stops. They hoped her parents and Jack, traveling on the same train, wouldn't miss them, for they did not intend to leave each other's arms for the duration of the trip.

A slightly panicked Mr. Jackson met them at the station. He couldn't find Prince and had been warned that the authorities would arrest Thaw, Cowdin, Prince, Buck, and Keeler if they tried to leave the country. They had to get on the *Saint Paul*, and go into hiding until it sailed or they were not going back to France. Thaw and Cowdin were waiting for them at the lobby of the Waldorf Astoria.

Elliot Cowdin tried to duck the attention lavished on him by his family and their society friends during his stay. Jackson had warned him and Bill Thaw not to let their notoriety get out of hand. Prince even wired messages to Cowdin and Thaw telling them to be prepared to head either to Canada or go incognito. Now he was nowhere to be found.

"Any sign of Prince?" Jackson asked while the porters dealt with the baggage.

"None, but don't worry. Nimmie can handle himself. I read about the ruckus they raised in Boston when he got home. He must have gone into hiding. He'll show up." Thaw said, with much more confidence than Jackson could muster.

"We can't wait too much longer. You four and you Miss—I mean Mrs. Keeler—need to come with me now. We are going to get you aboard ahead of time."

Michelle went through another tearful farewell with her parents in the cavernous ornate Waldorf lobby. It had been harder leaving the Keelers. At least her parents would be sailing on the originally scheduled ship the next week. The emotional whirlwind dizzied Michelle. She was close to exhaustion from lack of sleep. She dreaded Charlie's departure for Cazeaux and subsequent assignment to an operational squadron. She planned to make the most of every day at sea once she caught up on her rest.

An hour before they pulled up the passenger gangway Prince had still not shown up. Cowdin had been waylaid by a group of demonstrators. New York police were ready to lay hands on him when the crowd broke the cordon line, allowing Elliot to run to his father's waiting car and whiz off to Pier 50.

The last announcement directing visitors ashore forced Mr. Jackson to move to the gangway. He apologized to Thaw and the others for the way things had gotten out of hand. As he descended the ramp, a car pulled up and two men got out, both wearing heavy fur coats with hats pulled down over their faces. They ran up the gangway without slowing down. Soon the crowd at the railing swallowed them. One sidled up to Thaw whispering something.

"Prince! You son of a gun! Where the hell have you been?"

"Shush! See those cars behind mine?" Norman Prince said ducking back from the railing. "They are some thugs from Customs. If they suspect any of us are on board they will hold up the ship!"

A third figure, wearing the same fur coat and hat as Prince, stepped out of the door. The man lit a cigar, looked around, walked toward the gangway that had already been pulled back from the ship, shook his head demonstratively, and got back in the car. The car pulled off followed by the two others.

"That's cousin Bill down there and this is my older brother, Fred. We found out they were tailing me in Boston and decided to try to shake them by driving down here. They followed though. Fred is coming to fly too, but the agents were after me. They can't arrest us until we try to leave the country. We hoped they would see Bill's little charade there and think it was me. Looks like it worked."

"A bit too close, don't you think, Nimmie?" Bill Thaw asked. "Can you imagine our own country trying to keep us from going back? Hell, we are spending millions to support the Allies, and the Germans are sinking our ships. When are we going to wake up?"

"Not soon enough, Bill, not soon enough."

Chapter 32
Boats, Guns, and Bombs

Cazeaux, France, mid-January, 1916

The motor whirred as the speedboat spun at the end of the run and headed back in the other direction.

Da da da da da da! Da da da da da! Da da da da da da da!

Splashes in the water fell way short of the towed target. "*Levez! Il faut lever la mitrailleuse si vous desirez frapper la cible*!" shouted the gunnery instructor over the noise of the unmuffled outboard.

Charlie raised his aim as the instructor ordered, this time stitching a line across the canvas target before emptying the drum of the Lewis machine gun. In three days, he had hardly been able to hit anything. Where was Antonelli when he needed him?

Since their abbreviated trip to the States, Buck and Keeler had had a few days in Paris before reporting to the school at Cazeaux. Michelle obtained Fleury's blessing to continue to keep her suite in the Crillon in return for contining to look after their boys and serving as his administrative assistant.

Charlie and Jack went to Neuilly to talk to Doctor Gros and enlist Nurse Wilson to look after Jennifer when she arrived. Gros took them to the doctor's lounge where they could talk privately.

After congratulating Charlie on his marriage, he brought them up to date. Piatt Andrew had moved the ambulance headquarters to an old estate on Rue Raynouard in Passy on the Seine just west of the Trocadéro. They now quartered most of the volunteer nurses in the old rooms above the American Hospital now vacated by Piatt's drivers. Jennifer could stay there while she worked. Charlie wanted Jennifer to stay with Michelle, but Michelle wisely pointed out that the nurses worked long hours late into the night. Jennifer could stay with her anytime, but she would be better off at the hospital rather than commuting at odd hours in a city that would be at first very strange to her.

Jack hadn't stopped talking about Jennifer since leaving Saint Louis. Charlie, remembering Buck's dalliances with Marie de la Croix de Valois and Madame Walker, might have preferred her to meet Victor Chapman or Kiffin Rockwell, but Jack was a devout Catholic, and Charlie really liked him. It would be Jennifer's decision in any case. She'd told him to look out for Buck before he'd left. This surprised him nearly as much as what his father had said minutes earlier:

"Charlie, this isn't easy for me to say, but I've been wrong about you. Your uncles are your enemies now, and I'm sorry I don't care what happens to them, but I do care what happens to you. I'm proud, son, damned proud of you! You have a lovely bride. Take care of yourself and bring her back to us."

They actually embraced; something Charlie couldn't remember doing since he was a small boy. It brought tears to his eyes, and to his father's.

THE STUDENTS WERE HOUSED IN BISCARROSSE south of the northernmost of the two lakes on the Cazeaux firing center. Located on the Atlantic coast southeast of Bordeaux, the thinly inhabited region south of Archachon, and the famous Cap Ferrat, had long been used by the French military to test weapons. A small caserne on the *terrain militaire*, housed the school cadre. Cazeaux's mission was to teach machine gunnery. *Les mitrailleuses* had so dominated the early days of the conflict that traditional mounted cavalry seemed doomed. Ironically, this advance in the technology of warfare caused the brutal stagnation in the trenches of the western front.

Outstanding artillerymen since the time of Napoleon, the French quickly mastered the peculiarities of aerial gunnery. Cazeaux taught pilots and observer/machine-gunners the basics. No one pretended that aerial gunnery could be learned on the ground, but the evolving training system at Cazeaux earned good marks from the active escadrilles.

Classes covered the Vickers, Lewis, and Parabellum machine guns. Charlie had never been assigned to a machine gun crew. Antonelli's skillful recognition of his aiming problem had taken care of the left-handed quirks with rifles. Would he be able to learn similar tricks with machine guns?

They fired the weapons from tripods, bipods, and fixed pintles. Originally designed to train ground crews, all pilots and observers now had to qualify on the range. Jack thought the ground qualification to be almost a joke. "Heck, Charlie," he said after firing his ten meter zeroing rounds, "you can see the rounds hit the target. All you have to do is move the hose. Haven't you ever watered the grass? You just point the stream where you want it to go."

"If it were that simple why do we have to go to this course, Bucko?"

"That's pretty clear. I haven't watered the grass at a hundred miles an hour lately. I expect firing while moving will be a bit more challenging."

Ice formed near the shoreline of the lakeside range. It might be pleasant to visit in the summer, but the cold and the wind made their current work most uncomfortable. They started shooting at anchored buoys from fixed sites on the shore. Machine guns mounted on universal ball joints enabled them to be fired into the air as well as in any other direction. These were designed to train gunner-observers who flew in aircraft like the Caudron and Voisin. Target buoys at 100-meter intervals out to 1,000 meters taught the gunners to judge horizontal distances from known distances. The artillery officers in the class had no problem with this phase.

After the shoreline firing, the instructors sent out a safety boat to make sure the lake was clear before opening up the next phase. The school owned a small fleet of motorboats powered by American-built Evinrude motors. Familiar to Jack, the motors made an enormous amount of noise.

The Lewis machine guns on their boat were mounted on the bow and on the port gunwale. Two boats departed at the same time. The target boat towed a floating frame with a canvas target stretched across it. Some had various silhouettes of German airplanes in black or red. The towing boat ran out a line almost 300 meters long. Drivers were trained to keep their relative positions in order to keep the shooters from hitting the towboat. Starting out on parallel lines, the firers had to engage the target at a distance of between one hundred and two hundred meters. They thought it would be easy firing from the side gun, but Kiffin discovered keeping the gun steady extremely difficult in the rocking boat.

Later, they fired the forward machine gun. The towboat passed in front of them flying a red flag to indicate 'don't fire!' Once the target was at a distance of about 500 meters, the firing boat driver gunned the motor, aiming the boat at the moving target. Kiffin controlled only the trigger on the first run since the Lewis gun was locked in the forward position. He fired two bursts before the gun jammed. They'd been taught to tap the receiver with a mallet to try to free the jam. He hit the gun a couple of times and tried again unsuccessfully. The pass took only about thirty seconds. He was so frustrated that he wanted to throw the gun in the water. He'd only gotten off about ten rounds. Much to his surprise, ten little holes pierced the canvas. By waiting until the last second and getting very close, Kiffin had nailed the target, a lesson he would apply later.

Other runs simulated firing at oblique angles. This instruction approximated the relative motion and the ballistics involved in firing while moving. They learned about bullet drop over distance and the effect of relative winds on the cone of fire, that lethal imaginary circle in the air where the rounds were concentrated enough to achieve multiple hits. Beyond 200 meters, a number of factors, including barrel temperature, caused so much dispersion that hitting anything with any effect dropped significantly.

Jack enjoyed the classes and the theoretical side of aerial gunnery. He continued drawing homely analogies like the garden hose example to explain things to Charlie. Charlie, on the other hand, enjoyed puttering around with the firing mechanisms. He thought the way gas cylinders, feeding mechanisms, and rotating drums worked together to generate nearly 500 shots per minute was fascinating business. Kiffin just wanted to get it over with and go on to a squadron.

The three of them finished Cazeaux at the same time, weather waiving the flying portion of the course. They'd heard this was a blessing since they could only fire from old Caudrons or Farmans at fixed targets or those floating on the lake. Attempts to tow aerial targets behind other planes met with near disaster when a student became entangled in the towline during his firing run. The cable snapped, as did the Commandant of the school, a non-flyer. He put all such training on hold until the aviators could convince him they could do it safely.

NORMALLY NEWLY QUALIFIED CHASSE PILOTS WENT TO THE RGA at Plessis. The *Réserve Général Aéronautique* served as a clearinghouse for replacement pilots of all types. Le Plessis-Belleville, a small town northeast of Paris had four large grassy strips and a host of canvas hangars. The pilots flew under the supervision of an instruction team whose sole mission was to bring the men up to speed and to allow them to continue to build flight hours.

Jack Buck skipped RGA to report directly to Voisin Escadrille 97, the unit charged with the defense of Paris. V. 97 had the latest version of the Voisin with a forward firing machine gun mounted on the top of the single wing. No match for the Aviatiks, or the growing number of Fokker fighters the Germans sent up to protect their Taube and Gotha bombers, V. 97 could at least provide early warning and harass the bombers if they closed on Paris. The Boche fighters seldom accompanied the bombers or Zeppelins any farther forward than the front lines. The Germans flew these missions at night to avoid anti-aircraft fire and defensive fighters. V. 97, like most French squadrons, simply did not fly at night.

Jack stepped into his first line aircraft, a Voisin configured for combat, on January 25, 1916. He took off following a French Lieutenant. The observer who manned Jack's Lewis gun was no less than his old friend, *Sergent* Cartier, the man that Jack had learned so much from in his early ambulance days.

"*Allez, Jacques*," Cartier said. "We meet again, but this time my life is in your hands."

"Whatever are you doing here, Cartier?" Jack asked, puzzled at why an old motor sergeant would be manning a machine gun in an aviation unit.

"*Bonne question*!" Cartier smiled. He told Jack about a general call that went out to the whole French Army shortly after Jack had left SSU 2. The growing number of aviation escadrilles desperately needed mechanics and *personnel navigant*, people who could serve as observers or machine-gunners, to fill the ranks of the growing number of aviation squadrons.

Shortages forced many squadrons to man the machine guns with mechanics. The mechanic came back from a mission and still had to work on the airplane while the pilot went off to rest. It was a sore point that already affected the quality of maintenance. All the two-seater units in 1915 and 1916 suffered terrible shortages in observer-gunners. Some escadrille commanders combed local ground units looking for suitable volunteers among the more senior sergeants, reasoning that these men would need very little training to become good observers. Most of them already knew how to handle weapons.

Cartier told Jack that things just weren't the same after he and McConnell had left. Besides, Cartier said with a little gleam in his eye, the Army paid them a supplement for flying, and the food was better in Aviation.

Cartier's five months flying made him one of the more experienced observers. Their mission that day was to orient new pilots. V. 97 occupied a field just north of the city of Paris. Le Bourget, a small town known for its fine restaurants, had given its name to the nearby field. From a quiet little meadow where cows grazed lazily, the French Army had hewn out a sizable strip capable of handling at least four escadrilles. Voisin 97 had the distinction of being the only operational unit at Le Bourget.

The field served more as a depot and transfer station than as an *aérodrome de combat*. V. 97 shared the defense of Paris with a number of other escadrilles. Jack learned that many of the pilots in the squadron only stayed a few weeks before going on to more forward escadrilles. The lack of activity made V. 97 a good escadrille to wet the new pilot's feet. They had to be on their toes, but seldom got into harm's way. The officer commanding the unit had taken to sending his patrols up just before dawn and just before sundown in the hopes of catching the enemy skirting the dark.

Jack marked their key landmarks on his map. He had little difficulty handling the Voisin. He didn't delude himself for a second that this flight even approached the danger and challenge of a real combat mission. The only excitement occurred when they tested their machine guns over an open field east of Senlis. Cartier tapped Jack's shoulder just before firing a short burst. Jack activated his trigger causing the forward-firing Vickers to rip off about ten rounds, the highlight of an otherwise routine mission.

Cartier complimented Jack on his piloting skills. "I knew you would be a good *aviateur.* I could tell by the way you handled the ambulances. You know the *poilus* used to ask for you by name when they had to be evacuated? *Oui*! It's so!"

Jack laughed as he thought about all the ribbing he got from Kiffin and Charlie after their rough ride. It was nice to hear Cartier insist that Jack had been the best of the best in SSU 2.

Cartier also updated Jack on Dombasle. The captain, he swore, would never pursue the de la Croix widow for her money. Laughing at the thought, he told Jack that Dombasle had more money than he could ever spend. It relieved Jack enormously to realize that Dombasle was taking care of Marie which reminded him that Jennifer would be arriving in Paris in a couple of weeks.

ON JANUARY 29, THE GERMANS SENT A FLIGHT OF GOTHAS and Zeppelins to attack Paris. Observation balloons and ground stations reported the approaching formation at 7:30 that night, estimating its arrival over Paris around eight. Attacks on the city had not been too terribly effective. Parisians quickly blacked out the city whenever the siren, whistle, and bell system alerted the residents of a pending attack. Batteries of powerful searchlights ringed the city casting eerie shadows as their shafts of lights swept the skies. Paris national guard artillery batteries guarded the perimeter of Paris. Yet, not a single Zeppelin or airplane had been brought down.

All the pilots and crews of V. 97 turned out for the show, or *spectacle*, as they called it in French, to rail at their impotence, and cheer when the big guns began to boom. At Le Bourget, the men wondered what the target would be that night.

At half past eight, they began to drift back towards their quarters, tired of craning their necks. A few remained, slowly smoking cigarettes guarded in their cupped palms. No one got into the sandbagged shelters. They reasoned that the Germans were after Paris. Le Bourget seemed safe.

A blinding flash and deafening boom startled the men of the escadrille. A bomb had landed harmlessly in the woods east of the field igniting a small fire. Jack stared into the black skies wondering what it was like to navigate in the dark. Did they use lights in the cockpit? How did they stay upright? Being swallowed by clouds in broad daylight was terrifying enough.

Three more explosions rocked the ground in rapid succession, each closer to where the Voisins were tethered. A blast of hot wind flashed across the area when one of the bombs found a gasoline reservoir. The flames lit up the whole field. Jack could feel the heat from the fire. Now he thought he could see how they might identify targets. The fire must have made every airplane and hangar stand out clearly to the attackers. What was to keep them from continuing the destruction?

French artillery reports and subsequent explosions thousands of feet in the air added to the cacophony. Streams of light criss-crossed over the field, occasionally outlining the form of the bombers. Gothas, Jack thought, not mad at the Germans, fascinated at their bravery.

In minutes, it was over. Why hadn't they continued the attack? Maybe Le Bourget was not the eventual target. While the searchlights kept up their dance, the artillery tapered off. Jack could hear the crackling from the burning woods. He also thought he heard the familiar cries of wounded men. Dashing from the spot where he had been riveted during the attack, he ran towards the buildings where the squadron slept.

The wood smoke and crackling sounds he thought were coming from the distant woods engulfed one of the barracks! The wooden building had taken a direct hit. Jack hoped no one had been fool enough to stay in bed during the attack. By the time he got there, the fire had consumed most of the building. He remembered the fire Charlie had described at Avord. The thought of burning to death horrified him.

Sitting on the ground some distance from the building, a French soldier with a blanket over his shoulders shook with sobs. When Jack got closer, he saw that the man was the young mechanic who had started their motor that day. Asking if he'd been hurt, Jack knelt down beside the man. Getting no response, Jack lifted the blanket to see if the guy had been wounded or burned. The light from the dying fire flickered across the man's sooty, tear-streaked face. Jack couldn't see any injuries.

"*Si vous n'êtes pas blessé, pourquoi les larmes*?" Jack gently asked the man if he was not hurt then why the tears?

"*C'est Cartier. Le fou*!" Jack strained to hear. What about Cartier?

"*Il est mort, le pauvre*."

Cartier dead? No! Jack's mind screamed while his mouth failed to work. Masters, and now Cartier? He began to feel a rage welling up inside him. Earlier he had marveled at the German pilots' skills without feeling the slightest rancor that they were attacking *him, his friends.* Now he trembled in rage. He wanted to lash out. For the first time in his life he wanted to *kill.*

Chapter 33
An Antidote to Civilization

Le Plessis-Belleville, January 1916

The *Réserve Général Aéronautique* occupied one of the largest and most diversified aérodromes in France. Le Plessis-Belleville, sixty kilometers northeast of Paris, began as a *chasse* training field. After the Marne, the field served as a jumping off point for pilots en route to the front.

North of the town stood a small city of clapboard buildings, canvas hangars, and the assorted paraphernalia associated with aviation units. A railroad siding served both the town and RGA, nearly twice the size of Le Plessis in population. Fuel tanks and an ammunition dump straddled the rails a safe distance apart. Each was protected by earthen berms. From the air the conglomerate looked like a cavalry depot. Bessaneau hangars replaced stables, and motor parks took the place of wagon parks. The smithy had become the *atelier*, or machine shop, and what would have been a drill and parade field served as the landing strip.

Pilots and other aviation personnel wore the distinctive insignia of their *armes*, a bewildering *mélange* of colors and regimental symbols the Americans found impossible to master. Of all the branches, however, none were more distinctive or prouder than the cavalrymen. Something vestigial left over from the days of knights survived and flourished in this branch of aristocrats. Cavalrymen flyers often sported riding breeches, spurs, and flowing scarves reminiscent of those fixed to the lances by damsels before a medieval jousting match.

After signing in for duty, Keeler and Rockwell walked the short distance from the gate to the nearest hotel, an old dilapidated-looking brick building with a faded sign announcing: *L'Hôtel de la Bonne Rencontre*. Inside, the place was a bit seedy. The proprietress, Madame Rodel, reminded Charlie of a fading flower. She seemed to be somewhere past fifty. She wore her gray hair pulled back in a bun tightly enough to make her eyes bulge. They were kindly eyes all the same. Madame Rodel lit up when she discovered they were Americans.

"*Mais, c'est parfait*!" She announced. "*Connaissez-vous Raoul Lufbery*?" She asked excitedly.

"I know of him, Madame," Kiffin answered. "Luf enlisted in the Legion about the same time as I did, but he went right into aviation. Is he here?"

"Oh my, no, not here," she smiled as if remembering something very special about Lufbery. "He *was* here, last October. He is far more French than American, you know. So nice to me. I wanted to be his *marraine*, but he already had one in Chartres. Besides, my husband wouldn't approve, if you know what I mean." She snickered and Charlie swore she even winked.

Madame Rodel gave them what she said was her last room. She complained that the Army brought people to Le Plessis-Belleville for only a few days or weeks before sending them off to be killed. She couldn't keep up with the constant comings and goings. Kiffin and Charlie both wondered what had kept the old place going before the war. Maybe it had been a brothel? *Good Meeting Place.* Stands to reason, they told each other later, when she was out of earshot.

The officers manning the reception desks in the headquarters the next morning seemed casual to the point of listlessness. Charlie stood before a *Commandant* who looked to be about sixty. The old officer had to be a recalled reservist. He gave Charlie a packet of papers and directed him to a table to fill out the forms.

Kiffin soon joined him with his own stack of forms. "I tell you, Charlie, without all this paper, the French could have whipped the Germans a year ago."

"Does seem like they are fond of their *formulaires*," Charlie grimaced. "What if we played dumb or filled out a bunch of bogus information? Do you think anyone would notice?"

"Maybe not, but I'm not too eager to find out. Someone might think we're spies."

Next, they joined a group of other newcomers in one of the large canvas hangars that had been set up as a sort of theater. A bespectacled captain said that they could be at RGA for as little as days or as long as several months, depending on the demands of the line groups and escadrilles. "But don't worry. A major battle is shaping up near the French line of forts around Verdun," the captain announced.

In response to ever-changing needs, the French turned Le Plessis-Belleville into a sort of finishing school. Different sections made up of *moniteurs* and full support contingents could provide instruction in just about any aircraft currently used in the French Army. Experienced combat pilots came to RGA between assignments where their knowledge and experience were put to use to season the new arrivals.

Every day they posted lists showing the names of those pilots going to a particular escadrille. With over two hundred pilots at any given time, the first arrived could count on being the first to be assigned to a unit with few exceptions. Clerks also posted flying assignments for the day.

Charlie couldn't see any reason for hanging around for weeks waiting for an assignment. Why not let him stay in Paris, he thought? In just a few days they would be celebrating their one month anniversary.

"Listen, Charlie. The best thing for it is to keep as busy as possible," Kiffin said. "Let's get as many hours flying here as we can. I'm sure traipsing around in the sky will help to get your mind off Michelle. Think about what it will be like when we do go to a squadron. At least here we're less than an hour from Paris. She might be able to come here, so get that soppy hang-dog look off your face."

"That bad, huh, Kif?" Charlie said. "I didn't realize it showed so much. God, it hurts to be away from her! It almost makes me wish we hadn't gotten married yet."

"Bullshit, Keeler! Quit talking such drivel. It wouldn't be any different. You managed well enough for those months in the Legion. Don't go soft on me now."

"Thanks, friend, but let me tell you it's not the same. I can't say why, but, it's just not the same."

"I wasn't born yesterday, Charlie. You've discovered wedded bliss. You got along without it before, and you can now." Kiffin, no prude, had a *marraine*, a beautiful Parisienne named Alexis de Raneville. They were still getting to know each other, literally in body and soul.

"Believe me Herc, abstinence ain't terminal, even for married men."

Kiffin was right, of course.

Charlie drew a Nieuport for his first flight. He temporarily forgot Michelle in his excitement.

Kiffin got a Farman, not one of the old trainers, but one of the two-seater observation machines with the larger motor and wider wingspan.

He couldn't believe they would put him in the machine with no more instruction than verification that his logbook included Farmans. A moniteur walked around the aircraft with him to perform a perfunctory inspection, pointing out a few differences in the newer version. A lieutenant awaiting assignment as an observer came to occupy the second seat. They received maps and instructions not to fly too far north or east lest they enter the *zone de combat.* Kiffin took off after talking to the young lieutenant about what he wanted to do. The officer deferred completely to the American *sergent.*

Kiffin put the Farman through its paces. He took it up as high as it would go before stalling, reaching 6,000 meters. Then he executed a *vrille* that made the lieutenant get sick over the side. Recovering at 4,000 meters, he cut the motor and volplaned to 2,000 meters, dead sticking the Farman. The silence, except for the wind and the retching sounds of the poor lieutenant, made Kiffin feel like a bird. Restarting the motor, he decided to have mercy on the officer and just cruise around sightseeing. By the time he landed back at Plessis, the lieutenant had recovered enough to thank him and compliment him on his flying skills.

Charlie's experience in the Nieuport was entirely different. It began with a class on defensive maneuvers that covered how patrols of two or more aircraft could work together to ensure mutual protection. *Now we're talking!* Charlie told himself, remembering the flight with Kiffin and the near-collision with Johnson.

"The patrol leader is not only in *charge* of the patrol, but also the most likely one to acquire an enemy first if he's any good and does his job," the instructor intoned, relating examples of patrols being caught by surprise by superior numbers of German aircraft and being picked off one by one.

"Aerial skill notwithstanding," he explained, "the first to see the other has an advantage at the outset. The key is to see and not be seen. Every member of a patrol gets an assigned sector to search. The patrol lives or dies on the alertness of the team. The main thing to avoid if attacked is being separated from the rest of the patrol, but more importantly," he pointed out emphatically, "*don't get surprised*."

To teach this lesson, two groups of three Nieuports took off to form patrols at different ends of a ten by five mile box defined by red and white towers at each corner. Experienced patrol leaders led each group. The two patrols were to enter the box at opposite ends in search of the other. Once a patrol spotted the other, they would record the time and approximate position. Patrol leaders would attempt to maneuver into attack positions. If the discovered patrol didn't realize it had been spotted, chances were good that the other patrol could maneuver above and behind until they closed to machine gun range, claiming victory. If both patrols discovered each other, they were to execute evasive maneuvers to get back to the entrance to the box to repeat the whole drill.

The maneuver box lay well to the south of Le Plessis-Belleville between the villages of St. Mard and St. Mesmes. The road between the villages served as the western limit of the box. Charlie's patrol entered from the south. En route, the patrol leader, a captain about to be promoted to take over a group of several escadrilles, led his flight through a series of gentle formation maneuvers, all the time climbing. He told them that a height advantage at the outset could be worth almost as much as being the first to see the other patrol. He placed Charlie on the right with a search sector that covered from directly in front to directly behind their line of flight. He ordered the other pilot to scan the same sector to the left. He would cover both himself, as well as all that he could see above and below them.

Instead of entering the box in the middle, the captain edged the patrol onto the eastern edge. They cruised along for five minutes without seeing anything—or so Charlie thought. Soon they would reach the end of the box. *What a waste of time. How dumb*, Charlie thought.

Suddenly the captain executed a left climbing turn. Charlie couldn't see any sign of another aircraft. A ninety-degree turn to the left had them heading south! In seconds, the captain wagged his wings, pointed down, and dove. Charlie still didn't see anything. After losing several hundred feet and struggling to stay on the captain's right wing, Charlie began to make out the other patrol. His heart began pounding as he imagined closing in for the kill. Still undetected, the captain carried their dive right across the front of the other patrol causing it to scatter like a flushed covey of quail. *What fun!* Charlie thought, before remembering that this was no game and that those men in the other patrol would likely be dead.

At the mission debriefing, the other patrol went first. Their patrol leader, a young captain, described crossing into the box at the prescribed time and altitude. They flew straight ahead down the centerline seeing nothing. Just before reaching the southern limit of the box, he acknowledged that the other patrol bounced them, scattering his patrol.

Captain Féquant, Charlie's patrol leader, gave his debriefing more like a class than a simple description of what they had done. "Never do the expected," he said. "Anticipate what your opponent will do, and position yourself accordingly. Surprise, don't be surprised. Seize the high ground and attack from unexpected directions."

It all made so much sense in retrospect. Rather than bowl down the center of the box, Féquant had opted for one of the sides. Instead of meeting the other patrol head-on, Féquant had anticipated their arrival at a certain point and time, and had maneuvered to attack from above and behind.

"Remember, *mes amis*, this is an exercise," Féquant concluded. "Study your enemy and know yourself, but don't forget that in war, anything can happen. Today you were supposed to learn about defensive tactics. My apologies to the cadre, but in the air, in my humble opinion, the only defensive tactic worth a pile of *merde* is attack! Any questions?"

"*Mon capitaine*," Charlie began. "I understand everything you just said and everything we just did, but I don't think we played fair. Aren't there times when the enemy has an advantage on you and it would be better to avoid combat?"

Féquant regarded Charlie closely before responding. "Let me answer your second question first. Yes! However, let me remind all of you that avoiding combat is not a defensive tactic. It is a conscious decision, probably a prudent one. Notice that I never said to be foolhardy. The key is in what I told you about surprising and not being surprised.

"Now, was my attack fair? What do you think, Captain?" He asked the other patrol leader.

"Hell no, it wasn't fair!" The younger captain said, looking at his two nodding wingmen. "But," he continued, slowly turning to face Féquant, "war isn't about being fair. This isn't the playing field. No officials to call foul here. Ours is deadly business. No, Captain Féquant's attack wasn't fair. It was brilliant! He taught me a big lesson today about being predictable. *Mes respects, mon capitaine!"* He ended, saluting his fellow officer.

"*Bon*. Does that answer your questions, Mr. Keeler?" Féquant asked, gently, not expecting a response. Charlie just nodded, thinking about the curious interplay between the two captains. This training beat the dickens out of anything he had done until then. He couldn't wait to do another exercise, hopefully with Féquant. The man had something about him that inspired confidence. He reminded Charlie of Capitaine de Lattre and Antonelli.

At night, the men could hear the big guns booming in the distance. Le Plessis-Belleville wasn't that close to the front, but the Germans had started using huge cannon that could fire as much as seventy-five miles—enough to range even Paris.

"Charlie. Tell me about your patrol with that rat Rejik again. Every time I think about it I want to personally throttle a Hun," Kiffin said.

"You really hate the Germans," Charlie stated, rolling over and sitting up.

"At first I didn't. When we went into combat the first time back in the fall of '14 I imagined the German boys being pretty much like us. You know, scared guys just doing their duty. Then one of our corporals got caught between the lines. I was with the squad when it happened. Didn't I already tell you this?"

"If you did I must have been asleep. I did a helluva lot of that in the hospital when we used to trade tales, remember?"

"Yeah, more than we seem to get here!" Kiffin said, ducking involuntarily at the whistling passage of another Big Bertha round. "Anyway, we're behind a stone wall by this Chateau the first day we moved up to the lines. Near a hole in the wall a German patrol surprised us. I think they were as surprised as we were, because they fired wildly and began to run back to their lines. The corporal grabbed us and started after them. We got about a hundred meters from the wall when the Heinies started firing a machine gun. The corporal dropped, but he was still alive. He shouted for us to go back. I didn't want to leave him there, but he wouldn't let us move him. He didn't seem to be hurt that badly, but he knew that if we stayed there we would all be cut down.

"A sergeant sent one of the men to the regiment to ask for artillery support. What a joke! We were so green and so exhausted that any chance of coordinating artillery was out of the question. Besides, it was getting dark. We would go back for the corporal as soon as it got dark.

"Then we heard a hideous scream. We scrambled to the wall and strained to see in the failing light. There, not more than maybe two hundred yards away we could make out some figures up on the hill. They were laughing and stabbing the corporal over and over again. His cries stopped, but their cackling replaced it, taunting us. We fired everything we had in their direction, but kept hearing that mocking filthy laughter most of the rest of the night.

"I couldn't imagine what kind of monsters would torture a wounded man and laugh like that. I shook in fear and anger at our helplessness." Kiffin said before continuing pensively.

"Our resident poet, Alan Seeger, put it better than I could. He called it 'a diabolical cry, more like an animal's than a man's, a blood-curdling yell of mockery,' or something like that. He wrote it down too, saying he saw all the evolution of centuries leveled in that cry. He compared it to the yell of the warrior of the Stone Age over his fallen enemy and called it an 'antidote to civilization.'

"I knew from that moment that I was no longer a neutral volunteer serving out of some sense of honor and glory. I felt vengeful. I became engaged. It has taken me a while to stop seeing all Germans like those pigs, but, frankly Charlie; I have no sympathy for a race that can produce such evil."

Charlie tried to picture the situation and compared it with his own first combat experience. "You know, Kiffin, Rejik wasn't even a German, but his treachery had a similar effect on me. It made me hate war. It didn't bother me to kill him and the Huns, but I still don't hate Germans. Kinda hard to do when you are half German yourself, you know?"

"Damn! I didn't mean you, Charlie. I mean, you are American even if you have some German heritage." Rockwell stopped. After a minute or so, he began to reflect aloud.

"When I was a kid I remember my granddaddy Ayres telling stories about the War of Northern Aggression. He would get all worked up about the damned Yankees and make me see northerners as some kind of—what was the word I used earlier?—monsters. It never occurred to me that men on both sides of that bloody war were Germans, English, French, whatever. Just sitting here talking about it with you and realizing what I have allowed myself to feel makes me a little sad."

Charlie couldn't see Kiffin's face in the deepening shadows. "I forget about being German most of the time. Maybe I'm too young and naive. I never knew my grandparents on my father's side. Dad told me his father had been in the Franco-Prussian War. He wasn't pleased about me coming over here, but would you believe he told me he was proud of me fighting his brothers and fellow countrymen? Makes you think, doesn't it? Ah, Kif let's go to bed. All this heavy thinking makes me sleepy."

Chapter 34
Pour Les Siècles Des Siècles

Paris, January 31, 1916

Two other V. 97 men died in the bombing attack that terrible night. A Zeppelin bombed Paris at about the same time killing thirty civilians. Everyone in V. 97 swore oaths of vengeance. Jack asked to be one of the Cartier's pallbearers.

Most of V. 97 had to remain on duty at Le Bourget, so their commander arranged a funeral Mass and ceremony for the three men on Sunday before putting Cartier's coffin in a hearse for the drive to Paris the next morning. Madame Cartier accompanied the body in another car. Jack rode next to her. The widow sat stone-faced hugging her two boys who sobbed quietly.

At least a hundred mourners came to the graveside ceremony in the Père La Chaise Cemetery in Paris where the Cartier family shared plots with some of France's greatest poets and artists. Jack noticed dozens of men in the Ambulance uniform, and Piatt Andrew himself showed up with an ambulance full of flowers. Jack was surprised to see Jim McConnell in the crowd.

McConnell was finishing up his *chasse* qualification when he got word of Cartier's death. He got a short *permission* and caught a train for Paris arriving in time for the funeral that Monday morning.

Other friends joined Jack to carry the coffin to the waiting bier beside the grave. Jack watched the honor guard standing at attention waiting to fire their salute, thinking about doing that duty under more detached circumstances at Pau. The *aumonier*, the Catholic chaplain for the escadrille, said the prayers at the grave. The priest spoke of the kingdom of God and life everlasting, ending each prayer with the words, *pour les siècles des siècles*. Jack stood with the other pallbearers turning those words over in his head. *Forever and ever.* Looking at Cartier's bereft wife, Jack wondered how many more of these he would face before this craziness ended.

Jennifer, in Paris only days, had come to the funeral at Jack's invitation. He wasn't sure if it was such a good idea, but it was the only way he would get to see her. She came with Michelle, both of them wearing long black dresses with dark veils over their faces. Though they didn't know Cartier, all women dressed similarly for the too often repeated ceremonies held all over France since August of 1914.

"*Pour les siècles des siècles*, Amen," ended the chaplain, the signal for the firing squad. Jack kept looking at the little boys thinking how they would do without a father. Cartier's wife could always re-marry. She was a feisty little woman. The honor guard folded the French tricolor. When they handed it to him instead of to Madame Cartier, he didn't know what to do at first. Then he realized that they were giving him a chance to say a few words to the widow. Jack simply handed the folded flag to Madame Cartier saying how proud he was to have served with such a brave hero of France.

"*Merci*, Jack," she said. "Cartier was equally proud of you. Thank you for being here now. I will treasure the fact that my husband was buried with an American friend's assistance. You will always be welcome at our door."

Jack listened, hearing and understanding every word. At that moment, he could not have said whether she had spoken in English or French. He realized then that his two languages and his two countries had become as one.

He expected to have to return to Le Bourget almost immediately so he politely excused himself. He forgot about Jim McConnell, Piatt Andrew, and any other acquaintances in his rush to see Jennifer. She hugged him excitedly.

"Michelle says you have to go back, but perhaps we can come with you?" Jennifer asked.

"Yes, Jack," Michelle said joining them. "I have a motorcar from Fleury, a chauffeur, and a free afternoon. We can go to Le Bourget and maybe stay for a couple of hours."

"Splendid idea!" Jack exclaimed. "I'm not on the schedule until tonight."

Jack hadn't talked to Charlie since they'd left Cazeaux, so he anxiously asked about him once they were on the road. Both women replied at once.

Michelle brought him up to date on Charlie's news from RGA. "Apparently he and Rockwell are flying nearly all the time," she said.

Jack felt a little jealous. He had only flown ten hours in two weeks. He almost wished he were at Le Plessis-Belleville until he remembered he'd have missed the funeral and seeing Jennifer.

Jennifer told him about her work at Neuilly. "It is not very difficult so far since they only have me assisting the more experienced nurses. Oh, I almost forgot! I have something for you from Nurse Wilson." She pulled a framed photograph out of her bag and handed it to Jack. It was a picture of him getting his Croix de Guerre! How had she come by that?

At the entrance to the field at Le Bourget Jack left them in the automobile while he rushed off to find Lieutenant Granger to obtain permission to go into town for a couple of hours. He returned out of breath but beaming. "I have all afternoon! Let's go."

Michelle directed the driver to take them to *Le Cigogne*, a well-known restaurant in Le Bourget. They passed the rest of the afternoon eating and talking pleasantly as if no war darkened the horizon. Jennifer wanted to hear more about flying. Jack described his better flights at Pau, talking about dancing in the clouds with the snow-capped Pyrenees for a backdrop.

"You do sound like a writer, Jack," Michelle said. "Don't you think he has a way with words, Jennifer?"

Jennifer looked at Michelle for a long second before looking at Jack, almost dreamily, sighing, "he does have a way."

"When will I see you again?" he asked Jennifer at the gate to the field.

"That's up to you Jack. I could come again on a weekend. Michelle says there's a local train that stops here."

Would you? I mean, I would love to see you. Can I telephone the hospital? Does Sister Wilson still guard the telephones?"

"Please do call. Mildred Wilson has taken me under her generous wings. If you get her, she will be able to find me. Thank you for inviting me here. I was a little frightened at the cemetery, but I thought you were marvelous with Madame Cartier," she said warming and encouraging Jack.

"I have to go," Jack said. "Bye Michelle. Thanks for suggesting *The Stork*. The food was only a little less pleasant than the company. Give my respects to Monsieur Fleury." He leaned into the car to shake Michelle's hand, reaching over Jennifer. Then he pulled back and kissed Jennifer gently on the cheek. "*Au revoir, et à très bientôt*!"

BACK IN THE ESCADRILLE MESS, the building that served as both bar and dining room for V. 97 pilots and observers, Jack expected a subdued funereal atmosphere. On the contrary, he found the place hopping with action. The gramophone scratched out some French singer with a strong accordion background. Four men hovered at the pool table, and the little bar had a throng around it with men smoking and drinking. Nobody seemed to be mourning Cartier or the other two deceased NCOs. Probably better that way, Jack thought.

He wandered over to the bar and asked for an orange soda. As one of the duty crews, he had to stay awake until eleven that night. Even though they didn't fly missions after dark, the crews could take off to clear the field. Since the bombing attack, they had done two emergency evacuations, flying to the lighted field at Orly, south of Paris. These had been Jack's first attempts at night flying. Landing at night didn't seem too difficult on a lighted field. Judging height was challenging. He had bounced the Voisin to the ground very hard, but, fortunately, Gabriel Voisin's machines could take rough handling better than others.

Sitting on a stool at the end of the bar, he began to muse about the day, the funeral, and the conversation with Jennifer and Michelle in the restaurant. Suddenly he remembered that he hadn't even said hello to Jim McConnell! He didn't even think to look for Jim. He wondered how he could get a message to McConnell. He had to be at Cazeaux by now or back at Pau.

The routine at Le Bourget grated on Jack. He had entirely too much time on his hands, and they only flew at the most two hours a day. For one reason or another, the Germans seemed to have turned their attention to London and its environs, dropping incendiary devices from Zeppelins at night. For V. 97 it meant long hours of standing by and doing nothing. Jack wrote letters until his hand was sore and calluses formed on his middle finger where the pen rubbed. He got a call through to McConnell's school the day after the funeral, leaving a message. Dreaming about Jennifer helped him while away some hours.

Two of his fellow pilots received orders that week. One had instructions to return to Avord for a month of training on Nieuports. The other was bound for a line squadron near Compiègne, not too far to the north. Leaving V. 97 seemed to crush the Frenchmen. The defense of Paris was the perfect assignment. You seldom faced any enemy. The delights of the city were readily at hand. The duty never taxed flyers, and one could fly as little as one wanted.

These fellows puzzled Jack. He couldn't understand wanting to be held on the ground. There were men in flight school who were so afraid of flying that they went to great extremes to avoid having to get in an aircraft.

February wore on ever so slowly. Daily rain and gray skies didn't help the mood and morale of V. 97. The paths between the buildings rapidly turned into streams of mud that the men covered over with duckboards. Conditions on the flying field weren't so easy to fix. By filling the ruts with sand brought in from a nearby quarry, the workers just barely stayed ahead of the mud. What had been a grassy pasture now resembled a pigsty.

Flying when weather permitted entailed lengthy preparations to get the Voisins into position for take off. After each flight, ground personnel dragged the machines through the mud to the hangars where they cleaned them meticulously before putting them inside. Even a little accumulated mud on an undercarriage could affect the flying characteristics of the big Voisins. They were among the only airplanes built with metal instead of wood in their framework. Other than improved motors, the Voisin remained little changed from those in service in 1914. They were neither acrobatic nor fast, but they were reliable and stable in flight. A French pilot achieved one of the first recorded aerial victories in a Voisin against a German Aviatik. Those of V. 97 carried two machine-guns suited for defending against slow bombers or airships. Jack considered the mission and the machine a total bore, but Lieutenant Granger liked him and had refused to submit Jack's requests for transfer to a Nieuport escadrille.

Jennifer spent the first Saturday of February with Jack and took the last train back to Paris at nine o'clock in the evening. On the next and following weekends, she stayed overnight in the apartment Lieutenant Granger, maintained in town with his young wife. The Grangers treated Jack like an officer in spite of his sergeant rank. Jack's heroic feat at Pau had circulated quickly in the escadrille. Indeed, it was one of the reasons the lieutenant didn't want to let Jack go. He relished having an American in the unit, and a decorated one at that. But Granger saw how the repetitious duty and bad weather wore on Buck. He made a point of keeping him as busy as possible. His best idea was to put up the American girl to give them more time together.

"How do your parents handle both of you being over here, Jennifer?" Jack asked after attending Sunday mass with her at the old church in Le Bourget. "It must be almost too much for them."

She shuddered at the scene she had created when she finally announced her plans to leave. John Keeler hadn't gotten over Charlie's enlistment at the time. Letting his nineteen-year old daughter follow her brother bordered on sacrilegious to him. Angelique, on the other hand, took her daughter's part just as she had with Charlie. She told her husband that she too would go to France to volunteer if she could. Eventually, Michelle's gentle reassurances at the wedding that she and the Fleurys would look after Jennifer in Paris got John Keeler to back down.

"Dad changed his attitude then, Jack," she told him. "I was mortified at the friction I'd caused and the only major fight I'd seen my parents have. Dad actually gave me money. Charlie says dad told him he was proud of him. Something good is coming of all this."

"I'm glad you're here. Charlie told me what your dad said. He was very surprised."

"We all were. When the war started, dad was a wreck. He started drinking heavily and got really mean, especially to Charlie. He'd never been very supportive of him, acting like Charlie was a bum no matter what he did."

"I've seen that in some of the other volunteers. Seems that the fathers are seldom happy with their sons."

"Well, I don't know about that, but the change in dad was remarkable. I probably wouldn't be here were it not for the wedding, Michelle, and you, Jack Buck."

"Me?" he asked.

"You and your brother made an impression on them, especially dad. He told me he approved of your folks keeping Larry back. But, let me be honest. I wanted to come before I knew you. After we met, nothing could stop me."

Jack beamed at hearing that. Jennifer's work at the hospital matured her rapidly. The carefree young girl he had met and escorted up the aisle at Charlie's wedding seemed more serious each time they got together. It reminded him of how carrying his first wounded soldiers made him feel. When he mentioned it she took his arm and began to talk.

"It's not the wounds or the amputees, Jack, it's the gas victims. We can do so little for them. It's so frustrating to see men burned and blinded and barely able to breathe. Do you know what phosgene does to a man's lungs? It's horrible. They are burned and blistered *inside* where no doctor or nurse can go to ease their pain. I never learned about these things in nursing school. We saw burns—terrible burns—but never anything like what mustard gas does. Oh, Jack, how can men be so uncivilized?"

He knew she didn't expect an answer. He hadn't had to deal with gas victims during his time in the ambulance service, but drivers became detached or risked losing their minds. He had distanced himself almost clinically from the hideous things he had seen. His fertile imagination never let him fully turn off the natural curiosity that causes humans to stare and want to see the very things that make them sick. He'd never seen anybody at the instant a bullet or piece of shrapnel struck. He hadn't had a man's brains splattered on him as Charlie had described. He knew that the British and French were using gas just like the Germans. His intellect kept reminding him that this war was brutal, offering little in the way of the noble.

After seeing Jennifer off at the train station the night of the 13th he spotted a familiar face.

"Chouteau! Hey, Johnson! It's me, Jack Buck."

"Lord Almighty, you half frightened me out of my wits!" Johnson said, a big smile coming to his face as he recognized Buck. Jack had been quite the celebrity at Pau. Even though Johnson had started a full month before Buck, he had just finished Pau at the end of January and Cazeaux before reporting to V. 97.

"Let me help you with your sack," Jack said, excited to have another American coming into the escadrille. "I'm sure glad to see you. It's been kind of dull around here."

"Dull? Didn't I hear that you guys lost three men a couple of weeks ago?"

"Yeah, and one was old Cartier."

"No! Not the motor sergeant? How did he end up here? Do you have an ambulance section here?" Chouteau asked.

Jack explained on the ride back to the field. He told Johnson 'dull' in this case had nothing to do with being attacked, and everything to do with being impotent against a night flying enemy.

"Don't know about that, Buck, but I've seen a friend of yours at Pau."

"No kidding. Not Haviland?"

"The very same! He was just starting training when I left for Cazeaux.

"Clyde Balsley's coming here. He got a 72-hour pass in Paris. So it looks like you'll be having more American company."

"That's great Chouteau, but I'm afraid you guys won't like it here any more than me. You hear anything about the American squadron?"

"As a matter of fact, guess who showed up at Pau for chasse training before I left?"

"Bill Thaw and Nimmie Prince?"

"I can't even have a little surprise with you. Oh yeah, you were in the States with them on that famous promotion trip, weren't you? Well, wise guy, Prince wasn't there. He doesn't start for a couple more days. Thaw was alone."

"Were Charlie Keeler and Elliot Cowdin with them? Thaw and Prince were supposed to do *chasse* qualification as soon as we got back. I haven't talked to or heard from them since. Did Thaw tell you any news?"

"Well, according to him—and I'm just saying what he told me—some French guy named Flanders or something like that had just dropped a bomb on the bureaucracy. Apparently the French are about to approve the *Escadrille Américaine* because of this guy's intervention."

"I'll be damned! Flandin did it!" Jack shouted, nearly missing the turn for the gate. He told Johnson about how the Flandins had befriended him and Willis Haviland when they first arrived in France. "I just talked to Monsieur Flandin before coming here. Would you believe I asked him for help in getting the escadrille approved? He did it!" Jack whooped again, pounding on the steering wheel as he pulled to a stop at the headquarters.

Johnson, Balsley, and Buck, all veterans of the Ambulance Service, were reunited in V. 97. Jack welcomed the company, but the flying routine continued to drag. Lieutenant Granger kept throwing bones in Jack's direction to keep him happy. He had visions of making him into a flight leader and even trying to get him a sous-lieutenancy.

One of the tasks Granger assigned Jack was to ferry one of their machines back to Issy-les-Moulineaux for an overhaul. Jack would stay in Paris for the three or four days while the factory put the new Constantescu hydraulic interrupter mechanism on the Voisin and replaced the engine. Finally, the old birds would be able to shoot through the propeller.

Jack called the hospital as soon as Granger confirmed the mission. After talking to the formidable Wilson for a minute or two, he asked her to put Jennifer on the telephone. Jack told her not to come to Le Bourget that weekend. Something had come up, he said, purposely lowering his voice.

"What is it Jack? You don't have orders do you?" Jennifer said a little panicky.

"No, no, nothing like that. I'm coming there!" he burst out.

"Goodness, Jack Buck, don't you ever scare me like that again!"

"I'm sorry. Maybe you don't want me to come to Paris?"

"You're incorrigible, Buck! Of course I want you to come. When will you arrive?"

"Tomorrow. I'm flying in to Issy-les-Moulineaux to the Voisin factory. Do you know where that is?"

"I barely know where to find the bandages in this little hospital. Is it far from here?"

"No, maybe ten minutes. I'll be staying with the Flandins if they will have me. It won't be as cozy as the Granger's apartment, but I have four whole days. Do you think you can get some time off?"

"I don't know, Jack. I have Saturday and Sunday in any case. Can you come to get me after you get in?"

"With pleasure, mademoiselle. If you aren't there, I just might go out with Mildred Wilson. I hear she has a warm place in her heart for me."

"I'll be there. Sister Wilson sends her love," Jennifer said loudly enough for the other woman to hear.

Jack found Jennifer's sense of adventure and spontaneity refreshing and exciting. She was neither fragile nor retiring. Indeed, she was the most aggressive woman he'd ever met, not counting Mrs. Walker, who was aggressive in a different way.

Jennifer knew more about Jack than Jack knew about her. Charlie had tried to caution his sister without poisoning the way for Jack. She wasn't sure how to deal with his other romantic experiences, but he was nicer to her and treated her more respectfully than any other man she had known. Her striking blond hair and stunning good looks always drew admiring stares. She had grown weary of attention fixed on her physiognomy more than on her person. Jack made her feel different. She trusted him. Unlike some of the young men back in Saint Louis who had tried to paw her on a second date, Jack had been a perfect gentleman—almost to her vexation. *Well,* she remembered, *at least until she let him know it was all right to hold her.*

Jack's four-day pass started out with a near disaster.

Chapter 35
Out of the Sun, Pushing up Daisies in Hunland

Le Plessis-Belleville, February 21, 1916

"At 0715 hours this morning the Germans began an attack against our fortresses near the city of Verdun. The bombardment before the attack has only just stopped, making it at nine hours long, the longest of the war. Our forces are holding in spite of heavy losses," the bespectacled captain read the official report to the pilots and service personnel. He paused, removing his glasses and rubbing the bridge of his nose before continuing. "Aviation has not been able to influence this new battle yet due to foul, foggy, and rainy weather. Without aerial observation, our corps is blind. We have no special instructions as of this afternoon, but expect some reassignments in the next two days. No questions please," he finished, leaving the crowd murmuring.

"Looks like the fun's about to start Charlie," Kiffin said as they walked out of the hanger and lit up cigarettes.

"Certainly sounds ominous. Imagine a nine-hour prep? Those poor guys had to have taken a beating. My ears rang for days after the measly ten-minute preparation they dropped on us. Where's Verdun anyway?"

"I've never been there, but I think it is near Metz."

"Which is not far from Pont à Mousson where my unit was. Now that I think of it, I remember seeing a sign for Verdun on my way to Arras and your regiment. It had to be somewhere east of Metz. Boy, if the Germans get through there, they could cut France in half diagonally."

"Never happen, Charlie. Old Joffre beat them at the Marne and he'll do it again unless I miss my bets."

"You sure have a lot of confidence in the old man and the French." Charlie didn't share that feeling. He had seen the best and the worst of French soldiery in his stint in the legion. One thing he was sure of, the French wouldn't give up much of their precious ground and would spare no amount of blood to heave the Huns back.

"Something in their spirit has me convinced that they will prevail no matter what the cost," Kiffin said. "This probably means we'll be getting to line units soon."

"Does sound like that. I hope they don't split us up. What does Paul say about the all-American unit?"

He hasn't written much. A little preoccupied like someone else I know. I think I'm going to try to get some leave and go back to Paris to check up on him *and* my *marraine*."

"After this announcement, do you really think they will let you go?"

"It won't hurt to ask."

The next day Charlie saw his name on the assignment list for N. 65, a Nieuport escadrille. Kiffin's request for *permission* came through as well. Except for the trip to the States, he and Kiffin had been together for ten months.

Nieuport 65 occupied a field near Malzéville, northeast of Nancy. The escadrille was one of the newest in a line of units being formed almost daily by the French Army to meet demands fueled by the growing battle in the Verdun region. Charlie heard that its commander handpicked all of his pilots. Surprised and flattered, he wondered what had earned him such a distinction.

Charlie's pending reassignment meant he moved into the Nieuport acrobatic and gunnery section for his last flights. This section concentrated on refining skills, often from a list provided by the receiving escadrille commanders. N. 65 demanded high proficiency in patrol work.

Charlie reported to the Nieuport Section for a dawn patrol. He would be flying the third aircraft in a flight of five. Their mission was to protect two Caudron *réglage* or artillery adjustment aircraft. For this mission, the French were actually firing live artillery onto a range at Camp de Mailly some 100 kilometers east of Le Plessis-Belleville. The Caudrons would direct the fires of two batteries of 75-millimeter howitzers. Both aircraft and batteries were equipped with wireless sets, an experimental effort to improve on the older method of flying back to an observation post and dropping a message containing corrections. Balloon observers used wire to telegraph adjustments. Using radio made sense, but was limited for air use because of the bulk and weight of the transceivers.

The Caudrons took off first. Charlie's flight departed ten minutes later. Climbing to three thousand feet, the five Nieuports took up their respective positions in a line called *echelon left.* The leader formed the flight by dipping his left wings. Number two climbed and tucked in at a distance of about fifty yards from the leader. Charlie repeated the maneuver sliding up under number two's left wing. Numbers four and five did the same until the formation looked like a line slanting off to the left rear in a stair step stack below the patrol leader.

They continued their climb to four thousand feet where they caught up with the Caudrons. The Nieuport leader signaled with another wag of his wings, causing the flight to break up into three elements. The leader climbed to the base of the clouds keeping the other aircraft in sight. His job was to oversee the whole operation. In real combat, two fighters would perform this mission at the highest possible altitude to provide early warning of any enemy aircraft and drive them off if possible.

Number two in the flight, an aerial combat veteran, peeled off with Charlie to protect the northernmost Caudron. Numbers four and five went south with the remaining observation machine. The Caudrons descended to 1,000 feet to be able to make out the targets in the impact area, in this case, empty petrol barrels stacked randomly and painted brightly in different colors. Once in position, the observers radioed a Morse Code message to initiate firing.

Charlie and his element leader went to 2,000 feet and took up a wide orbit in the opposite direction of their Caudron below them. Their job was to intercept any intruders and keep them away from the Caudron long enough for the observation machine to escape to the safety of friendly territory. In practice, the observation machines seldom strayed very far over enemy lines, preferring to remain over the French anti-aircraft batteries. The protection aircraft had to keep an eye out for enemy pursuit aircraft as well as each other and other friendly machines. Given all the moving elements, the mission was complex even without enemy intervention.

Though the orbit routine quickly bored Charlie, he was fascinated by the way the Caudrons were able to direct the artillery. He could see the target area and make out the stack of blue target drums. The first pair of rounds landed well to the northwest of the target. Charlie realized from his classes that this was short and left of the target along the firing direction of the howitzers. The Caudron radioed its correction. The next pair of rounds landed southeast of the target—now over and right on the gun-target line.

This is what the artillerymen called *bracketing* the target. The observer thought he had it close enough, Charlie noted when six rounds landed in the fire for effect volley. At least one struck the barrels, but the rest landed to the northwest. Charlie, noting the time, groaned that they still had an hour on station. As he droned on, he began to imagine the barrels as real soldiers. Having been on the receiving end of artillery, he shuddered in his seat at the destruction men wrought upon other men.

The mission ended with a long and detailed critique. Representatives from the artillery unit came to discuss results with the observers. The flight leader and overall mission commander began the post-mission debriefing.

"What seemed to most of you like a cakewalk this morning, was really a very complex mission. By keeping its respective parts separate, each of the elements of the mission—the artillery, the observers, and the cover aircraft—performed their jobs somewhat independently. We, of course, left out the anti-aircraft artillery today, but don't forget it has an important role both in protection and in signaling. Before I turn to the leaders for comments, let me remind you, especially you *chasse* pilots, that there was no enemy to disturb your lazy circling. How many of you saw other aircraft during the mission, other than ours, that is?"

No hands went up. All looked at each other knowing the captain had to have a reason to ask, assuming the air had been cleared for their training mission.

"Just as I thought. I noted *twenty-three* different aircraft above and below us, en route, on station, and on the way back. Most were within two kilometers. Had any of them been Boches, they could easily have interfered in our little show. Even the combat veterans among you need to keep this in mind. When you get so focused on your mission that you are no longer able to see anything else, you won't." He let that sink in before adding, "And that will be the guy that gets you."

The chatter in the room increased when the captain stepped down. None could believe there had been that many other aircraft that close to them. It humbled Charlie. He felt arrogant and guilty. He told himself he had to wake up and pay attention no matter what the situation.

That afternoon the same five Nieuports flew another escort and protection mission. This time they were to protect a photographic reconnaissance machine, a specially modified Henri Farman two-engine biplace mounting a large camera on the side of the fuselage near the observer. The Nieuports broke up into flights of two and three. Because the slower Farman would be over 'enemy' territory for a good twenty minutes, the chasse aircraft were there to keep enemy fighters away.

For this mission, the French threw in another twist, an 'enemy' patrol of two Morane Saulniers whose mission was to get the Farman. While armed, no one was to fire except in the case of self-defense against a clearly identified enemy.

The flight formed over Plessis and split into two for the escort mission. Charlie followed with the mission commander. They climbed to 6,000 feet where they could watch the rest of the flight and pick off any intruders attempting to attack the Farman. The Aube River ran east to west in the mission sector, simulating the front lines, and the Chateau de Fontainebleau, southeast of Paris was the reconnaissance objective.

During its time over the lines, the Farman was not unlike a stray sheep. Should the wolves discover it, it would be easy prey. Charlie's team, like shepherds and sheep dogs would drive off attackers.

Arriving at the Aube River, Charlie stretched his imagination to see it as a trench line. Everything looked so peaceful from 6,000 feet. The low flight of three Nieuports maintained its position off the left wing of the Farman only 1,000 feet below them. Charlie and the other chasse pilots vowed not to be caught sleeping this time. All of them craned their necks in search of the Morane Saulniers. Charlie counted dots in the air off to the west, probably traffic going into the field south of Paris. He also noted a flight of Nieuports thousands of feet above them going in the opposite direction.

The Farman flew straight for the magnificent grounds and park around Fontainebleau. He should be getting some good photographs, Charlie thought. He looked west for any other aircraft, but the descending sun blinded him. Wondering if the captain was thinking the same thing, Charlie tried to get the officer's attention by sliding up on his leader's left side and wagging his wings, pointing into the sun.

Just as the Farman over flew the chateau, a Morane-Saulnier dove down from the west out of the sun. The lower trio of Nieuports reacted slowly, barely cutting the attacker off before he got within range of the Farman. Meanwhile, Charlie and the Captain turned into the sun to try to find the other Morane. Charlie began to worry that they would run head-on into the other 'enemy.' He couldn't see forward except by shielding his eyes with a free hand. He had all he could to stay on the captain's wing. His concerns about colliding with the Morane Saulnier continued to grow when all of a sudden the other Nieuport rolled right and dove sharply away.

Charlie initially thought the captain was turning to avoid collision. If he followed, he could fly right into the Morane. When he didn't see an approaching aircraft, Charlie realized that the captain hadn't been turning to avoid collision, but to pursue the other 'enemy.' Evidently, the other aircraft had begun its attack on the Farman when the lower flight began its attack on the first Morane Saulnier. This second attacker knew there were two other Nieuports out there, but he hung in the sun as long as possible in order to get an unobstructed run on the Farman. He almost made it, too.

The captain avoided turning in front of Charlie. His dive and steep turn brought him around but some distance from the attacking Morane. He pressed his machine to its limits hoping to cut off the Morane pilot, but he had lost too much time in the turn.

Charlie dove left towards the Farman. He only eased out of the power dive when he felt the Nieuport Bébé buck, a sure sign that the wing fabric would soon peel off. He could see the Farman, now turning for the Aube to the north. No sign of the captain. The other three Nieuports were mixing it up with the first attacker who was screaming south as fast as he could. Charlie searched for the other enemy plane. He adjusted his dive and turned back a little to the right when he saw Morane Saulnier number two diving on the Farman! The Farman observer waved his gun in the direction of the pursuing Morane Saulnier, but close to 2,000 yards still separated them, too far for their weapons to do much to each other.

Charlie closed on the Morane Saulnier in seconds. He held the other aircraft in his sights for a good ten seconds before pulling up performing an Immelman turn that gave him another hundred feet advantage and reversed his course. By the time he closed for a second attack, the Morane had gotten into range of the Farman, but Charlie again crept up on the rear and zeroed in on the other aircraft from a distance at which he couldn't possibly miss. By then, the Morane Saulnier pilot noticed Charlie and the captain who had caught up and joined in the attack. Convinced he had beaten them to the prize, the Morane pilot wagged his wings and broke off the engagement.

Charlie landed, sweating profusely. His flight suit was soaked. He remembered the frigid air at 6000 feet and couldn't ever remember feeling warm. What had caused the sweating? He also noticed his pulse seemed to be racing, not unlike it had during the fateful patrol between the trench lines over a year earlier. Obviously, he had been fired up during the mission. The signs were all there. He felt drained.

At the critique, the second Morane Saulnier pilot argued hotly with the crew of the Farman, telling them they were dead. When the captain took over to begin the formal debriefing, his first question wasn't who had 'won' the conflict, but how many other non-mission aircraft the crews had seen. After all the excitement of the chase and hide and seek, the pilots looked at each other as if the captain was crazy.

"At 1615, I saw a flight of three Nieuports at about 8,000 feet going north," Charlie said, consulting his kneepad. "At 1620 I noted considerable aerial activity to our west, probably over the field at Orly. During our disengagement," he stopped to look at his pad again, "I think I saw some Voisins, at least two, well to our south. Could be students from Buc on their navigation triangles."

"Bravo Keeler! Anyone else?" The Captain looked around shaking his head and clucking his tongue. "Gentlemen, I told you this morning to keep your eyes open, and to be careful not to get too focused on the mission. Keeler here not only listened, but he saved the day. Our friend Lieutenant Gaston very nearly got the Farman, but he would have been dead long before he could have pulled the trigger thanks to Keeler."

Charlie had only fired once from an aircraft due to his truncated course at Cazeaux, so he welcomed the chance to ground fire on a bad weather day. The motors weren't even started. Crews rolled them to the firing station, oriented the machines so that the guns were pointed down range and turned them over to the pilots.

He carefully verified the rounds in the magazine on his Lewis gun, mounted dead center on the upper wing. He chambered a round by pulling back on the charging handle. Sliding back down into the pilot's seat, he tested the tension on the Bowden cable, an ingenious system of pulleys and eyelets that enabled the pilot to fire the weapon from a button on the control stick. Satisfied all was in order he raised his left hand indicating that he was about to fire. He squeezed off a four or five round burst and released the trigger before firing another shorter three round volley. There were only 47 rounds in the magazine of a Lewis machine gun. It took just over six seconds to empty the drum of its .303 ammunition, so the pilots learned to fire short bursts.

For their last flights before joining their units, the Nieuport section leader, *Capitaine* Franck, devised a series of tightly controlled dogfights. In the morning, the pilots had to fight one-on-one, usually against an experienced cadre member. Franck told them they would try two-on-one and three-on-one in the afternoon if the morning went well.

Charlie drew the captain as his first opponent. Franck told him not to think about whom he was fighting, but about what he was trying to accomplish. No question of choice here of whether or not to fight. No chance of evasion. No sneaking up on the other. They would take off together, climb to 10,000 feet, and engage in combat. The only rule all had to follow was to remain at least 50 yards from the other aircraft. They exchanged signals for breaking off the engagement and indicating emergencies.

Charlie harbored no illusions about beating the captain. He just hoped to hold his own. Once level at 10,000, Franck signaled the beginning of the first combat. When they pulled apart, Franck's Nieuport suddenly whipped up until it hung on the propeller, motionless for a long second or two. Charlie raced past and wing-slipped to the right to try to catch the captain in his inevitable descent.

Franck did descend, tail-first until he dropped the nose and began a screaming dive. Charlie raced to keep up, gaining slightly. Just as the Nieuport entered his sights, it zoomed upward. Charlie watched Franck loop over the top of him and lock onto his tail. If he stayed there, he would be done for. Instead of doing the expected, a sharp maneuver to the right capitalizing on the torque of the motor, Charlie abruptly pulled up, causing his Nieuport to point at the sky in much the same way as Franck's maneuver. The captain undershot Keeler who, still copying his superior, slid back on his tail, dove, and whipped around in a loop that placed him on the captain's tail.

Franck saw this last maneuver with only a few seconds to spare before Charlie would have been in range. This time he twisted to the right in a corkscrew that caused him to lose almost five hundred feet, throwing off Charlie's aim. Franck then struggled for altitude while Charlie again closed in for the kill. Thinking he had the captain, Charlie held off just one second too many. He couldn't believe Franck could drop so quickly, but the other Nieuport stalled and tumbled off in a spin. The only way he could keep up would be to do the same thing.

Franck leveled off at 2,000 feet and took his bearings. He'd lost Charlie in the spin. It is simply too difficult to overcome the forces on one's body in such a violent maneuver. Where did Keeler go?

Charlie kept an eye on Franck's Nieuport as best he could during his own spin. When he saw the captain begin to pull out hundreds of feet below him, he centered his controls. As his altimeter approached 2,000 he saw the other Nieuport making "S" turns, obviously looking above and below for Charlie. Since they were at the same level, Franck missed seeing Charlie for several critical moments. Just as he rolled out of one of his turns, he caught the flash of the sun glinting off Charlie's windscreen. The kid was on his tail! How long had he been there? Signaling to break it off, Franck pointed his machine back at RGA, leading his conqueror back.

"You are a natural, Keeler. When you bring all of your skills and talents to bear, there aren't many who can touch you. Tell me, had you done any of those maneuvers before? Not the standard stuff, the tail slide into a loop, you know."

"*Non, mon capitaine*. I only copied you. I knew I could neither outsmart nor outfly you, but I could follow your lead. You could say that you taught me to beat you this time. I know it is just a fluke."

"Not at all, my young American friend. You are the first ever to get on my tail and stay there. I have eight Boches confirmed and at least as many pushing up daisies in Hunland that nobody saw. Never have I been so relentlessly pursued. It must be your youth. My reactions aren't as fast as yours anymore. Mark me closely, Keeler. You are very good. I am proud to have flown with you. Now get out of here. Forget about this afternoon. I can't deal with being killed twice in one day. Good luck in N. 65. Gonnet-Thomas will take good care of you. He ought to. He doesn't know what he is getting yet. *Bonne chance, et à bientôt*."

Charlie fairly floated to the Bonne Rencontre to pack up his things and wait for Kiffin. He telephoned Michelle to tell her he was done and on his way. She sounded especially excited, saying something about having some news for him. Kiffin showed up just in time to catch the three P.M. train for Paris.

Chapter 36
Unfriendly Fire in the City of Light

Paris, February 25, 1916

The news of the start of the Verdun battles caused a real stir in V. 97. Those doing their best to avoid combat were alarmed. Others, like Jack and his fellow Americans, were excited that they might now be able to get to a line unit.

Both Johnson and Balsley came to Jack's section. Lieutenant Granger gave Jack the mission of orienting them. Here he was, not even a college graduate, giving an alumnus of the great University of Virginia an orientation on the defense of the great city of Paris!

Johnson was as self-effacing as Mac. Balsley turned out to be close to Jack's age. He had attended the University of Texas without graduating. They hadn't seen much of each other in the Ambulance Service because Clyde arrived two months after Jack and had spent a good deal of time in Paris as a mechanic before going out as a driver. Jack liked Clyde right away. Everybody did. The guy had absolutely no pretense about him. He smiled easily and brightly. His handsome features, full mustache, and gangly posture combined with a Texas twang to make a most pleasant impression.

Jack took Clyde up in the observer's seat of one of the escadrille Voisins. He pointed out the key landmarks around the field before landing and taking Chouteau up for the same quick orientation. Next, they linked up with their observer/gunners for a longer flight. Jack briefed their route of flight, reminding Johnson and Balsley of the landing pattern at Le

Bourget in the event that they were separated. He asked the observers, all experienced men, to point out anything of interest during the flight.

They flew north to Compiègne and then southeast in the direction of Soissons. Jack was careful to stay in their operational area of responsibility and not drift too far in the direction of the front lines. From Soissons, he turned south to Chateau Thierry and then back east to the city before angling northwest to Le Bourget for the landing. Back on the ground, both Balsley and Johnson professed themselves impressed.

Friday the 25th, Jack departed Le Bourget in the Voisin for Issy-les-Moulineaux. Since direct flights over Paris proper were forbidden except for very specific reasons, Jack planned his flight around the north and west sides of the city. He'd calculated it to be a thirty-minute flight. He'd packed the observer's station with his gear and some trading materials the mechanics had given him to take to Issy. He flew west for ten minutes from Le Bourget until he spotted the big loop of the Seine River northwest of the city. When he turned south, he could make out the Eiffel Tower, the Arch of Triumph, and Montmartre. Expecting a quiet and eventless flight, Jack relaxed and tried to identify the places on the ground that he had frequented during his ambulance days.

Nearing the suburb town of Neuilly, Jack saw the white building of the American Hospital across the river. He had to stay on the west or left bank of the Seine. He kept the distinctive fortress on the top of Mont Valérien to his right between him and the river. Letting down to 500 feet he aimed at the Pont de Saint Cloud, his final reference point before landing at Issy-les-Moulineaux just southeast of a loop in the Seine. A loud pop and a puff of white smoke startled him. Another bang and flash to his left front followed closely by two more just to his front shook the Voisin. Damn! They're firing at *me!*

Looking right towards Mont Valérien he saw a stream of tracers lacing up in his direction. *Lord Almighty,* he thought, *they must think I'm a Boche.* Flipping the Voisin on its side, he hoped the big cocardes would be clearly visible on the undersides of his wings. Instead of stopping, the firing increased, pinging on the metal struts of the Voisin as rounds found their target. More anti-aircraft fire rocked his craft. He felt something hot against his back. Reaching behind he fetched a still hot piece of shrapnel sticking through his wicker seat.

Enough of this horseshit! his mind screamed. He dove the Voisin down over the river and jumped over the rooftops of Boulogne. The firing stopped. He cut the motor just as he cleared the trees. Dropping onto the small field, a mixture of gendarmes and armed soldiers rushed out to surround him. *What in the hell is going on?*

An aging gendarme, brandishing a shaking revolver, ordered him to descend. Soldiers ringed the Voisin. Other gendarmes grabbed him as he got out and held his arms lest he try to set the machine on fire.

"*Je suis sergent Buck de l'Escadrille V. 97*!" he protested to unheeding ears. The gendarmes handled him roughly looking for his weapon. Jack didn't even have a pistol. The pilots in V. 97 drew them for operational missions. Since Jack was going to be on administrative leave while the machine was modified, he had come unarmed.

Once they got him into the security building and finished searching him, they discovered his *carnet de vol*, his French Pilot's logbook, and license.

"*Mais, c'est un Français, celui là*," one of the gendarmes observed. Finally, the lieutenant colonel in charge of the military facility arrived. He had just come from the aircraft.

"There has been a terrible mistake, *sergent*," the colonel began. "A general alert went out last night that the Germans had captured some of our aircraft intact and that they were going to try to infiltrate our defenses and bomb the Palais Royal or bridges on the Seine. Our panicky National Guard reported your flight over Neuilly. No one thought to check with us. They opened fire and dispatched a security team here when they saw you coming down. It didn't help that your aircraft has no markings on the bottom or sides."

"No markings! But how could that be?" Jack said, unaware that the escadrille mechanics had stripped the markings in preparation for a new paint job. They counted over forty holes in the aircraft including the one from the *éclat* that had heated up Jack's backside. He found a deep crease in his left boot from a round that must have passed through the cockpit. Even after the mistake had been cleared up, the old gendarme didn't seem convinced until he learned that Jack was an American.

"Monsieur, I am so sorry. I was so set to capture a German spy. You had an accent and that blond hair. I was sure we had a live Boche."

"Think nothing of it, *grandpère*. I'm just glad I *wasn't* your Boche. I'm sure it would have gone badly for me otherwise."

The excitement over, and the damage limited to the aircraft and the pride of the trigger-happy defenders of Paris, the colonel asked Jack to join them for lunch. Jack declined, asking only to be taken to the American Hospital.

"*Bien sûr, sergent*. You are hurt?" the colonel asked, alarm in his voice.

Jack quickly reassured him he was not injured, in spite of the number of rounds that had hit the Voisin.

Because of the damage, the officer was not sure they could have it ready for Jack in four days. He promised to notify Jack's escadrille. Jack pictured with some amusement how the officers and men of V. 97 would react when they learned that he'd been shot up on a milk run!

Mildred Wilson came around the reception desk to give Jack a hug. "Mr. Buck! You are a sight for sore eyes. Come to take that lovesick girl off my hands for a few days, are you? Good, good. What is this I hear about you being the source of all that shooting and fireworks this morning?"

"That? Oh, it was nothing," Jack said. "Let me look at you. Why, you have lost weight! Just as beautiful as ever!" He kissed her cheek and skipped away deftly before she could bear hug him like she had with Pavelka. "Now where might I find the lovely Miss Keeler?"

"I'm here, Jack!" He heard her voice behind a screen. Jennifer stepped out in her nurse's uniform. It was the first time he had seen her in it, and he swore she looked like an angel. "Miss Wilson, do I have your leave to depart with this man?"

Mildred Wilson smiled brightly. "Miss Keeler, we got along without you before. I think we can manage for a few days without you now. How long will you be here, Jack?"

"Four days at the least. Now that they turned my machine into a sieve, I may get a couple of extra days, but I won't know that until Monday."

"A sieve, huh? And nothing happened, right? Oh, you men! Very well. Jennifer please call in Monday, but I don't want to see you here until this young man has to leave."

He took her straight to the Flandins for lunch. Pierre insisted on meeting her and readily agreed to put Jack up during his stay in Paris. After lunch, Jack would take Jennifer to the Crillon to see Michelle and Charlie. For the moment, all he wanted to do was savor her beauty, and hold her hand.

"SO MICHELLE, MY DEAR SWEET WIFE, WHAT NEWS HAVE YOU?" Charlie sank in the armchair pulling Michelle down onto his lap.

"Remember our first honeymoon night?" Michelle squirmed on Charlie's lap in a manner that left no doubt of her desire for him.

"What part," he asked, "the crowded train, the bumpy ride?"

"No silly. What did I tell you before our first lovemaking?"

"Let's see. Something romantic for sure. You liked my chest. That's it. You said you were glad I wasn't hairy as an ape!"

She punched him playfully in the chest and put on a little girl frown.

"You really don't remember, do you?" She said, pouting.

"Well, you did say we could make a baby.... Michelle! Is that what you are getting at?" Charlie became very agitated, taking her face between his hands, looking tenderly into her eyes.

She looked down and nodded very slowly, bringing her eyes up to his to see how he reacted. Her expression looked so apprehensive that Charlie feared she might not be well. He held her face in his left hand and stroked her hair with his right.

"So it's true! We are going to be parents! I am going to be a father! Oh Michelle, Michelle, are you all right?"

"You aren't upset?" she asked. "It's all right with you, I mean."

"Upset? Good grief, how could I be upset? This is great news! I just don't know what to say."

"I haven't told anyone, not even Jennifer. I saw the doctor after I missed my last period. It's only a week now. I couldn't wait to tell you, but I couldn't do it by mail or telephone. If you had not been coming here this weekend, I would have come to you. Are you sure you don't mind? I will get fat you know."

"Michelle, I will always love you no matter how you look. I didn't realize it could happen so quickly. I guess I imagined us settling down with children after the war..." he let his voice trail off.

"Not the best of times to be bringing babes into the world, is it husband? What do you want, a boy or a girl?"

"A boy, of course, but I'll settle for a girl. I really never thought about it. Shouldn't we be celebrating?"

"We are. First, you are going to help me out of these clothes so that you can see me while I'm still skinny. Then we are going to, you know.... Later, we dine with the Fleurys, Jack and your sister, and make our little announcement. Sound good to you?"

She kept squirming in his lap, which added to the sexual tension and encouraged him even more. It was time to act, not to talk. He felt an almost spiritual sense of excitement as he took Michelle slowly and lovingly. She had to reassure him that he wouldn't hurt her or the baby. Her responsiveness and energy testified to that.

MADAME FLEURY LOOKED FORWARD TO MEETING JACK BUCK. She already treated Charlie like a son, though only ten years separated them. Michelle had been with the family so long that Béatrice Fleury thought of her like a younger sister. If Buck was anything like Keeler, she knew she would approve.

When she wasn't off to Le Bourget visiting Jack, Jennifer Keeler spent much of her free time with Michelle. Madame Fleury found the polite young woman refreshingly naive. Jennifer's efforts to master French were coming along slowly, but Béatrice Fleury enjoyed speaking English. Béatrice, daughter of the Count de Beauvais, had lived a very sheltered life, protected first by her father's title and money, and then by the fortune Alexandre Fleury amassed before they were married. She overcompensated in doing numerous charitable acts and volunteering her time. It put a strain on Fleury's security team. Since the attack on Michelle and Charlie, he'd had to double the force.

Jennifer showed Jack the way to the Fleury suite in the Crillon. The trappings of wealth fascinated Jack. Neither envious, nor overly impressed, he was learning the difference between good taste and tawdriness. At the Flandins' everything had its place, and Berangère's arranging made their wealth seem subtle, understated. While only in the Walker's place for several hours, he had noticed the almost deliberate ostentation. Everything spoke of recent wealth. He seldom noticed such things as statues and classic paintings, but in Claudine Walker's salon, they all but screamed to be seen.

A muscular, dark-haired man greeted them and smiled pleasantly upon recognizing Jennifer. Jack expected a much older man.

"This is Paul, one of the security men I mentioned. He's a Russian expatriate, but he speaks some French."

"Bonjour, Paul," Jack said offering his hand. The Russian didn't take his eyes off Jennifer. He wasn't purposely ignoring Jack, but it was obvious he considered Jennifer's companion an unwanted intruder.

"I guess he doesn't like me," Jack moved just a little too fast for the Russian's taste and found himself pinned to the door with his right arm bent painfully up behind his back. Jennifer shrieked, which brought Béatrice Fleury and Alexandre rushing into the foyer.

"An intruder?" Fleury asked, seeing only the back of a man in uniform. He quickly realized that Buck had run afoul of Paul Koniatev, the hotheaded bodyguard. Fleury immediately ordered the man to release Jack, apologizing profusely. He assumed the Russian thought he was doing his job. Fleury didn't get cross, noticing that Jack didn't seem to be hurt. Jack was embarrassed at being taken out so quickly. Rather than make a scene, he politely offered his hand again to Koniatev. The Russian scowled, and left the room.

"I'm terribly sorry, Jack. This is no way to be introduced to my home and family. I will have to speak to Paul. He is very protective, but far too quick to resort to violence. With all our young men in service, we have to use foreigners far too often. What Koniatev lacks in social graces he more than makes up for in vigilance."

"Forget it, Monsieur Fleury. No harm done and no offense taken. I think your man is sweet on Jennifer. I must be very unwelcome in his eyes."

"Ah, yes. It seems that all our security people are interested in Miss Keeler's welfare," Béatrice Fleury interceded before introducing herself to Jack.

Jack almost did a double take. She was a brunette version of Claudine Walker! He sputtered the word *enchanté,* resisting the urge to rub his eyes.

"What's the matter, Jack? You look as if you have seen a ghost." Jennifer said; thinking that Koniatev may have shaken Jack up more than it first appeared.

Just then, Michelle came out with the two Fleury boys to see what all the fuss was about.

"Ah, Jack, our best man…is something amiss?"

Alexandre quickly explained the tousle with Koniatev.

"I told you, Alexandre!" Michelle said. "He leers at me, Jennifer and Madame. He may be a great bodyguard, but I've said from the start that he is going to be trouble. I'm sorry he attacked you, Jack. He almost did the same thing to Charlie."

"I'll bet Charlie decked him," Jack laughed, trying to relieve the tension.

"Actually, I had to step between them to protect my husband." Michelle said provoking a laugh from all of them at the ludicrous image.

"Enough of this," Béatrice Fleury said. "We may want to let Paul go, Alex. But, for now, let's try to show Jack a little more hospitality."

Jack followed obediently, still dazzled by the resemblance of Madame Fleury and Claudine Walker. They could be sisters! If she was, would Claudine betray him?

"Where is Charlie?" Jennifer asked, not having seen him since he left for Le Plessis-Belleville.

"He went ahead to the restaurant," Fleury answered. "He's meeting an American Army officer from your Embassy." Fleury had reserved a large table for six at *Maxim's,* just around the corner from the Crillon.

"Major Parker met us the night we returned to Paris, Alexandre. Don't you remember? He is attached to the American Observation Mission. He works out of the American Embassy now. I think Charlie just wanted to pay a friendly visit, but Parker told him he had something to discuss," Michelle explained.

Presently, Michelle and Béatrice took Jack's arms and led him into the apartment. He glanced around at the furnishings and wall hangings.

This was a hotel after all, but it seemed that the Fleurys had imparted their own flavor to the decor. Indeed, it had a very orderly but lived-in look. The boys' room was impeccable except for a single toy on the floor. They offered a chair in the *salon à séjour*, or living room, and stuck a glass of champagne in his hand. Jennifer sat down beside him and rubbed the arm Koniatev had twisted. Jack's head was still spinning.

Maxim's took them less than five minutes to reach on foot from the Crillon. Jack looked for Koniatev, but a different security agent had come on duty. If he could get the Russian alone, he thought he might be able to make a friend. The man couldn't be faulted for liking the women. If he was equally protective in a real threat, Jack thought, the Fleurys were in good hands.

Jennifer slipped away from him and rushed to her brother. Standing at the table with Charlie, the man in the uniform of an American Army officer smiled at the group and introduced himself in impeccable French. Fleury asked him to stay for supper, but Frank Parker declined, saying he was meeting his wife in Neuilly for dinner with another American couple.

As Jennifer and Charlie separated, she picked up Parker's last comment.

"Oh, I'm sorry, Major, I'm Jennifer. Did I hear you say Neuilly?"

"Hello, Miss Keeler. Charlie told me you were beautiful, but the word doesn't seem adequate to the reality. I wish *my* Jennifer were here to meet you all. Maybe we will see each other another time. You work at the American Hospital? Perhaps you have met Christine Wheeler? She does volunteer work there."

"Mrs. Wheeler is an angel. I have learned more from her than all my lessons in nursing school. What a coincidence that you should know her. Isn't her husband a doctor? I remember her saying he'd been wounded fighting in the Foreign Legion. Imagine a medical doctor joining guys like my lunkhead brother to carry a rifle?"

"Oh sisterly love, how fleeting you are," Charlie interjected.

"We heard about your glorious entrance to the city, Jack," Parker said smiling and shaking Jack's hand. "They were getting ready to evacuate the Embassy when you landed at Issy."

"Seriously?" Jack said, genuinely surprised the incident had reached such proportions. "Excuse me, Major. It is nice to meet you, sir. Is the United States any closer to getting into this war?"

"If the Germans sink any more civilian ships we may have a different situation, but for now, I'm afraid we remain on the sidelines. I've been talking to Charlie about flying. Perhaps we can talk sometime. Please look me up." Parker took his leave.

After he left Jack leaned over to Charlie to ask what the major wanted.

"He says the French are working on the issue of an American squadron at the highest levels. Parker thinks they have already approved the concept. Maybe we will be together after all, Jack."

"I just know I have to get out of V. 97. We grow moss on our tires. I fly only a couple of hours every other day. That little fracas today got my heart going again. If it weren't for Jennifer, I think I would die of boredom."

"I'm on orders to N. 65." Charlie told him.

"You lucky dog! A Nieuport escadrille too! How did you do it?"

"Nothing I did myself. Plessis is a real hole. I've gotten some good training there, but you aren't missing anything at RGA. Kiffin will still be there for a while. Have you talked to him or Paul?"

"Are you kidding? After the forces of Paris failed to bring me down, I wasn't about to let anything else hold me back from fair Jennifer. What news do they have?"

"I don't know, but I think they are in cahoots with Doctor Gros. Ever wonder how they will decide which of us will go to the American unit?"

"Charlie, we are talking too much business here," Jack observed.

A waiter came to take drink orders. Jack whispered to Charlie, "I will be damned upset if they don't take both of us and Rockwell and Chapman, too. Thaw is a sure choice and Cowdin too, since they have been flying longer than the rest of us. Let's talk about this later, okay?"

Jack hardly noticed the food, a wonderful menu ordered ahead of time by Fleury. Jennifer sat across from him. Their eyes locked in an almost physical embrace of dancing gestures.

After the last of the dishes from the main course disappeared, Charlie and Michelle asked for everyone's attention.

"We want to tell you something special," Charlie said in English.

"Something we hope will bring you as much joy as it has us," Michelle added in French.

"Michelle is expecting."

"We are going to be parents."

Fleury slapped Charlie on the back and Béatrice kissed Michelle's bright cheeks. Jennifer's smile suffused her face with joy. Only Jack seemed subdued. Jennifer noticed his reticence.

Later that night, after the Fleurys retired and the Keeler couple moved to their room, Jennifer sat with Jack in the foyer. She was staying in the

Fleurys' guest room, her home away from the hospital dormitory. It was their first truly private moment since he'd arrived.

"A strange night for you and a very unusual day, isn't it Jack?"

"You could say that. I'm still recovering from being nearly shot down by our own people, wrestled by a Russian bear, taunted by a beautiful blond, and shocked by my best friends." He didn't add the surprise of Madame Fleury's resemblance to Claudine, but it still troubled him.

"Why shocked, Jack? People do have babies after all. What's so strange about that?" She held his hand and nuzzled her cheek against his shoulder.

"Charlie and I are the same age. I just can't picture myself becoming a father now. Something about this stupid war makes imagining tomorrow difficult let alone nine months from now."

Jack stood up and took Jennifer in his arms. Kissing her first on her forehead, he let his lips find hers. They held onto each other, eventually sinking back onto the couch. Jack wanted to prolong this fluttering joy. Sometime in the midst of a kiss, Jack's mind crossed an imaginary boundary. His body had led him into the arms of Marie and then Claudine. Now he felt a powerful restraint.

They lost track of time. The night guard disturbed them during one of his rounds. At two-thirty, Jack reluctantly pulled himself away and said he was going to leave. They kept this up for at least another hour, kissing and holding on to each other. It took Jack all his remaining energy to get up and say a final good night. Jennifer felt like a limp rag doll willing to do anything he wanted.

Only after he stepped out into the cold early morning air did Jack recover some of his composure. He floated the four blocks to the Flandin residence. Pierre insisted that he could come in at any hour. Jack let himself in and quietly wended his way back to the familiar room he had used on several other visits. He barely unbuttoned his tunic and slid off his shoes when he dropped off to sleep.

Soon he began to dream. He saw Marie and Dombasle with a whole brood of children. Then he ran into a naked Claudine, arms outstretched, chasing him. He woke, or thought he woke, to find himself standing at the open gravesite of someone important to him. He couldn't figure out who it was. He looked at the faces around the freshly dug grave, but all the men looked the same and all the women were covered in black with veils over their faces.

The graveyard scene dissolved. He thought he was awake, though he realized, or thought he realized, that he was still in bed somewhere. Deeply asleep again, Jack began to see people who had died. First, he saw his grandfather, a man he never knew since he died before Jack was born. Then he met and talked to Chérie de la Croix de Valois. She smiled brightly and handed him a flower, telling him not to worry. George Masters appeared wearing clerical vestments. He blessed Jack. Jack fought his way to consciousness some time later, checked his watch, and forced himself to remember where he was.

At nine, Pierre Flandin knocked to ask Jack if he would like breakfast. Jack roused himself and uttered, "*Oui, merci.*" He sank back on the pillow trying to sort out the meaning of his crazy dreams. He languished a few more minutes, thinking about Jennifer and their embraces, but his reverie was clouded by the lingering images. He'd have to write it down.

He cleaned up and joined Flandin. The older man smiled and shook his hand, asking whether it would be French or English that morning.

"French, I think," Jack said.

"You look a bit worn out Jack. Has the flying been that demanding?"

"No, not at all, unless you count being attacked by the Paris National Guard."

"What a disaster! If they had shot you down at least we could rest assured they were competent. How glad I am you were not hurt."

They continued their conversation over coffee and fresh baguettes. Berangère was at the market, Pierre explained, and Isabelle remained in the South of France under a physician's care. They discussed Haviland, now almost through flight training. Jack let Pierre know that he really appreciated his intervention in trying to get the American squadron approved.

"You know about that then?" Flandin asked.

"Not really. One of the Americans mentioned your name. We were just talking last night about which of the Americans would get to go to such a unit."

"I cannot tell you that. All I did was plant a bug in the ear of the Minister of War. He is a good man, if a little slow. Getting Americans into a separate unit, I told him, would have the effect of telling the world whose side your country is on in this mess."

Jack pumped Pierre for more information until Berangère returned. She wanted him to stay the day, but he took his leave, thanking them and promising to come back later with Jennifer. Mentioning her name made him even more eager to get back to the Crillon. He wouldn't let Koniatev get the jump on him twice.

Chapter 37
L'Escadrille Américaine Finalement Approuvé

Malzéville, March 1916

Nieuport 65 had only been in existence for several weeks when Charlie reported. He got a warm welcome and a cup of coffee, and then found himself on his own. He decided to take a walk around the escadrille. Maybe he would run into someone he knew. At the flight line men were painting distinctive unit insignia of a Grim Reaper on the new Nieuport 11's.

Charlie soon learned that his assignment was no accident. The commanding officer, Lieutenant Gonnet-Thomas, came from the same *promotion* or class at Saint Cyr as Capitaine de Lattre, Charlie's first French commander. The lieutenant said he would be happy to have an entire squadron made up of American pilots, but urgency in his current mission limited his recruiting efforts. Getting Keeler was a major plus. Charlie not only had great marks from flight training, but he was a decorated veteran of infantry fighting. Gonnet-Thomas knew that men who had been in the thick of the ground fight were more sympathetic with the plight of the poilu. They would fight harder. Charlie's reputation and the fact that he was already a *sergent* earmarked him for patrol leader and potential commissioning.

Charlie soon met and exceeded Gonnet-Thomas's expectations. By the end of March, Gonnet-Thomas put Keeler up as a patrol leader. In ten combats, Keeler had acquitted himself well. He had at least one probable victory, though no official credit was possible because the Boche went down deep in German-held territory. Charlie attacked with a measured deliberateness.

Charlie was not the only American in N. 65. Elliot Cowdin arrived the day after Charlie. This was Cowdin's third Nieuport escadrille since October. He'd gone to N. 38 for about a month and then transferred to N. 49 just before their trip to the United States. Charlie found it hard to warm to Cowdin. The man didn't seem to encourage friendship, perhaps because of the difference in age and station in life. Elliot kept to himself when he wasn't trying to impress the officers.

Cowdin also caused Gonnet-Thomas a bit of discomfort. While the man had come from N 49 with nothing but positive reports, something in his demeanor both in the air and on the ground wasn't right. Cowdin, like Charlie, was already a *sergent,* but unlike Keeler, who had earned his rank on the ground, Cowdin got his for hours of flight. Where Charlie was affable and a natural leader, Cowdin was content to let others bear responsibility and make decisions. Perhaps the single most irritating thing Gonnet-Thomas saw in Cowdin was his boastfulness and propensity for currying favor.

Louis Gonnet-Thomas was particularly happy to get Bill Thaw at the end of March. Now he had the most Americans in a single escadrille in the entire French Army. Thaw had been with him in Capitaine Brocard's escadrille. Brocard met Thaw before the war at one of the international flying competitions and had helped get Thaw, Hall and James Bach into aviation back in December 1914.

The lieutenant remembered Bach especially. The man had indirectly cost him his captaincy. Bach, unfortunately, now languished as a German prisoner, the first American captured by the Germans. Gonnet-Thomas had given Jimmy Bach and a French *sergent* named Mangeot a difficult mission that turned sour on them. The two flew a pair of specially trained saboteurs across the lines to a point in German-held territory. The saboteurs, dressed in civilian clothes and familiar with the region, had the mission of blowing up a key rail terminal and bridge. Bach and Mangeot landed without problem, discharging their passengers and then repositioning for takeoff. Bach got off and circled the field to wait for Mangeot. Mangeot's Caudron failed to clear the trees and crashed. Bach immediately landed and loaded up the unhurt French pilot. Bach's second takeoff met with the same fate as Mangeot's first. The two, still unhurt, managed to evade the Germans for several hours. When the Germans caught them, they questioned them about the second seats in their smashed aircraft. Both then were charged with espionage and tried. The trial received enough attention that Bach's fate became common knowledge, especially after his acquittal. Gonnet-Thomas still felt a twinge of guilt for his part in Bach's abbreviated aviation career.

Bill Thaw came from *chasse* training after a short stop in Paris. He brought Charlie a box packed by Michelle and Jennifer.

"Finally, the French have approved forming an all-American escadrille from men already flying with combat units. It's a good thing I did my *chasse* training now or I wouldn't be one of those chosen."

"Are they sending them here like you?" Cowdin asked. "Kind of makes sense, doesn't it? I mean with three of us here and all."

"I don't think so. N. 65 is already engaged, trained, and doing a tough job. I think they are trying to organize something from the ground up," Bill Thaw answered.

"Will we all go? Who decides?" Charlie asked.

He was happy to see Thaw arrive. Unlike Elliot Cowdin, Thaw never flaunted his wealth. Since marrying Michelle, Charlie had entered a new stratum of society, but the change was subtle. Thaw made him feel comfortable. If Jack, Bill Thaw, Rockwell, and McConnell got to come, it would be almost perfect. Chapman too, he thought. Charlie wished Antonelli had gone into Aviation.

"I don't know, but Charlie," Thaw asked, "what did Michelle send? Are you sure she doesn't have a sister? Too bad you don't have another sister, too. Why do guys like you and Buck have all the luck?" Thaw, who had a beautiful French *petite amie* back in Paris, was just being pleasant.

April brought some of the heaviest fighting around Verdun. N. 65 began flying three patrols daily after moving to a field northeast of Suippes. Gonnet-Thomas now had a bit of a dilemma. Both Cowdin and Thaw had more flying hours than Keeler. Thaw was clearly one of the most experienced pilots and an excellent leader, but he had just come from *chasse* training. He wanted to make Keeler *chef de patrouille*, patrol leader, a step away from becoming an officer. He decided to give Charlie the afternoon patrol on April 3. Gonnet-Thomas himself would fly one of the Nieuports and his most senior NCO would fly the other. If Keeler performed as expected, Gonnet-Thomas intended to recommend him for promotion to *adjutant*.

At 10,000 feet Charlie turned northeast, crossing the Meuse and the lines just north of Verdun. He'd briefed a route that would put them over the most frequently used corridor for the German patrols supporting the Verdun battle. A mixture of Pfalz and Albatros fighters harassed the French observation machines regularly in this sector.

Charlie began a slow left-hand turn to initiate the mission. They were setting up the equivalent of an ambush in the air. Instead of hiding in trees or foliage along a known path and waiting until the enemy entered the kill zone to open fire, Charlie tucked his flight up against a bank of clouds and dodged in and out of the wispy fringes. The location of French observation flights and balloons helped predict where the jastas would try to penetrate. Charlie expected the enemy to operate from about 8,000 feet. Friendly photographic missions worked between four and six thousand feet.

After seeing nothing for the first twenty minutes on station, Gonnet-Thomas was afraid Keeler wasn't going to get to show his stuff. Then Charlie's Nieuport wagged a quick 'follow me' and shot up into the cloud layer. Flying blind with only occasional glimpses of the ground required total concentration, especially for those following. Charlie kept his movements slow while in the clouds. His 180-degree reversal and descent out of the clouds were equally smooth. When they emerged in a shallow dive Gonnet-Thomas could make out Charlie's prey, a flight of four Albatros fighters, now only a couple of kilometers away and no more than five hundred feet below them.

Charlie's clever move into the clouds kept the patrol from being detected. His reversal, timed to put them on the Germans' tails, worked out perfectly. Though outnumbered, the patrol had total surprise on its side. As agreed, Charlie would open fire on the rearmost enemy while the adjutant and Gonnet-Thomas attacked from the sides. Once the German's reacted, it would be every man for himself. Charlie waited to spring the ambush until he was only one hundred meters behind the unsuspecting Albatros. He hit his trigger and watched the lethal stream of bullets pour into the fuselage. The shots alerted the German who immediately fell off his left wing, trailing smoke. Charlie decided not to follow him down. He attacked the lead aircraft instead, lacing its left wings until the Lewis stopped firing.

Gonnet-Thomas and the adjutant took on the remaining two while the fourth Albatros either fell to Charlie or quit the fight. When Charlie shot his last round at the leader the other two were too busy to see what he was doing. Charlie rocked the Lewis gun back on its hinged arc, reached up into the slipstream with his left hand, and twisted the drum loose. Happily, it came off at his first attempt. Only twenty seconds elapsed between his last shot and the magazine pulling free. At that instant, rounds began to spatter against his upper wing, one tearing the empty magazine from his hand. Not having time to reload his spare, Charlie turned into his attacker, hoping to cut off his line of flight. Whipping his head around, he saw not one but two Albatros fighters on his tail!

Charlie cranked the Bébé hard to the right and down, extracting as much assistance from the motor's torque as he could. The maneuver caused his pursuers to overshoot him. By the time they had reacted and returned to the attack, Charlie had reloaded the Lewis gun. He let them get close enough to open fire before pulling abruptly up and looping over the top to arrive on the tail of one of the Germans at the end of the loop. A burst of about ten rounds sent the first enemy into a spin with flames coming from the upper wing. *Must have hit his gas*, Charlie thought. *Thirty-seven rounds left in this can. Have to make every one count.*

Kicking hard on the rudder bar brought the nose to the left enough to engage the second Albatros. This one did not intend to stand still. Charlie's first volley went wide. The Albatros nosed down and turned to run for home. Charlie followed, trying to draw another bead on the fleeing enemy. He fired a longer burst. The German showed no sign of being hit and none of wanting to fight. Charlie tried one more volley until the Lewis stopped abruptly. While banging on the receiver with his mallet, Charlie searched the skies for other aircraft. He'd lost his patrol and he was about to lose his Albatros. Cursing under his breath, he checked the time. He had less than thirty minutes fuel remaining. Time to break it off.

Charlie landed at Suippes with barely enough fuel to taxi to parking. He felt terrible for having lost Gonnet-Thomas and the adjutant, hoping they had landed safely.

"The lieutenant! Where's the commander?" he asked the mechanic helping him down.

"Why, he and the adjutant have been back for almost twenty minutes. They will be happy to see you, Keeler. Congratulations! You have two confirmed already. Did you get any more?"

When Charlie dropped off to sleep that night, he had reason to be proud as well as tired. Gonnet-Thomas swore he'd never seen such skill in the air. Instead of losing his patrol, Charlie had flushed a large ten-ship flight headed for the French balloon line. The first four they'd bounced were the high cover for the other six. In downing two of them, Charlie had forced the Germans to abandon their attack. Gonnet-Thomas and the adjutant chased the others down to 6,000 feet. The Germans tried to lure them into a fight with the other six. Instead, the flight of six broke up into twos. Apparently, one pair went after Charlie after he had brought his second ship down. Not seeing this, Gonnet-Thomas lost sight of Keeler's aircraft and departed reluctantly with thirty minutes fuel remaining. Keeler's performance that day earned him two palms to his Croix de Guerre.

In the next several days, the pace began to tell on the pilots. A corporal in Thaw's flight smashed up his Nieuport when he overshot the field at

Suippes in the dwindling twilight. The man broke his collarbone and received a serious slash on his left cheek. On April 5 the escadrille lost its first pilot in a combat over Etain. In a week, they lost two more.

Charlie's skills sharpened on every flight. Where he could pick out another aircraft at about a mile's distance when he arrived in the escadrille, he now regularly detected and identified machines as friend or foe at distances of up to three to five miles. Unfortunately, at least for Gonnet-Thomas and N. 65, they were about to lose Charlie and his compatriots.

"FINALLY!" JACK SHOUTED, WAVING THE ORDERS POSTING HIM and Balsley to the *Réserve Général Aéronautique.* "Clyde, get your things, we leave today!"

Jack returned to V. 97 with the refurbished Voisin after five glorious days in Paris. They ate fabulously. The Flandins gave them tickets for the Opéra one night. More importantly to the young couple, they fell hopelessly in love.

Charlie left for his new squadron on February 27, so Jack went out of his way to include Michelle in their outings. Michelle handled Charlie's posting to a combat escadrille better than Jack expected. When the time came for Jack to leave, he felt terrible. The thought of being separated from Jennifer drove him to distraction. *How did Michelle and Charlie deal with their separations?* Jack wondered.

During a quiet moment when he was alone with Michelle after Charlie left, Jack screwed up the courage to ask her if Madame Fleury had a sister, perhaps a twin.

"You have met Mrs. Walker then?" Michelle asked. "Claudine married that lout and hasn't been the same since. Béatrice is her sister. Not twins, though the resemblance is remarkable. Why didn't you mention this to her yourself, Jack?" she asked a little coyly.

Jack fidgeted. Michelle feigned shock that Jack might have fallen into the clutches of the lascivious Claudine. He tried to shrink, feeling guilt and shame while being thankful that Jennifer wasn't there. His flushed face gave him away. What would Michelle think of him now?

"I am outraged, Jack Buck!" Michelle said, playing him along and prolonging his discomfort.

"I'm sorry Michelle, how did you guess so quickly?" Jack asked, his head hanging in genuine shame and remorse.

"I didn't have to guess, you silly oaf. Claudine is the black sheep of the Beauvais family. She wasn't always that way, but that ass Walker turned her into a real predator. Her prey is younger, virile men. When they moved to Pau and the war started, Claudine became like a cat in heat. Don't worry, Jack, I won't say anything to Jennifer. What could I tell her? You still haven't told me what happened. I don't even want to hear. Whatever it was, don't blame yourself. Béatrice thinks Walker will eventually kill her sister if Claudine doesn't do herself in. The woman is unbalanced."

ON MARCH 6, THE GERMANS LAUNCHED THEIR SECOND MAJOR ATTACK against Hill 304 and Mort Homme, names that would become well known. Throughout the first two weeks of March, Jack, Chouteau Johnson, and Clyde Balsley pestered the escadrille commander. None of their requests for transfer left Le Bourget, but at mid-month the situation changed.

The collective efforts of Norman Prince, Bill Thaw, Frasier Curtis, Dr. Gros, and the Vanderbilts, finally succeeded after more than a year of wallowing in the French bureaucratic quagmire. Flandin's prodding of the Minister of War, Millerand, led to the replacement of General Hirschauer as the head of French Aviation with Colonel Henri Jacques Regnier. Hirschauer had agreed in principle to the idea of creating an American unit and even gave it a name, *l'Escadrille Américaine*, but he failed to act on the decision. Regnier not only embraced the idea, but pushed it through the General Headquarters in a record two weeks. On March 14, 1916, he informed Jarousse de Sillac and Dr. Gros, the official heads of the Franco-American Committee, of the approval.

Jarousse de Sillac proposed forming the committee way back in July of 1915. His idea was to assist all Americans flying for France. Gros threw his support behind the idea, suggesting that de Sillac act as President. Mrs. Vanderbilt quickly wrote out a check for $5,000 to support the committee and egged her husband on to contribute another $10,000. De Sillac wisely named William K. Vanderbilt as the Honorary President of the Committee. Gros became the Vice-President as well as attending physician. Eventually some twenty-three influential Americans and Frenchmen participated in the effort. Theodore Roosevelt even wired supporting words and funds. The recalcitrant Hirschauer earned honorary membership along with Robert Bacon. Pierre Flandin joined the committee, but would not accept a position as an officer in order to retain his ability to operate freely in government circles.

At that time there were twenty-two Americans in flight training or in squadrons, not counting the unfortunate James Bach in a POW camp somewhere in Germany. Soon the committee approved enlistment bonuses, prize money for victories or awards, and a supplement to the meager French salary for *all* Americans flying with the French. With momentum building on the organization of the American Escadrille, de

Sillac's committee amassed funds to make their contribution to the welfare of the young American volunteers a significant reality.

Between March 14 and April 20, 1916, the official organizational date of N. 124, *l'Escadrille Américaine*, two parallel efforts advanced the event. Capitaine Georges Thénault volunteered to command the unit, joining de Sillac and Gros in selecting candidates for the escadrille. Initially, there was room for up to nine pilots.

Gros presented the committee's recommendations to Capitaine Thénault in early April. Thénault accepted the recommendations. Thaw, Prince, Cowdin, Rockwell, Bert Hall, James McConnell, Victor Chapman, Jack Buck, and Charlie Keeler were his selections. With the exception of Buck, Keeler, and Hall, all of these men came from prominent and wealthy American families. Of course, Thénault's encounter with Jack influenced Buck's selection.

Colonel Regnier briefed the twenty-nine-year old captain on his special mission. Thénault, Regnier explained, would get a complete issue of new equipment and have his choice of the latest aircraft coming out of the factories. For the first month of the escadrille's existence, Thénault would train and equip the unit while keeping it out of harm's way.

"The first American you lose will be a shock to the entire world and will get so much attention that we may be pressured to break up the escadrille," Regnier explained. "I want you to operate just as the rest of our chasse units, but go slow at first. Use your judgment on disciplinary matters. You know why we have formed this escadrille. Get us some good results, and the publicity will take care of itself. Just remember that you and your valiant volunteers will be under everyone's magnifying glass. When you have problems, see the group commander, and he will get to me if I need to intervene. *Bonne chance*, Georges."

With Regnier's backing, Thénault launched a flurry of orders and requisitions for personnel and equipment. He quickly selected an old friend and former cavalryman, Lieutenant Alfred de Laage de Meux, as his second in command. Snatched from his observation squadron, C. 30, de Laage reported immediately to Paris. Thénault arranged for their first assignment to a quiet sector of the front not far from the Swiss border.

JACK'S ORDERS TO RGA INCLUDED A SUPPLEMENT further assigning him to N. 124.

"It's a new escadrille, Jack," Lieutenant Granger explained, smiling at the American who was so hot for combat. "They will be the *Escadrille Américaine*, your all-American squadron. *Ça vous plaît, mon ami*?"

"Very much, *lieutenant*, but why aren't Balsley and Johnson on the supplement with me?"

Granger didn't know, suggesting that there might be a limit to the number of aircraft. They were probably taking the most experienced first. Why, Jack asked him, did he have to go to RGA if he already had orders to the escadrille? Granger said something about Nieuport refresher training. "After all, Monsieur Buck, you have been flying these old buses for months. A Bébé might take you a little while to get used to again.

CHARLIE REPORTED TO GONNET-THOMAS after the morning mission in support of the French counterattack on the Fortress of Vaux, April 2. When he heard the commander wanted to see him, he began to worry. *What could it be? Not something about Michelle!* Charlie tried his damnedest not to let such thoughts cripple him. Once in the air he seldom had to worry about being distracted, but as soon as he touched the ground, mission stress gave way to worrying about his pregnant wife.

Knocking on the commanding officer's door, Charlie heard a booming "*Entrez*!" In the room stood, Thaw, Cowdin, and Gonnet-Thomas who was pacing angrily behind his desk. Every few seconds Gonnet-Thomas muttered "*merde,*" or something stronger. Obviously, the French officer had a burr under his saddle that somehow involved his three Americans.

"*Sacrebleu*!" Gonnet-Thomas spouted, stopping and sinking into his chair. "How can they do this to me?"

None of the Americans dared ask what was troubling Gonnet-Thomas. He'd finally been promoted to captain. What could be bothering him? They waited silently, stiffly at attention.

"*Repos*!" Gonnet-Thomas commanded, allowing them to relax. "What do you know about this?" He said, holding up a handful of papers. "I am to release the three of you *tout de suite* to return to Paris for reassignment to N. 124, *l'Escadrille Américaine. Ils sont fous, les vaches*! How can I function if I have to give up three pilots all at once, and two of you patrol leaders?"

Glancing at each other, the Americans' smiles provoked another tirade by Gonnet-Thomas. He finally calmed down enough to congratulate them on realizing their dream. His loss would be France's gain, he admitted.

Outside the office the three whooped and hollered, and raced out of the building. Thaw suggested going to the communications center to see if they could get a line to Paris. He wanted to call Dr. Gros to find out who the rest of the pilots were.

"By God, this is great!" Thaw exclaimed. "Together in an American outfit! It's too good to be true." It made them heady to think of themselves as being on the vanguard of true American support of the war, but they had little idea of how much of a wave their little ripple would produce.

Chapter 38
Willingly to Death's Door

Paris, April 16, 1916

Jennifer, Jennifer, what is the matter? Nothing has happened to Michelle or Charlie, I hope?"

"I just missed you Jack. I always cry when I'm happy. You had better get used to it." She wore a blue hat with a dark blue ribbon. She'd arranged her hair to curl up and under just above the high-collared blue dress creating a marvelous contrast of fair skin and golden hair between two fields of blue. Her eyes were only slightly reddened from her tears and offset by the slightest touch of bluish makeup that made them seem larger than normal.

"You look like an angel, Jennifer. All that beautiful blue to match the bright sky. I can almost see you sitting on one of those billowy white clouds waving as I fly by."

"Let's forget the war, Jack. Michelle says Charlie leaves Tuesday with the rest of you. It's just not enough time. What a mess you've made of an otherwise sensible Saint Louis girl. I can hardly bear being away from you."

"There, at least you've stopped crying. We are attracting a crowd. Are we going inside?" Jack said, marveling at the reaction his return to Paris produced in her.

The two locked arms as they moved into the lobby of the Crillon where Charlie and Michelle waited for them with Kiffin Rockwell, Jim McConnell, and Victor Chapman. Jack saw that Michelle was just beginning to show the infant growing within her. He introduced Jennifer to the others, stopping at McConnell and unashamedly throwing his arms around his old friend.

"So we meet again, Bucko!" Jim McConnell smiled.

"Why are you guys all here? What a pleasant surprise!"

Charlie filled Jack in. "We're meeting Thaw, Cowdin, Bert Hall, and Norman Prince in about an hour. Then we go to a farewell dinner at Alice Weeks' apartment."

Jack remembered the woman whose son had been killed in the Foreign Legion. They called her *Madame Légionnaire*. Her door was always open to Americans passing through Paris.

Jack looked at Jennifer and wondered when they would have any time alone. She just smiled at him and never let go of his hand.

"Now I understand why you were so preoccupied," McConnell said, chiding Jack for not even saying hello at Cartier's funeral.

"Guess who my last instructor was at Avord?" McConnell asked the crowd. No one answered.

"Bert Hall, of all people! Why that guy can spin such malarkey that you never know what to believe. Imagine him teaching me to fly a Nieuport. To hear Bert, he practically invented the tactics they now teach.

"Victor, didn't you have Hall for a while too?"

"Yes, but you know how Nieuport instruction works. Bert gives this big speech in broken French, waves his hands in the patterns he wants you to follow, tells another tale, and then plops down in a canvas folding chair with a glass of pinard or pastis while you go off confused as hell about what you are supposed to do," he chuckled and poked McConnell. "Tell them what happened to you."

"Well," McConnell began, "old Bert got himself all worked up one afternoon—a tot too many at lunch I think—and decides he has to demonstrate the maneuver we were supposed to be doing. I think the only reason the French put him there was to speak English to us Americans, but he insisted on mangling French with us as well as with the poor French students. When he gets a few under his belt, his French improves markedly. Anyway, he climbs into one of the Nieuports and fires it up. We all backed away, anticipating tragedy.

"Off he screams into the air, not the least bit wobbly. He loops the loop and barrel rolls right over our heads and then flutters in dead stick to a perfect landing. Impressed, we all run over to his aircraft only to find him sound asleep with one hand on the stick and the other in his crotch. He woke when we tried to pull him out, worried that he might have passed out from the violence of the maneuver. Instead, he stands up unsteadily in the cockpit and continues the story of his last victory. One of the French students went up next and tried to do the same maneuver Bert had done, only to tear off his undercarriage when landing too fast. I guess he wasn't smart enough to pass out on final approach."

The men laughed uproariously. Hall had already become somewhat of a legend, though he never really drank anything. He would undoubtedly be an interesting addition to the escadrille.

Charlie related Jack's story about being shot up and nearly arrested by the old gendarme. When Prince, Thaw, Cowdin, and Hall walked in, the group broke up into another paroxysm of laughs.

"Well, we are in good spirits here, aren't we?" Prince observed. No one offered to explain. Thaw checked the time and said they'd better be leaving. Michelle, Charlie, Jennifer, and Jack piled into one of Fleury's automobiles with the ubiquitous bodyguard and chauffeur. Jack noticed it was Koniatev at the wheel. They met at Mrs. Weeks' apartment at 80 rue Boissière.

When Charlie and the others arrived, they were surprised to find Larry Rumsey, Clyde Balsley, and Chouteau Johnson already there. Rumsey and Johnson had recently left V. 97 en route to RGA. Balsley hoped to be added to the roster with the others and had obtained a short leave to Paris for that purpose.

The whole evening went extremely well. Michelle and Jennifer helped Alice and her staff serve the tables. Naturally, almost all conversation revolved around the new escadrille. Thaw extolled the virtues of Thénault. Jack, who had received his wings from Thénault, added his endorsement.

"There's another dinner tomorrow night at *La Bourdelaise* for all of us," Prince announced. "That's why we have all been brought back here. Thénault will be there along with some members of the Franco-American Committee. I think we will get our marching orders then. Sorry, Michelle and Jennifer. We will have to pull your men away from you for this."

Jennifer whispered to Jack that she wanted him to stay with her that night. From that moment on, he could think of nothing else. He couldn't stay at the Crillon without raising the suspicions of Charlie and Michelle, and, there was Koniatev waiting in the car. He couldn't take her to the Flandins, and a hotel room would be tawdry. Jennifer solved his dilemma on the way home after leaving Mrs. Weeks.

"I have to work the day shift tomorrow," she said when they got in the car. "Do you think the driver could take me to the hospital tonight? Jack can ride along and the driver can drop him at Flandins on the way back."

"I thought you had the day off?" Michelle asked, unraveling from a deep kiss with Charlie.

"Mrs. Wheeler asked me to take her shift for a couple of hours."

"Paul, any problem dropping Miss Keeler and Mr. Buck off after you leave us at the hotel? There's another security man there and I'll have Mr. Keeler with me." Koniatev shook his head, his inscrutable scowl hiding his real feelings.

Jack expected trouble from the Russian when he didn't get back in the car at the hospital, but Koniatev was actually pleased to return without the American. Jennifer spirited Jack up the stairs out of the sight of the night shift head nurse. The third floor was divided into small rooms for the nurses. Jennifer quietly opened her door. It was past two in the morning. She hadn't fibbed about working part of the day shift. She *would* take Jennifer Wheeler's place, but not until noon.

Once inside the darkened room, Jennifer reached for Jack and hugged him closely. Soon they were kissing deeply and longingly, the fatigue of the long day forgotten in their passion. She pulled away to light a candle, leaving the electric light off. Also, off came the hat and the blue ribbon holding her blond hair in place. They resumed kissing, sinking down on the single bed. Neither spoke. Jack began to worry. In spite of his throbbing excitement, he pulled away.

"Jennifer," he whispered, "what are we going to do?"

Her hand slipped from his shoulder and landed in his lap inadvertently, brushing against his hardness. "Oooh! You are so obvious. I mean, can you tell from touching me how excited I am?"

"Jennifer, is this right for us?"

"Answer me, Jack. Don't you know I want you as much as you want me?" She moved his hand to the bodice of the high-necked blue dress. Through the fabric and the stays he could feel the peak of her breast, hard like he was, eager for release. When his hand pushed against her she moaned.

"Jennifer, I, I, I can't do this," Jack sputtered.

"Can't, or don't want to?" She asked.

"You can tell yourself that I both *can* and *want* to, but I don't think we should."

"What, Jack?" She said pulling away from him slightly, her passion cooling with every word of their conversation. "I am not your first woman, am I?"

"Gosh, I've never talked about this with anyone, let alone a girl. Oh, Jennifer. I'm no innocent. It's hard for me to tell you this, but I have been with women, two of them, since I've been over here."

"Did you love them?"

"No, I mean, yes and no." The flickering light of the candle made him feel like he was in the confessional at home in Our Lady of Victory Catholic Church. "There was a widow I met almost a year ago. I'd brought her dead daughter back to her on my ambulance. We didn't see each other for a long time and then I found myself back in the same town. I ran into her totally by accident and we ended going out on a picnic. She was about to enter a convent, Jennifer. *Seriously.* Somehow, things got away from us. We became lovers. She thought of me as her savior. Isn't that a laugh?"

Jennifer just sat, twirling a curl of her hair around a finger.

"Her in-laws treated her badly and tried to force us to marry in order to cheat her out of her inheritance from her dead husband. There is nothing left between us but a fond memory, but I think we helped each other."

"And the other time?"

"Wait a minute, Jennifer. Do I have to spill my guts with nothing from you?"

Laughing, Jennifer looked teasingly at him.

"Don't make fun of me. This isn't easy. Have you been with a man?" He really didn't want to know, not knowing how he would react.

"You are so serious. All right, here are the sordid details. My cousin kissed me and touched me down there when I was about ten. I thought I would die. It was so exciting and so dreadfully sinful. I never let him near me again, but there was something there that made me—how can I express this? It made me aware of my needs. I had many suitors in high school. Most of them were so afraid of Charlie that they didn't even dare try to kiss me. In nursing school, another student introduced me to a college senior who was so sophisticated and so good-looking that I almost fell into his lap without a fight. He turned out to be a cad. We never got beyond wrestling matches, and, once Charlie found out the guy had been pawing me, he broke his nose.

"There was a doctor in nursing school. He acted like he had no interest in any of us girls. All of the nursing students worshipped him. He was single, attractive, and very aloof. I ignored him better than most. I think that was why he began to show interest in me. I was only eighteen, and this guy was already a doctor. He took me to the best restaurant in Saint Louis and treated me like a high society lady.

"We went out for almost two months before he even kissed me. Just before Charlie and Michelle's wedding, he asked me to marry him. I asked him to give me some time to think about it. He agreed, but told me it was time that we moved on to the next 'plane' as he called it. He was smooth and very suave. Before I could protest, he had some of my clothes off, and it was clear to me it wasn't for a physical examination. I decided to go along for a little bit. After all, I was the only nurse this paragon pursued. Maybe he was sincere in his suit.

"I let him take all my clothes off, Jack. Then he disrobed himself. We were in one of the examination rooms with all the lights blazing…."

"Jennifer, you don't have to tell me anymore."

"No, I want you to hear it all. I love you, Jack Buck, and I don't want to lose you because of some stupid misunderstanding.

"So, there we are naked. He touches me almost clinically, like he's admiring an anatomical dummy. Then the esteemed doctor grabbed my head and forced me down to his crotch. He was strong, but I am stronger. I grabbed his testicles and jerked. For that reason, my good man, I am still a virgin. It's not a state in which I prefer to remain, Mr. Buck. That is, if your intentions are noble, and marriage be your goal, I am yours, here and now."

Jack could not believe his ears. Not a word of rebuke, and such unabashed honesty. *Jack, Jack. What are you getting yourself into?*

"What's the matter, Mr. Buck? Are you shocked by a modern woman speaking so frankly about these things?"

"I guess it is a bit much for me to digest. What was it you said? Is that from a play or something? *If your intentions be marriage....* Are we that far along? God knows I love you, but we have only known each other four months."

"Jack, you've transported the sorry wreckage of the battlefield, and I've had my hands in their dying entrails. How much time do we have? You leave in a couple of days for your precious *Escadrille Américaine*. How long will it be before you or Charlie and the others start getting killed?"

"We don't talk like that, Jennifer. The guys consider it bad luck. I never looked at it that way. I guess we all think we're invincible. I really don't see me dying in this war. I don't know why, but I almost *know* I won't be killed. I wish I felt the same way about some of my friends…" He stopped, wishing he hadn't said that, lest she intuit his fear for Charlie.

"You, your friends, and tens of thousands of others face death every day. We only get to help alleviate pain and patch up the hurt. Can't you see what I am telling you? I love you, and I've decided to give myself to you if you will have me, marriage or not. Do you want to finish what we started, or do you want to think and talk some more? It's already three in the morning. We have almost nine hours until either of us will be missed.

"Are you worried about committing a sin? Isn't that a bit ludicrous in light of what you just told me? Did that inhibit you with the widow?"

"It's not the same, Jennifer. She wasn't a virgin. She was not, at least at first, anyone important to me. She was just a woman in need."

"Well, I am a virgin, for whatever that is worth, and I hope I am important to you. Can't you give me at least as much as you gave her? Don't you think I am a 'woman in need'?"

Jack was in a velvet corner. He smarted at his obvious hypocrisy, but wanted to think of Jennifer like an eggshell, like priceless crystal. He actually thought about leaving, but Jennifer had other ideas, and other ploys to overcome his reluctance.

MONDAY, APRIL 17, DAWNED BRIGHT AND SUNNY IN PARIS. Charlie woke with his arm draped over Michelle's slightly swelling belly. Not far away Jack Buck woke full of the deepest love he'd ever felt. Both men rose early, leaving their women to sleep a little longer.

Charlie went out to flex his limbs and stretch. He was used to regular exercise and had made it almost a ritual. Jack slipped out of the room and down the back stairs of the hospital.

Jack hadn't slept but an hour or two, but he felt so refreshed that he began to trot in the direction of the Flandins. Neuilly was a good three miles west of Saint Augustin. He covered the distance in about twenty-five minutes.

Charlie ran past the Madeleine and decided to keep going until he worked up a sweat. In less than five minutes, he was approaching the big church at Saint Augustin. Only a few vendors were on the streets. He saw another man walking and breathing heavily as if he had just run a race. As he got closer, he recognized Jack and shouted out a greeting.

Holy Lord, guide me! Jack prayed.

"Jack, imagine finding you out getting exercise at this hour. So you got Jennifer back all right last night?"

"Of course," Jack replied thinking how ironic her brother's words sounded.

"Big dinner tonight. Prince says that most of us will be leaving right away for a place called Luxeuil-les-Bains. Have you heard of it?"

Thankful to be able to change the subject, Jack remembered seeing the name on the maps of the region around Bois le Prêtre and Dieulouard. "It's almost on the Swiss border. I wonder why they would send us there?"

The two friends stepped into an open cafe and ordered coffee and croissants. Going their separate ways, the two agreed to meet that afternoon after Jennifer got off her shift. Jack just didn't know what to feel with his new lover's brother. It occurred to him that Koniatev had probably guessed at their tryst. The bastard would take great pleasure in telling Charlie. He'd better be very careful.

At the restaurant that night, the designated members of N. 124, and a number of others who hoped to join it later, were the honored guests of the Franco-American Committee. Paul Rockwell attended, though his application for flight training had been repeatedly denied. A Frenchman named Michel seemed out of place. He was Norman Prince's mechanic, money in evidence.

Jarousse de Sillac opened the evening with a toast to the *Escadrille Américaine.* Doctor Gros toasted the French. William Vanderbilt asked them to raise their glasses to themselves and all the brave American volunteers now serving this noble cause.

Georges Thénault took the floor to tell them about the next several days of the new outfit. They needed to be at Luxeuil by the 20th, but their machines might not arrive for several days.

"This is Lieutenant de Laage, my second. I know you will get to know him well. Thénault addressed the other Americans present. "Rest assured gentlemen, that I will do everything in my power to bring you along as soon as I can."

This brought loud shouts and hurrahs. Seldom have men gone so willingly to death's door.

Part Six

Into the Fray

Stand to your glasses, steady.
The world is a world of lies;
A cup to the dead already
And here is to the next that dies.

Leighton Brewer, *Riders of the Sky*

Chapter 39
More Than a Pampered Vacation

Luxeuil-les-Bains, Spring, 1916

Charlie and Jack departed the Gare de l'Est for Luxeuil Wednesday morning, April 20, leaving two very passionate women in tears. Michelle spent five days with Charlie, while Jack had managed to steal only hours alone with Jennifer. Michelle could see something in Jennifer's face. She wondered if her husband knew or suspected as she did that his friend and his sister were now lovers.

Charlie couldn't decide whether he should stay in French service, or resign and take Michelle back to the United States to have their child. She adamantly refused to be the cause of his quitting the army. Charlie kept reminding her that he didn't have to stay in uniform. Others had left with less reason. His arguments sounded half-hearted to her.

"Remember all that rhetoric you used on me about how committed you had become? I am going to be fine here. When my time comes, Mums will come to help me through the delivery. Thanks to the Fleurys, I already have a room reserved in the same hospital where their children were born, The *Saint Louis*—isn't that rich?

"I know you could be wounded or killed, God forbid, but I accepted that before we married. If you really want to put my mind at ease you will stop worrying me with all your protectiveness."

Charlie wished he could spirit Michelle away to Saint Louis to his mother's care. But contemplating her out of France without him was unbearable. He worried that the de Vincents would be traveling when the baby was due in September. Michelle told him to quit conjuring up problems where there were none. In the end, they agreed to maintain the status quo. After all, how could he resign now that the American Escadrille existed?

ELLIOT COWDIN SAT ACROSS FROM CHARLIE AND JACK. Since his short time in N. 65 with Thaw and Keeler, Cowdin had become especially friendly, but Jack still had reservations about him. Since his arrival in France, Elliot hadn't stayed with anything for more than two months. He left the Ambulance after just six weeks. In one year of flying, he had been in four escadrilles. Jack wondered why.

To help pass the train ride, they played bridge with a French officer en route to the bombing escadrille at Luxeuil. Jack had learned the game in the Ambulance Service while Charlie had played with his parents from a very young age. Jack, still very much the novice, paired with the lieutenant. After four hands, the men began to talk more freely, their play becoming somewhat desultory.

The lieutenant said. "Ever been to Luxeuil?" None of the Americans had. "Baths and warm springs there have been in use continuously since the Romans occupied the area. Supposed to soothe aches and pains."

They talked and played nearly two hours trying to figure what kinds of missions they might get so close to the Swiss border. Cowdin got up to walk around and find something to drink. The lieutenant left Jack and Charlie alone.

"I'm going to get some sleep," Charlie said, "but before I doze off, can I ask you something, Jack?"

Jack had been thinking about how to tell him about Jennifer. He just nodded, speculating that maybe Charlie would ask him outright.

"I'm worried about Michelle."

Jack replied a little over exuberantly. "And I was afraid you were going to chew me out for bidding spades in that last hand."

"No, seriously, Jack. If something happens to me, promise you will look after her and the child until they can get settled. Maybe they should go to Saint Louis or England. If I go west I want to make sure they have someone looking out for them."

"What are you worried about? Even if we both buy the farm, she has her family and the Fleurys. It's kind of hoodoo to jinx yourself that way."

"Yeah, you're probably right, but promise me anyway."

"Okay, all right, but this is nonsense. I don't know why you need to start rattling those death chains. I for one have no intention of giving my life for France or even good old America should she ever jump in here."

"It's not that I am afraid of dying, Jack. I get these premonitions sometimes, you know? Oh, bugger it all!" Charlie said, changing the subject. "By the way, congratulations."

"Congratulations? Jack asked a little too quickly.

"For winning Jennifer."

"I love her Charlie," Jack said, defensively, wondering how much Charlie suspected.

"I know. She told me about your night in the hospital. You're lucky I found out from her and not someone else or I would have had to kick your Minnesotan butt."

"She told you? Mother of God! She told you everything?"

"We have never kept anything from each other since we were kids. She told me you are lovers, Jack. She said she twisted your arm and that she practically had to attack you before you would lay a hand on her. Like I said, congratulations. You wouldn't believe the string of broken hearts she left back in Saint Louis. Do you think I would ask you to look after Michelle if I didn't trust you?"

Jack sunk back and shook his head. The siblings were so like each other in temperament. Neither of them minced words. They said exactly what they thought as it came into their heads. It was one of the reasons he liked Charlie so much.

"Maybe after this damned war, we too can marry. If we do, you'll stand up for us, won't you?"

"You betcha, Jack. If I'm still standing, that is…."

IT TOOK TWELVE HOURS TO COVER THE DISTANCE from Paris to Luxeuil. Stops at Provins, Troyes, Langres, and Vesoul, where they had to change trains, brought progressively more evidence of war, evidence that curiously dwindled when they turned south for Luxeuil. Lieutenant de Laage waited for them beside a huge touring car with lights blazing.

"*Allons, mes amis, on va casser la croute*!" de Laage said after getting them settled in the hotel.

In the twilight, they approached a building with walls timbered in the Alsatian manner emblazoned with a lighted sign stating *Pomme d'Or.* The candlelit dining room smelled of roasting meats, fresh bread, and the faintly musty tang of wine casks.

Chapman, McConnell, Rockwell, and Capitaine Thénault were finishing up their meal. All rose to greet the newcomers with enthusiasm. "By the good Lord, boys, it's happening," Chapman said, pounding Charlie and Jack on the back.

"Prince is already here visiting a family friend," McConnell said.

"Bill Thaw comes tomorrow, and Bert Hall sometime next week," Thénault added. "You'll be taking your meals here at the Pomme d'Or, *mes amis*. Try not to tear the place up or fool with the waitresses," he added, more than a little seriously. Thénault smiled at Buck, remembering that incredible day at Pau.

Auguste Groscolas, a short florid cheeked man with a waxed mustache, introduced his wife and daughters, asking what he could bring them. One of the girls, a dark-haired beauty, stared very boldly at Kiffin Rockwell. When they left the room to get the meals for Charlie, Jack and Cowdin, the men all kidded Kiffin that he had another admirer to fend off.

"And a pretty one at that," he replied. "Just be lucky you guys have such ugly pusses." Changing the subject, Kiffin turned to Thénault and asked what they would be doing until their airplanes arrived.

"We will fish and hunt, no?" Thénault said looking at his classmate from Saint Cyr, Alfred de Laage de Meux, with an uncharacteristic twinkle in his eye.

"And swim, hike, climb some mountains, *n'est-ce pas*?" de Laage replied.

The Americans looked from one officer to the other. After a bit, de Laage, smiling at their discomfiture, explained their plan.

"*Alors*, we inspect what we have now and get settled while we wait. We scout out possible emergency landing fields and get familiar with the terrain around Luxeuil," he added, noting they had several touring cars for the task.

Thénault knew better than to waste their time making work, but he was unsure how to handle the rambunctious Americans. He told them they could pick mushrooms, fish, or have picnics with the local girls whenever they weren't conducting a reconnaissance. Jack winced at this last comment, remembering his last picnic of that sort.

McConnell laughed, "Sounds like they're fattening us up for the kill."

Thénault, missing the idiom, fired off a question at de Laage that made the Americans chuckle. Thénault bristled immediately and instituted the rule that they could speak English at supper and French at lunch. Offenders would have to cough up fines of ten sous for the escadrille bar fund.*

Buck, Cowdin, and Keeler attacked the juicy leg of mutton with vigor. Steamed new potatoes, and perfectly cooked white asparagus with

---

*About a quarter U.S.

a creamy butter sauce completed the meal. They sopped up the juices and sauce with chunks of fresh bread, and liberally whetted their travel-parched throats with a rich burgundy wine. Jack and Charlie both agreed that this hearty fare was more to their liking than the pretentious Paris cuisine. Cowdin looked askance at the remark, but he didn't halt his attack on a thick piece of flavorful mutton.

Bill Thaw arrived on the last train that night. As the senior American, he got a room with the officers in the *Lion d'Or*, a hotel near the *Pomme d'Or*. He protested to Thénault to no avail. Bill Thaw always made a conscious effort to treat his fellows as equals, but he was a sous lieutenant.

The next day, the men explored their surroundings. Luxeuil, reduced to only three thousand inhabitants since August 1914, provided an idyllic setting for the birth of the American Escadrille. Jack saw black draping over some doors and windows announcing the loss of a loved one. Despite the lack of men, the town teemed with activity. Women of every age went about their business. Young children played in the town square where a couple of older men tossed balls at pins on an open field. They noticed an old priest, evidently the curé of one of the two churches in the town, leading a group of school-aged children into a classroom. Over fifty miles to the north the war raged, yet the outward calm of Luxeuil-les-Bains belied its reality.

Luxeuil was off the main roads and high enough in the Vosges to provide breathtaking panoramic views almost to the Swiss border, about thirty-five miles to the east. Stands of oaks, poplars, and pines surrounded the town. Yellow rapeseed flowers made the fields around the town glow with a buttery hue. Lavender also bloomed in the warm spring weather. A silvery lacework of streams threaded through the area. Monsieur Groscolas swore they all were thick with trout, not having been fished for more than a year. At the baths near their villa, steam rose from the bubbling springs. A hint of sulfur tinged the air.

"Mac was right, Charlie," Kiffin noted as they made their way on foot to the airfield. "They are fattening us up."

"It's the poet in him, Kiffin," Jack observed. "You wouldn't believe the way he can describe something."

"I just hope we don't sit around on our duffs for too long or, American Escadrille be hanged, I'm going to find some action somewhere." Jack looked at the fire in Kiffin's eyes, uncomfortable that he didn't share his friend's zeal.

Following de Laage's instructions, they headed south towards the adjoining village of Saint Sauveur. Crossing two bridges over swift little streams, they passed a valley nestling a pond into which the two streams emptied. They walked farther on the *Route Départmentale* 64 until reaching a smaller road with the typical stubby gravestone-like concrete marker, painted red on the top and white on the bottom with D 270 in black lettering.

Soon they came upon a very large open field with a line of Maurice Farman bombers parked at the southern edge. The grass was freshly mown. On the northern side of the field, they saw an impressive array of very new-looking equipment and vehicles. Jim McConnell joined them.

"You remember how we had to walk six miles just to do our laundry at Pau?" He asked. "Imagine being driven here in a staff car by the captain? Such luxury! It almost makes me feel guilty."

The display before them demonstrated the magnitude of the effort the French put into organizing N. 124. Tents stood in the trees across the road from the field. Jack counted fifteen brand-new Fiat trucks, parked combat-style against the tree line with their noses pointed out. Cartier and Dombasle had always insisted he never park nose-in lest he have to pull out in a hurry.

Stacks of supplies of every sort rested on wooden pallets, covered with canvas. Thénault's office, a pre-fabricated building, lay on the ground awaiting assembly. Non-perishable food, bundles of rags, hundreds of gasoline barrels, and smaller barrels of castor oil, occupied another opening in the woods beside the field. It was an imposing collection, but they were in for an even more impressive sight at the noon formation.

NCOs assembled the men into two platoons while de Laage mustered the pilots in preparation for the first of the few formal formations Nieuport 124 would stand. After taking de Laage's salute, Thénault told them to look around and to get to know each other.

He named each of the American pilots and had them step forward to be recognized. Then he introduced the rest of the men by section to the Americans. First the mechanics, the men assigned to care for their airplanes, followed by the chauffeurs, the armorers, motorcyclists, telephone operators, radio operators, brancardiers, and clerks. All told, there were seventy men there to support the flyers. The numbers would change, but Thénault pointed out the ten-to-one ratio to emphasize the importance of their endeavor.

At precisely noon, Thénault ordered the escadrille to attention and had Lieutenant de Laage read the order officially activating N. 124 as the Escadrille Américaine.

Bert Hall's arrival completed the complement of pilots. Things had been relatively calm until Bert's arrival. Somehow, his presence changed the dynamics, sowing the first seeds of conflict in their ranks. But, at the end of April the mood remained festive and boisterous. Hall's tall tales competed with Thénault's jangling attacks on the old upright in the Pomme d'Or in setting people's teeth on edge.

Without planes the pilots made excursions to the front in unit vehicles. Their captain worried about inactivity dulling the men, but he would soon have to worry more about throttling their youthful enthusiasm.

THE RESTAURANT AT THE POMME D'OR BOASTED A ROOM outfitted with a full-sized pool table, the piano, and several worn overstuffed chairs The Americans wasted no time making it their *popote*, or escadrille hangout.

"Mac, pardon my prying, but what are you writing now?" Jack Buck asked Jim McConnell.

"You aren't prying Jack. I am just making notes, kinda like sketches. I wish I could draw or paint, but I try to capture things with words instead."

"We all notice. Does it come easy for you?"

"College helped, of course. I wasn't a very studious type. Raising hell seemed to be much more fun."

"I can't see you playing pranks, Jim. You know I want to write, but I don't seem to know what to say."

"I doubt it, Jack. Life is such a great teacher. You have more going for you than most, just from what you have done and seen over here. Think about it. Does anyone from your class at the University of Minnesota have a brevet from the French Army? Can any of your friends describe hauling wounded men in an ambulance in wartime? How many of them speak another language, or know another culture like you do now?"

"Few, I suppose. The letters I get from home are a little dull compared to our life here. Everyone seems to be standing still back there while we're running at top speed. I try to write about it, but when you describe something or tell a story, it just seems to come to life."

"Well, I have no secret potion. I did pay attention in my English lit classes and loved Shakespeare. At *Beaux-Arts,* the *professeurs* taught us to see things, really see things in a new light. Putting them into words, especially in French—a language I knew poorly at first—became a labor of love. I found new and better ways of saying things. Haven't you noticed how sometimes it is easier to express your thoughts in French than in English? I paint in words instead of with a brush."

"Anything I can read? You know, pick up some techniques and some new words?"

"Jack, don't think about technique. It just makes you mechanical. We learned to *feel* things instead of just describing what appears physically. Sometimes, when I have a few glasses of wine in me, I really *see* what they were trying to tell us. You let yourself float above the scene like a butterfly. I can't tell you how to write. Everyone has his own way. Mine isn't necessarily better than yours. The simple act of writing seems to develop a life of its own. Just do it. Oh, and read, read, read," Mac said, stopping to light a pipe.

"All the things I learned about verse, about iambic pentameter, alliteration, and rhyme just run together in my head. I don't even think about them now. I often wonder if the authors of the classics really thought about the imagery that our professors taught us to see. With so many experts reading so much into what Shakespeare said, who knows what he really meant?

"Read everything you can get your hands on and never stop reading. I've learned as much reading on my own as I did in all four years at Charlottesville.

"You'd be surprised how much you can learn from others too. A while back a *Crapouillard* gunner told me this tale. I translated it," he said, handing Jack a sheet of paper.

> I tell you, you laugh to see it. I shoot my torpille. She goes turning slowly over and over through the air and then drops right in the trench. Oh you see 'em go up. Legs and arms and heads. Rifles, helmets and sacks. All go up at once. Once I saw a whole boche go up. Perfectly good Boche. Only one leg missing. He went up. Way up thirty meters. Yes, and I would laugh, damn 'em. And, the more mangled they are the better I'd like it. I would take keen delight in a string of German ears. They cut the throats of some of our comrades the other day and stuck their heads up over the trench on bayonets. Les salauds.

Jack finished and looked up, "Jim, are we going to become like that?"

"Savage isn't it? War seems to suspend humanity. That gunner is probably a good Catholic like you. See anything Christian in that? If he lives, he'll probably go back to his village, raise children, and think nothing of it. I sent that little story to Marcelle. She may have shown it to Jennifer. You know, the women get a pretty tough hide after a while."

"Pity, isn't it?" Jack said. "All that we hold true about love, beauty, faith, hope reduced to butchery. Did Marcelle respond?"

"Yeah. She said she'd never show that to her parents or tell them where she got it. I wasn't thinking too clearly when I sent it."

BERT HALL SEEMED TO TAKE OVER THE *POPOTE*. He mixed up a batch of Manhattans every evening in a big pail. After serving everybody, Bert would begin spinning a tale about his service with such and such pasha in Turkey or some other exotic place. Amusing at first, the stories soon became repetitive and inconsistent. Bill Thaw seemed to encourage Hall, getting a kick out of the blatant exaggerations. Kiffin also had a warm spot in his heart for the braggart. The three were squad mates in the Legion at the beginning of the war. Charlie and Jack tolerated him, while some of the others began to scoff at Hall's graceless boasting.

Thénault took them out in the touring car the first several days on excursions as far away as Vittel where another escadrille had a field. He made them mark every field larger than 300 meters long on their maps as possible landing points. Thénault's dry instruction might have practical value, but his delivery challenged even Jack, who had more reason to like the man who had pinned on his wings than anyone.

Lieutenant de Laage, on the other hand, inspired the men. Without warning, he would leap from the car, rifle in hand, and chase after a rabbit. Soon he had all of them bringing guns along for sport. They seldom bagged anything, but the exercise and romping in the woods certainly broke the ennui. It didn't hurt that a well-meaning American benefactor, William Chanler, upon learning of their lack of machine guns, sent enough Browning 12-gauge shotguns for every pilot to be able to have one in his aircraft. Chanler's noble and impractical gesture lent little to their aerial efforts, but much to their ground pursuits.

Bill Thaw convinced Keeler and Buck to join him in a quest for the fat trout Groscolas had mentioned. Bill bought a fly rod and all the other necessary gear in town. Charlie had never fly-fished. Jack had never gone after trout. When they arrived at the recommended pool in the bend of one of the nearby streams, the two novices trailed along to observe.

Thaw began whipping the heavy line over his head, feeding it out as he tried to place the horse-tailed fly into the pool. Though a little out of practice, he managed to land the lure on the water at the pool's edge. Each time it touched the water he gave a little jerk causing it to pop up simulating a real bug. On his fifth cast a big splash startled Keeler and Buck, who were idly dangling their bare feet in the water on the bank. Soon Bill was working his bent rod up and down the bank, shouting for them to get out of the way. Jack grabbed the net Bill had bought and traipsed after him.

"Get away Charlie!" Bill shouted as he sidestepped on the edge of the stream. Keeler slipped and fell into the water splashing about and laughing loudly. They had polished off two bottles of the local *Bourgogne* with their lunch. Jack almost doubled up in laughter at Charlie's antics. Meanwhile, Thaw played the fish. As he brought it closer to the bank, Jack stepped out with the net, intending to help land the monster—surely a monster from how it bent the rod.

Once in the water, Buck himself slipped on the rocks and fell unceremoniously on his bottom. That made two flailing bodies in the water not counting the hapless fish. Thaw's expression of intense concentration dissolved into uncontrolled laughter. He nonetheless kept the tip of the rod up, holding the fish just off the stream's edge. With a big heave, he pulled the 'monster' out of the water and whipped the rod toward the bank. A six-inch half-pounder sailed through the air slapping Buck on the cheek, knocking him back down just he was struggling to his feet.

Keeler, dripping wet, raced to grab the wriggling fish. He got a hand on the line, lost his balance, and plummeted down the bank once again. Thaw was laughing so hard that he dropped the rod, sinking down on his haunches. The two heroes waded out of the water. Charlie held the startled trout in his wrestler's grip, making the fish's eyes bulge. The three of them lay back on the grass, panting in laughter. The unfortunate fish finally spit out the hook on the fly and slithered out of Charlie's hand, plopping neatly back into the water, only a little worse for wear. They decided it was time to open their third bottle of burgundy before tackling another of Groscola's 'monsters.'

After supper that night Hall asked if they had any luck. The three fishermen only smiled and began laughing. Bert claimed to have landed a five-pounder barehanded in the stream out behind their aérodrome. After their adventure with Thaw, Bert's surely exaggerated tale only produced more mirth. Almost on cue, however, old Groscolas came in with a very large trout wrapped in newspaper. He wanted to know if Monsieur Hall wanted the fish filleted and fried for breakfast or served at supper the next night.

AS APRIL ENDED, THÉNAULT'S FRANTIC MESSAGES begging for airplanes finally produced results. On May 1, a convoy of trucks arrived bearing six new Nieuport Bébés disassembled in crates. A crew of mechanics came along from the factory at Issy les-Moulineaux to put them back together. All the pilots pitched in excitedly.

Charlie couldn't believe it when he saw Stephane supervising the unloading. Rockwell remembered meeting Stephane at Villacoublay the day he showed them the very airplanes they were about to put together.

Thénault had strong reason to get the machines flying. Shortly after arriving at Luxeuil he'd met Capitaine Happe, the commander of the bombing escadrille already at the field. Thénault brought several of the Americans with him to see the 'Red Corsair.' Happe professed great joy at their arrival, telling them he could use their help as soon as possible.

On his desk Jack noticed eight red leather boxes. Seeing his curiosity, Happe told them they contained the Croix de Guerre medals for the pilots and gunners he'd lost on his last bombing incursion into Germany. The redheaded, red-bearded Happe's escadrille had flown their slow Maurice Farman pushers against targets as far away as the Zeppelin base in Friedrichshafen on the north shore of Lake Constance. The medals and the urgency Happe conveyed served as a sober reminder to the Americans that they were there for more than a pampered vacation.

A bewildering array of steel tapes, calipers, wire twisting pliers, and tension measuring devices were part of the assembly process. Stephane personally oversaw fueling the first Nieuport 11 and topping off the castor oil reservoir. After verifying it was securely chocked, he climbed in the cockpit. One of the Issy crew turned the prop slowly to charge the cylinders with fuel and air while Stephane kept the magneto switch off with the throttle full open. On his signal, the mechanic gave a sharp heave to the prop as Stephane turned on the switch. The 80 horsepower Gnome rotary roared into life sending up a cloud of bluish white smoke from the preservative mixture left in the rotating cylinders. Satisfied that the motor was running smoothly, Stephane cut the ignition with the switch on the control stick and released it quickly. The motor burped off and picked up again just as designed. As it ran, two factory mechanics checked for leaks and unusual vibrations. Everything had to be tightened and secured with cotter pins or safety wire to keep the vibrations from working nuts and cables loose. After running the motor for ten minutes, Stephane shut it down and climbed out of the cockpit.

Riggers went to work checking cable tensions and verifying the movement of the controls. Thénault himself stood by waiting. He would fly the first machine. He grumbled to de Laage and Thaw about the fact that they still hadn't yet sent the machine guns. "Damnation! How are we to fight with stingerless bees?" he asked in frustration. When the Issy crew finished, Stephane signaled Thénault that he could take it up.

While Thénault taxied to the end of the strip and took off for a turn about the field, the ground crews hurriedly rushed to a second ship to repeat the process. Ten minutes later, the captain landed. He spoke quickly with Stephane before leaving the field to fire off yet another telegram demanding his weapons.

Lieutenant de Laage got the second Bébé, repeating Thénault's test flight with a flourish of acrobatics that had Stephane wincing. "One does not do that with a new machine!" he complained to Bill Thaw who was waiting patiently for the third bird to pass its run up checks. Landing perfectly, de Laage came out of the Nieuport with a big smile on his face.

"*Parfait*!" he said, shaking Stephane's hand. "How long until the others are ready?"

Stephane admonished the lieutenant for his antics in the air, informing him that all the Nieuports required *réglage*, adjustment, before such maneuvers. Laughing, de Laage patted the chief mechanic's shoulder, and strode off jauntily.

Before Stephane and his team loaded up for the long trip back to Paris, Thénault organized a *pot* to celebrate the organization of *l'Escadrille Américaine*. Madame Groscolas and her daughters arrived at the field in one of the escadrille automobiles loaded with food and drink. A Fiat truck pulled up with Monsieur Groscolas himself in the front with the driver. Out came a load of bottles, baskets with plates and silver from the hotel. Charlie told Jack that it must have cost a fortune.

"Nimmie threw in a pile of francs and so did Victor. There are some definite advantages to being rich, aren't there?" Jack observed.

"Reminds me of the story of how Victor once tried to pay a surgeon to save one of his Legion buddies," Charlie said.

"You're kidding! I haven't heard about that."

"The doctor wouldn't take the 100,000 francs Vic offered. He said it was impossible, and, of course, Vic's friend died. I'm sure Chapman cried. Sometimes even money isn't enough. What a gesture, though."

"You guys talking about me?" Chapman said coming up from behind them with a sandwich of ham and butter in a fresh baguette. "Better get over there and get something before the Paris bunch finishes it off."

"Fat chance of that! Did you see the load old Groscolas brought in that truck? We heard you might have had something to do with paying for this. Makes us poor folk a little ashamed," Charlie said good-naturedly.

"Go dig in and don't worry about who paid for it. There's a *pâté de compagne* Madame Groscolas made that you don't want to miss."

Though the men lined up three deep waiting to fill their plates, there was no sign of anything running out. While waiting, Charlie told Jack that the French really knew how to put on the dog. Jack couldn't agree more. He grabbed a couple of bottles of cold beer and handed one to Charlie.

Kiffin joined them commenting about the difference between the Legion and Aviation. Charlie hadn't forgotten his time in the trenches. Neither had Hall, Thaw and Chapman, the other infantry vets.

"It wasn't so bad in the Ambulance, but we never had a feast like this, even when we got our new Fords, did we Jack?" McConnell said. Cowdin, McConnell, and Buck were the only Ambulance men so far in N. 124. A little friendly rivalry had already begun to develop between the former drivers and the ex-legionnaires. Prince had entered aviation directly, so he acted as referee.

Sunday, Chapman woke Charlie and Jack and invited them to Mass. Victor's mother had been a devout Catholic, though his father and stepmother attended Presbyterian services. Victor never missed Mass on Sunday even during his time in the Legion. One of the *aumoniers* always said Mass for the poilus, even on the front lines under bombardment. Buck and Keeler hadn't been quite as observant, but they shook off the effects of the long night of drinking and eating to go with Victor that morning.

Jack could finally understand the priest's sermon. Afterwards, they talked about how the Mass wasn't discernibly different in Luxeuil from anywhere else in France or in the United States. The Latin prayers were the same.

"Do you guys believe that the Protestants are all going to Hell?" Charlie asked them on the walk back to the villa.

"I certainly hope not," Jack began. "My dad's Lutheran, but he is more Christian than many a so-called good Catholic back home. I can't believe that God would send dad to Hell."

"Sometimes I think my father is already in Hell," Chapman said. "I heard you two talking about being rich yesterday. I may have money, but you have fathers that love you and that you love. That's rich to me. I just wish my father would show me that he cares for me. He never seems to approve of me."

"Me too," Charlie said, "though my dad sure seems to have changed since I got married."

Chapman observed that talking to Prince, Cowdin, and Thaw about their families was a little like comparing physiques. Prince's father was one of the richest men in America. Thaw's owned a good deal of Pittsburgh, and Cowdin's famous polo player father was a wealthy manufacturer.

"You know what? After the initial posturing and subtle high class bragging, we all discovered that we had quite a bit in common other than money."

"Your families know each other?" Jack asked.

"Not really. I guess they may have some common business acquaintances, but that's not what we share. We all almost hate our fathers. Isn't that a pity? Prince had to enroll in the flying school in Marblehead under an alias just to keep his father from finding out about it. Elliot's dad disapproved of him coming to France, and so did Thaw's. You should have heard the great John Jay Chapman howl when I told him I was going to enlist."

"It's funny, Vic. I always wondered why guys with so much money would join the Foreign Legion," Charlie said.

"I don't know about anybody else, but I just wanted to get away. I could never please him. I love my stepmother Alce all right, but I always feel like my father just tolerates me. Anyway, back to the original question. Protestants going to Hell, Charlie? No doubt a slew of Catholics will be there to keep them company." They all laughed. It began to rain so they ducked into the Pomme d'Or to see if they could find some coffee and breakfast.

The rain continued for the rest of the week, dampening Thénault's hopes to launch their first patrol. As it was, the machine guns still hadn't arrived. The men of the new N. 124, *l'Escadrille Américaine*, suffered one of many interminable weeks of inactivity that peppered their existence.

Tempers flared. Drinking, a regular pastime, almost a ritual, even for those who weren't drinkers before, fueled the friction. Some became maudlin after several drinks while others got combative. Bert Hall's daily Manhattan potion didn't help matters much, but Jack noticed that Bert didn't partake of his own concoction. Chapman hardly drank either.

Charlie pined for Michelle, writing her every day.

Jack missed Jennifer and tried to write a few lines every night before he went to bed. He often fell asleep with a line scratched across the paper. In the morning he could barely recognize his handwriting and admonished himself to cut back on the booze. Yet, as evening approached he gravitated to the *popote*, his resolve forgotten.

He had only mailed three letters in the two weeks they'd been there. Jennifer wrote her brother to ask if Jack was all right. Charlie thought about talking to Jack about drinking so hard, but would have felt hypocritical.

"Jack, when was your last letter to Jennifer?"

"She said something, right? I don't have a prayer with you two ganging up on me. Oh, what the hell! Okay, I've been a slug. Too much great wine and cognac, and this damned idleness. I'll write her tonight, but not because you are sticking your nose in, Keeler. Is there anything I can keep private between Jennifer and I?

"Calm down, Jack. I'm not the enemy here. I think I'm going to back off the liquor too. It's just too easy to get sloshed every night. I even like Bert's Manhattans, but two of them on top of the wine with dinner, and I'm ready to dance. Did I tell you about stepping on Madame Fleury's toes...?"

Charlie's attempt at humor took the edge off Jack's anger. Jack felt like a selfish dope. Remembering how disgusted he'd been with Red Rumsey at Pau when the New Yorker overdid his drinking, he resolved to cut back. It was never hard when he was busy flying. *Damn this inactivity*!

For Jack and the rest of the escadrille, things were about to change.

Chapter 40
Mavericks

Luxeuil-les-Bains, mid-May, 1916

Thénault assembled the pilots at his newly-finished office on the field on Friday, May 12. He felt energized by the thrill of having men under his command again. The weather was breaking up and Saturday promised to be a fine day. He paced back and forth before a map of the region rubbing his hands together, either in anticipation or because he was cold. With the French, one could never tell.

"At dawn we launch our first patrol. I've decided to have *Sergent* Rockwell lead this patrol. *Caporal* Chapman, *Sergent* McConnell, Lieutenant Thaw and I will fly the other machines," Thénault paused, seeing the looks of disappointment. "The rest of you will get your chance, so enough of the *gueule*." He said with his hand in the air.

Jack really felt *la gueule*—French for 'make a long face.' He wondered why Thénault hadn't picked Charlie to lead the patrol. Jack bit his lip. It wasn't his responsibility to question the captain's judgment.

Thénault drew them together over a carefully constructed terrain map of the patrol route and began to describe the mission. He put paper models of airplanes on the map, each with the name of the pilot written on a wing. He traced the route with a riding crop. Chapman and McConnell would flank Rockwell in the lead. He placed the paper planes with his and Thaw's names behind and on either side of the formation, telling them that he and the lieutenant would be like shepherds watching over the other three. He admonished them to stay together and not, in any case, to allow themselves to drift too far to the east or north. Gesturing with the crop he said, "*Nord les Boches, est la Suisse, tous les deux interdit pour le moment.*"

Everyone turned out for this first patrol Saturday morning. It was warm and clear at the field. Those flying had arrived an hour earlier to check over their machines. The Issy crew had modified Thénault's Nieuport before they left. They'd brought one 110 horsepower motor as a spare in case one of the six eighty horsepower motors proved bad. When the captain found out they had the bigger motor he ordered Stephane to mount it in his aircraft. It would turn out to be a propitious decision.

Rockwell, lamenting their lack of armament, said, "No matter what the damned captain says, if I see a Boche, I go for him." Charlie tried to point out that they needed some time to get used to working together before risking combat, but Kiffin just looked at him stone-faced. The steely determination of this young man from Asheville, North Carolina, impressed Charlie, but it also made him worry about his friend.

Jack and Charlie ate breakfast with the ground crews who had brewed up a great pot of hot chocolate to go with their baguettes and confiture. Bert Hall asked if he could *sidle up*, as he put it. Charlie said of course, and Jack braced himself for another yarn.

"You hail from Saint Louie, right Charlie? Ever hear of Higginsville?"

"That's up in the Ozarks, isn't it?"

"Yep, my ole' man ended up there, though I claim Kaintuck. Ever get homesick, you two? Nope, I suppose not what with you married, Charlie, and Jack 'ere dating yer sister."

The two younger men began to wonder where Hall was drifting. He hadn't talked about others or shown much interest in their backgrounds in the past.

"Well, I do. I mean, I do get homesick. I've been wandering about like a vagabond for so long that I don't even know where to call home. Something in me, I guess. Anyways, I jes wondered if you too young'uns felt like me."

"You're such an old fart, Bert?" Charlie began.

"Naw, you know what I mean. I'm just more experienced, though you got me on being married Keeler. Haven't given that a try yet."

"Bert, where is this going?" Jack asked, a little impatiently.

"Just friendly conversation, Bucko. Don't get'cher dander up on me. Why is it that you Swedes have no patience?"

"What *are* you trying to say, Bert?" Charlie asked.

"I don't know exactly. I don't have many friends, you know. Oh, I've got a bunch of acquaintances, but most people just put up with me. You two fellows seem so friendly to everyone. The way you stick together. I, well, I..."

"Need a friend?" Jack finished Hall's sentence, curious how the big talker would work around this.

"Yeah. Matter of fact. Kif's already agreed to take care of my stuff if I go west. I thought it would be nice if I sorta hedged my bets by recruiting one of you two. Whad'dya think?"

"Better ask Jack, Bertie. I already have him looking after me."

"How about it Buck? Will you back Kiffin up?"

"Sure. But why are you guys getting so morbid?"

"Jack, my boy," Hall started, putting his arm through Buck's as they walked out to the landing area, "I been shot at, chased, jailed, beat up, robbed, cheated, you name it. It's just plain old common sense to plan for the future."

"You old codger. You'll probably outlive us all."

"Mebbe so, mebbe so."

They settled in one of the rest tents to wait for the patrol to return. Without an audience Hall wasn't such a bad guy. He was an inveterate bull artist, but there seemed to be a streak of humanity in him. Bert Hall acted genuinely pleased to have Buck promise to pack up his things and send them to an address in Paris.

An hour passed, then another thirty minutes. The *mécaniciens* were waiting when Hall, Keeler and Buck returned to the strip. Knowing the flight would be low on fuel in minutes, the men anxiously scanned the sky. Soon the distinctive high-pitched whine of the Le Rhônes eased their concern.

Rockwell landed first followed by the rest of the patrol. Thénault got out of his Nieuport looking very agitated. Without saying a word, he walked briskly to his office. Charlie grabbed Kiffin first, asking him how it went. Rockwell smiled, saying "great," without offering any details. Thaw gathered them up saying the captain wanted to do a debriefing with all the pilots. McConnell, looking a little sheepish, confided to Jack that he had gotten lost and gone over Switzerland. He expected to hear about it from Thénault.

"*Mes amis Américains*," Thénault said, a stern look on his face, "*ça va pas*! This will never do. Who can tell me what went wrong?"

"The overcast caused the flight to scatter, *mon capitaine*," Rockwell answered. "But, after you were able to run Mac back into the formation, I think things went splendidly."

"Your attacks on the Archie puffs were amusing, Kif, I have to admit," Thaw said casually, tapping the ash from his cigarette. Rockwell had led McConnell and Chapman in some diving charges at the dissipating black smoke of the German antiaircraft shells that exploded harmlessly beneath them.

"The run on Habsheim wasn't such a good idea with us not having weapons, I suppose, but the damned Huns didn't take up the challenge anyway," Chapman threw in.

"All in all, a pretty good first patrol, *non*, mon capitaine?" Rockwell asked with the defiant look of a schoolboy facing a dare on the playground.

Thénault's frustration couldn't last in the face of their enthusiasm. Rather than conduct a detailed debriefing, he just pointed out that they needed to learn to work together to better support each other.

Charlie was excited because the Lewis machine guns arrived late Saturday and he was designated to lead the first armed patrol on Monday. Sunday the mechanics and armorers mounted and test-fired the six weapons on the upper wings of the Bébés. Charlie, Jack, Hall, and Cowdin went down to the field to fire and register their Lewis guns before doing their patrol briefing with Lieutenant de Laage.

Since their arrival at Luxeuil, German observation machines boldly circled their field during broad daylight. After the Nieuports arrived, the flights stopped. In addition to the Fokkers known to be at Habsheim, a Gotha Jasta operated from fields near Müllheim just across the Rhine River. Happe's crews wanted to bomb the field, but they needed better information. Charlie's mission was to escort a photographic machine from the Army Corps during its passage over the lines.

Charlie's patrol consisted of Buck, Cowdin, Hall, and Prince. The first two would fly on Keeler's wings with Prince and Hall trailing. Lieutenant de Laage would follow in Thénault's 110 horsepower machine, but Keeler was in charge of the patrol.

To rendezvous with the slower observation machine over Thann, they took off at first light. Fuel management was critical. They couldn't go all the way to Müllheim and make it back to Luxeuil with enough time to linger should they have to fend off any Huns. Charlie flew almost due east into the sun bringing the patrol up to 10,000 feet. Just west of Thann he spotted their photographic machine. Overtaking it, they took up their planned positions on either side and above the lumbering modified Farman. Continuing east with the sun right in their faces, Charlie easily made out the city of Mulhouse and the Rhine Valley just beyond it. Black puffs burst well below them almost lethargically as if the desultory gunners didn't care to be bothered. This would surely alert the Fokkers at Habsheim.

If the Fokkers attacked the Farman when it was over its target, Charlie could do little to help. He looked down at Germany wishing his father's country had never started this infernal war. Cowdin signaled engine trouble and turned to head back to Luxeuil. The remaining pilots held station. Elliot could find his way back on his own. The sun made seeing the Farman extremely difficult. Keeping their eyes out for Fokkers, the flight almost flew right into the observation machine as it approached the lines.

Still no sign of the enemy, Charlie thought. As much as he wanted to mix it up with the Boches, he couldn't mess up the reconnaissance mission. Apparently, the Germans weren't accustomed to Nieuports flying over their territory, though Rockwell's taunting them at Habsheim on Saturday should have been warning enough.

Once over friendly territory, Charlie finally began to relax a little. The Farman held them back with its 40 kilometer per hour speed deficit over the Nieuports, but they cleared the danger zone with no sightings of enemy fights.

Back at Luxeuil, de Laage congratulated Keeler on a job well done. Cowdin had returned safely, and the patrol landed without a shot fired. A call from Vittel an hour later informed them that the Farman had landed as well. The crew promised some great pictures. Everybody seemed pleased and in great spirits.

Though weather closed in and shut down flying the next day, that night they heard the droning of the Gothas over the field. It must have been the German's response to their mission. The sound of the engines faded almost as quickly as the men heard it. Must be heading for a different target, they all commented, resuming their nightly routines.

For the pilots this meant lounging around the *popote* at the Pomme d'Or. That afternoon a crew from Paris had come in with a truckload of movie-making equipment. They'd set up in the popote and shot some film of the men playing billiards. The camera team had to stay the night, so they livened up the evening with tales of filming actresses who thought nothing of showing their bloomers or more. The team hoped to get some film of the escadrille flying the next day.

Wednesday, May 17, started out poorly with a low ceiling and drizzle, but by noon, it cleared up enough for the film crew to shoot some footage on the field. Hall volunteered to fly a little demonstration for them, which Thénault readily approved. He'd been encouraged to take every advantage of publicity for the escadrille. Getting Hall up in the air would keep him away from the movie folks.

Later in the afternoon Jack went up with Thaw and Prince to poke their heads over the lines to see if they could bag one of the observation machines that had been popping up over the field for the last several days. They returned after almost two hours without seeing a thing. That night Hall's Manhattans warmed up the camera people who offered to bring back some of their more risqué movies and even some of the actresses. Several muffled explosions shattered their reverie. Rushing outside, the pilots could see the blue flames of the Gotha exhausts. Tracers streamed up from the machine guns protecting the field.

Buck took the wheel of Thénault's car as the captain and three others piled in for the wild ride to the field. By the time they arrived the attack had stopped. Several bombs had hit the field, but none of the Nieuports appeared damaged.

"*Bon! Merci. Et les hommes*?" Capitaine Thénault asked the adjudant, hoping nobody had been hurt. The NCO said he didn't know for sure. Before he finished, one of the motorcyclists rode up and reported to the captain. It was so dark that he had trouble finding them on the field. He'd just gone up to the town to fetch them, he said breathlessly. There were casualties.

In the dark and confusion, section leaders had trouble getting their men together for a headcount. No one dared use lights that might attract more bombs. The sergeant in charge of the mechanics came over to the knot of men around the captain, crying audibly. "*Les pauvres. Mes petits mécanos. Quatre morts, mon capitaine. Quatre dont Jonchre, le votre.*"

Four dead mechanics, one of them the captain's! The news quickly spread as most of the rest of the escadrille assembled at the field. All four men had been out in the open watching the bombers curiously. A single bomb fell in their midst pulverizing them. To men accustomed as they were to war, death, and maiming, this random act of violence boiled their blood. There was little sleep for anyone that night. Jack voluntarily helped the brancardiers with the grisly task of gathering up the remains. He had seen so much of it in the Ambulance Service that he knew he could handle it better than their young friends could. When he got back to his room at nearly 3 A.M., Jack sank onto his bed and prayed, thinking about Cartier, Masters, little Chérie and the four men whose pieces lay in boxes at the field that night.

With the Germans drawing the first blood, emotions ran very high in the escadrille the next day. Kiffin Rockwell, never known for his calm acceptance of anything he didn't like, fretted and fumed until Thénault agreed to let him fly up to the lines to look for the enemy. Rockwell took off alone and went to the same spot where Charlie's flight had met the Farman near Thann. He pushed the Nieuport up to 12,000 feet, crossing the lines and looking for a fight. When he landed nearly two hours later, French ground observers had already confirmed his victory over a German machine that had crashed just over the German lines.

As their first official victory, the event called for celebration, if subdued a bit by the loss of the four mechanics. Thénault's first action was to assemble the pilots and get Kiffin to give an account of his combat.

"My motor began to misfire so I turned back towards our lines. Below me I spotted a Hun two-seater heading back to Germany. I dove on him, forgetting about my engine trouble. His observer fired first. I think he put a couple rounds in my machine, but I waited to get closer. When I could make out the observer's face, I pressed the trigger. It must have been only about 50 meters. The Lewis stopped dead after only about four rounds—just like at Cazeaux, remember Charlie? I broke hard to the left to avoid hitting the Boche. When I looked back, the observer's gun pointed straight up. He must have sunk into his cockpit. The pilot seemed to be drooped over the edge of his station. The enemy plane fell off on one wing and plummeted, smoking, in the direction of the German lines. I suddenly remembered my failing engine and low fuel. I really wanted to follow the bugger down, but I broke off and headed home. Somehow, the motor held out. *C'est tout, mes amis*."

"Bravo Kiffin! That's the stuff!" Thaw shouted.

"Our first confirmed. You should be proud," Prince added.

"Atta boy!" Hall said, honestly proud of Rockwell.

"Does justice to our boys, at least a little, doesn't it?" de Laage observed, pulling on his mustache in his usual manner.

Rockwell cabled his brother that very day, and the next day a bottle of eighty-year old bourbon arrived via the *poste*. Paul wrote: *You earned this, Kiffin. Use it as you see fit.*

Kiffin opened the bottle that night and poured a small tot. "Let this very American whiskey be the mead we sip after each victory. *Vive la France! Vive les Etats-Unis*!" Thus began a tradition that would last almost a year before they emptied the bottle.

While Rockwell rejoiced in public, he confided to Charlie that he'd almost retched once he'd landed and realized that two men had fallen to their death. This greatly relieved Charlie. Kiffin's lust to avenge the dead mechanics had seemed reckless.

With a touch of extravagance, Thénault submitted Rockwell for the *Médaille Militaire*. The mere act of submission was enough to guarantee some award. Georges Thénault saw a chance to curry Rockwell's favor and gain some publicity at the same time.

The Rockwell's were among the first Americans to offer their services for France. Kiffin, more than Paul, drove the pair into the Legion. He had all the makings of Lancelot. Kiffin was chivalrous with the women, competitive with the men, zealous for the cause, and as hot-tempered and impatient a man as Thénault had ever met. It made him think about his Americans.

The *Section Aéronautique* authorized his escadrille as many as ten airplanes with up to twelve pilots. He requisitioned three more pilots and four Nieuports knowing that he would eventually have to replace casualties. After signing the *Carnet de Jour*, the daily report submitted to headquarters, listing the men killed in the bombing attack, he turned to the pilot's files.

Bill Thaw had served with him in C. 42. Thénault had been instrumental in getting Thaw's lieutenancy. Though young, Thaw was a solid asset with natural leadership traits. He was also a friend. Thénault numbered few men in that category. His stiff nature discouraged people from becoming close. Alfred de Laage de Meux, on the other hand, was a perfect foil to him. Their friendship dated back to Saint Cyr. He knew he could count on his two officers.

Prince's record included his Aero Club of America pilot certificate. Thénault knew that Norman Prince had many ties in wealthy and influential circles. The man was aloof and a bit aristocratic, a characteristic unusual among the Americans. Prince was clearly officer material, though he had yet to prove himself in the unit. Thénault chalked him up as a definite asset.

What a difference between Victor Chapman and Prince, Thénault thought as he picked up the thin file. *Chapman's* connections included two of the men on the Franco-American Committee. Thénault appreciated the efforts of that body in getting the escadrille approved. Chapman was a little green as an aviator, but he made up for this with enthusiasm. Thénault smiled as he thought about the morally straight Chapman. With more like him he wouldn't have to worry about trouble on the ground. Chapman was headstrong though, like his friend Rockwell. *Mavericks*, he thought, recalling the word the American cowboys he admired used for wild horses.

James McConnell's record from flight school listed him as Mac Connell. Thénault would never get the name right thereafter. Now here was a man he liked and trusted. Not at all arrogant or full of himself, Mac was a rock. Mac was close to most of the others, especially Buck. Thénault knew that McConnell drank pretty hard, though he seldom showed the effects.

Jack Buck had none of the pedigree of the others, but he seemed to be the fastest learner and the hardest worker of all the pilots. His impossible survival in the crippled Caudron had made a lasting impression on Georges Thénault. Here was a man who should be groomed for command. He was young and hadn't had much *chasse* experience, but he was a natural pilot. If he survived his first combats in the air, Thénault predicted a brilliant career for Buck. Remarkable the way the *gosse* spoke French, Thénault reflected.

Elliot Cowdin was an enigma. Cowdin always seemed to be promoting something—usually himself. He had a hand in getting the escadrille approved and in recruiting McConnell and Buck, but Cowdin seemed to lack something in the way of motivation. His marks from flight school were average, and, like Prince, Cowdin had an American flying license from before the war. Cowdin's file included evaluations from his previous escadrilles, VB. 108, N. 38, N. 49, and N. 65. Thénault scanned these, recognizing the signatures of three of the four commanders. All had written "*bon pilote, apte au combat*." Why, he wondered, if Cowdin was a 'good pilot apt for combat,' did his commanders let him go to other units? He scribbled some question marks beside Cowdin's name. Elliot had given him and de Laage expensive bottles of champagne the day after he arrived. He would bear watching.

Of all the Americans, Thénault had the most reservations about Bert Hall. He would not have accepted Hall but for Thaw's endorsement. Hall's record from flying training was mottled. His *moniteur* from Pau had written: "Claimed flying experience. Smashed up two machines. Admitted never having flown. Possible saboteur." Yet Hall had a confirmed victory with MS. 38, and had good reports from his time as an instructor at Avord. What gave Thénault pause was the way Hall alienated his countrymen. If it weren't for Thaw, Rockwell, Keeler and Buck, Hall might end up getting trounced. More question marks.

That left *Keeler*. His records from the Legion and flight training were impeccable. He had citations from no less than Capitaine de Lattre, now a *Commandant* commanding one of the battalions in the 170th Infantry, the *Hirondelles de la Mort*. Keeler already had the *Médaille Militaire* in addition to two awards of the *Croix de Guerre*. Clearly a very brave man and a fighter. As young as he was, Keeler was the only married pilot among the Americans which could be an asset or a liability. Another candidate for sous-lieutenant. How many would the Army allow him to recommend for promotion? In addition to Thaw, he listed Prince, Rockwell, Buck, and Keeler as next in line. McConnell would be a great officer. However, Thénault concluded, if he got them all promoted, he was sure to lose most of them to another unit.

"So," he said aloud as he stacked the files, "five out of nine are leaders. One maverick and two question marks. One already an officer. I *am* blessed."

Blessed though he might be, Thénault faced some serious challenges. A clerk handed him a telegram ordering the escadrille to a field near Bar-le-Duc. A month to the day from their arrival at Luxeuil *l'Escadrille Américaine* set off for Behonne where they would spend the whole summer laboring over the bubbling cauldron of Verdun.

Chapter 41
Bloody Strings of Victories

Late Spring 1916

Rain kept the escadrille on the ground. It was just as well since they had to put their efforts into packing for the move. Most of the ground personnel welcomed the orders to leave. The funeral for their fellows and the thought that Luxeuil might be jinxed worked powerfully on their minds. The pilots, on the other hand, regretted the move. Kiffin had developed a slight crush on the Groscolas daughter whose hero worship shook even his attachment to the formidable Madame de Raneville waiting patiently for him in Paris. All of them enjoyed the comfortable surroundings and idyllic atmosphere, though most knew that the pampered existence couldn't last.

Lieutenant de Laage recruited McConnell and Cowdin to help supervise the ground movement. The others would fly to the new field at Behonne, leaving the captain and Prince to drive in one of the touring cars. Charlie led the first flight with Rockwell and Chapman. Thaw took the second with Buck and Hall. Thénault authorized them to make one patrol over the lines before proceeding to Behonne.

Rockwell's victory inspired debates over who would get the next Boche and who would be the first ace in the escadrille. Chapman didn't want to talk about it. He broke away from the flight on a wild goose chase on their way to Bar-le-Duc. Keeler saw him dive on a German two-seater. He held his altitude, disappointed to see that Rockwell too had broken off to join Chapman. He contemplated joining them, but, remembering Féquant's warning never to do the expected, he waited, circling at altitude. Once Chapman began his attack, a flight of five Fokkers came screaming out of the overcast to protect the observation machine. They hadn't seen Keeler's Nieuport so their leader probably liked the odds of six to two. Rockwell never got close to the biplace, becoming occupied with two Fokkers hot on his tail. Chapman seemed to be repeating Kiffin's feat of knocking down the observation machine until the Fokkers entered the picture.

Charlie sized up the situation and decided to try to distract the three Fokkers now locking onto Victor, leaving Rockwell to contend with his two assailants. The observation machine dove away firing, and returned in haste to the German lines. Victor performed some impressive acrobatics in twisting away from the first of the three Fokkers. By then, Charlie loosed a long stream of bullets into the third Fokker that dove to join the two-seater in a dash to safety.

Chapman's machine gun jammed. Charlie closed in firing, sending one Fokker into an uncontrolled dive. He didn't have time to follow it down. The other Fokker now attacked Chapman who was frantically trying to clear his jam. Charlie turned on that German and emptied his drum from about two hundred yards. Too far for a kill, his fire did scare off the Fokker.

While Charlie struggled to change his drum, he searched the skies for Rockwell. Signaling Chapman to leave, Charlie zoomed skyward to recover some of the altitude lost in the fight with Victor's attackers. He came up to 8,000 feet where he found a Nieuport—probably Rockwell's—doing a great loop with one Fokker in front of him and another on his tail. All three were firing, but the tight loop kept any of their rounds from connecting. Charlie's arrival broke up the aerial Ferris wheel. These Germans decided to turn tail. Kiffin had exhausted his ammunition. Later he would discover he had also taken hits in his fuel tank. It was time to head on to Behonne.

Charlie knew how close a call their headlong charge on the two-seater had been and was trying to think of a way to tell his overzealous friends. After landing, he went to Victor's Nieuport where Chapman and his mechanic, Bley, were counting the holes. Rockwell made it in on fumes, his motor quitting before he could even taxi to parking. Charlie walked over to Rockwell's Nieuport, seeing even from a distance that it too was peppered with holes.

"Kiffin, a mighty close call wouldn't you say?"

"I should have gotten those two! Thanks for jumping in, though. I was out of bullets, you know."

"Let's go over to talk to Victor. We need to talk." Rockwell followed him without saying anything. They found Victor smiling with Bley, smoking a cigarette as if nothing had happened.

"It was my turn to lead today, guys. Why did you break off without my signal? I could have predicted the biplace would have some protection. Useless risk and damned close call."

Chapman's smile never faltered. "Come on, Charlie. The Hun was easy prey, and we made it back in one piece."

"I still think I could have gotten one of those Fokkers," Kiffin said, not in the least ruffled by Charlie's criticism. "Charlie did a good job getting them off you too, didn't he, Vic?" He threw in as a conciliatory bone.

"I'll say! Hey, Charlie, why the stern looks? All's well that ends well."

Charlie tried to tell them something of what he had learned from Féquant. He praised their aggressiveness, but failed to convince them that their attack was imprudent. Rather than prolong the point he gave it up.

Thaw's flight returned thirty minutes after them. They too flew up to the lines looking for a fight, encountering nothing.

"How did it go?" Thaw asked, looking at Charlie's serious expression and noticing the holes in Chapman's machine. "A bit of a fight, I see."

"Bill, could you tell these two pig heads that you don't automatically go after a lone observation machine without verifying it doesn't have an escort?"

"Charlie's right, you know. Lost a good pilot in N. 65 who did that very thing and got tangled up with the three Fokkers protecting his intended victim. Not playing the odds. Which one of you took the bait?"

"I went first," Chapman said, still smiling.

"And I joined him. Gotta admit it was a good thing Charlie held back to shake off the Fokkers, but, hell's bells! We're here to get the Boches, aren't we?" Rockwell insisted.

"Or be gotten by them," Hall observed wryly. "It's a little like poker, you know. You have to know when to hold them and when to throw them in. What were the odds in this fracas, Charlie?"

Hall was an unexpected ally. "Five Fokkers and the biplace to our three. Not bad if we had the upper hand, but they got the jump on Vic and Kif, and we had all we could to escape with our skins."

"Well, what's done is done. Doesn't look like the damage is too bad. I agree with you, Charlie, and so does the captain. We have to learn to work together. Let's go see where we're going to be living. I could use something wet, preferably strong. What do you say?" Thaw ended the discussion diplomatically and led them off to find de Laage.

THE MOVE BROUGHT N. 124 TOGETHER WITH TWO other escadrilles, already on the large field at Behonne just over a mile north of Bar-le-Duc. It also brought them closer to the battle at Verdun, the reason for their move. Bar-le-Duc had about 10,000 residents before the war. It sat astride a major railroad and highway linking it to Paris. More importantly, the twenty-two foot wide road already known as the *Voie Sacrée*, the Holy or Sacred Way, proceeded northeast out of Bar-le-Duc, passing the field at Behonne and continuing to the rear trench lines of the Verdun battlefield.

The *Voie Sacrée* was the French Army's aorta. By May, the nearly four-month battle at Verdun kept the way throbbing with a vital flow of men and materiel. The Americans couldn't help noticing the cloud of dust raised by the unbroken line of vehicles, horses, and men clogging the road.

Thénault knew the commanders of the other escadrilles on the field. He'd secured a comfortable villa between Behonne and Bar-le-Duc for the *Escadrille Américaine*. With that, he'd continued the precedent set at Luxeuil. It would be difficult to face the harsh conditions of other fields, but Thénault didn't care as much about living conditions as he did about getting his unit integrated into the fight raging over Verdun. They would miss Groscolas' hospitality, but they were still living in style.

Jack asked Prince what he thought of the way the French commandeered rooms and whole buildings in many cases for soldiers.

"Not quite in keeping with our Bill of Rights, is it Jack? I could quote it to you, but I'm sure you know the gist of the Third Amendment. Don't know that we would put up with it in the States, but the same thing happened during what Kiffin calls the 'War of Northern Aggression.' Think about it. Most of the inhabitants close to the front are staying at their own risk. Back during the Marne battle some of these towns changed hands several times. You don't suppose the Germans scrupled to take over a morsel of property, do you? I'd wager that the homeowners are almost happy to house soldiers. It must give them a little sense of security. Besides, the lawyer in me says they will demand compensation and probably get it when this war ends."

"Provided the Allies win," Buck commented. "Anything but a sure thing with the way Verdun is going."

Prince looked askance, stroking his mustache before agreeing with Jack. "No, you're right there, but I've no doubt our country will be in this before long. It could decide the issue."

"Nimmie, what do suppose happens to us *if* and when the United States enters the war?"

"Commissions, I'd say, and command of the first American squadrons. Only sensible thing to do. Some of us may even go higher. I wouldn't be surprised if Bill gets his majority, already being an officer in the French Army."

"I hope you're right. With all your education and experience the Army would be dumb to leave you only a captain."

Laughing, Prince poked Jack and said: "You flatter me Bucko, but you, Keeler, Chapman, McConnell, and Rockwell are sure bets to command at least a squadron. I may be considered too old to fly. Thanks for talking to me. I've been beginning to think I was somewhat of a pariah."

THE ESCADRILLE WAS NOW WITHIN EARSHOT OF THE BATTLE raging some thirty miles to their northeast. They knew that General Pétain took over the Army Group of the Center at the beginning of May, effectively moving the old war-horse, Joffre, upstairs and out of the tactical arena. Pétain had given his previous command to another firebrand named Nivelle. Nivelle's touted offensive chewed up men almost faster than they could be pushed up the *Voie Sacrée*. At the same time, pilots and observers fell at alarming rates—seventy out of two hundred killed in less than a month.

Every attack began with an artillery duel orchestrated in large part by Farman and Caudron observation machines on the French side, L.V.G.s and Aviatiks on the German. Nearly continuous bombardment by the numerically superior German artillery drove the French to compensate with accurate counter battery fires. The balloon and airplane observers were the bane of German artillerymen because devastatingly accurate barrages of the French 155-millimeter howitzers silenced many a German battery pinpointed from the air.

To keep those observation platforms in the air the French needed continuous coverage from the pursuit escadrilles. Aviation headquarters located at Bar-le-Duc issued daily orders with blocks of time and altitude assigned to the various escadrilles within range of Verdun. For N. 124 this meant a daily patrol at dawn at 12,000 feet, and another near dusk at 6,000 feet. In between, Thénault allowed his pilots to fly missions in pairs or alone at altitudes of their choosing. In spite of the volume of air traffic concentrated over the battle, there was limited coordination between flying units. Headquarters counted on the assigned altitudes and blocks of times to keep various escadrilles from interfering with each other.

Anti-aircraft artillery was another matter. Ground commanders knew the assigned altitude layers for routine patrols and observation circuits were at 1,000, 6,000, and 12,000 feet. Identifying friendly aircraft took up a great deal of training time for the gunners and observers in those batteries. Not only did they have a mission of shooting down enemy airplanes, but the anti-aircraft artillery also signaled other batteries, friendly air, and ground forces with certain pre-arranged messages like the one that turned back the Flandin's bombing raid. German AA shells gave off an oily black smoke while the French bursts were white.

Thénault took off with Rockwell, Hall, and Keeler on their first patrol the morning of May 22. He crossed the lines en route to Etain northeast of Verdun. In spite of orders to await his signal, Thénault saw Hall break off and dive on a lone Aviatik crossing the lines below them. Seeing Bert's intentions, Keeler stayed with the captain in spite of his desire to go down and help Hall. Bert must have found the dish a bit too rich. He continued his dive past the hail of bullets from the Aviatik's observer before working his way up to rejoin the patrol. All made it back unharmed.

Thaw led the afternoon patrol with Buck, Hall, Rockwell, and Prince. Jack took off last in Thénault's 110 horsepower Nieuport. Their mission that afternoon was to protect a Farman circling over Fort Douaumont adjusting artillery. Again, Hall broke away in pursuit of a lone Aviatik. This time, by previous agreement, Buck peeled off and accompanied Hall. Bert's first rounds alerted the Germans who turned and made a mad dash for their lines. Hall, heedless of enemy fighters on the German side of the line, zoomed to 12,000 feet, keeping the Aviatik in sight. His diving fire caught the observer by surprise. He slumped in his cockpit either dead or seriously wounded. Jack kept above Hall's combat looking out for Boche Fokkers. He saw none, but did see Hall's target Aviatik flutter away out of control and tumble towards the ground near Malancourt. He had gotten Bert's attention and managed to coax him back as they passed through three thousand feet following the Aviatik down.

That night the escadrille celebrated Hall's victory in spite of Thaw's admonishment for failing to follow orders and stay in patrol. Bert, the culprit on both patrols, sheepishly kidded Thaw that he was getting to be an old fuddy-duddy.

Overhearing this, Keeler elbowed Hall hard enough to elicit a wince.

"What happened to your sage advice to Kiffin and Victor the other day, you old coot? I'm surprised at you. If I didn't know better, I'd say you were trying to run up a string of victories," Charlie chided.

"Looks like there's plenty to be had, Charlie my boy. One more and I'm up to you. Worried I'll pass you up?"

"Hell, no, and you ought to know me better than that. I just think we are courting disaster like a bunch of pig-headed individualists out dueling for sport."

Thaw pulled Charlie away and whispered that he was wasting his time on Weston Bert Hall if he thought he was going to change the man in any way. "You just have to tolerate him and take what he says with a grain of salt. Let's not dampen the celebration. I think you're right, but some of us are going to have to learn it the hard way."

The next day they got their chance.

Charlie and Jack were on the scheduled morning patrol with Thénault, de Laage, Thaw, Rockwell, and Chapman. It would be the first time the entire leadership of the escadrille went up together. They'd picked up a seventh Nieuport, one of the N-17 models with a 120 horsepower motor, from an escadrille converting to Nieuport 27's.

Earlier that morning, Thaw and Rockwell had gone out by themselves. Thaw barely had time to tell them he had shot down a Fokker monoplane before he got refueled to join the patrol. Three victories! Now every pilot wanted to add his name to the list of victors, oblivious to Thénault's order not to attack without his signal.

Charlie's engine began to sputter once they reached station near Etain, so he reluctantly turned back. As he left the nearly perfect V formation, he spotted a flight of twelve German two-seaters far below heading toward the lines. With his engine still running roughly, he was not about to mix it up with such a crowd. He began to lose altitude. One of the other Nieuports in the formation saw him pull away and must have thought Charlie was going after the two-seaters. It looked like either Chapman or Rockwell. Charlie cringed at the thought that they might have misinterpreted his trouble as a signal to attack.

With no other choice, Keeler continued back, wondering if he would make it over the lines before his motor quit. The fracas behind him got very interesting very fast, but Charlie would have to wait to hear about it until later. As he nursed the Bébé along, descending involuntarily due to the motor cutting in and out of its own accord, Charlie saw a lone L.V.G., a two-seater like the one Rockwell had downed, lazily circling, evidently adjusting fires on Fort Tavannes, just across the lines. All he had to do was dive straight ahead to get the L.V.G. in his sights. Looking around and overhead, he couldn't see any covering aircraft. He held his fire hoping the observer was too busy with his artillery work to notice an approaching Nieuport.

When the L.V.G. began its slow turn back towards German lines, Charlie adjusted his flight path to stay behind and out of the pilot's line of sight. It worked. He was able to close to under 150 yards before the startled observer began to swing his machine gun up in Charlie's direction. Charlie's first burst nailed the observer. Charlie knew he had only one pass. He couldn't maneuver lest he come down in no man's land when his sick motor quit. Every round counted. He pressed the trigger a second time catching the pilot. The L.V.G. nosed down under full power and headed south parallel with the lines. Charlie was tempted to follow it, but wisely decided to continue for Behonne. When his motor quit completely on approach, he thanked God he hadn't gone after the two-seater.

At the field Prince, Cowdin and Hall were the only other pilots no longer airborne. Charlie quickly told them he'd left the flight with motor trouble. He remembered seeing someone diving for a large flight of observation machines, but he couldn't account for their actions.

"You wouldn't be the Nieuport we just got a call about from the observation post near Fort Tavannes, now would you?" Prince asked.

"I came back that way and had a little scrap. Why? What did they want?"

Hall let out a whoop and slapped Charlie on the back. "That's four confirmed Keeler! One more to be our first ace!"

"Congratulations, Charlie," Cowdin said, genuine admiration on his face. "With a bloody bum motor to boot!"

Prince shook Charlie's hand and explained that the observation post confirmed an L.V.G. crashing just yards from the Fort. "They saw your victory, Charlie. It's another confirmation!"

Charlie smiled slightly. "Those unlucky bastards practically flew into my sights. It was almost too easy."

"*Deux de moins qui mangent la soupe ce soir*," Hall said, quoting the popular phrase before continuing in typical Hall fashion, "I wouldn't cry in my soup over them."

Clever Bert, Charlie thought, *two less to eat soup tonight. I wonder if either of them has a Frau or fraulein or even some kinder back in Germany.* He began to feel a little nauseous, excusing himself and rushing to Thénault's office for a drink of water.

The four of them waited together. The first to land was Kiffin. He came out of his cockpit streaming blood from his face and vile Legion invectives from his mouth. Thénault taxied up next and rushed over to check on Rockwell. Chapman landed and descended from his Bébé clutching a bleeding left arm.

"A scratch, I tell you," he said seeing and hearing Kiffin. "Where's Jack and Thaw?" he asked as they watched de Laage's plane come in and taxi over.

Thénault asked de Laage the same question. The lieutenant said he'd seen Thaw in a running fight with the Aviatiks obviously getting the worst of it when Buck passed through, breaking up the circle and throwing off their aim. Thaw appeared to be hit, and Buck might have taken some rounds as well. The two of them dropped out of sight and he'd had to break off in order to make it back himself. All of them were low on fuel.

Thénault and the others spent an anxious afternoon waiting for word on their two missing pilots. Charlie was beside himself that Jack might have gone down. They returned to the villa after Thénault's calls produced no results, reluctantly leaving the field and going for dinner, a dinner Charlie couldn't possibly enjoy. When his mission mates learned of his victory, they broke out Rockwell's whiskey and told him it was his turn for a shot.

"Not until we get word on Bill and Jack," Charlie said, sinking even further down in his chair. The phone rang in the Villa causing them all to jump.

Thénault's face lit up as he repeated what he'd heard for the waiting pilots. "They're both alive. Went down together near Fort Tavannes close to where Charlie's L.V.G. crashed. They're in a field hospital at Dieue. Who's coming with me besides Charlie?" Rockwell and Chapman had to return to the dressing station to have their wounds re-bandaged. The rest piled into the staff car and drove the thirty miles to the hospital.

Charlie almost knocked Thénault over in his dash for the reception desk. His haste was of no avail because the orderly manning the desk would not release any information to anyone but a commanding officer. Thénault stepped up and asked after Thaw and Buck.

"Ah, les *Américains*!" the orderly said. He led them to an officer's ward where they found Bill Thaw sitting up on a bed with his arm wrapped in plaster. Charlie looked around for Jack, and didn't see him. Maybe they put him in an enlisted ward. He asked Bill, hoping Jack's absence didn't mean something more serious.

"He's right here. They think he's an officer. Should be too, if you ask me," Thaw said, pointing to the man in the bed beside him with a foot all bandaged and a swath of bandages over his whole head and face.

"I got hit above the right elbow. It felt like an ax blow. I was surprised the arm was still there. Couldn't move it or feel anything after the initial shock. I started feeling woozy almost right away, and could see that I was losing a lot of blood. One of the Aviatiks took after me when I fell out of the fight and headed towards our lines. That was when Jack saved my life. He killed the observer who had kept up a stream of lead after catching me in the arm. With Jack in the game, the Aviatik bugged out.

"I didn't know that Jack had been hit in the foot, and that his motor was about to die from fuel exhaustion. He stayed with me all the way down. I don't remember landing. I passed out. Woke up with some poilus pulling me out of the Bébé. Not far behind me I saw another Nieuport with its nose stuck in a shell hole. Jack's.

"We got here a couple of hours ago. Jack hit his head on the cowling when the Nieuport nosed over. He's got an ugly crease in his forehead that bled like hell. Seeing double too." Thaw turned his head to Thénault. "Captain, the man deserves at least the *Médaille*. I think he got the Aviatik too. I tell you, he saved my sorry ass. What a fight!"

Thaw lay back exhausted from the effort and loss of blood. Both he and Buck were being sent to Neuilly the next day. Charlie got permission to stay until Jack woke. They'd send a car for him if he couldn't hitch a ride back to Behonne. The orderly assured them that Keeler could ride with the wounded to the train station at Bar-le-Duc if he didn't mind spending the night at the hospital. Thénault wrote up an *Ordre de Mission*, making it official. The others returned to Behonne.

Charlie sat between the two beds and thought about the day's activities. Thaw's morning victory, his own later in the morning, and Jack's probable victory had cost them four wounded. In one day, they'd lost two airplanes and at least two pilots in less than two hours. He couldn't wait for one of his two sleeping friends to tell him what had happened after he'd left. At least they would get to go back to Paris to recover. Jennifer would surely take personal interest in Jack's care. Suddenly, Charlie felt very tired and very old. His head drooped and bobbed until a very overworked nurse came and stuck a pillow against the arm of the chair. He didn't wake until Thaw shook him at suppertime.

"Charlie, Jack's awake. See if you can get him to talk a little. He suffered a concussion."

Charlie went over and put his hand on Jack's. "Hey Bucko, what do you have to say for yourself?"

"Charlie? God my head hurts! Am I blind? Why do they have all these bandages on my eyes?"

"You hit your head pretty hard right above your eyebrows. The bandages are to keep the blood out of your eyes and face."

"You OK? I saw you turn around. Lord what a hornet's nest we fell into!"

"I'm fine. Don't bother talking if it hurts. Looks like you and Bill are getting a free trip to the American Hospital. I'm sure a certain nurse there will be happy to see you."

"Yeah, but with us out who's going to cover the extra patrols?"

"Hear that, Bill? A hole in his foot and a cracked skull and he's worried about who's flying his missions!"

"Jack, I know I thanked you when they brought you in, but in case you didn't hear me then, I owe you my life." Thaw said with more emotion than either of them had heard from him before.

"When you turned around and headed back, Chapman or Rockwell thought it was a signal to attack. They dove one after the other on the Aviatiks. The rest of the escadrille followed," Thaw said. "I knew Thénault would be thoroughly steamed."

"Boy am I glad to hear Rockwell and Chapman made it back," Jack said after Charlie informed them that Rockwell had a face full of glass, wood, and metal splinters from the explosive bullet that shattered his instrument panel. Chapman's wound was less serious.

Thaw said the Aviatiks circled like a wagon train being attacked by Indians. Each machine's observers covered nearly every possible quadrant. It was pure hell flying through that formation. He and other others were lucky to get out at all.

"Adds to our reputation for not following orders. Thank goodness nobody got killed," Charlie observed.

"I know you are right about using our heads and working together," Thaw said, repeating something he himself told Keeler before. "I just think some of us are not cut out for working in formation."

"You two will have plenty of time to think about it. Get some rest. I am riding into town with you and will see you off at the railway station. Helluva price to pay for a trip to Paris."

WITH TWO ON THE WAY TO THE HOSPITAL and more Nieuport 17's showing up, Thénault needed more pilots. The day Thaw, Buck, Chapman and Rockwell were wounded, a short feisty man with a polyglot accent reported from the Réserve Général. Gervais Raoul Lufbery, no stranger to some of the N. 124 men, was upset to learn that Thaw was out of action. All the excitement that day had everybody so tied up that few could pay much attention to the newcomer. Lufbery plopped his bags in Thénault's office and took a walk up and down the field at Behonne. Every once and a while a mechanic or pilot from one of the French squadrons would glance up and shout, *"Beh oui! Bienvenue Luf!"*

Lufbery had already made a name for himself, and some knew him from the beginning of the war when he had served as Marc Pourpe's mechanic until the adventurous pilot died in a crash. Born and raised in France, Luf's American citizenship derived from his father who had deposited Raoul with relatives in France after the death of his first wife. After remarrying, the senior Lufbery returned to settle in Wallingford, Connecticut. Raoul's two-year stint in the US Army included service in the Philippines further tying him to his adopted country, but he remained a man caught between two cultures. Lufbery had virtually circled the globe in search of adventure. Linking up with Pourpe, a pre-war exhibition pilot, began one of the deepest friendships he had ever had.

Having maintained Pourpe's Morane Parasol for nearly two years on tour in Calcutta, Indo-China, Egypt and most of North Africa, Lufbery really knew the plane inside and out. On the way back to France in 1914, Pourpe learned of the war. It was an easy decision for Luf to follow Pourpe into the Army. There was a bit of a problem with his citizenship. Lufbery had to enlist in the Foreign Legion first in order to be detached to Pourpe. Thus, Lufbery became the first American to serve in French aviation.

Pourpe's death in an airplane accident devastated Lufbery. He immediately volunteered for flight training after nearly a year as a mechanic. Finishing flight school in September 1915, Lufbery, now a corporal, began flying with VB. 106, a Voisin bombing escadrille. It was there that he met Bill Thaw, and Norman Prince.

Something in Lufbery churned for action. Flying a slow bomber and only occasionally getting into aerial combat made him restless. He asked for Nieuport training at about the time Prince and Thaw were finishing their *chasse* instruction late in March 1916.

Lufbery reported to the Nieuport division at RGA. In spite of his superb knowledge of the mechanics of airplanes, Luf proved at first a little too heavy-handed with the sensitive Nieuports. So many candidates wanted to become *chasse* pilots that the instructors could turn pilots away in a flash. When Luf heard he was a candidate for *radiation*—French for getting kicked out—he redoubled his efforts. Lufbery surprised his instructors by completing the course on May 22, 1916.

Lufbery felt more French than American. Going to the American escadrille wasn't his first choice. He wanted to join the Storks, the most famous group whose ranks included France's Ace of Aces, Charles Guynemer.

Thénault returned from the hospital at Dieue at about the time Lufbery wandered back into the captain's office. Georges Thénault had a lot on his mind. Seeing the swarthy short corporal with pilot wings, he assumed he was a French replacement in the wrong place. Lufbery even spoke French like the native he was. Thénault seemed preoccupied. Only when Luf dropped his orders on the desk did Thénault finally take notice. He smiled and welcomed Lufbery somewhat curtly. Luf, ever sensitive to any wrong, took an instant dislike to the commander.

Later Lieutenant de Laage took the escadrille's first 'new' pilot to his room in the escadrille villa. Lufbery asked de Laage why the captain had such a large broomstick up his ass. The loyal lieutenant couldn't suppress a little chuckle before admonishing Lufbery not to say anything like that within earshot of anyone else. He held back on his usual spiel about doing one's job and not drinking too much. This French-American vet was at least a year or two older than both Thénault and himself. Instead, he explained how the captain was probably preoccupied with Thaw, Buck, and the other wounded men. Luf said nothing, deciding that at least the lieutenant was okay.

Buck and Thaw's evacuation left the remaining N. 124 pilots to take up the slack. Lufbery readily agreed to join the morning mission with de Laage, Prince, and Hall. Lieutenant de Laage spent nearly an hour briefing them. He kept reminding them that everything had gone to hell in a hand basket earlier because of lack of discipline. Instead of worrying about each other and picking the right moment to fight, the recklessness of a few drew them all into a grinder.

"Remember, we are here to guard our territory, our observation machines, and ourselves. It we lose two pilots a day to foolhardy jousts against superior numbers, there won't be enough of us left to do the mission," he said reaching deeply into his English repertoire to make this point. "If you survive your first week of combat, you will probably make it a month. If you are still flying after a month, chances are good you will last six months."

Prince, Hall, and Lufbery, tallying up their months of flying, realized de Laage was pronouncing them survivors, but talk about discipline and staying together didn't sit well with Lufbery. He preferred to look out for himself and not count on others. He wouldn't hesitate to help a fellow on a patrol, but, to his way of thinking, formations were for bombers. He agreed with de Laage about not taking on more than you could chew. Going after a flight of twelve with half their numbers was reckless.

Thénault's curtness with Lufbery stemmed in part from frustration at having little or no control over his American pilots. Maintaining balance while trying to form a cohesive team would elude Georges Thénault no matter how hard he tried. Lufbery would be a special case from the day he arrived.

Keeler made it back to Behonne in time to see the morning patrol return. He'd met Lufbery in Paris. Charlie remembered the man as an incredible raconteur. The difference between Luf's stories and Hall's lay in more than the telling, though Lufbery's English was seasoned with international flavors. Luf was never the center of his stories. It was always someone else. Even when telling about winning an award for marksmanship in the American Army, he downplayed his accomplishment. Bert Hall, in contrast, would never miss a chance to embellish his stories and his role in them. The two men were as different as night and day.

"*Rien à signaler*—nothing significant to report" de Laage wrote in the escadrille book after the eventless mission. The patrols the next two days submitted negative reports in spite of the stepped up German offensive. Chapman and Rockwell refused to be grounded by their superficial wounds. Both flew the two daily patrols as well as at least one in between. Charlie too logged up to six hours a day. The Germans he spotted traveled in packs of eight to ten and stayed on the German side of the lines, taunting the French aviators.

Charlie instinctively liked flying with Lufbery. He went out of his way to make the colorful man welcome. Lufbery was fearless. With a few more hours under his belt in Nieuports, Charlie predicted great results.

On May 29, Clyde Balsley and Chouteau Johnson joined N. 124. They'd been checked out on Nieuports at Plessis, and arrived raring to go. Charlie didn't know Balsley, though Jack said he was a swell fellow. Chouteau, he'd almost crossed paths with fatally at Pau, but he hadn't seen Johnson since returning from the States. He was anxious to tell Chouteau about meeting his parents in Saint Louis.

Thénault told Keeler, "Take another pilot out with the new men and do the 12,000 foot patrol." Charlie had to choose between Lufbery and McConnell. Mac had more Nieuport experience and knew the region.

Charlie took off at six that evening. Balsley's motor wouldn't start so he never got off. Johnson took up the left wing and McConnell the right. At 12,000 feet they could see more than twenty miles in every direction. Edging the flight over the lines, Charlie tried to make sure Johnson got a good look at the trace of the trenches. Artillery had largely obliterated the main forts, making them nearly invisible from the air. The lack of air action in the last several days led the French headquarters to believe another major offensive was brewing. According to the analysts, when the observation machines started reappearing, the offensive would be close behind.

While pleasantly warm on the ground, the air at 12,000 feet was frigid. Charlie pulled the muffler Michelle had sent him tighter around the bottom of his face. There was just enough of a trace of her scent in the wool to make him relish every breath. At the end of seventy minutes of circling and enjoying the pre-summer sunset, Charlie led his flight back to Behonne. "Nothing significant to report." *Just as well*, he thought, *Johnson doesn't need a baptism of fire on his first flight.*

The N. 124 pilots didn't complain about fatigue under the pressure of the two-a-day missions, but the toll showed in their haggard faces.

Cowdin seldom flew extra missions. After some friendly kidding in the popote, Elliot began to complain of headaches. Hall's Manhattans might have something to do with them, but his comrades sipped from the same pail without noticeable effects.

Rain gave them a welcome break. Charlie called Michelle to see if she'd gotten to see Jack and Bill Thaw.

"My health is fine, thank you for not asking, if you count getting bigger than a cow as healthy."

"Lord, Michelle, I'm sorry. I guess I'm just tired. We're hitting it hard here, but it's raining today. I'm glad you're fine. You know I love you."

"Yes, and yes to your original question too. Thaw will be in a cast for a while. Jack's wounds will heal in time, but the concussion affected his vision and is still giving him headaches." He ran a great risk of getting an infection, but Jennifer was delighted to be able to spend so much time caring for him. Thaw's arm required complicated surgery. He might not recover full use of the arm, but the doctors were sure both of them could get back to flying in a couple of weeks.

"Keep the letters coming, darling," Charlie said before ending their conversation. "I live for your words and the smell of your perfume."

Just as Charlie left the *téléphonist's* office, he looked up to see a flight of Gotha bombers passing overhead. Remembering the disaster at Luxeuil, he raced back to get the soldier out of the office in time for both of them to dive into a sandbagged bunker. The young corporal needed little encouragement. All over the field, others were taking cover. Anti-aircraft machine guns barked, but instead of Behonne, the Germans dropped their loads on Bar-le-Duc that first day of June 1916. It pained the men of N. 124 to learn that forty civilians died in the attack. Somehow, they felt responsible for attracting the bombers.

That day the artillery preparation for the renewed German ground attack shook the earth for several hours all the way to Behonne. Waves of field gray clambered across the torn and dusty expanse between the two forces. French machine guns and artillery mowed them down viciously, but on came the distinctive coal-bucketed heads overwhelming some of the defenders. In a week Fort Vaux fell, but the French poured men into counterattacks. The carnage exceeded the human mind's ability to comprehend—one hundred thousand dead or wounded in one day. Somehow, the French Army held at Verdun.

The weather, on the other hand, did not hold. Heavy rains, low overcast, and fog set in almost as if the hand of God wanted to put out the fires on the ground. Flying was out of the question. With some of the biggest fighting of the war going on only thirty miles away, the Americans in N.

124 huddled in their villa waiting for the weather to clear. On Thursday, June 8, Thénault allowed Lufbery to take off to check the ceiling. Luf returned in thirty minutes never having gotten more than five miles from the field and a hundred feet above the ground.

The next day, Dudley Hill arrived. During the weather down time, Thénault and de Laage drove to RGA to check out the crop of new pilots awaiting assignment. The only two Americans they found were Hill and Didier Masson. Both struck Thénault as ideal candidates for his escadrille. Hill he could almost take back on the spot, but Masson had some more Nieuport flying to finish before he could leave. Thénault laid claim to both men and returned to Behonne.

On June 15, the weather let up enough for regular patrols. Rockwell, Chapman, and McConnell made patrols that afternoon, happily shaking off the gloom and boredom of being ground-bound for so many days. Innumerable shell holes now filled with water made the ground sparkle like a diamond-studded tiara when the sun glanced off the pools. Much to the Americans' chagrin, no enemy aircraft seemed to be aloft.

Thénault gathered the escadrille for a briefing Friday evening. The German effort to cross the Meuse River threatened to collapse the Verdun defenses. The escadrille's mission for the next day was to guard the near bank of the river and to prevent German observation machines from concentrating artillery against French defenses. The captain, de Laage, Chapman and Balsley, would make the morning patrol. Keeler, Prince, Cowdin and Rockwell would take the evening mission. Thénault made it very clear that they were not to cross the river for any reason.

In the air the morning of June 17, Thénault looked about content to see the flight in tight formation as they approached the lines near the little village of Champ. In that sector the lines ran roughly west to east while the Meuse flows generally south to north. A large bend in the river formed a loop sticking out like a big tongue pointing at the hotly contested Mort Homme hill to the west. N. 124's mission was to remain west of this loop. Almost at the moment of crossing the lines, Chapman spotted a big A.E.G. twin-motor bomber slicing across the "tongue" of the loop. He didn't hesitate for more than a second, breaking off, and crossing the river against Thénault's strict orders.

Victor didn't think about orders. He only saw an enemy winging its way into friendly territory. His dive on the A.E.G. gained no surprise at all. The gunner in the rear opened up on Chapman, following his attacker's flight path all the way through Victor's first pass. The German dove away escaping to safety before the Nieuport could close to firing distance. Victor rejoined the flight that continued on the west side of the river, patrolling up and down without any action for another hour.

Finally, Thénault signaled end of mission. All turned to join him but Chapman. Remembering Thénault's encouragement to fly independent missions, Victor thought nothing of breaking off after the fruitless morning flight and striking off on his own.

He landed for fuel just behind Verdun at one of the fields marked on his map. Heading back for the lines, he couldn't seem to find any Boches. They found him. Five Fokkers gave Chapman more than he could handle. He twisted and turned to get out of their lines of fire. As he approached friendly lines, he thought he might shake them when a bullet crashed through the empennage shattering wood and ripping canvas. It ricocheted, tearing through Victor's leather helmet, furrowing a deep crease in his skull. Blood flooded his face and filled his goggles.

Victor felt the Nieuport fall into a deadly spin. Blood blurred his vision and the machine seemed not to respond to his movements. He tore the goggles from his face feeling a searing pain as the strap scraped against the fresh wound. Wiping his eyes he tried to get his bearings. At that point, he noticed that the control rod for his right aileron flopped freely in the air from the top wing. A bullet must have severed the rod. No wonder the machine felt out of control. The ground approached dizzyingly. He had to do something.

Grasping the end of the rod with his right hand where it entered the wing, he centered the aileron and pulled back on the stick at the same time. Slowly the Nieuport recovered from the spin and went into a shallow dive. He could just control flight by flying with his left hand while manipulating the control rod with his right. The blood seemed to have either stopped or was being blown back by the wind. He was a little surprised not to feel much pain.

Victor landed at Froids, one of the forward-most airfields just inside French lines. The medics helped him from his machine and cleaned up the wound before wrapping layer after layer of gauze until the dressing towered above Chapman's head. He perched his cap precariously on top of the pile making him look more than a little ludicrous. The commander of N. 67 at Froids, Capitaine Saint-Sauver, gave Victor a ride in his own vehicle back to Behonne. Not knowing it was pointless, Saint-Sauver ordered Victor not to fly until his wound healed.

"*MONSIEUR* CHAPMAN," THENAULT BEGAN SERIOUSLY. "I am told you may have encountered the great Oswald Boelcke in your little combat. You are lucky to be here if that is the case. Boelcke has close to twenty victories. I should ask you why you violated my orders and left the patrol this morning, but I am too happy to have you back. You must go to the hospital to have your wound treated."

Laughing, Victor said it was nothing at all. "Just get me a new airplane, mon Capitaine, and I will go get your Boelcke for you. And make it one of the 120 horsepower ones, *s'il vous plaît*." He saluted and turned to leave before Thénault could say another word.

At the end of the second full month of Thénault's command of l'Escadrille Américaine, he resigned himself to his powerlessness over the headstrong Americans. He could rant, rave and fume at them, or try to channel their boundless energy into something productive. It caused him tremendous anxiety since it ran counter to everything he'd ever learned in uniform.

Balsley's first mission across the lines was uneventful, making Clyde all the more eager to get up and have a go at the Boches himself. He got his chance that Sunday morning at just before six when he took off with Thénault in a flight of seven, the most N. 124 had launched to date. The captain wasn't surprised to see three of them break off just as they crossed the lines, probably with mechanical difficulties. He could see from the markings that he still had Rockwell, Prince, and Balsley.

At 15,000 feet, the sight of at least forty German airplanes wending their way towards the lines made them huddle in closer to each other for security. Even higher, another flight of Aviatiks, maybe fifteen, circled like vultures. There weren't enough Nieuport escadrilles in the entire sector to match this number of enemy planes. Thénault had to think about saving his patrol.

When a flight of Fokkers detached itself from the larger gaggle and attacked Thénault's little formation, the fracas rapidly devolved into an every man for himself affair. Prince found himself pursued by a Fokker that poured deadly accurate fire into his machine. When a bullet singed the right side of his head and sliced open the leather of his helmet, he dove in terror for his own lines.

Thénault and Rockwell saw Prince's predicament but were powerless to respond due to the number of other attackers now annoyingly buzzing about them like bees dislodged from their nest. Thinking Balsley was right behind them; Thénault too dove for safety, and headed back for Behonne with Rockwell for once following his leader. Only when they began their approach did they notice the absent Texan. On the ground, Prince, shaking like a leaf, joined them. The other three had returned equally rattled. It was as if they collectively came to the realization that they were impotent against such numbers.

Their brazen bravado and sense of invincibility took a bitter swill of reality that morning. Most would recover when the adrenaline levels returned to normal, but, for the moment, the pilots of N. 124 all shared the bilious taste of abject terror.

Balsley's absence didn't help matters at all. Thénault immediately directed calls to adjoining fields to see if he had landed. He called around to the field hospitals. A forward military hospital at Vadelaincourt had indeed picked up an American 'officer' and still had him there. Thénault didn't worry about them calling Corporal Balsley an officer, but, afraid he might have lost his first pilot, he raced off to the hospital with Chapman and de Laage.

They found Balsley in an officer's ward feverish and only barely conscious. He had taken an explosive bullet in the right hip. The doctor told them he had pulled nearly a half kilogram of pieces out of Balsley's abdomen. The American had severely perforated intestines and a shattered hip. He was too critical to move. Between the loss of blood, the danger of infection and the holes in his intestines, the doctors already called Balsley a "sad case." Chapman recognized the military medicine's euphemism for a goner. The doctor in the Legion clearing station had said the same about his friend when he refused Victor's 100,000 francs. Victor felt tears welling up in his eyes.

Clyde rallied a little to say hello before they left. All of them were anxious to get clear of the charnel house. It stunk of mud and unwashed bodies, carbolic, feces, and other smells that they didn't want to identify. Flies filled the ward defying the flypaper the orderlies had tacked to the windows and over the doors. Men were brought in on stretchers during their short visit. Others were carried out on the same stretchers covered with sheets, bound for the freshly dug graves outside the building. Balsley begged for something to drink. The doctor refused, but told them the patient could suck on oranges.

The next day Chapman loaded a bag of oranges in his Nieuport before the morning mission. He had paid dearly for the fruit, but it was just a small gesture for the kind-hearted Chapman. After the mission, he landed at the field nearest Vadelaincourt. He walked into the ward just as a group of senior officers moving from bed to bed approached Balsley. Victor watched as they pinned a *Médaille Militaire* on Balsley's hospital frock.

As the colonel turned to go to the next bed, Clyde looked up and said in English: "I'm not going to die!" The officers looked surprised, though they understood what he'd said. Smiling, they said nothing and moved on to the next bed.

"No, Clyde, you're not going to die. What made you say that?" Victor asked.

"Oh, hi Vic!" Balsley said wincing. "I've seen them pin these medals on guys only minutes before they carted them out with a sheet over their head. I'm going to have to disappoint them."

"That's the spirit! Hey, I brought you some oranges. You can suck on them according to the doctor. I'd keep them close to my nose too. God, it reeks in here!"

"I know. You get used to it. They are too overworked here to clean up the place. I wish they'd get me out of here, but they had to open me up again this morning." He held up a jar full of metal pieces that he said they'd taken out of him.

"I can't stay too long," Victor said, "but what do you remember about your flight? I want to go out this afternoon and bag one of those Huns for you."

Balsley tired quickly because of the morphine, but he did manage to tell Chapman that he'd gotten off one round when the Lewis gun jammed. Just then two Aviatiks latched onto him like glue. He tried to shake them by diving into a cloud but their bullets followed him into the foggy mist. He'd rolled inverted hoping to throw off their aim when the explosive bullet slammed into his side. He couldn't feel his leg, thinking it had been shot off. After unjamming the rudder by pulling at his useless right leg, he'd been able to pull out of the spin he'd entered. He told Victor that it was incredible that he felt no pain whatsoever. He grimaced just then when a sharp wave of pain rose up above the medicine and coursed through his body.

"Take it easy. You don't need to tell me the rest."

"No, no. It's okay," Balsley said, wiping the sweat from his brow and breathing deeply before continuing. "I crash landed upside down between the lines. Even when I unbuckled and fell to the ground, I didn't feel anything. I knew I was hurt, but the leg was still there, thank God. I dragged myself about ten feet away from the machine hoping the Boches hadn't zeroed in on it already with their artillery. When the poilus came and started dragging me to the trenches, the pain hit me like a monster. I must have passed out since the next thing I remember is waking up in this stink hole." The memory must have stirred up more pain for Clyde shuddered and closed his eyes tightly.

Chapman took Clyde's hand and told him they'd get him out of there as soon as possible. He promised to come back in a couple of days with more oranges. Before he finished, Balsley was sound asleep. More determined than ever to down one of the evil Germans using the illegal explosive bullets, Chapman returned to his Nieuport and set off on yet another solitary hunt.

Chapter 42
Sweet Convalescence

Paris, June 1916

Jennifer brushed a blond curl back from her cheek as she leaned over Jack's bed to put the thermometer into his mouth. He was sleeping so soundly that she didn't want to wake him. His chart showed no increase in temperature in two days, a very good sign that his body was not fighting an infection. Just as she touched the glass tube to his lips he woke with a start, grabbing her wrist. He'd been dreaming of his last flight. The bump on his head now gave him frequent headaches. Aspirin helped a little, but he still got dizzy from time to time. For a second or two before he came fully awake, he waved Jennifer's outstretched arm in tight little circles much as he would have moved the control stick in his Nieuport. He didn't make a sound or thrash about, but he kept pressing down on Jennifer's small wrist with his thumb, almost painfully.

"Jack! It's me, Jennifer. Wake up and let go of my wrist. You're hurting me!"

"What? Hurting you? What was I doing?" Jack asked looking very confused.

"Flying my arm, you big lummox of a Swede! You were dreaming. Look at the bruise you made on my wrist. Was that the trigger you were pressing so hard?"

"Gee, Jennifer. I'm sorry. I didn't mean to hurt you." He sat up and took the thermometer from her, placing it dutifully under his tongue while stroking her wrist gently.

"Did you get him?" Jennifer asked.

"Geh hoom?" He mumbled with the thermometer in his mouth.

"The German you were fighting in your dream."

Jack looked at her strangely, not comprehending her for several seconds. When he caught her drift, he admitted he didn't even remember dreaming. In the past, he'd told her about his nightmares. Most of the time they involved torn up bloodied bodies and not being able to wash the blood from his hands. He hadn't dreamt of flying, or at least he didn't remember dreams like that.

Jennifer had been at his side every free moment in the hospital. Nurse Wilson made sure that Jennifer's assignment included Jack's ward. Mildred also looked after Bill Thaw until he was released on local convalescent leave. Thaw's arm was on the mend. He no longer needed to be bed-ridden. He itched to go back to the escadrille, but the doctors wouldn't take the cast off which meant he wouldn't be able to fly anyway. Now that Jack was getting on his feet a little, Thaw came back to walk with him when he could pry Buck away from Jennifer.

Jack still couldn't put much weight on his wounded foot, but he refused to be wheeled around in a chair. He used crutches to go to physical therapy and walk around the hospital as often as possible. Jennifer knew it was the best thing for him so she didn't object or treat him like some of the other nurses who tended to mother the wounded. She hardly ever left the hospital grounds now that Jack was there. When she got off her shift, she went to see him. They dealt bridge hands and practiced bidding until they were almost thinking alike. Sometimes Jennifer would read to Jack whose headaches made it hard for him to focus his eyes for any length of time.

Some of the other patients grumbled about his special treatment, but they thought that Buck was engaged to the beautiful blond nurse. Just having her on the floor or in their ward increased their envy of Buck's good fortune. Jennifer looked ravishing in her uniform. The white that covered her from head to toe couldn't hide her figure. More than once Jack had noticed some of his ward mates practically drooling when she leaned over a bed tightening the white uniform over her round bottom. Instead of getting jealous or angry, he counted his good fortune and hoped the view brought a little joy to the lonely men on the ward.

In spite of the time he spent with Jennifer, Jack was restless. He received updates on the escadrille from Paul Rockwell who visited several times a week. Kiffin had gotten his second victory but couldn't get it confirmed. He learned that Balsley and Johnson were now in N. 124 and that Dudley Hill signed in on June 9. Paul kept after Jack to write things down while he was recuperating. Jack couldn't concentrate at first, but he had filled a small notebook with descriptions of the men in the *Escadrille Américaine* that Paul wanted to send off to his editor.

Michelle visited even more often than Paul Rockwell, often coming with Madame Fleury, the woman Jack found disturbingly reminiscent of Claudine Walker. Michelle now wore loose-fitting dresses to accommodate her growing waistline. She didn't seem to slow down because of the pregnancy, and, according to Jennifer, never complained of discomfort but always of looking fat. He never failed to tell Michelle how beautiful she looked, pointing out the admiring stares she attracted from the men on the ward. She passed on news from Charlie who wrote her about his flights, carefully avoiding any mention of danger or friction in the escadrille.

Charlie wrote Jack as well, telling him what he wouldn't write to Michelle. His last letter, posted June 20, told of Chapman and Balsley's wounds. Balsley, he wrote, would probably end up living at Neuilly for a good long time. He was still in danger of losing his right leg or they might have sent him there sooner. Victor burned the candle at both ends as usual. Only Rockwell took more chances. Charlie flew just as many missions, but he seldom came back with as many holes in his machine. He said that Thénault was seething because no one would follow his orders to stay together. Some thought their commander was more interested in nice formations than in killing Germans. Hall was carrying his load. Prince, McConnell and de Laage flew together fairly often. Only Cowdin, of the original members, seemed to be dragging his feet. The new men were good. He told Jack that Hill asked after him often. Masson had just arrived the day before he wrote so Charlie couldn't say much about him.

THREE WEEKS IN THE HOSPITAL WAS THREE WEEKS TOO MANY FOR JACK. Even Jennifer's loving ministrations couldn't stem his irritability and frequent depression. Medically, there was no more the doctors could do for him. His wound had closed and no longer suppurated. He was clearly out of danger of infection. Though still painful due to the torn muscles, Jack could put some weight on the foot for extended walks with a cane. Only the headaches and insomnia caused the doctors continued concern.

"It's never easy to tell with concussions, Jennifer," Doctor Gros said when she asked why Jack hadn't been discharged. "His vision is back to normal—a good sign indeed—but the headaches become so debilitating at times that putting him back flying could be disastrous." Gros told her about the French specialist from the Pasteur Institute that he'd asked to examine Buck. "If my esteemed colleague is right, Jack might benefit from a fortnight in the south of France. Something about getting away from Paris, the hospital, the rain and the war, he says, along with large doses of sun, should do the trick."

The psychiatrist approved Jack's convalescence, recommending monitoring by a colleague then serving with the Navy in Provence. This gave Jennifer an excuse to volunteer to be Jack's nurse companion. She didn't ask Nurse Wilson. She *told* her she was leaving for two weeks. Mildred Wilson never liked losing any of her staff, especially without notice. Jennifer was a special case. The older woman, childless and widowed, looked at Miss Keeler like a daughter.

Jack hated his mood swings and the excruciating headaches that brought them on. He particularly hated being cross with Jennifer. The psychiatrist's suggestion of sun and rest seemed ludicrous to Jack, but he was willing to try anything. Gros arranged for Jack's transportation and lodging at a small naval base in the town of Fréjus located about halfway between Marseilles and Nice on the Mediterranean. The base had a small dispensary. The doctor in residence was the naval reservist the Paris doctor had in mind to follow Jack.

Jennifer secured official traveling papers for Sergent Buck and herself, *l'Assistante Médicale*, from the French Army administrative representative at the hospital. Gros gave her a small satchel with several medicines that might be helpful, including a vial of Laudanum in case Jack's headaches became intolerable. Michelle and Madame Fleury came to the Gare de Lyon to see them off.

The farther south the overnight train rolled, the more they felt themselves distanced from the war. Jack had been in southwest France while at Pau, but neither of them had seen Provence. They slept sitting up in each other's arms for much of the trip. When they woke the train was leaving Valence somewhere in the Rhône River valley. The sun painted the eastern sky pink as it peeked up over the tops of the Maritime Alps. Great fields of purple *lavande* alternated with others in the brilliant yellow Jack recognized as rapeseed, *colza* in French. Had they not been cooped up in the rail car with its close air and coal smoke odor, they might have been able to smell the lavender.

From Valence, the train sped south through Avignon, then on to Aix-en-Provence. Whenever they stopped, Jennifer went to find the nearest lavatory. She fastidiously avoided the little booths at the ends of some of the rail cars. At Aix she picked up some croissants in the gare and barely made it back before the train began to move again. Jack's foot ached from not being elevated so he stayed put in their compartment during her forays.

Departing Aix they continued east through the rocky hills of the Var. Jack saw neat vineyards nestled between clusters of red-roofed pink-stuccoed buildings tucked onto hillsides or planted on the flat plain of the valley through which the tracks ran. He hadn't had any headaches since they got on the train. Maybe his sore foot kept his mind off them. Just being with Jennifer, away from the prying eyes at the hospital, was like an elixir itself.

They arrived at the station that served Fréjus and Saint-Raphaël at about ten that morning. Jack used a cane. Jennifer still wore her nurse's garb since, technically, she was traveling as Jack's medical attendant. As a result, the French sailor sent to meet them had no problem identifying the Americans. He led them to a military sedan and asked if they wanted to see a little of the area before going to the base. Jack said no. They were travel-weary and feeling the need for a hot bath to scrub away the lingering coal smell.

The driver headed south from the gare for the road along the beach. He turned right on the road and slowed down enough for his passengers to observe the growing numbers of sun bathers gathering on the long expanse of sand between the two towns. It only took minutes to arrive at the gate of the base, itself located on the beach. A sailor armed with a Lebel rifle waved them through. Taking them directly to the dispensary, the driver told them he would wait for them and take them to their quarters after they had seen the *médecin chef.*

Jack thought the base looked very sleepy. As far from the trenches as one could be in France proper even with Austria and Italy fighting several hundred miles to the east, Provence seemed untouched by the war. He noted that the dispensary and other buildings on the base were new, and there were stacks of building materials nearby.

A few sailors sat in a corridor waiting to be seen on sick call. Jack expected to wait in line, but the orderly at the desk took his name and escorted him to one of the treatment rooms, telling them the doctor would be with them in a few minutes. No sooner had he closed the door than a small man with black hair and a full black mustache burst in, his white coat flapping behind him. His smile crinkled the corners of his eyes. In very passable English, he told Jack to sit on the table. Jennifer handed him the envelope containing Jack's chart and Doctor Gros's orders. The doctor sized up the beautiful, if a bit disheveled, nurse with an appreciative eye.

"*Bon, alors*. Let me introduce myself. I am Doctor Alfred Lascasse, Stanford '08. Your Doctor Gros has already filled me in. You are *Sergent* Jack Buck, of course, and this lovely lady has to be Miss Keeler. *Enchanté, mademoiselle*. It is good to be able to speak English again. You don't mind? Of course not. I am delighted to be at your service."

Taken aback by the man's ebullience, both Jack and Jennifer remained mute. Lascasse wore the four stripes of a commandant, a major in the Army, though Jack had no idea what the naval equivalent was. After checking Jack's foot, Lascasse clucked his tongue a couple of times. He manipulated the foot to see if Jack responded in pain at the gentle turns and twists. Satisfied that the wound was healing properly, he left the dressing off.

"No shoes or socks for a week, and walk on the sand for at least an hour every day and your foot will be as good as new. You swim?" He asked, not waiting for an answer. "You must walk in the water and swim as much as you like. It will be good for your foot and help you to recover your strength and motion."

Lascasse then examined Jack's eyes before giving him a simple vision test. He checked Jack's reflexes and listened to his heart. Jack wondered what it all had to do with his foot and his headaches. Finally, the man told Jack to get dressed.

"You are very healthy, Mister Buck. Now if we can get rid of those headaches and your blurred vision, we should be able to get you flying in a couple of days."

"But doctor," Jack protested, "I have two weeks congé."

"You do indeed! But did you see the aeroplanes when you came on base?"

"No, I thought this was a navy base."

"Yes, of course. We have just opened a small field here for our Naval Aviation. I don't know what kind of machines they are, but when you are ready you may go up with one of our pilots to verify that your headaches aren't going to keep you from flying.

Jennifer smiled, seeing Gros's hand in this new twist on their situation. How clever of the doctor to put them in a place where Jack could fly. She already knew how antsy Buck got from inactivity. He was so eager to get back to the escadrille that it pained him to distraction that his headaches were all that kept him from being released. She could have kissed Lascasse for the news, but the man wasn't done with his surprises.

"We have a small cottage intended for the commanding officer of the base that is empty for the next month. It is very sparsely furnished, but I'm sure you will find it comfortable. It is within walking distance of the beach. Do you object to being lodged in the same building?" He asked with a raised eyebrow and—Jack thought—a knowing smirk.

Their driver took them to the quarters and helped bring in their bags. He showed them the military telephone on a table at the entryway, explaining that they could ring the *standard*, the switchboard, and the operator would connect them with the dispatcher for a vehicle to take them anywhere. Lascasse had told them he wanted to see Jack in three days to see if he could clear him to fly. Meanwhile, he'd ordered the swimming and walking therapy and no medication except for the most severe headaches.

Once alone, the two looked at each other in total disbelief. Other than a few furtive nights in Jennifer's cramped room above the hospital, they had had no privacy at Neuilly. Now they were thrown together in the most agreeable of circumstances for a full two weeks. If only Jack's nightmares and headaches would relent.

A quick turn about the two-bedroom cottage only increased their anticipation. Lascasse had said *sparsely furnished* for good reason. They found two beds, two nightstands, a table and four chairs, and a small kitchen area with a sink and a gas-fired two-burner stove. In a cabinet over the stove a set of dishes marked with French Naval insignia stood waiting to be used. Jennifer located a couple of pots and pans and some utensils. The only thing missing was food. They put their suitcases on the beds in the two separate rooms and began to wonder where they could bathe and take care of personal hygiene needs. The military telephone began to ring with a raspy irregular rattle. Jack picked it up. It was Lascasse asking if all was in order. Jack didn't dare ask for anything else lest the dream be shattered.

"An orderly will be there in a few minutes with some necessaries compliments of the base commander. He is living comfortably in a villa in town so he is pleased that his cottage will be put to some good use. You will find a bathroom behind the cottage. It is a bit primitive, but there is a shower. I hope you find our little hotel to your liking. *A bientôt*!"

"Can you believe this, Jennifer? I don't think the generals and admirals get such treatment. Whatever makes me deserve it?"

"Nothing I can think of," she said coquettishly.

He grabbed her and pulled her to him in an embrace full of passion. Kissing her on the eyes and then on her cheeks, Jack felt his excitement increasing more rapidly than ever. She returned his kiss and moaned deep in her throat. He wanted to take her there and would have moved to one of the beds had a knock at the door not interrupted them.

The sailor at the door carried a large wooden box covered with a white cloth. He asked them if he could come in and set it down before he went for the second. Jack took the box and set it on the table while Jennifer peered under the cloth to see what it contained.

After the man left the second crate, they examined the contents. One box was filled with cans of food and bottles of various drinks. The other contained towels, sheets and more bottles. The two of them sank into the chairs shaking their heads. Something just didn't track. Neither of them wanted to burst the bubble of their extraordinary good fortune, but both realized that something or someone had gone well beyond Doctor Gros's demands on their behalf. They talked it over for a few minutes without coming up with an answer. Something nagged at Jennifer, something Charlie had told her about his crossing on the *Rochambeau* and their cousin's help. She couldn't recall what he had said, but she did remember that the cousin, Claude Toussaint, came from Saint-Raphaël.

Going back in the kitchen Jennifer opened the cabinet with the dishes and glasses. Something had caught her eye when they'd glanced in there the first time. She reached in and pulled out the only tankard. It was a simple beer mug like she's seen in Saint Louis at the October fests, except this one was solid silver. What had looked unusual was the engraving. In the cabinet, she could only make out an outline, but it looked familiar. Now she examined the tankard under the light and saw that it bore the same crest that her mother had on a few pieces she'd managed to retain from her family.

"Jack, I can't say for sure, but I think I see something a little strange here. Remember Charlie's story about our cousin Toussaint on the *Rochambeau*? I don't know a lot about the family other than that they totally disowned my mother when she married my father. I wonder if any of this might have something to do with my mother's family."

"You're not serious? How would anyone connect me to your family? We've only known each other a short time."

"I don't know, Jack. I don't suppose we should look a gift horse in the mouth, but maybe we should make some inquiries. If the family is involved, maybe putting the two of us together in this compromising situation has a dark purpose."

"Ruin your reputation? That sort of thing?"

"You know me well enough by now that I don't much care about reputation. Who seduced whom my dear Jack? No. Scandalous as our behavior might seem to prudish eyes, I consider us as good as married already. Heck, we might even be able to make it legal down here and rob any rumormongers of their ammunition."

"And give up your big wedding?"

"Jack, I am not the little girl that came over here with stars in her eyes. A big wedding seems terribly out of place in these times. Look at you and Bill Thaw. How long before one of you gets killed? You and I barely know each other, but the circumstances have made us fall in love. Dad always used to say that anything worth doing is worth doing well. I agree. We need to make the most of the moment."

"You aren't worried about a little trap being set by the Toussaints?"

"Only slightly. Remember Charlie telling how cousin Claude helped him out on the ship? Maybe he's behind this. Wouldn't that be rich?"

FOR THE NEXT SEVERAL DAYS THEY FELL INTO A PLEASANT ROUTINE. They supped on the provisions in the cottage. They walked on the beach until sundown and went back to the cottage to crowd their bodies onto the narrow military bed. Jack wished he had never met Claudine Walker and regretted becoming Marie's lover. He felt a little sullied each time he thought about it, but Jennifer was so open and so understanding that he began to forget.

Jennifer watched her cycle closely, knowing from her nursing training when she was most fertile and when it should be safe to make love. Their first coupling she'd known had been during a safe time. Now, by happy chance she was again past the period when pregnancy was most likely. She knew that Jack loved children as she did and that they would welcome them under the right circumstances. Pregnancy now would be awkward.

On their walks they talked about their families, favorite memories, and the people they liked the most apart from their relatives. Jennifer made him tell the whole Masters story twice. She was intrigued by the fact that he was a priest. Masters' defrocking prompted her to ask Jack if he felt guilty about what they were doing. Buck quickly said no, but she could tell that it troubled him all the same.

Nevertheless, he could tell that she was a very strong woman to have such a sure moral compass. Instead of dithering about sin and damnation, she seized the moment. She even went to communion without the slightest hesitation when they attended Mass at the magnificent cathedral that Sunday in Saint-Raphaël. When he asked her how she felt about going against the Church's teachings, about receiving communion when in a state of mortal sin, she punched him playfully in the stomach saying: "It's no more sin or mortal than a Jew eating pork."

Jack had to think about that. He knew a few men from the ambulance service who were Jewish. They'd eaten whatever the rest of them had eaten, often the ham or bacon that were staples of the military mess. According to their religious laws eating pork or anything not prepared according to strict kosher regulations was strictly forbidden. Jennifer saw him struggling with her analogy.

"Think about it, Jack. Who made the kosher laws? Who were they made for and why?"

"How do you know so much about this?"

"I had a Jewish roommate in nursing school. She explained the Leviticus laws in medical terms. In the days of the Old Testament, the Jews were smart enough to make the connection between what they ate and their health. The prohibition against pork didn't come from the fact that pigs are swinish, according to Rachael. She said people got trichinosis only from pork. The disgusting worms and violent sickness and death made them see the animal as poison, *unclean* in their language. Soon they began to apply more and more rules to cleanliness and preparation of what they ate. As Rachael pointed out, it became more ritual than necessity. That Gentiles could eat pork without dying didn't matter. It was a rule they claimed came from Yahweh himself, though it was a rule made by man for man's purposes."

"Not the same as the commandments, all the same. They came from God if we are to believe the Bible. *Thou shalt not commit adultery* is hardly the same as a dietary law."

"Is that what you think we are doing? No. Your little affair with the woman in Pau was adultery in the classic sense, though I think God will forgive you, considering the Walker woman's pressures."

"Jennifer! How do you know about that?" Jack asked genuinely shocked and ashamed at the same time.

"The same way Charlie knows we are lovers. Don't be so shocked. I had to know about you before I threw myself at you. Charlie and I learned long ago that the best way to take care of each other was to be totally honest with each other. We really have no secrets. Charlie wouldn't have told me about your affairs if I hadn't made him. He was sketchy on the details, but he made it clear that he thinks the world of you. Would I be here if I thought otherwise?"

Their discussions weren't always so serious. Jack learned that Jennifer had a tremendous sense of humor. He loved to hear her laugh. She saw that he brightened when she laughed and cavorted in front of him on the beach and that he began to frown and get melancholy when they dwelt on serious subjects. His headaches had almost completed relented and never recurred on their walks.

Jack shut the war out completely when they set out for the beach. He savored the sight of Jennifer in her bathing outfit, modest as it was. She had such lovely legs that he delighted in getting her to walk in front of him just so he could appreciate their beauty. In the intimacy of the bedroom he began to memorize her curves and sensitive spots, but on the beach he could admire her more visually. He not only forgot about the war in the hot sun and cooling waters of the Fréjus bay. He also forgot his headaches.

The efficient French Army postal service delivered a bundle of mail on the third day of his convalescence. His mother sent a long letter with colored drawings from both of his sisters. Her tone of concern at the news of his wounds made him feel a little homesick. She had been closer to him than any other person in the world. Even with her meager education, his mother's wisdom and good judgment were like rocks of refuge for Jack. His father was fine, she wrote. Jack didn't expect to get anything from his father. Ockie was a man of very few words. He didn't even answer the letters they got from Norway and Sweden. He gave them to his mother who answered for him. Jack knew it embarrassed his father to not be able to write in English or speak it correctly. To his credit, Ockie read everything he could get his hands on in his effort to improve his vocabulary. Jack's mother wrote for both of them and for Larry as well. Larry had written only a handful of letters. He told Jack he had nothing interesting to say. According to their mother, Larry wanted to enlist in the Army as soon as he turned eighteen. Jack imagined his brother aching to get into the border conflict now brewing down in Mexico.

The American Hospital forwarded Jennifer's mail as well. She had told her parents about her engagement to Jack Buck. They wrote back with enthusiastic congratulations. Both her parents had liked the Buck boys from the moment they stepped off the train for Charlie's wedding. Their only negative note had to do with the wedding. The Keeler parents made it clear they wanted to have a big wedding for their only daughter. Jennifer told Jack that they might have to get married secretly and celebrate it again formally for her family at a later date.

True to his prediction, Doctor Lascasse cleared Jack to go up for a flight three days after his arrival, a Saturday. Jennifer went with him to the field to meet the pilot that would be flying the old Farman pusher. They noticed a lot of activity at the field including the flashy staff car parked next to the Farman. Jack still used the cane, but he could now walk without a noticeable limp. When he and Jennifer started towards the airplane, the staff car raced over to pick them up. The driver apologized for not coming for them at the cottage, saying that the commanding officer had pressing business.

At the Farman a mechanic saluted when they pulled up, embarrassing Jack. *Maybe he is saluting Jennifer*, he thought. A man already in flying garb was just finishing his walk around inspection of the machine. He came over to greet them. Jack saw the five stripes on his flying jacket, realizing that the man was the equivalent of a lieutenant colonel! He had never flown with so senior a pilot. He saluted instinctively.

"*Finalement*!" the man began. "Finally we get to meet. I am Claude Toussaint, *ma cousine, enchanté*." He bowed, taking Jennifer's hand and bringing it to his lips.

"Why am I not surprised to find you here?" Jennifer asked, far more composed than Jack who stood silently trying to absorb the fact that she, not he, might have been the cause of their special treatment.

Later they would learn that Claude Toussaint had managed to escape the maritime service and get reinstated on active naval duty right after the *Rochambeau* docked in January 1915. He'd applied for aviation training in the small but growing naval arm and gone through flight training in the Army schools.

Toussaint shook Jack's hand vigorously. He seemed to know much more about Buck than Jack would have expected.

"So you are Charlie's best man. Did you know that my cousin was actually jealous of me on the voyage, thinking I had designs on the fair Michelle? I could see they were headed for marriage and now you, too! *Merveilleux*! You are wondering how I know this? Charlie wrote that you were coming. He didn't know that I was now commanding this measly little station, but he did ask me to do what I could for you. I'm sorry I couldn't greet you sooner. I have been on a mission in Italy to observe their aviation."

Jack listened and sized up the man who had been their benefactor. He was exactly the same size as Charlie and built just as strongly. There the similarity ended. Toussaint had coal black hair and an equally black neatly trimmed mustache. His eyes were a deep brown that would have made him look like an undertaker if they weren't so lively and animated. He spoke English, like some other French officers, with a pronounced British accent. All this made a favorable impression on Jack, but the most striking thing was Toussaint's resemblance to Claudine Walker and Madame Fleury.

"So we fly? How long has it been since you piloted a Farman? No matter. This one has dual controls. You take the pilot's seat. Treat me like a passenger. If you need any help just tap me on the shoulder."

Jennifer went to sit in the sedan while they went through their run up and taxied into position to take off. She wasn't worried about Jack. He hadn't complained of headaches or nightmares for the last two days. While she waited, she tried to get some more information about her cousin from his driver. It was a bit of a challenge since he spoke no English and her French was still very rudimentary.

Jack asked Toussaint before they started the motor where he was to fly. "Anywhere you want, my friend." They had no maps. Jack supposed the French officer knew his way around.

He set off to the north for about ten minutes to get a better look at the city of Fréjus and its Roman ruins. The dominant feature of the ancient town was the steeple of the church on top of the hill at the center of the town. Jack drifted left to better see the coliseum to the west of the town. He then followed the road to the north to where it intersected the remains of an aqueduct whose arches seemed to trace a line to the hills north of the city. Jack reasoned that the Romans must have used them to bring fresh water down from the mountains.

The sky was absolutely clear. The deep blue color impressed Jack. He continued the slow climb to the north until reaching the first foothills and the last of the identifiable archways of the aqueduct. He then turned west and flew over the line of hills called the *Esterel*. Little villages dotted the hillsides, their red roofs and pinkish white walls blending in beautifully with the countryside. Jack wanted to follow the tracks to the west to see what they looked like from the air. As he passed a massive reddish rock formation he picked up the line of the tracks paralleling the *Route Nationale*. He hopped across the ridge of mountains that lay between the valley and the coast and headed south towards the water. When he took off it had been nine in the morning. The Farman carried nearly three hours of fuel. If Toussaint didn't object, Jack intended to use as much of that as he could.

Being in the air again exhilarated Jack in a way that surprised him. He always enjoyed flying even in the moments of gut-wrenching terror that had marked some of his more challenging flights. Being up in a new area in the circumstances he currently enjoyed only added to his sense of thrill. He thought about Jennifer watching them take off, knowing that Jack was at the controls. It wasn't showing off, but she was the first person he really cared about, other than his fellow pilots, who had seen him fly. He'd often wished his parents, Larry, and his sisters could see him flying. In the back of his head he realized he was being evaluated for medical competence, but he was enjoying the scenery and the feel of the old Farman far too much to worry about the headaches.

Crossing the Massif des Maures he came upon the coast and the breathtaking view of the blue Mediterranean. No other airplanes seemed to be in the area. He felt an incredible sense of independence and peace, forgetting for the moment about the officer in the front seat. He descended to about one hundred feet and turned east to follow the coast. As he looked down into the water he saw startling color combinations. The azure of the deeper water offshore had a cast several shades darker than the sky. Closer in where he could make out the bottom, the water varied from blue to green with phosphorescent transitions. In close to the shore the water was crystal clear. He thought he could see schools of fish in some of the pools along the rocky cliffs.

The shoreline varied from irregular indentations with sharp drop-offs to stretches of sandy beaches. At first he noticed no man-made features and admired the pristine purity of the coastline. Pines and scrub oaks grew right up to the edges of the promontories. As he rounded the cape and followed the inlet he crossed a village with a sheltered harbor bristling with masts from dozens of boats of all types. Toussaint turned around and shouted "Saint Tropez!" as they turned back east. Soon he saw an even larger city spreading northward from a long beach. Again numerous boats lay at moorings in a series of small inlets and harbors. "Saint Maxime!" Toussaint hollered. They'd been up no more than forty minutes. So far Jack felt no ill effects from the experience.

Seeing the big curve of the Fréjus Bay coming up, he decided to try getting some altitude. If anything was going to trigger his headaches, the thinner cooler air might do it. The Farman climbed laboriously making no more than five hundred feet in ten minutes. Over the water of the bay his forward motion seemed to have stopped. It was a strange sensation. Jack had to keep looking for landmarks to reassure himself he was moving forward. At a thousand meters they had not gone any farther east than the airfield at Fréjus, one of the few landmarks familiar to Jack.

He continued to climb straight ahead following the coast. He saw the cathedral at Saint-Raphaël with its prominent dome. It looked tiny compared to its impressive massiveness on the ground. All along the coast, beaches dotted the shoreline. Some were long and wide like the one at Fréjus, but most were small indentations that seemed to be hewn from the living rocks jutting out into the sea. At two thousand meters objects on the ground were no longer discernible. Jack thought the Farman could make it almost to five thousand meters, but the slow climb and the retreating landscape discouraged going higher. He let the machine level out at three thousand and began to pull back slowly on the stick until the Farman shuddered and shook uncomfortably. His airspeed dropped below the stall speed causing the wings to waffle in the disturbed airflow before the machine fell into a *vrille*. Fortunately, Toussaint anticipated the maneuver. He even put his hands up behind his head locking his gloved fingers together in a manner that reassured Jack that he was the only one flying the Farman.

The spin progressed rapidly, dropping them five hundred meters in a matter of forty seconds. Jack let it go, holding in just enough right rudder to impede recovery. He felt fine in spite of the gyrations of the falling, twisting Farman. He let the controls come to the middle at one thousand meters which produced the expected result of slowing and stopping the spin. Soon they were descending in a shallow dive straight ahead along the beach.

"*Cannes*," Toussaint shouted pointing down at the relatively large group of buildings tucked up against the hill and tumbling down to the water's edge. Jack had only the vaguest notion of the geography of the area. He remembered only that the large city of Nice lay somewhere east of them. He thought he'd go at least that far before turning around and retracing their path at low altitude. It was so clear that he could see at least thirty kilometers. The farther east they flew the more the buildings were clustered together. He thought he'd reached Nice after passing a long line of large hotel-like buildings, but Toussaint didn't make his usual announcement, so Jack pressed on a little longer, level now at about three hundred meters. Jack saw an impressive harbor with hundreds of sailing craft of all sizes tied up to a complex network of slips. He'd been concentrating on the shoreline so much that he didn't see the two large ships at anchor south of the city.

Toussaint turned and waved his hand in front of his face pointing to the controls and then to himself. Jack nodded and let go, feeling the French officer's touch before totally releasing the stick. Toussaint turned, pointing the Farman directly at the larger of the two gray shapes. He dove down to less than a hundred meters above the water moving farther and farther out to sea. Jack felt a slight twinge of queasiness from being so far from land. It was a new experience, a little like being in the clouds except there was a definite horizon where the water joined the sky. Judging distances, he could see, would be difficult in that environment. He looked back over his shoulder surprised to see how close the shoreline still seemed. Looking forward again produced a sense of discomfort, but frequent scans out to the horizon and back to the land helped him overcome the uneasiness.

The ship Toussaint aimed for took on more form until Jack could make out the numbers 373 on the side near the bow. They descended even more and approached the ship from the left front. When within about one kilometer, Jack could see the huge guns and dozens of blue-clad men moving about on the deck. Now the ship, a cruiser even bigger than the *H.M.S. Reliant,* dwarfed them. Toussaint maneuvered closer, wagging his wings to calm any uneasy gunner on the ship. He continued his approach until they were abeam the midship stacks. He circled the cruiser one time at less than a hundred meters horizontal distance. Jack thought they could have dropped a good number of bombs had the ship been an enemy. Surely someone had given some thought to that idea. He wondered how the machine guns on board the ship would do in fending off an aerial attack.

Toussaint closed in even closer passing the ship on the port side. Jack now saw men manning machine gun stations tracking their flight. If Toussaint made a hostile move Jack didn't doubt they would end up in the drink. How could they miss the slow-flying Farman at that range? If he were going to attack a ship, Jack decided, he would do it from altitude. He would dive until in range of his bombs or machine guns, drop or fire and zoom up as fast as he could. With a whole flight attacking in that manner he thought they could overwhelm a ship's defenses.

Looping around to the starboard, Toussaint wagged his wings as they passed the bridge. Maybe he knew the captain or some of the officers on the cruiser. When they cleared the bow moving away from the ship, Toussaint raised his hand pointing at Jack who took the controls back, seeing both of the French officer's hands go up in the air as a signal.

They made their way back to the coastline and Jack stayed low feeling the increased sense of speed as objects sped by them. He saw figures on the beach, colorful umbrellas, and children racing down to the water and then back. How incongruous this idyllic scene appeared in the shadow of the warships just offshore.

A headwind slowed their return flight giving them more time to survey the scenery below them. A number of mansions stood on various promontories looking out over the water. Jack saw swimming pools and tennis courts by some of them, wondering who owned them and if the war had touched them. As they got closer to Saint-Raphaël he saw one villa very close to the water with its own inlet and a large sailboat tied up to a private pier. A pool was set into the stone on an outcropping between the manicured lawn and the beach. As they passed overhead, a woman lying on a towel at poolside rolled over to look up at them. Her nakedness seemed illusory at first glance. She made no attempt to cover herself and even waved. Jack couldn't help staring. At that distance he couldn't see if she was old or young, pretty or homely, but he could definitely tell it was a woman. Her breasts stood out prominently. He had to tear his eyes from her to concentrate on flying, noticing that he had lost a good fifty feet and drifted considerably closer to the pool in his ogling.

Passing the beach in front of Saint-Raphaël and seeing the familiar *Cathédrale*, Jack began to look for the base and the wind direction. So far all of his flying motions had been largely automatic. He could tell the wind was from the west. The airfield lay almost directly north to south.

Crosswind landings in the Farman were discouraged. He lined up over the water and aimed to touchdown on the near end of the field with his nose as much into the wind as he could manage. The Farman's slow speed made the landing run relatively short. Jack tensed up a little before cutting the motor for the landing. Toussaint had his fingers laced behind his head again. At least the man trusted him.

The angle of approach Jack had chosen took them almost directly over the beach cottage. He wondered if Jennifer had returned there or waited for them at the field. They touched down with a slight bounce and rolled no more than fifty meters in the soft grass. Jack forgot to let the motor start back up on their final approach so they couldn't taxi back to park. Before he could get unbuckled and stand up in the cockpit, the black staff car arrived and Jennifer stepped out, her blond hair blowing in the breeze. Jack forgot about the flying for an instant as he remembered the naked woman. He realized that he couldn't wait to get Jennifer back to the cottage. He could be sure that part of him was working normally.

Toussaint came around and patted Jack on the back saying "Well done, very well done! You'll have to teach me some of those maneuvers while you are here."

"Maneuvers? What maneuvers sir?"

"The observation technique at the pool, for example. I would like to do that again myself." He laughed and patted Jack again, winking before Jennifer came within earshot. "Seriously, you are a good touch. Any problems with the head?"

"No. Thank you, sir. What *do* I call you anyway? It isn't 'colonel' in the Navy, is it?"

"*Capitaine de Vaisseau* is the official title, though that seems a little funny for a pilot. I also hold the title of *Commandant de base*, so most people here call me '*Mon Commandant*' which you will recognize as 'major' in English instead of colonel. Confusing isn't it? If you didn't get a headache flying, I can promise you one trying to figure out our ranks and insignias. Just call me 'sir' if you like when we are on duty. Otherwise Claude will do."

"So, how did my patient do? Any problems in the air?" Jennifer asked, after picking up the end of their last exchange.

"Not a *soupçon* of a headache. You'll have to ask your cousin about the flying side of it, but I really felt great in the air. The scenery is great too," Jack said casting a sidelong glance at Toussaint.

Claude joined them for the ride to the cottage. He told Jennifer that he'd never flown with a better pilot. He only touched the controls for the spin around the cruiser. One of his missions was to help train the ship's company to shoot at airplanes. The Austrians had already attacked some Allied ships in the Adriatic, he explained. When they got to the cottage Toussaint reassured himself they had everything they needed before inviting them to dinner at his villa that evening. He said the driver would pick them up at seven.

Once inside Jack pulled Jennifer to him and said he had just restored himself spiritually and needed some physical therapy to complete the cure. "Are you sure you didn't know your cousin was going to be here?"

"Not a hint of it. Incredible coincidence, isn't it? Do you want to talk then or take some therapy?"

"Therapy first. Then we can talk." She obliged him with a kiss before leading him into the bed they now shared. They forgot about lunch. It was hot in the room even with the window open. Afterwards, slippery with sweat, Jennifer suggested a swim to clean off and cool down. Jack, remembering the nude figure, wondered if Jennifer would be bold enough to sunbathe without clothes. He wouldn't mind as long as he was the only one there to watch.

The drive to Toussaint's villa that evening allowed Jack to see part of the shoreline he'd flown over that day from a different perspective. They drove along the beach road until reaching Saint-Raphaël where a jog in the road circled a small boat haven. Then they resumed following the beach until it ended with a large rock formation. About 500 meters offshore a small island caught their eyes. It had a crenellated square stone tower that had to date back to the Middle Ages. The road climbed and twisted as it mounted the Esterel east of Saint-Raphaël. They could still see the water off to their right, but a number of trees and some buildings blocked the view most of the time. They had moved inland some due to the increasingly rugged shoreline.

The driver turned into a large paved driveway and stopped at the double wrought iron gates. He got out and unlocked the gates, swinging them in for the car to pass. Jack tried to relate the terrain to what he'd seen on the flight, but the different perspective made it difficult. Trees lined both sides of the driveway. After the heat of the afternoon the evening air felt soft, caressing. They could feel the slight breeze and smell the flowers that seemed to be growing everywhere. Descending to the villa they parked on the circular drive before the entryway. The driver came around to open the door waiting for them to descend from the car. Jack wondered what the sailor would be doing while they were there, hoping he would get to eat something himself.

Toussaint, wearing an open collar white shirt, came to the door to greet them personally and guide them through the villa to the terrace on the seaside of the house. A stone walkway led to a stretch of grass that ended at a large swimming pool nearly at the water's edge. Looking to see Jack's reaction, Claude led them to a table at the side of the pool and asked them to sit down. He excused himself and returned to the house.

Jack looked back at the house and realized now that this was the very place that they had flown over earlier. No wonder the woman had waved. Was it Toussaint's wife? Jack decided he didn't need to tell Jennifer about the sunbather that he expected to meet in a few minutes.

Claude reappeared carrying a tray with drinks, a woman on his arm. Jack stared at the lady wearing a light blue sun dress and wondered if she was the same one he'd seen naked by the pool. Up close he could see she was certainly proportioned similarly. She had light brown hair now gathered in a knot on top of her head with tendril curls hanging down on either side of her cheeks. The overall effect of her deeply tanned skin, the light dress, and her hair, was stunning. She smiled as Claude introduced her to Jennifer and then Jack.

"Perhaps Monsieur Buck has seen me already, *non*?" She said in lilting French.

Shaking his head, Jack could only mutter "*Enchanté, Madame*" as he blushed. Jennifer, not understanding this exchange, looked a little confused. Claude decided to let her in on their little secret.

"Marie is an artist's model I met on my last voyage on the *Rochambeau*, the same trip where I met your brother, Jennifer. We have been married one year. She has not given up her work, modeling for some of the painters and sculptors that come here for the sun and good clay. She is fond of swimming to stay in shape and takes as much sun as she can to keep her complexion evenly colored—*everywhere*—if you get what I mean. We flew over here today. Marie may have shocked Mister Buck waving as she did with no clothes on. She is a little embarrassed now, since she thought it was only me in the Farman."

Jennifer looked at Jack who seemed to be blushing even more. She laughed at his discomfiture. Turning back to shake Marie's hand, Jennifer told her she was a very beautiful woman. She could see why she was a model. The awkward moment passed smoothly because of Jennifer's laughter.

"You don't look at all like your brother," Marie said with Jack translating. "He reminded me of Claude, but you are too beautiful to be compared with such brutes."

Jennifer smiled even more as they sat down by the pool and drank chilled champagne while appreciating the colorful setting sun and its reflection on the sea. Marie spoke no English whatsoever. In deference to her they switched to French. Jennifer gamely tried to hold her own in conversation, but she often had to resort to English, requiring Jack to translate for Marie.

He tried to avoid staring at Marie and visualizing her as he'd seen her that morning. Jennifer whispered that his tongue was hanging out which snapped him out of his reverie. It bothered him that Toussaint's wife so titillated him when he had Jennifer sitting there right beside him. Jennifer was far more attractive even to his prejudiced eye. Marie had noticeable squint lines at the corners of her eyes and a few creases around her mouth that showed her age, perhaps from too much sun. She had to be in her thirties—about Claudine Walker's age, he thought reflexively. Yet, somehow his sight of her in the altogether made him feel a sense of intimacy with her that was entirely out of place.

They moved back to the terrace for dinner. Marie, it turned out, was not only a model, but also an excellent cook. She had prepared roasted chicken perfumed with fresh rosemary. She served a rice dish redolent of saffron with little pieces of roasted red peppers offsetting the golden yellow of the grains. There was no evidence of servants in sight. Jack wondered if Toussaint had domestic help. In reality, Marie valued her privacy when home alone. She was used to keeping house, a task she'd done as a girl for her father and three brothers after her mother died. Claude, if truth be known, could afford a whole platoon of help.

During dinner Claude filled them in on his activities since leaving the merchant service. Jack discovered they'd been at Pau at the same time. Incredibly, Toussaint had been the naval officer that had flown the Morane Parasol that Charlie had flown. Claude had ended up in the hospital with influenza for almost four weeks. He didn't know about Charlie's flight and near mid-air collision. He was surprised to find out that Buck and Keeler were there at the same time.

Jennifer wanted to know more about the mysterious Toussaint family. Unlike Charlie who carefully avoided the subject on the ship, Jennifer still felt the shame and pain her mother described from her disinheritance. What kind of family would treat a daughter so cruelly? She couldn't form the question in French, so she asked simply and carefully if Claude knew anything about the affair.

"I'm afraid I don't know very much," he began in English. "My parents never talked about it. Father is at least ten years older than your mother. He sided with our grandparents when they decided to exile Angelique. There are two other siblings, you know?"

Jennifer shook her head. She only knew that her mother was the youngest.

"We have an aunt and an uncle. Aunt Sophie married a Cuirassier in a grand affair when I was just ten. I think our grandparents expected your mother to do the same. Uncle Bertrand went in the Army. He is a colonel now somewhere near Arras. He was wounded early in the war, but recovered in time to take part in the May offensive last year. He has two grown children—our cousins. One of them even married an American. Perhaps you heard of them, Jack? They live outside of Pau. Walker is the name. Claudine is a wild one. I'm surprised Uncle Bertrand didn't disown her like his parents did Angelique. Apparently Walker has money of his own though, and there was some rather funny business that the family doesn't talk about."

Jennifer looked at Jack who had gone totally white at the news that Claudine Walker was Jennifer and Charlie's cousin. The contrast between his earlier blush and his current blanching did not escape his dinner companions.

"Are you all right, Mister Buck?" Marie asked.

"Perhaps we should go back now, Jack? You don't look well at all," Jennifer said, not making the connection as quickly as Jack.

"No, I'll be fine. Perhaps another glass of water Madame Toussaint?"

"Of course. Claude? Is there any reason why Mister Buck can't call me Marie? I cannot get used to 'madame' this, and 'madame' that. It makes me feel so old." She poured Jack a glass of water as Claude waved an approval at the use of first names. He studied Jack to see what might have caused his reaction.

"Perhaps you have met the Walkers, Jack?"

Jack had recovered some of his composure. He carefully set the water glass down and then took a healthy drink of the Côtes de Provence rosé they'd served with the chicken. "I have met them. They were among the people that put on our Thanksgiving dinner last fall. I wasn't at their table. Charlie sat with them. I'm afraid Mister Walker behaved poorly. A bit too much to drink." He looked furtively at Jennifer.

"I've heard the old boy tipples regularly. How did you find cousin Claudine? I remember she is quite striking."

Jack squirmed visibly at his seat. Jennifer by now made the connection and couldn't help bringing her hand to her mouth to stifle a little shriek.

"First one and now the other!" Marie observed. "We mustn't upset our guests so, Claude. Let's talk about something else. No, let's not talk at all. You take Jack in for a brandy and Jennifer and I will clear up here. We'll have coffee inside afterwards."

It was dark on the terrace except for the light from several candles in glass lanterns. The night air was close. It had become very calm. The high pitched sound of the *cigales* continued to pierce the night, a sure sign that the temperature had remained high. In the enclosure of the Toussaint villa garden wild herbs contributed a fragrance that mixed with the sea air. All this was lost on Jack.

Once inside, the men moved to a room full of nautical artifacts gathered by Claude over his years at sea. Jack picked up a brass telescope, less out of interest than out of a need to do something with his hands. Claude poured two snifters of cognac, handing one to Jack without even asking if he wanted it.

"Your face is a window on your soul my friend. From bright red to white as a sheet. Women have a great effect on you I see."

"I'm sorry if I have caused any problems."

"Not at all. I'm at fault. First, I didn't tell you that the lady waving at us was my wife. Then I embarrassed you with my mention of Claudine—you see I know something of her peccadilloes. That oaf of a husband she has is no match for her energy. If I haven't missed my guess you too were swept into her net, were you not?"

Jack simply couldn't understand how Toussaint or anyone else could have divined his debacle with Claudine Walker. Rather than fuel the fire, especially with this man he'd only just met, he didn't answer. He looked over the top of the glass as the heady aroma wafted up from the cognac. Amazing, he thought. Here he was sipping brandy with a senior officer who just happened to be the cousin of two of the only three women Jack had slept with in his whole life. Just over a year ago he remembered nearly choking on the same deep amber fluid in Flandin's study. He worried about what Jennifer would think when she realized that his affair in Pau was with her cousin. Toussaint was either a very good guesser, or Jack was as transparent as a jellyfish.

"Sir, I have so much to thank you for. The coincidences have been a little much for me. Please excuse my poor self-control."

"Well, I doubt I would be able to react much differently in the same circumstances. Don't let it bother you so much."

"We, Jennifer and I, are planning to marry sometime soon. I hope you can get away to come to the wedding. Have you spent any time in America?"

"Why congratulations!" Claude said lifting his glass. "New Orleans and New York are much like Paris to me. I have spent nearly as much time in each of them. If I can be there for your wedding I will. Let's go see how the girls are doing."

The rest of the evening passed relatively smoothly with no further mention of Jack's blushing and blanching or the reasons for them. Before the driver took them back, Toussaint promised to get together again to fill Jennifer in on the Toussaint mystery as best he could. He also asked Jack if he wanted to fly some more. Jack's immediate enthusiastic answer was exactly what Claude expected.

Jennifer remained uncharacteristically quiet in the car. Back at the cottage, Jack worried that she would be angry with him. While she might not consider it important now, Madame Claudine Walker was her cousin. He had never seen Jennifer angry. Now he braced himself for a storm.

"Talk to me, Jennifer," he said, once they entered the little cottage that seemed somewhat dingy after the Toussaint villa.

"Give me a little more time, Jack. I know all this happened before you met me. I have never met, nor did I even know cousin Claudine. Charlie sat with her that Thanksgiving. Is that right?"

"He handed her off to me innocently enough. He probably still doesn't realize she's a relative. Hey! That makes Madame Fleury her sister! There must be quite a story behind the Beauvais and Toussaint families." Jack said all this, thankful to have something to steer things away from him.

They went to bed as it was very late and Jennifer clearly didn't want to talk more. Much to Jack's surprise she was even more ardent in their lovemaking. Before they went to sleep, she poked him in the side and said he'd better not be fooling around with any other women, least of all any of her relatives.

With that, Jack laid back relieved, thankful, and very much more in love with the woman beside him. He couldn't undo what he had done with Madame Walker or Marie de la Croix de Valois. Now that it was all in the open he could at least put it behind him. The mystery of Jennifer's family in France, however, piqued his imagination. As he slipped into sleep he thought he had the answer, but sleep overcame him before he could put his finger on this thought or another, more disturbing by far, that nagged him deep in the background.

Chapter 43
Victor Goes West

Bar-le-Duc, June 1916

As Jack began his convalescence *l'Escadrille Américaine* continued to support the mammoth struggle at Verdun. Balsley still lay in the horrible conditions of Vadelaincourt, alternating between feverish incoherence and absolute agony. The doctors vacillated at the same pace in deciding the fate of his right leg. The damage to his hip alone was enough to guarantee some crippling. Keeping the wound clean proved nearly impossible. Three times the attending surgeon prepared to remove Clyde's leg only to have Balsley protest so violently that a check of the circulation and feeling in his lower leg and foot verified that the leg could be saved. Clyde suffered agonizing thirst continuously. He sucked on a soaked muslin rag until Chapman's oranges gave him a better alternative.

Victor Chapman visited every day with Charlie Keeler and often Jim McConnell. Clyde didn't know it, but his mates leaned very heavily on the doctor who wanted to amputate. Victor, deciding that money wasn't enough, resorted to threats. The harassed surgeon took the wild-eyed American's promise to apply his saw to one of the doctor's own appendages quite seriously. The two large men that came with Chapman looked every bit capable of holding him down for the one called Chapman to do the deed. Balsley began to receive more consideration than the usual patients passing through the butcher shop at Vadelaincourt. Even at that, he awoke one morning with two corpses on the cots on either side of him.

The place revolted Charlie Keeler. A heavy pall of death hung over the whole area competing for dominance with the nauseating odor. He hoped they could get Balsley out of there soon, but at the end of a week, Clyde was the longest surviving patient in the transient facility. The doctor still refused to release him to Paris because of the constant threat of infection. Balsley's wound was not healing properly. Charlie could see that keeping him there was doing no good. He, Chapman and McConnell appealed to Thénault to intervene to get the American out of the charnel house. Thénault himself agreed. He protested to the head of the hospital who pulled rank on him and told him to mind his own business. Georges then lodged an official request in channels, despairing that Balsley might die before the system could react.

Patrols the week of 19 to 22 June produced no further casualties, but no victories either. Didier Masson's arrival brought their numbers back up to enough to fly the available machines. Thénault found himself more and more tied down in keeping up with administrative chores. He spent hours on reports, the dreaded letters to the families of the mechanics killed at Luxeuil, and the running battle to keep the escadrille's airplanes mechanically sound. Georges kept up a constant demand on the system for newer equipment. His argument that his escadrille was unique reached the right ears more often than he realized. Already Aviation General Headquarters scheduled N. 124, only two months in existence, for new Nieuport 17s. Thénault tore himself away for at least one patrol a day, but allowed de Laage to take on more and more of the day-to-day mission planning.

On June 23, Thénault led Rockwell, McConnell, and Keeler on an unscheduled morning mission over the same area where Thaw and Buck had fought. Fort Souville, one in the line of contested forts that were still in French hands, came under German attack early that day. A call to all aviation units to step up their activity in the area to relieve the pressure produced by German artillery gave added impetus to their patrol.

Chapman's head wound had hardly healed, but he refused to remain on the ground. Thénault ordered him to report to the infirmary to have his dressing changed every day. Victor cleverly interpreted the captain's order as permission to *fly* to the hospital to visit Balsley. He procured another bag of the precious oranges that Thursday afternoon and planned to fly to Vadelaincourt the next morning. However, when Thénault's patrol took off, Victor decided to tag along at least as far as the hospital near the front. Thénault thought nothing of the additional Nieuport since Chapman had already told him of his intentions.

When the patrol reached Fort Souville, the N. 124 pilots searched for German observation machines directing artillery. Their hunt didn't take long. Not more than two kilometers north of the Fort a pair of Aviatiks buzzed along secure in the faith that their Fokker cover would fend off any attackers. Thénault, wise to the bait and trap strategy, held the patrol at altitude looking for the inevitable Fokkers. Out of the corner of his eye he saw one of his Nieuports dive on one of the Aviatiks. Before he could react, a flight of eight Fokker E-III's entered the fray. The Germans focused on the first attacker driving the Nieuport off while scattering Thénault's neat formation.

Each American latched onto one or two Eindekkers in the macabre aerial ballet now so common over the mire of the trenches. Thénault drew three of the Fokkers himself; managing to pull them away on a climbing chase he hoped to end with a dive for French lines. That left Rockwell with one potential victim. His Eindekker dashed for the safety of German territory, trying to shake the persistent Nieuport, surprised that the French pilot hadn't fired. Kiffin patiently closed the distance. He ignored the fact that he was dangerously low and well over the lines. When he reached less than 100 meters he squeezed the trigger. The Lewis didn't fail him this time. The monoplane burst into flames so suddenly that Rockwell had to pull up violently to avoid the conflagration.

Keeler and McConnell had their hands full with the remaining E-III's. Mac desperately maneuvered to get out of the cone of fire of his pursuer. He tried every acrobatic he knew, but the German seemed to be sewn to his tail. Bullets whizzed close enough to hear them pass through the struts and wires. This fellow was good, though he had hit nothing critical on Mac's machine. Jim's frustration at not being able to shake his tail led him to a move that surely saved his life. He cut the engine, which caused the Eindekker to overshoot him. Now Mac became the pursuer. He didn't hesitate to let the Boche know how angry he was at the hammering he'd gotten. Mac emptied the drum as fast as the Lewis could fire. For some exasperating reason none of his rounds found their mark. The German pilot must have realized McConnell was out of ammunition. Rather than trying to resume the fight, Oswald Boelcke wagged his wings in a salute and dove away.

Charlie found himself pitched into the middle of the three remaining E-III's. He wondered how they could hit him without hitting each other. Their numerical advantage working against them, Charlie culled one away before the other two could make the turn to rejoin the fight. He let a short burst go in the direction of the Eindekker. When the left wing separated from the German machine, Charlie almost forgot the pair now closing on his tail. He zoomed skyward and reversed course in a whipping maneuver that put him above and behind the two other Fokkers. When he pressed the trigger release, nothing happened. He didn't feel any resistance in the lever so he looked up to the machine gun and noticed the firing cable hanging loose, probably severed by one of the German bullets. He reached up to fire the Lewis with the loose cable. Two rounds exploded instantly in the receiver. The explosion blew the weapon to pieces, most of which flew away harmlessly from the Nieuport. At least one fragment, however, penetrated the small reserve fuel tank spewing gasoline in Charlie's face. Were it not for his goggles, he would have been blinded. The super-cooled fuel burned his face, causing him to flinch involuntarily and duck the flow of gas. The nourrice emptied in seconds. Meanwhile, Charlie lost the E-III's. Charlie alone with Michelle's muffler now full of the noxious smell of the gasoline and castor oil mixture, headed south for Behonne, gagging.

Less than an hour after the patrol staggered back to Behonne the Americans began to worry about Chapman. Thénault had seen him last diving away from the Aviatik. He'd hoped Victor went on with his oranges to Vadelaincourt. A call to the hospital dashed that hope. Kiffin's claimed Eindekker raised spirits a little even if getting confirmation was next to impossible. Charlie's victory, on the other hand, happened in plain view of the poilus. It was his fifth, making him the escadrille's first confirmed ace.

Louis Bley, Victor's mechanic, didn't give up hope. He'd seen Chapman come in long after the others many times. He stood at the field staring off into the northern skies until the sun began to set. Tears streamed from Bley's eyes as he stood there motionless for hours unwilling to believe his pilot had "gone west."

Thénault called every front line observation post in search of news of Chapman. He received confirmation of Keeler's victory from no less than three units on the line. At about nine o'clock the phone rang in his office. Most of the escadrille pilots were there anxiously waiting for Victor's return. They hoped he'd just landed at another field as he had so many other times. By that hour, though, they began to realize that he or one of the other units would have called had he simply put in somewhere else. Still, they consoled themselves, hoping he had holed up in the trenches. Less appealing, but at least holding a shred of hope for their beloved Victor, he might be a prisoner. The call confirmed their worst fears. A Farman pilot on the line told Thénault that he'd seen a blue Nieuport engaged in combat with some Fokkers. It had gone down well behind the lines. There was no chance the pilot survived, the Farman pilot said remorsefully.

Elliot Cowdin left earlier with another bag of oranges and some chocolate for Balsley. He told Clyde that Chapman couldn't get off that day. Cowdin didn't know yet that Victor was dead, but he feared the worse. Balsley accepted the oranges gratefully.

That night the escadrille popote was uncharacteristically silent. Cowdin began to complain of stomach pains and faintness and went off to bed. Charlie and the others knew the New Yorker was deeply affected by Chapman's death, but so were the rest of them. Kiffin Rockwell, Chapman's roommate, sat in the room they shared, chain-smoking and vowing that he wouldn't rest until he brought down at least two Boches for Victor.

Michelle's ruined muffler saved Keeler from worse troubles, but the wool had absorbed enough of the noxious fumes which he in turn breathed that he threw up soon after he landed. He couldn't eat supper. The exposed skin outside the muffler and goggles began to redden and itch. His lips swelled up and cracked. The group medic at Behonne, an aspirant with the unlikely name of Smith, applied petroleum jelly to Charlie's face.

Smith, a medical student drafted in 1915, was the son of a British businessman and a Frenchwoman of some renown on the stage in Paris. Born in France and attending the Catholic University in Angers, young Smith became 'recruit Smith' in spite of protesting his British citizenship. Since he had finished most of his medical training, the French made him an aspirant, a grade given to men about to become officers, most often because of special qualifications. Smith had his hands full with the escadrilles at Behonne. He could only do so much for the seriously wounded or injured. Keeler's gasoline poisoning wouldn't last long, but Cowdin's illness seemed to come from something other than physical causes.

At about 11 that night the escadrille got a call from the hospital that Balsley was dying. McConnell, Rockwell, Smith and Thénault jumped in the car and rushed to the hospital. When they arrived, they found Balsley sitting up reading a paper! Sending Smith to find out the reason for the frantic call, Thénault and the others left the shed and headed back to the car. None of the men had the heart to tell Clyde of Victor's fate. Smith came to tell them Clyde had become feverish the night before. He was on the verge of dying when the fever broke. Now the doctors thought they needed to watch him a little longer.

"And what do you say?" Thénault asked.

"Get him the hell out of there before it is too late, *mon capitaine*."

Back at Vadelaincourt a wounded French officer placed in the bed next to Balsley sat reading a newspaper account of the previous day's aerial activity. He read about Chapman's death and turned to ask the American beside him if he knew a man named Chapman. Clyde brightened, thinking the officer knew Victor.

"*Il est mort*," the French officer said, ignorant of Clyde's friendship with Chapman. Balsley's silent tears wetted his straw-filled pillow for several hours.

Charlie spent a miserable night with the taste of raw gasoline still lingering in his mouth and aspirating its fumes with every breath. In the morning he got up and washed his puffy face before going down to try to eat something. Determined to make the dawn mission, he downed a bowl of hot chocolate and half a baguette. On his way to the field he doubled over and retched up the measly little breakfast. Undaunted, he continued to his plane only to be overcome again by nausea and the need to throw up when he got a whiff of the gasoline fumes mixed with castor oil. Rockwell saw his friend nobly trying to overcome the sickness. He went over and persuaded Keeler to go back to bed at least for the rest of the morning.

"If you feel up to it, come on a mission with Lufbery and me after lunch."

The mention of lunch got Charlie to gagging again. He stumbled away from the flight line and headed back to bed, tumbling onto his mattress and dropping off for twelve straight hours of sleep. When he awoke, he felt famished. Distressed at missing the afternoon mission, he sat up too quickly only to feel the room spinning. Smith came by to look in on him, finding Keeler sitting on the side of the bed holding his head.

"Nasty stuff, petrol, what?" Smith said in his father's clipped British accent.

"It's got to be more than that. I can't believe how sick I felt earlier."

"Let me look at your face," Smith said kneeling beside Charlie. "Much better. Good. No blisters. Sometimes the mechanics come to me with blisters all over their hands and arms from fuel spills. Still feeling nauseated, eh?"

"Haven't kept anything down since lunch yesterday. I think I'm just hungry."

Charlie stood up a little unsteadily. Smith took him down to the popote where some of the others were finishing supper.

"You look like you got the short end of the stick there, Keeler," Bert Hall said from his station behind the bar. "Maybe a shot of my concoction would do him good, doc?"

"Leave him alone, Hall. What he needs is some fresh air and something to eat."

"You look as bad as I feel, Charlie," Red Rumsey said. Rumsey had been hitting the Manhattans hard every night. His speech was slurred and he looked pretty done in himself. Charlie looked around for Rockwell and Lufbery and asked if they were back yet.

"Just now landed," Nimmie Prince said, looking up from a book and blowing a cloud of fragrant blue smoke from his pipe. "Good thing you got some rest and didn't try to go with them, Charlie. Tomorrow's another day."

"Charlie, here's a plate of spaghetti and some soup the cook whipped up. Why don't you sit down here and give it a try?" Dudley Hill said, pulling a chair back from the table.

"Thanks, Dud." Charlie took the seat and sipped at the soup, thankful it didn't make him want to throw up again. "Anybody heard from the Captain about a service for Victor?" he asked.

"We're all to go to Paris for the July 4th ceremonies. I think they're planning a memorial service at the American Church," Prince said.

"Wonder if Jack Buck has heard about Victor yet?" Charlie said as he tackled the noodles with increasing vigor.

"The lieutenant sent a wire to Fréjus. I didn't know you had relatives there, Charlie. De Laage says the commander at the naval base there is your cousin."

"So Jack knows," Charlie said, thinking about his friend's reaction to the news. "Yeah, a long-lost cousin. Hey, you came over on the *Rochambeau* too, Nimmie. Claude used to be the navigator. I think he left the ship for naval aviation before your trip."

"Ah, the *Rochambeau*! What a crossing. One of my best. Elliot came over on that trip too, you know? Come to think of it there was some chatter about some bigger than life American hero on his way to kick the Kaiser's fanny. No one you know, right, Charlie?" Norman smiled, knowing full well it was Keeler.

"Any other American volunteers on that voyage?" Hill asked.

"A young fellow from Ossining by the name of Genet. Ever heard the name?"

"Any relation to the 'Citizen Genet' the French sent us after their revolution?" Charlie asked, perking up even more with his stomach filling.

"The same. Edmond was his first name. He's a great-great-great grandson, I think. Had his heart set on the Legion. I'm surprised you didn't get to know him."

"I'm not. I didn't get to know Vic until Avord. Hey, I'd wager Genet knew him if he was in the other regiment. Is he still in the Legion?"

"Don't know. He's a good kid. Not more than nineteen or twenty. Hope he's all right," Prince answered.

Charlie asked for more food. The French cook came out with a plate of cold meat and more bread. He also stuck a bottle of burgundy on the table in front of Keeler, observing that a little rouge was good for whatever ails you. Charlie finished eating and dabbed the cloth at his sore lips. He began to feel a little uneasy again, but not physically. He'd been so sick that he hadn't had time to think about Victor's death. All their comfortable surroundings closed in on him. He longed for Rockwell and Buck's presence. They were all close. The others all liked Victor as well, but Hall had never hit it off with the straight-laced Chapman, and Hill and Rumsey barely knew him.

Charlie thought about Michelle, knowing that she would have learned of Chapman's death from Fleury. That meant she would be worrying about him all the more. At least he would get to see her if Prince's prediction that they were all going to Paris in a week panned out.

Thénault came in with de Laage, Rockwell, McConnell, and Lufbery, their faces revealing their lack of success on the day's patrols. Kiffin and Mac were happy to see Keeler there finishing some food. Thénault noticed Rumsey's advancing inebriation with some concern. He expected the men to blow off some steam with their first loss. It was time to keep them active. He got everybody's attention and announced the schedule for the next several days.

"We will still do the twice daily routine missions at dawn and dusk. I have asked de Laage to organize two more patrols during the day. I want N. 124 to begin to carry more of the mission load here. We are set for a *prise d'armes* this coming Saturday. It would be nice to be able to pin on a couple more medals for additional victories. It's the best way for us to honor Victor as well. You will all be authorized 48 hours pass in Paris after the ceremony to attend a memorial for Chapman on the fourth. Lieutenant de Laage will be taking over for me for a week while I take some leave myself." He paused to see if anyone had any questions. "Isn't it time to recognize Keeler's victory, de Laage?"

Charlie was used to the French manner of addressing each other by last names, but he still found it strange that fellow officers didn't use first names. He personally detested being called Keeler. Hall produced the bourbon from behind the bar, pouring a shot glass for Charlie. All the men stood as they passed the precious fluid from hand to hand until Charlie took the glass and held it up before them. "Not to my victory but to Victor!" He took his drink quickly as they all echoed "to Victor!"

For the next week, every N. 124 pilot flew every available plane as often as four times a day. While they got into scraps on nearly every mission, additional victories eluded the escadrille. Lufbery noted that just about everyone suffered at least one jam or weapon malfunction on every mission. He studied the others and watched the way the armorers handled the ammunition. Charlie's exploded receiver had gotten the armorer's attention. A double feed from the drum of a Lewis machine gun could only happen with defective bullets or a bad drum. Lufbery began to personally inspect every bullet loaded into his drums, rejecting any with the slightest flaws. By the end of the week he had solved the jamming problem at least for himself, though he still hadn't scored his first victory.

Every *prise d'armes* or formation under arms meant they had to stand an inspection. The Americans sported a colorful collection of uniforms. Thénault and de Laage always came out impeccably dressed, their medals gleaming. The French enlisted personnel, especially the mechanics, seemed transformed at these affairs. Men whose greasy overalls and unkempt hygiene were constant trademarks on the flight line became regular military fashion plates for a leave or inspection. To their credit, the French officers didn't enforce standards too vigorously for the American pilots.

A French *Général de Division* wearing three stars on his sleeves and on his gold-braided Kepi, presided at the ceremony. Four escadrilles now occupied the field at Behonne. The older French escadrilles seemed to have dozens of men lined up to receive awards. It was almost embarrassing for N. 124 to have only four pilots called forward for recognition. Bill Thaw, back from the hospital with his arm in a sling, joined Bert Hall, Charlie Keeler, and Kiffin Rockwell in the ranks of the honorees. Bill, received the Legion of Honor, an award normally reserved for officers. Charlie, a sergeant, got a second award of the Médaille Militaire instead. Hall and Rockwell also received the Military Medal. Jack Buck and Chapman were mentioned in orders as recipients of the Croix de Guerre. Norman Prince and Jim McConnell were cited in orders. By the time the announcer finished listing the awards for N. 124 the Americans realized that their escadrille had received more citations than all the units combined. Hall, Keeler and Prince also advanced to *adjudant*, the highest enlisted rank. Buck's formal promotion to that grade would have to wait until he returned. Rockwell and McConnell became permanent sergeants.

Charlie didn't feel special or particularly proud to be called an Ace. He grieved not only for Chapman, but also for the German pilots whose deaths he'd caused. Yet, even the grief of the escadrille at its first loss couldn't completely dampen the American's excitement at their upcoming four-day pass. Only Elliot Cowdin decided not to take the pass. He struggled with himself and the growing physical afflictions that he knew came from fear.

He had to stay behind and fly at least once more. Best to do it after his compatriots left, he reasoned.

Chapter 44
Best of the Best

Paris, July 4, 1916

For the second time in two years all available Americans serving in France gathered in the capital for the celebration of the American Declaration of Independence, the one hundred and fortieth. French authorities continued a major effort in diplomatic channels to draw the Americans into the war. The sinking of the liner *Lusitania* the previous year, and continued German attacks on civilian vessels on the high seas had persuaded a large number of Americans that their real interests lay in supporting the Allies.

In mid-1916 the number of Americans in volunteer service to France climbed to over three hundred. Many filled the ranks of the growing Ambulance Service. Almost seventy shared the lot of the poilus in the infantry. Over forty-five now flew with French escadrilles or were in flight training. This relatively large contingent escaped neither American nor German attention. Formal protests by the German government grew in timbre and frequency. American newspapers and magazines portrayed the volunteers heroically.

The Franco-American Committee worked tirelessly both in France and in the United States. William K. Vanderbilt's open support of the committee persuaded many of his fellow millionaire friends to throw their lots in on the side of the French and British. Reports of the frightful losses on both sides at Verdun shocked many Americans, reinforcing their resistance to getting mired in the bloody war.

Nearly 180 volunteers from the Legion, Aviation, and the Ambulance Service converged on Paris for the July 4 celebration. Along with the traditional wreath-laying at the statue of Lafayette, a small parade would wind around Washington's statue and work its way to the Place de la Concorde. Victor Chapman's memorial service at the American Church would follow.

Bill Thaw couldn't convince Thénault that he could fly as well with one arm as with two, so he had to ride the train back with the others to Paris. On the way he filled them in. All their favorite watering holes were still there, he assured them, and none had given any indication of going dry. Bill pumped Prince, Hall and Keeler for news. He discerned the growing friction between Prince and Rockwell. Lufbery stayed quiet, but Bill made a point of talking to him to get his impressions of the escadrille, especially of its leadership.

"It isn't my place to say," Lufbery began in his unique accent, "but I think your captain prefers to fly a desk."

Thaw didn't give any sign of agreeing or disagreeing. He decided against defending Thénault who he knew did his best for N. 124 for the most part. He asked Luf's opinion on the flying that he'd seen. As the oldest member of the escadrille and one with the longest overall aviation experience, Thaw knew Lufbery saw things others wouldn't notice.

"As good as any I've seen. Could use more care in preparing the machines. Couple of hotheads in the ranks. Don't know the new guys." Lufbery didn't waste words or mention names. He knew and trusted Thaw, but the man *was* an officer.

Bill was happy to learn that Balsley was at last being sent to Neuilly. He asked after Cowdin, getting a mixed reaction. "What is it with Elliot, Charlie?" He asked sitting next to Keeler.

"That *médecin aspirant* fellow, Smith, says Cowdin's nerves are shot. His ulcers and other ailments are real enough, but what makes him an invalid is mostly here," Charlie said, pointing to his head.

"Then he should be grounded instead of making another mission or two."

"Remember how you felt, Bill, when Thénault refused to let you stay and fly one-armed? You knew in your heart you could do it—and probably could too—but the captain was right not to let you stay. Elliot's not as lucky as you are. He doesn't know if he can do it. Old Thénault is right to let him give it a go."

"Save face, that sort of thing?"

"Something like that. Does it make sense to you, *lieutenant*?"

"Cut it out Charlie. It's always going to be 'Bill' to you guys. You seem to be a pretty good judge of character." Thaw fingered the medal still hanging on his tunic, thinking that Charlie deserved it more than him.

"Not always," Charlie said, remembering Rejik's treachery.

When they got to Paris the men scattered as if a bomb had fallen in their midst. They knew where to be and at what time. Some agreed to meet at Harry's Bar or the Chatham. Charlie didn't have to make that choice. Michelle picked him up at the gare with yet another driver.

"Charlie," she said after their long embrace, "let me introduce Nguyen Gho." The small dark-haired man bowed slightly and took Charlie's hand in a very firm grip. "Nguyen is a medical doctor in his country of Laos. He is unable to return to his family and unable to practice here in France. Alexandre hired him to look after me."

Charlie looked at the man with renewed interest and respect. How could he be a doctor and not be in French service? He trusted Fleury's judgment implicitly. It gave him great comfort to know that Michelle had such care readily available.

Michelle looked radiant. Her red tresses seemed to shine even more, and her green eyes twinkled in the bright sunlight. Charlie noted that the dress she'd chosen artfully hid her pregnancy. Its high waist didn't hide her enlarged bosom, stirring the smoldering fire in Charlie's belly. She linked her arm in his for the short walk to the car. Anxious for news of Jennifer and Jack, Charlie waited until they took their seats to ask.

"My word! You don't know then? They are coming back early. When Jack found out about Victor Chapman he simply couldn't wait to go back to the escadrille. They will be on the train from Lyon tonight. Jennifer says Jack is almost as good as new. He is sleeping well and doesn't have the headaches."

"How about his foot?" Charlie asked.

"Good enough for him to be flying every minute he wasn't walking the beach with Jennifer. Wouldn't you like to see Claude and Marie again? It seems like ages since our days on the ship."

"Sure nice of them to look after Jack. I can't wait to see how Jennifer reacted to the surprise of meeting Toussaint."

"I've been thinking about something infinitely more interesting myself," Michelle said, stroking his cheek. "But are you sure you want such a cow?"

"More than ever. You are everything good to me in this ugly war. I think about you every minute that I'm not flying, and many that I am—though I shouldn't. By the way, I could use a new muffler, and you're the prettiest cow I've ever seen." She nuzzled closer and said nothing. Their enforced separation during this time of her pregnancy tried them both.

TOUSSAINT TOLD JACK ABOUT VICTOR'S DEATH. A daily dispatch listed aviation casualties. Victor Chapman's name included his citizenship and unit. Claude always kept an eye on N. 124. He knew about Charlie's nomination for the Legion of Honor, and other facts that cropped up in *Le Rapport Quotidian du Service Aéronautique*.

Stunned by the unwelcome news, Jack Buck didn't know how to react. His first thought was to return immediately to the front to be with the others and to do whatever he could. He thought Rockwell must be devastated, not to mention Charlie, and Vic's devoted mechanic Bley. He felt like he had just gotten to know Chapman. The man was so vital, so full of life. How could he be dead?

Jack remembered how he felt facing death: the calm, untroubled, almost joyful emotion. After seeing so many die, so many lifeless bodies piled like meat in a butcher shop, Jack hadn't become fatalistic or jaded like so many others. It hadn't fully hit him until his vision of little Chérie during the time the Caudron came apart around him. From that moment on, death truly held no sting for him as it said in scripture. Yet, it still stung when it happened to others.

Jennifer watched Jack's reaction to the news closely. She knew his religious convictions, but they didn't talk much about that. Instead of wanting to go back to kill the Germans who had taken his friend, Jack wanted to go back to help the friends he'd left behind. She remembered the kind way he had helped Cartier's widow at the funeral. Jack may have been susceptible to other women's charms in ways she didn't like, but those indiscretions were all part of the compassionate, sensitive man she was learning to love more than ever.

Jack's convalescent leave still had a week to run when the news of Victor's death reached them. Though his recovery in the first week had been remarkable, Doctor Lascasse was not about to let Buck go in only one week. Jack pleaded with Lascasse, fearful he might miss Victor's funeral.

He tried to fly every day. The more he flew the fewer were his incidences of blurred vision and dizziness. By the end of June and nine full days in Fréjus, even Lascasse had to agree that the American was fit for full flight duty.

Claude Toussaint found several additional opportunities to get together with them socially. He introduced them to the mayor of Fréjus who quickly took them to meet his chief of police, a jovial man named Marquette, who spoke English with an American accent.

After a quick explanation of his American mother and French father, Marquette took it upon himself to see to it that the young couple saw everything of interest in the area. "Napoleon landed here on his triumphant return from Egypt. The baptismal font in our church is housed in perhaps the oldest Christian building in Europe. You've seen the ruins. Did you know that Julius Caesar himself established a rest camp for his legions near here?" said the indefatigable Marquette. He apparently didn't have enough criminal activity to keep him from personally escorting them and keeping up a running account of what they were seeing.

While Jack flew and Toussaint worked at the base, Jennifer found Marie Toussaint to be a willing shopping companion. The older woman delighted in going from shop to shop in the small shopping areas of Saint-Raphaël. She kept up a steady stream of French with Jennifer, the shopkeepers, or whomever they met. When they'd exhausted the town's meager offerings Marie insisted they make a trip to Nice. While Jennifer only understood parts of what Marie said, she was amused at how much Marie loved clothes.

A day before they were scheduled to return to Paris, Jack accompanied the ladies on one of their excursions. He could now walk and wear normal footgear, though he had to sit down and rest his foot frequently. After an hour of watching them moving things around on hangar racks in Saint Maxime, Jack found the prospect of lunch very appealing.

Jennifer tried to carry her end of the conversations with Marie, but her vocabulary didn't allow much more than an exchange of pleasantries. This frustrated Jennifer because she wanted to ask Marie what she knew about Claude's family. Toussaint himself either dodged the subject or didn't want to spoil the ambiance of the young couple's stay with unpleasant information.

Marie blissfully continued her running monologue with Jennifer even though Jack was there and could understand everything she said. At lunch Marie began talking about the Beauvais family. Jennifer caught a little of what she said. Jack could have translated, but Madame Toussaint didn't slow down, so he listened patiently to what he suspected was just gossip anyway.

"The Beauvais women have always been among the most beautiful in Europe. I knew some of them before I met Claude—older women who in their prime had modeled for Lautrec in his studio at Montmartre. They were a snooty lot until their family's comeuppance in 1913," Marie went on without stopping to see if either of her companions understood or were trying to follow her. Jack noticed Jennifer stifle a yawn. He was curious though how one family could produce two gorgeous women like Claudine and Béatrice who were so different in personality.

The meal almost forgotten, Jack listened in fascination to the incredible story of the Beauvais-Toussaint alliance. By the time they finished their lunch, Jack was eager to tell Jennifer what she might not have understood.

Emile Toussaint, Jennifer's maternal grandfather, broke with his family's tradition of serving on the sea and went into business in Marseilles shortly after the end of the Franco-Prussian War. Marie didn't know the details, but apparently Emile made a lot of money in a short time. By then he'd married and began to have the first of their five children. Angelique, Charlie and Jennifer's mother, was the youngest. Toussaint's business dealt with some sort of trade tied to the Port of Marseilles. Legitimate at first, Emile found that he had to pay off certain members of the growing *milieu*, organized crime bosses that controlled the unions as well as vice traffic in the region.

André Jean-Jacques de Beauvais, Béatrice and Claudine's father, owned one of the major shipping companies located in Marseilles along with several others along the Mediterranean Coast. Labor feuds over wages, hours and working conditions flared up frequently. Beauvais, who dropped the 'de' legally to show his Republican loyalties, found it useful to pay local police and crime bosses a small stipend to keep the unions from getting out of hand. Strikes in 1881 and 1885 cost Beauvais—and by extension, men like Toussaint—tens of thousands of francs. Neither of the businessmen saw any moral dilemma in their payoffs.

Apparently, Marie explained, the de Beauvais family had a history of mental illness. André's daughters seemed untouched by the heritage. His son, Jean-Claude, however, suffered from periodic bouts of some kind of mental disorder. André put the boy to work in Marseilles where Jean-Claude discovered the seamier side of life and got himself into trouble well before turning twenty.

Marie skipped over many details that Jack tried to bridge in the retelling to Jennifer. Toussaint and Beauvais formed a partnership in 1886 that gave them control of nearly all maritime traffic in Marseilles. The two families became allied socially as well. Emile even presented himself as a candidate for mayor in 1888, losing by a small margin to the opponent backed by the unions. Béatrice attended the university in Avignon, doing so well that her professors recommended that she pursue further studies in Paris. Jack guessed that she met Fleury during that time. Claudine, on the other hand, had some of her brother's wildness hidden by her girlish beauty. She didn't do well in school and leapt at the chance to escape the family when Harry Walker came along.

Jean-Claude was André's only hope to take over the business, but the young man's episodic bouts of mental illness and rowdy behavior made it unlikely he could follow his father. A favorable marriage to a strong woman might solve the problem. Angelique Toussaint, at eighteen a bright beautiful girl, seemed a good candidate. The parents arranged the marriage without consulting either Jean-Claude or Angelique. Beauvais agreed to establish trusts for any children they might have, and Toussaint offered Angelique's inheritance from her maternal grandparents as dowry.

Angelique couldn't stand Jean-Claude let alone the thought of marrying him. She stood up to her parents in what must have produced some terrible arguments.

Jennifer sat listening to Jack retelling Marie's account with her mouth hanging open. She interrupted several times to ask him what certain phrases meant, surprised at how much she had understood after all. When she tried to imagine her mother at eighteen she felt a sense of pride welling up in her.

Emile Toussaint, thinking marriages arranged by the parents perfectly acceptable, threatened to disown Angelique if she gave them any trouble. Frantic and hopeless, Angelique stowed away on a German freighter bound for New Orleans.

Toussaint had done a little detective work of his own. When Jennifer asked about their grandparents on her mother's side, he told her they'd both died before the century ended. Their name, he said, was one they might have heard: *Pétain*.

Jennifer boarded the train for Paris with Jack at midday on June 30. She'd found the Toussaint revelations fascinating insights on her mother, but nothing more.

"VICTOR CHAPMAN REPRESENTS THE BEST OF EVERYTHING AMERICA has to offer. His courage frightened lesser men. He embraced with his whole being the cause of freedom he had grown to love from his youngest years. Victor's generosity is already legendary. He gave freely of everything he had from time to wealth, always putting others first. Many of you know how his high ideals illuminated the way for others, but few could know how much this young man loved God except by the love he showed to others. He was physically strong but he never bullied. He was artistically talented though he never bragged. He was as morally straight as we weak humans could ever hope to be in this world of temptation."

Charlie could make out most of the Catholic priest's words. He looked around at the solemn faces, seeing the family in the front left pews, black, veiled, and shaking quietly with sobs. He hadn't met Alce, Victor's stepmother, but she stood out next to Victor's father. She was taller and straighter than the others in the pew. Her posture seemed to emulate the priest's words about her beloved stepson. Grey-bearded John Jay Chapman, fully six inches shorter than his wife, stood with his left arm folded behind his back, the sleeve pinned back. It covered the missing hand he'd burned to the knuckles after thrashing an innocent man whom he suspected of courting his wife. Such extreme passion both before and after the incident led to the amputation of the hand. Victor had told him of his father's self-mutilation. Charlie couldn't sense the sternness of the man, but he felt Victor's intimidation. He wondered if the son's selfless sacrifice finally placated the uncompromising father.

Jack fought back tears as his eyes kept wandering back to the Chapman pew. The family may be wealthy, he thought, but they have suffered greatly. He knew about Victor's real mother's death, his brother's drowning, and his father's extremism. Victor's death must be even more unbearable to them.

The church at Quai d'Orsay was full of mourners. The priest was second to speak after the Protestant pastor of the American Church. Considering Vic's powerful Catholic faith, Jack found it ironic that the family would insist on a Protestant service. At least, he thought with some Christian piety, the Chapman's allowed the French priest to deliver Victor's eulogy. Jack clung to Jennifer and her to him throughout the service. All the N. 124 personnel banded together naturally. Many of Chapman's legion friends clumped in little knots throughout the crowded church.

A memorial service like Chapman's only half fills the figurative bellies of the starving mourners. His physical absence made their sorrow incomplete. Some foolishly held out hope that he would come back. Others simply denied his death. *Habeas Corpus.* Without a body, death wasn't a legal fact.

Victor's family, familiar with the finality of death, harbored no such fantasies. John Jay himself felt anger at his lack of feelings. Why, he thought, didn't the loss of his eldest son produce the terrible anguish he'd felt at the loss of Jay? Had he been able to see into his soul, he would have known that Victor was dead to him from the day young Jay had drowned. His inability to see life in any more than two dimensions denied him the soothing escape of rationalization.

Kiffin Rockwell sat in the row with his escadrille mates, but his mind was somewhere else entirely. Victor was his best and closest friend—even closer than his beloved brother, Paul. Chapman's attack on life closely matched Kiffin Rockwell's. He tolerated no equivocation, and he suffered fools poorly, though he had a ready smile and a warm nature. Victor's death close upon Balsley's crash brought the possibility of death or serious injury perilously close to all of them. Kiffin thought of his own death with disdain and brash indifference. Like Victor had insisted, death was nothing more than a passage into another life, a life without rancor, without war. Rockwell was anything but fatalistic or suicidal, but Victor's philosophy made death seem insignificant, even honorable.

Chouteau Johnson's reaction to Chapman's death surprised Charlie Keeler. He'd gotten the impression that Johnson was what his father called 'hoity-toity,' one of the uppity South Saint Louis crowd. Charlie, try as he might, just couldn't help jumping to premature conclusions and overreacting to imagined wrongs. Chouteau genuinely mourned Victor, making the sign of the cross at the end of every prayer. He'd been wrong in his assessments of Toussaint and Rejik, but he felt sure that Johnson wasn't just putting on a show.

The mourners left that bright summer day with all their various feelings and thoughts pouring out onto the banks of the Seine as they themselves emerged from the dark confines of the church. It was as though the entire congregation spilled its collective sorrow down the banks into the nearby river. The deep blue of the midday sky seemed to bleach out the moroseness, but Jack Buck struggled with the feeling that the memorial service was over too soon. It didn't seem right that folks could smile and laugh and talk about heading to Harry's Bar.

"Jack," Charlie said as they descended the steps with Michelle and Jennifer, "strange isn't it? I mean, others will die. It just seems like they will be forgotten all so quickly."

"I was thinking along the same lines. Vic's family won't forget him. Did you see the look in his father's eye? If ever a man was at war within himself," Jack said, "Mr. Chapman sure looks the part."

"His mother is certainly an impressive woman," Jennifer observed.

"Stepmother, isn't it?" Michelle corrected her.

"She acted more aggrieved than his real father. Why is it that men feel like they have to hide their feelings?" Jennifer asked.

Charlie said, "In Mr. Chapman's case, I think he's not hiding his feelings so much as he just doesn't know them. Victor always said he could never please his father. Now that he's dead he may have finally forced the great John Jay to see how wonderful a son he had."

The two young couples rebounded quickly in spite of their deep feelings. Chapman himself had insisted that life was for the living. After losing his mother and brother, Victor told them, he'd cried until there were no more tears. He'd prayed until the words ran together. Slowly he began to accept the losses though he could never escape the feeling that somehow he was responsible, especially in his brother's drowning. Guilt, he told them, was every bit as painful as grief, except it never went away completely. He railed against the 'eat, drink, and be merry' practiced by so many soldiers. He would ask them rhetorically: "Isn't life worth more than debauchery?" Even Rockwell shrank before his friend's high moral stance, but all of them agreed with him, at least in principle.

Keeler and Buck got on the train for Bar-le-Duc with heavy hearts. Michelle's approaching delivery made it awfully difficult for Charlie to return to Behonne, and Fréjus had spoiled Jack and Jennifer. The ride back gave the men time to reflect. As the train progressed, they both found their feelings changing subtly from lament to anticipation. They were going back to work, back to the air they both loved, and the war they both hated.

Chapter 45
Revenge and Rockets

Behonne, July and August, 1916

The men of *l'Escadrille Américaine* entered July intent on avenging Chapman who lay dead somewhere on the German side of the lines. Three of their number languished in hospitals, and one seemed to be coming apart.

Elliot Cowdin forced himself to take the mission on July 4 with Lieutenant de Laage and Red Rumsey who had missed the train to Paris and lost his pass. The three took off to fly the dawn patrol on one of the clearest days they had seen in six weeks.

When they crossed the lines north of Douaumont in search of German observation machines, Cowdin began to shake and shiver in the cockpit of his Nieuport. To his credit he kept his place behind and to the right of de Laage. The Lieutenant already had a reputation for sniffing out the enemy—knowledge of small comfort to the rattled Cowdin.

Alfred de Laage breathed fire in the air. He rode his Nieuport as he would one of the mounts of his cavalry days with all the fury and abandon of his hard-charging forebears. Early in the war de Laage led his mounted section on a reconnaissance straight into the scything fires of the German machine guns. Wounded in the thigh and thrown from his dying horse, he fell to the ground where he would surely die or be captured were it not for his faithful orderly, Jean Dressy. The young corporal galloped to his lieutenant, snatched him up on the run and carried him from the advancing enemy. The experience solidified the two men's dedication to each other at the same time that it presaged an end to classical cavalry tactics in modern warfare.

When de Laage traded horses for airplanes, he gave up nothing of his hell bent for leather upbringing. No fool, however, he mastered pursuit flying in much the same way he had mastered equestrian skills. He knew the value of surprise and good reconnaissance innately, and tried to apply cavalry tactics in the air with some success. As often as not, de Laage found the enemy before they found him. He seldom hesitated in the face of superior odds to take advantage of surprise. For this reason, some of the pilots in N. 124 considered flying a patrol with de Laage to be high adventure at the very least. The lieutenant had but one credited victory for all of his wildness, but he had never been shot down or lost a member of a patrol he led. He was as skilled at getting out of a mess as he was at finding one.

Over the Meuse River on the German side of the lines de Laage's patrol stumbled on a pair of slow-moving L.V.G.s. The two-seater observation machines were directing artillery into the French defenses near Fort Douaumont. After checking the immediate area for Fokker defenders, de Laage signaled the attack with an abrupt dive. Red Rumsey went for the second L.V.G., while de Laage took on the first. Cowdin held back reasoning correctly that he would follow one or the other depending on their success or failure.

Elliot's quivering stopped when the engagement began. He scanned the skies overhead and behind while the other two pressed their attacks. He was beginning to feel like he had conquered his personal devil when two Fokkers appeared seemingly out of thin air. Knowing he should take them on, Cowdin immediately climbed and maneuvered to meet the diving enemies. His heart fluttered and his limbs felt weak but he didn't falter. One of the Fokkers peeled off to pursue the other Nieuports, leaving Cowdin to face the other. He felt a flood of relief at having to deal with only one.

Elliot was a good pilot and an excellent shot. Though he had only one victory, his skills in the air had never been in question. The Fokker made the first pass unleashing a burst that narrowly missed his Nieuport. Cowdin whipped the machine into a loop that placed him on the Fokker's tail and closed to less than a hundred meters before firing. Almost at the instant he pressed the trigger the Fokker flipped over on its back and tucked its nose avoiding Elliot's fire. Before he could redress his machine Cowdin found the Fokker on his own tail. Without thinking, he executed a sharp turn to the right, dragging his assailant closely behind but throwing off the German's fire. For the next five or ten minutes the two traded positions in violent maneuvers that took them well to the east of their meeting point and farther away from the flight of the L.V.G.s then under attack by de Laage and Rumsey.

Cowdin realized he was running short of ammunition and not achieving many hits on the Fokker. On one of his passes he grasped the spare drum and prepared to switch out the empty while above and behind the Fokker. His momentary distraction was enough for his opponent to reverse the pursuit and resume firing. A *clack clack clack* sound alerted Cowdin to the renewed danger but not in time to prevent the spare drum from being shot out of his outstretched hand. The shock numbed his left hand. A warm wetness flowed down his legs. Now the shivers and fluttering returned with a vengeance all their own. All he could think of was to escape.

They had lost altitude in their dual—enough so that Cowdin could see he was very near French lines. He dove, driving the Nieuport down and again to the right in the hope that the German wouldn't cross the lines. A quick glance over his shoulder increased his fear greatly. Now the Fokker was tailing him at less than fifty meters. Why he wasn't firing puzzled Cowdin. He shook so violently that he could barely control the Nieuport. He told himself that if he ever made it to the ground he would never fly again. For some unknown reason the German pilot either couldn't fire or decided not to shoot down the French aviator who had been so worthy an opponent moments earlier.

Cowdin continued his flight to the south, expecting a fatal slug at any moment. Maneuver didn't seem to work as the Fokker kept pace with his every move. Then, as quickly as the German had appeared on his tail in the first of their gyrations, he disappeared. Elliot couldn't believe his luck. His soaked pants began to cool off rapidly. He even had a moment to feel embarrassed at his incontinence.

Back on the ground he had to be helped from the cockpit by two mechanics. When they got him out and on his feet, Cowdin realized that he'd survived the ordeal and was indeed on the ground. He tore off his goggles and helmet and walked away unsteadily, intending never to return to the flight line as a pilot. The mechanics sponged the urine smell from the wicker seat. Cowdin was not the first pilot to foul his own cockpit.

Meanwhile the furious combat over Douaumont continued. Rumsey and de Laage had fired all their ammunition into the L.V.G.s to no effect whatsoever. The other Fokker split them up forcing them to egress and return separately. On the return flight de Laage saw another Nieuport with a blue Fokker in pursuit. He thought he recognized the distinctive markings of the famous German ace Oswald Boelcke. Why he wasn't firing at what was surely Cowdin's Nieuport could only be explained by lack of ammunition. Just the same, the German boldly continued his pursuit well into French territory until he executed an abrupt Immelman turn, leaving Cowdin.

"*Quelle chance, mon ami*!" de Laage said when he caught up with Cowdin who was slowly making his way off the field hoping no one would notice the urine now staining his coverall. "That was surely Boelcke on your tail. Few have come back to tell of a fight with him. *Mes respects*!"

Cowdin simply nodded and rushed away to change his clothes. The knowledge that the great Boelcke had chased him provoked a rumbling in his bowels and he feared he would further dirty his pants if he didn't get away in a hurry.

The next day he left the field for a binge in Bar-le-Duc. He got into a brawl and ended up spending the night in the gendarmerie under arrest. When the authorities delivered him to Behonne, de Laage kindly overlooked the incident. Two days later Cowdin disappeared again and didn't stumble back for another day and a half. This time de Laage warned him that he would place him under arrest on the field if it happened again. By then, the rest of the men were back.

The press of missions masked Cowdin's misbehavior at first. He complained of chest pains and refused to go near a Nieuport. Rockwell was tempted to punch the New Yorker in the nose for shirking his duty. Even Bert Hall, the perennial pariah, disdained to associate with Cowdin. With morale already hitting bottom, de Laage convinced Cowdin to submit his resignation papers. De Laage held them until Thénault returned, hoping whatever ailed Cowdin wasn't contagious.

From those first unfortunate mechanics killed in the bombing at Luxeuil, to the pilots wounded in the air, to Chapman's death, to Cowdin's breakdown; N. 124 had run the gamut of losses in its very short existence. As soon as the men returned from the short stay in Paris they knew they had changed. N. 124 had been bloodied. Luxeuil was long behind them. Sister escadrilles suffered as much and more in the days they'd been at Behonne. What rankled the Americans was their failure to exact like payment from the Boches. For N. 124 early July brought no verified victories in a bewildering series of fierce aerial combats.

By the middle of the month the mood in the unit was black. Bill Thaw came back *sans* cast bringing their numbers back up to twelve. Thaw's return proved fortuitous to morale. His ebullient character and open friendliness to all was palliative. The strain of flying two and three and sometimes four missions daily exacted a toll. When patrols returned day after day empty-handed with machines riddled with holes, that toll grew exponentially. Some began to wonder who would be the next one to crack.

Without the exhilaration of a victory to compensate for their doldrums, the men of *l'Escadrille Américaine* began to think their unit was jinxed. Thaw was astonished at the change in attitude and increased friction that had grown since his absence.

Rockwell himself chafed as much as anyone at the lack of success. He blamed the officers for their lack of aggressiveness though he knew de Laage drove as hard as any of them. He already contemplated asking for transfer to a French squadron. He'd done the same in the Legion when his first regiment began to falter and rub him the wrong way. Only Charlie Keeler kept Kiffin from going to the captain with his transfer request.

Charlie was a natural leader. His unassuming modest demeanor endeared him to all, just as his powerful physique impressed his fellow men. He presented no threat to the established chain of command, so Thénault let Keeler have free reign, giving him tough patrols in the air and additional tasks on the ground.

The captain wanted to improve morale by getting his men promoted as rapidly as possible. But, in contrast to the rank-conscious French, rank didn't seem to matter to the Americans. He had his clerk prepare the paperwork to put Keeler, Buck, and Rockwell in for lieutenancy. Prince, older and presumably more mature, was a logical choice as well, but he just didn't ring true with the other Americans. Thaw would say nothing against Prince, but he equally avoided praising the man. Prince talked as if he were the sole inspiration for the American squadron and the first to suggest it. This irked Bill Thaw who knew he had a hand in the event.

Even without Thaw's unreserved endorsement, Thénault thought, Norman Prince would make an excellent officer. Since James McConnell got separated from the first aerial patrol back in May, Georges Thénault thought Mac was less adept than some of the others. Despite Jimmy's subsequent superb performance in the air and his ready acceptance by all on the ground, McConnell—perhaps because of his modesty—didn't rise in N. 124 as he had in the Ambulance Service.

For his part, McConnell was quite content to remain a sergeant and to fly his share and more of the patrols. He saw much less need of leadership in the group assembled now at Behonne than he'd observed at Neuilly back when he and Buck were getting started with the ambulance service. All these men had been through the French flight schools. Some had flown in other squadrons. The new man, Didier Masson, had even flown what he claimed was the only airplane in the Mexican Army. What need of leaders had they except to get them up for missions and to run interference with the higher authorities? For all Jim McConnell's powerful sense of observation, he, like most of his compatriots, failed to see the real value of an inspirational leader on the ground. Lieutenant de Laage came closest to filling this role for the escadrille, but de Laage was as much of an individualist as the headstrong Rockwell. Jim McConnell seldom thought about the issue. The upheaval of the battlefield at Verdun mesmerized him. He was also suffering from early symptoms of rheumatoid arthritis that made him stiff and pain-ridden at times.

When Thénault returned from his leave in mid-July he found the men in a foul mood. Querying de Laage only produced an account of the past week's missions, the lack of victories, and the disturbing news that their nemesis, Boelcke, may have driven Cowdin over the edge. Thénault knew the other escadrilles in the group were recording kills, but they were also suffering losses at a faster rate than his unit. He sat slumped at his desk on Bastille Day trying to think of a plan of attack on the morale issue when an old student and friend showed up at the door of his office.

Before him, leaning lightly on a cane, stood Lieutenant Charles Eugène Jules Marie Nungesser. Thénault rose to greet him noticing that the younger man had changed in outward appearance. New scars now furrowed his rugged handsome face. Even his wavy blond hair seemed parted unnaturally from a recent wound. Nungesser's slight list came from one leg being a full inch shorter than the other. Thénault knew his former pupil was one of France's leading aces with nine confirmed kills. That Nungesser had been banged up in the process didn't surprise Thénault. What did impress him was the double row of medals on Charles' stylish black tunic. At the rate he'd been going Nungesser was on his way to becoming the most highly decorated man in the French Army.

Nungesser saluted and said he was reporting for duty if his old friend would have him. In reality, the dashing lieutenant should have been convalescing in a Paris hospital. His last adventure ended with a bullet in the mouth that broke his previously shattered jaw a second time. Nungesser now had broken nearly every bone in his body and lost most of his teeth. He never stayed down for any longer than the minimum recovery time. It astounded the doctors as well as his escadrille that he could absorb so much punishment, jump back in the cockpit, and go on to score more victories in his debilitated state.

Thénault took Nungesser to the villa to introduce him to the American pilots. Many already knew the man or at least of his feats. When the exuberant Frenchman smiled, his double row of gold teeth flashed, competing with the colorful double row of ribbons and medals on his chest. Nungesser immediately began to regale the gathered pilots with tales of his last victory—not in the air, but in a bistro in Paris with an elegant lady curious about his battered physique. He told them how he numbered his various injuries by the teeth he'd lost. A different man might seem overly full of himself, but Nungesser managed to relate his accomplishments without braggadocio. His presence in the popote wafted through the room like a breath of fresh air. Maybe he could change the streak of bad luck of the escadrille.

While only partially recovered from his latest injuries, Nungesser insisted on flying missions. He'd even arrived in his Nieuport with its distinctive skull and crossbones over a coffin flanked by two candles superimposed on a black heart. A few of the Americans had their own distinctive markings, but none as bizarre as Nungesser's. Immediately Hall began to paint "BERT" in twelve inch letters on the left side of his Nieuport, and "TREB" on the right. He explained that he wanted the Huns to be able to read his name coming or going. The new fashion trend took wings as each pilot proudly sought a distinctive design of his own.

Finally breaking the long dry spell for N. 124 on July 21, Nungesser downed a German after a short combat with the Aviatik and a Fokker. Never at a loss for a reason to drink a toast, this victory called for a celebration. It made for a wild night of drinking and singing in the villa. Over the next several days, Hall, Rockwell, and de Laage, achieved victories. Hall's came in full view of the poilus. He'd carefully noted the time on the watch he'd won at cards just to be sure.

Rockwell still seethed about the German two-seater he'd brought to the ground in flames on the same day as de Laage's victory back on June 27, before the leave in Paris. Kiffin's victory couldn't be confirmed by the required two impartial observers. It angered Rockwell then and he continued to unfairly blame the lieutenant. The thought that kept rattling about in his mind was that had he been an officer no one would have questioned his victory.

With the injustice of it all still fermenting in his heart, the next episode did nothing to calm his anger. After coming back from leave, he and de Laage attacked a German machine and followed it down. The two-seater looked to be in a deadly tailspin. Yet, the German pilot recovered just above ground level and sailed away safely. Ironically, ground observers called to verify credit for the victory. When de Laage and Rockwell honestly reported that the German had escaped, two other French pilots laid claim to the victory. It was almost more than the fiercely idealistic Rockwell could handle. At least his current kill could not be contested.

On the last day of the month of July Lufbery finally logged his first kill. He'd carefully stalked a biplace and closed to within 50 meters before firing. The enemy aircraft began to careen crazily as a lick of flame sprang from the fuselage. Lufbery was sure he'd hit the pilot because the hapless gunner thrashed about in the flaming plane all the way to the ground. It sickened Lufbery, causing him to reaffirm his vow never to ride out a fire. He told his mates he'd jump first.

Two weeks later Lufbery scored the escadrille's second double victory. This prompted the taciturn Thénault to rush to headquarters to put the American in for the *Médaille Militaire*. The gesture tempered Lufbery's antipathy towards the captain considerably.

Jack tried to fly every patrol with Nungesser who used many of the same techniques in the air that he'd seen Charlie Keeler employ. The other pilot also watching Nungesser closely was Raoul Lufbery. On Tuesday, August 8, Lufbery went up alone once again and came back with his fourth confirmed victory.

That same afternoon Buck, Keeler and Nungesser chewed up a flight of six Fokkers sending at least four down to their deaths. Not a single one could be confirmed as their fight took place out of sight of both ground and balloon observers. Nungesser took the news of the non-confirmation nonchalantly, telling Buck and Keeler that he had as many unconfirmed kills as confirmed and didn't care who counted. Charles Nungesser may have been a little less than candid in this statement. He was already a contender for the coveted title of "Ace of Aces" with his ten victories. Though not a braggart, Nungesser was a proud man. That was why he wore all his decorations even in the air. Charlie found this aspect of the likable Frenchman a bit distasteful but mentioned it to no one, not even Jack.

Prince labored tirelessly trying to find the key to becoming an ace. When he found out about an innovation that might help him add to his score, he pursued it with a passion. Observation balloons on both sides of the line defied downing by conventional fires. Even incendiary bullets failed more often than not. A French officer named Le Prieur devised a system of rockets he hoped would spell the end to the balloons. Nothing more than simple devices similar to fireworks used for displays, the rockets had to be launched either en masse or very close to their target to achieve any effect. A volatile powder charge propelled them at great speed for a relatively short range. They exploded with a fiery burst at the apogee of their trajectory. To down a balloon they only had to pierce the skin. Inherently inaccurate, firing them from the ground proved futile. Firing them from mounts under the wings of an airplane provided some chance of success.

Norman Prince pounced on the idea and persuaded Thénault to let him try out the Le Prieurs. He took McConnell along for cover from above. Norman, using the battery-powered solenoid his mechanics had crafted, fired his six rockets into the fabric of one of the German Drachen over the lines. At first he zoomed up and away disappointed at the results. Looking back over his shoulder, however, he saw a greasy-looking cloud of black smoke where his victim had been. The rockets worked! The normally reserved Prince felt as excited as a child shooting off bottle rockets on the Fourth of July back in Boston. He was so eager to get back to claim the victory that he almost landed on top of James McConnell. When the dust settled, their crazy gyrations on the ground rendered both machines *hors de combat*. Thankfully, neither of them was hurt.

Nungesser continued to fly at least one mission a day, but his most significant contribution was the turn-about in the escadrille's morale since his arrival. He kept the pilots on edge every night with yet another story of one of his fights. Nungesser had to be in incredible pain, but he'd acquired a taste for Hall's Manhattans that seemed to ease his discomfort and loosen his tongue. He took a shine to Jack Buck who in some ways looked like a taller, undamaged version of Nungesser. Jack's French also attracted the officer who appreciated the fact that Buck had neither studied the language nor lived in France before the war. Thénault told his old pupil about Buck's unbelievable landing of the Caudron at Pau. Having survived six near-fatal crashes, Nungesser admired what Jack had done as a mere student.

Paul Pavelka joined them at Behonne on August 11. Paul had spent several days in Paris with Paul Rockwell before reporting for duty. He knew Kiffin was a candidate for becoming an officer, and it pained him to think that his old friend from the Plain of Artois might leave the noble ranks of the soldiers. Pavelka had seen both good and bad officers. The sous-lieutenants in the Legion could not be beat for bravery, though every one he had known was dead.

Charlie Keeler took great delight in getting Pavelka back in their old circle. They had to arm wrestle within minutes of seeing each other. Charlie acted challenged, but his recovered strength made the smaller Pavelka no match for him. After getting Paul settled in his room, Charlie took him to the field to make his first flight. Paul protested as soon as he saw the disreputable Nieuport Thénault had assigned him. It was the same one Prince had wrecked earlier when he tried to mix it up with Mac. While Louis Bley had repaired the machine, it still looked a wreck, and the blotches of oil and grease splattered all over the fuselage didn't help its appearance.

"Charlie, you're supposed to be influential around here. Why don't you tell the captain that I shouldn't get a hoodooed machine?"

"If you believe that nonsense I'm afraid you are in for a nasty introduction to the glorious reality of the American Escadrille. First off, I don't have any special influence in the least. Second, we don't hold with that baloney of jinxes. A man would go crazy if he swallowed that bunk. Listen, Louis Bley put that machine in flying order. It is probably better than half the others are mechanically."

On his first flight, with Keeler showing him the ropes, Pavelka saw the truth in what Charlie had told him. The Nieuport was tighter than any he had flown in training. Even the machine gun functioned flawlessly. Just the same, Pavelka had a feeling that his mottled mount was bad luck. The next day, he went on the dawn patrol with Buck and McConnell. They wandered east to Etain in search of prey. On the way back, not having flushed even a single German, the patrol split up for a little free hunting near the front lines. Pavelka found an L.V.G. and dived on it immediately. His gun jammed on the first pass. He climbed and tried to bang the machine gun with the mallet readily available in a holster on the right side of the cockpit. His banging couldn't have been that loud or fast! Alarmed, he looked ahead to see flames pouring from his motor. Something had broken loose or had been hit causing raw fuel to come into contact with the whirling hot cylinders.

The flames grew in intensity singeing his face. He jammed in right rudder and slipped the Nieuport for all he could. It seemed to work for the flames went off to the left though they now licked the doped fabric of the wings flaring them into shreds of sparkling brilliance that might have been pretty in other circumstances. He had lost enough altitude to begin to distinguish details on the ground. If he held the slip the entire left bank of wings would disintegrate in flames. He punched in left rudder, thankful that the Nieuport still responded to his efforts. Now the flames whipped over his head and began to devour the right wings. Even after cutting the engine and fuel flow, the fire continued to grow in intensity. Pavelka didn't panic even when the heat seared his face as the flames switched sides. He discerned a marshy area below him and decided to ride it out. Jumping from the flaming plane never crossed his mind.

As soon as he straightened out to land, the flames scorched his face, forcing him to duck down behind the cowling and land blindly straight ahead. The Nieuport plopped into the marsh and plowed ahead without turning over. Pavelka unfastened his belt even before it stopped moving and clambered over the side falling face first in the slimy smelly ooze of the swamp.

The tempting coolness made him want to lie immersed in the muck until the roar of the flames renewed his sense of urgency. He extracted himself, trying to run awkwardly in the clinging mud. A blast and wave of heat drove him back face down into the mire when the remaining fumes in his fuel tank exploded. Remembering the Germans shelled downed machines in No Man's Land, he forced himself to struggle away even farther. Moments later German rounds, guided by the column of smoke, began to pelt the stricken Nieuport.

Pavelka then found himself being tugged and pulled into a trench by some poilus. Only then did he realize how seriously his hands and face were burned. The mud kept the pain at bay for a little while, but soon huge blisters rose on the exposed skin unprotected by his half-melted goggles. Paul's last thoughts before passing out were that he was finally rid of the hoodooed machine. Were he able to realize it, he might have appreciated that he was one of only a handful of aviators to survive what they called a 'flamer.' Maybe the machine wasn't so jinxed after all.

All were sorry to see the French hero leave. When Nungesser's convalescence technically ended in mid-August, he returned to his escadrille, N. 65, to continue to relentlessly run up his score. Buck was sure that few others could rival him in the race if Nungesser could stay out of the hospital.

The spate of victories sparked by Nungesser renewed the effort by the rest of the escadrille. Norman Prince didn't want for effort, but he just didn't seem to be able to get credit for the kills he was sure he had earned. Finally on August 23 Prince succeeded, though the "victory" would be questioned later. Exasperated by the French confirmation system, Norman tackled an Aviatik and tried to work their fight over the lines in view of the balloon line. He succeeded in either disabling the weapons on the Aviatik or the Germans had run out of ammunition. Seeing a chance he'd never thought of before; Norman decided to try to force the Aviatik to land inside French lines. A series of threatening gestures and a few bursts from the Lewis gun persuaded the somewhat inept German crew to follow the crazy French pilot's directions. The terrified pilot landed unharmed in a field near Verdun where poilus soon captured him and the observer before they could set fire to their machine. Prince quaffed his shot of the dwindling supply of Rockwell's bourbon with great relish.

Even Rumsey flew sober and showed great courage in the air, but he had little luck. Chouteau Johnson became another stalwart on patrol though he too couldn't seem to bag his first German. Dud Hill showed the most promise from Charlie Keeler's perspective. Hill paid close attention to the more experienced flyers. He liked to fly on the patrols Keeler led, and he always followed Charlie's lead. This didn't keep him from showing his aggressiveness. On one patrol in late July, Hill pursued an Albatros so closely that the German crash-landed in No Man's Land doing very little damage to the machine or its two occupants. Much to his disappointment, the French listed Hill's victory as 'unofficial,' denying him credit.

Didier Masson, much like Lufbery, had every right to feel superior to his younger escadrille mates. Instead, he made no effort to advance himself. His sense of humor and tenaciousness became apparent almost as soon as he arrived. Thénault appreciated the calming influence Masson had on the escadrille. His courage in the air manifested itself as he flew more missions, but he wasn't flashy or out to run up his numbers. Because of his years in America, Didier was considered an American though he had never applied for citizenship. Like Lufbery, his English was fluent, if accented and a bit less colorful.

While the victories bolstered the flagging morale in N. 124, they also exacerbated the internal frictions. The men aligned naturally with others of the same ilk. Thus the rough edged Bert Hall's linking with Rumsey wasn't as strange a match as it might otherwise seem. Hall's legion comradeship with Thaw and Rockwell explained their friendship—an otherwise strange bedfellow relationship given the vastly different backgrounds of the three men. Age and social standing didn't seem to factor much for most of the men, Prince excluded.

One night after a tour of Bar-le-Duc's various bars and cafés, Hall and Rumsey returned late to the villa arm-in-arm with Rumsey singing about an old English king who'd lost his wits. They mounted the stairs of their villa with some difficulty since Rumsey kept insisting he wasn't ready to call it a night. At the top Hall let his attention wander as he reached for his key. Red tumbled noisily down the stairs in the loose-limbed attitude of a truly drunken man. Hall rushed down the stairs fearing the worse.

"That you Bertie, you old bozo?" Rumsey said sitting on the landing, "I could have fallen down these gawdam stairs!" Hall laughed and half-dragged the uninjured Rumsey back up the stairs, putting him in his bed. Red was snoring loudly before Bert left the room.

Raoul Lufbery still had a tough time seeing the captain in a different light from his first impressions. He wasn't alone in his reservations. Rockwell continued to harbor negative feelings of his own. He and Bert Hall groused from time to time that the captain made little effort to get them credit for their victories. Kiffin might have had some justification for thinking this, but Bert Hall's roguish self-promotion made everybody skeptical of his claims.

Not so curiously, given his nature, Bill Thaw could relate as well to his fellow officers as to his fellow Americans. He would bear no criticism of Georges Thénault without deflecting it. Alfred de Laage took the same stance, and the universally liked lieutenant kept everyone but Kiffin Rockwell fairly happy with the status quo. Kiffin *liked* de Laage, but he resented the fact that officers seemed to have to strive much less for verification of their combat victories.

Rockwell had turned the corner from a purely idealistic warrior to a man who thinks his accomplishments amount to little without medals and other kudos to show for them. He often filled his letters, especially those to Paul in Paris, with acrimonious statements.

Thénault had tolerated Cowdin's bootlicking and shirking. When the captain approved Cowdin's dismissal, he gained a little ground in the ranks of his critics. In fairness, Georges Thénault labored diligently trying to get his men credit for their victories. He frequently jumped in one of their staff cars with two or three others and at least one camera to go up to the lines to try to obtain verification or pictures. Yet, even with that, Thénault remained distant from the men of the escadrille.

Thaw and de Laage were the hubs of the escadrille. Thénault still drove the chariot, but his lieutenants carried the load. Thénault, a very accomplished pilot, struggled to find the right balance for himself.

Thénault recognized his lack of charisma. He would try to be 'one of the guys,' as much as it went against his grain. His one entrée with the men was his faithful dog, Fram. Fram, a large German Shepherd, gamboled about the escadrille whenever she wasn't at Thénault's side. He played with her for hours, teaching her a retinue of tricks that always impressed visitors. One of his favorites—totally out of character for the strait-laced Thénault—was Fram's ability to leap into the air and snatch the headgear off a man neatly without even touching his body. Whenever he got her to perform the maneuver on an unsuspecting senior officer, Georges's esteem in the unit rose measurably.

As August waned, with Nungesser's influence fading and Cowdin gone but not forgotten, the pilots were ripe for something uplifting. A British squadron sent two of their BE-5 crews to Behonne to study French tactics. One crew consisted of two Scotsmen. When they landed and traipsed up to the escadrille operations shack wearing their distinctive tams, Thénault couldn't resist the temptation to demonstrate Fram's fondness for hats. He'd trained her to respond to no more than his gestures. Thus, he caught one of the Scots completely by surprise. Fram leapt from Thénault's side without warning, flew through the air and ripped the tam o' shanter off the head of the bald machine-gunner, all without laying a paw on him. Mechanics and pilots alike broke into uproarious laughter as the short, stout gunner set off after the capricious dog. On Thénault's command, which he held off for as long as he could, Fram came and deposited the wet but otherwise undamaged black wool hat with its checkered trim at his feet.

Even the Scottish pilot roared at the spectacle. His gunner let loose with a string of invectives lacking any hint of an 'h' sound and totally foreign to all within hearing. With his hat restored to his bald pate in a misshapen form, more laughter rippled through the observers. That night at the popote the story circulated repeatedly at the poor gunner's expense. He played along, trading drinks with Rumsey and Lufbery while scowling menacingly below his bushy red eyebrows. Much mirth and drink made for one of the best night's sleep in N. 124 in many weeks.

August had nearly ended when Bert Hall scored another victory. Of all the Americans, Hall's claims were the most questioned. He commiserated with Kiffin Rockwell on the subject, but his brazen boasting made it inevitable that others would doubt his word. On the 28th Bert was lucky enough to have Keeler on his patrol to verify his claim.

They'd flushed a covey of Fokkers guarding some observation machines just north of the Meuse above the hill named Mort Homme. Though the odds were four to two, Keeler succeeded in driving off one of the enemy with a long burst at close range. Smoke streamed from the Fokker that continued to fly almost normally. Hall aggressively went after two Fokkers flying closely together for mutual defense, while Charlie chased the remaining German. Having sent his Fokker to the ground, Charlie rejoined Bert Hall. Hall had scared off one of his prey and was harassing the last of the German patrol. Charlie arrived in time to see Bert send a fatal stream of bullets into the pilot of the Fokker. The machine seemed to hang for a pregnant moment before tumbling and falling just on the other side of the German lines. There should be no question that day of Hall's claim.

August saw a decrease in activity as the Battle of the Somme began to draw off German resources, but things were looking up for the escadrille. The men were busy. Their pilots had achieved some renown at Behonne even among the more experienced French escadrilles. Newspaper reporters began to flock to the unique all-American unit. The doldrums of the summer were over. But, the war was far from over and its vicious jaws were closing on N. 124.

Part Seven

Anguish and Accolades

"The best and bravest of us all is no more."
Captain Georges Thénault

Chapter 46
And the Last Enemy is Death

Behonne, early September 1916

Jack Buck moved into Chapman's bed shortly after he returned to duty in July, pointing out that Victor had 'willed' him his sleeping bag. Kiffin Rockwell welcomed the company. Jack harbored no illusions about filling Victor Chapman big shoes, but he did want to cultivate Kiffin's friendship.

"Jack, you seem to take Vic's death better than me. We were close, but you know that. You were too. I just can't believe he's gone. He was so full of life! Where does that go?"

Jack fidgeted on the bed. What could he say? From his first encounter with dying poilus, death both intrigued and appalled him. He had held the hands of dying men at the moment they expired. He often evoked the smiling mask of beautiful little Chérie. He'd placed his hand in her gaping wound and had scooped up the disembodied flesh of the bomb-shredded mechanics at Luxeuil. He'd choked on the decaying gangrenous and offal smells of countless clearing stations. He'd help place the once bubbly Cartier, charred and blistered, in his coffin.

As a way of coping over the months, Jack developed a philosophy about death. Somehow, he couldn't see courage and death bound tightly together. While Kiffin extolled the virtue of dying a glorious death in combat, Buck found the philosophy far too fatalistic. Death seemed capricious. Most blithely believed the bullet hadn't been cast with their name on it.

"Our faith helps, I suppose. Remember the priest's comments about our fleshy resurrection? Vic believed in that. He told me he almost looked forward to the day he could see Jay and his mother."

Kiffin didn't share the Catholicism that had linked Chapman, Keeler and Buck. Raised Presbyterian, the Rockwell clan saw the world in rather absolute terms. For that reason Kiffin scorned the brawling, whoring manner of the ruffians in the Legion. He detested it even more in the men who entered aviation, a chivalrous service in his mind.

"Well, I don't know what I believe about all that. For me life here is what matters. That's why I can't understand you being so calm. I'm full of rage. *I want to skin some Boches*," he said in a low intense whisper, snuffing out a cigarette in his bare hand before smashing his fist into it

Rockwell's increasing moodiness bothered Jack. "Listen, Kif. I loved Victor as much as any of you. I'll miss him as much too. I just can't dwell on death or give it the upper hand. Death's finality is so much crap to me. Believe me, I'm not cold or numb to the pain of losing someone. Like it or not, Rockwell, Chapman wasn't the first and won't be the last of us to go west."

"Yeah, and if I have anything to say about it, the next will be one of the Kaiser's boys. Kill the lamp, willya? I'm flying at first light. All this philosophy is fine and I know you believe what you're saying, but *I* have to do something about it."

In eighteen months in France, as he looked back over all that he had experienced, Jack saw himself rising and falling with the tide of events. He thought of himself like the cattails back home by Shingle Creek bending with the slightest breeze, not brittle, not breaking. He tried to sleep, but Rockwell's question troubled him. Was he becoming indifferent?

Three of his friends were dead. Masters and Chapman had, in their own ways, fulfilled their purposes, their callings in life, but poor Cartier? Kiffin had once said, "The man who enters this war should consider himself dead from that moment. Every day thereafter that he lives should be accounted as so much good luck—as so much to be grateful for."

Jack struggled with this thought. It struck him like a hammer's blow that so many of these so-called heroes might be forgotten. The meat grinder of Verdun left little room to recognize great feats of individual courage or glory. An unfinished prayer trailed off as he drifted into a troubled sleep.

The next day Jack flew the dawn patrol with Rockwell. Once over the line of forts he pictured the battlefield as a struggling mass of ants working instinctively, mindlessly at its relentless macabre task. The whole battle made little sense when he looked only at a few of the ants, but when he could visualize the massive swarm as one body, he could see the death struggle over the miserable anthills collectively called Verdun. He shuddered, terrified at the anonymity of those sacrificing their bodies to the blood-sodden soil.

Maybe Kiffin was right about dying honorably for a good cause. *But we're not ants!* His mind screamed. The difference, Jack concluded, was in the tears of parents, widows, brothers, sisters, and friends. Perhaps ants didn't mourn the loss of their companions crushed underfoot or devoured by predators. Men did mourn, remember, and try to learn from those who died. The difference was belief in God and in the life to come. In that light, maybe being remembered by the living wasn't all that important.

He tried to conjure up the feeling of total acceptance and peace he had experienced as the Caudron came apart underneath him at Pau. A big black puff of smoke burst close enough to shake him from his reverie. He banked sharply to the right into another oily cloud. Seconds earlier it would have torn his Nieuport to pieces. Climb or dive? They had his altitude nailed! Up seemed smarter. Climb he did, right into another cloud of black put there not by the Germans but by the hand of God.

Lord Almighty! Jack screamed as the towering thundercloud buffeted his machine making up and down meaningless words. The altimeter, his mind shouted! By now centrifugal forces told him he was either spinning or upside down. Let go of the controls? That was the corrective action for spins, but something told him it wouldn't help. The belts bit into his shoulders hard and pressed against his waist. If he throttled back he'd lose altitude, but, again instinct warned him. Instead, he slammed the *balai* to the left.

After feeling his weight shift, he pushed the stick forward slowly. Noticing the pressure loosen on the belts and straining to see the fogged glass of the altimeter, Jack determined that he was now in a shallow dive. The buffeting hadn't let up. The needle on the gauge fluctuated crazily. Now he had something else to worry about. He'd been on the German side of the lines heading north when Archie forced him to climb. How long had he been up and how far had he gone over the lines? The compass had been spinning and now wobbled too much to be reliable. He had to get out of the soup now!

Granite clouds! His gut churned when he remembered the instructors joking about flying into mountains. The Vosges weren't that high here, but he had no idea how much altitude he'd lost. Thunderclouds often dipped close to the ground spouting lightning. That was all he needed now. He could have kicked himself for daydreaming. Low on fuel, flying blind, lost. “Well, Jack Buck,” he said to himself, “you’ve got a choice of going west or *going west*,” chuckling through his fear.

He backed off the throttle trying to sense his attitude and keep from stalling. Suddenly, the bottom fell out! He felt his body rise in the seat as the Nieuport fell. Throttle! Dare he raise the nose? Mountain currents were like this, he thought. Damn! He was in a thundercloud. The violent buffeting and sudden climbs and drops were what they’d warned students to avoid in towering cumulus clouds. Shit! Jennifer! Jesus!

Jack fought his inclination to climb to get out of the descending column of air. Down was good, he hoped. He wanted to get down on the ground so badly that he could taste dirt. This wasn’t like the Caudron. At least then he could see what was happening and do something about it. Now he was totally at the mercy of nature, God, or whatever demon grasped his fragile mount.

It had been dark as soon as he entered the cloud, dark and clammy. Other than the sounds of the engine and the straining guy wires, he heard nothing unusual. His skin tingled, no it stung! Snow? Hailstones? After avoiding being hit by shrapnel, to be downed by a hunk of frozen water would be humiliating. Down!

Light? He thought the clouds might be thinning. But no! The next flash nearly blinded him and the crashing sound reverberated through the Nieuport enough to shake it apart. Lord, he’d had it. *Mom, dad, bye.* He all but surrendered to the forces of the storm. What could he do to battle them? Dive! Get smashed by hail or fried by lightning. Not today, he decided. He’d take his chances on kissing Mother Earth even if it was a crushing embrace.

Jack broke out in a full power dive a mere two hundred feet above the ground with the fabric of his upper wing peeling back. He didn’t have time to think about where he was or the possibility of capture. He had to arrest the descent with no time or space to play with, and not too abruptly lest he lose the upper wing. He pulled back on the stick and throttle at the same time, slowly increasing pressure to the back. At less than a hundred feet, trees flashed by in a blur. More backward pressure! The ground now rushed up and he could see the flashes of rifles from men in the trenches. Throttle full back gave him full power, his only chance of arresting the descent being to fly out of it. He was at the level of the telephone wires strung haphazardly from broken trees and tripods no more than twenty to thirty feet high. Great! Survive the thunderstorm and get decapitated by wires. What the hell? Holes appeared in his wings! It was the German rifles flashing!

Jack Buck felt a sting behind his left ear and reached up to brush at it. He'd leveled off only inches above the mounds of dirt and sandbags. His hand was covered with blood, but he felt no pain whatsoever. Enough was enough! He roared up and winged over with his Lewis gun blazing, raking the bastards in the trench. All he needed now was to run out of gas, and sure enough, the Le Rhône sputtered. He continued to fire with his right hand while switching to the *nourrice* with his left. Fifteen minutes max if the damn tank had anything in it at all. Good and gracious God, he thought, any more trials? Death? Hell, death would be easy compared to this.

He zoomed skyward to gain as much altitude as possible for the dash to friendly lines. More Archie puffs followed him, naturally. It wouldn't surprise him now if his wheels fell off. Somehow he cleared the lines and was still airborne. Nothing looked familiar, but he knew he'd been going away from the gunfire and black puffs. He was just low enough to make out the horizon blue uniforms of the poilus. Thank You Lord! Now to find a place to….

The motor quit. So much for picking a place. He held the nose up as long as he could before stalling. Straight ahead he saw a road crowded with trucks and troops—the *Voie Sacré*? "Boys, look out! He settled onto the narrow shoulder barely missing a squad of poilus marching to the front. The Nieuport bumped to a stop upright less than a foot from probably the only remaining standing fencepost in the Verdun region.

Jack slumped in the seat, drained. Shouts and hands grabbing at him roused him slightly. He had to unfasten the buckles on the belts or they were going to tear his arms off. By the time he'd gotten free of the machine his mind had cleared and his breathing returned to normal. He walked around the once perfect little Bébé to assess the damage. If he had any adrenalin left or any ability to be shocked more he might have fainted or puked.

Bley would later count over a hundred bullet holes. The fabric on the upper wing was shredded and the struts holding it on cracked. A pinhole in the *nourrice*, the reserve tank, had let most of its contents evaporate. They would determine that something small had hit it with enough force to dent and penetrate. Hail, most likely. Every wire and turnbuckle was stretched, strained and loosened well beyond airworthiness, and both tires had been ripped apart by small arms fire. The space into which Jack had landed was too small for them to get a truck in to tow the Nieuport out. They had to disassemble it on the spot.

Jack rode back to Behonne on an empty supply truck. On the way they stopped an ambulance to get his head bandaged. After his string of mishaps Jack was tickled to see the markings of the American Ambulance Service on the Model T.

"Mr. Buck!" The young driver shouted. "Damned glad to see you! Why they're still talking about you in Section Two. Ladies man and hero they say. Just my kind of guy!"

"Slow down fellow," Jack said as a brancardier cleaned out the wound. "You're in Section Two, Dombasle's outfit?"

"Williams, sir, from Wyoming. I was in the second bunch of Yale guys. You know, the ones you trained?"

Jack looked at the man's young smooth cheeks and placed him at all of nineteen or twenty. Was he ever that young? "Don't bother with the sir stuff, Williams. I can't believe you recognized me."

"Well, you look older and a lot dirtier with all that oil around your eyes, but your picture goes with us wherever we go. Yours and McConnell's. Masters too. Your crew is legendary."

That night Jack wrote until his fingers hurt and his head began to droop with the heaviness of sleep. Looking over at Kiffin, who had come back frustrated and gone straight to bed, Jack extinguished the light and fell asleep almost immediately, a prayer on his lips, his last thoughts of Jennifer.

THE BATTLE OF THE SOMME RAGING IN THE NORTH SINCE JUNE continued to draw attention away from the waning Verdun conflict. Indeed, British General Haig's reason for launching the battle came largely as a result of the French appeal for relief from the pressure at Verdun. By September French papers already spoke of the *victory*. Those who had fought there knew that the recapture of a few useless forts hardly constituted victory. There was little mention of the hundreds of thousands dead on both sides or of the threats of mutiny in French ranks.

The pace slowed for N. 124 as the Germans shifted more forces to the north. Why fly two and three patrols daily if the enemy wasn't there to meet you? Morale slipped. The weather didn't help. Cold winds, rain and heavily overcast skies made conditions miserable and kept them grounded for days.

Kiffin was already upset not to be flying and avenging Victor's death when more bad news hit him. "Jack. Listen to this," he said, reading from a letter he'd just received. "*If you are in this thing at all, it is best to be in to the limit. And this is the supreme experience*."

"Who sent that? Sounds like someone from the same school as you."

"It's from Alan Seeger's mother. Remember the poet I told you about? Alan was one of the first killed in the Somme offensive. She sent Alan's last letter. He wrote that. 'Supreme experience.' God rest his soul. That man could write! What a waste!"

Kiffin showed him a letter he was sending to his mother that only made Jack all the more uneasy.

> Now, I don't want you to worry about me. If I die, I want you to know that I have died as every man ought to die, fighting for what is right. I don't feel that I am fighting for France alone, but for the cause of humanity, the greatest of all causes.

"Damnation, Kiffin! Your mother's going to have a heart attack when she reads that."

"Not mom. No. You don't understand our ways, Jack. Grandfather Ayres said it best when he told us about Antietam. He said there was no greater thing than to lay down your life for your country."

"Come on, Kiffin. That's just a bastardization of scripture. 'As every man ought to die?' What kind of horse manure is that? Weren't there more killed at Antietam than in any other American battle? Besides, your grandfather died peacefully in bed, didn't he? Jesus, you scare me. It sounds like you—well, do you have a death wish?"

Rockwell never really answered that last question.

"Charlie, I think Kiffin's taking the cause too seriously. Has he said anything to you?"

"Showed me Seeger's letter. Scary thinking the man must have known he was going to die."

"Yeah, but did Kiffin show you what he wrote to his mother?"

"Why should he? It's none of my business. I've got enough to worry about myself."

Charlie's preoccupation with Michelle's imminent delivery made him touchy. He spent so much time trying to get through on the unreliable telephone lines that Thénault decided to send him back to Paris on leave. The captain expected orders to move N. 124 almost any day since the Somme battle now drew most of the French escadrilles to the north.

Jack was relieved to see Charlie head back to Michelle. In the last several weeks he and Charlie had spent very little time together. Thénault selected one of them or Rockwell to lead different patrols daily until things tapered off. Often the only time the whole escadrille was together was at the midday meal. Even the gatherings in the bar at night thinned out as men succumbed to exhaustion.

"Well, go take care of Michelle and that baby. You've earned a break. Thénault thinks we'll be moving soon, so we may meet again at a different field," Jack told him as he departed.

Charlie shared Rockwell's sense of glory and honor. But, to Jack, Seeger and the other creative men like him would write no more poems, play no more music, build no more edifices, cure no more illnesses. If he could do anything about it, Jack decided with firm determination, he was going to survive.

The foul weather threw the men together so that old ills, real and perceived, blossomed into volatile disputes that nearly drove some of the men to blows. Cowdin's ass kissing and shirking had been a catalyst for trouble. Few regretted his departure, some less than others.

"Mac, why Chapman?" Rockwell asked. I mean why not Cowdin, for example?"

"I hear you, Kif, but don't go playing God on us. Elliot was no Victor Chapman, but who among us is?" Jim McConnell counseled.

With Cowdin out of the way, Norman Prince's thinly veiled attempts to shoulder himself into a position of influence with Thénault and de Laage stood out even more. Rockwell, Bert Hall, Pavelka, and Keeler all questioned his claimed August 23 victory. They'd been on patrol at the time and hadn't seen Prince's victim go down. The rest of the men, Buck chief among them, were willing to give Prince the benefit of the doubt. Thénault threw fuel on the fire by accepting the claim and putting Prince in for a *Médaille Militaire*. Then Prince vehemently argued five days later that Bert Hall's victory that morning was so much smoke.

This ratcheted up the tension. Kiffin, who bristled at any injustice, was outraged by Thénault's decision to submit Prince for the medal while not even giving Hall credit for his victory. Friction between the hotheaded Rockwell and Prince and Thénault was reaching a bursting point. Kiffin exploded when called for violating Thénault's rule against speaking French in the popote at the dinner meal. They kept up the custom of speaking nothing but French at lunch and English at supper.

"I'll be goddamned if I pay the fine!" Kiffin asserted. "The damned article is in *French*!" He'd been quoting an article about his friend Seeger's death. His outburst teetered on outright disrespect.

Buck had all he could do to keep his friend from thrashing Prince when the patrician Bostonian backed the captain insisting that rules were rules. Seething, Kiffin stormed away from the table.

Kiffin complained to Jack and wrote Paul that night saying he was close to leaving the escadrille if things didn't change. Jack prayed for better weather so they could get back in the air. At least when they were flying regular missions the men got along and didn't squabble.

In thirty-four combats Rockwell had downed at least three Germans though only one was confirmed. Kiffin was tired, but he kept flying two or three missions a day until the weather kept them down.

Rockwell differed starkly from his Legion friend Bert Hall. Hall boasted of his accumulated hours because it got him promoted and earned him bonuses from the Franco-American Committee. Kiffin received the same monetary awards, but he was more interested in killing as many Germans as he could. Yet he wrote his brother privately that he wanted to get the Legion of Honor and his lieutenancy regardless of how conceited it might seem.

Bert Hall, the street-wise former Paris taxi driver, didn't try to be a troublemaker—it came naturally. He was automatically at odds with Prince.

"Kif, don't forget our pact. If one of us goes west, the other sets things right with Prince," Hall said out of earshot of everyone but Buck. Jack didn't know what 'set things right' meant, but it couldn't be anything good.

One night at the end of a numbing week of inactivity, the men were all gathered in the popote after supper. Hall took a seat at one of the tables where four others were beginning to deal poker hands. Bert had won a little something from every member of the escadrille. He could usually read his opponents' guileless faces while masking his own expressions. When he raked in his second pot some of the others came over to watch.

Prince walked over and said, "I'd keep my eyes on Hall if I were you guys."

Bert stood up. "Mind your own fuckin' business, Norman."

"Watch your tongue, Hall," Prince snarled. The two squared off with Hall standing half a head taller. Red Rumsey, the least likely peacemaker on hand, resolved the conflict by stumbling into and toppling the table sending cards and francs flying. Rumsey tugged at Hall and Prince to catch his balance pulling them together as they struggled to keep their footing. The whole popote broke into much needed laughter. Prince and Hall ended up on either arm of the wobbly Rumsey. That's the way Thénault found them when he entered the room.

"*Alors, mes amis*," he began, looking a bit confused by the commotion and overturned table. "We may be heading north next week. We are to get the new Nieuport 17 soon. I expect orders any day."

"Where might we be going, captain?" Thaw asked. They moved to the map where Thénault pointed out the fields now shared by the Brits and the French in the Somme sector. He hoped they would stay with the group soon to be taken over by a friend of his named Féquant. Were Keeler there, he would have been very pleased to learn that his teacher at GDE might be his new group commander.

The next day the weather broke late in the morning. Prince got off on a mission with Buck and Rumsey at midday. By the time they returned two more German Aviatiks lay in pieces. One went to Norman Prince and the other to Jack. Confirmation awaited them at the field. On the evening patrol Kiffin downed his second confirmed Boche in a very short combat over Douaumont. That night he described his fight to Jack who had just finished telling the story of his successful patrol and second victory.

"I tried to get close, you know. The bus was purring like a cat. My mouse was one of the Fokker pursuit airplanes, painted gray on top and white underneath. He looked like a mouse. We spun around in circles for minutes before the German leveled off and headed north towards his lines. He must have thought I quit too. I couldn't get any closer than about 200 yards no matter how I coaxed my machine. Were you cold this afternoon, Jack? God, my cheeks were numb! I was about to give it up, but decided to give the Hun something to remember me by. I mashed the trigger and worked the stream of tracers up into his fuselage, never thinking I could hit him at that range. All of a sudden his nose dropped like a lead weight and I zoomed right over the top of him as he headed for the ground. He was not yet into German territory so I dared to follow him down. He fell so fast that I couldn't keep up even in a full power dive. I was afraid he was playing possum, my little mouse, and I didn't want him sneaking back into his hole when I looked away. I wasn't watching for any other aircraft because we were going down too quickly for anyone to catch us. Thank God, too. I got so fixed on my prey that I almost followed him into the ground. He must have died and fallen forward on the stick during my long range firing pass. Jack, it was so fantastic and awful at once to watch him plow in below me. I barely redressed in time to clear the wire myself. He just disintegrated…" Kiffin's voice trailed off.

Jack knew that Kiffin wanted to be the escadrille's next officer. He had more time in the trenches than Bill Thaw and more time in the air than everybody but Keeler. Charlie might earn the next lieutenancy because of his five victories and proven leadership, but Kiffin thought he deserved it just as much. He never spoke badly of Keeler. The decision was in their commander's hands, but Kiffin didn't hold Thénault very high in his esteem at the moment. Kiffin would just have to prove himself to all of them.

Chapter 47
Bye Bébés, New Baby

Paris, September 1916

Charlie took a suite of two rooms in the Hôtel Roosevelt next to the de Vincents who were in Paris for Michelle's delivery. Fleury picked up the tab after insisting that the young couple shouldn't have to share the "maid's" quarters in the Crillon. Michelle didn't seem close to term. Only naked did she look truly pregnant to Charlie. Clothed or not, he found her so radiant that he felt little of the drive to return to the front that had plagued him on other visits.

Major Frank Parker and his wife were also in the Roosevelt. Parker had befriended Keeler earlier. The U.S. Army officer now served as an observer attached to the Embassy. Because of his profound interest in the American Escadrille and in the role of aviation in the war, Charlie enjoyed talking to him. They dined together in the hotel restaurant, with Michelle and Mrs. Parker exchanging gossip about Paris life.

One of Parker's acquaintances was another American named Edmond Genet, a former legionnaire presently in flight training at the school near Versailles called Buc. Taking advantage of the proximity of the school to Paris, Parker made several trips to see Genet. Edmond had connected with Alice Weeks, *Madame Légionnaire*, like most of the other Americans. Through her he learned that Charlie Keeler was in town awaiting the birth of his first child.

The young New Yorker was full of energy and enthusiasm. It pleased Keeler to learn that Genet had chosen aviation. When he found out

Edmond often stayed in the same hotel, he thought he'd try to recruit the young American for Nieuport 124. Parker aided him in this goal by inviting Genet to lunch.

Parker told them that the United States was on the verge of entering the war. The sinking of the *Lusitania* had provoked outrage and strong pressure that was weakening President Wilson's antiwar posture. Genet seemed disturbed by this information. He confided to Charlie later that he'd deserted from the U.S. Navy to join the Foreign Legion. Charlie couldn't believe that the boyish Genet was old enough to have served in the Navy. Edmond explained that he had lied about his age to enlist hoping to get into the Naval Academy. When the appointment didn't come through, he decided to throw his lot in with the French.

The two young men hit it off immediately. Genet's unabashed enthusiasm recharged Charlie. He introduced Edmond to Michelle who also warmed to the young patriot. Genet's desertion was safe with the Keelers. He told them that he was about to tell Major Parker and try to seek some sort of reconciliation or pardon. He was determined to be one of the first to fly for America if she entered the war.

The Keelers agreed to keep in touch with him at Buc and to invite him to the christening. Genet's smile at this was so brilliant that Charlie dubbed him *Smiler*, a nickname that would stick.

Michelle, technically two weeks past her due date, gave no sign of entering labor. She felt fine and didn't seem impeded at all by the pregnancy, but Charlie worried that he might not get to stay for the birth. Word from Paul Rockwell, relaying news from Kiffin, was that the escadrille would be moving in mid-September. Charlie's leave was for only a week. He feared being pulled away any day.

Then on September 12, Michelle announced that it was time. She had been feeling contractions for several hours early that morning. They were erratic as yet, but she was sure the baby was on its way. Her father ordered a taxi that very morning against his wife's advice. "These things can take time, *mon cher*." She reminded him of her prolonged labor with Michelle's older brother, her first-born.

Over her protests, in the absence of Dr. Gho, who had finally been drafted into the Army, de Vincent rushed his daughter to L'Hôpital Saint-Louis with Charlie anxiously holding her hand in the taxi. They arrived and were greeted by Fleury's personal—and appropriately named—physician, Doctor Animant. Michelle wasn't feeling any contractions at the moment and the last one had been hours earlier, but Animant went ahead and admitted her. Charlie was too nervous to help with the admission paperwork. Thankfully, her father saw to that detail. Keeler held her hand the whole time and bothered her to no end with his persistent questions about her well being.

Michelle had listened carefully to her mother's instructions on what to expect, but the first strong contraction caught her unprepared. Soon she began to feel the waves coming only minutes apart. Animant stayed close. Charlie dabbed her brow with a damp cloth and pushed her auburn curls to the side when she leaned forward in some agony.

At nine that evening Animant moved her to the delivery room. Charlie wanted to stay, but hospital policy didn't allow it. He and Michelle's father took up watch in the waiting room with Mrs. de Vincent trying to calm the two nervous chain-smoking men.

At a few minutes past midnight September 12th Doctor Animant came out of the delivery room to announce the birth of a healthy three-kilo baby boy. De Vincent rapidly converted the weight into six pounds, seven ounces and began thumping his son-in-law on the back in congratulations.

"You can go in to see your wife," Animant told Charlie, "but she might be a little groggy from the anesthesia." The French used chloroform and ether to assist women in labor. Charlie entered the room noting the beatific look on his lovely wife's exhausted face. Her hair was matted with sweat and her skin a bit pale but she was conscious, if lethargic.

Charlie kissed her on the forehead and leaned close to tell her how proud he was of her. She could barely whisper but he understood her question. She wanted to know about the baby.

"Animant says our son is a strapping young man," Charlie told her, kissing her again on the forehead and feeling the most overwhelming sense of love and gratitude that he could imagine. "I am going to see him in the nursery in a few minutes. Are you all right?"

"You American bumpkin!" She managed, rallying a little. "If I had known how much it would hurt I might have punched you in anticipation. Oh, but it is over! A boy! Shall we call him Charles like you or would you prefer Michael, after me?"

"Mike it is, my dear!" *Charles* or *Michael* seemed appropriate for a boy. When Charlie got to see little Michael Keeler an hour later, he was moved to tears. With all the death and destruction wrought by the war, he saw the birth as an incredible blessing, a reaffirmation of life.

He toyed with naming the boy Victor in honor of Chapman, but quickly decided that this child should bear the name of the archangel instead. He remembered the words "let the dead bury the dead" from the Bible. While the phrase puzzled him, he thought naming the boy after a dead friend would be unnecessarily melodramatic. *Let our son be a new being untouched by this filthy war,* he thought.

Charlie cabled his family when the *Poste* opened that morning. He also tried to get word to N. 124. He wanted to stay until he could bring Michelle and the baby home.

Fleury came with Béatrice to offer the young parents a furnished apartment in the Crillon. He hoped that Michelle would be able to continue in his service, but he wanted to be sure that she and her American husband had a place they could call their own. Georges de Vincent offered to pay the rent, but Fleury refused to hear of it. Charlie, remembering arriving penniless in France, counted his blessings yet again.

"How ever can I repay you for your generosity, Monsieur Fleury?" Charlie asked, still unable to call his benefactor by his first name.

"You have, my friend. You already have," Fleury responded gently tapping the medals on Charlie's tunic.

As they began to leave the hospital after Michelle and Michael's discharge, the young couple was greeted by a group of familiar faces. Rockwell, Buck, Pavelka and de Laage all stood on the steps, each holding flowers or a wrapped gift. "They said you were going home today, but we hoped to catch you before you left the hospital," De Laage spoke for the group. "Thénault wanted to be here himself, but he sends this," he said handing Michelle a small silver spoon wrapped in cellophane with a blue ribbon. Already engraved on the spoon were the date, September 12, 1916, and Michael's name, though spelled *Michel* in the French manner.

"*Merci, Lieutenant*! But what are you all doing here in Paris?" Charlie asked anxiously.

"Leave, Charlie. *Congé. Permission.* Just like you. By the way, yours is extended until we leave here for God knows where, God knows when," Jack explained, smiling.

"I wrote Paul to let you know, but I don't think he got the letter until today," Kiffin said, shaking Charlie's hand and bending to kiss Michelle.

"So this is to be my godchild?" Jack said, feeling the rush of warmth he'd felt when he first held his baby sister. "Speaking of godparents, where's Jennifer? I thought she would be here. I never got a chance to let her know I was coming."

"Day shift at Neuilly, Jack. The place is a zoo with all the casualties from the Somme," Charlie explained.

"She gets off at three. Boy, will she be glad to see you! Now we can have the baptism with both of you here," Michelle said, gently taking the baby back from Jack. "You sure know your way around these little ones, Jack. I liked the way you supported his head."

"Mom raised me right. I babysat my sisters, you know," Jack said, a little embarrassed.

"Make someone a great wife," quipped Pavelka.

Jack rushed off without commenting, hoping to catch Jennifer between rounds. Kiffin and Paul Pavelka set off for Alice Weeks' house where some of the other American volunteers were staying. Alfred de Laage went to visit an aging uncle.

They had left the Nieuport Bébés at Behonne expecting to pick up new Nieuport 17's at the depot at Le Bourget before their return to combat. Thénault still hadn't told them, or didn't know their destination. They had four days during which the men scattered like so many shot dropped from a height. Every night they would run into each other in pairs or groups of three or four at the various bars frequented by many French aviators. The main hang out was the *Chatham* on Daunou Street, but they also made the rounds of *Harry's Bar* and the *Continental Hotel*.

Almost every one of the Americans had a *marraine* or even more than one, as in the case of Bert Hall. They often spent the late evening and morning hours with these women when they didn't take them to the bars. Few rose until late in the morning. Alice Weeks' place was the unofficial headquarters. Her cook had mastered good old American-style flapjacks so most of the unattached men made it a point to eat a late breakfast there before setting off on whatever business the day offered.

One day Bill Thaw suggested a trip out to the Nieuport factory at Issy-les-Moulineaux. Even Charlie and Jack broke away for this, anxious to see the new machines and learn something about them. Charlie also hoped to see his old friend Stephane.

The Nieuport 17 had the Vickers synchronized machine gun in place of the familiar Lewis gun. The belt-fed Vickers would be within easy reach on the cowling in front of the pilot should he need to clear a jam or reload a belt. Gone would be the crazy gymnastics with the Lewis on the upper wing with its cranky drum. Finally they could match the Germans with their synchronized guns.

When they arrived at Issy, Prince, Lufbery, Hill, and Thaw followed Keeler and Buck into the long building that served as the assembly line. The banana oil smell of the dope used on the wings was stronger here than they had ever smelled it. Jack remarked that it smelled good at first but got nauseating after a while.

"Sounds a lot like one of my old girlfriends," Lufbery noted, evoking chuckles.

There was action everywhere on the floor. It didn't look like any assembly line to Thaw who had been to the Ford plant in Detroit. The bare framework of the fuselages and wings stood on sawhorses at crazy angles in varying degrees of completion. Jack, who had an eye for fine woodworking, ran his hands appreciatively over the joinery and smooth surfaces. The small amount of metalwork in the planes surprised Dudley Hill whose father manufactured stoves. Stephane, greeting them and congratulating Charlie on the birth, led them down the line past a large group of women stitching Irish linen for the coverings. The women never even glanced up from their busy hand or machine stitching. Whether they were young or old, pretty or not was well concealed by scarves holding their hair back out of their eyes.

At the other end of the hangar-like building stood two machines covered with fabric, waiting doping. It never ceased to amaze Jack how the cloth now hanging rather loosely in wrinkles would tighten drum-hard after doping. Another completed machine at the end of the line was evidently Stephane's destination.

Once they arrived and stopped, he began to describe the differences between the 17 and its predecessor, the 11 or Bébé. While the two versions looked similar, the 17 had a little more than two additional feet of wingspan and two more square meters of lifting surface. This added some weight, he explained, but to compensate, the old 80 horsepower Le Rhône on most of the Bébés had been replaced with a 120 horsepower motor.

Lufbery, the old mechanic and native French speaker, picked up on other little details as he peppered Stephane with questions. They learned that the 17 could reach 10,000 feet in nine minutes, nearly doubling the rate of climb of the Bébé. It could also go to 17,400 feet, 2,400 feet higher than its predecessor. Like all pursuit pilots they wanted to know how fast it could go. Stephane produced a chart that showed maximum speeds at different altitudes. It had figures in both kilometers and miles per hour. The numbers said that the Bébé would achieve 97 miles per hour at sea level whereas the 17 would go 110 at 6,560 feet. He said these were conservative manufacturer's numbers. He'd personally flown in a two-place derivative of the 17 at more than 122 MPH.

"But can she maneuver?" Charlie wondered out loud.

"Remember the problem with the wing skin coming off in a dive in the Bébé?" Stephane asked. "*Fini, terminé*, no more."

It all sounded great to the Americans, but Lufbery wanted to know how long could it stay up, pointing out that the added weight and capabilities had to be paid for somewhere. Stephane agreed, but he told them that the weight difference was less than a hundred pounds unloaded.

"With that," he explained, "the machine can still carry almost two hundred pounds more than the Bébé." This meant more fuel and more ammunition and more pilot gear. But it also meant a loss of nearly thirty minutes duration in the air—what the French called *autonomie*.

Before they left the factory they asked Stephane if their escadrille was indeed on the list to receive 17's. Eventually all the frontline units would get them, he assured them, but he didn't see N. 124 on the current list. Maybe there had been a mistake, or maybe the escadrille was going back to Behonne to their trusty old Bébés. Thaw led the confused and disappointed bunch away from Issy after bidding farewell to the affable Stephane. "The drinks are on me. I dragged you out here. Let's go see if we can find the captain and learn where we are going."

At the Chatham they found Hall, the Rockwell's, and a new man named Robert Lockerbie Rockwell, distantly related to Paul and Kiffin. He looked to be at least thirty. His shock of dark hair and heavy mustache combined with deep-set eyes gave him a somewhat menacing look, but when he talked, his eyes sparkled. Hall told them that the new Rockwell was a genuine medical doctor and a pre-war aviator. This got them all interested. Apparently, Robert "Doc" Rockwell had indeed been practicing medicine before completing French flight training. He would be going with them as their latest addition.

Thénault wasn't in the bar when they arrived, but someone sent word to him that most of the escadrille was assembled there awaiting news on their next posting. While they waited, Dudley Hill ran across an ad in the *Herald* for a lion cub. The men began debating the value of mascots and decided that Fram and his fellow dogs needed a little competition and company. They took up a collection for the asking price with all contributing enough to make 500 francs. Thaw threw in Bert Hall's part since Bert claimed a shortage of funds. Bill then deputized Buck and Hill to accompany him to the address in the advertisement. A Brazilian dentist owned the exotic animal that he had brought over on a trip from Africa. The little cub bothered his patients, he said, so he had to part with it.

Jack cradled the cub for the trip back to Chatham's while Thaw and Hill tentatively petted the animal whose minuteness made it seem harmless. When they arrived and put it on the floor the male cub peed a little puddle as if to baptize the bar, and then curled up at Lufbery's feet and promptly went to sleep.

Now the men tried to decide what to name the lion. Lufbery lifted his glass and said: "He's the color of my drink and probably just as strong. Let's call him Whiskey!" No one debated his suggestion since it made great sense. Luf dribbled a couple of drops on the cub's head in an irreverent baptism.

Since it was the last night of their leave in Paris, Charlie and Jack were anxious to get back to their women. Neither would have dreamed of taking them to the regular watering holes, even though Chatham's, Harry's and the Continental were all considered classy joints. A bout of fisticuffs was not uncommon in any establishment in wartime Paris when the men got juiced up and began questioning each other's pedigree. Additionally, many of the ladies who frequented the clubs were somewhat less than reputable. Michelle wanted to join them that night, but the baby put up too much of a fuss. Jennifer kept Michelle company.

Georges Thénault prolonged making his trip to Chatham's as long as he reasonably could. His news was discouraging. He dreaded the men's reaction. Not only were they not going north to the Somme, but also they weren't getting new machines. Worse still, they were going back to Luxeuil. As nice as the place had been, it would seem like a backwater to the men who knew they'd been sent there originally because it was a quiet sector and they were a green escadrille. The return would be seen as a slap in the face. He wondered how to put the move in a favorable light.

He found the group in a great mood of anticipation and excitement. To his surprise the news provoked only a few moans and complaints. He explained the renewed bombing effort they were being sent to assist with in the most glowing terms he could muster. In the end it sounded like the outcome of the war depended on their protection of the bombers. Most of them knew better from reading the papers, but what were they to do? Buck and Keeler begged to be excused and ran most of the way back to the Crillon each trying to outdistance the other.

Charlie simply wanted to get back to be with his wife and baby. Keeler sensed the change in both himself and Michelle. He even felt a little jealous of the little tyke because of the way he dominated his mother's time. Becoming a father marked a major watershed for Charlie. He knew he couldn't count on the generosity of the Fleurys and de Vincents forever. He would have to provide for Michelle and their child. Now the thought of "after the war" had ominous overtones to him.

"Okay, when and where, Mr. Buck?" Jennifer asked Jack, standing with her hands on her hips, putting him on the spot. He was at a loss to respond. He'd never formally proposed to her. He just wasn't sure about how to go about the process.

As they discussed this in hushed tones in Fleury's drawing room, Fleury came in and asked if they knew how marriages were done in France. Getting a puzzled look from both, Fleury began to enlighten them.

"I've watched you two every time you come here. You are smitted. Or is it smitten? It's none of my business. Anyway, one must be married in a civil service in France. This is the legal part of the affair. Many choose to sanctify it in a church, but it is not legally necessary. If you are interested in a civil marriage here in Paris, I might be able to assist you. You could go to America to celebrate the sacrament with your families. You know, after all, marriage is only a covenant between two people. It is none of my business, of course," he finished, looking from one to the other.

They looked at each other and smiled at the simplicity of his solution. Jack could ask for another leave. He'd saved enough for the passage and he thought he could get some money from home. Meanwhile they agreed to let Fleury explore the possibility of a civil marriage of two Americans in France.

The next morning the escadrille trickled into the Gare de l'Est from points all over Paris. The entire glass-domed station seemed to throb with the enormous number of poilus coming and going, meeting sweethearts, wives and friends. Their train sat at its appointed quai, the engine noisily getting up a head of steam. Tearful good-byes abounded, but few were as touching as that of the young Keeler couple. Michelle came to the station in the most fashionable dress she could find that would show off her nearly recovered figure. She pushed a pram with little Michael quietly cooing with the swaying motion. Charlie held her free hand and stopped every several yards to embrace her. When it came time to board, conductors moved up and down the siding yelling *en voiture, en voiture, s'il vous plaît!* The rest of the N. 124 men scrambled into their car leaving Jack kissing Jennifer, and Charlie holding Michelle and the baby at the same time. Lufbery reached out the open door to tap Buck on the shoulder, and Kiffin actually climbed down to pry the Keelers apart moments before the train started moving.

Inside the car another drama played out. Bill Thaw boarded with his small bag on his shoulder and a furry bundle under his left arm. He moved to a seat and set the sleeping Whiskey in his lap. A conductor punching tickets paused to look more closely at the buff-colored quadruped. Punching Thaw's ticket he asked:

"*Quel type d'animal, Monsieur*?"

Thaw didn't bat an eyelash when he answered in French that it was a dog, an African dog. Whiskey was about the size of a lapdog. The conductor leaned over to look more closely. The cub chose that moment to stretch and yawn a precocious roar while exposing his large claws.

"*Mais, cet un lion! Un véritable lion*!" the startled conductor shouted. Thaw bore the information that he would have to get off the train with a smile. Whiskey, now fully awake and somehow aware that the conversation was about him, let loose a credible—if high-pitched—roar that sent several admiring ladies and curious on-lookers scrambling. Bill didn't need to clear a path to get to the door.

The train pulled away while Thaw went off in search of a suitable container for the new mascot. He would turn up the next day with Whiskey no worse for wear in spite of his ignominious voyage as cargo.

Chapter 48
Nightmares Realized

Luxeuil-les-Bains, September 1916

The Groscolas' welcomed the Americans back to the *Pomme d'Or* like long lost family members. Monsieur Groscolas confided that it had been rather dull since their departure. His daughters found Whiskey to be an irresistible pet. They delighted in feeding the little cub milk from a bottle. Before long the young lion would think he was part of the family. Even the dogs, Fram chief among them, took to the feline with parental protectiveness.

Catherine Groscolas, the eldest daughter who found Kiffin more irresistible than the lion, brightened visibly when the American entered the parlor. "Ah, she is still here, my little Catherine," Kiffin said as he playfully swept her into his arms and planted the traditional kisses on either cheek. Their relationship was little more than a flirtatious game for Rockwell, but it did lighten the otherwise somber mood in the escadrille at the prospect of being shuffled out of the main action.

In spite of the disappointment of going back to what they considered a backwater, the men were very pleased to find out they were after all getting new Nieuport 17's, several of which were already on the familiar field awaiting the escadrille. They learned that Capitaine Happe was still at his bombing raids, raids that had apparently taken on greater importance. Instead of one or two flights of four to six bombers, Happe was now mounting attacks with as many as thirty or forty bombers from six different escadrilles on three different fields. N. 124 joined the

British and Canadian escadrilles at Luxeuil with the role of protecting the vulnerable bombers as they crossed the dangerous strip along the Rhine so well defended by the Germans.

Unlike the Germans, the French and British had yet to take up bombing civilian population centers without an ostensible military target. Bombing objectives were still largely industrial works. Allied bomber crews also confined most of their raids to the daylight hours whereas the Gothas and other German machines attacked at night.

Navigation was more difficult at night to be sure, but the German command cared less for precision than for the overall effect of their bombing. The civilian populace on the Allied side of the lines was slow to appreciate the way their brightly lit towns and villages attracted bombs. Neither side could measure the effectiveness of their attacks very accurately. Both squelched reports in newspapers or deliberately manipulated them in order to diminish the toll an enemy might claim to have inflicted. Though the raids on both sides produced little long-range effect on the outcome of any given battle, or on the war, they did disrupt communications, interrupt or hinder industry, and take the war into the homelands of the belligerents.

The Nieuport escadrilles and British Sopwith Two-Strutter squadrons detailed to protect the bombers considered their mission to be a half-measure at best. While they did succeed in keeping German fighters off the bombers for part of the flight, the limited range of the pursuit aircraft meant they had to leave to refuel, exposing the bombers for the most hazardous segment of the flight over enemy territory. Pursuit pilots rankled at this and at the constraints placed on them in the escort mission. They found it very difficult to get motivated for this type of mission, especially when the success or failure of the bombing raids was measured only in the number of bombers that made it back to their aérodromes. To units used to assessing themselves by their victories, every bomber lost—regardless of the reason—counted against them. Even the passionate and sincere appreciation expressed by the crews in escadrilles under Capitaine Happe did little to stem the feeling of uselessness.

Nevertheless, returning to Luxeuil with its comfortable surroundings and familiar faces couldn't be all bad. Jack might get a chance to look in on Dombasle and his bride, Marie—the de la Croix de Valois widow. He knew the ambulance section had returned to their old sector in the Vosges Mountains. He hoped she was happy.

Keeler nursed mixed feelings about returning. He was ripe for action, but the thought of escorting lumbering bombers didn't thrill him. He and Rockwell both made it known that they would prefer regular patrols in a more active zone. Lufbery, now rivaling Keeler for kills, was more circumspect. "There'll be plenty of opportunities to get killed here just like up on the Somme. Don't you worry about that."

Charlie thought the older man brooded an awful lot. Whiskey seemed to take to Luf. When he wasn't flying, Lufbery could be found sitting with the cub playing as if it was an overgrown kitten. He seemed driven by a sense of revenge that others couldn't share or fathom. They all knew about Luf's friend Pourpe who had died, not at the hands of the Germans, but in an accident. What made Raoul act like he had a personal grudge to settle with the Germans?

Jack Buck's mental assessment of his escadrille mates changed often. Thénault, he deemed an old school officer, brought up in an aristocratic manner, or at least trying to live up to one. Alfred de Laage, though every bit the image of an aristocratic cavalryman, didn't have any of the airs of his Saint Cyr classmate. Because of his fluent English and total lack of sense of rank, de Laage inspired confidence in all the men. Even Rockwell, who still harbored anger at de Laage's privileged rank, admitted he couldn't help but like the man.

Bill Thaw seemed the ideal bridge between them and the other officers. He was at ease with everyone regardless of their rank or job. The mechanics practically worshipped him for the kind way he treated them. Only Lufbery stood higher in their eyes for his knowledge of their jobs and his detailed attention to maintenance. But Lufbery wasn't an officer.

This distinction meant more to the French than to the Americans. The pilots, most enlisted like the non-flying mechanics, drivers and cooks; enjoyed a special status. Officers were in another class altogether. The French soldier, unlike his American counterpart, would never think to question an officer's authority, at least not in earshot of another officer or senior non-com. They might disagree or dislike this captain or that major, but the officers were *officers*.

Jack found it ironic that a society so proud of its revolution and the toppling of the oppressive monarchy could so easily fall into these sorts of class distinctions. An officer had to have authority and the ability to demand unquestioned obedience in combat to be sure. What puzzled him was how some men seemed born to the task of leading and how others mastered it reluctantly. Thaw fell into the latter group whereas de Laage was a natural. Kiffin seemed to lack one of the essential characteristics Jack thought an officer must have—loyalty. Rockwell always seemed on the verge of bolting from the escadrille.

The 17's already available at Luxeuil mounted the fully synchronized Vickers belt-fed machine gun which fired through the propeller. All of the pilots were anxious to give both the aircraft and its gun a try. Charlie drew the first patrol to scout the primary and alternate routes for the big bombing raid, try to attract any enemy fighter action, and determine what active anti-aircraft positions covered the planned crossing sites. The eventual bombing target was kept secret even from the escort escadrilles.

Charlie selected Jack and Kiffin for his patrol, since they would be the other flight leaders for the escort mission. Lieutenants de Laage and Thaw would take another patrol out that afternoon to verify the morning patrol's information. When the remaining Nieuport 17's arrived, Thénault planned a rehearsal with the entire escadrille in the air—a rare event in the life of N. 124.

Keeler led his flight north to the planned rendezvous point with the British bombers over Hartmanskopfweiler. From there they turned east and flew the ingress route offsetting it and varying their headings so as to confuse any ground observers as to their actual plans. Jack flew the left wingman position in full view of the rest of the flight. When he signaled the turn-around point they'd calculated to allow enough fuel to make it back with a ten minute reserve, they would execute their egress regardless of the actual location.

Kiffin got the task of covering the flight and watching out for enemy aircraft. He flew loosely in the slot behind Keeler and to the right of Buck where he could see the whole flight and concentrate on the skies over, around and behind them.

Charlie concentrated on navigating to make the most of their limited range. It wasn't possible to set up a refueling site closer to the lines for the Nieuports to top off, or to set up a relay to extend their coverage. Unnecessary maneuvers or diversion from the flight path would only waste fuel and further limit the time they could escort the bombers. The critical time, all agreed would come during the ten minutes they were over the front lines. At that time the Germans would be alerted to the coming raid and scrambling to get their own fighters up to break up the enemy flight.

Jack came up with the idea of dividing the airspace around the flight into quarters with the direction of flight being 12 o'clock. Their Nieuports and three flights of Strutters would divide the clock into fifteen-minute segments. That way a single enemy flight wouldn't split up the whole escort.

This coordinated effort was one of the most sophisticated N. 124 had yet undertaken, but Charlie's patrol didn't go at all as planned. Kiffin thought he saw an enemy bus and broke off immediately. He didn't care much for the idea of a dry run rehearsal for a futile raid escort when there were real live German targets out there. When Kiffin disappeared, Charlie didn't notice until they began their egress. He was frustrated that he couldn't even keep three aircraft together for a simple reconnaissance. What would happen when dozens of machines were airborne at the same time?

Thaw and de Laage marked their maps before taking off with Prince, Hill, Lufbery, and Didier Masson to repeat the reconnaissance. They drew some fire from ground artillery near the Rhine River. Lufbery spotted an Albatros circling over a field not marked on their maps. He wanted to break off and explore, but Bill Thaw had made it clear that any such action might compromise the eventual mission. If they were attacked, it would be a different story. Luf bit his lip and hoped the Germans took the bait. They didn't.

While the escadrille awaited the arrival of the remaining Nieuports, Thénault allowed them to fly periodic patrols to see what they might be able to drum up. Lufbery and Rockwell took advantage of this flying at least twice each day. A cold kept Keeler from joining them. It gave him time to reflect on more than a year and a half of serving the French.

Charlie was a different man from those first days on the *Rochambeau* when he had been ready to take offense at anything and anybody. Michelle accounted for much of the change, but so did the life and death struggle he'd found himself in almost from his first day in French uniform.

He'd always been competitive. He liked the way his strength and agility enabled him to succeed in wrestling. He thrived on excitement. When he tackled the would-be robber in New Orleans, he never gave a thought to the danger. Rejik produced a different kind of thrill, one of total outrage and anger. At the moment of discovering Rejik's treachery he felt such a powerful drive to action that he literally felt impervious to bullets.

In the air he experienced similar stimulation. In a way it was akin to the height of sexual passion. How incongruous the two extremes! One threatened death while the other fostered life. Both engendered primal surges of energy so explosive that they seemed to shatter one into tiny pieces. In those fractions of moments Charlie's senses became more powerful than his muscles. At the instant of pulling the trigger and seeing a German machine burst into flames his brain screamed a primitive warrior's victory cry while hormones coursed through his bloodstream preparing him for yet another engagement.

"Jack, it's like an elixir poured from the chalice," he said after one flight. "It's so heady a brew that I can't wait for a second swallow. What does your poetic mind think of that?"

"It's not something you can draw on forever, Charlie," Jack said, remembering how depleted he felt after a harrowing combat.

"You know, Jack, I love it and hate it at the same time." He shuddered to think how much he craved adventure.

He lay on the bed wiping his runny nose, his mind working feverishly. If there was anything he wished he could change about himself it was his ability to visualize what lurked around the next corner. Too often, he imagined the worse, wound himself up for the fight, got poised to spring, only to embarrass the hell out of himself by overreacting. Thank goodness Michelle had learned to deal with this.

The atmosphere in the escadrille confused and chagrined him. He saw no threat in the competition for victories, and he couldn't get worked up about the foibles of guys like Hall, Prince, and Cowdin. He had a strong sense of balance and justice. This enabled him to give the oddballs a chance to prove themselves. It had backfired with Rejik, but he wasn't about to change.

Injustice inflamed him almost as much as it did Kiffin Rockwell, but it was always for the other guy's suffering rather than for his own. He envied Jack Buck and Jim McConnell their ability and desire to write things down. It seemed therapeutic to both of them. Kiffin used letters to vent his frustrations. Charlie's missives were weak strings of words recording nothing more than events. He couldn't even write a meaningful love letter to Michelle. He needed a Cyrano.

Even when he wrote home to say he'd won the *Croix de Guerre*, he'd recounted it in such a modest and unexciting manner that his father didn't realize that his son had been awarded a medal for heroism. His mother had to explain it to John Keeler, the well-educated schoolteacher who had dumped everything German about himself when he fled for America. The Prussian passion for medals like the coveted *Pour le Mérite,* the famous Blue Max, meant absolutely nothing to him. His ignorance of the panoply of French ribbons was natural.

Thinking about his father reminded Charlie of Victor Chapman. The elder Chapman had visited the escadrille and written twice to Charlie asking for anecdotes about his son. How ironic that the man who was such a stranger and antagonist to Victor in life wanted to build shrines to his son after losing him.

Prince too complained about his father, and it was no secret that Elliot Cowdin's aberrant behavior was in part a revolt against his "perfect" father. Charlie felt some of the hostility toward his father that his fellow pilots carried like heavy anvils. Fortunately, it had abated with his wedding.

While he continued to sniffle and ponder these thoughts he finally began to fall asleep, the distant sounds of revving rotary motors and the high pitched scream of landing airplanes blending with ragtime music jangling continuously down the hall. Images of Michelle and the baby appeared fuzzily. He tried to focus on them but in his slumber he began to dream.

He woke unsettled, his nose running, confused about where he was and totally disoriented. Though it was very cool in the room he was sweating profusely. His pillow was drenched. It was dark in the room and little light came in through the drawn shade. He sat up and shook his head to clear it, feeling dizzy and falling back on the wet pillow with the room spinning. He couldn't understand feeling like he was drunk when he hadn't touched anything in days. Soon he slipped back into the dream, almost as if he needed to finish whatever he'd been doing before he woke.

He was back in Saint Louis being chased by the police after throwing rocks at a warehouse. The police wore rounded Bobby hats. The hats turned into coal bucket German helmets when his pursuers began to fire their rifles at him. Running beside him was another boy—Rejik or someone who looked just like him! The cops were gaining on them when Rejik stopped, a sardonic smile on his face. Charlie's feet kept going but he felt like he was running in knee-deep water.

Now he was nearing a cliff in a place he didn't recognize. Rejik was running with the police. He could see their uniforms though it was dark. They were field gray soldier uniforms. At the cliff's edge with nowhere to turn he plunged blindly into the air with no thought of surviving the fall.

He smelled the sickening sweet odor of burned castor oil. He was not falling but flying! The sky turned brighter than day and flashed on and off revealing glimpses of his pursuers—three Fokkers firing. Rejik's sinister smile curled under goggles unable to mask his identity. Charlie hoped for help. Two Nieuports materialized out of the ether. Though they were too far away to recognize, somehow he knew they were Rockwell and Prince. Both fell in beside him in flight from the Germans—now six in number, all firing incessantly.

Charlie felt his rage rising. First Rockwell's plane dropped and spun to the ground, and then Prince's crashed though it was dark and he couldn't tell if the landing was survivable. Charlie felt the bullets impacting all over his machine and wondered how long he had to live. In a violent gut-wrenching maneuver, he reversed course. He madly mashed the trigger and walked a stream of bullets from left to right and back again against the line of German planes. They all fell but one.

In another flash, he saw yet one more Nieuport, an old Bébé. It was Victor's bus! Charlie fairly shouted for joy at seeing his old friend back. The lone Fokker gave up his chase to turn on the newcomer. Soon Chapman's plane fell into a nosedive. The eerie light flared again long enough for Charlie to clearly see Victor plow into the ground.

The Fokker did an obscene victory roll right over Victor's broken machine. Charlie could easily see the still snarling smile of Rejik. *I'll ram the bastard!* Tears clouded his goggles. Kiffin gone. Prince down and probably dead. And now Victor dying all over again.

With all his might he hurled his machine at the unswerving Fokker. Time slowed unnaturally. They had to be closing at over two hundred miles an hour, but they seemed to hang repelled as like poles of a magnet no matter how hard they were pushed together. Charlie's fury grew intolerable. He screamed at the top of his voice when the power holding them apart suddenly lifted. Hurtling the remaining distance, he felt all the tension fall away with the imminent collision.

With a wrenching motion Charlie woke. He ran from the room in his pajamas and bounded down the stairs before coming fully awake. Madame Groscolas gasped as he streaked through the kitchen knocking bowls off the counters and nearly tearing the door off its hinges. Whiskey followed him out the door thinking he wanted to play. The cold air shocked Keeler awake just as the lion club lashed out a playful paw scraping Charlie's calf.

Whiskey brought him back to reality. By then two of the night owls, summoned by the startled woman, came to see what the ruckus was about—Rockwell and Prince, an unlikely pair, grabbed Keeler as he began to sag.

"He's burning up!" Prince shouted.

"*Appelé le médecin, Madame*!" Rockwell demanded at almost the same time.

"Hey, I'm all right. Just dizzy! What a dream! Kiffin! Nimmie! You're both OK! Thank God. How's Victor? I saw him go down..." his voice trailed off.

"This man is very sick, *mon capitaine*!" Aspirant Smith told them after they had settled Charlie back in his room. "He needs to go to a hospital. Influenza or pneumonia, I think. He's strong. A weaker man might have already died. Waste no time!"

Jack Buck drove the staff car with Thaw and Rockwell riding along to wipe Keeler's feverish brow. Jack had been to nearly every hospital in the region. He took them to Capernaum about ten miles distant. Charlie received immediate attention. The admitting nurse looked familiar to

Jack. She was heavier, maybe pregnant, but he couldn't deny that it was Marie Françoise de la Croix de Valois—*Dombasle* now. She showed no sign of recognizing Jack at first, busying herself with the patient. Thaw slipped out for a smoke with Rockwell. Neither of them could stand the smell of hospitals.

Once his friends were out of earshot, Marie took Jack's arm and guided him back to the reception area. She said nothing until they were seated. Slowly, deliberately, she asked him why he had never written. Not waiting for an answer, she waved a hand in the air flashing a wedding band and diamond. "Now," she explained in her regional accent, "I am married to your friend and old boss."

Jack only smiled.

"You *are* married, then, and expecting a child too?" he asked gently and politely. She nodded, smiling, impressed by his improved French.

Thaw agreed to let Jack stay at the hospital until Charlie's condition could be better determined. Thaw and Rockwell returned to N. 124 to rest up for the morning's mission.

THEY ARRIVED AT THE *POMME D'OR* TIRED AND unsettled by Keeler's sudden turn for the worse. Everybody looked up to Charlie. His strength and feats in the Legion had long been the stuff of legend. To see him brought down by a simple cold made the others think about their own vulnerability, and not only to disease. Most of them feared injury far more than death. Clyde Balsley's ordeal was never far from their minds. "When it comes I want it to be swift and final," whispered more than one pilot.

Kiffin wished Jack had come back with them that night. He felt like talking. Buck understood him, and didn't judge. He listened, read and wrote in his journal. Talking to him made Kiffin feel like an older brother. Jack didn't idolize him, but the younger man did seem to hang on his words.

Though it was late, he knocked on Paul Pavelka's door. With Charlie gone, Skipper would also be alone that night. He found his friend smoking a pipe and scratching out a letter.

"Hey Kif! Aren't you doing the eight o'clock? You oughta be in bed!"

"Yeah, Skipper. Can't sleep. Rotten luck about Charlie. He's too strong to let this keep him down long though. Got a minute?" Paul smiled, knowing he didn't need to answer. Since he and Rockwell had been in the charge at Artois, they shared something beyond words. Kiffin sat on the stripped bed where Charlie slept.

"Madame Groscolas took the bedding and burned it. Can you believe that? She says Keeler can have their very best when he gets back, but she doesn't want any of the rest of us to get whatever he's got."

"Makes sense, I suppose," Kiffin's voice trailed off. They sat silent for a few minutes before he started up again. "Listen, Paul. I already told Jack this, but he's with Keeler. If I go down I want to be buried where I hit. Take any money you find on me and drink to the destruction of the damned Boche."

Paul decided not to say anything in response. He kept thinking about the party that they'd had two days earlier to celebrate Kiffin's twenty-fourth birthday. Rockwell made a big speech thanking Thénault for the birthday gift of the five new Nieuport 17's. Kiffin later told Paul, "The son of a bitch ain't half as bad as I used to think."

Kiffin took one of the short, thick cigarettes from the blue *Gitane* pack. After a long pull, Rockwell felt a slight dizziness. He got up and started for the door, turning back to see Pavelka lift his head and wave goodnight.

Kiffin tried to sleep, but his mind wouldn't stop racing. He'd scored his second official victory on September 9. It was high time he got the remaining three. Once he got to be an officer, he could get the Legion of Honor. All he needed to complete his goal would be to become an ace. He finally dozed off with visions of Boche buses in his sights.

At six, an orderly knocked gently on his door and brought in a steaming cup of coffee. Kiffin felt like he hadn't slept at all, but he was raring to go just the same. He caught a ride to the field with Lufbery, his wingman for the morning mission. They were going to try to stir up the nest of fighters between Colmar and Habsheim that had been so effective against Happe's bombers and the British machines.

"Here's your birthday present, Rockwell." Lufbery said with a smile when they approached the two waiting Nieuport 17's. It would be their first flight in the new machines and both were anxious to see what they could do with the Vickers machine gun.

"It's supposed to be faster and able to climb quicker, Luf. If you can't keep up I'll see you when we get back." Rockwell said sticking an elbow in Lufbery's ribs.

"Watch that *sergent*!" Lufbery protested playfully. "I've flattened many a man for less, and I gotta get my licks in before they make you a gawdamned *lewtnant*."

They agreed to rendezvous about five miles north of the field to test their guns before heading east toward Habsheim. Kiffin liked the feel of the 17. He put it through its paces all the way to their agreed upon meeting point. Lufbery trailed at a safe distance. He seldom wasted energy leading up to a fight in the air. Rockwell mashed his trigger sending an unbroken stream of lead into space. He looked at the bullet-filled belt and wondered how they ever managed with the old Lewis drums. Even still, he felt reassured by the extra Lewis on the upper wing, mounted there by his mechanic just in case. Lufbery closed up only to wag a signal of trouble with his gun. He pointed down to the field at Fontaine indicating his intention to land and resolve the problem.

Kiffin followed Luf down and circled overhead before heading back up to where they'd seen the Albatros. Rockwell marveled at the rate of climb. In only minutes he reached 11,000 feet over Rodern. Back in April he'd downed the first Boche for N. 124 over that very region. Maybe he'd get his third on this mission. All thoughts of dying for the cause and of friends spending his money on drinks gave way to the thrill of his lone hunt.

Well below he made out not an Albatros, but an Aviatik two-seater going in the other direction heading for the lines. Nosing over, Kiffin dove rapidly on his quarry like an osprey after a fish. Rockwell closed the distance in a quarter of the time it had taken him to climb to altitude. As was his style, he flew directly at the two-seater holding his fire until the last possible minute, ignoring the threat of the rear gunner that had proven so lethal to others. He saw the observer swing his gun around and up to try to get off a volley before the two planes collided. Kiffin pressed the trigger; sure he had the German.

The Nieuport hung close to the Aviatik. To a French artillery captain watching the combat from the ground, it looked like the German plane had to have been mortally damaged, but it was the French plane that dropped. With full power applied, the nose plummeted to the vertical, ripping the wings from one side of the fuselage. They drifted slowly to the ground like plucked feathers while the remainder of the stricken machine streaked to earth with tremendous speed, plowing deeply into a flowered field. Soldiers from the captain's 75-millimeter battery rushed to the wreck to pull the aviator away before the German shells could fall. The poilus found a handsome young man in a black tunic covered with blood, a gaping hole bigger than a tumbler at the base of his throat. Dragging the limp body away, they easily concluded that this *aviateur* had been killed instantly by an explosive round. *This one's war is over at least,* they told each other.

Lufbery hadn't finished refueling and clearing his jam before he got word of Rockwell's death. Sick with grief and furious with anger, Lufbery took off again and flew directly to the enemy field at Habsheim where he all but landed trying to pick a fight. No one gave him the satisfaction. He left reluctantly after nearly an hour of taunting maneuvers right over the field, disgusted with the Boche airmen who wouldn't rise to the challenge. Raoul Lufbery now had justification for being a ruthless killing machine in the air. No longer would there be a question of whose death he tried to avenge.

When word arrived at N. 124, the entire escadrille turned out stunned and shocked at the loss. Lufbery came in, his oily face streaked with tears. Others returned from their patrols to hear the grim news. Thénault loaded Pavelka and Didier Masson in the sedan and set off for the place where Rockwell went down. Paul told the captain of Kiffin's wish to be buried where he fell, but that was impossible. Instead, they would bring Rockwell back to Luxeuil.

Thénault kept saying over and over again, "When Rockwell was in the air, no German passed." It reminded Pavelka of the Legion mantra "*Ils ne passeront pas.*" *No one gets by us.* Thénault wept openly when he saw Kiffin's body. "The best and bravest of us is no more." He would be heard saying the same thing at the funeral two days later. His reactions weren't lost on Lufbery and the others. Suddenly, they realized how totally committed this otherwise taciturn French officer was to his Americans.

Buck arrived at the *Pomme d'Or* from the hospital full of apprehension. Charlie had sat up early that morning and grabbed his arm with surprising strength. "Kiffin!" He moaned. "Victor and Prince too!" The doctor muttered something about delirium, but Jack felt a tingling shiver he couldn't ignore. He hitched a ride back to Luxeuil on a truck loaded with potatoes from a nearby field. When he entered the dining room he saw right away that something was wrong.

Thaw was first to notice him. He went up quietly to Buck and took his arm. "It's Kiffin, Jack. Took a bullet this morning. The captain's out with Skipper and Didier to pick him up." Bill Thaw's face was so infinitely sympathetic. Jack wondered if anyone had notified Paul Rockwell. Bill told him he could call from the hotel phone.

It wasn't a call he looked forward to making, but there was no point in waiting for the captain to return. He got the older Rockwell at his desk with the *Daily News*. Jack paused to let Paul absorb the awful news. When Rockwell didn't answer for a long uncomfortable moment, Jack squirmed, trying to imagine how he would feel if he heard that his brother Larry had been killed. He was afraid their connection had been broken. Then Paul said in a dolorous voice: "Thank you, Jack. I know how much you two meant to each other. I have to cable the folks. Please tell the captain not to allow any funeral until I can get there."

"I'll let Mrs. Weeks know and our other friends in Paris, Paul. You take care of your parents and yourself." Anything else Jack might say seemed empty. *God give them who sorrow strength,* he prayed silently to himself.

Two days later, September 25, the entire town of Luxeuil and just about every available military unit in the region turned out for the funeral. Charlie refused to remain in bed, convincing Jack to spirit him away from the hospital to be there. He was weak and still had trouble breathing. Though the doctors were amazed at his rapid recovery, they refused to discharge him. Under military law he was technically absent without leave. Both he and Buck could get into major trouble, but neither cared. Jack didn't tell Charlie that Michelle and Jennifer were riding the train with Paul Rockwell to attend the obsequies until he got him away from Capernaum. Jack worried about Charlie's partial recovery, but figured the best medicine for him would be to see his wife and sister.

Another person showed up unexpectedly for the funeral: U.S. Army Major Frank Parker. He descended from the train in uniform with Paul Rockwell, Jennifer and Michelle close behind. Rockwell wore a black suit and a black bowler. Jack thought he looked great for someone who had just lost a younger brother, though he really didn't know what a grieving brother should look like.

Jennifer's appearance took his breath away. He recognized the outfit from Cartier's funeral when he had first begun to court her in earnest. Her bright blond hair, fair complexion with the faintest of makeup and brilliant blue eyes presented the only color peeking out from the black veil over her hat. The women took one look at Charlie and quickly scolded both of them. Charlie smiled through his pallor and sniffles and refused to let them hug him lest they get whatever he was fighting. Michelle ordered her husband to bed in his room at the *Pomme d'Or* until the funeral. Pavelka moved to Jack's room, feeling just a little uneasy at taking Kiffin's bed, though Rockwell's things had already been packed for Paul to take back to Paris.

No missions left Luxeuil from ten to noon. A cortege stretching nearly three-quarters of a mile wound its way through the streets of the old town accompanying the coffin draped with a French flag. Flowers appeared from everywhere piled on the casket until they were nearly a foot deep covering the flag. Sister escadrilles from neighboring fields flew low over the cortege dropping more flowers. Paul Rockwell walked behind the caisson bearing his brother's body. Every member of N. 124, led prominently by Capitaine Thénault, marched behind Rockwell. Happe's escadrilles, resplendent in a rainbow of different uniforms, marched behind the flamboyant red-bearded Red Corsair. The British followed with pipers sounding mournful keening sounds.

Given Charlie's condition, he and the women went ahead in the escadrille sedan to the burial site on the edge of Luxeuil. Paul Rockwell consented to a non-denominational Christian burial presided over by a military chaplain as long as there were no "papist rituals, incense, and Latin gibberish." He and Kiffin had talked this out on the way to France back in August 1914, more than two years earlier. In case one of them died, they agreed, the other would see to the burial as close to the place of death as possible.

After both of them had been wounded and participated in dozens of burials, Kiffin especially began to think the post-mortem activities made no difference to him in the least. Jim McConnell shared this attitude. He'd written: "If you need to do a Christian burial, I guess I could tolerate it." Mac wasn't there now, but he sent a cable from the hospital consoling Paul and the rest of the members of the escadrille, charging them to get out there and kill some more Boches to make up for the loss.

Paul Rockwell asked the British chaplain to conduct the service. It was hard to find a French *aumonier* that wasn't Catholic. Georges Thénault himself did a moving eulogy in both French and English. He recited the same words he'd mentioned to the men on learning of Kiffin's fate: "Where Rockwell went, no Germans passed." He ended by presenting Paul with the galons of a sous-Lieutenant, the rank to which Kiffin rose posthumously. He promised to send along the *Légion d'Honneur* as soon as it could be approved.

Thénault ended with his earlier words that "The best and the bravest of us is no more." A slight commotion interrupted him in mid-sentence as the military commander of the region, *Général de Division* Davout, a descendant of the famous Napoleonic commander, arrived with a small entourage. All the officers and men stiffened into positions of attention, awed that such a luminary would show. Davout asked Thénault's permission to speak briefly. He simply went up to Paul Rockwell, kissed him on both cheeks and presented him with the impressive medal on a bright red ribbon of a Chevalier of the Legion of Honor. Davout saluted smartly, turned to the men of the escadrille and saluted them, and said "*Vive l'Amérique, Vive la France*!" This dramatic gesture impressed everyone present, ending the ceremony with the kind of panache only the French could manage.

Frank Parker, no stranger to France, was used to such grandeur and pageantry from his time as a student at the Cavalry School at Saumur. What struck him was the fact that this general made such an effort for a mere sergeant, albeit an officer in death. Parker's task in France was to observe military operations and gather as much useful information as he could. While the United States remained steadfastly neutral, a few far-sighted officers in the War Department saw American involvement in the European conflict as inevitable. Since the Franco-Prussian War, American military thinkers largely discounted the French as sorry shadows of the Napoleonic giants that had dominated the beginning of the previous century. Now the French seemed at least equal to the Kaiser's Teutonic Goliath at Verdun and the Somme.

Parker was one of a handful of professional officers capable of unbiased observation of the situation. In spite of the low opinion of the French as a fighting force before the war, American schools still taught French military tactics, French artillery and engineer techniques, and French campaigns from the early Nineteenth Century. At West Point, French was more popular than any other language. Parker had excelled in both French and German as a cadet. He had a fine mind and a keen sense of subtleties, especially in reading people. Davout's appearance at *Sergent* Rockwell's funeral was no accident. It wasn't the first sign he had seen of the French courting the Americans, but it was one of the most touching.

Parker eased Davout's aide aside, a cavalry classmate he knew from Saumur. The captain reminded him of his troubles with *dressage*. Frank Parker had been a mediocre horseman at West Point. He gave it his best shot while at Saumur, rising to the astounding level of being eligible for the *Carrousel*, the annual competition. The aide had won the competition. Parker laughed when reminded of his defeat, before gently steering the conversation to Davout's sudden interest in a mere aviator's death.

"Ah, it is something that the headquarters watches now very closely," the captain stated. "Did you know that you have close to two hundred Americans in our uniform? There are these in Nieuport 124 plus a score or so in aviation schools, several in flying squadrons, and the rest on the ground with our troops either in the infantry or ambulance service." Parker, knowing these details from the Embassy, still acted surprised.

"That many? Why, we are soon to take over the French Army with those numbers," he chided the proud aide.

Ignoring the jibe, the captain confided that every American killed, as sad as the loss might be, increased the chances that the United States would enter the war on France's side. "My general knows this. He likes Americans. He wants to see you here because he doesn't think we can break the stalemate without you." Hearing this uncharacteristic admittance made Parker realize just how important his own work could be in smoothly integrating American forces if ever committed to this war.

Parker felt out of place among the grieving pilots, so he took the rest of the day to travel to Davout's headquarters where he was treated to a grand lunch. Davout himself took time after lunch to brief Parker on the dispositions of the support forces in the sector. Because Parker represented the United States, a neutral country, and even a potential enemy, Davout and his staff would say nothing about frontline troop units or other sensitive intelligence. This amused Parker who already had detailed information from the military attachés at the Embassy. Davout knew this as well, so the little cat and mouse game was no secret to either of them.

While this *pas de deux* played out, another proceeded at Capernaum Hospital when Jack and the ladies returned Keeler for his remaining convalescence. The hospital commander, wearing the four stripes of a *commandant* or major, threw a small fit about the unauthorized absence, threatening to place Keeler and Buck under arrest. Capernaum was one of several civilian facilities commandeered by the French government for military casualties. Most of the doctors and nurses originally working there had remained on duty, but the administration of the hospital had been under a military officer for over a year. The apoplectic commander ranted about statistics, his ruined reputation, how he'd never had anyone voluntarily leave the hospital grounds in the past.

Charlie was too tired to protest and too distraught by the funeral to give a damn what the doctor said. Jack was embarrassed for both of them and upset that this little martinet had decided to throw his fit in front of Jennifer and Michelle. He was steaming up and close to doing a Lufbery number on the major when Marie Dombasle came to the rescue.

Stepping between the doctor and Jack, Marie rattled off a string of invectives ranging from the appalling inefficiency of the military running the hospital to the incompetence of *certain* surgeons there present. This turned the hospital commander white as a sheet.

Michelle and Jennifer led Charlie to a seat and sat down, tired from the journey and emotionally drained by Rockwell's moving funeral. Jennifer noted Jack's clenched fists and hoped he didn't decide to resolve the matter physically. After they were settled, she looked over again and saw Jack had relaxed as the attractive, apparently pregnant, nurse continued browbeating the snotty doctor. Before long the man came over to them and apologized for his outburst.

"I couldn't know that Monsieur le sergent Keeler was now an officer and holder of the *Légion d'Honneur*. Please to forgive me," he said haltingly in broken English, his face reddening. He turned on his heel and escaped. Whatever Marie had said to him had sure changed his tune.

"What was he saying about Charlie being an officer, Jack?" Jennifer asked. She looked even better to him now with the hat and veil off, though he could tell she was tired. He needed to get them a place to rest, and the *Pomme d'Or* was out of the question. He didn't want them around in case the mood got too melancholy and somber or in the event the men began to raise hell and blow off steam.

"What? I missed that. All I know is that Marie here let the air out of that old windbag." He stopped to introduce Marie. After the introduction, Marie again took over, getting a wheelchair to take Charlie to his bed. Keeler didn't protest. He was nearly asleep as it was. Not even Michelle's presence could keep him awake. Marie checked his temperature, nodding and smiling to find it only mildly elevated.

She asked them to stay a minute until she had gotten Charlie in his bed. Michelle and Jack conversed with Marie in rapid French leaving Jennifer a little bewildered. She saw something in the proprietary manner of the French nurse with Jack that suggested more than mere acquaintance. It then dawned on her that this might be the Marie he had told her about. *The widow who had lost her daughter.*

While they waited, Michelle asked again about what Marie had said to convince the doctor that Charlie was an officer. Jack didn't know where she got the idea, and he hoped it wouldn't backfire when the commander found out the truth.

"*Eh bien*, Jack!" A voice boomed. A short compact man with the same number of stripes as the irate doctor strode quickly into the waiting room and hugged Buck enthusiastically. "*Désolé, mon ami*," he said, offering his condolences on Rockwell's death. "*Mais, félicitations aussi*!" Dombasle congratulated Jack, pointing to the article in the local paper about the funeral. "*Finalement, tu sera un officier*!"

"Excuse me, Jack." Michelle said on hearing the words that Jack was now to be an officer. Dombasle, Jack explained, had been his commanding officer in the Ambulance. He was Marie's husband. Jack didn't have the faintest idea about the officer issue.

Marie returned and kissed her husband with obvious affection. In the confusion of introductions and surprises Jack finally looked at the article Dombasle had mentioned. After the description of the 'grandest funeral ever conducted in the Luxeuil region,' the story mentioned *l'Escadrille Américaine*, N. 124, and its return to the region. Something followed about the general named Davout and how he had arrived in time to award Rockwell the Legion of Honor. It went on to say that one other American pilot would be similarly honored at a later date, and that he and another had been selected for sous-Lieutenant. Jack's eyes flew so fast over the page that he almost missed Charlie's name and then his own. They were both there! Marie had known all along!

Jack felt uncomfortable about his good fortune at this time of sorrow. Dombasle wouldn't allow him to mope. He insisted that they all pile into his motorcar. Michelle protested that she wanted to stay with Charlie, but Marie convinced her that he would sleep for hours. They could bring her back later that night. Besides, she explained, he might be strong enough for a legal convalescent leave in a day or two. She might be able take him back to Paris with her. That settled, they departed for a restaurant in a nearby town close to Dombasle's new headquarters.

"You must be very proud, Madame Keeler. And you too Mademoiselle Keeler." Marie said in carefully annunciated French. She reached over the seat to offer her hand to Jack. He was numb. Unlike Rockwell who literally lusted for the galons of a sous-Lieutenant, Jack had seldom even given it a second thought for himself. Charlie's earning the Legion of Honor really said something. Only a handful of French officers earned this distinction. Even the intrepid Lieutenant de Laage had yet to gain the precious red ribbon. While these thoughts rolled through his mind, he shook Marie's hand and accepted her congratulations.

Suddenly, the car seemed far too small for him. Marie's touch threw him back to their first embrace, and he literally cringed at the situation he now found himself in. Jennifer must know, he thought. What could she be thinking? First Madame Toussaint's revelation of his liaison with Claudine Walker; now meeting face-to-face with the first of his lovers. He felt a strange sense of guilt at a time that he should either be thinking about Rockwell or rejoicing about his promotion. It could be a long afternoon.

JACK EASED HIS LONG LIMBS INTO THE COCKPIT FOR HIS FIRST PATROL in a Nieuport 17 at dawn the next day. He felt relieved to be away from Jennifer, Michelle, Marie and her husband. Life had gotten so damned complicated so damned quick. He longed for the simplicity of man and machine and the uncompromising demands of aerial combat.

After dinner the night before, they'd deposited Michelle at the hospital on the way to the Dombasle quarters, a neat farmhouse next to his command post. Jennifer accepted their invitation to spend the night there. Jack didn't protest though he was disappointed that he wouldn't be able to be with her. He hoped his tryst with Marie wouldn't come up in his absence. Dombasle's driver drove him back to Luxeuil.

Paul Rockwell came out to see the morning patrol depart. He had always wanted to fly himself, but the doctors wouldn't allow it. He wanted to see Jack off and to wish him luck before he left. "Jack, Kiffin left this envelope for you. I don't know what's in it, but I'm sure you'll appreciate the fact that he thought a lot of you. Take better care of yourself than my brother did of himself. I don't want to lose another 'brother' in this bloody war."

Jack had all he could to fight back the tears upon hearing those last words. He departed on his mission determined all the more to make it through the war. Rodern passed under his right wing. Kiffin's wreck was now totally obliterated by shellfire, but a burned out area marked the spot where he'd crashed. At ten thousand feet Jack spotted a pair of black dots far to the east. Continuing his climb, he wagged a signal to Dudley Hill pointing to the distant enemy. Hill waved back. They rose another two thousand feet to the base of the thin wispy cirrus clouds, continuing towards the east.

The two specks resolved themselves into three as they closed the distance. Jack began looking for a fourth and spotted it above and behind the other three. By staying in the base of the clouds, they were nearly invisible to the Albatroses. He watched them approach from below and continue blissfully on their westerly heading. Even the cover machine cruised well beneath them. At the precise moment that the four Boches passed underneath, Jack reversed course and dove on the cover bird. Hill went after the hindmost of the other three. If they could dispatch these two quickly, they would even the odds.

Jack gave Dud a little more time to close the gap before he fired himself. His first burst went a little in front of the Albatros, but some rounds must have hit the motor. The German plane dropped rapidly, obviously dead-sticking. Jack let him go. This German wouldn't interfere with the remaining combat.

Hill's fires seemed ineffective. His target did an Immelmann in an attempt to get up and behind Dud. This placed the unlucky German dead in Jack's sights. Jack couldn't miss. Now Hill locked onto the tail of the leftmost Albatros that had tried to escape by turning and diving to the left. The remaining German, now fully alert to the threat, looped the loop, a maneuver that caused Jack to shoot past him and have to reverse course to resume the attack. Hill and his enemy continued to descend until Jack lost sight of them. He and the last Albatros were on their own.

While he'd been searching for Dud, the German had sneaked up underneath and behind Jack, unleashing a volley that tore away part of the vertical stabilizer but missed anything vital. Jack punched in right rudder and dipped his nose down and to the right in order to get out of that line of fire. At the same time he pulled the stick hard into his stomach feeling the propeller bite at the air as the nose dropped slightly. If the Nieuport didn't catch and climb, he was sure to lose. For an interminable moment, he thought of Kiffin and then of Jennifer, waiting to see if the machine would respond to his harsh demands. If he was going to die, so be it.

The Nieuport 17 snatched great gulps of air, snarled into a sharp climb and twisted in response to Jack's motions. The Albatros, unable to match the violent maneuver, rolled inverted and screamed for the safety of German lines. Jack was having none of that. He too flipped the 17 on its back and traced the path of the plunging Albatros. Both machines whipped themselves upright to regain control of the dive. Jack worried about the wings. Word had it that they tore off just as easily as in the Bébés in violent dives. He dare not ease up the dive or he would lose the Albatros. Instead he tried slipping a little rudder first one way and then skidding a little in the other direction to accelerate his rate of descent. In the process, on one of his swings from left to right he found the German machine in his sights. He was so excited that he could barely activate the trigger on the Vickers on time. When he did, the enemy bus came apart right before his eyes!

When Jack landed at Luxeuil, he didn't see Hill's plane anywhere on the field. He raced into operations to learn that Hill had force-landed at Fontaine. The men in operations congratulated him on his double kill. Both had already been confirmed. Jack had four victories, one short of being an ace.

While Jack and Hill flew their mission, Didier Masson offered to take Paul Rockwell up in the hopes that giving him a ride might take his mind off Kiffin's death. He succeeded in his goal, but in a most unpleasant manner. Once airborne, the new oil radiator sprung a leak spewing hot castor oil back into the cockpit of the escadrille's only two-seater. Masson wiped his goggles, choked a little on the nauseating grease and beat a hasty retreat back to the ground. Paul fared poorly in the back seat. Unused to the noxious castor oil, he gagged until he had to vomit. Once on the ground, he had lost all interest in flying for some time to come. After they cleaned up they returned to the field to meet Buck. Masson borrowed a motorcar and offered to drop Jack in town before taking Paul out to Rodern to look at Kiffin's wreck.

Jack found Bill Thaw sitting with Jennifer at a table in the café down the street from the *Pomme d'Or*. Jennifer seemed her radiant self again. Thaw had her laughing with stories about Whiskey, Lufbery, and Red Rumsey. He suggested riding out to see Keeler at the hospital, something that surprised Jack since Thaw's aversion to hospitals bordered on the neurotic.

They arrived at midday. News of Jack's double victory preceded them via an ambulance driver who had witnessed the combat. Charlie sat up when they entered his room, looking much better, and apparently trying to get out of bed to congratulate his friend. Michelle pushed him back on the pillows.

Charlie asked after Paul Rockwell and would have laughed at the comic flight with Masson had circumstances been different. Jack reached in his pocket and pulled out a silver cigarette case that Charlie instantly recognized from his near disaster in the Penguin at Avord so long ago.

"Kiffin left instructions that you were to get this."

Turning it over and over in his hand, Charlie looked from Jack to Michelle and said the words Kiffin himself had said, "He gave his life for Lafayette and Rochambeau."

Chapter 49
No After the War?

Luxeuil-les-Bains, early October 1916

"Damn this weather! *Il fait mauvais encore*!" Lufbery bellowed as he poked his head out of the *Pomme d'Or*. Not only was the weather miserable, but only two hundred rounds of Vickers ammunition remained in the escadrille, all drawn by Lufbery. Luf pounded the breakfast table asking what in the hell he could do to avenge Rockwell under these circumstances.

No one could offer an answer.

Charlie departed Capernaum for two weeks of mandatory convalescence the day after Kiffin's funeral. Thénault pointed out that they still lacked all their aircraft and ammunition. In spite of the build-up for the bombing mission, no one knew when or where the mission would go, not even Capitaine Happe. Thénault was due for leave himself. He made Keeler feel a little better in saying he was going to take off too. Jack and the others remained behind struggling with yet another period of doldrums.

Bert Hall, Kiffin's choice to right the wrongs they'd blamed largely on Norman Prince, took off for Paris even before Rockwell's funeral. He turned up in certain salons trying to peddle the story of Rockwell's last flight. When this filtered back to Luxeuil, everybody was up in arms, including Jack Buck. Bert Hall returned on Monday, October 2, to an almost universal cold shoulder from the unit. When he tried to serve his traditional batch of Manhattans, only Rumsey took a glass. Red, already loose from wine by then, didn't give a hang where his next drink came from.

Didier Masson tried to lighten up the mood with tales of his exploits in Mexico, surprising the men with a story about his onetime hot Mexican wife. He suggested getting some lumber and hiring some carpenters to go out and put a fence around Kiffin's grave. Pavelka and Buck took him up on this, anxious to get away from the tension in the *Pomme d'Or*. Bert Hall's offer of help earned him another blast of cold stares. He retreated to his room, nursing his hurts and wondering how much longer he would last in the escadrille.

When the men arrived at the small gravesite on the edge of town they couldn't believe their eyes. A neat white picket fence already surrounded the grave, and many flower arrangements adorned the site. Jack found a groundskeeper working on another grave and asked who had done Rockwell's. Checking with the florist, they could only extract the fact that an anonymous benefactor had ordered the work and provided funds to keep flowers on the grave. All the man would admit was that it was a lady from Paris claiming to be a cousin of Rockwell's. No amount of coaxing could get him to say more.

Most of the pilots in the Sopwith two-strutter squadrons that made up Number 3 Wing at Luxeuil were Canadians. They were fully equipped and armed allowing them to carefully rehearse tight formations every day they could fly. At night and during the long bad weather periods the Canadians mingled readily with the men of N. 124. They whiled away at dice or poker in one of several games going on constantly. The *Yanks* were mostly high rollers. A few limited themselves to the penny ante games with five-franc top bets, but most played at the unlimited stakes tables. The Brits and Canadians found the likeable Yanks an unruly lot. How such an undisciplined group survived under French command amused the dickens out of the more stiffly starched British.

The weather let up enough for Lufbery and Prince to go up with their limited ammunition on Saturday the seventh. They returned frustrated after two hours dodging clouds without seeing a single German bus.

Beginning the next Monday, a series of events eased the ennui. First, General Headquarters released the remaining Nieuports. Then a train loaded with the long-awaited shipment of .303 caliber Vickers belted ammunition arrived. Finally, the morning of the tenth dawned clear. After weeks of the soupy fog, seeing blue sky and sunshine lifted spirits more than anything else could.

Norman Prince, fuming quietly at Buck's elevation to Lieutenant, took off that morning intent on getting another victory to demonstrate his prowess and prove once and for all that he, sophisticated scion of the Prince empire, deserved to be an officer. Norman was a complex study of patrician and plebe rolled into one. At the same time, he couldn't escape his silver-spooned upbringing. Used to getting his way and coddled with the best life could offer, Prince adjusted poorly to the military at first. He'd run afoul of his mates in N. 124, especially Hall and Rockwell, by disdaining their accomplishments.

When Kiffin died Prince decided to try to change things by becoming the next American ace. He had to swallow his pride, but he eventually appreciated Thénault's wisdom in picking Buck and Keeler over him. They were younger and quicker and, most importantly, liked by all. *So be it,* he told himself, *I'll just get out there and earn my stripe in the air.*

That day, Prince came back with a readily confirmed victory over an Aviatik, one similar to Rockwell's assailant. As the first victory since Rockwell went down, this earned him unaccustomed praise in the popote that night. "Old Nimmie! I knew he would be the one to avenge Kiffin," Rumsey announced, making a formal and dignified toast at dinner. Prince almost refused to take his shot of the Rockwell bourbon, but the men cheered him on. Bert Hall sat quietly in a corner feeling ostracized and a little bitter in light of past goings on between Prince and Rockwell. Even Buck toasted Nimmie heartily, casting a caring glance at the old reprobate, Hall.

Alfred de Laage interrupted the victory celebration to announce Prince's nomination for Lieutenant and the confirmation of the long-awaited mission for the morrow. Jack marveled at how quickly old hostilities evaporated with good news and a real task at hand. He hoped to nudge Hall back into the fold. No sense in Bert feeling left out any longer. He'd done no real harm with trying to capitalize on Rockwell's instant fame. No one should have been surprised. Hall was only being his self-promoting self. Ironic, Jack thought. It was the very reason they had railed against Prince. *Oh frail frame we humans form….*

As much build-up on this mission as they'd seen, the men of N. 124 couldn't believe they still hadn't gotten their remaining aircraft by the day of the mission. Happe announced the final target the night before. The bombers were going for the massive Mauser works at Oberndorf, a town close to a hundred miles from the border. The Camel Strutters, well armed for self-protection, wouldn't need escorts. All three squadrons of Number 3 Wing's half-strutters carried bombs. One consisted of single-seat Camels mounting synchronized Vickers machine guns. The other two carried a bombardier-gunner armed with a Lewis machine gun mounted on a clever ring assembly enabling coverage of most of the rear sector.

No. 3 practiced tight formations to take advantage of their armaments and gain the best possible protection from intruders. Their swift machines made them fair matches for the German E-III's and Albatroses. For that reason, No. 3 Wing got the mission of providing a layer of cover above Happe's slower Breguets and Farmans.

L'Escadrille Américaine, the sole French pursuit unit available for protection, had only five Nieuports for the mission. According to the British colonel who had given the mission briefing in impeccable French, this raid could bring the war to an early end. If the factory could be demolished, it would take the Germans many months to restore production of their rifles. In that time, the British and French offensive would drive them back into Germany.

Rockwell's death stirred up the press both in Europe and in the United States. German papers wailed shrilly about the so-called neutral Americans fighting on the French side of the conflict. Some American papers called for all the volunteers to return to the United States to aid in the current conflict in Mexico. This amused Masson who knew the Mexicans still didn't have any kind of an Air Force. It also riled up the Americans who resented the implication that they were somehow betraying their own country by fighting for the French.

One result of the unsolicited attention was the adoption of the term *l'Escadrille Américaine* as the unofficial name of N. 124. It made the pilots swell up with pride. They weren't the only Americans flying for the French, but they were the only intact unit.

On the twelfth, six bombing escadrilles, four from Luxeuil and two from other fields, took off at 1300 hours. Happe's ancient, but carefully maintained Farmans, and the newer Breguets lumbered off the ground with their heavy burdens. Neither type could make more than 65 miles per hour loaded, so they had to depart ahead of the Strutters. Caudrons took up the lead in the flight of sixty aircraft from three nations.

With Thénault, McConnell, and Keeler absent; de Laage had his choice of Thaw, Buck, Lufbery, Masson, Prince, Johnson, Doc Rockwell, Rumsey, Dudley Hill and Bert Hall to fill five seats. Hall purportedly had taken to having teeth pulled to get out of missions. Red Rumsey didn't seem to care. Doc Rockwell was too new and unfamiliar with the region. Hill and Johnson were good solid choices, but Thaw and de Laage opted for Prince, Lufbery and Buck with Didier Masson flying a borrowed Nieuport as a spare.

Thaw led the flight, leaving a full ten minutes after the French bombers. Masson was the only escadrille pilot left on the field at two o'clock that afternoon. As he waited he noticed the only other aircraft on the field besides his borrowed Nieuport was a wrecked British Camel two strutter, the victim of an inept landing in poor weather a week earlier. Didier Masson had a terrible premonition that something would go wrong. He fought the urge to take off immediately. As the only spare, he had to stay put at least until the escadrille returned to refuel for the egress.

The flight took almost twenty minutes to get formed over Fontaine, the closest Allied field to the border. Once together it provided one of the most impressive displays of air power in the Great War. Over sixty airplanes crossed the Rhine into Germany at 3 P.M. N. 124's meager presence seemed terribly inadequate. Upon crossing the border their Nieuports could remain with the flight for no more than thirty minutes. For that critical half-hour, they would give any Boche intruders hell. If only they had been able to fuel up closer to the border, they could have stayed with the flight all the way to the target.

Jack's flight had difficulty keeping position on the slower bombers. Even though they had practiced cutting the motor off and on while flying a combination of serpentine motions with porpoise-like rises and falls, the speedy Nieuport 17's disliked being constrained to just above their stall speed. Above and slightly ahead of the French planes the tight V's of V's of No. 3 Wing stretched as far as the eye could see. Shimmering below them the wide expanse of the Rhine struck a placid scenic pose that Jack could imagine McConnell describing with his artist's eye. With the sun at their back for the ingress, the escadrille had the advantage over any Huns that rose to greet them—at least initially.

Thaw and de Laage expected to get the first action since Buck's lead flight was likely to flush the Germans, but would clear the border before the enemy could react. Straining to turn behind and look overhead, Jack saw Thaw maintaining a steady position and not signaling enemy action. Good for the time being. Most of them expected the return to be more dangerous. By then, the whole German command would be alerted to the raid, and, if the bombing was successful, eager to avenge the loss of their *Mauserwerks*.

At 1630 hours the Nieuports reluctantly peeled off to head back to refuel. Not a single German threatened the ingress.

Jack's flight refueled at Fontaine in record time. Ground crews positioned multiple barrels of aviation gasoline on the periphery of their field allowing up to fifteen airplanes to refuel simultaneously. He taxied into position to take off, but realized that if he took off then he would be too early. Even if the bombers were right on schedule, they would not be within thirty minutes of the Rhine for another three quarters of an hour. He cut his engine after making sure he was clear of the landing area.

Getting ahead of the schedule hadn't been anticipated. He climbed out to tell the others of his intentions. By the time he'd gotten back to the last Nieuport, it was almost time to go again.

Aloft at six P.M., Buck strained to see either the returning Strutters or Happe's distinctive Farman birdcages. The sun was now setting behind them. It was going to be a close run between darkness and the end of the mission.

Out of the corner of his eye he caught movement. Above and behind not more than a mile distant, small dots suggesting individual airplanes alerted Jack. Could it be one of the Strutter squadrons? Jack had to decide in an instant whether to investigate or continue. The bombers couldn't be that far west. He couldn't take the chance. Wagging his wings and pointing skyward with his left hand, he zoomed upward pushing the Nieuport to altitude with all he could. If the other flight was hostile every bit of altitude counted.

He scanned the horizon to the east, charged the Vickers, and reached up to put his hand on the extra Lewis gun as if to reassure himself it was still there. He hadn't done any more than test fire the Vickers. The Lewis gave him a sense of comfort. At least he knew what it could do in a fight. The other flight mirrored their movements. Either it was a friendly escadrille still unsure of Jack's identity, or they were Boches. He steeled himself for a fight.

The distance dwindled between them enough for Jack to see the menacing black crosses on the wings. Both formations climbed on opposite legs of a triangle whose apex would bring them together. Eight Fokker E-III's! Almost two-to-one odds. Jack's heart sank. Not only were they outnumbered, but the Germans had the sun behind them. He sharpened his climb as much as the Nieuport would handle until his path was nearly vertical, admiring the power of the new machine. Seconds later he had the lead Fokker, also fighting for height, in his sight.

Jack pressed the Vickers' trigger feeling the shudder as the machine gun rattled the fuselage with its powerful recoil. The E-III did a wingover maneuver he hadn't seen before, sliding neatly out of his cone of fire. Soon his focus was on nothing but the enemy bus whipping wildly just out of reach. He followed every movement as they approached the apogee of their climb, hung momentarily parallel to each other and then fell off together gyrating down trying to get each other into a line of fire. Vaguely aware of the others in the flight, Jack hoped they were able to cull out individual Germans rather than tangling with two or three at a time. This thought probably saved his life, for a second E-III let rip a volley at close range stitching a line in his wing before he could twist away. Jack felt the hopelessness of this uneven combat, wondering how the others were doing when his original target passed inadvertently belly toward him only a hundreds yards away. *Where was Masson?*

His Vickers roared its throaty music and stopped after only seven or eight rounds. The Boche had to be hit, but it continued to climb across his path. He had just enough time to activate the Lewis spurting out a volley that caught the tail section before the German reacted, tucking down and to the left to try to get out of the way.

Jack felt rather than saw the second aircraft on his tail. Abandoning the first, he turned sharply to the right, tucking the nose to throw off the aim of his pursuer. Below him two E-III's troubled another Nieuport. He fired wildly in that direction shaking one off. Simultaneously, he hammered on the Vickers hoping to get it back in action. All around him French and German machines pirouetted in an unorchestrated dance reminiscent of a disturbed beehive. He counted three Germans still in sight. Whatever happened to the others didn't matter. At least two Nieuports remained in the fray, but he couldn't be sure. Unloosing the jam he tried the Vickers again while pointing at the cockpit of an E-III firing a deadly stream into Thaw's Nieuport. Jack's rounds found their mark. The Albatros tumbled still spraying the sky with rounds, definitely out of the fight.

A sharp sting in his left shoulder announced the arrival of one of the remaining Boches. He instinctively reached for his shoulder, grabbing the stick with his left hand. Blood covered his right glove, but the wound had to be shallow for his left arm still functioned normally. Ignoring the pain, he pulled the stick back into his stomach looping the Nieuport neatly until it was on the tail of the same machine that had hit him. Before he could fire, the Fokker literally exploded in flames hot enough to be felt on his exposed cheeks. *Un de moins qui mange la soupe ce soir,* he thought, wondering which of the others had knocked him out. Three to two!

Jack's flight now had the advantage. Grimly, he maneuvered onto the tail of a pure black E-III, intent on downing yet another. Before he could fire, the German pilot entered a vrille, spinning rapidly down and away from Jack. The remaining Boche joined his buddy in a precipitous dive. Rather than pursue them, Jack leveled off hoping Thaw, de Laage, Prince and Lufbery were close behind him. These Huns were no longer a threat to the bombers. It was time to try to find the strike force. Jack counted the Nieuports. Only four! Afraid the fire had taken Thaw's life, bitter bile rose in Jack's throat.

With the light fading he began to despair of ever finding the bombers. Below them, well to the south, Jack thought he saw a flight of Farmans coming out of the east. *Only two!* Where were the rest? It was getting so dark that only a sliver of the sun remained above the horizon behind them. If they didn't pick up the remaining bombers they would have to turn back and feel their way to the ground somewhere. He realized that the Germans were similarly strapped. Their mission was over for all practical purposes. He barely had fuel to make Fontaine or one of the other French fields.

Jack's shoulder throbbed. Inspecting it he could see a splotch of darkness on his arm, but it was too dark to see more. He lifted his left arm, feeling a sharp stab of pain. Still a good sign, he reasoned, nothing broken, and he still had movement. He remembered a small emergency field at Corcieux and decided to land there. Checking behind him, he made out two other Nieuports loosely following him.

Corcieux was little more than a grassy clearing in a wooded copse. In broad daylight it would challenge all but the most skilled pilots. Jack wasted no time setting up for a steep approach. His Nieuport bounced hard and rolled near the end of the strip with Jack's clumsy one-handed landing. Satisfied he was clear of the landing area, Jack undid the wide belt with his good right arm. He stood up normally but began to black out from loss of blood. Before he could fall from the cockpit, friendly hands lowered him to the ground to a waiting stretcher.

Lufbery came in next. Luf's vision was nearly perfect. He too landed hard. His Nieuport rolled to a stop short of Jack's. He gunned the motor and angled the plane off the landing area to make room for Prince. It was too dark to see the men carting Buck away. Lufbery wasn't worried about the young Minnesotan. Prince, on the other hand, couldn't judge depth for beans. His landings were little more than controlled crashes in the best of conditions. Raoul anxiously scanned the approach end listening for the Le Rhône's familiar hum.

Prince was only seconds behind. He saw Lufbery's Nieuport disappear into the black hole where they knew Corcieux to be, but he could only make out flickers and sparks of light on the ground. These assured him he was in the right place. He blipped the motor off in a position he thought was well above the trees on the approach end of the small field. His machine settled, reaching for the ground. Norman made out the darker trees at the edge of the clearing passing below him as he crossed them onto the lighter grass. Committed now to landing, he further lowered the nose intending to drive the Nieuport into the ground, so thankful for having cleared the obstacles. Prince had gotten at least one Fokker that evening. He looked forward to getting back to Luxeuil to get his confirmation.

Abruptly, his machine seemed to come to a complete stop in mid-air. He knew he wasn't on the ground, but what happened next was so fast, that he couldn't have described it had he tried. An electrical cable stretched just above the treetops between two poles caught his undercarriage. He had slowed enough so that the cable neither broke nor sheered off the wheels. Instead, it snatched the descending Nieuport like a frog's tongue lashing out for a fly. Though slowed, the forward momentum of Prince's plane caused the tail to snap sharply upward. At fifty feet up, Prince's seat belt also snapped, propelling the bantam Massachusetts man through the air to a bone-breaking collision with the ground while the Nieuport cartwheeled ahead of him.

Lufbery raced to Prince sure the man was seriously hurt. Norman looked up and recognized Luf. "By God, Luf, get them to put out some lights so that no other unlucky bastard does this."

Brancardiers appeared with a stretcher and gingerly loaded Prince into the back of an ambulance. Lufbery got in with them and held Norman's hand on the ride to the hospital. Prince began to sing between clenched teeth to try to forget the pain. At the hospital, Buck, his left shoulder and arm swathed with fresh bandages, rose unsteadily when they arrived. Luf reluctantly let the doctors take over and went to join Jack to tell him what had happened.

Jack's wound was not serious, but he had lost quite a lot of blood due to the violence of his maneuvers. He was drinking glass after glass of milk and orange juice following the doctor's orders at Gérardmer, the small country hospital closest to Corcieux. He asked Luf to call Luxeuil to see if the others made it back and let them know where they were. While Lufbery called, the doctor attending Prince came out to tell them their friend had two badly broken legs and some internal bleeding, maybe a cracked rib or two. He should live, the doctor said.

The next day the men pieced together the results of the mission as best they could. Of Happe's thirty bombers, only six made it back to Luxeuil intact. Fifteen lay scattered somewhere in the sixty-mile corridor from Oberndorf back to the border where the E-III's had savaged the return flight. Ten Strutters met a similar fate. N. 124 lost Prince's plane which had torn itself to pieces as it tumbled end-for-end down the strip at Corcieux. Thaw and de Laage made it back to Fontaine. Already, Buck, Prince and Lufbery had gotten confirmed victories during the flight. Luf and Jack became the escadrille's second and third aces—officially.

"So, did we knock out the Mauser factory?" The British account of the attack told of the Strutters releasing their loads one after the other directly over the buildings of the factory. Happe reported dropping their entire load through the thick clouds of black smoke churned up by the Strutter's bombs. No one could see the actual damage they'd inflicted below, but none of the pilots doubted they'd busted up the place enough to keep it out of action for some time to come. They tallied later that 9,548 pounds of bombs pummeled the factory and its environs.

"Jack, me boy. They tell me I can take you back to Luxeuil. It's what I'm here for, grounded as I am with this damned toothache. You ready to leave, Bucko?"

Jack had begun to share Prince's disdain for Bert Hall's antics. Hall would always be Hall, a man totally lacking in integrity or conscience. Nimmie Prince abounded in those two characteristics. In a way, Jack thought of Hall as a sort of Falstaffian character. He wasn't rotund like Shakespeare's player, but he did exhibit some of the roughshod tomfoolery of Toby Belch from *Twelve Night*. He could easily hear Bert uttering the Falstaff's line in *Henry IV*: "Nothing's wrong but seeing makes it so." Bert had gone too far in alienating his mates.

When Hall walked into the ward, Jack felt a pang of guilt at what he'd been thinking, remembering the pact he'd made with Kiffin and Hall.

"Want to check on Nimmie first. Hey, thanks for coming up here Bert. I..."

"Don't mention it, Jack. You know, I've been thinking I ought to move on. Longest I've been in one unit over here. Reckon I've worn out my welcome, don't you? Too bad about Prince getting busted up. Go check on him if you want. Doubt he'd want to see old Hall."

Prince was propped up on some pillows with both legs swathed with plaster. He was so heavily sedated that he didn't respond to Jack's voice. Jack didn't dare try to shake Prince's hand not knowing the extent of his injuries. As badly injured as he was, Norman's face looked untouched. Jack left, confident that the tough New Englander would be back before long.

No sooner had they gotten back to Luxeuil than the hospital rang the escadrille to report Prince's slipping into a coma with a blood clot lodged in his brain. Thénault, newly returned from Biarritz, loaded up a contingent of pilots and headed up the road to Gérardmer. He stopped at Happe's office on the way out to tell him what had happened. Félix Happe, already sickened by the loss of nearly a third of his command, nevertheless jumped in his own staff car to accompany them.

At the hospital, Happe pinned the *Légion d'Honneur* on Prince's pajamas after promoting him to Lieutenant. When Prince died Sunday, October 15, the escadrille grimly prepared for yet another funeral.

Chapman, Rockwell, Prince. Brave and noble young men. In its short five-month's existence, *l'Escadrille Américaine* had paid dearly with its blood. Balsley out of commission for months, Thaw's elbow poorly mended. Buck wounded twice. McConnell and Keeler hospitalized. How much longer would it be before the war claimed the next of their dwindling numbers?

Everyone wondered if he would be next. Luf summed it up when a reporter came and asked the new ace what he would do after the war. "After the war? For a fighter pilot there is no after the war."

Chapter 50
A Cachet, Mascots and Mishaps

Cachy, October 1916

"About time we get into some real action," Dudley Hill said. "Time to leave this lap of luxury and veil of tears," Buck threw in, responding to Thénault's announcement of their impending move up to join the Battle of the Somme.

"Hope the chateaux up there are warm and cozy," Rumsey observed.

"Chateaux?" de Laage laughed. "We'll be lucky to have holes already dug to live in around Cachy. Don't you know that some of those villages up there have changed hands two or more times? I doubt if our Boche friends left one stone upon another."

"Can we take one of Groscolas' daughters?" someone asked, more than half-seriously.

"Don't you worry," another observed. "The captain has done great by us so far."

More discussion and debate on the possibilities continued as the news settled on them that in two days they were to leave the comfort of the *Pomme d'Or* for whatever awaited them in Cachy. The veterans like Thaw who had served in other escadrilles knew *l'Escadrille Américaine* had led such a pampered existence that anything less would produce considerable wailing and gnashing of teeth.

Bill Thaw didn't mind slipping back into the Legion lifestyle as long as he didn't have to make forced marches and carry a seventy-pound pack. His voice of reason tempered some of the speculation. Had it not, the shock of Cachy, so soon after laying Prince in the ground, might have unraveled the escadrille's already shaky morale.

Charlie Keeler cut his convalescence short to attend the Prince funeral accompanied by Paul Rockwell and Doctor Gros. This was Gros's third visit to the escadrille. All the way there on the train, Gros lamented the passing of Norman Prince. "It was Prince, Thaw and me that got this unit going," he told Charlie for the fourth or fifth time.

Keeler's recovery from influenza and a brush with pneumonia taxed him as much as his earlier wounds. His cheeks were sunken. He'd lost at least ten pounds of muscle weight. Gros personally agreed to this trip to serve as the attending physician. Charlie's challenge included heavy doses of the doctor's self-important monologues. He learned that the Franco-American Committee now oversaw what they called the *Franco-American Flying Corps.*

Not a 'corps' in any true sense of organization, in addition to the men in *l'Escadrille Américaine* there were some fifty-four others either in active escadrilles or in flight training. Gros told him that the numbers were growing daily, especially since Kiffin Rockwell's death got such sensational newspaper coverage in the States. Charlie groaned inside to think that Kiffin's funeral less than a month ago would be so closely followed by Norman Prince's.

He listened to the doctor with more than polite attention. Keeler had benefited from the "Corps" more than any other American pilot to date. As a result of his award of the *Croix de Guerre* and *Médaille Militaire* in July, he'd gotten the equivalent of $300 from the organization—one hundred for the cross and two for the medal. He also received 1,000 francs for each of his five victories. Together these added up to the princely sum of $1,000. He would receive an additional $300 for the Legion of Honor. His eight citations in orders earned him $50 each. In less than six months with the escadrille, Charlie had totaled $2,000 over and above his regular pay. He'd earned as much as his father made in a whole year teaching!

Getting these bonuses almost embarrassed him, but he could hardly turn them down. Fleury's generosity and the de Vincent's contributions felt like charity to him, but he needed every cent they provided. He didn't plan to depend on the generosity of the Fleury's and de Vincent's forever. Officer pay would help.

Money didn't keep guys like Chapman and Prince alive. *There were far more important things*, he reasoned, his father's words echoing in his head as Gros droned on. Charlie deposited most of the money in the bank closest to the Crillon, adding both Michelle's and Jennifer's names to the account. Jennifer never asked him for money. The volunteers at the hospital could get by on almost nothing.

Michelle gave Jennifer some apparel she could no longer wear since the pregnancy. She also gave Jennifer *carnets*, books of tickets for the metro or buses. Fleury made these available as part of the family security arrangement. He didn't want anyone caught without means of transportation. Michelle still enjoyed his protection since she continued to look after the boys and some of his secretarial needs.

Michelle appreciated Charlie's gnawing concern at being dependent on Fleury and her parents. She had no independent source of income. She would share her parents' estate with her brothers, but dreaded that event. Accustomed to the lifestyle of *une grande parisienne*, Michelle was now the wife of an American and mother of an infant whose citizenship could be French, English or American if not all three. As long as the status quo prevailed, they were fine. If ever Fleury's patronage or her parents' generosity faltered, Michelle knew the challenges she and Charlie would have to face.

Prince's funeral was only slightly less impressive than Kiffin's. The turnout was similar and the mood equally somber, but, coming so soon after the Rockwell catharsis, the various displays of respect failed to move the Americans in the same way. There were planes dropping flowers, and as many different uniforms as September 25, but the subtle difference came in part from the fact that Kiffin had been killed in combat while Prince died after an accident. Buck and Keeler weren't the only ones to notice the difference, but they kept their observations between them. The acrimony between Prince, Hall and Rockwell had been poisonous, pushing the old hands into different camps.

Remembering his dream, Charlie confided to Jack that he couldn't bear to see the friction continue with both Kiffin and Prince gone. Jack told him about his 'pact' with Bert Hall, adding that Bert himself was acting strange and already talking about leaving of his own accord before getting thrown out of the escadrille.

"What the hell is Thénault doing about this, anyway, Jack? It's nice to make Kiffin and Nimmie Lieutenants in their graves. Do you suppose our promotions are no more than invitations to join our friends in the ground? Damn! I can't believe this. Tell me what's been going on while I was gone. Doctor Gros says that even Happe is getting canned! After all that he has done, what is this madness?"

Buck gave Charlie a rundown on the Oberndorf raid. Happe as the overall group commander, even though still a captain, took all the heat for the losses. Rumor had it that Happe would be going back to the Infantry.

"A Swiss woman reportedly saw the factory in ruins shortly after the raid, but she wasn't enough of a witness to justify declaring a victory. There were six downed Germans credited, including one each for Luf and Nimmie. Mine wasn't confirmed, and I don't give a damn."

Losing two key pilots in such a short time shook *l'Escadrille Américaine*. Tempers, already frayed like dangerously exposed wires, quickly shorted with the least bump. The pending move was the best thing for them. Some said that, as nice as Luxeuil was for living, it wasn't nice enough for dying. The area had claimed four mechanics and two pilots in the small escadrille. The superstitious were glad to be leaving.

Had they known what waited for them at Cachy, even the superstitious might have changed their minds about Luxeuil. The order to move came on the 17th. Two days later the escadrille launched its planes for the long flight that took them two thirds of the way from the southeastern end of the lines near Switzerland towards the other end of the line anchored on the North Sea near Dunkirk. Still short of Nieuport 17's, more than half the pilots had to ride the train through Paris. Thénault granted them a two-day layover. Having just come from Paris, Charlie volunteered to fly, but Thénault refused to let him after seeing how gaunt he looked. Instead, Hall, Rumsey, Masson and Hill would fly with de Laage leading.

Thaw looked forward to an interlude in Paris. He wanted to see Jim McConnell, but, more importantly, his sister now lived in Paris. Mrs. Lawrence Slade, née Thaw, represented one of Bill's only links to the family. Her husband conducted much of his business in Europe, representing several of the larger steel mills in the Pittsburgh region. Bill had helped them settle in back in September. Now he wanted to see how they'd adapted to wartime Paris and see if Sally had any news from their parents, especially anything she could tell him about their younger brother, Blair.

Jack simply hoped for some time alone with Jennifer Keeler. Chouteau Johnson was talking about a trip to the States in November. Jack had leave time built up since his last voyage. He had saved his award money and had enough for passage for himself and Jennifer. If she was willing, he intended to take her back to Saint Louis and marry her in the same church as Charlie and Michelle. He didn't care who could make it. Jack doubted Michelle would want to go back with the baby. Chouteau could stand in for Charlie, if necessary. He hoped his folks would make the trip from Minneapolis for the wedding.

In Paris a big surprise awaited Jack Buck. First, Frederick H. Prince, Jr., Norman's older brother, got his orders to join N. 124, and then Robert Soubiran, an acquaintance of several of the Legion veterans, joined along with Jack's old friend, Willis Haviland. Although he and Buck kept track of each other, neither knew until the last minute that Willis was coming to N. 124. Willis represented a piece of the past. It would be great to spend some time catching up.

After several false starts the N. 124 pilots in Paris were ordered to pickup new aircraft at Le Bourget for the flight to Cachy. There they learned of Rumsey's mishap during the flight from Luxeuil to Cachy. It had all the makings of an Elizabethan comic tragedy. Rumsey showed up for the flight tanked up almost fuller than his Nieuport. He'd been hitting the bottle more and more to overcome the jitters. That morning he was shaky enough for some to suggest he shouldn't fly, but sober enough to convince de Laage he could make the flight. They took off on the first leg for Paris and arrived without incident at a field outside the city. The next morning de Laage briefed them to take off and rally over the field to fly together to Cachy. Rumsey, again tipsy, insisted he could fly in spite of several of the pilots urging him to give it a rest and come up with the rest later.

Over the field they waited for Rumsey for several circuits before deciding to go on thinking he'd come to his senses and landed rather than try to fly drunk. When he didn't show up as it got dark they put out flares and really began to worry. The French dispatcher then told them what he found to be an almost hilarious tale.

"Your man set down at Delouzé, a field well inside our lines west of Cachy. He must have been pretty confused," the man said with a smile while he put his thumb to his nose and curled his fingers closed in the French gesture for inebriation. "He thought he was in Germany! Before he could be 'captured,'" the man began to snicker almost uncontrollably, "he remembered his training! He torched the poor machine. Oh you Americans!"

The Nieuport burned up on the field. Jack listened in sad disgust as the man finished. It was bad enough to lose a precious machine let alone have the French laughing at them because they were Americans. He was angry with Rumsey, but he knew it would do no good. Alcohol touched most of them. This was the second time Jack had been embarrassed because of Rumsey's drinking. If the French officers didn't do something this time he would.

Cachy lay in wait like a rude blow from a hidden foe. As the escadrille men trickled in via train, truck and plane, they discovered a place more inhospitable than they could have imagined. Not only were there no rooms in waiting hotels, but the accommodations lacked even the most rudimentary conveniences. Hastily erected tar-papered wooden buildings surrounded the field at Cachy Wood, nine miles south of Amiens. By the time N. 124 arrived, winter made a premature appearance. The rains and wind lashed the open field saturating the ground and turning it into a slimy muck the consistency of library paste and the color of dirty chocolate. The building assigned to the pilots leaked in dozens of places. Inside it was bereft of even the least stick of furniture.

No messing facilities existed for N. 124. The other escadrilles, already settled in on the field, were a little better situated. As the newest sous-Lieutenants, Jack and Charlie drew the job of solving the lodging problems. Bill Thaw went to find Thénault to ask what arrangements there were for the men to eat. He took Pavelka along. Both of them were shocked to see that Thénault had moved in with the Group 13 commander, Commandant Féquant. While not a palace, their building was warm and sported running water. It was more distressing to hear Georges Thénault tell them to forage around the other escadrilles until they could set up their own *popote*. N. 124 was now part of *Groupe de Combat 13*. Maybe they could piggy-back on one of the French escadrilles, but the two Americans left scratching their heads dismayed by their own commander.

Charlie wanted to go see Féquant himself. Surely Philippe Féquant, who had set such a great example at Plessis, teaching Charlie innovative tactics while putting junior officers in their places, wouldn't allow shoddy treatment of the Americans. Thaw told him Féquant was there when the captain told them to fend for themselves. "Don't waste your time rocking the boat too soon, Charlie. I think Thénault took a lashing for Red's escapade. He's probably sore at us. We'll work this out ourselves."

There were eight escadrilles on the field. At first, sharing facilities and eating at different units gave the Americans a chance to get to know their French compatriots better. Before long though, they felt like sponges. Thénault spent most of his time with Féquant. Neither seemed concerned with the welfare of the Americans. Bill Thaw and Alfred de Laage did what they could to deflect criticism. Buck and Keeler absorbed much of the heat. Rain, fog, wind and cold temperatures kept the escadrille on the ground for the better part of the rest of October. The men devised ways to improve the barracks, sealing the cracks and leaks and adding touches to increase their comfort.

Thaw, ever one of the men, officer or not, conspired with the group to circumvent the apparent indifference of the chain of command. He tapped Didier Masson for an unauthorized trip with him to Paris leaving Keeler and Buck to cover for them. Thaw went directly to Gros and told him of their plight. The good doctor reluctantly secured a sum from the coffers of the Franco-American Flying Corps, bitching loudly about not being able to feed the whole damned corps with their limited funds.

Thaw then secured a large sedan from his brother-in-law. Masson located the cooking utensils and provisions he would need to set up a decent mess. They loaded the provender along with a boozy former sauce cook from the Ritz hotel. The latter, bearing the name of Sampson, agreed to come if they promised to keep him fed and charged with good wine. Didier became *chef de popote,* seeing his main job as keeping Sampson happy and not too drunk.

"Good old Bill," Rumsey chimed when they began unloading the sedan. "Look at the booze!"

Red got the job of supervising setting up the best bar at Cachy in a tent adjacent to their barracks. Jack said it was tantamount to putting the fox in the hen house, but even Charlie wanted to give Red a chance. Red was now somewhat of a folk hero. Some pilots wondered if they would have the sang-froid to set fire to their buses if they were captured. So what if Rumsey was fifty miles inside friendly lines? As far as he was concerned, regardless of how foggy his booze soaked brain might be, he was in German territory.

Masson tended to the cooking arrangements with the ever so colorful Sampson's help. Sampson's big brushy mustache reminded the Americans of silent movie villains. His first meal that very night established him as more magician than villain. Even in the unrefined crude kitchen they'd rigged up after stocking the bar, Sampson worked miracles with the chicken and vegetables Masson provided. He called it *coq au vin*, and it was pretty apparent during the meal that the chicken wasn't the only one stewed with wine that night.

The salubrious effect of getting control over their feeding arrangements went far toward improving the mental attitude of the escadrille. Getting the rest of their Nieuports and a role in the big Battle of the Somme went even further. Their *Groupe de Combat 13* also included Nieuport escadrilles 15, 84, and 65. Sharing the huge field were the famous Storks, *les Cigognes, Groupe de Combat 12,* made up of four other Nieuport escadrilles under the command of Commandant Brocard, Thaw's old friend and benefactor. One of the storks, Georges Guynemer in N. 3, already had eighteen victories. Guynemer was the same age as Keeler and Buck, the youngsters in N. 124. This heartened the Americans, as yet unaccustomed to their new status as officers.

Over a period of several days the men added dividers to the barracks and plastered the walls with colorful and risqué posters from Paris. Taking the lead from the Cigognes with their distinctive storks emblazoned on the fuselages of their Nieuports in various attitudes of flight, the Americans began looking for something unique to symbolize their unit.

"How about a flag or something with stars and stripes?" Soubiran suggested.

"Some pinhead bastards would call it as a brazen violation of neutrality," Charlie grumbled.

"What's more American than an Indian?" Thaw asked. They put it to a vote. Charlie tried to draw an Indianhead from memory, but disliked the results. Suchet, one of their mechanics, fished an empty box bearing the Savage Arms Company logo out of his tool bag. A good deal of rifle and pistol ammunition came from American companies. A colorful trademark Seminole Indian with a huge hooked nose provided the first model for the escadrille symbol. Suchet proudly began painting a relatively crude facsimile on the sides of their airplanes. The subtle transformation from an anonymous French escadrille into the proudly proclaimed *l'Escadrille Américaine* sparked their pride. All the recognition in the papers did nothing to make them stand out physically. Along with Whiskey and the other mascots, the Indianhead gave N. 124 a cachet, a trademark.

The Seminole was just about the only thing standardized in N. 124, and that loosely, considering Suchet's inexpert application of red, blue, yellow and orange paints. When word of a visit by British General Hugh Trenchard, Chief of the Royal Flying Corps, hit Cachy, Thénault wondered where he could hide the bulk of his pilots.

No two wore the same uniform. When they donned ties, the only standard applied was to be different from every other necktie in the escadrille. Dozens of pictures snapped by the men themselves and by visiting news photographers revealed a veritable forest of different headgear. The standard box-like *kepi* with its stiff shiny bill came in a variety of colors designed to delineate branches of the Army. Long pocket-like caps that folded flat were favorites since they could be tucked in a jacket during flight. A few thought the traditional floppy beret worn by the Alpine troops made a dashing statement.

The Americans irreverently combined uniform items according to whimsical fancy. Hall favored the black engineer tunic with its sharp red stripe. Kiffin had worn the same uniform, but neither Hall nor Rockwell had the least connection with the engineers. If the headgear at one end of the body had to be different from everybody else's so too did the footgear. It was almost more than the strait-laced captain could handle.

Thénault purposefully avoided ordering formations for anything but the most necessary affairs. He was now up to fourteen pilots, no two of which were even similarly attired. Trenchard's visit might prove an embarrassment to the brass at Cachy. Georges Thénault was beginning to feel even more distance developing between him and the Americans.

To his credit, Féquant took time to tell Thénault form was less important than substance. He said that as long as the escadrille continued to do its job he wouldn't make waves about its peculiarities. Implicit in his words, Georges suspected, was the warning that outright disrespect wouldn't be tolerated.

When the rest of the Nieuports arrived on October 30th, several of the men, recalling that Jack's birthday was the 31st, carelessly joked that he was getting the same birthday present as Kiffin Rockwell. Jack recoiled. How could they be so insensitive? He turned away and made a concealed sign of the cross as if to ward off evil. Instantly he felt ashamed of himself for being so superstitious. "Yeah," he replied, "but I hope I can use mine more than once."

The next day he got his chance. They took off in two flights of three with barely enough visibility and ceiling to gain sufficient altitude to perform a patrol. Thénault led Luf and Dud Hill on a wide circle over the lines seeing nothing in the wispy clouds. Thaw took Buck and Johnson in the other direction and stumbled on a German two-seater trying to work artillery missions along their sector. Giving chase and firing their Vickers, the three Nieuports quickly drove the German bus off. After the long dry spell of not flying at all, they all returned to Cachy somewhat rejuvenated though frustrated by their lack of a victory.

Thaw and Johnson started packing immediately after the mission for a 21-day leave to America. Jack asked Thénault if he could join them. The captain waved nonchalantly mumbling under his breath but not raising an objection. It was enough for Jack.

He rang Michelle in Paris asking her to notify Jennifer they were leaving the next day. "What about Charlie, Jack? He'll miss his sister's wedding and won't get to be your best man!" Jack told her Charlie wouldn't leave Europe without her and Michael for any reason, and had insisted that they go ahead without him.

So it was that Chouteau Johnson became Buck's surrogate best man. Jack could hardly believe it when his mother and father showed up the day before the wedding. Larry stayed back with the girls just so their parents could come. Larry was very disappointed, but he sent his best wishes and a letter telling Jack how proud he was of his big brother, the French officer.

John and Angelique Keeler, well prepared by Jennifer and Charlie for the inevitable wedding, were nevertheless overwhelmed with the 'loss' of their last child. Neither of them could see it any other way. Not only was

Jennifer going back to the hospital in Neuilly, but she now belonged to this young man they barely knew.

The night before the wedding the men got together at Chouteau Johnson's parents' huge mansion just outside of Saint Louis. John Keeler was impressed and so was Jack's father. Chout had prepared Jack ahead of time.

His father, David Dick Johnson had been a Captain in the U.S. Army and a graduate of West Point. He'd married Anne Victoire Chouteau, a direct descendant of the founder of the city. The Johnsons had amassed both a fortune and an impressive collection of original art.

They had a magnificent meal of Kansas City steaks, roasted potatoes, and vegetable compote of extraordinary flavor and texture. After dinner Keeler, the Bucks, and the Johnsons—Charles, Chouteau's father, and Fabrice, an uncle—moved into a heavily paneled room with a vaulted ceiling and two walls covered with leather-bound books.

"I bet you have read every one, Chout." Jack kidded, provoking Fabrice to great belly laughs that shook his immense girth causing his watch fob and chain to bob up and down. Chouteau quickly explained that instead of reading every book, he had scribbled something in every single one of them during a long rainy day when he was eight.

"It's nothing to brag about," David Johnson began somewhat seriously.

"You can say that again!" Fabrice choked out, still laughing at some inside joke. "Little Chouteau was ten before the family discovered his artwork, and only then because a book knocked off the shelf by a maid while dusting fell open to Chout's crude drawing." David Dick Johnson reddened but forced a smile anyway, shaking a finger at his brother for letting the family cat out of the bag. Reading might not have been their long suit, but the Johnson's definitely knew how to make money.

Jack noticed that Chouteau and his father got along quite well. The contrast to the conflicts reported by Chapman, Cowdin, Hill, Prince and Thaw made him wonder what was different. Victor's father was nearly certifiably insane considering the bizarre self-amputation. The other fathers shared only great ambition and some status in society. Jack hadn't suffered the sense of inferiority Charlie experienced on the *Rochambeau* among the wealthy gentlemen. He was observant enough to notice how much social status meant to men like Norman Prince. If you had it, Jack determined, you wore it like a comfortable pair of shoes. If you'd only just gained it the shoes bit the foot. If you didn't have it at all, you had no shoes.

David Dick Johnson seemed to be like the French saying, 'a man comfortable in his skin.' He affected no pretensions. His military record wasn't remarkable, but his study of his wife's family gave lie to the idea that he was unlettered in any way.

While the book incident embarrassed the elder Johnson, at least he and his brother could laugh about it. Jack doubted that Prince's or Thaw's fathers laughed at much of anything.

When Chouteau's father related the story of the Marquis de Lafayette's 1825 visit to Saint Louis, pointing out that Lafayette had stayed in that very house, it didn't come across as bragging. Instead, it reinforced their linkage to the French for whom his son and Jack were fighting.

Later in the evening while relaxing with fine cigars and even finer cognac, John Keeler fidgeted toying with some unspoken worry.

"Sir, I assure you I will take care of Jennifer," Jack intoned, trying to assuage the elder Keeler. Later John Keeler put his arm around Jack's shoulders on the way out telling him he knew Jack would take care of her, but that he'd better take damned good care of himself lest he break Jennifer's heart.

"Oh, one more thing," John Keeler said for everyone to hear. "Keep an eye on Charlie too, Jack."

The wedding was a lower key repeat of Charlie and Michelle's. Ockie Buck lightened the mood at the short reception by singing an Old Norse song in his deep baritone. He and Jack's mother danced polkas and schottisches until the young couple had to leave.

There was barely enough time to make it back to New York for the return passage. Like Charlie and Michelle, they spent their honeymoon on the train back to New York. By then they had learned each other's bodies well enough to make every moment together an exquisite memory. Once aboard the *Saint Paul* for the return trip, her eyes promised it would be a lovely voyage.

When they parted in Paris days before Thanksgiving, Jennifer told Jack that she could very well be pregnant. He beamed at the possibility which reinforced his intent to survive.

CHARLIE RETURNED TO FLYING AT THE SAME TIME AS JIM MCCONNELL. Mac had to pull lots of strings to get the doctors to release him. His back continued to nag him causing excruciating pain from all but the smallest motions. Charlie, on the other hand, felt fine. He had regained his appetite. It didn't take Sampson's fare long to relieve Keeler's sallowness.

Incessant rains in October frustrated their efforts at laying duckboards between buildings, tents and hangars. Most of the non-flying personnel took to wearing wooden clogs rather than boots. Even the pilots appreciated the utility of the *sabots* that at least kept their feet dry. Since they couldn't fly in them, the mechanics took the wooden shoes back to the Bessaneau hangars and lined them up on a bench. After several colossal mix-ups some of the pilots painted their initials or other designs on their sabots.

The day Buck, Thaw and Johnson left for the States, Bert Hall walked up to the dining shack and stood in the door. The pilots stopped eating and talking. Some of them had banded together to complain to Thénault about Bert's behavior. He owed money and wrote rubber checks. On top of continuing suspicion of his cheating at cards, they'd had enough. Bill Thaw normally stood up for his old Legion buddy, but he was on leave.

"You bastards haven't heard the last of me," Hall announced after telling them he was leaving. Charlie started to get up to at least say good bye, but de Laage touched his sleeve telling him to let Hall go. In his wake several "good riddances" rippled around the room. It occurred to Charlie that letting Hall go marked a watershed.

Cowdin had left ostensibly for health reasons and no one shed a tear at his departure. Bert Hall was a good pilot. He too wouldn't be missed, but somehow losing its black sheep made the old escadrille lose some of its character. That the captain made no effort to retain Hall, already an Adjudant and one of the original volunteers, made it clear that they were going to play more by the rules.

Keeler had maintained a respectful distance from de Laage in the past. He found his new status a bit uncomfortable. With his restraining touch in the mess shack when Hall departed, Alfred de Laage de Meux let Charlie in on the fact that he too was no longer just one of the guys.

"Remember how I greet the new pilots and tell them that they have to toe the line?" de Laage asked, further revealing his mastery of colloquial English. I try to sound firm and authoritative as we learned at Saint-Cyr. Our captain doesn't have to try. He *lives* authority. This is why he is our commander and I am but a Lieutenant." He dropped his eyes momentarily, almost imperceptibly; a signal of some embarrassment, Charlie wondered?

"I love to fly. I enjoy the hunt, the thrill of combat. To my seniors I am—how do you say it—a loose cannon, no? I should have had my own escadrille more than a year ago, and I could have had it if I didn't ask to stay here to help Georges with you Americans. He needs someone who can relate to you. He is a good man and a great officer, but he is basically shy. Headquarters told him when he accepted this command that he couldn't treat it like just any escadrille. Do you have any idea how difficult it is for him?"

Charlie's interest piqued. Up until then he had subscribed to the 'we-they' tradition that separated most officers from the enlisted men. Thaw, of course, was an exception. This man, on the other hand, never let the side down. As friendly and open as a person could be, de Laage nevertheless remained an officer. He didn't have to lord anything over anyone or put on airs. He simply carried himself with the dignity and decorum that came from his training and upbringing as a cavalryman.

"Charlie, you've seen other escadrilles. You spent your time in the Legion. Our little group is such a departure from French Army norms that it taxes the very imagination. Why, look at how the Brits ride their men and guard their privileges. They think we are amusing if not downright outrageous. Remember how Cowdin got away with murder until the end of the summer? Never happen in a regular escadrille. And Hall's dodging missions? Court martial material anywhere else. Luf's arrest in Chartres? Had he been in the Storks—back to the trenches. We are in a special category, my American friend. Even Kiffin, God rest his soul, walked a tight line with our traditional authority. Old Georges bit holes in his tongue over that headstrong young hero."

"Lieutenant, you don't need to tell me all this, you know...."

"Call me de Laage, Charlie. It's our way. I call all of you by your first names because you Americans hate being referred to as Keeler, Buck, Hill, Hall and whatever. Do you see what I'm trying to tell you? Bert Hall didn't leave because he had to. Thénault didn't have the heart to kick him out. The new pilots don't understand our history. You, Jack, Bill and I have to—what's the expression—sit on the lid? That's it."

"You are talking about Féquant more than Thénault, aren't you?"

"I suppose. It's a different situation being part of a *Groupe de Combat*. We either adapt or we get split up. There's some talk about that already. Something in the air about German protests to our being the *American Squadron*. Féquant says we might have to change the name to *Escadrille des Volontaires*."

"Shit! I mean. I'm sorry sir. What a pile of horse manure!"

"Don't call me *sir*! You won't let your friends call you sir. Do you want them to think we have different standards?" de Laage laughed, recognizing the irony of his statement in light of everything he'd said earlier. Charlie looked at him quizzically before going on.

"I flew under Féquant at Plessis. He's one of the best teachers and leaders I have ever met. I sure hope he isn't behind the idea of breaking us up."

"I don't know. I don't think so, but Georges is definitely nervous now that we aren't an independent unit. I think you need to listen to something, Charlie. Maybe I can make you see how things are."

Charlie absorbed de Laage's comments, sometimes surprising the French officer with an observation of his own. On the subject of leadership, Keeler exuded the best of the ideals de Laage had had drummed into him at Saint Cyr. *Set the example.* Charlie couldn't understand why Thénault didn't fly as often as the others. He even voiced a reserved comment on how the captain let the men fend for themselves when they got to Cachy.

Their conversation stretched over several days with de Laage taking time to educate Charlie on the role of the officer, the requirements of being part of a larger effort, and the subtleties of palace politics, even among junior officers. To his credit, de Laage never once disparaged his superiors, especially Thénault. In fact, he told Keeler how happy he was to have such a straight arrow as a boss. Charlie, sensitive to nuances of language, was impressed that de Laage chose that metaphor. The more he listened, the more he realized that N. 124 was an anomaly. As well as it might do in combat, it existed at the pleasure of the French Army. Some things needed to change, and he and Buck would have to do their parts to make it happen.

While Jack, Chouteau and Bill Thaw were away, the new pilots flew every day. For the first time they had more planes than pilots. Keeler and de Laage alternated taking at least one of the new pilots on patrols. Soubiran proved to be a rock. The man stuck to the flight like glue, but never hesitated to take on an opponent when necessary. Willis Haviland also impressed them. His was a steady hand. He oozed reliability. Prince's brother was as different a person as one could be from a sibling. Frederick was so easy-going and affable that a few days before he left even Bert Hall wondered out loud if Freddie came from the same family as Norman. This didn't endear Hall to anyone, but he'd only expressed what everyone else noticed.

"*Allez, "écoutez mes amis,*" de Laage began on their first mission day. "We will be flying much as at Bar-le-Duc, three flights daily. The big difference is we are now part of the Group which means more coordination and less free-lancing."

Naturally the men groaned. They would receive their assignments the night before in order to have time to coordinate with the other escadrilles. Their group had two major responsibilities. One was to defend the balloons and observation aircraft close to the lines. This was the task of the low and mid-altitude patrols. The other was to hunt enemy aircraft. Each mission demanded different tactics, and at Cachy that meant working with the rest of the group.

With Chapman, Rockwell and Prince gone, the remaining hotheaded independent-minded pilot was Lufbery. It was the same characteristic that distinguished the French aces in the other escadrilles at Cachy; men like Duellin, Guynemer and Dorme. They could go their own way as long as they kept running up their victories. Lufbery understood this, at least subliminally. He never refused a mission. After a regular mission, he would set off on his own to prowl the lines for hours.

Cachy was much closer to the front lines than any other field N. 124 had occupied. As a result, the field attracted German bombers regularly. Most of the time these raids were more nuisance than danger. Often the men had barely turned in, huddling under blankets, still wearing their flying clothes for warmth, when the siren announced another visit by the damned Boches.

"If you stay in bed, Charlie, so will the others," de Laage warned. He'd get up and roust the whole lot of them, leading the way to the sandbagged shelters carved into the mucky ground. For about thirty minutes the pilots would shiver and bitch until the all clear siren. They seldom heard the rumbling of the bombers. Sometimes explosions rocked the far end of the field, doing little actual damage. The next morning crews filled in the craters as necessary. Pilots, already tired from their disturbed sleep, cursed the bombing but could do little to stop it, but not all of the raids were harmless.

The Storks were getting new aircraft and had switched about half of their Nieuport 17's for Spads. Guynemer hung on to his trusty Nieuport that he'd named *Vieux Charles*. It was hangared nightly along with most of the rest of the aircraft at Cachy. A chance bomb scored a direct hit on that very hangar on November 13. Efforts to douse the resulting fire were futile. *Vieux Charles* was destroyed. Guynemer promptly christened a new Spad as the new Vieux Charles, but the loss still stung him deeply.

"Charlie, we've got to do something about this bombing," Pavelka said the next day. "I think Bley has an idea of how to light the instruments so we can go up to give those Boche bastards what for. Any problem with me testing it?"

"Dicey stuff flying at night, Skipper. We can't even light the flares to recover a plane for fear of guiding the bombers here. Even if you can get up and fly without getting lost, all you have to shoot at—all that you can see, I mean—is the exhaust of their motors. You know how hard it is to see them from the ground. And there are all those trigger-happy gunners down here peppering the whole sky with their fires. What's to keep them from plugging one of their own?"

Keeler saw the long look on Pavelka's face and realized how stodgy he sounded. After a short pause he resumed on a brighter note. "Having said all that, I don't see why you can't give it a try. If you have any success, we might get ourselves a new mission. Go see de Laage, though. He needs to know if we are going to try something new like this."

By rigging a small propeller to a bicycle generator, Bley's device produced enough power to light small bulbs in front of the revolutions counter, the altimeter and the compass. The only problem was that the aircraft had to be going at least forty miles an hour before the generator spun up enough. That meant no lights for the take-off. Since one focused outside the cockpit during take-off anyway, Pavelka wasn't concerned. He looked forward to trying the system the next time the bombers appeared.

He got his chance the day after the raid on the Storks. Racing to his waiting Nieuport, Pavelka took off into the blackest of nights and climbed straight ahead until the generator caused the bulbs to flicker and then shine brightly—for about three minutes. Horrified when they went out completely, Paul wondered why Keeler had given in so easily. He could see the flashes of the artillery and the occasional searchlight beam sweeping the sky. This was just enough to let him know which way was up.

Lieutenant de Laage lifted off minutes later with a similar system. He'd applauded Pavelka's initiative. Never one to let a subordinate do something he wouldn't do himself, he'd ordered his own Nieuport to be outfitted with Bley's device.

Paul searched the sky for the other aircraft without luck. He futilely tried to light his cigarette lighter. Every spark of light stood out in the inky darkness. Some seemed to be moving. The German bombers? Quickly he thought about turning around and trying to find the field at Cachy. Not a single light on the blacked-out field gave him a clue. He continued to the north in the direction of Amiens whose lights faintly glowed on the horizon. Maybe he could land there. As he approached the city it disappeared like an illusion. Hearing his motor must have triggered a blackout on the ground. Soon artillery and machine gun fire flashed up in his direction. Giving up hope of landing there, Paul calculated that he could stay up for close to two more hours. He'd left the ground at around 4:30. Dawn started sometime between six and seven.

Cursing his luck, Bley's failed invention, and Keeler for letting him go, Pavelka searched for clues on his altitude and attitude. When he felt pressure on his right buttock a little left stick and right rudder seemed to level him off. This was true seat of the pants flying, and Pavelka didn't like it one bit. He couldn't even see his watch to keep track of the time. For all he knew he could be flying directly into German-held territory. He shivered in the cockpit from both the cold and the thought of running out of fuel on the wrong side of the lines. If that happened he hoped the damned lighter would work long enough for him to burn the Nieuport before he became a prisoner.

After what seemed like many hours of aimless wandering about the featureless sky, Pavelka had run out of ideas at about the same time that he was about to run out of gas. *What a pity*, he thought. *Here he was a survivor of a dreaded flamer and he might have to burn a perfectly good airplane.*

His eyes ached from straining to see light, any kind of light. Somehow, they adapted to the dark enough for him to see darker patches on the ground. Trees, he reasoned. The lighter areas must be open fields. He toyed with the idea of shooting for one of those patches when the first faint glow of dawn began to define a sliver of horizon. *Only a few more minutes*, he prayed. Urging the Nieuport on, he listened to the drone of the rotary even closer, fully expecting it to choke and quit at any second.

He thought he heard something, a burp or catch. But the motor kept going. A pinkish tinge now cast faint shadows. In another five minutes he might be able to see well enough to land normally. A field! No question about it and no choice for him either. He drove the Nieuport towards the ground hoping it was a friendly field, but fingering his lighter just in case.

With his landing assured, Paul began to relax ever so slightly. Just then the motor sputtered to a halt. Already in a glide for landing, he deadsticked it onto the field. Before the Nieuport finished its short landing roll, he unbuckled and prepared to jump. Some figures came running in his direction. Limey tin hats! Brits! He'd done it again!

The sleepy-eyed soldiers guarding the field were surprised to see the French colors and Indianhead symbol in the growing light. "Mighty strange time to pay a visit, mate," one of them said. Paul's response in English surprised them even more. He'd landed, they told him, at Martainville.

It wasn't an airfield after all. Paul noticed a nearby chateau and asked the soldiers whose it was. "The colonel's, Yank. 'Upon my word e'll be pleased to meet yer lordship."

The colonel came out of the chateau just as Paul walked up.

"Had breakfast, chap?"

"No sir, but would you have a bit of petrol for my plane?" The colonel told him it might be arranged. They went to breakfast with Pavelka silently thanking his lucky stars.

Three days later the fog lifted enough for Paul to fly the thirty miles back to Cachy.

Lieutenant de Laage had had better success with Bley's lights that night. He didn't find any enemy during his ever-widening circles over Cachy, but his lights held up long enough for him to find his way back and make a landing at first light. He worried about Pavelka, but only slightly less than Charlie Keeler did. He rang every field within two hundred miles trying to locate his friend. Later that morning, the British headquarters reported Pavelka's dilemma, giving much relief to Charlie.

When Paul finally returned, his nerves settled by the cozy treatment of the Brits, he compared notes with de Laage. As terrified as he had been, he still believed they could fight at night. The two of them improved the system and began to make regular night patrols.

THANKSGIVING FELL ON NOVEMBER 23 IN 1916. Charlie sent letters to his folks that he hoped would arrive before Jennifer and Jack had to begin their return trip. In one addressed to Jack he congratulated Buck on winning Jennifer and apologized again for not being able to be there for the wedding. He included the latest news from the unit, telling about Hall's departure. He wrote: "If you can make it back before Thanksgiving, pick up a turkey in Paris. Sampson says he knows how to fix it American-style."

Charlie's letter to Jennifer consisted of a poem he'd started to fashion painstakingly when she and Jack started seeing each other:

Sister

Sorry for pulling your pigtails that night
You shouldn't have screamed so loud
Sorry for tickling you so hard at six
Wish you didn't tell on me for that.

Who will pull your pigtails now?
Will you scream, will you laugh?
Who will you tattle on or get in trouble?
Will you forget me now that you are grown?

I won't forget you or let you go
Though a friend now has your heart.
I will still pull your pigtails in my dreams
And tickle you until you scream.

Aren't brothers wonderful?

It didn't rhyme and it wasn't mushy. He outlined his words forming a sort of vase. Somehow, he knew she would get the message even without him saying it outright. He loved her and he was happy for her.

Pavelka was anxious to see how Sampson's cooking compared with the British meals he'd been enjoying. He told them about 'bubbles and squeak,' and 'bangers.' They laughed at Skipper's rendition of a Cockney accent. The men had dressed up the shack and even added a pot-bellied stove now glowing cherry red, creating an almost cozy atmosphere for the homecoming.

Rumsey stood to toast Skipper's return but noticed Whiskey chewing on something before he could finish the toast. His hat! His new $20 hat dripping with the lion's saliva and looking like a sieve. Rumsey had his usual snoot full before dinner so he was a little shaky. He threw his half-full glass at the animal missing him but getting Whiskey to look up lazily before returning his attention to the tasty wool and leather.

Red reached for the nearest weapon, a heavy walking stick leaning against the coal bucket by the stove. He whacked Whiskey on the head dislodging the ruined hat. Everybody had been laughing at Rumsey's plight. When the lion got up unsteadily and wobbled off into a corner someone noticed blood on the floor.

"Look what you've done, ya damned lush!" Emil Marshal said. Marshal was the only non-pilot of the Americans. Somehow he'd enlisted in aviation and missed all the schools, arriving directly at Cachy to join N. 124. When they tried to get him into flight instruction the doctors turned him down because of blindness in one eye. Marshal had a choice of returning to the Legion where he'd been an excellent and well-decorated bomb-thrower, or staying with *l'Escadrille Américaine*. Thénault agreed to keep him as an administrative clerk. Emil didn't like it much, but he stayed. He hadn't lost the coarseness of his Legion days. Not only that, but he had taken a shine to the mascot, an oddball like him.

Rumsey was shaken by the outburst. He held his drenched and perforated hat at arm's length and dropped the stick with a loud clang. On closer examination they discovered that he'd put out Whiskey's right eye. Red actually started crying and rushed from the shack. The next day he broke out in a rash. Just before Thanksgiving he started getting the shakes.

Thaw, Buck and Johnson pulled in to Cachy Thanksgiving Day. No holiday in France, only the Americans considered it a special day. Bill had a fresh batch of liquor. Johnson brought stuff to restock the larder. Jack had the biggest turkey he could find in Paris, a scrawny bird by American standards. It reassured Charlie that his letters had gotten through. More importantly, he now had a brother-in-law. The two men hugged unselfconsciously. Charlie could hardly wait to hear all about the wedding.

Whiskey's disfigured eye made Bill Thaw sick and angry. After hearing the account from Lufbery who told him to "go easy on the kid," Bill calmed down and gingerly petted the wounded animal. Surprisingly, Whiskey didn't seem to mind the injury nearly as much as the gauze they'd taped over the eye. The animal pawed it off so many times that they contemplated hobbling him. Bill wouldn't hear of it. Whiskey still walked a little funny, but, other than the disfigurement, fared better than Rumsey.

Sampson made a very credible Thanksgiving feast *à la française*—meaning with baguettes, cheese, and lots of wine. For some of them it was their third such holiday away from home. Féquant had given N. 124 no missions that day in honor of the event. Thénault, in turn invited the group commander to be the honored guest at the meal. It was a festive evening undaunted by Rumsey's absence. Red hardly left his cot now except to use the privy.

Jack remembered Red's dunking in the Pau River in flight school. The man had been heading for trouble from the get go. Buck suggested sending Red back to Paris for a couple of weeks to get dried out and see if he could get over the rash and shakes. Féquant shook his head. "He leaves tomorrow," he said somewhat sadly. "His nerves are shot. I can't let him stay and fly in this condition. Captain Thénault signed the discharge papers this morning. Sorry men."

Jack also thought about his Thanksgiving at Pau a mere year ago. Claudine Walker seemed tawdry, cheap. He thought of Kiffin's rescuing him and nearly falling into her naked arms. He stood up glass in hand and proposed a toast.

"We have all lost friends since coming over here. Few went more nobly than Victor Chapman, Kiffin Rockwell and Norman Prince. Lift your glasses, men, and drink to their memory. As Kiffin said, they did their part for Lafayette. May we never forget them!"

"To Victor, Kiffin and Nimmie!" Keeler boomed picking up the toast from Jack. Glasses clinked. Eyes moistened. Rather than becoming somber they chattered even more to mask their own feelings of vulnerability. Lufbery tossed his glass at the potbellied stove, startling everybody.

"The hell! Eeet's a fireplace, no?" He said with a smirk, provoking laughter at both his expression and accent. Nobody followed suit, probably to keep glass from flying everywhere.

"To N.124, *l'Escadrille Américaine*!" Philippe Féquant said, standing, commanding rather than demanding attention. "To the best damned American squadron in France!" He finished with a flourish and a twinkle in his eye. No one was drunk enough not to realize they were the *only* American squadron in France or anywhere in Europe.

"I regret to make one announcement you will not like. No longer can we use the term 'American Escadrille.' Our German friends think your country is still neutral and they are jealous of us having an American squadron. Until further notice N. 124 will be known as N. 124 or *l'Escadrille des Volontaires*, a name dreamed up by a bureaucrat no doubt. Maybe you can come up with something better." With that, he bid them farewell with a warning that the missions were back on in the morning. The men began to drift off, full of Sampson's feast, sated on good red burgundy, and—for the most part—terribly homesick.

Chapter 51
Lafayette *Finalement*

Cachy, December 8, 1916

Twang! Jack heard and felt the familiar snap of overstretched bracing wires. It was Pau all over again, except that now the Nieuport 17, unlike the old Caudron, whipped completely over with the loss of the support holding the right upper aileron's attaching point. One more flip followed by the nose climbing sent the machine into a spin. Jack had started his combat with the L.V.G. at 12,000 feet. He could barely hold his head still enough to see that he'd already dropped to less than two thousand. So violent were the gyrations that Jack felt the first signs of nausea since he'd started flying.

Releasing the controls didn't produce the hoped-for exit from the *vrille*. With the right aileron flapping wildly, the lifting surfaces couldn't get a grip on the air. Jack remembered Chapman grabbing the loose end of a control rod and getting his Bébé down by holding it in his powerful grip. It was his only chance. Reaching up with his right arm for the upper wing he confirmed what he already knew. He could never reach the aileron out on the end of the wing. Climbing out of the cockpit would mean certain death. Jack felt again the sense of futility at fighting the inevitable. This time he didn't feel the calmness or see the faces of the dead. It was more of a feeling of excruciating helplessness. The ground raced closer, blurred and dark. His last thought was no thought at all. Then black silence.

"*Mon Lieutenant! Reveillez! C'est l'heure*!"

Shaking him gently, the figure insisted in a loud whisper that it was time to get up. *Up,* he wondered? He was late? Eventually, his eyes adjusted to the dim light. He felt absolutely nothing except for extreme fatigue. He could even move his head and arms, though his legs seemed to be pinned down.

"Ou sommes nous?" He asked.

"Cachy, Lieutenant. Allez y!"

Get going? The plane must be destroyed. Certainly the Germans won't waste artillery on it. Cachy? How in the hell did he get back to Cachy from going down over the lines at the Somme? I must be hurt, he concluded. *They brought me back. I must have passed out.*

He sat up without pain or too much effort. Then he noticed that his legs were pinned under a blanket. He tried to move his left leg and found it was numb. The right one responded. As his head cleared he recognized the barracks at Cachy, not a hospital. Then he made out the scarred face of his personal mechanic, Brancard. What luck! He'd gone down at a friendly field and even his own crew chief was there to rescue him.

Ever so slowly, Jack came awake, rising through layers like veils being pulled aside, until he came to full consciousness. He was in his own cot in his own barracks! What the hell had happened? Slowly, it dawned on him that he had been dreaming. The whole combat and crash had been a conjured up image of his troubled sleep. As he tried to shake off the cobwebs, he marveled at the reality of the image so fresh in his memory.

Jack rose and dressed for the morning mission, shaken by the nightmare.

At 6:10 A.M., strapped firmly in the cockpit of his Nieuport, Jack still felt the cloying effects of the dream. It was too real! Every sensation was so poignant. It had taken two cups of coffee and a blast of the cold air outside to fully accept it as a dream. When Brancard turned the propeller to charge the cylinders, Jack concluded he was indeed among the living. He went through the pre-takeoff preparations mechanically.

Over the lines he looked left and right to see his wingmen, Soubiran and Haviland. Time to tango, he thought, further suppressing the lingering sensation that he had done this in his troubled sleep. They had the 8,000-foot patrol—3,000 meters. The sky glowed with the rising sun and wispy clouds. Jack breathed deeply of the castor oil-laced air trying to erase the lingering image of his dream.

Spotting a flight of L.V.G.s, Jack wagged his wings and plunged on the enemy. *It isn't the dream,* he reassured himself. *We're at 8,000 feet, not 12,000.* Still, the feeling of having done this made him hesitant and tentative. A burst of rounds from the observer of the first L.V.G. shocked him from his reverie. He mashed the trigger at less than two hundred meters from the German plane. Nothing happened! The lumbering two-seater proceeded blissfully on its course as if Jack was nothing more than an irritating mosquito. Redressing his Nieuport, Jack watched to see if Soubiran or Haviland had better luck. Both zoomed by him and climbed to altitude as if tied one to the other.

Irritated at the audacity of the L.V.G.s, Jack resumed the attack, diving again on the lead biplace with both the Lewis and Vickers cranking out their rhythmic tune. Neither gun failed. Yet, the L.V.G. continued unhindered. His sense of *déja vu* returned. Turning his head to the right the arriving flight of five Fokkers startled him.

The odds were against them. He didn't have time to think. The L.V.G.s lumbered on indifferently, no doubt thankful for their rescuers. Jack pointed his plane at the nearest Fokker. In seconds they closed to firing range. Still feeling the sense of having done this, Jack let loose his first volley. Missing completely, he dove down and to the right to avoid the oncoming German. Total confusion ensued as the three Nieuports danced and dodged in all dimensions with the five German fighters. Twice Jack fired the Lewis from the upper wing in the habit he'd learned in the Bébés. Each time the rounds streaked to the target without evident effect. On his third encounter Jack employed the Vickers but fired underneath. Rounds slammed into his machine as the Germans found their mark. He twisted and turned to get out of their line of fire.

A Nieuport burst into flames, coming apart and falling in pieces. *Soubiran or Haviland*? Jack wondered, feeling sick. A black object flew under him. The wing from a Fokker? For a brief second Jack had time to look around. Now he saw that there were at least two other Nieuports in the fight. Someone had joined them! He attacked the nearest Fokker drilling it with a stream of Vickers fire. Nothing happened. *Damn!* He was sure of his aim. Why hadn't it fallen?

Sweat fogged his goggles. In spite of the bitter cold air, he was hot and close to hyperventilating. Another Fokker announced its presence with a rafale of fire that stitched his lower right wing. Pulling back on the stick, he attempted a loop to escape and possibly reverse from chased to chaser, but the German mimicked the maneuver. Thinking of the others in the flight, Jack pondered going after another enemy and hoping for the best with his pursuer. Rounds hammering into his fuselage quickly put that thought out of his mind.

All his wagging and wiggling seemed to throw off the German's aim, but he just couldn't shake the tenacious enemy. He blipped the motor off, punched in full right rudder, and pulled the stick back and to the left. This forced the Fokker to scream past him and float away and above as his own plane plummeted into the spin that he'd purposefully induced. Sure he would soon hear the twang of the wire that snapped in his dream; Jack released the controls and centered the rudder. Nothing! Falling like a leaf, Jack remembered he hadn't let the engine restart! The Le Rhône roared back into action when he released the interrupt button. This brought him out of the spin.

Confident the dream was nothing more than his overworked imagination. Jack climbed for all he was worth to regain contact with the fight still swirling above him. It took several minutes to mount the thousand feet he'd lost in his spin. The Lewis drum was empty. Reaching down between his legs, he retrieved the spare. He loosened the seatbelt and stretched up to replace the empty while holding the stick between his legs. So far so good.

Approaching 8,000 feet, Jack singled out one of the Fokkers pursuing a Nieuport that looked like one of theirs. He aimed his nose at it, waiting the interminable seconds it took to close the distance. When the wingspan of the Fokker filled the sight ring he pressed the Vickers trigger. The machine gun barked and bucked in its mount spewing at least thirty rounds in the direction of the enemy plane. In a flash the Fokker broke contact in a violent uncontrolled dive towards the ground. Whether Jack had hit it wasn't clear. Too much was happening for him to break off and follow it down.

A quick twist of his head and scan of the sky told him there were still many airplanes engaged in fights for survival. Where did they all come from? He counted four Nieuports and at least that many Fokkers. They must have stumbled into someone else's fight. He joined a Nieuport with the Indianhead symbol in its attack on a sole Fokker. *Must be Haviland,* he thought, fearing Soubiran had gone down earlier. The two French planes were too much for the Fokker pilot. He dove frantically for his own lines. They let him go, thinking the odds were still uneven. They weren't. Three German planes of the original five were gone—possibly shot down. Now he counted not five but seven Nieuports. The others all marked with the white stork of N. 3.

Each of the three remaining Fokkers had two Nieuports serenading them with the music of machine gun fire. One, brightly painted in yellow, seemed to wiggle like a lady trying to get out of a tight girdle. Jack aimed at that one, but before he could fire, the German rolled inverted and dove at full speed for the ground. After pondering chasing it for a second or two, Jack decided it was time to head back. His fuel was now down to just enough to make it home—barely. He broke away from the party still raging in that spot of the sky. Behind him he noted not one, but two N.124 aircraft were following his lead. Soubiran must have made it! Whose Nieuport went down in flames?

They landed in formation. Jack felt elated and relieved that his dream hadn't played out. He also felt relieved that he'd brought back both the new pilots on his first patrol as a sous-Lieutenant. Then, as he remembered the downed Nieuport, he realized that his own hesitation and efforts at self-preservation probably contributed to the pilot's death. It left a lingering feeling that something wasn't quite right.

"Lord almighty, Jack what a thrill!" Willis came up slapping him on the back. "You saved my sorry ass too, my scandahoovian friend."

Soubiran also rushed up to congratulate Buck. "Did you see the way that Fokker exploded? You sent him to hell in a flash, Jack! God I wish I could shoot like that. Nice of the Storks to jump in, wasn't it?"

"Yeah. Any idea who bit the dust in that flamer?" Jack asked, a little flummoxed by their praise.

"Someone went down from our side? I didn't see that, did you Bob?" Haviland asked.

Soubiran's face was flushed from the flight and the exhilaration of the fight. He shook his head in answer to the question. They would have to check at group headquarters to find out the day's losses.

"You guys go get cleaned up and meet me for lunch in an hour. I'll head over to group." Jack didn't think he was giving orders, but he did catch the tone in his own voice. Haviland was not only older and more experienced in life, but he was also his first friend in France. He would have to watch being too bossy and full of himself now that he wore the stripe of a Lieutenant.

At group headquarters Jack ran into Capitaine Thénault. Since his return and promotion, he had had little contact with their commander other than the Thanksgiving dinner. "Jack. Good job today. I see you made it back with both your pigeons. Duellin tells me you got a Fokker too. Congratulations! That's five isn't it?"

"But, *mon capitaine*, it won't be confirmed. We were over German territory. No ground observer confirmation, no victory."

"Ah, but you forget, Monsieur Buck, another escadrille can verify your claim and it has already been done!"

After all the fuss in diplomatic channels about the name they'd been using, the men kicked it about before endorsing Bill Thaw's idea that they use Lafayette's name in their title. Kiffin had often referred to the young hero of the American Revolution. Chouteau Johnson reminded them about

Lafayette's visit to Saint Louis in 1825. The more they discussed it the more they liked the idea.

"Dr. Gros likes the name," Thaw said. "He might have come up with it at the same time as me, but let's run it up the flagpole." In what had to be the most remarkably quick decision in the history of French bureaucracy, General Headquarters issued a directive on 2 December 1916, canceling the earlier order to utilize *l'Escadrille des Volontaires* and approving the title *l'Escadrille Lafayette.* It was official. They were the Lafayette Escadrille, and Jack's first victory since the renaming made him the squadron's fourth ace.

On December 8, Jack was more interested in the lost Nieuport than in getting another victory. Nungesser had taught him a very important lesson about fame and glory:

"Every time I get a victory or add a medal to my collection I light a candle in the church for the sorry Boche that I killed." Nungesser said. "They put us in the newspapers and shoot newsreels of Guynemer and the other aces. It is well and good. The women like it. Who doesn't want to be thought a hero? But my success is another man's failure or death. Is this something I can gloat about? Maybe it will help shorten the war. I like that. Maybe it is inevitable in war that we must kill our enemies. But to glory in their deaths makes me sick. They put us in newspapers, Jack, but they put our victims in the ground."

By the end of the day they still didn't know which plane went down in the morning combat. Apparently it came from a different field, for everyone at Cachy had landed or been accounted for that night. Later they would learn that a British Nieuport all the way from a field in Belgium had stumbled on their fight, hopelessly lost and nearly out of fuel. The pilot, Anthony de Vincent, Second Lieutenant, Royal Flying Corps, had a curiously French name. Jack knew Michelle Keeler had brothers. Could this be the same man? He didn't look forward to asking Charlie.

"She has two brothers," he stated. "I think the youngest is still in school, and the older, Alain, is in an infantry regiment on the Somme," Charlie said in response to Jack's tentative question.

"Would the younger be Anthony by any chance?" Jack asked, hoping he was wrong.

"Yeah! Tony, they call him. Wants to fly. Thinks I'm some kind of bloody hero according to Michelle. Hey! How did you know his name?"

"Charlie, I'm not sure. Maybe there is another Anthony de Vincent. We just found out the identity of the pilot of the Nieuport that went down during our combat this morning. It was Second Lieutenant Anthony de Vincent. Your brother-in-law couldn't be a Lieutenant in the RFC already, right?" Keeler absorbed this information quietly without visible reaction. Then he raced away saying he had to find a telephone.

Left alone, Jack absorbed this reality. The sense of something out of kilter returned. During the first minutes of that day's combat, Jack had been preoccupied with his dream and his vow to survive. Now he began to think that his hesitation had cost a man's life. He'd been firing like a rookie, well out of range, afraid to get closer lest he get hit. What in heaven's name was de Vincent doing there? *Oh God. Am I becoming an embusqué?* Jack shuddered at the thought of being a shirker, the cause of de Vincent's death.

"Michelle? It's me, of course. Yes, I'm fine. Listen. I don't want to alarm you, but has your brother joined the RFC?" In minutes Michelle confirmed Charlie's fears. Jack, standing over his shoulder could tell right off that the man killed that morning was Charlie's brother-in-law. Would Charlie tell her now or wait until the official confirmation came through channels? How could he explain the question if he didn't tell her? Jack decided to move away and let his friend handle it his own way.

Charlie came out of the *téléphonist's* shack looking terribly forlorn. "I never even met the guy Jack! Why do I feel so broken up?"

"He's your wife's brother. What do you expect? How do you suppose Jennifer would feel if she just learned you were killed? How do you think I would feel? You better go see if Thénault will let you go be with her. She's going to need you. Damn, Charlie, it's my fault."

"Your fault? That's crazy! How could you have known who he was or why he was there?"

"I had this dream. I thought I was going to buy the farm today. I just didn't do my job."

"And got a credited kill? What's the matter with you, Jack? Don't you go getting dopey on me now. Good grief, a dream! You too? We need to talk about that. Don't be stupid and blame yourself. I'm going to see Thénault. You all right?"

"Yeah. I'll be okay. I'm sorry about de Vincent. What a sorry coincidence."

Anthony de Vincent's remains could not be recovered even had there been anything to recover. His aircraft literally exploded at altitude and fell in burning pieces all over German-held territory. At the family's request, the British officials agreed to a memorial service at the Cathédrale Notre Dame in Paris the week before Christmas. Since there was no body, there was no real urgency, so the family would have time to prepare and gather both English and French relatives for the service. Thénault graciously granted a week's leave to both Keeler and Buck, though he was wont to let his best flight leaders go at the same time.

1916 crawled to an end without bringing any indication of an end of the war that now gripped much of the world. The United States wrapped up its little foray into Mexico but stuck closely to the neutrality that brought President Wilson to office in the first place. Yet, hope remained for the beleaguered allies. The tragic sinking of the passenger liner *Lusitania* had American blood boiling. French and English diplomatic efforts continued unabated in the effort to get the Americans to commit. The Lafayette Escadrille, renamed to avoid diplomatic friction, now became the darling of the international press. German protests notwithstanding, N. 124's propaganda impact began to rival its combat contributions.

Chapter 52
Beginnings and Endings

Paris, December 1916

Michelle knew she had to break the news to her parents though she prayed Charlie might be wrong. *Oh Tony, Tony, Tony,* she pined in her heart. Eighteen! Tony literally worshipped Charlie and wanted to do everything he could to be just like Keeler. The man that won his sister had to be special, he told her, and he wanted to be just as special.

Michelle's world had been full of challenges. Nothing she had done since finishing school had been normal or easy. Going to work for Fleury tossed her into an unfamiliar lap of luxury. She missed her family dearly though the Fleurys treated her as a family member. She had developed her sassiness and independence to protect herself. She hated the fact that her natural good looks inspired lechery and made her vulnerable to physical attack.

At sixteen she had ventured into London unaccompanied to attend a piano recital. She'd taken public transportation out of necessity and convenience. On the crowded omnibus she'd been compelled to stand. A man jostled her and apologized after looking a little too long into her innocent green eyes. Then she felt something brush against her bodice. Some people got off the bus making a little room. Michelle tried to move away from the man, but a flood of passengers crowded on at the next stop. Now she felt something pressing against her hip. Looking down, she was startled to see the man rubbing his crotch against her, his fly undone. How could he do this in public?

She screamed and tried to pull away. Panicky, she screamed again, this time yelling rape. The man disappeared as the driver brought the vehicle to an abrupt stop. Her explanation of the cries for help only infuriated the driver and other passengers. No one else had seen the man expose himself. If a man could expose himself and behave like that on a crowded bus, what was to stop him in a secluded place? Ultimately, however, the experience on the bus made her feel vulnerable, violated.

Her father bristled upon hearing what had happened. “Next time, Michelle, don’t scream. Just reach down and squeeze the bastard’s balls until he turns blue.” Her mother cringed at the image, but she understood what Michelle was feeling. Anthony, hearing it all, told her he would protect her next time and every time. It was a brotherly gesture totally impracticable given their different paths and his youth, but it did endear him to her.

Unlike their older brother, Alain, an exuberant athletic type, Anthony was slight of build and reserved. Alain now sported the three pips of a captain. He wrote long descriptive letters from the front. To him everything was very much the pitch at Eton where he had excelled at cricket. War was just another game with bigger stakes. Michelle never doubted that Alain would emerge from the war, intact and swaggering.

Anthony excelled in academics, but shied away from sports. He too could have attended Eton, but chose instead a lesser-known public school closer to home. Where Alain had sailed into Sandhurst, Anthony showed no interest in the military. When Michelle heard from her mother that Anthony had volunteered for an air cadet program, she didn’t worry much. He was only seventeen. Surely they would keep him in flying school long enough for the war to end. At least that was what she had thought in early 1915, as she and Charlie became serious.

She’d written Anthony about Charlie’s exploits in the Legion and then about his becoming a pilot and the first ace of the American squadron. She didn’t realize how much her younger brother worshipped her and how much the man she loved became an idol to him.

Anthony could never compete with Alain athletically. His marks throughout school were superior to his older brother’s. When Alain donned the dashing uniform of the Royal Welsh fusiliers, their parent’s pride made Anthony shrink with envy. Only Michelle seemed unimpressed. She loved Alain and all his bluster, but she saw it for what it was. The six years that separated the brothers made it difficult to share any common ground. Michelle fell between them.

Anthony's death caught Michelle totally by surprise. Until last May she didn't even know that he had finished flight training. Indeed, she secretly hoped he would wash out of the strictly regimented program. Instead, Anthony excelled in training, jumped a class and graduated first in the class. He qualified for a commission. How ironic, she thought, that Anthony could overcome his frailty and achieve the rank of Lieutenant at only eighteen years old. He even beat Alain to that grade. He beat him to the grave too, she thought, weeping quietly while rocking Michael, struggling with how to inform her parents.

Ringing London seemed such a cold way to break the news, but Michelle worried that the official telegram would arrive at their door before she could get the word to her father. She couldn't leave Michael.

Fleury solved the problem for her. He now maintained an aerial courier service between London and Paris. He would put one of his men on the next flight with whatever letter she wished delivered to her father's office. It would then fall to de Vincent to inform his wife.

Michelle did call Jennifer. She needed a friend. Jennifer left the hospital before the afternoon report, an hour before her shift ended. When she arrived she found Michelle rocking in a dark room, the baby asleep in her arms.

"Let me put him down, Michelle," she said gently. "You just sit there. I'll make some tea. For the next hour the two women commiserated, cried, hugged each other and tried to compose the letter Michelle would write her father. In the end Jennifer dictated the missive to the distraught Michelle who could barely write the words. They finished it and sealed it in time to hand it to the messenger sent by Fleury who was none other than Stephane, their old driver and bodyguard!

"*Oui, c'est moi, Madame. Mes condoléances*," Stephane said embracing Michelle. Jennifer hadn't met the man but knew him by reputation from Charlie's first letters. Fleury had picked the perfect person to deliver the terrible news. Stephane had not only driven the de Vincents and Fleurys on many occasions; he had also saved Michelle and Charlie from the attackers in the Métro.

DECEMBER 8 IN CATHOLIC FRANCE IS A RELIGIOUS HOLIDAY of some import. It is the Feast of the Immaculate Conception of Mary. Catholics learn in school that Mary was born without the stain of Original Sin. The feast commemorates this article of faith. In England the Protestant children often confused this event with Mary's virginal conception, something many of them learned to consider as papist idolatry.

Tony de Vincent came home more than once with a bloody nose and torn clothes after an argument with his classmates over this issue.

Georges de Vincent sat at his desk staring at the calendar while tenderly holding the single sheet of stationery Stephane had delivered moments earlier. Anthony had died on December 8. The boy Georges secretly loved more than anyone in the world, including his wife and other children, had gone to God on the day they celebrated Mary's being without sin. How appropriate, he thought. He had expected Tony to enter the seminary. The boy had a religious calling so strong and so evident in his every fiber that only the war could divert him from the cause.

Tony's success in flight training didn't surprise his father. When the young man applied himself to anything, he achieved success. That he didn't appear to be athletic was not from lack of potential. Tony simply had little interest in games. He gave the impression of frailty because of his slight build, but he was well coordinated and strong from hours of swimming on his own.

Georges knew he had to leave the office to go home to Janet with this terrible news. Before he left, he rang the switchboard and placed a call to Michelle.

"*Merci, ma cheri*. It was better to hear from you. There is no doubt then?" Michelle would have loved to grasp that straw, but she wisely replied, no. They spoke for a few more minutes on the scratchy cross-channel line. Georges resisted the temptation to wish it had been Alain instead of Anthony. Alain, he could handle. The boy literally attacked life with all the vigor he could manage. He had lived a full life even at the tender age of twenty-four. Now he shuddered to think he could lose his remaining son as well. Thanking God for his grandson, he gathered the note from Michelle and headed for the tube.

THE WEEK AFTER DE VINCENT'S DEATH, a fog closed in on the Somme shutting out the light from dawn to dusk and making flight impossible. With the fog came a penetrating cold that made life in the trenches even more intolerable. In such visibility ground operations became nearly as hazardous as flight. Small patrols got turned around in No Man's Land and arrived back at their own lines where, as often as not, they were greeted by gunfire.

Both sides suspended maneuvers, opting instead for unobserved artillery fires dropped on known or suspected enemy positions. When the targets were close to the lines, short rounds and blow-back of shrapnel took a toll on friendly troops. The enforced inactivity gave the illusion that the war might not only be on hold, but might be over soon. Many hoped that Christmas 1916 would inspire the leaders to call a halt.

Verdun came to an official end with the French final attack on December 16 on a narrow front. Learning of the success of this last battle, the chatter in the Lafayette barracks was optimistic.

"Home by Christmas! Sounds marvelous to me." Dudley Hill, the reluctant warrior, said.

"Never make it by Christmas, Dud, but maybe this gawdamned war might end."

"If that's the case," someone else added, "then why do they keep sending us replacements?"

Ronald Hoskier, who had joined them on December 11, was a very good-looking, intense man whose hairline had receded early. Hoskier came to the Lafayette via the Ambulance service. Both his parents served in France as well. His father now commanded a section of the Norton-Harjes Ambulance, and his mother worked in Paris as a Red Cross volunteer. Jack Buck learned that Mrs. Hoskier worked at the American Hospital from time to time. Surely she knew Jennifer.

Ron was born in New Jersey. Newcomers had to give their life history almost the first day of their arrival. The escadrille pilots learned that Hoskier had attended Harvard but hadn't graduated. His father was British by birth and rich from a short successful career in banking.

"I like to write," he said, a skill his father cultivated as well.

"You've joined one of the writingest bunch of pilots on the front," Jim McConnell told him.

"Ever meet Jennifer Keeler in Paris, Ron?" Buck asked.

"Goes by Buck now," Hoskier exclaimed in mock surprise, adjusting the beret he affected to cover his bare pate, "Too bad she didn't meet me first. What a handsome woman! Here, Jack. She sent these with me," he said handing a packet of books and letters to Buck.

Hoskier brought news of other Americans in flight training. The most recent arrivals, Haviland and Soubiran, knew many of the men who had trained with Hoskier.

"You know that Jim McConnell just wrote a book on Americans flying in France," Jack told Hoskier. "I wish you had a chance to read it. Dudley Hill left for the states with it the day after you arrived."

"Who is his publisher, do you know?"

"Doubleday."

"No kidding? Dad uses them, too."

Jack didn't detect any father-son friction here. It verified his theory that wealth alone couldn't account for what he'd observed in Chapman, Cowdin, Hill, Prince and Thaw.

December 18 was a very cold Monday in Paris. Getting Notre Dame for the memorial service was no easy task and totally out of the question on a weekend. Georges de Vincent had to pull a number of ecclesiastic strings. His son was a *British* officer, the prelate explained. They normally agreed to funeral Masses for only the most senior French officers. The earnest prelate explained that there was no class privilege involved, just too many men dying every day. He would take the matter up with the bishop, but it would be prudent to schedule the service at another church.

Fleury paid a personal visit to the bishop. He pointed out the large contribution made by Renault to the cathedral upkeep fund, suggesting that it might be increased now with all the extra work the factory down the river was getting. The bishop smiled at the obvious bribe. "Trouble yourself no more, Monsieur Fleury, and don't worry about increasing your contributions. I have agreed to do this service myself as a personal favor to an old friend of their family, Archbishop McGuire. He and I served at the Vatican together some years ago. It seems that young de Vincent was one of his acolytes and a candidate for the priesthood."

Thénault told Buck and Keeler to take the whole week off and stay the weekend as well. "*Alors*," he said, "stay for Christmas too. With this weather we won't be doing much flying anyway. Take care of your families. I need you back here to help me run this motley crew."

At 10:00 o'clock A.M., December 18, 1916, the bells of Notre Dame tolled the hour of the beginning of the memorial service for Anthony de Vincent, Full Lieutenant (posthumous), Royal Flying Corps, deceased, remains not recovered. Archbishop McGuire, over seventy years old, came to concelebrate the funeral Mass with his old friend, the Bishop of Paris. McGuire noted that Georges and Janet de Vincent had been married in the cathedral some twenty-five years earlier by his friend's predecessor. Beginnings and endings, he thought, already composing the words he would say.

Alain was back from the front on emergency leave. The de Vincents, as usual, were guests of the Fleurys in the Crillon. A large contingent of de Vincent relatives from Normandy arrived for the service. From England the Caldwell side of the family sent three uncles, the only ones too old to be in uniform. Anthony's regiment, based a mere seventy miles from Paris, spared a full contingent of forty officers and men in full dress. Fleury declared the day off for any of his workers who attended the service. Consequently, the pews in the massive Notre Dame were full to overflowing.

Charlie met Alain de Vincent for the first time the day before the ceremony when he and Jack arrived by train from Amiens. The British officer struck him instantly as one of those men who swagger better than they fight. It wasn't fair, he knew, to make such a quick judgment, but the way Alain looked down his nose at Charlie's wrinkled tunic made him edgy. Alain's uniform was impeccable, of course. He was cordial enough. *Lord, the man looks like a masculine version of Michelle.* Charlie thought.

Jack saw the exchange between the brothers-in-law, drawing the same conclusions as Charlie. He also noticed an uncanny resemblance to Ferguson, the blowhard he and Haviland encountered on the *Reliant.* The curly red hair was the only real physical resemblance, Jack knew, but something about Alain's demeanor said 'I'm better than you, and *you* ought to know it.'

The reunion with their ladies and of Charlie with his infant son could only be slightly dampened by the sad occasion. Seeing Charlie with little Michael looked almost amusing. Charlie's forearms were as thick as the baby's body. Jack loved babies. His day would come, he thought, but not before the end of the war. After their initial hope that Jennifer might be pregnant they decided it wouldn't be right to bring a child into such a troubled world with the ever-present possibility of Jack dying in combat. Michelle and Charlie saw it differently.

Michelle missed Charlie as much as he did her. Her physical recovery from the delivery hadn't taken that long, but the doctor forbade marital relations until six weeks after the birth. They started kissing on the elevator. Michelle had to twist awkwardly to keep Michael from being crushed between them. Charlie too made allowances for the baby who slept quietly. Once in the room, Michelle gently laid Michael in his crib and drew the curtain around it to shut out the light. She unbuttoned the top of her blouse and returned to Charlie with the tops of her breasts inviting his gaze, his touch and his lips. In frantic seconds they had each other's clothes off, stopping only long enough to kiss each newly revealed part.

Michelle pulled Charlie down on top of her as she fell on the bed. There were tears streaming down her face.

"I've hurt you?" he asked still partly out of breath. "It's your brother. I'm so sorry. I've been too selfish."

"Don't be a fool, Charlie. I am crying from joy. Pure ecstatic joy. I've missed you so much these last weeks. I even wonder sometimes if Tony didn't wander into your zone just to give us a reason to get back together. He was that way, you know."

"Stop, darling. You are punishing yourself. If I made you feel half as good as I feel then I think we aren't going to get much sleep tonight."

"Or any night until you have to leave."

What a confusing time, Charlie thought. *How am I supposed to feel? How do I behave? Michelle is grieving. What does she need me to do?*

The answers to those questions came in action. So many things were happening at once that Charlie became entangled handling the English uncles while Jennifer took charge of the baby. Michelle, Alain and their parents met with the bishop and Archbishop McGuire an hour before the memorial service. Jack got tagged with meeting the late arriving de Vincent relatives and getting them to the church. He had a lettered sign he held up to attract their attention at the Gare Saint Lazare. There were two families coming in from Caen that morning. He had never seen them. All he knew was that Madame de Vincent, reputedly a *comtesse* of old royal stock, was coming with one of the families.

Michelle's grandmother was at least seventy-five. Jack expected a stooped wrinkled lady. Instead, a woman dressed in black silk with perfectly coiffed dark brown hair and eyes that made you forget anything else you saw, addressed him formally in French. He couldn't believe it was the grandmother. She looked to be in her forties, but then Jack was no judge of age. After the briefest of introductions, she took his arm and motioned to the others carrying their few things to follow. Jack protested that there was a second family to meet. Madame la Comtesse waved a gloved hand to one of the younger men in the party, and he peeled off to wait for the others.

Inside the cavernous cathedral a crowd of close to seven hundred filled the pews. Jack saw every type and variety of uniform from *ambulancier,* to Legionnaire. Many in the crowd looked like workers. He escorted the comtesse to the front, sensing the impact she had on the crowd. Some whispers suggested she'd been recognized. Jack left her in the pew with the immediate family and sat with Jennifer in the next one back. Who was this mysterious woman?

Jennifer looked as good as ever. Black made her shine. She wore the slightest of color on her cheeks and lips. She'd pinned her hair up underneath yet another of those hats so much in vogue. A veil hid her face, creating an aura of intrigue. He wondered how many more funerals would draw them together during the war. He took her hand

Charlie followed the de Vincents with Michelle on his arm. Janet held Georges' arm on one side and Alain's on the other. When they were seated the organ boomed a reverberating fanfare and everybody rose to greet the procession. The Archbishop led with the Bishop of Paris on his left. At least fifteen priests trailed side-by-side followed by deacons with their single sash over the right shoulder. Next came the acolytes, young men aspiring to become priests, and then an honor guard from Number 43 Squadron, Tony's unit. Such a dazzling display of clergy was worthy of a state funeral, Jack thought. *There is more than money behind this, he surmised. Perhaps the countess has something to do with the pageantry.*

A High Mass back in Minnesota took just about an hour depending on the length of the sermon. This Mass seemed interminable. The bishops blessed the altar, the family, the people and each other with holy water. Then they circled the altar with the censer dispensing the familiar fragrant smoke that always made Jack think of his First Communion. He realized now that the whole building of his old parish would fit in the sanctuary of this cathedral. Instead of sermons there were eulogies done first by Alain in English, then by the Bishop of Paris in French, and finally by McGuire in English.

Alain's words were correct and well delivered, but there was little spark or passion in them. He was *keeping up the side* as they said. Both Charlie and Jack decided their first impression of Alain was correct. Instead of sympathy, both felt somewhat disappointed.

The French bishop's focus was on the sacrifice this young man made for a noble cause. He compared Tony to Joan of Arc who also died in flames for France. It was stretching things, Jack thought, remembering that Joan fought the English and was executed by the French clergy for heresy.

McGuire got up last and held them in thrall for at least twenty minutes. He related every year of Anthony's life to each of the sacraments the young man had received. "Tony was marked by God at birth and claimed for Him in Baptism. I only poured the water and said the words." When the archbishop finished and sat down, Jack half expected the crowd to break into applause. Instead of feeling moroseness and grief, McGuire had depicted Tony as *everyman*, one all present could relate to.

Tony hadn't died gloriously, McGuire reminded them. He'd been lost after all. But he did die a glorious death, the Archbishop explained, in that he had fulfilled his own dreams to the best of his ability. "He didn't become the priest he wanted to be, but he did learn to fly like his admired brother-in-law." Charlie squirmed visibly at this reference. "And he did become an officer like his beloved brother."

McGuire's ending made Jack feel chills. He said: "Tony, remember us in your prayers. We have to go on in this life, young and old, with all our crosses to bear. You are free. You are there in Paradise enjoying Christ's presence. Pray for us, Tony, that we might be worthy to join you when our time comes."

To hear an Archbishop say this unsettled Jack. All his life he had admired—almost envied—the clergy for their possession of the keys to the kingdom of heaven—what he saw as an unblemished dedication of their lives to God. Masters had helped him see priests as men with their own failings, but he still had the feeling that the practicing clergy had a corner on salvation.

McGuire had just put salvation into another light. Even an Archbishop, steeped in the church, dedicated to God, could ask to be worthy to join a young man in heaven. It still didn't make sense to Buck, but he knew he'd learned something there that he would have to make part of his life. At least he would need to ponder it more.

Charlie absorbed much of the same message from McGuire's eulogy. He watched the elder de Vincents to see their reaction. Janet was quiet and unfathomable behind her veil. Georges had set his jaw during Alain's formula eulogy and hadn't relaxed it until McGuire ended. Michelle, who had cried for hours after getting the official confirmation, could cry no more. McGuire's words seemed to be aimed at her, if not at all of them. His exhortation to live the best life one could was nothing new to Michelle. She'd grown up hearing McGuire preach the same message. She accepted and believed in it already.

Hearing the old priest ask Tony to pray for them made her want to laugh out loud. Considering the chastising she and Tony had gotten after their Saturday confessions, she wondered what McGuire had done that was bad enough for him to seek Tony's help in getting to heaven. She truly believed her brother was in heaven. She would miss him, but she knew he was happier now than he had ever been in life.

In spite of the solemnity and formality of the procession and the Mass, the entire mood was different than it had been at Chapman's service in the American Church. Victor's, Rockwell's and Prince's funerals had been occasions of unbearable sadness. Thanks to McGuire, the service for Anthony de Vincent left them with a sense of hope as they emerged from the cavern of the dark cathedral with lightness in their steps.

The de Vincents' had only begun to grieve, of course. They had lost a son and a brother. Though all too common throughout Europe in the past two years, the pain of loss remained unique and poignant to each and every family. Now, the Battle of the Somme devoured British (and German) lives at rates exceeding even the toll of the horror of Verdun.

Christmas, a week hence, would take some of the edge off the sorrow. It was the first time that Charlie could spend the holiday with his in-laws. They remained in Paris for the occasion.

Alain's reticence tolled the sole sour note. He fumed about Keeler's marrying Michelle without any input from him. While he respected the man's appearance, obvious fitness, and array of medals, Charlie simply lacked the pedigree Alain valued. Charlie and Michelle were too busy to notice.

At Fleury's suggestion Georges de Vincent and his wife organized a Christmas feast. Their surprise guests gave Jack Buck great pleasure as well as a little trepidation. Now Deputy Minister of War and a member of the newly renamed Lafayette Flying Corps Committee, Pierre Flandin made his appearance at *Maxim's* with his wife and daughter. Jack's trepidation sprang only from a fear that their daughter might make a scene. Isabelle wore a very provocative gown whose décolletage, as usual, showed her bosom to its best advantage. Jack had told Jennifer about their insignificant romance. Isabelle's previous instability worried him. Jennifer admired the French girl's obvious beauty. If she felt any jealousy, Jack couldn't detect it.

The evening turned out very pleasant for all. Alain, on his last day of leave, appeared in his dress uniform. He dazzled Isabelle. The two couldn't keep their eyes off each other for the entire evening.

Michelle entrusted Michael to the Fleurys' nursemaid, a young woman who was more of an *au pair* than a babysitter. She had taken on many of Michelle's duties with the boys since the baby. Michelle felt truly free for the first time in months.

The Bucks remained absorbed in each other, resisting Fleury's attempt to seat them separately in French style at the table. Jack did talk at length to Flandin. Pierre informed him that it was only a matter of time until the Americans declared war on Austria and Germany. Berangère, as stunningly attired as her buxom daughter, fawned over Jennifer. Jennifer's French was still rudimentary, but one would never know it from the way the two women jabbered. Both the Flandins insisted that Jack bring Jennifer by their apartment the next day.

Watching Alain and Isabelle made Jack slightly uncomfortable. He didn't like the British officer. Isabelle wasn't his responsibility, but he knew how much she had suffered at Jacques-Antoine's death. Surely she was transferring affection to the dashing captain. Jack struggled within himself about talking to Flandin. He really had nothing to say against Alain. In the end, he told Jennifer he would hope for the best.

Charlie ended up across the table from his brother-in-law. Alain bantered politely enough until he asked Charlie if he knew any Americans in British service. Keeler didn't, but he thought Jack might have met some on the *Reliant.* Alain proceeded to berate the Americans he knew, one in particular. "The man is all wind and bag, I say. Present company excepted, of course. He is a sorry specimen of a Yank."

Charlie chose to deflect this to Jack, sitting several places down the table with Jennifer. When he got Buck's attention, Jack was surprised by the question.

"Americans with the Brits?" I thought we gave up citizenship if we joined the British Army?"

"Just so. Few exceptions though. This fellow I mention seems to have found one of them."

"What's his name, Alain? Chances are we don't know him, but who knows?

"Chap by the name of Ferguson, a bantam rooster of a type. Says he wants to fly. I'd be pleased to see him go up and never come down."

"Ferguson! A red-headed fellow, like you but shorter?"

"The same. Not a friend of yours, Buck? Meaning no offense." Alain temporized.

"No. We sailed here together. You've described him to a tee." Jack chuckled inside at the fact that Alain had reminded him of Ferguson. Talk about the pot calling the kettle black, he thought.

"In fairness, I do know a Yank who acquitted himself well with our artillery battery. *Hall*, James Hall. Have you met him? I think he did find his way into French Aviation. Jolly good chap! Speaks the King's English with the best of us."

The conversation made both Charlie and Jack think twice about Alain. He wasn't nearly as shallow as he first appeared. Had he damned all Americans, it would only have confirmed their suspicions.

LIKE MOST HOLIDAYS, CHRISTMAS ENDED TOO SOON FOR SOME and not soon enough for others. The de Vincents were bedraggled. They were anxious to get back to London. Georges insisted on going back to work despite Fleury's encouragement to take a month of vacation. Janet simply wanted to spend some time alone. Anthony was her baby. She needed to take leave of him in her own time.

Alain, on the other hand, asked for an extension on his leave in order to get to know Isabelle better. His regiment had pulled off the line. He received confirmation on Christmas Day that he could stay an additional three days.

For the Keeler and Buck couples another parting loomed darkly. Charlie and Michelle glowed in young parenthood. Jennifer savored Jack in their private moments. She set out to convince him that he was more than capable of meeting her needs—over and over again. Like many wartime lovers, they'd learned to snatch at brief moments together and make them last. Both Michelle and Jennifer told their husbands privately that they knew they could be killed at any time. Somehow their strength helped Buck and Keeler to return reinvigorated to the challenges of Cachy.

Catching the train back to Amiens the day after Christmas, Jack and Charlie looked back at the past seven days wondering where they had gone. On the train, Jack read that Joffre, the famous big man who headed the French Army, had been promoted to *Maréchal*, Field Marshall, the highest rank in France. The article was kind to the aging soldier, but it didn't hide the fact that Joffre's promotion came on the day of his retirement—more of an honorary grade and, the writer implied, a way to get the man out of the way. General Nivelle, the man who engineered the recapture of Fort Douaumont now commanded the Armies. Charlie told him that these moves at the top, according to Fleury, meant the war wasn't going as well as some would think. "Talk in Paris is that if we Americans don't come in to shore up the Allies soon, Britain and France will have all they can to hold on for another year." This was not good news for two young newlyweds.

"I hate this war, Charlie."

"You, me, and any sane person."

Chapter 53
Spads and Bad Press

Cachy, December 1916

The winter by all reports was the coldest ever experienced in the region. Mechanics had to drain the oil after every mission and keep it warm in the hangars near electric heaters. Pilots wore extra layers of clothing making them look like puffed-up mannequins. Sleep in the poorly heated drafty barracks became a chore. Most of the men wore their flying garments to keep warm. Lufbery even resorted to sleeping with the malodorous Whiskey for the warmth the animal offered.

If the cold was bad on the ground it was worse at altitude. Many pilots came back with the exposed parts of their faces white with frostbite. When they thawed painfully, the skin turned black and peeled off in disgusting layers. Conditions knew no politics. The Germans suffered the same privations and pain. Missions continued on flyable weather days, but some pilots on both sides lacked the stomach for aggressive action.

Jack started spending more of the down time mingling with the mechanics and pilots of the other escadrilles at Cachy. He enjoyed picking up the idiom peculiar to Frenchmen from different parts of the country. Certain expressions and locutions marked their origins as Midi (the southern part of France closest to Italy where Jack had already distinguished the soft singsong Provençal accent), or Basque—the harsher tones of the independence-minded folks from the Pyrenees nearest to Spain. This region, not far from Pau, was also familiar to Buck. The Parisians used a rapidly fired patois. Jack's time with the Ambulance had imbued him with the linguistic characteristics of the hardy people in northwestern France. In the northeast, where he had met Marie de la Croix de Valois, the local dialect seemed tinged with traces of guttural German. Jack learned that he had a parrot-like capability to echo the tones of whatever locale he visited after only a short period of hearing people talk.

The Storks were still receiving SPADs though some of their aces expressed trepidation about the newer machine. While there, Jack admired the Spad's lines and the robust look of its simple rigging. The Hispano-Suiza motor wasn't a rotary. It was more like the automobile engines he had worked on, though considerably more powerful. Spa. 3, the designation the Storks now held, even had a two-seat version of the Spad. Jack persuaded one of the pilots to take him up on a short orientation flight just to see what the machine felt like.

On December 27 they had one of the first good days to fly in weeks. Jack got the back seat. It had a set of flight controls that could be removed and stowed so the gunner-observer didn't interfere with the pilot's actions in the front seat. Their mechanic left the controls in position at Jack's request. Buck noticed right away that the enlisted men treated him differently now that he was an officer. He didn't like it. In N. 124 where almost all of them had started out enlisted, the mechanics and other ground personnel changed very little in their reaction to the new officers. Both Buck and Keeler made it clear that they didn't want to be treated any differently. Yet, in other units where they weren't known, the rank they wore visibly affected other soldiers.

All pilots, regardless of rank, seemed to get deference from the men who maintained their machines. Sergent de Castres had been a *moniteur* at Pau. He hadn't flown with Jack, but he knew him by reputation. Jack's discomfort came as well from the fact that de Castres was at least ten years older, an experienced pilot who refused a commission or even promotion to Adjudant so he could remain a regular line pilot.

After walking around the Spad together, de Castres took a few minutes to explain the operation of the duplicate engine controls. He showed Jack where the extra drum for the swivel-mounted Lewis gun was stored. "Of course, mon Lieutenant, you know the operation of the Lewis," De Castres said with a Gallic wave of his hand. They would not be crossing the lines or seeking combat on their flight, he explained, but one never knew.

Jack expected to simply ride along and maybe get a chance to test the controls a little in the air. Instead, de Castres completed the startup and flight control checks and then turned around in his cockpit to point to Jack, indicating that the American was to take off and fly the machine from the start.

Fearing an embarrassing mistake, Jack tried to shake his head and point back at de Castres, but the French sergeant had already turned back around and signaled for the chock blocks to be removed. *What the hell?* Jack thought. *The controls are all the same. What can I mess up? De Castres will have his hands close to the front controls.*

Jack pulled the throttle enough to get the Spad moving. It was less sensitive than the rotaries that operated at one speed only. With the Hisso—the mechanic's name for the motor—one could advance or retard the throttle through a whole range of speeds. Jack lined up on the familiar field before beginning the takeoff roll. He expected to feel de Castres' hands following him on the controls, but was startled to see the Frenchman had laced his gloved fingers behind his head! *Confident SOB,* Jack thought, realizing it was show time for the American Lieutenant. If he blew it, they would be talking about it for days to come. *Curious the man would use the same gesture practiced by Claude Toussaint*, Jack mused as he began the takeoff roll.

Thinking the throttle a little sluggish in getting started, Jack pulled it to the stop in one quick motion. Two hundred horses worth of power surged the machine forward. Jack toyed with throttling back, but thought better of it when the Spad didn't lighten up as quickly as the Nieuport 17. Carrying more fuel, two pilots, and three machine guns, this airplane outweighed the 17 by almost a half ton. The tail came up slowly as they picked up speed. Jack gingerly pulled back on the stick to see if the wheels would break ground. He still had plenty of room to clear the trees at the end of the strip. His inclination was to jerk the stick back and see what the Spad could do. After all, it was supposed to be able to out climb anything on the Western Front.

As they broke ground, Jack prepared to apply left pressure and left rudder to compensate for engine torque as he did in the Nieuports. It was an automatic reaction. The result was an uncoordinated turn to the left at very low altitude. *Damn,* he remembered, *this isn't a rotary!* He eased the controls back to neutral and continued a gentle climb straight ahead. Now de Castres came alive. He began scanning and searching above and around them as they inched up to the agreed cruising altitude of five thousand feet. If they were to run into an enemy, de Castres would have to take the controls to be able to engage with the synchronized forward-firing twin Vickers. He looked back and circled his hand vertically and horizontally, telling Buck to put the machine through its paces.

Now that he had a basic feel for the Spad, Jack tried a few simple maneuvers: a climbing left turn, a descending 180-degree turn to his original heading. He had to admit that the Spad was smooth and stable.

Without having to compensate as much for engine torque, control responses were regular and balanced in most directions. It would be a good firing platform. Sitting in the back obstructed his vision to the front and below. He didn't relish trying to land from that seat, but de Castres signaled for him to circle the field and land. The engine was much louder than the high-pitched Gnomes and Le Clergets. It was nearly impossible to converse between the two cockpits. Jack did as instructed descending to traffic pattern altitude without reducing his speed. In the Nieuport they simply blipped the interrupt switch to reduce power and lose speed. Reluctantly, he eased the throttle in a hair to see if he could slow down some and continue his descent.

Craning his neck over the side to the left and right, Buck struggled to see the ground and get aligned with the field. Visual cues forward were impossible, so he had to rely on what he could see to the sides. He was lined up fine and coming down on a decent glide slope, but it seemed awfully fast to him. Pulling back on the stick only made the Spad level off or porpoise up. He would have to reduce power soon and a lot. After being so tentative and gentle up to that point, Jack decided to make a bold reduction. He pushed the throttle handle in all the way to the stop. Silence! Horrified, Jack watched the propeller spin freely as the motor no longer pulled them along. A dead stick landing on his first flight in the blind back seat didn't strike him as the joy ride he'd anticipated. Looking for help from up front, de Castres had again laced his hands behind his head! This man was either crazy or brave or both.

As soon as the engine quit the nose of the Spad tried to drop. There was a heavy moment of gravity out there in front of him. He would need to toy with the attitude to keep forward speed while holding the nose up just below stalling. Trial and error quickly taught him when the new airplane wanted to fly and when it wanted to drop. Jack wondered if he could restart the engine somehow. The Nieuports easily cranked back up from the wind turning the propeller. All one had to do was release the interrupt switch which reapplied the spark. Idiotic to try in any machine at this altitude. He would have to land.

Jack had no feel for the Spad's ability to glide. If he pulled the nose up too far he'd stop his forward speed sure enough, but he'd also cause the Spad to fall like a rock. If he came in too fast the machine could bounce or catch something on the ground and flip inverted. McConnell's wrenched back and Prince's death came from such a flip. Even if he didn't flip, the Spad could either ground loop or smash into something or overshoot the landing area and crash into the trees. His options were few. He had to do it right.

Jack cleared the trees at the landing threshold and saw out of the corner of his eye that he was below a hundred feet. Nose it over or hold it off? From countless other landings in his Nieuport, he had a pretty good idea what the surface was like and how many feet of the four thousand foot strip he had left. Jack decided to let the Spad set itself down. He'd heard stories of single-seaters floating to perfect landings with a dead pilot in the cockpit not touching the controls.

He had made the only choice that would work, though he wouldn't know that until the wheels touched down smoothly. Jack even guided the rolling Spad back to the front of the hangar from which they'd started, coasting to a bumpy stop in front of the astonished mechanic. They'd only been airborne fifteen minutes. Had they had an engine failure?

After unstrapping, de Castres came back and climbed up on the left of Jack's cockpit. He reached down beside Jack to the throttle handle to pull it through its range of motion. Without a word, de Castres pushed it in as Jack had and smiled. Then he said his first words: "As I suspected. The damned lever is supposed to lock at the idle position so we can't cut the engine inadvertently. Your *lever* is not right." In French it sounded almost like a crude reference to Jack's male organ. (*Le votre n'est pas bon.)*

"*Magnifique, mon Lieutenant*! I hope they are right that you are coming to fly with us. I have never felt more comfortable in the air with another. Are you sure you have not flown the Spad?" Jack tried to absorb the sergeant's words, all of which he'd clearly understood. His throttle had been improperly rigged. He should not have been able to kill the engine. Okay. That wasn't his fault. Coming to fly with them? What could that mean? Was de Castres testing him for Capitaine Duellin? Surely they wouldn't pull him from the Lafayette now. Now he began to see why de Castres had so demonstratively stretched his hands behind his head. He clearly wanted Buck to know he was on his own. Jack wondered how far the little instructor would have let him go before trying to save the airplane and their lives.

Back at N. 124, Jack sought out Thénault. He explained the morning flight and what had happened, extolling the virtues of the Spad. Then he asked if there were plans to move him out of the Lafayette Escadrille.

"No!" Thénault said, a little too vehemently. "Where did you get this idea? *Mon Dieu*, I cannot be losing my most experienced men now." Calming down, the captain explained that Duellin had lost a flight leader and had Guynemer taking leave to overcome the effects of the weather on an old wound. Féquant asked each of the other escadrilles to lend Duellin an experienced *chef de patrouille*. He and Keeler were his first choices. Thénault wanted one of them to observe the way Duellin handled his flights and worked with the new Spads. Eventually, Georges told Jack, the Lafayette Escadrille would become Spa. 124. "Yours is the better French, mon ami. Unless you really object...."

"*Non, mon capitaine*," Jack replied rapidly. He didn't want to give the impression of turning down any mission. "I will be coming back soon?" he asked, hoping to get some reassurance he wouldn't be shuffled off for good.

Thénault promised no more than three weeks. He said Duellin would love to steal one of his Americans, but Féquant would not allow it.

That settled, Jack asked when. The reply surprised him. Thénault said next week, the first of the year. The little flight with de Castres was looking more and more like a set up to him. Could they have purposefully rigged the throttle that way to see how he would handle it? He would have to play that one close to his chest. *Three weeks*. At least he didn't have to move his things. They all lived within three-quarters of a mile of each other at Cachy. He would have to eat with them, an unpleasant thought considering Masson and Sampson ran such an Epicurean delight in the Lafayette mess.

Lufbery got his sixth victory during Buck's test flight of the Spad. This put Luf in the lead for victories in the Lafayette which now boasted four aces with Jack's confirmation of December 9. To put this in perspective, Lufbery reminded them that Georges Guynemer scored his twenty-sixth kill the same day. He had more personal confirmed victories in twelve months than the whole of N. 124 in its eight months on the front.

News of these victories after the long dry spell drew reporters from Paris like honey draws flies. Early in their existence, Thénault had encouraged the visits. Part of his unofficial mission was to parade his unit in such a way that it might help sway America to France's side. As some of the articles became wildly distorted and sometimes maligning to the young men in N. 124, the Americans were wary of reporters.

Newsmen seemed to fall into two classes. The sensationalists succumbed to any malarkey foisted on them in the field and printed it as gospel. A Pittsburgh reporter even wrote that Bill Thaw shot down two Germans before being forced down behind the lines. According to this writer, Thaw drove off a full squad of German infantrymen by taking his machine gun off the airplane and letting them have it from his hip. He then restarted his Nieuport, took off and decimated the enemy infantry with bombs and machine gun fire before returning to safety. Thaw was amused. It wouldn't occur to most readers that it was impossible to start your own Nieuport let alone remove a machine gun to fire it by hand. The mere mention of bombs should have been a clue to anyone even remotely familiar with pursuit aviation.

The other class of writers may have been less gullible and more credible in what they wrote, but they were also more dangerous and critical. This made them more respected. It also made the officers wary when one of them showed up at the escadrille. Paul Rockwell numbered among this latter class, but he was a known friend. The man who arrived on December 28 wasn't known at all. He stood about five foot nine, rising constantly on his toes in an attempt to seem taller. He wore a straw boater, a common hat in the city but totally out of place on the field at Cachy. Around his neck hung a boxy Kodak. When news of his arrival at the guarded entrance reached N. 124, Keeler answered the call. Thénault, de Laage and Thaw were on missions. He had to greet the reporter, a task he welcomed about as much as a toothache.

Charlie took his time in the futile hope the reporter would find something else to do. He met the man at the door of the shack that served as the escadrille command post. Emil Marshal looked up from the report he was working on and winked knowingly at Charlie as if to say "better you than me."

"Keeler," he said not wanting to volunteer any more lest it end up in print.

"Ferguson," the man replied lifting his boater slightly to reveal a shock of curly red hair. "I'm told the Americans have a couple of aces in your squadron, Lieutenant. Any chance of talking to any of them?"

Charlie's antennae were already tuned. *Ferguson? Where had he heard that name? Looks a little like Alain. That's it! Alain had mentioned an American in British service. Could this be the same guy? How in the hell did he get to be a reporter?* "With what paper did you say?"

"Ah, no newspaper, Lieutenant," Ferguson said. "I'm what you call 'free-lance.' Hey, you speak pretty good English for a frog. Ever been to America?"

"Born and raised in Saint Louis. And you?" Charlie said wincing at the word frog.

Ferguson looked genuinely surprised as if it wasn't possible for Keeler to be both American and an officer. "Yes, of course. Harvard. Boston's my home. Doing an article for the *Globe.* Had a stint with the limey Artillery. Bloody bunch of rotters, them! Hoped to see some real Americans to get some of the snooty taste out of my mouth."

The guy seemed harmless enough. Charlie decided to relax a little and see how it played out. If this was the same Ferguson Jack ran into on the *Reliant*, Buck and Haviland might like to get a piece of him. "Let's walk down to the line, Ferguson. There's a couple of pilots down there you might like to meet."

They walked through the mud with Keeler purposefully choosing his path to avoid the duckboards. He had his sabots to keep him somewhat dry. Ferguson's high-topped button shoes were soon covered with slime. When they got to the hangar Charlie hailed Bley and asked if Buck or Haviland were in the area. Ferguson didn't understand French and missed the names in the quick sentence. Bley turned after an exaggerated salute and went to find the pilots.

"The captain's on a mission with Bill Thaw and Lieutenant de Laage, our second in command. Maybe you'd like to meet one of the other flight leaders?"

"Is that what you are Lieutenant? I'm really interested in talking to aces, not your officers, begging your pardon." Ferguson's arrogance could have rubbed Charlie the wrong way, but he kept his cool, hoping Willis Haviland or Jack Buck showed up to see if this was their old shipmate.

"Charlie," Buck said, coming over wiping his hands on an oily rag, "you looking for me?" Jack wore a mechanic's coveralls with no insignia. He had been helping his mechanic service his motor.

"Got a reporter here wants to talk to an ace. Got any of them hanging around?" Charlie said, his earnest tone masking his sarcasm.

Buck took a look at the man with the plaid Mackinaw jacket and boater perched jauntily on his carrot top. He did a quick double take on recognizing Ferguson. Two years in France hadn't diminished his memory of their three weeks at sea. "I'll be a son of a bitch! Ferguson! Why I'd heard the Brits gave you the boot. What the hell are you doing here? A reporter? That's rich!"

"Excuse me, Lieutenant, who is this filthy-mouthed soldier?"

"Why, Ferguson, don't you recognize an ace when you see one? This is Jack Buck, sous-Lieutenant, French Army, holder of six Croix de Guerre, and, if my memory holds, an acquaintance of yours of sorts." It was Ferguson's turn to do a double take. He looked hard at Buck, squinting and screwing up his face at the mistake he'd made.

"Keeler, you need me for something?" another voice said from behind them. Willis Haviland came up in full flying gear. He had the midday mission that was departing in twenty minutes.

Ferguson was still off balance absorbing the fact of Buck's presence. Willis' appearance nearly totally unnerved him. "I, I, um, I.... By God it is you two! I'll be damned! I thought I read something about a Buck in the paper, but I never connected it with you. Haviland! Damn. I didn't think I'd see the likes of you two again. Pilots? Damn!"

"You guys take as much time as you like. Seems like old buddies need to get caught up. Willis, I'll take your mission if you like."

"No! I mean, let me do it, Charlie. I don't need to waste time on this guy."

"No way to treat a guest, Haviland. Go ahead. I'm sure Mr. Ferguson will want to hang around and have dinner with us tonight," Charlie said feigning mild anger. Jack was going over to Spa. 3 soon. A little excitement in the popote might do them all a bit of good. Remembering the fun they'd had with the Scottish pilot and his gunner, Charlie looked forward to Ferguson turning slowly on the spit that night.

In the end it wasn't such a good idea. Neither Haviland nor Buck cared to even talk to Ferguson, leaving him to Bley to show around the field at Cachy. Ferguson made it clear that he wanted to spend some time with some *real* aces, implying that Jack's five victories barely qualified. Bley's English was very limited. He made it clear enough that Keeler, Buck and Lufbery were not only bona fide aces, but that all three had scored a number of victories that couldn't be confirmed. This still didn't impress Ferguson whose idea of aerial combat was limited to what he'd read. His artillery unit had been in the line for ten weeks, but they'd only seen pursuit aircraft en route to or from their actual missions.

Supper that evening proved less mirthful than Charlie had hoped. Ferguson didn't drink or smoke or play cards, so few of the men felt like socializing with him before the meal. Buck arrived cleaned up in his black tunic wearing only his wings and none of his ribbons. Though he looked sharp, he apparently didn't fit the image Ferguson had of an ace. When Thénault announced the fact that N. 124 had more combat hours over the front than any other escadrille at Cachy, Ferguson copied it down on his notepad, but still acted bored. Lufbery bristled at the so-called reporter. He remained as polite as he could but snickered when Ferguson asked if he could interview him in private.

"You should talk to Lieutenant Keeler or Lieutenant Buck if you want to talk to real heroes. Keeler has more decorations than any of us, including our other officers. He was our first ace. Buck can fly circles around most of us. He just brought in a Spad with a dead motor on his first flight. Why don't you talk to one of them?"

In the end, no one gave Ferguson an interview. He got tired of asking Lufbery. He wouldn't talk to Buck, and actually went out of his way to avoid Haviland. Keeler left with Thénault for group headquarters to get the next day's missions, and Ferguson begged to go along. He'd picked up on the fact that there were some 'aces of aces' in the French escadrilles. Maybe he could get an interview with Guynemer or Dorme. He was wasting his time with the Americans. They all seemed too flippant for him, though a few like Robert Rockwell wore class rings from reputable colleges.

The next day Ferguson showed up at Spa. 3. He would have considerable trouble communicating in an all-French unit, but it didn't matter to him. He planned on filling up the space in his article with some color of his own anyway. When Duellin insisted that an escort accompany him, Ferguson acquiesced. He'd only been 'reporting' for a month or two. His only instinct was to go for the top dogs and the hottest stories. He wasn't worried about being manipulated or steered around to see only what the unit wanted him to see. After all, he was so much smarter than they were—or so he thought.

Buck reported for duty that morning only to find that his first mission was to play nursemaid to Ferguson. Jack shouldn't have been surprised at Duellin's decision. Duellin told him that Féquant approved Ferguson's visit. The commander wanted him handled well, Duellin explained. As the only native English speaker, Buck would be responsible for making sure the reporter came away with a good impression. Jack almost gagged on hearing this.

His spirits rose considerably when the weather lifted allowing scheduled missions to depart. This gave him an excuse to leave Ferguson on the flight line watching take offs and recoveries. Jack went to find the little instructor pilot, de Castres, to see if the dual-seater might be made available to take *an important visitor* on an orientation ride. At first de Castres balked, insisting that the man was a civilian and a foreigner. "What happens if I kill the bastard?" he asked Jack. "An international incident, that's what!" Buck convinced de Castres that the group commander himself wanted this reporter to see as much as possible. Finally, the instructor pilot agreed.

"This is Sergent de Castres, Ferguson. He is the senior instructor in the group and the highest time pilot at Cachy. He will be giving you a ride in this Spad. Of course, you've already flown?" Ferguson acted like he didn't hear the question. His bragging on the *Reliant* about already being a pilot and about having to have a college degree to learn to fly had already come back to haunt him.

Continuing on in French which he translated back to English loosely for Ferguson's sake, Jack told de Castres that the American reporter was very interested in the way dogfights took place. He *was* already a pilot, Buck stated, again getting no denial from Ferguson. Show him some acrobatics if you like, Jack said, translating it back literally. Ferguson's naturally ruddy complexion seemed to glow in the cold morning air. Jack wasn't sure, but he thought he'd detected a bit of a blush and shudder. *Well,* he thought, *de Castres will give him a great flight. If he is a pilot, he ought to enjoy the Spad's stability and power. On the other hand, seeing that red hair atop a green face would make my day. Shame on you, Buck!*

Thirty minutes later the Spad settled on the field. No head showed in the back cockpit! *My God!* Jack worried. *Didn't I get him strapped in right? There'll be hell to pay if old Fergy fell out. Shit!* Racing over to the Spad Jack waited a second or two while the mechanic chocked the wheels. He climbed up on the lower left wing root intending to ask de Castres where he'd deposited his passenger. It was possible that the sergeant landed to let Ferguson out to pee or something. Instead, Jack saw a ball of plaid Mackinaw curled up on the wicker seat of the rear cockpit that was fouled with vomit from one end to the other. With the motor off he could hear faint moaning. Stifling his own urge to gag at the stench, Jack poked at the form down deep in the seat. Ferguson, not feeling the motion of the Spad any longer, dared look up. Jack had gotten his secret wish. If ever a face was green, Ferguson's pale shade most closely met the description.

Jack didn't feel any elation at Ferguson's discomfiture. Instead, he rebuked himself for being so petty and vengeful.

They were able to get rid of the pesky man more easily than the traces of Ferguson's breakfast in the rear cockpit. Any satisfaction Jack might have felt was quickly dashed three weeks later as he got ready to return to N. 124. Ferguson had managed to write a diatribe decrying the lousy state of French Aviation training. He'd gotten the article printed in the Paris version of the English language *Herald* along with several major papers in the States.

New York Herald (Paris Edition)
January 1, 1917

Aces and Spaces

By Amory S. Ferguson

On a recent visit to a French Combat group at _____ _this reporter had the opportunity to observe French aerial operations on an actual mission. A pilot himself, this observer found nearly every aspect of French flight operations lacking. This broad brush has unfortunately tainted the so-called Lafayette Escadrille, part of the same Groupe de Combat. Much to the credit of the individual pilots, several notable high-scoring aces seem to have overcome the poor training of French units in general. Lieutenant Guynemer stands highest with 26 victories and a handful of others have the five or more victories necessary to be designated an ace. N. 124, the official title of the Lafayette Escadrille, claims to have three aces, but only Sergent Raoul Lufbery, more French than American, seems to have a valid claim. After nearly a year in the Royal Fusiliers Artillery, I have never seen such shoddy discipline and poor military decorum. In two days at _____ I never saw two uniforms the same. Most were filthy. The men slog through the mud on purpose. Officers and enlisted address each other by first names. Aircraft maintenance is so poor that on a combat flight in a new Spad two-seater, this reporter was thrown from one side to the other of the cockpit as the pilot fought to regain control of his wildly flailing machine. My pilot, purported to be the senior instructor pilot in the group, had to terminate the flight early due to technical difficulties. If the American Army ever does join the forces united against Germany, I hope it takes its flight instruction from the professional British rather than from the slipshod French. To the friends and family of any Americans attached to the so-called Lafayette Escadrille, I send a message of hope. The unit is so green that the French don't even let it get near the front. These boys only have to survive the rotten conditions in the French Army in order to be fit to get retrained by American forces should they enter the conflict. That day cannot come soon enough based on my observations. The French, if the Group I visited is any example, are in a sorry state of decay. They hold a hand of aces and spaces I wouldn't bet on.

Chapter 54
Hails and Farewells

Cachy, January 1917

"If I see that little red-headed shit I hope his insurance is paid up, 'cause I'm gonna squeeze the piss out of his carrot top and then use his shriveled balls—assuming he has any at all—to wipe up the mess," Skipper Pavelka said waving the week-old newspaper over his head.

"Get in the queue, mon ami. It is I who will do the squeezing," Lufbery said, a wild look in his eyes.

Haviland said: "I wish I'd thrown him over the side. Can you imagine the audacity? 'Too green to let near the front.' I don't know how he got this drivel by a reputable publisher. Mac, is it worthwhile trying to answer this trash? Defend our good name and that of the French?"

"I doubt it would do any good or harm to tell you the truth. There's enough sensible stuff in print to make Ferguson's whiny story stick out like a sore thumb. I say let it go. I know you guys are hot, but let the truth speak for us." McConnell hadn't heard yet from his publisher about the manuscript he'd sent with Dudley Hill. He had high hopes *Flying for France* would get printed relatively quickly. It would go a long way towards putting Ferguson's crap in the proper hole.

"Nevertheless," Jack said, feeling the most responsible for Ferguson's diatribe against the French, "I'm going to write something for Paul Rockwell to look at in answer to this unmitigated slander. Maybe Paul can get it stuck on a prominent page. Maybe I should write it myself as a letter to the editor of the *Herald*."

"And give that bastard the satisfaction that he had gotten to you and the rest of us?" Charlie said, also feeling responsible for Ferguson's treatment. "I'm the one that took him 'slogging through the mud on purpose.' Ruined his pretty shoes. I suppose I'd be a little mad after that myself."

"What irks me," Bill Thaw said, never having met Ferguson himself, "is that this turd dares criticize the French. I've flown with just about every nationality over here before the war and none could match the French. The Brits have some fine pilots, but that goes for the Germans as well. Now some fancy pants American officers are going to look at this article and take it as gospel. Lord have mercy!"

"Too true, Bill," Doc Rockwell agreed. "All it takes is a sniff for some of the stupid regulars to make a foolish decision. I saw it as an intern with some visiting medical officers. Someone had told them that French medical school is less rigorous than ours in America. Never mind Louis Pasteur or Madame Curie, those dopes came here criticizing everything."

"Well, no sense getting all worked up about a few lines in a newspaper, is there?" Chouteau Johnson offered trying to placate the men. "In a few days it will all blow over anyway. We know the truth about the French and our own unit. It's all that really matters, isn't it?"

"Eeet's fine to say Chouteau, but I will still pluck the pigeon's feathers if ever I get my hands on him!" Lufbery made a wringing motion with his hands and then suggested chopping Ferguson up into Whiskey-sized meals. Everyone got a little chuckle out of the image of the docile lion munching on bits of Ferguson.

"Speaking of our favorite people. Did you guys hear about old Bert Hall?" Freddie Prince asked. "He stayed over in N. 103 until last week. I heard he got himself assigned to the French mission to Roumania."

"I wonder if that's better for the Roumanians or for the Turks." Hoskier said. He knew Bert Hall only by reputation.

"Say what you may, Hall's still a damned good pilot. He may be a rogue and scalawag, but he can fly and fight when he wants to," Buck, about the only one who would take Hall's part, reminded them.

"Yeah, Jack, I guess you're right, but what's old Bertie going to pull when he runs out of teeth?" Lufbery interjected bringing on even more laughter. As angry as they were, the men of the Lafayette Escadrille never missed a chance to laugh. In their circumstances, laughter was the only consistent palliative to the numbing cold and constant threat of death or injury.

During Jack's tour with the Storks the Lafayette languished at Cachy unable to fly except for short sorties during the irregular breaks in the weather. Every morning a thick fog blanketed the field, preventing flights. Often the fog didn't lift until mid-afternoon if at all, and then the ceilings were, as often as not, too low to allow combat operations. Ironically, the nights were often clear and cold which brought out the inevitable German bombers. Pavelka and de Laage still flew night patrols, but they never seemed to do more than keep the bombers away from Cachy. Amiens still took major damage nearly every night.

Hall's purported assignment to Roumania coincided with a general request for combat pilots to volunteer for service in Salonika. Due to the prolonged stagnation on the Western Front, actions in the Middle East and the Balkans took on greater importance. Few of the men knew the terrain or situation in that exotic region of the world. Everyone assumed it would be considerably warmer. This tempted Lufbery, McConnell and others who suffered from arthritis or rheumatism aggravated by the dampness and chill.

While flight action lagged, N. 124 still managed to pick up two new pilots in January. Hoskier had come before Christmas as a replacement for Bert Hall. Edmond Genet and Edwin Parsons came within a week of each other, more as bonuses than replacements.

Genet signed in the same day Jack came back from Spa. 3. His grand entrance established him straight off as someone to contend with. A low fog hung over the field touching the treetops and giving no sign of lifting in the dead calm chill. They heard the sound of a Nieuport approaching and wondered what fool was up on such a forbidding day. Returning to their individual activities no one noticed when the sound of the motor died. Several minutes later the men in the barracks were totally startled when the door burst open.

"A Lieutenant! Great day in heaven! I'm honored, sir!" Genet spurted with his usual boyish enthusiasm when he saw Jack.

"Smiler! That was you? Holy cow! Who let you take off anyway? Does Keeler know you were coming? He bugged the dickens out of the captain to make sure we got you."

Genet walked into the popote that night with so much sparkle and pep that the ambiance brightened up markedly. He went from man to man calling out their name and saying something he'd picked up in flight training or from his legion friends. The latest arrivals were, of course, familiar to him from the schools. The others he knew by reputation. Keeler still couldn't get over how young Genet looked. As one of the few old timers who had met him, he stood up to make a formal introduction that included Genet's lineage as a direct descendant of the first representative of France to the United States.

In several days, Genet's enthusiasm countered the dourness of the barracks. He scoured the field for large pieces of cardboard from packing materials and began to line the walls of the barracks both to shut out the drafts and to provide a canvas for his artwork. Since flying opportunities were scarce, Genet scrounged up paints and brushes and began to decorate the walls with scenes of Indians, dogfights between Escadrille pilots and black German airplanes, and various other scenes. Genet was like a breath of fresh air sweeping through N. 124.

With Genet's arrival, the escadrille went over the authorized number of pilots for the first time. Even after Rumsey's departure and Hall's transfer, there were usually just as many pilots as there were aircraft to fly. Now there were more, so it fell to N. 124 to cough up someone for Salonika. Luf and Mac really couldn't bring themselves to leave. Skipper Pavelka, on the other hand, had been such a rolling stone for so long that the opportunity to go somewhere else and do something different caught his fancy.

Kiffin Rockwell's death severely affected Pavelka. Only Charlie Keeler had been closer to Skipper. Kiffin's last night in the room in Luxeuil haunted Pavelka. He kept thinking he should have said something else or tried to get Kiffin to stay on the ground. He didn't show it, but he felt devastated by the thought that he contributed to Rockwell's death. It had been months, but he couldn't shake the feeling that he was jinxed.

When the request for volunteers to go to the Army of the Orient arrived in December, Paul Pavelka quietly put his name in for consideration. He didn't tell anybody. Thénault agreed to keep it to himself. When his orders arrived on January 22, Paul fessed up to Buck and Keeler. He was departing the next day for Marseilles with subsequent sailing for the Orient. The men had a tearful farewell party for him that night. Everyone swore to keep in touch via the surprisingly good *Poste Militaire*. Skipper told Jack and Charlie that he hoped they would be able to put an end to the bickering and in fighting in the escadrille.

"I look forward to joining N. 391. They say it's more than 180 kilometers from true civilization and that they fly every day. Just what the doctor ordered. *A bientôt mes amis*."

Almost before Skipper's absence really impacted on his friends, Edwin C. "Ted" Parsons reported for duty. Where Genet was all boyish enthusiasm, Parsons was more the playboy type. Impeccably decked out, Parsons gave the impression of a fop, one of the 'boulevard aviators' who preyed on young women while never getting near the front. He would soon prove to be anything but.

Parsons enlisted in aviation at the same time as Genet and Hoskier. The three naturally chummed together, but proved as different as three men could be during their first days in the escadrille. Charlie latched onto Genet as one of the regulars for his flights while Jack laid claim to Hoskier and Parsons. Such alignments were generally meaningless since the escadrille mixed missions and flights daily, but it did give Keeler and Buck the chance to get to know the new men better.

When Parsons told about his Mexican excursion, Didier Masson jumped in with great interest and some skepticism. Soon the two had confirmed their independent experiences flying during the Mexican Revolution on different sides. Both Masson and Parsons flew the single rickety machine owned by their respective employers. In Ted's case it was a Curtiss biplane ill-suited for combat. Masson got a Martin pusher also built in the United States. While the two exchanged stories the others listened in fascination.

"I was on Pancho Villa's side, but the *guerreros* didn't trust gringos for shit. Villa made a fellow from Martinique named Jeff de Villa fly with me just to keep me in line. I don't know if they were related, but Jeff was a major and I got to be a captain. The first chance I got to get back on our side of the border I resigned, but not before trying to teach a couple of Mexicans to fly," Parsons chuckled heartily at the memory. Masson smiled knowingly as Parsons continued. "They were very brave warriors on the ground. It only took me one flight with one of them to convince both to stick to horses."

"On General Obregon's side, things were very similar." Didier Masson threw in. "I quit for two reasons. First, they never paid me on time, and second, I wouldn't drop bombs on cities. I did try to sink the *Federale's* fleet of three ships with pipe bombs. Boy, did they make big splashes!"

"You sunk ships with bombs?" Genet, the one-time sailor, asked incredulously. "You could have even dropped them on my ship off of Vera Cruz!"

"Not to worry, my young friend. We never hit a thing. The bombs just made big impressive splashes," Masson concluded, looking curiously at Genet.

Jack felt humbled by the fact that so many of them had been in some kind of military service while he was still puttering around at the University of Minnesota and delivering newsprint. Lufbery's incredible adventures, including time in the Philippines in American uniform, made Jack feel all the more insignificant. He kept thinking about the kind of men attracted to the *Service Aéronautique*. Most made no bones about the fact they were out for adventure.

Parsons told them about how his father wouldn't give him money for the passage. Another father-son conflict, Jack noted. Edwin worked his way over on a horse transport. Having heard the stories from the men on the *Carpathia* during his own crossing, Jack could imagine the horrors of that trip. When Parsons named the ship he'd bummed passage on as a phony veterinarian, Jack laughed long and hard.

Charlie Keeler felt some of the same insecurity that plagued Jack. He respected the experiences of others, but realized that the past was just that—passed. Even the most experienced of pre-war pilots like Lufbery's Marc Pourpe bought the farm. Charlie remembered the senior non-coms in the Legion telling him how much a fit and energetic leader made up for all the experience in the world. Charlie found himself feeling protective of little Genet, one of the few men in the escadrille younger than him. With people looking up to him and counting on him for guidance and leadership, Keeler didn't allow himself the luxury of self-doubt.

The day after Parsons signed in, orders arrived to move to another field at a place called Ravenel near the town of Saint-Just en Chaussée. Word was that they were to lay low in preparation for a big offensive. Looking at the map, the men verified Ravenel's location about thirty miles nearer to Paris than they were at Cachy. Visions of sorties to the capital during whatever "laying low" might mean excited both the old hands and the newcomers.

They were in for a big surprise.

Part Eight

Purest Spirit of Sacrifice

"The American Escadrille...during very heavy combat with heavy losses...has gained the deepest admiration of its leaders and its fellow French escadrilles...."

Pétain, Maréchal des Armées

Chapter 55
Misery Shared

Ravenel, St. Just-en-Chaussée, January 26, 1917

Parsons' stories of his Mexican adventures had the men laughing all the way into the next day. Laughter, however, soon died out. Whereas the luxury of Luxeuil made Cachy seem close to hell, Cachy looked like heaven to the first arrivals at Ravenel.

Thénault sent Sergent Bley to Ravenel, the small village east of Saint Just, with a quartering party. Their field was supposed to be between the two towns. Louis Bley took Sampson, the cook; Lucien Capouillet, their supply sergeant; and Emil Marshall, the American clerk. They arrived in three vehicles the French called *tracteurs,* though they were nothing more than small Renault trucks with towing pintles. On the trailers were an entire kitchen and a *bac souple*, a rubberized canvas bag filled with fuel for the Nieuports.

Leaving the main road at Saint Just-en-Chaussée, they headed to Ravenel about two miles to the east. Cachy had had several wooden framed buildings and a large number of tents to shelter the men in the muddy field. The field outside the tiny village of Ravenel had only the mud.

They did find dugouts, apparently excavated for their use as bomb shelters. The grassy strip looked untouched except for recent ruts of a Nieuport's landing gear. Bley checked the map just to make sure he wasn't in the wrong place. No one from *Groupe 13* waited to greet them. A single stone building stood at one end of the strip. They pulled up there hoping to find someone to verify that they were supposed to be there; convinced any fool could see that this place couldn't handle an escadrille let alone five. The building was empty, but a sign read: *Réserver au Quartier Général du Groupe 13.*

"Naturellement," Bley muttered to Marshall.

Sampson stomped about muttering *"Mon Dieu, mon Dieu, quelle bêtise, quelle connerie*!" He preferred the warm kitchens of a Parisian hotel to any primitive setting, though he had adapted well enough to the building at Cachy. Here he envisioned weeks before they could erect a proper building. A cold rain added to his frustration.

Bley sent Capouillet to position the fuel bladder on the far side of the field. At least they could refuel the arriving aircraft. He then took Marshall on a reconnaissance of the woods, leaving the sputtering chef, Sampson. Their trek confirmed that the ground was soft and saturated under a thin crust of frosty soil. Snagged branches of dead trees impeded movement on foot and would need to be cleared to allow a vehicle through. While Bley digested this unfavorable information they heard the first of the Nieuports circling the field, checking the wind. That would be Lufbery though he wished it were one of the lieutenants. They might not know any better than him what to do, but any decisions they made would take the heat off him.

Lufbery made a very low pass of the field to check the surface. Satisfied, he circled once and set up for an approach into the wind. Bley, watching from the ground, wondered about the weather at Cachy. If it was raining here, the ceiling had to be pretty low everywhere. He had visions of escadrille airplanes scattered all over the region, and secretly hoped for just that. He dreaded the wailing and gnashing of teeth he knew the pilots would raise when they arrived at this godforsaken place.

As the day progressed, the remaining available Nieuports from N. 124 landed at roughly fifteen-minute intervals. Enormous confusion arose on where to park the eleven machines, leading Lufbery to declare the affair a first class goat screw. Fortunately, no other escadrilles would arrive that day or the chaos would have been absolute.

Sampson, fortified by his stock of 'cooking wine,' had achieved that state called 'three sheets to the wind.' Nevertheless, he had prepared dozens of sandwiches of ham and butter or Camembert spread on split baguettes. These tasty morsels were the only bright spot as the rain turned to snow.

Compounding their misery, N. 124, like other French escadrilles, had very few tents and none of the large Bessaneau hangar tents. The Army Corps supplied most canvas in the area where they were located. This detail had been overlooked when the headquarters sent N. 124 to what looked like a great location on the map.

Georges Thénault entrusted the move to Lieutenant de Laage. This usually resourceful officer arrived by vehicle in mid-afternoon to discover the bewildering mess that was Ravenel. He set off immediately for the Supply and Transport Regiment to try to eke out support personnel to move some old Bessaneau hangars from Cachy. He found the regiment's command post had moved. Apparently, a German counter offensive had achieved enough of a penetration to cause the entire Corps to move. De Laage would get no assistance from them.

Passing back through Saint Just, a town with its own railroad siding, de Laage decided to take a closer look at Ravenel a little further to the east. The sleepy village consisted of a small collection of buildings typical of the region. None showed any effects of the war, though not a soul walked the cobbled streets, and all the shutters were fastened shut. De Laage spied a long trailer laden with sawn planks. Supposing it a quartermaster load abandoned in the move, the lieutenant decided to at least ask before commandeering the lumber.

When no one responded to his knocks and shouts, he directed his driver to back the truck up to the trailer. Thankful that nearly every vehicle manufactured in France had standard-sized equipment, they hooked up the load and departed.

They pulled up to the field at the same time Thénault stepped out of the Nieuport that he had flown in from Cachy. By then Bley had managed to erect the now rickety prefabricated office they had dragged through four moves for the captain's use. Thénault invited all the officers to share it until better accommodations could be arranged. Thaw and de Laage accepted, but Keeler refused, claiming to like sleeping under the stars as long as no one was shooting at him.

In fact, Charlie still felt like the enlisted man he was at the beginning. Jack too knew the way they would feel if all the officers slept high and dry while the rest fended for themselves.

"I'll stick with my little lean-to captain." Jack said, trying not to sound sanctimonious.

The rain stopped suddenly and just as suddenly the temperature plummeted. In a wink of the eye tree branches bare of leaves were coated with a thin layer of glistening ice. Thénault decided to fly back to Cachy to see what he could work out with Féquant. He was sure the Commandant would send at least one of the hangar tents once he realized the conditions at Ravenel.

It had been a futile hope. Even were Féquant able to provide the additional support—which he wasn't—he had five escadrilles and a growing panic at Army headquarters as the German offensive took shape. He sent only encouragement and permission to scour the region for whatever they might need—a provident ruling in light of de Laage's lumber heist.

Meanwhile snow began to fall like a white curtain lowering, extinguishing the last light of day. Keeler and Buck huddled together under Jack's waterproof cover, a gift from his cousin Annette. Neither felt like sleeping. Both were chilled to the bone from standing around with nothing to do for hours after arriving. They began to commiserate.

"Jack. I'm not saying all your philosophizing is a bunch of hooey, and I'm not saying that it isn't, but what do you make of this balls-up of a day?" Charlie said pulling a blanket around his broad shoulders.

"What's to say? It's not the first time the captain let us down, and I doubt if it will be the last."

"I don't blame Thénault. I was up at Féquant's headquarters when old Georges showed up to ask for help. I've never seen him that way. He didn't yell or carry on, but he gave the Commandant what for all the same. You know how I respect Féquant. I waited to see if he would ream the captain. Instead, he apologized. 'Give me a few days,' he said. 'I'll get something out of the old man,' he said. I think he was referring to the division commander. Have you ever seen him? I mean up close?"

"Féquant?"

"No, you dope, the division commander."

"Why the division? I thought we belonged to the Army Corps, not the division," Jack replied.

"Guiscard, the Brigadier, owns this piece of ground as well as Cachy. His is a reserve division. Rear area troops. Mostly men too old to serve in the trenches. Guiscard must be sixty-five. I heard he squeaks when he walks. Something about an articulated wooden leg, but appropriate all the same."

"Because he's tight?"

"Like a drum. Corps tolerates him because he doesn't ask for anything. Why should he when his division lives off the land? Anyway, Féquant can't get normal supplies because Guiscard won't issue them except to frontline regiments. Most of the things he hoards are useless in the trenches—tents, cots, and the like. I was thinking that it sounded an awful lot like your theory about paternal difficulties."

"You're pulling my leg, Charlie. You never paid much attention to that stuff before," Jack said scrunching down in Victor Chapman's sleeping bag.

"Think about it, Jack. Say Guiscard is old man Prince or Thaw or Chapman or any one of them. He's got more money than Croesus but refuses to let his wayward sons—we aviators—get any more than peanuts. It's his way of controlling us."

"When did you dream that up, Charlie?" Jack said, slowly digesting his friend's interpretation of the classic father-son conflict. "You know, it almost works too if you look at the blokes in the front lines as Guiscard's favorite sons." Jack stopped and lit up a cigarette. He'd avoided drinking, but he didn't see any harm in indulging in that other adult vice, tobacco, especially since Larry had sent him the *Lucky Strikes.*

"Suppose we turned the war over to all the fathers—the old ones, you know, not guys like you, Charlie—and grandfathers. I mean it's their generation on both sides that started this in the first place. Why not let all us youngsters go home and let the old fogies sort it out?"

"Wouldn't last a fortnight in the trenches," Charlie said, shivering as he tried to imagine his father in uniform. "It's a funny picture, though. Sort of like the idea of letting the outcome be decided with a hand of cards. Never happen, though. Too much blood and too much pride at stake." He stopped and waited for a response.

"Is that bag warm, Jack? Maybe I'll get Michelle to send me one." Not hearing anything, he realized that Jack must be asleep. He took the cigarette out of Jack's hand and flicked it into the thin layer of snow in front of them. Charlie watched it go out and then stared straight ahead into the darkness for several long minutes until the darkness gave way to oblivion.

In just under two weeks the men of the Lafayette Escadrille turned the miserable patch of woods into a small city of dugouts, ramshackle tarpapered shacks, tents of every imaginable shape, and a burgeoning network of duckboard sidewalks. Féquant's tacit approval resulted in some imaginative scrounging that accounted for the conglomeration.

When others arrived, the French pilots envied the Americans their makeshift shelters. Sampson delighted in serving hot meals to the other escadrilles from his new kitchen fashioned from de Laage's planks. While far from cozy, Ravenel was already an operational aérodrome even if snow, fog and rain precluded full combat operations.

DURING THE FIGHTING IN LATE DECEMBER 1916 THE GERMANS PUSHED WEST against the lines astride the Somme River after British General Haig's offensive had lost steam. Now the Kaiser drove his forces hard in the hopes of splitting the British and French. Only the bitter winter kept him from achieving his goal. By then the end of the Battle of Verdun freed up large numbers of French regiments which poured north to stem the German advance. The lines stabilized in January

1917. The Germans consolidated their gains and the Allies seemed content in the age-old tradition of armies to suspend some operations for the winter.

Opposite Ravenel, on the German side of the lines just out of the long range French and British artillery, Jasta 6 hunkered down at Eppeville on a field not unlike the one the Lafayette Escadrille now occupied. Jasta 6 was one of four squadrons that formed the main group opposing the French *Groupe de Combat 13*. Hauptmann Oskar Waldrep, Georges Thénault's German counterpart, commanded twelve of the new highly maneuverable Fokker DR-1 triplanes. He counted three aces under his orders; men who had achieved the ten victories the Germans required for this distinction.

Waldrep had flown under Oswald Boelcke's command for a year before rising to captain and getting his own squadron. Boelcke had taught him respect for their opponents and a certain restraint that saved lives while, ironically, running up the score of victories. Too many glory hounds, Boelcke would tell them, raced headlong into a fight because they had superior numbers. Numbers alone, he insisted, were not enough to insure success. In fact, the young major pointed out, numbers often work against you in aerial combat unless efforts are carefully coordinated.

Bringing these and other lessons to J6, Waldrep had spent the hectic autumn months honing tactics. He hoped his flight leaders had the necessary vision and imagination to picture three dimensional ambushes, long range decoys, use of cloud and sun to cover flight elements, and a variety of other techniques he wanted to try. J6 wasn't yet a flashy, newsworthy squadron like the ones of the Flying Circus. It had no dazzling heroes of the Fatherland like the rising star, young Baron Manfred Von Richthofen, Boelcke's other protégé. Yet, Waldrep believed in himself and in his men. He didn't suspect that one of his officers failed to share this conviction.

Lieutenant Johann Keller, aged twenty-three, plowed his Fokker into the soft wet grass cursing the captain's choice of landing fields once again. *How could the man be so thick?* Keller wondered. It amazed him that the great Boelcke would recommend such a sheepherder for *Hauptmann* let alone command of a Jasta.

Keller came from a long line of Prussian officers all of whom served in the cavalry. His transition to aviation was easy though under curious circumstances. In less than ten months as a flyer he had carefully built a reputation as a formidable ace.

Keller disliked what he saw as Waldrep's lock-step application of Boelcke's tactics. To him it smacked of drill field maneuvers—blind repetition of rote commands and movements. These had their place in parades, but not in the fluid field of aerial fighting. Even though he didn't care a wit for tactics, Johann Keller enjoyed the superior feeling of knowing he was better than his captain in most every respect. Keller was a master of self-deceit.

Waldrep also earned Keller's disdain for being an infantry officer who had risen from the ranks. While the captain flew as well as any in the squadron, Keller thought he lacked initiative and acted naive. Waldrep's six victories all came under Boelcke's supervision. Keller dismissed them out of hand. His personal tally was impressive, if contrived. He *had* shot down—or at least shot *at*—two enemy aircraft, though his official count was 12. Keller had convinced himself that the ten others, 'victories' he'd manufactured without ever getting close enough to an enemy to cause or receive harm, were valid.

Keller faulted the handsome blond officer for his lack of pedigree as well. Waldrep came from a burg in Bavaria named Bad Windsheim. His forebears were farmers. Waldrep's possession of a degree from the University of Munich mattered little to Keller.

Keller thought himself to be attractive to the ladies in a very masculine sense. His rugged features were marred by a deep furrow that ran from his forehead to the corner of his mouth, a scar given him by a Cuirassier's saber after the Battle of the Marne. He considered the scar a badge of courage, but had to admit that looking at it took some getting used to, even for other men.

How he'd earned the scar didn't matter as long as his countrymen believed he had killed the French colonel as he had claimed. Keller's facile memory enabled him to believe even the most preposterous of the claims he made. In the event, the colonel, a wounded prisoner, had seized his saber back and slashed the irksome German lieutenant guarding him before making a remarkable escape on horseback. Such facts would do little to enhance Keller's image. *Toussaint*, a dying French NCO had called the colonel. *Vive Toussaint!* He'd managed to shout before he died. Keller silently thanked the colonel for sparing his life and earning him his first Iron Cross as well as the wound stripe.

Coasting to a rough stop, Keller barked an order at one of the enlisted crew. *Have to keep them on their toes.* He hoped for the captain to go down in combat. As the senior lieutenant in the Jasta, he would surely take over, a prospect he both coveted and dreaded. It would make it easier for him to cultivate his reputation. Avoiding danger would be a challenge. He only had to maintain the ruse until he could rise into a General Staff position where his uncle could more effectively manage his career. Keller hated flying, though he had mastered it out of necessity. It had served his purposes well.

BOTH THE LAFAYETTE ESCADRILLE AND WALDREP'S JASTA 6 had moved at about the same time. Uncannily, both moves were onto unprepared fields where foot, vehicle and aircraft traffic rapidly turned grass or plowed fields into viscous mud. Freezing temperatures at night solidified the soil into ridges that could puncture tires. Iced over puddles on the fields made movement, even by foot, challenging. Both sides devised ways to drag heavy timbers over the landing areas to smooth the ground out enough for takeoffs and landings. Tons of straw scattered every day absorbed some of the moisture, but the cycle of freezing and thawing exhausted efforts to combat the muck.

At Cachy the Lafayette men had learned to roll with the punches the cruel environment landed, but Ravenel sapped their strength and morale, sucking at it much like the mud pulled at their boots. Had they known that their German opponents were warm and comfortable in commandeered French buildings, they would have been even more outraged at their plight.

Their only escape was to fly the rare mission the weather grudgingly permitted. Then the mud and dampness could be temporarily left behind. Even in the air, however, nature exacted her toll. Every hour in the freezing blast of cold air was an endurance challenge. Men's limbs stiffened. Reactions slowed. When they did find an enemy the ensuing engagement seemed to play out in slow motion. Both opponents were almost as lethargic as a housefly slowed by the cold.

Many days the temperature dipped well below freezing, frustrating the mechanics' efforts to keep engine oil from congealing. Combined with the abhorrent conditions of the field, these cold snaps all but brought flight operations to a standstill. Since N. 124's general mission was to lay low in anticipation of an upcoming offensive, this idleness suited the higher command, if not the American pilots.

Just the same, like soldiers in every army throughout history, they found ways to pass the time. Cards appeared at every opportunity. Bridge actually supplanted poker in popularity. Bets could still be laid on the games, but the stakes didn't deplete an individual's funds as quickly as poker, and careful pairing insured that partners won almost as often as they lost.

Bridge, many found, challenged them to concentrate and made the time pass more quickly. Bert Hall, one of the best players, never wanted for a partner before he left. Now Lufbery seemed to hold the title of bridgemaster. When he paired with Charlie Keeler, the two were nearly unbeatable. Jack was still learning the game, but doing well enough at bidding to be eagerly accepted as a partner by more experienced players.

Chess also kept them busy. At least twenty sets existed in N. 124, many with hand carved pieces in rare woods or ivory. Jack was amazed at how well the polyglot group played these sophisticated games. Many of the mechanics played both bridge and chess. Minor tournaments helped break the boredom. Many missed the billiards table back at Luxeuil, evoking a distant nostalgic memory of better times with friendly old faces like Kiffin Rockwell and Victor Chapman bent over the table sighting down a cue stick.

In Jasta 6 the games were nearly identical. Had the two units realized this, someone might have tried to organize a tournament in lieu of aerial combat. Charlie laughed when he imagined it. "Winner take all. Best of three games, your best man against ours." How much more civilized it would be to resolve the current war over cards or chessboards.

Chapter 56
A Good Stiff Lip for the Old Pal's Sake

Ravenel, St. Just-en-Chaussée, February 1917

Days of inactivity set many to conjecturing openly about their eventual fates. As volunteers, the Americans knew they could leave or change their situations more easily than their French counterparts. Escape offered relief if one could bear the shame. Ironically, the very act of volunteering made quitting all the more distasteful. What may have started out as a lark, a thrilling pursuit of adventure, had turned for most of them into a commitment sealed with the blood of fallen friends.

The *cause* paled beside their commitment to the escadrille. Rather than becoming embittered and cynical about the idiocy of the war, they measured themselves against each other. Eliot Cowdin and Red Rumsey left under questionable medical conditions, but they had tried at least to get along. Bert Hall departed under pressure. After he popped up flying in another French escadrille, his old mates shrugged it off. Skipper Pavelka's transfer to Salonika didn't raise an eyebrow since he was still flying in combat. Most were more horrified of letting others down than of injury or death.

Jim McConnell exemplified the devotion most of them felt. He could easily obtain a medical release from the French and honorably return to America to pursue his writing career. Mac wouldn't even begin to entertain such a thought. With examples like him and Nungesser constantly returning to combat in spite of incredible pain and discomfort, how could the healthy men shirk?

The French Army's request for experienced combat pilots to serve as instructors appealed to the restless Didier Masson. Masson, renowned at Cachy for the miracle of the N. 124 popote, found the setback of Ravenel disheartening and injurious to his health. Coming down with a bout of the flu similar to Charlie's, Masson applied for release as soon as he was well enough. He obtained permission to proceed to Avord by the middle of February. Though maintained on the Lafayette roster, Masson would serve at Avord where at least he would be flying every day.

Freddie Prince, a mere three and a half-month veteran of the Lafayette Escadrille, reluctantly succumbed to pressure from his family to become an instructor. He received orders to depart for Pau before the end of February. Prince had made a few friends, but found living in his brother's shadow oppressive. His father's letters were shrill in their demand that he get himself out of the front lines. Freddie spoke to Charlie and Jack separately about his desire to stay, but both of them told him to go if he could. Jack was most sympathetic.

"I've been sort of studying the way some guys get along with their families. You know Chapman had some of the same friction with his dad that Nimmie had with yours. In a way I think they both stuck their necks out too far on purpose. Maybe they didn't think it consciously, but I think they needed to impress their fathers so much that only something of epic heroic proportion would do. You are a good pilot, Freddie. There are lots of Americans in the flying schools. Just think how much you could do for them. We'll get others here in no time. Your family's paid a big price already."

Freddie got essentially the same message from Charlie. Keeler pointed out that if the United States entered the war, the Army would need instructors. The crowd of pilots likely to arrive in France would overwhelm the schools. Prince could be the seed money for resolving this inevitable problem. "Besides, somebody will have to run interference with the French," he elaborated, referring to the tangled bureaucracy and language differences that Prince might help to unravel.

In the end, Prince accepted posting to Pau. It was close to his childhood home and it got his family off his back. He still felt like he'd let his friends in the Lafayette Escadrille down, but maybe Charlie was right. Maybe he could make a difference when America entered the war. He personally doubted it would be more than weeks before this occurred.

Charlie and Jack read everything they could get their hands on, passing dime novels and magazines back and forth. When they weren't reading they were writing. "What is it with you Buck?" Charlie would ask good-naturedly. "You never stop writing. I run out of words before getting a half page done."

The dismal conditions and paucity of news from Jennifer reduced Jack to the deepest despair he had ever felt. Though he tried to hide it on the outside, Jack felt sullen and very moody. He began to worry irrationally that Jennifer would succumb to the charms of some flashy patient at the hospital or one of the boulevard *embusqués*. He felt so far away and so unable to influence her. Though his insecurity had little foundation, the combined effects of foul weather and enforced idleness caused his mind to run amuck.

He began to worry that she would lose interest in him. These black thoughts were new and unwelcome. He wrote feverishly. Letters to Jennifer, letters to Paul Rockwell, descriptions of his flights, anything to get his mind off worrying.

Jack began to indulge in flights of nostalgia during the lulls in flying. Great blue lakes sparkling through fragrant pines filled his mind's eye. Imagining arriving at Sugar Lake on Independence Day, one of his family's outings of the year, Jack could almost feel the heat of the Minnesota summer sun. He raced barefoot to the water's edge to splash in the clear water. He grabbed a handful of the creamy foam that the gentle waves pushed up and dropped to his knees to look at the small shells nestled in the sand among the colorful pebbles. Silvery flashes caught his eye—schools of minnows.

Racing to the trap they'd driven out in, he grabbed his cane pole, the can of worms he'd dug behind the house the night before, and called to Larry, his seven-year-old brother. He could taste fried chicken and potato salad, and smell the sunfish they would catch and fry in the big iron skillet over the aromatic open fire.

One night Jack dozed off with these pleasant memories enveloping him, protecting him. Water dripping through the porous roof of the pilot's hut brought him awake and back to the unpleasant reality of Ravenel. For several long moments, Jack wondered why things had to change from those halcyon days. Slowly he shook the childish, maudlin longing, mentally upbraiding himself for his weakness.

At times he thought about the British soldier he had transported more than a year ago. The man, neither young nor old, was terribly wounded. He had gripped Jack's hand and thanked him over and over again. Jack tried to remain detached with all the wounded, but this Englishman's gratitude had moved him.

Some weeks later he happened upon the same soldier while transporting men from an evacuation hospital to another hospital near Paris. On seeing Jack the man called him over. "Give me your name, sir," he begged. "I will endeavor to write you." Jack saw that the man was in a very bad way. He wrote his name and unit on a sheet of paper thinking he would never hear from this man again. Jack was headed for flight school at the time anyway.

At Pau, shortly before going to gunnery training, Jack received a letter posted from Paris. In it he found a poem that he kept carefully folded in a waterproof envelope ever since. He would pull it out when he started feeling sorry for himself or depressed. He pulled it out and read it again now:

THE EVERYDAY OF WAR
(Hospital, Versailles, November, 1915.)

A hand is crippled, a leg is gone,
And fighting's past for me,
The empty hours crawl slowly on;
How they flew where I used to be!
Empty hours in the empty days,
And empty months crawl by,
The brown battalions go their way,
And here at the Base I lie!

I dream of the grasses the dew-drops drench,
And the earth with the soft rain wet,
I dream of the curve of a winding trench,
And a loop-holed parapet;
The sister wraps my bandage again,
Oh, gentle the sister's hand,
But the smart of a restless longing, vain,
She cannot understand.

At night I can see the trench once more,
And the dug-out candle lit,
The shadows it throws on wall and floor
Form and flutter and flit.
Over the trenches the night-shades fall

And the questing bullet pings,
And a brazier glows by the dug-out wall,
Where the bubbling mess-tin sings.

I dream of the long, white, sleepy night
Where the fir-lined roadway runs
Up to the shell-scarred fields of fight
And the loud-voiced earnest guns;
The rolling limber and jolting cart
The khaki-clad platoon,
The eager eye and the stout young heart,
And the silver-sandalled moon.

But here I'm kept to the narrow bed,
A maimed and broken thing --
Never a long day's march ahead
Where brown battalions swing.
But though time drags by like a wounded snake
Where the young life's lure's denied,
A good stiff lip for the old pal's sake,
And the old battalion's pride!

Jack had tried to look up the Tommy twice while in Paris to thank him for the poem and to wish him the best. There was no name signed, and no forwarding address. Every time he read the poem he marveled at the man's pluck and at his continued dedication to his mates and unit. It shamed Jack to think he was whimpering inside like a homesick child when this man could write of 'A good stiff lip for the old pal's sake.' The poem always snapped him out of his funk. He needed company. He needed action. He had to stop brooding.

While Ravenel was supposed to be a place of repose for the group, missions still arrived daily. The front seemed to be weaving like a snake at the end of a handler's stick. With every advance and retreat the squadrons assigned to that sector jumped into action. First against the artillery regulating machines, then the balloons.

N. 124 configured three of their Nieuport 17's to carry the *Le Prieur* rockets used earlier by Norman Prince and Chouteau Johnson. Firing the incendiary pyrotechnics at the ubiquitous German gasbags became the priority mission for Jack's flight. He chose the new pilots to fly cover while Johnson and Hill, recently returned from leave and an appendectomy in the States respectively, mounted the rocket attacks. Soubiran and

Haviland protested that they too should mount rockets. Everyone wanted to get a piece of the balloon busting effort. Downing a balloon was as much an aerial victory as shooting down a German bus, and often more dangerous.

Every time the escadrille shot down an observation airplane it got another citation, for these enemy platforms spelled death to the frontline troops. But airplanes rarely carried the new, excessively heavy, wireless machines that made it possible to adjust fires directly from the air. Balloons did. Both sides also used telephone to link the balloons to the ground. Both protected the crews in the vulnerable baskets with heavy anti-aircraft artillery and regularly scheduled fighter protection.

Whenever a fight loomed, both sides manned their ground crews at double shifts to rapidly reel in the tethered balloons and to keep up steady machine gun and artillery fire to discourage aerial attack. Observers wore parachutes and jumped to safety when threatened. Jack had seen the contraption the French attached to a raised wheel on a truck to speed up bringing down the balloons. He saw right away the danger of the cable jumping the spool and getting tangled in the axle. As for parachutes, Jack saw men jump from the German balloons and wondered why pilots didn't have the same capability.

The Germans called their gasbags *drachen*, German for kite, which they certainly resembled at the end of tethering cables. The word also comes from the Greek for dragon; one of the Harvard sages informed them. It was an appropriate nickname for the balloons that brought so much fire to the battlefield. The French called them *saucisses,* meaning sausages. By the end of 1916, pilots considered attacking balloons high adventure if not suicidal.

Le Prieur rockets were notoriously unreliable. They left their racks in a swooshing flash and streaked into the air on whatever trajectory the launching platform had set. When fired from the stable and unmoving ground, the rockets could be made to fall within several hundred meters of their target. Fired in sufficient numbers this inherent inaccuracy didn't matter. From a flying Nieuport, however, the impact of the rockets was seldom less than a hundred meters from the aim point unless delivered dangerously close to the target.

Johnson's experience with Norman Prince attacking drachens months earlier had been frustrating. He watched incredulously as five of the rockets streaked up and down trailing white smoke on paths nowhere near his aim point. The other three flew true. Though they seemed to pierce the gasbag, they continued unexploded to some unknown destination. Redressing, he fired all his incendiary rounds into his prey with no apparent effect.

Dudley Hill's munitions made no more of an impact than Johnson's during the escadrille's later experiment. The Germans pulled their drachen down intact so fast that their parachute-equipped observers didn't trouble to jump. Evidently, the Germans were not impressed.

Buck came up with the idea of attacking the balloon and the ground crews at the same time. He volunteered his flight to make the hazardous attack on the well-armed artillery. Jack reasoned that the agitated gunners would be so busy protecting the balloons that his fighters might be able to disrupt their fires.

He directed Johnson and Hill to attack in their established manner. He intended to strafe the machine gun emplacements and the artillery batteries at the moment they focused on his aerial team. While this placed the rocketeers at considerable hazard, Jack hoped to overwhelm the defenses with multiple attacks.

Lieutenant de Laage applauded the initiative. He decided to fly the ground attack with Jack, rightly perceiving that it was the more dangerous of the two missions. Most aviators knew that flight below 1,000 feet placed them in what was known as the 'dead man's curve,' a murderous region because of enemy small arms fire. At low altitude engine failure or any other malfunction left little room for recovery.

Happy to get off the dismal field on a mission, Jack literally soared airborne leaving his morbid thoughts and fantasy flights on the ground. He quickly checked his guns while looking about for the other aircraft. Soubiran and Haviland had left first to take up a high patrol looking out for enemy fighters. Johnson's Nieuport preceded Jack's, with Dudley Hill close behind. Buck and de Laage followed, giving the others minutes to climb to attack altitude. The balloon line they were attacking lay close to the Oise River north of Compiègne. It took only minutes to reach the target area.

Jack watched Johnson and Hill split up going for two of the large balloons. No sooner had they arrived than the German artillery began to pepper the sky with black bursts. Nearby balloons began precipitous descents, struggling to get out of the way. Jack saw Chouteau's first rocket flare from under the wing. Tracers arced up in his direction. Hill launched on another balloon, coming up from underneath. Jack worried that Dud would catch a tethering wire, but he had other things to worry about then.

Diving from three thousand feet, he and de Laage aimed their machines at the source of the tracers first. Coming in on them gave Jack the sensation of plunging into a galaxy. Huge balls of fire streamed up at him perilously close. At three hundred feet he pressed the trigger of the Vickers pummeling the ground around the machine gun emplacement quenching their fires. Nearby de Laage worked on the 77-millimeter battery position. Men scattered in every direction.

High above them Hill's rockets found their mark, splashing one of the giant balloons. Johnson zoomed up and away from the conflagration with smoke and ashes lashing his face. Jack made a second pass on the ground emplacements only to receive a handful of rounds in the underbelly of his machine. Alerted now, the defenders kept their stations until the very last minute. Jack's fusillade, combined with that of de Laage, served their purposes, but the guns were soon back in action. Jack found himself wishing for some powerful explosives to drop on the enemy.

Reassured that Hill and Johnson were clear, both de Laage and Buck regained altitude to get out of the fusillade of ground fire. The patrol then returned to Ravenel while Soubiran and Haviland continued their high patrol without seeing anything.

Jack snagged a tire on landing and ground looped to a smashing stop at the tree line; his Nieuport damaged beyond repair. Lufbery brought his machine back with so many holes and broken spars that it too had to be written off. On the bright side, he had scored a double victory. Dud Hill broke his undercarriage on a frozen hillock, narrowly escaping injury when his Nieuport flipped and came to a rest upside down.

Parsons took off on a mission and soon found himself engulfed in a sudden snowstorm. He related the event that night, reestablishing himself as one of their more accomplished storytellers.

"It was eerie. I could see the edge of the cloud, but I was sure I'd pass underneath. I was about to call it a day and head back when I began to feel snow pelting my cheeks. It was like being in a blizzard. I could duck down to get out of the stinging wet, but it was fascinating to watch the snowflakes swirl in the prop wash and speed by me. I thought I could descend easily to get out of it, but when I looked at the altimeter I was horrified to find I was climbing! A glance at the spinning compass needle really shook my bones. I was so discombobulated that I was sure I was a goner. I let go of everything like they taught in the schools, hoping things would settle down. Then I felt the seat belt straining against my churning gut. Was I hanging upside down? I braced myself thinking I'd hit the ground at any minute when I broke out in a patch of glorious blue! Grabbing the controls I wanted to kiss the sun, I was so excited at being out of that maelstrom. Then I realized that I had no idea where I was! Imagine my renewed fear when I tried to recall how long I'd been up there. My mind was still spinning and my stomach upset, but I just pointed the bus west and hoped I ran out of gas before I got to the Channel. Drowning appealed a whole lot less than smashing into the ground. Then I spotted a glimpse of the ground through the wispy clouds and plunged into the hole regardless of where I might be. An unfamiliar field beckoned. Feeling like I was about to foul my pants, I abandoned my fears of being captured in favor of regaining Mother Earth and relieving my straining bladder and bowels. It was Mesnil-St. Georges, of course, and you know the rest."

"A perfect description of my bout in the thunderstorm," Jack observed. "Let that be a lesson to all of you new guys. Let's not make it any easier on the Boches."

As they wrote off Nieuport 17's and a few powerful 27's inherited from French escadrilles, the Lafayette Escadrille began to receive its first Spads. Thénault gave Jack the task of providing qualification instruction for those designated to fly the new machines.

"The Spad VII is easier to fly than a Nieuport because of its stability. One gets the impression of being in a Pullman car after hours in a boxcar. You have to be careful with the throttle," he explained, recalling for them the way he had inadvertently killed the motor at low altitude. "Just remember '*la manette dans la poche,*' and you won't go wrong. Pull that throttle all the way and only ease it back to reduce power. Check the stop on the ground. This 180 horsepower bus is able to reach close to 120 miles per hour at 6,500 feet. Take some time looking at the Hispano-Suiza and notice how much heavier it is than the Gnome and other rotaries. It has eight cylinders arranged in two banks of four in a V. Like a car it has a radiator for cooling. This adds to the weight, but the added displacement gives it the extra power."

"Hey, professor," one of the pilots quipped, "just how heavy is it?"

"1,550 pounds at takeoff with a full fuel and ammunition load and a driver about half your size." Jack answered without missing a beat. He enjoyed this and he clearly knew his stuff.

Normally the new machines went to the leaders first. Thénault ordered the first three to de Laage, Thaw and Buck. He flew fewer missions since they'd joined Group 13, allowing the lieutenants to plan and lead the flights more and more often. Thaw and de Laage regularly recruited Keeler, Buck or Lufbery to take flights of their own. Luf's mounting score clearly marked him as one to follow.

What little formation flying they did in N. 124 was achieved by maintaining a certain view on the aircraft one was following. The structure of the Spad wasn't significantly different from that of the Nieuport other than in the larger vertical stabilizer. Speed differences and climbing differentials disappeared when one pilot flew 'off' another as long as the faster machine compensated for its slower brethren. Some enjoyed the challenge of formation flying, but most thought it to be excessively demanding, dangerous, and largely pointless. Fortunately for them, unlike the British, the French Army agreed about this when it came to *chasse* machines—what the men called *battle aircraft*.

One of the few attractions of Ravenel laid waiting in the brush and undergrowth surrounding the field in small uncultivated copses of trees. Early one morning Robert Soubiran took one of the Browning shotguns and set off to see what he might bag to supplement their larder. Soubiran easily passed for a French poilu both in appearance and habit as well as language. He returned from his first expedition with three rabbits swinging from his leather belt swearing he would bring in some of the delicious looking deer on his next trip.

"Monsieur must take care," Sampson said in one of his more sober moments. "If you shoot so many holes in these poor animals, Sampson will only be able to produce a lead laden stew. Mind you the local gendarmes as well," he added, shaking a fat finger.

"Whatever for?" Soubiran answered. "Have they nothing better to do in this war than to chase poachers?"

"*Je ne sais rien*," Sampson answered with a Gallic shrug and a wagging finger.

The next day Soubiran again sortied at dawn armed with slugs for the Browning shotgun aiming to fell a deer or two. At just before eight when the first mission was getting off in the late-lifting fog, a clatter in the recently finished barracks woke the remaining men. Two local gendarmes, their blue uniforms covered with brambles, stood in the doorway stopped only by Lufbery in his underwear. Luf, never overly fond of authorities, even these old men in the quasi-military gendarmerie, let them know that they were disturbing the rest of some very tired pilots.

"We chased a man back this way who had been shooting in the woods…" the shorter of the wizened old gendarmes wheezed, still out of breath. "I think he came into your building, monsieur."

"Fuck your chase," Lufbery said in French. "Do you not see the sleeping pilots? Get the hell out of here or the shooting you hear will be directed at your fat old asses."

The gendarmes looked over his shoulder and shook their heads, but they made no move to try to enter the barracks. Soon they turned and left more or less quietly. In a few minutes the remaining pilots sat up laughing and cheering Lufbery's insolence.

One blanket remained in place on a cot at the end of the room. Soubiran's. Lufbery shuffled down there. He ripped the blanket away and looked at the fully clothed Soubiran and the long Browning the American tried to tuck back under the blanket.

"Ah, ze flics had reason!" Lufbery shouted. "Zees sonufabeech should be arrested, *n'est-ce pas*? Should we call dem back?" Luf's feigned anger dissipated as his mouth curled into an involuntary smile at Soubiran's discomfiture. Soon he asked if there would be venison for dinner or not.

Bobby Soubiran was already pushing thirty. Seeing him hiding under the covers like a schoolboy brought great mirth to the assembly and made for even greater stories at dinner that night—rabbit, not venison.

Haviland observed that Jack had changed from the green, young wide-eyed boy he remembered in Flandin's parlor so long ago. Where he had been a lanky sinewy raw-boned towhead, he was now more filled out, more muscular. Maybe it was the uniform. Jack's youthful enthusiasm hadn't abated much, but Willis noticed Buck brooding by himself more and more. His face looked careworn.

Everyone told Haviland he was their Beau Brummell, a lady-killer, a man with his choice of *les jeunes filles*. These comments flattered him, but still left him a touch envious of the two younger men, Keeler and Buck.

Willis had many opportunities to marry. Isabelle Flandin attracted him, though she was now engaged to Keeler's brother-in-law, the English captain. If he had run into a blond as attractive as Jennifer or a redheaded beauty like Michelle Keeler, he might have taken the plunge. To date he'd found women to be pretty or bright, seldom both.

Willis didn't know Buck or Keeler as well as Parsons, Bobby Soubiran and Freddie Prince, all of whom had been in the flight schools with him. The fact that his fellow Minnesotan was now an officer also contributed to Haviland's changed perception of Buck. Listening to either Charlie or Jack briefing a flight mission was humbling.

During his short stint in the Navy, Willis Haviland developed an innate respect for good leaders. Having rank didn't automatically confer leadership talent. He'd seen some lousy officers. He had trouble adjusting to the casual informality between the officers and the men. It was more like a fraternity house than a military organization. It wasn't that he wanted to change anything, but he found it difficult even chatting with the officers. These guys were responsible for sending and leading men into combat. Though Thaw, Keeler and Buck maintained no airs and all three chummed around easily with the rest of the men, Haviland still kept a respectful distance.

For his part, Jack wanted to get to know Willis better. He couldn't understand why the man seemed to hold back. "Charlie," he asked one night before they turned in, "do you ever get the feeling that some of the new guys are, well, *distant*? I mean, I don't know how to describe it."

"You mean Havvy, don't you?"

"Yeah, but Bobby Soubiran too, and the guys just coming in. Are we pariahs now that we are officers? It doesn't make sense in this outfit. Look at the way everyone loves Bill Thaw. Do you thing I'm acting hoity-toity?"

Laughing, Charlie Keeler poked Jack in the side before putting his arm around his shoulder. "Hoity-toity?" Charlie chuckled out loud at hearing one of his father's expressions. "Not a chance, Bucko. You do get a little intense and didactic at times, but you haven't got a conceited bone in your body."

"Didactic? God, aren't you the one to talk? And intense too, huh?" Buck looked surprised and confused by what Keeler found so funny. "But, seriously, how are we supposed to act? Look at Thénault and de Laage. Nobody gets too familiar with them."

"Not since Cowdin left and Prince died, anyway. I've got my own theory on this. We—you and I anyway—are officers in name only. Sure, we rate salutes and we can give orders, but no one actually expects us to *really* lead anything bigger than a flight of three to six planes. We did that as sergeants. What difference is there now? I think the rank is more honorary and an incentive to others, at least in this unit. The trouble is the new guys don't know this. They have been taught to respect officers and follow orders. In the Legion officers were gods. One could get shot for disobeying even the lowliest Lieutenant."

"Before the poor son of a bitch got killed, you mean. This definitely isn't the Legion, Charlie." They had talked about this several times before in trying to teach each other how to act once they had become lieutenants. Thaw told them not to take their ranks too seriously. He was so casual about his own stature that even the new men got on with him right away. Something about Bill Thaw said 'one of the guys.' He led his share of patrols and took part in teaching the newcomers, but he remained 'Bill' or 'Old Bill' to everyone.

Jack looked to de Laage for a model to emulate. Bill was Bill. Alfred de Laage de Meux was a thoroughbred. He didn't even have to try to lead to get men to listen to him. He was a natural leader and an inspiration. Whenever a group of them started bitching about something all de Laage had to do was show up to make them feel guilty for their lack of dedication. Jack saw the same characteristic in Charlie Keeler. Charlie told him that, before he realized Charlie was married, Major Parker suggested he should apply for West Point. He'd said Charlie could finish college that way and continue flying afterwards.

Of the original members of N. 124, three were dead, one still hospitalized, two invalided out, and two transferred. Jimmy McConnell had so much trouble with his back that he had spent almost as much time in the hospital as he had in the field with the unit. He still had to be helped up and into his cockpit. Johnson and Lufbery were Adjudants, the most senior enlisted rank. So were Dudley Hill and Didier Masson. Most of the rest were sergeants except for the latest arrivals.

Lufbery, older and more experienced in life, was in a class by himself. No one really knew Luf, though many claimed he was their best friend. Masson too stood out for his maturity and rich past. Like Lufbery, though, he made little effort to influence others or make decisions. Now he and Freddie Prince were leaving.

The shortest month of the year seemed to drag on forever. It was hard on morale, but after Lufbery's double victory, Féquant put the American in for France's highest honor. Though only an adjudant, Lufbery's proven skill warranted recognition. In record time the coveted award came back through channels approved. Féquant came down to N. 124 on Friday, February 23.

Féquant found the men huddled around a glowing stove banging their hands together and wondering why the captain had ordered them all to gather. The lieutenants snapped to attention on seeing Féquant and tried to get the milling body of men to do the same with hilarious results. Any semblance of order or standing in ranks could only be achieved when someone lined them up for a photograph. Soubiran, never caught without a weapon or a camera, rose to the occasion. He triggered his flash. Instantly the men lined up facing his camera. Realizing Féquant's presence and seeing the officers at attention, some of veterans put on their hats and stiffed in Legion manner. Slowly the rest of the Americans stopped fidgeting and assumed some degree of military posture. Someone stopped the gramophone in the middle of *Pretty Baby.*

Féquant smiled at the whole circus-like affair. He wasn't one for pomp and circumstance in the combat zone of advance. The Americans did their job in the air. That's what mattered to him. If he started picking nits now he would likely destroy one of his best escadrilles.

He put them at ease before announcing his reason for coming. "Normally, these things take months to get through our tangled bureaucracy," he said in French. "Somehow this award arrived in days with instructions to me to award it immediately. I am to dispense with the usual *prise d'armes*, much to your collective disappointment, I'm sure." This brought chuckles.

There were so many ceremonies in flight school that one had only to utter *prise d'armes* to get a line started at the dispensary.

Thénault called them to attention and read the order awarding Lufbery the *Légion d'Honneur* along with the citation extolling his bravery and skill in bringing down two German aircraft in one combat. Lufbery stood dutifully, his face expressionless, as Féquant draped the red ribbon over his head. The simple medal dangling neatly on Luf's chest was that of *chevalier*, the first grade of the Legion of Honor. In addition to the Military Medal he'd earned earlier, he had seven palms on his *Croix de Guerre* making him the top ace in N. 124. Lufbery didn't even flinch when Féquant placed his hands on his shoulders and proceeded to kiss him first on the right and then on the left cheek. This brought some snickers from the ranks followed by uproarious applause.

The men crowded around Lufbery, slapping his back and shaking his hand. He smiled throughout this, turning to hug Keeler when Charlie, the only other living American in N. 124 to hold the Legion of Honor, came up saying something about them now being brothers with Rockwell and Norman Prince.

The ceremony occasioned a *pot.* Champagne appeared, apparently provided by the Group. Féquant's orders said nothing about limiting the celebration after the award. He drew his saber—he'd arrived in full officer's dress uniform—and neatly decapitated the first bottle with a sharp glancing blow, revealing considerable expertise at the task. Soon corks popped everywhere. If the award didn't boost morale, the champagne sure would.

After Féquant's short speech praising the Americans, the entire body of men cheered in one voice: "*Vive l'Amérique, Vive la France, Vive Féquant.*" He was impressed. Later he would playfully ask Thénault how he could get them to cheer in unison when he couldn't get any two of them to wear the same uniform.

Before the end of February, two replacements arrived to fill the holes left by Masson and Freddie Prince. In addition to Dud Hill, Smiler Genet, Ted Parsons, Willis Haviland, Bobby Soubiran, and Ron Hoskier, the Lafayette Escadrille roster now had five officers and fourteen enlisted pilots. Stephen Sohier Bigelow and Walter Lovell became American volunteer numbers 24 and 25.

Bigelow had been in the schools with Genet, Parsons and Hoskier, but he went to a different French escadrille before gaining a slot in the Lafayette. Stephen, an alumnus of Harvard like Norman Prince, had tasted military life in the United States. Similar to McConnell, who had served as a lieutenant in the National Guard, Bigelow went through officer training at Plattsburg in New York. Lured by the articles he read in newspapers and magazines, he quit reserve officer training and sailed for France to enlist in the Foreign Legion in the hopes of getting to fly.

On one of the few flying days of February the tall slender youth from Massachusetts plowed into the mud at Ravenel and demolished yet another of the escadrille's Nieuports. It was Monday, February 26, the same day Walter Lovell signed in.

Jack knew Lovell from his time in SSU 2. Walt also came from Massachusetts. Jack could always detect the Massachusetts guys from the funny way they talked. It amused him that Americans could speak with such a refined almost British air. Lovell had done well in the Ambulance Service, winning a *Croix de Guerre*. Jack thought Walter was a lot like Jimmy McConnell. They were about the same age. Both were solidly built, and both would give you the shirt off their back. He was delighted to find out Lovell was joining them.

Now that Bill Thaw had joined de Laage and Thénault in the recruiting effort, the men had more say on those they knew or knew about. One exception was a fellow known to several of them including Thaw. He was doing everything he could to get into N. 124. His tortuous path derived from his relatively advanced age—41. In spite of French efforts to discourage him or fail him in training, Edward Hinkle persevered.

When Thaw learned Hinkle was available, he petitioned Dr. Gros to intervene with the French to obtain an exception on the age ceiling of twenty-eight years-old set for combat pilots. Hinkle had attended the schools with most of the later replacements including Genet. All spoke highly of him.

This wasn't the case with another Lafayette Escadrille candidate, Thomas Hewitt. Genet remembered "Jerry" Hewitt smashing up plane after plane at Pau in spite of excellent marks on aerial maneuvers. When asked if anyone knew Hewitt, several responded neutrally, not wanting to hurt the man's chances. Smiler kept his own counsel as well, though he would regret it later.

The demand for troops on the Russian front caused the Germans to slowly withdraw behind what would be called the Hindenburg Line as February 1917 dripped and froze its way into history. N. 124 had logged fewer than fifty hours flying and only ten combats. Along with Lufbery's double victory they could only count Hill's balloon at the cost of five destroyed Nieuports—all from accidents. Two men had left and two came in. No one mourned the passing of February.

JASTA 6 FINISHED FEBRUARY WITH EVEN FEWER AERIAL COMBATS and only one victory—a French biplace credited to their commander. In spite of tight censorship and very limited mail, Jasta 6 occasionally received copies of *Le Figaro* or *Le Monde* taken from captured French soldiers or sent by relatives in neutral countries. When they got the weekend edition from the end of February, some of the officers pounced on the article about the American pilot receiving France's highest honor. Lufbery was no stranger to the frontline pilots. Just as the French knew about Immelmann, Boelcke, and the rising ace, Richthofen, German pilots knew about their more accomplished adversaries.

Keeler and Lufbery made the news more than once. While it wasn't clear that they were in the same squadron, the Germans knew they were American volunteers. N. 124 was well known as the single American escadrille. The fuss about its name had made headlines in the German press. Waldrep, who could read French, put the facts and dates together and determined that the famous *Lafayette Escadrille* was indeed the unit opposite them on a field somewhere near Saint Just-en Chaussée. It was good to put a face or name on the enemy, he reasoned. At their daily mission briefing March 1, he announced his conclusion that the two machines from a sister Jasta shot down on the same day in February were the same ones for which Lufbery was awarded the Legion of Honor.

"It is only reasonable to assume that this Lufbery is one of the Lafayette Escadrille men and that his squadron is our main opponent." When he made this statement he saw a flicker of disbelief on Lieutenant Keller's face. Maybe it was more than just disbelief? Keller had been acting strangely around him, almost as if he didn't want to be close to the captain for some reason.

No one asked questions. Waldrep went on to explain that they should try to identify the American planes and see if there were distinguishing characteristics either in how they looked or fought.

"I am sure the Fatherland will reward any who brings down an American. It is looking like the Americans will join the British and French soon. Let's get a head start on knocking them down."

This challenge inspired Keller. He might be able to escape the cold and hasten his elevation to the general staff if he could claim a victory over an American. He thought back to his time in the trenches after recovering from the saber wound that made him a minor hero. It had been wet and cold like this most of the time. Keller winced whenever he remembered the patrol he had lost early in 1915. He had been lucky to survive and keep his commission after that fiasco. Thank goodness for his uncle on the

General Staff. Keller relived that night frequently even though he tried to suppress the memory.

They had been in the lines for two days when guards brought a deserter from one of the Legion regiments to the company command post in the early morning hours. The man, speaking in accented German, said he wanted to show his commitment to the German cause by leading them to the French patrol that he'd abandoned. He promised them the American volunteer leading the patrol.

Keller, motivated by a deep hatred of anything American, volunteered to lead an ambush patrol. He was not thinking heroics but easy fame. With the deserter along as insurance, he hoped to trap the French as they tried to exit. Keller kept a loaded Luger pointed at the scum who called himself Rejik.

On their way through the wire they encountered one of the French soldiers, alive but immobile with a trench knife stuck in his neck. Keller rolled the man over and pulled the pin on one of their potato masher grenades, positioning it so that if the man moved or was moved he'd be blown to bits. Working quickly they then set up where Rejik told them the French patrol would come out.

According to Rejik, his patrol's mission was to find the seam between two German units. Their penetration point was very near such a boundary. If the deserter was right, the Germans would easily round up the patrol and perhaps capture some of them alive. Keller drooled at the prospect of capturing an American.

Keller and his men were startled when a figure popped out of the wire a good ten yards away. They didn't have time to reorient their weapons before the madman cut them to pieces. Since Keller had his pistol on Rejik, the man's body was between him and the crazy French soldier. The bullet that killed Rejik went right through his body and lodged in Keller's shoulder. Though not seriously hurt, Keller decided to play dead in case the wild killer decided to come over and finish them off.

When Keller dragged himself back to his lines his commander charged him with dereliction of duty, threatening to shoot him himself for losing an entire patrol and coming back with just a little hole in his shoulder. There had been talk of a court martial. Only the intervention of his other uncle saved him. After dressing his minor wound, Keller was quietly shipped off to flight training.

Much later, on seeing the news of American volunteers with the French, Keller began to fantasize that he might run into the madman who so nearly ended his career and his life. Keller knew he was becoming obsessed with a highly unlikely coincidence. In fact, his usually dormant conscience fed his fears.

Once Keller got into a combat flight unit he found it surprisingly easy to obtain credit for kills. As a Prussian officer his word was never questioned. He always provided enough evidence to make his claims plausible.

Keller usually worked by himself to avoid witnesses. All he had to do was hold back and watch a fight in progress. Often a French or English pilot would kill one of the Germans before being crippled and turning for safety. Keller would then follow at a safe distance, fire off all his ammunition blindly and then return to claim the victory. In Jasta 6 he was considered a miracle man. How he could come back from such hot combat with no holes in his plane baffled and impressed the other pilots.

Keller envied Waldrep because the man was a bona fide hero. Keller was thankful the man was gullible enough to swallow most of his phony claims. Waldrep gave no indication of suspecting his lieutenant of anything nefarious—or so Keller thought.

Keller's fellow pilots had no reason to doubt his claims at first. He'd come to Jasta 6 with eight victories credited in other units. His four in Jasta 6 had all taken place on lone missions. The captain allowed Keller to fly alone because of the reputation he'd brought to the unit. After all, the lieutenant wore the Iron Cross for his actions on the Marne.

On regular patrols Keller held his position until a fight started. Then he broke away on his private chases. Some of the sergeant pilots were suspicious. Why did the lieutenant always peel off just at the moment a combat started? Where did he go?

Waldrep wasn't as easily duped as his lieutenant thought. As Jasta leader it was his business to keep track of his flight leaders. He'd noticed Keller's disappearing act one too many times to think the man was actually off fighting on his own. Every machine except for Keller's in Jasta 6 bore multiple patches from numerous combats. Waldrep decided to give his arrogant subordinate a chance to prove himself—or enough rope to hang himself—as soon as the weather allowed regular operations.

Chapter 57
A Birthday, a Jilting, and a Stunning Loss

Ravenel, St. Just-en-Chaussée, March 3, 1917

The last of the Lafayette Escadrille men moved into the clapboard barracks hastily erected by French engineers. Getting above ground and out of the dirt brought some life back into the escadrille. Genet once again began the task of decorating the walls with bright drawings of Indianheads, planes in flight, and mountain scenes. Edmond Genet refused to be depressed. His bubbly attitude began to rub off on others including Buck.

Jennifer wrote nearly every day. Her missives were filled with newsy information about the goings on in Paris and her work at the hospital. For such a passionate lover, Jack was perplexed by her lack of romantic flair. He longed for a word or two, but she avoided anything intimate in her writing.

He on the other hand had penned the most erotic of letters. In words richly poetic for their suggestiveness, he wrote of his desire to caress her slender waist using it as a foil for all the other curves he longed to touch. Why she hadn't replied in kind did nothing for his insecurity.

Charlie told him that censors in the various *Bureaux de Postes* read all the mail sent to the front. "Michelle even watches what she writes."

Jack wondered what the censors made of his letters. "If they read my letters and understand English I hope it gives them a kick."

Jennifer wrote somewhat wistfully that she was not pregnant. Jack spent hours poring over her letters searching for affirmation of her continued commitment to him. Charlie told him he couldn't see the forest for the trees.

"Jennifer is a one-man woman, you fool. She loves you for God knows whatever reason. Why you have to question that and mope about here drives me crazy."

"Why waste my time telling you, Charlie? You're just like her. No frills, no nonsense. Just the facts."

Charlie laughed at his friend's illogical response. "So you don't like the fact that she loves you? Or is it that she is a one-man woman? Come on you thickheaded Swede. What more do you want?"

"You are absolutely right. I just miss her so much."

"I seem to remember a friend telling me the same thing after my first separation from Michelle once we were married." Charlie linked his arm in Jack's and led him over to the escadrille's bar.

The buzz in the popote turned over and over to what would happen if the United States entered the war. A newspaper back home suggested that any Americans already flying in France might be commissioned in the Navy. At this Genet's ears perked up.

"It's an idea born from anger at unrestricted submarine warfare. Imagine trying to sink submarines with airplanes!" Rockwell said, shaking his head.

"Not entirely crazy, Doc," Haviland observed. "Have to find a way to get planes out to sea and able to operate off ships. Last time I was on leave I heard some French naval officers talking about how they used balloons to some effect."

"You'll not see me volunteering for the Navy," Jack interjected. "Havvy doesn't seem to remember our lovely little séjour on His Majesty's Ship *Reliant.* Luf, you spent some time at sea. What do you think about aviation and navies?" Jack asked, hoping the rumor about putting them in the Navy got debunked. Lufbery only looked up and turned a thumb down, apparently not wanting to waste words on such nonsense.

"Anyone want to drop in on the Legion regiment?" Thaw asked when Keeler walked in. He told them the remnants of the First and Second Regiments had been pulled together and were now encamped in the third line of trenches only five miles from Ravenel. Genet, Keeler, Soubiran and Buck climbed into the escadrille sedan with Thaw navigating while Jack drove.

It was late in the afternoon when they pulled up to the Regimental Command Post. The first man they met was an officer Charlie immediately recognized. "*Bonjour, mon capitaine*!" Charlie shouted jumping from the vehicle.

"*Commandant, monsieur,*" Antonelli answered before he recognized the lieutenant with aviator wings.

"*Pardonnez-moi,*" Charlie started to say, thinking he might be mistaken. Antonelli smiled, squinting as if he didn't believe his eyes. He walked up to Keeler, placed his hands on the taller man's shoulders and then slid them down to the upper arms feeling for the muscles he once remembered.

"*C'est toi Keeler? C'est toi?*" he said again in disbelief. The others watched and waited. Antonelli invited them to stay for supper. He was now the second in command to a new colonel none of them knew. Thaw just hoped it wasn't Colonel Passard, the one who had threatened to shoot him back in September, 1914, when he'd sat rubbing his sore feet during a march to the front. Genet found an acquaintance from his legion days, an Italian sergeant who had been with him at Bois de Sabot. Soubiran grabbed Genet and his friend and headed off to the NCO mess, leaving the officers, avoiding a potentially awkward situation.

Antonelli brought Charlie up to date on the men they'd gone into the lines with before the unit was disbanded. Only three of the original company survived including de Lattre and Antonelli. De Lattre was now a Lieutenant Colonel with his own regiment in a regular infantry division located somewhere around the Chemin des Dames.

"So who is the third, Tony?" Charlie asked, using the nickname for the first time.

"*You*, my friend!"

They passed a pleasant three hours with other hardened veteran survivors before finding Genet and Soubiran for the trip back to Ravenel. In the car Jack couldn't help commenting on how the legionnaires never stopped praising the aviators while the pilots kept complimenting the legionnaires. "I've never seen such a mutual admiration society. We need to get them to come to our popote to help with our sagging morale." The others were quiet, trying to absorb the fact that so few of their acquaintances remained.

The next day Genet gave them all a fright when he failed to return from the morning mission. He had gone up to the lines near Ham and Saint Quentin at nine. He had to climb to 12,000 feet to get clear of the clouds. Finding nothing up there he got a bearing for Ravenel, but lost all contact with the ground. He turned south knowing it would take him away from the lines and German-held territory. Seeing he was low on fuel he dove into the first hole he could find and landed at a field south of Paris!

Genet, undaunted by the harrowing experience, took off again only to become hopelessly embroiled in the clouds. He felt his way to the ground again landing at Le Bourget. Anxious to get home, he ignored recommendations to wait on better weather and set off on his way north, unknowingly passing Ravenel. Recognizing Amiens he landed again and lunched at a British squadron. By then the weather improved. It became a lovely Sunday afternoon so he took his time getting back, landing at two o'clock that afternoon. Everyone was so glad to see him that he escaped any censure for failing to inform the escadrille of his whereabouts.

Weather kept them on the ground for most of the rest of that week, though Jack did get up for one mission with Genet, Johnson and Bigelow. After they landed Genet confided in Jack that he'd been trying to run up his hours to twenty so he could become a *sergent.*

"I can't wait for the United States to get into the war, but I'm afraid I might have some problems. At least I can stay with the French. It will be better as a sergeant or officer."

"But Smiler, why would you have problems? I'm sure you will make an excellent lieutenant or even captain in our army," Jack replied, without letting on that he knew about Edmond's past.

"I deserted from the Navy, Jack," Genet blurted out.

Rather than try to respond or act surprised, Jack simply draped an arm over Genet's shoulder and guided him to the escadrille orderly room.

"Emil, fix up two leave requests for the weekend for Genet and me."

Jack took the requests along with Haviland's seven-day leave, and turned them over to de Laage. De Laage glanced at them and smiled. He signed all three telling Jack he would make sure the captain wouldn't miss him. "Monsieur Buck, you walk around here with that hang dog look much longer and we are all going to get depressed. Bon voyage!"

That Friday the three Americans caught the number 2-26 train from St. Just and arrived in Paris at 5:45 P.M. In his haste, Jack hadn't alerted Jennifer. On the train he and Haviland tried to buck up young Genet. It didn't take much with the ebullient young man. Genet agreed to meet the Parkers for supper at the Roosevelt.

Jack found Jennifer at the Crillon attending to little Michael. Fleury had asked Michelle to work late on a report. Jennifer was so startled when the maid showed Jack in that she woke the baby in her arms. The scene moved Jack very much. That night they decided to try for a child of their own, regardless of the war. They secluded themselves for most of the rest of the weekend with that aim in mind. Aside from church and an unfruitful walk to the Flandin's apartment, the young couple kept to themselves.

Monday, Jack met Genet at the Gare du Nord in time to catch the 1:15 P.M. train back to St. Just. Neither of them wanted to return. Jack had spent the morning visiting with Michelle. Jennifer was on shift at Neuilly. It was the first time they had really gotten to talk during the weekend. She gave Jack some things to take to Charlie. "These letters won't be censored, Jack, so don't lose them. Oh! I forgot. This is from Jennifer," she said handing him a small packet of envelopes.

On the train the two young men talked little. Jack didn't know what to say. He knew Edmond was troubled by not hearing from his girlfriend. He also knew that Edmond had asked Major Parker to assist in getting his desertion from the Navy erased. If Genet brought either subject up, Jack wasn't sure what he'd say. Meanwhile, he closed his eyes to savor the memories of his more intimate moments with Jennifer.

They got back to Ravenel just before supper in time to learn that another Spad had been delivered and would go to Johnson. Genet's face betrayed his feelings on hearing this. He'd hoped he would get the next new machine. Johnson didn't seem to have much taste for combat anymore in Edmond's eyes. Why didn't the officers see this and give him a Spad? Adding to his frustration, Thénault assigned Johnson's old Nieuport to Genet. Jack watched Genet's reactions to this news. The kid was getting more than his share of challenges.

Finally alone, Jack anxiously opened the first envelope.

Dearest Jack,

Michelle suggested writing these to avoid prying eyes. I hate not being able to write what I want, and I can't seem to say it when you are here.

You know I love you and I know you love me. Please don't blush at what you read in this note and in the next two. You might want to wait to read the others later—savor them so to speak.

Now to my point....

Jack didn't blush, but he was glad he was alone. Her words heated the pages in his hand and stirred his loins almost as much as if she'd been there. She outdid his fumbling attempts at erotic writing, making him wonder just how she came up with such thoughts. The first letter filled two pages. He was tempted to read the other two on the spot but didn't. He would be rereading them every day anyway.

MARCH 14 BEGAN WITH AN ENORMOUS RUMBLE OF HEAVY shelling in the distance. It continued all morning long. All leaves were cancelled. The long-awaited Nivelle offensive was underway.

According to the papers, March 1917 was colder than any other March recorded. Parsons froze a toe on a mission with Jack in spite of triple woolen socks and insulated boots. Ted couldn't walk for a week. On that same flight, Jack led Hinkle into a fight with two DR 1's. They were astonished when one of the pair pulled away and raced off to a safe distance before they even began the engagement. "Pop", the name they gave Hinkle, the oldest man in the escadrille, chased after this Fokker while Jack wrestled the other two to a draw, all three running out of ammunition before parting with a wave. After the mission Hinkle asked Jack if he had run into other Germans who refused to fight.

"Happens all the time, Pop," Jack replied. "I chased an Albatros for nearly an hour once. I think the Germans rely on numbers more than us. Fritz won't stand and fight if the odds are against him or even, for that matter. There are exceptions, but most of the Germans try to stay on their side of the lines. I've only run into a few who are as aggressive as Charlie Keeler or Lufbery. You have to watch out for tricks, too. More often than not a guy running is trying to lead you into trouble. Was the Fokker you chased marked in any way?"

"It was hard to miss. All yellow with a red band around all three wings."

"Mine was bright blue. I only caught a glimpse of yours. Yellow and red, you say? Luf chased one like that last month. Said it turned tail before he fired his first rounds."

"I was scared shitless going up against the triplane. All you guys say that they work in groups. I kept looking for his buddies, but he seemed to be alone. I couldn't catch him. Didn't want to waste rounds out of range. What a pity. I was starting to feel like a real fighter too."

"You're doing fine, Pop. That Boche doesn't have the bit in his mouth, if you take my meaning. Don't count on others to be so complacent." Buck checked himself. This man was almost as old as his father. *How combat levels the classes and the generations*, he thought. *Well, these guys look to us for guidance. God help me!*

"You ought to have that ear looked at. I thought everybody who grew up in Minnesota was immune to frostbite. Your ear is all red and starting to swell."

"Yes sir. Remember I was only a kid in your state. In my old age I have forgotten all I knew about surviving in the Arctic," Hinkle said with a pained expression as he touched the affected ear.

On the 15th de Laage headed to Paris to pick up another Spad. Keeler led the morning patrol and Buck took the afternoon mission, patrolling for two hours between Roye and Noyon without any action. "Heck of an offensive, Jack," Genet commented when they landed. "Looks like the Germans aren't coming out to play. You don't suppose they saw this one coming?"

"You're kidding, of course, Smiler. Nivelle's made such a circus of his big show that I wouldn't be surprised if the Germans were selling tickets for ringside seats."

Between missions Harold Willis, an architect by trade and training, undertook the task of dressing up the escadrille logo. He learned that the anniversary of the organization of the escadrille was March 17, the day the French approved forming an all American unit. He wanted to produce a new and improved Indian Chief in honor of the event.

Willis was another ambulance veteran who had served in SSU 2 with McConnell and Haviland before joining aviation. Jack remembered Willis nursing his wounded ambulance to safety with a leaky radiator full of wine. They hadn't gotten to know each other then. Jack heard that Hal Willis had a tyrannical father.

It continued to amaze Jack that so many sought adventure in fleeing paternal pressures. Parsons fought his father's efforts to bring him into the insurance business, leaving home as soon as he graduated from college. Willis, on the other hand, had been employed as an architect and faced a comfortable life before his precipitous flight to join the ambulance service.

"Humbling, isn't it?" Charlie observed. "Here we are young nobodies wearing officer's ranks, and on come these talented highly-educated men. If only our country would get off its dead duff, we could fill the air with men such as these."

Friday night they entertained a British lieutenant named Sheridan who had gotten lost and landed at their field. There was a moment of great laughter when Sheridan recognized Genet from his unscheduled visit to the British squadron days before. At supper Sheridan admitted to knowing Anthony de Vincent. He took a lot of ribbing for the tendency of Brit pilots to get lost. When Sheridan learned that Keeler was de Vincent's brother-in-law, he reacted instantly.

"You're the bloke with the Legion of Honor! Blimey! Have we heard about you! You and Lufbery. Where's that fellow? I'd like to shake your hands before you Yanks get me too drunk."

Lufbery came in late, having spent the last two hours painstakingly checking every bullet in the belts going into his two Vickers for the next day's mission. He was in a rare mood that night. They played Sheridan for all he was worth until the young lieutenant began to sing in a very loud voice. Keeler trundled him off to de Laage's cot before things got any further out of hand. When Charlie returned, Jack motioned him over and poured a little cognac in a glass, pushing it over to Keeler.

"I like the new men a lot. Willis is a whip. Did you see what he did to the stencil for our planes?" Jack said.

"Made a limp Seminole into a screaming Sioux. Ought to warm your Minnesota heart to see the warriors that gave your state such a hard time painted on our planes."

"Your education is showing again, Charlie. Where do you come up with these jewels?"

"Listen, do you like the new Sioux or not?" Charlie said with an edge to his voice.

"Are we getting touchy?" Jack bristled, the cognac beginning to take hold.

Charlie looked at him quizzically. He took a minute to collect himself and then said: "I'm sorry Jack. I shouldn't snap like that. It's just that I miss my kid and his mother."

"Ah ha! So you feel the sting like—what did you call me—a thickheaded Swede?"

"You are a bit didactic, by the way. Do you ever listen to yourself talking about motors and the workings of the Spad? We have an architect and bona fide engineers like Hinkle on board and who is the expert? A damned Swede from Minn-e-so-ta. Beat that."

"And you, the great wounded scholar who never finished college using eight-bit words like didactic. What a pair of greenhorns we are. At least we'll have something to tell our kids about when this is over."

"God willing, Jack. You know as well as I do that some of us aren't going to make it. Now that we are flying every day it's just a matter of time. It tears my gut to think about any of our friends buying the farm. I'd give up this officer crap in a heartbeat not to be the one sending someone like Mac to his death."

"Shsssh!" Jack said, waving his finger in front of his mouth unsteadily. "Mustn't spout such poppycock. Touch wood, Herc!" Both made a show of touching the table to avoid bad luck.

"Let's get to bed, Bucko. We have the morning go, and I'm beat."

Saturday morning's mission proved as uneventful as the previous day's. Jack had a cognac hangover, his first in months, and he didn't like it a bit. His mouth was dry and felt cottony as if it had been impregnated with dry cleaning solution. Even the shock of the cold air at altitude did little to alleviate his discomfort. He wondered how he'd managed to drink so much in the past without the least effect in the morning. Now he cursed the bottle again, swearing he wouldn't touch a drop. Almost as if to punish himself, he guided the flight back to refuel and took off again with Charlie for a little independent hunting.

"A Zeppelin! Coming our way!" shouted Emil Marshall, running up to them after they landed the second time that morning.

"Who's ready to go?" Jack asked.

"Parsons and Willis are running up for the afternoon patrol. Should I tell them to go after the Zep?"

"Just tell them to look for it. What in the hell is a Zeppelin doing around here anyway? I thought they were after London." Charlie exclaimed.

An artillery unit had relayed the message. Apparently one of the big steerable airships was drifting out of control over the lines. It would be a sitting duck if they could find it. Charlie and Jack raced to the hangar. They arrived just in time to see Parsons and Willis take off.

"Let them go for it, Charlie," Jack said. "If it is disabled it will be drifting back toward Germany faster than we can get up to give chase. Besides, we've already flown two missions today. You need a rest."

"You too, Bucko. Look at the bags under your eyes! I just wish one of the more experienced guys were up now. Parsons is good, but he has only done three real patrols and one of them in a snowstorm. This is what? Willis's second? If the Boches get their fighters up to protect the Zeppelin, they're going to have a nasty party."

Neither of their Spads was refueled or rearmed in any event. Jack tried to borrow McConnell's Nieuport, but it blew a seal during run up. Charlie raced to the other end of the line looking for another ready aircraft to no avail. In the end Parsons and Willis were too late. Artillery did the job for them. The two Americans swooped down over the still smoking skeleton of the downed Zeppelin before heading back.

Every day rolled into the next like waves hitting the shore. Holidays and weekends passed without much notice. Willis finished his design stencil for the fierce-looking Sioux in time for the escadrille anniversary, but was disappointed that no one acted interested in celebrating the event. The old timers of the original N. 124 couldn't agree on a fitting day to mark the anniversary. March 17 was the *official* day on paper only. April 20, the day they arrived at Luxeuil, or the day of their maiden flight on May 13, 1916, were arguably better milestones, while others suggested the day Rockwell downed their first German airplane, May 18. The debate on the proper day and a certain superstition about celebrating any anniversaries caused the 'official' date to pass without fanfare. N. 124 underwent a slow rebirth until the number of Spads exceeded the older Nieuports and they became SPA. 124.

Another event almost slipped by when James McConnell turned thirty on March 14. Mac didn't say anything, but Jack remembered the date from their first sortie with the American Ambulance. He produced a *petit gateau* he'd purchased at Fouchet's in Paris. He gave it to McConnell at breakfast before the morning mission.

"You're a jewel, Buck! A real diamond in the rough. Imagine remembering my birthday!" Mac said he thought the war might kill him.

"Knock it off Jim," Keeler insisted. "Enjoy your birthday, old man. Who knows how many any of us have to celebrate?"

McConnell didn't brood, but he seemed to have a sense of foreboding.

Jack chimed in, "Let's toast the escadrille and your birthday in style, Jim. Look at what we've done! We've made an African cat an American and kicked some Heinies into Hades. Not bad for a year."

Thénault used the birthday as an excuse to keep McConnell on the ground to give him some rest.

By Monday, March 19, McConnell insisted on flying. He still walked with great difficulty because of the pain in his lower back. Just the same he smiled gamely after two mechanics lifted and lowered him into the cockpit of the Nieuport marked with large letters spelling "MAC," and the white footprint of the Hotfoot Society. Keeler led that morning with Genet, McConnell, and Parsons on the patrol. They were supposed to gather information on German ground forces and interdict any observation machines they detected.

Keeler took off at ten A.M. followed by Mac and Genet. Parsons departed last but lost his motor and landed straight-ahead about two kilometers from the field. Seeing Parsons down safely, Keeler took up the lead with the remaining two planes. Charlie's Spad sported the new insignia along with his trademark green and red diamond emblazoned with a gold "C" in the green half and a "M" in the red. He'd originally wanted a heart with his and Michelle's initials, but after seeing the black heart and coffin used by Nungesser, he opted for a diamond. Genet's blue, white and red chevron topped by a white star was barely dry on the Nieuport he inherited from Johnson. Mac's "MAC" stood out clearly. Thénault never got 'McConnell' spelled right because of that three-letter symbol.

They penetrated German lines, dodging the low scudding clouds. A few miles west of Ham, a French city in German hands, Charlie spotted two German biplanes circling lazily just inside German lines. Genet dove immediately on the first of the two, with McConnell close behind aiming for the second. Charlie worried about Mac being able to twist and turn his head enough to see any attackers, so he hung back looking for the inevitable fighters lurking somewhere above them. He lost sight of Genet and Mac for a second when a flight of three DR-1 Fokker triplanes screamed into the fray.

Keeler decided to try to draw off these latecomers and let Mac and Genet deal with the two-seaters. As soon as he zoomed up at the attackers one of the Fokkers peeled away. Ignoring it, Charlie fired off twenty rounds at the lead Fokker. It immediately started trailing smoke before dropping like a rock.

Charlie worried that the bright yellow plane that had broken away would go after Mac and Smiler. Craning his neck above and around him for a glimpse of it, he almost missed the third triplane lining up to attack him. He whipped the Spad into a violent chandelle pointing straight up before snapping it around above and behind his former attacker. Still thinking about the missing Fokker, Charlie let loose a burst of ten to fifteen rounds. The second triplane wobbled in his sights and fell off on a wing before disappearing from sight into a cloud.

Charlie scanned every cloud for other planes. At some distance he could distinguish the bright yellow plane against a charcoal colored cloud. The man was heading north. Knowing he could never catch it at that distance, he reluctantly turned back to see how Mac and Genet were doing.

Clouds limited his forward vision and mist coated his goggles. He searched in vain for the others for almost twenty minutes, circling back over the area where he had left them.

Finding no sign of the German two-seaters either, Charlie assumed they'd been driven off. He hoped Mac and Genet had made it back all right. Charlie didn't give a second thought to the fact that he had likely scored two more victories unseen by anyone but the victims.

He had barely rolled to a stop at Ravenel when Genet raced up to his Spad with a bloody kerchief held to his cheek.

"Sir! Did you see Mac? I lost him in the fight. He hasn't come back."

"Smiler, how many times do I have to tell you not to call me sir?" Charlie said peeling off his helmet. "No. I didn't see anyone. Mac's not with you? What happened to you guys?"

Genet was visibly upset and in obvious pain. Tears flowed from his blue eyes from pain or from fear for Jimmy McConnell. He had a nasty gash on his cheek carved by the bullet fragment that had shattered his instrument console.

Buck, Thaw and Thénault pulled up in a vehicle at about the same time, anxious to get a report on the mission. Keeler told them what he'd seen. After telling of his own combat and the mysterious yellow Fokker, he turned to Genet, asking gently if Edmond felt up to giving a report.

"I lost Mac when the fight started. We both came into range of the observers at the same time. Those gunners were vicious accurate. I was hit right away. I kept at the attack as best I could, but blood got in my eyes and filled up my goggles. I couldn't see until I ripped them off." Genet made the same motion of pulling off his goggles, pulling off the cloth on his cheek in the process. Jack grabbed a compress from the first aid kit in the car and pushed it against Genet's wound.

"When I got the goggles off I found I was alone. No sight of the Germans or of Jimmy. God, I hope he landed somewhere else! It was murder out there. Lieutenant Keeler got a Fokker before it could get to us. I saw it crash. God knows what would have happened if those triplanes had gotten to us. Captain, we have to find Jimmy. I, I…" His tears flowed freely.

Buck took him away to get a medic to bandage the wound properly. The others rushed to operations to get on the telephone.

The day ended without word from the frontlines or from other fields. Knowing they had been over enemy lines, there was some hope that Mac had landed safely and had been made a prisoner. Charlie was sick to his stomach at the thought of losing McConnell, his own words about sending someone like Mac to his death ringing in his head.

If Jimmy was a prisoner, Charlie hoped he wasn't hurt. With his bad back, any other injuries would make it especially difficult. As much as they dreaded being captured, they knew that the Germans treated pilots better than other prisoners in the hopes they would get similar treatment.

They talked about the yellow triplane later that night. From Hinkle's account, it had to be the same one. Pop told him what Jack had said about the German not having the bit in his mouth.

"I'll say," Charlie observed. "If that Fritz had stayed and fought I might not be here myself."

KELLER SHOT OFF HIS AMMUNITION WHILE FLEEING THE FRENCH sharpshooter that had downed his two wingmen. When he landed at Jasta 6's field, south of Ham, Waldrep came out hoping for news of the other two pilots, two experienced sergeants, one of whom had expressed concern about Keller's disappearing act.

"Herr Hauptmann, I regret to report that both fell in combat this morning. We attacked three French fighters, the new SPADs I think, that were harassing our observation machines. Kleinschmidt fought bravely before getting hit. I was engaged myself and didn't see where he went down. Corporal Weiss didn't have a chance. Two of the enemy attacked him at once while I battled the third SPAD. My opponent burst into flames." Keller said, looking earnestly sorry for the loss of the two others and not even flinching in fabricating another victory for himself.

"I see you weren't hit. Amazing! We lose two good pilots, one a senior NCO, and you come away unscathed, claiming a victory. Unbelievable," Waldrep sighed shaking his head.

"I have been very lucky, sir."

"Yes. Very. Well, that is your thirteenth, isn't it Keller? I hope you aren't superstitious. SPADs you say? Hmm. How did you find them in combat?"

"It was very cloudy and everything happened too quickly for me to truly assess the new enemy machines. They do seem to be faster than the Nieuport, much faster than our triplanes." Keller remembered worrying that the French plane would catch him from the way it closed the distance before giving up the chase. He had to be careful to render as accurate a report as possible. The aircraft they were protecting were well enough occupied that he didn't think they saw his premature departure, but there was a chance someone on the ground could refute his claim. He doubted the stupid captain would check any further, but there was always a chance.

"It is curious, isn't it that you were five to their three, on our side of the lines and we lose two to their one?" Waldrep scratched his short blond hair looking carefully at Keller's face to see the lieutenant's reaction. He'd already gotten a report from the artillery of a French *Nieuport* coming down, but it was claimed by the L.V.G.s. He would have to play this one close to his heart. Keller, if he was dissimulating, revealed nothing on his ugly scarred face.

"As I reported, the visibility was bad. We lost sight of each other several times."

"Perhaps that explains it. Pity about Kleinschmidt. He was to get a field promotion to warrant officer tomorrow. Write up your patrol report, lieutenant. I have to see if we recovered their bodies. Then I will write yet more letters to next of kin." Waldrep fixed Keller with steely blue eyes waiting for his subordinate to salute and leave.

For all his guile and practiced deception, Keller reacted a touch too slowly, unable to muster respect for Waldrep or his rank. When he did snap his heels together and salute he detected a dangerous look on the captain's face. It was time to lay low. He would need to be more careful.

GENET'S WOUND BLED PROFUSELY, BUT A DOCTOR CAREFULLY stitched it closed and treated it to fight infection. It would not be disfiguring, the military doctor reassured him. Genet would be attracting the women in a couple of weeks if not sooner with his badge of courage. Edmond Genet found this assurance both empty and ironic.

Genet couldn't shake the feeling that his friend had sacrificed his life for him. Mac's fate plagued him. Jimmy McConnell had treated him like a younger brother. Mac hovered over Genet on patrols.

The doctor's comment called to mind the letter he'd gotten from his beloved Gertrude several days ago. In nearly a year of combat he had written her every day. She had not responded for months. He'd written his mother and brothers to inquire after her. Then, out of the blue he got the long awaited letter. He'd tucked it in his breast pocket and held onto it all that day until he could savor her words alone.

His anticipation turned to horror when he read her terse words. Gertrude had met another man and gotten engaged. Genet's devastation was as complete as any young man's could be. He had been introduced to some of the prettiest and most available women in France in the past year and he had turned away every one of them in favor of his precious Gertrude. Her faithlessness shook him to his very soul. A deeply religious young man, Genet begged God to make it different.

A loving letter from his mother only confirmed the news. She wrote that Gertrude had actually married a clergyman less than a month earlier. The mails were so slow. His mother's letter was six weeks old. All the time he had pined for her she had been in the arms of another! It was almost too much for him to take.

Genet had all but sworn off liquor after a bad binge at Pau. After getting the terrible news, he hit the bottle. It caused McConnell to gently probe enough to hear the sad tale of Gertrude. He was the only one Edmond had told. Now Jimmy was probably a prisoner, or worse, dead

Buck learned about Gertrude from Mac. Jimmy thought it best to let one of the officers know lest the news affect Genet's ability to fly. Seeing Smiler in tears and pain now moved Jack profoundly. Jack tried to imagine his brother bearing so much in such a short period of time. Larry, about Genet's age, would hold up, he guessed. Larry was tough. So was Edmond Genet, but Jack decided to make a point of keeping an even closer eye on the younger man.

Jack tried at first to keep Genet on the ground, but the young man was bent on revenge. He begged to fly and convinced the doctor to clear him in spite of the danger of reopening the wound. Thénault thought of ordering Genet to the hospital, but Buck convinced him that Edmond needed to get back in the saddle as soon as possible. Thaw backed him. So did Keeler. Genet went up again on the twenty-third.

Buck led the flight. They went back to the place where they thought Mac might have gone down. It was too cloudy to see anything clearly. No Germans were in the air either. Genet's bitterness at not being able to strike back at the enemy showed plainly on his face upon their return. He'd gotten so sick from his earlier bout with gin that he swore off the booze again.

That night Féquant received a call from a cavalry unit returning from a place called *Détroit Bleu*. They'd found a wrecked Nieuport with McConnell's tail number and the stripped body of the pilot lying beside it. The Commandant went to Spa. 124 to inform Thénault. They solemnly drove out to recover the body. The silence in the escadrille rang louder than church bells that night.

Alerted earlier, Paul Rockwell showed up to take responsibility for McConnell's effects. He said he'd never had a better friend short of his brother Kiffin. Paul found Edmond Genet suffering, thinking he was responsible for Mac's death. Rockwell worried about his diminutive and inconsolable friend.

"Paul, I lost my girl and now Mac. I feel worst than worthless."

"Come on Edmond. You're made of stronger steel than that. You know damned well that Jim shouldn't have been flying in his shape. You didn't let him down then. Don't let him down now." Paul said before leaving.

Mac's death hit the escadrille like a slow but inexorable avalanche. Buck mourned the fellow that had led him on his first ambulance missions and who encouraged him to write from his heart. Keeler remembered McConnell's influence at Avord so long ago, thinking he might not have finished flight school without Jim's encouragement. Emil Marshall loved McConnell for the way he had never looked down on him as a non-flyer. He wrote a friend saying: "All I can do is to always remember him as the best and the bravest comrade one could have wished."

This was powerful praise for an extraordinary man, but the most unusual testament to McConnell was soon to come.

PARIS USUALLY RESET THE CLOCKS FOR THE COMBATANTS. Returning from the horrors of combat, the wiles and ways of the City of Light softened the reality of the war raging less than a hundred miles away. McConnell's memorial was sobering, but it couldn't hamper merrymaking.

The testimonials were so familiar now that Jack thought he knew them by heart. He'd heard Masters praised in similar terms and even Cartier's French service echoed with the same ringing praises.

Jack remembered the day they'd gotten the ambulance stuck and lost the French artilleryman. McConnell almost cried when they took the man's body to be buried. He told Jack that he had to do something more to help in this war. Now he too was buried in France. Had he done enough yet?

Even though the words of the service were familiar and glowing, they didn't mean nearly as much as the simple presence of so many people crowding into the American Church that day. Jack recognized American Ambassador Sharp. Doctor Gros was there with just about every member of the Lafayette Flying Corps Board of Directors including Pierre Flandin, who nodded solemnly to Jack when he saw him.

Jennifer pointed out Nurse Wilson. It was the first time either of them had seen her out of her white uniform. A. Piatt Andrew headed up a contingent of at least fifty members of the American Ambulance, only a few of whom Jack recognized. They looked terribly young to him. He searched for Alejandro, hoping their old leader was in the group. Not seeing him, Jack felt tears welling up in his eyes, the memories of their first days together with Mac at Neuilly flooding back on him.

Jack's struggle with the meaning of death usually ended with him concluding that only the living really mattered. All extolled the greatness of the fallen man. Having heard Rockwell praised as the 'best and the bravest of us all,' Jack knew how futile it was to try to use words to characterize men like McConnell, Chapman and Rockwell.

He couldn't help comparing the three. Were they truly better than Prince or young de Vincent, Cartier, or the hundreds of thousands on both sides whose blood nourished the hallowed ground where they fell? Masters' face kept swimming into his mind's eye. *No greater sacrifice is there than to lay down one's life for another.*

Perhaps the greatest testament to Jimmy Mac came with the appearance of three beautiful women, including the formidable Marcelle Guérin. Jennifer, hanging on Jack's arm for all she was worth, couldn't believe what she'd overheard. Each of the women claimed to be Jimmy's fiancée!

"You'd better not have another woman lurking out there somewhere," she whispered half seriously to Jack. "I'll claw her eyes out and that's not the half of what I will do to you." It was just the right touch of humor that he needed to keep from bawling like a baby.

Michelle clung to Charlie just as hard. Both young wives suppressed thoughts of the ever-present threat of losing their husbands brought so much closer by every death in the Lafayette Escadrille.

Michelle begged Charlie to be more careful. Unlike Genet who tormented himself about Mac's death, Charlie knew better than to think that he could protect everyone in his patrols. Therein lay madness. Yet, he worried that he was becoming callous and fatalistic. He saw the tears in Jack's eyes. Where were his own? Charlie gripped Michelle's hand and tried to pray. Even that failed him.

McConnell's death, like Chapman's, Rockwell's, and Prince's, laid them low, but it couldn't keep them down. Soon other news would brighten their horizons with the promise of a speedier end to the infernal war.

IF JACK HAD ANY FURTHER WORRIES ABOUT JENNIFER, they dissolved in the heat of their incessant passionate lovemaking. Just when he thought she'd had enough or that he was drained, she enveloped him again with renewed vigor doing one of the things she'd written him in those passionate letters. She gave him a bracelet engraved with their wedding date and the words "*Ensemble éternellement.*" She made him feel so wanted, so needed that he almost had to fight the sweet suffocation.

Jennifer had always been strong-willed and independent. She knew that it was ridiculous to feel lonely or helpless, though both emotions laid siege to her heart. She overcame them in the all-consuming tasks she performed at the hospital where she was seldom alone and always exhausted. Even her rare free moments were spent with Michelle and little Michael.

Jennifer's energy had been boundless from the beginning. During their courtship she thought nothing of working a twelve-hour shift and then partying with Jack almost until the next shift started. She could keep up that pace physically, but she further drained her emotional reserves day in and day out in trying to buoy up wounded soldiers.

She got on marvelously with Michelle and Michael. The two women from such different cultural backgrounds proved perfect companions. Michelle, for all her sophisticated education and cosmopolitan experience of the world, still didn't understand Americans. Charlie's enigmatic mood swings and periods of silence frustrated her. Jennifer was also alarmed to see her brother so serious.

Michelle misinterpreted his lethargy. Concerned that childbirth had marred her figure and made her unattractive to him, Michelle donned black net stockings and a tight black bustier to try to get his attention. She worried that Charlie would be offended, but Jennifer suggested the lingerie, telling Michelle she was going to do the same thing with Jack.

"You are much more beautiful than the trollops on the stage at the *Moulin Rouge*, but you can tantalize me like this any time." Charlie said admiring her.

Michelle purred and whispered things in an exaggerated French accent that drove Charlie wild. She turned away from him leaning back to ask if he liked what he saw. Keeler had seen her in the altogether many times. He loved the look of her body, especially her long shapely legs. Seeing her this way re-ignited his smoldering fires.

Michelle had learned much about her husband from his sister. She realized that her hold on him was as permanent as anything could be in this world. However, she found that motherhood was different from tending someone else's children. She couldn't put Michael out of her mind like she did the Fleury children when engaged in something else.

She had a feeling that Charlie resented the boy's demands on her. He was affectionate enough with the child and seemed comfortable holding and caring for Michael, feeding him and changing his nappies. Yet, when it came time to go to bed, Charlie became very impatient if she dallied or went to check on the baby. This hurt her and brought her to tears as she sat brushing her hair. Like Charlie though, she resolved to put a happy face on every moment and treat each as if it was to be their last.

THE OTHER AMERICANS IN SPA. 124 SPENT THEIR LIMITED TIME IN Paris in pursuit of the numerous numbing pleasures of the City of Light. Whether with a *marraine* or another willing *jeune fille*, a favorite pastime was drinking or striving to achieve satisfaction horizontally. Dud Hill and Willis Haviland weren't even looking for girls on their evening stroll through the Bois de Boulogne.

The air was warm and the sky clear. They could smell the blossoms on the trees and bushes. Another strong and heady odor wafted their way. They discovered that it emanated from an extremely well endowed young lady who appeared from the edge of the woods and opened her blouse for them to see her substantial breasts. The girl appeared to be about eighteen. Her face was deftly painted to make her look older. Under the gaslight she looked breathtaking to both of the Americans, but they kept on walking. She cooed that she would make them both feel heavenly on her little blanket if they were interested. Both men wondered if they would have resisted were they alone.

A few steps further brought them face to face—literally abreast—of another slightly older woman beckoning from the bushes. The young leaves on the branches failed to conceal her unadorned charms. She posed almost Venus-like. Their urge to avert their eyes seemed ludicrous in the circumstances, so they simply stared, motionless on the sidewalk for several moments. Finally, Haviland suggested crossing to the other side of the street.

"And miss the free show, Havvy? Have you lost your senses?" Hill said, voicing what they both felt.

"No, Dud, but I am not sure I can handle much more of this temptation. Have you any idea of where we might locate some more legitimate female companions?"

"Not without paying I'm afraid, my friend. If you want to try your luck with one such as these I can meet you at Madame Weeks'."

"I am not that desperate yet, Mr. Hill, if you please. I just thought you might have made the acquaintance of some decent girls instead of these *poules*."

"Are you, the most handsome man in the escadrille, asking me, the half-blind dullard of the unit, where to find women? Hell, Havvy, you were just back here for a whole week. Why didn't you line something up then?"

"Forget it, Dud. I guess seeing those girls just got me going. Let's head over to Alice Weeks' and see what's stirring. Maybe the guys there have had better luck."

What the men couldn't or didn't get in the arms of charming women, they more than made up for in alcoholic libations. Champagne was often the poison of choice. Many thought they could drink it like soda pop. More than one attested to its potency the next day when they woke with dry mouths and throbbing heads.

Just about any other kind of liquid refreshment could be had for a pittance. Since they had access to a well-stocked bar at Ravenel, liquor in Paris couldn't compete with the allure of the gentler sex. Booze, on the other hand, didn't bite back, slap or give them social diseases. For that convoluted reason, many spent their entire leave in a semi-stupor. Some mixed the two, often finding themselves in a strange bed with a strange woman the next morning. Usually, the couple laughed a lot and forgot about it. Such was wartime Paris.

Thaw made the extraordinary effort of bringing the lion Whiskey to the city. The mascot's milky eye bothered visitors. He wanted to find an eye doctor or someone who might be able to fashion a suitable glass replacement eye.

Paris had one of the most elaborate directories of services and telephone numbers Thaw had ever seen. After bouncing through three eye doctors, he hit upon an Argentine doctor who agreed to at least see the animal.

The receptionist nearly fainted when she saw the lion on a leash. "*Madré de Dios*!" the doctor exclaimed when Thaw and Soubiran came into the examining room with the lion. Bobby held the leash they'd fashioned from some harnesses. Whiskey simply walked into the anteroom, put his head down to smell the floor, and settled comfortably on the tiles.

"There is nothing I can do for your animal, monsieur. I have the eyes for men and women, but nothing so big. You will have to go somewhere else." Almost as if sensing the doctor's comment, Whiskey growled his deepest displeasure. The Argentine jumped at least a foot in the air before turning on his heels and scrambling out of the room.

Undismayed, Bill went to another office. This shop had grown with the war. Many men returned from the front with holes where their eyes used to be. The doctor employed a skilled glassworker who could work miracles with artificial eyes. The lion cub was fully-grown except for the lack of the mane. After several delicate and tentative measurements the doctor announced: "*Bon*, it can be done. It will be fifteen hundred francs."

Thaw, rich beyond concern about money, screamed in loud protest that the lion had only cost five hundred francs in the first place. He wasn't above haggling if necessary, but he knew he was playing with other men's money as well as his own.

"*Désolé, monsieur.* I must insist on this payment now or you can take your patient elsewhere."

Bill Thaw hated men like the doctor. His normally cool disposition gave way to anger. Soubiran intervened before Thaw could vent his rage.

Speaking in rapid vernacular French, Soubiran told the doctor that the lion was the mascot of the most famous, most important, and *only* American unit in the French Army. If the lion continued to appear in public with a disfigured eye socket the French nation would know right away that France didn't give a damn about its supporters. Citing the recent articles that indicated America's imminent entry into the conflict, Soubiran pointed out that literally thousands of soldiers would need eye treatment in no time at all. Only the most competent and most respected eye doctor would get this business. If Doctor Spitiesse refused to treat the glorious lion of the famous American squadron he could be assured of not getting a single American patient in the hectic months to come.

Whiskey's new eye—obtained for the princely sum of a mere one hundred francs—improved his appearance markedly, but did little for his disposition. Thaw decided to mount another hunting expedition.

At the Crillon for lunch, Thaw asked Keeler to accompany him on an "urban safari" to find a companion for Whiskey. Charlie readily agreed, feeling a little guilty for wanting to get away from his son's screaming every time Michelle left the room.

That night they came back to the Crillon with a female lion cub in a small dog crate. Thaw convinced the concierge to store the crate and its occupant in a basement overnight. The next day he, Keeler and Soubiran were taking the train north to St Just to rejoin the unit.

Chapter 58
L'attaque À Outrance

Ravenel, early April, 1917

Arriving after a trip of only ninety minutes, the trio recovered both of the lions in their cages and waited for an escadrille vehicle. Jack Buck, who had come up with Haviland and Hoskier on an earlier train, showed up with one of the trucks. When introduced to the newest mascot, Jack learned that they had yet to name her.

"What's that drink the Scot called a damned abomination? Whiskey and soda? Remember how he swore it was criminal to put anything in a good whiskey?"

"Yeah, Jack, but that was 'whisky' without the 'e' he was talking about." Thaw replied, calling attention to one of the differences between American and Canadian whiskeys and true Scotch.

"What could be more natural then to call her 'Soda' since our Whiskey is with the 'e?" Jack suggested, feeling very clever.

"Soda it is!" Thaw said slapping Jack on the back. "Why didn't you think of that, Bobby?"

"Why pick on me, Bill?" Soubiran asked.

"I'd never have thought it either. Jack's the writer you know," Keeler said. "Jack, get this rattletrap moving so we can shake the dust off and get settled."

"Yeah, let's go." Thaw added. "I can't wait to see how the guys react to Soda and her beau's new eye."

At Ravenel Whiskey's artificial eye turned out to be a sensational success. People weren't satisfied to see a lion cub in captivity. They wanted to see this special animal that slept with men and wore an artificial eye. Soda proved to be a bit more feisty and difficult to handle, several commented.

"Just like a woman," Lufbery observed. He appeared to be one of the few that could handle her without getting scratched.

Charlie noted three new faces at supper that night. Kenneth Marr introduced himself as 'Siwash,' the name he'd picked up as a sourdough in Alaska. *Another adventurer,* Charlie mused.

He thought he recognized the next guy who said his name was Bill Dugan, a friend of Genet's. Smiler, his face swollen from the unhealed wounds, stood up to say that 'Duke' had fought beside him at Horseshoe Woods, enough to establish Dugan's pedigree.

The third guy looked really sharp. This had to be Hewitt; the fellow they'd asked Genet, Parsons and Hoskier about earlier. His sharply creased black uniform and handsome features bespoke confidence. He introduced himself as a New Yorker and former Norton Ambulance driver.

The pair of animals and the new volunteers competed for attention with talk about America entering the war. The prospect excited everyone. Genet, especially agitated, hung on every word, every snippet of a rumor. Major Parker told him that the government would probably pardon his desertion. Parker said there was a two year limitation on prosecuting deserters. Genet's second year ended the previous January.

Genet, preoccupied with this issue, resisted expressing his misgivings about Hewitt. As much as he wanted to serve under the Stars and Stripes, Edmond had already decided to stay with the French should his name not be cleared of the AWOL charge.

Edmond Genet, one of the most faithful and ingenuous diarists in the Lafayette Escadrille, recorded what he saw every day. Depending on his new friendship with Buck, he asked Jack to read his entry for April 2. It was a scathing account of the McConnell memorial ceremony at the American Church of the Holy Trinity on *l'Avenue de l'Alma*. Among his words were *too long, disorganized, and shameful eyesores* speaking of the American Ambulance contingent.

"Smiler, I was touched by all those folks showing up. You know I was in the Ambulance myself. That crowd Gros and Piatt Andrew brought over must be the latest wave of college boys. I didn't recognize any of them. They didn't know Mac, didn't want to be there, and were anxious to get out of the church to prowl the city. I wouldn't be so hard on them," he said, pausing to see Genet's reaction.

"I'm thinking about all the other services we've attended in the last couple of years. Bishop Bhrent wouldn't have been Mac's choice to deliver the sermon. Hell, Jimmy even wrote that he didn't have any religion. I think his exact words were that he could 'stand the performance,' if we found it necessary. Anyway, what I was thinking was that those memorials aren't for the poor dead guy. What does he care? They're for us, for his buddies, his family and loved ones.

"Don't go burying yourself either," Jack commented with concern after reading the line that read: *Perhaps there will be such a service held for me soon, but if there is I pray the American Ambulance will fail to be represented.* He looked at Genet's troubled expression and thought for a fleeting second that Edmond knew something was coming. Jack quickly shook the thought, but not before recalling Mac's moodiness days before his death.

"Yeah, yeah. All the same I want both the tricolor *and* Stars and Stripes on my box," Genet said more than half seriously. Then, changing the subject abruptly, he said, "Jack, you and Charlie are really lucky stiffs having such sweethearts for wives. Mac's three 'fiancées' sure threw me for a loop. Here I've been carrying a flame for my dear sweet Gertrude for over two years, not fooling around with anyone over here, and she up and marries some piker back home."

"It stinks Edmond. I wanted to talk to you about it before, but Mac didn't want you to know he'd told Charlie and me. God it must hurt to be betrayed like that! I had something like that happen to me once." He paused, thinking out loud. "My mom always said 'there's plenty of fish in the sea.' She also told me there was someone out there made for me and that I would know it when I found her. Mom was right on both counts. Think about it. I saw your friend Helen with you. She's a beauty! What about her?"

"Gone to England with her family. Gosh Jack, she just turned seventeen!"

"Yeah, and you are on what side of twenty? She's fond of you. I could see that right away. Can't imagine why any girl wouldn't be with that innocent look on your baby face. Well, the bruises and bandages don't look so swell now, but you have your whole life to live. Cheer up! That's what Mac would have wanted." Jack heard what he was saying almost as if someone else had said it. He hoped he was right in Genet's case.

While Jack talked to Genet, Charlie pumped Thénault with questions. Georges had returned early from Paris to meet with Féquant. *Groupe de Combat 13* was now attached to the French Fifth Army. America's entry into the war was still rumor while the reality of the Nivelle Offensive now bogging down on the Somme had the brass worried.

Indeed Robert Nivelle, now Commander-in-Chief of the French Army, had openly boasted of his massive attack, unwittingly giving the Germans plenty of warning and time to improve their offenses. Nivelle had distinguished himself at Verdun before Joffre's forced removal. Pétain took over the defenses and stabilized the situation in the late fall of 1916. He was then promoted while Nivelle took charge of the retaking of Douaumont, the hotly contested fort whose recapture marked the official end of the battle of Verdun.

Nivelle's success propelled him into Joffre's position. The French were desperate for a miracle worker, and the enormously confident Nivelle captured their imagination with his fiery rhetoric. Meanwhile, Pétain received command of the Center Army Group.

Moves such as these meant little to the men on the ground and even less to the flyers whose concerns were more prosaic. Féquant answered to the Fifth Army headquarters where he received sector boundaries and aerial mission priorities. Boundaries and the trace of the front lines were vital information to the pilots.

Since moving to Ravenel, Group 13 got nothing but reconnaissance missions. Other escadrilles specifically dedicated to this mission couldn't provide enough information fast enough. Some Nieuports and Spads were fitted with cameras the pilots could operate with remote cables. The Lafayette men didn't much go for the mission. Technically they weren't supposed to seek aerial combat during a reconnaissance mission. Most simply ignored this rule.

"As far as we're concerned," Parsons told Thénault, "offensive or defensive, our mission is to attack, attack, attack! After all that's why we're called *chasse*, right?"

So far, aviation's contribution had been far from decisive, but the senior ground commanders had learned how much leverage could be gained by concentrating bombers, observers and fighters. When the Germans attacked they invariably poured everything they had into the effort, including aviation. Since Joffre embraced aviation early in the war, woe unto the French corps commander who failed to consider the aerial component.

Keeler had learned not to expect great revelations from Féquant or Thénault. Generally the leaders did their best to explain the tactical situation, but for the most part they brought back limited details, either because they filtered them themselves, or the details didn't exist. For that reason, Thénault's briefing on April 4 was both a surprise and somewhat of a revelation.

"The Boches have withdrawn to here," he pointed out on the map. The line his finger traced cut off the large bulge that had included the French city of Ham. "It is called their *Hindenburg Line.* Captured papers indicate that the Germans have had to send a number of divisions to the Russian front forcing them to shorten their lines by straightening them. Of course, this makes them less vulnerable to flanking attacks as well.

"We know their aviation was concentrated almost directly opposite us near the town of Ham. They have since moved to stay behind their lines. We think we know where they are. I even know the number of one of their Jastas and the name of its commander." Thénault's eyes twinkled as he waited for this to sink in. "One of his pilots crashed on our side the day Jim died. Before he expired, the German asked us to deliver a message to his unit."

Up to that point, nothing seemed terribly unusual in the briefing. It was a common enough practice. Thénault did surprise them when he said that he personally wanted to deliver the message.

"I want to drop a note indicating that Flight Sergeant Kleinschmidt died in action. It will be a damned sight better than what the bloody Boches did for poor Mac."

"Are we supposed to drop flowers and a wreath and maybe a bottle of champagne, mon Capitaine?" Charlie asked, sarcastically.

Thénault controlled his pained expression carefully, choosing to ignore the remark and continue. "I want a flight of three to take the morning patrol. I will carry the message personally. We will cross the lines at 5,000 meters and try to pinpoint this Jasta. It shouldn't be too difficult since—as you have noticed—many of their Fokkers are very brightly colored. Our deceased friend gave pretty good coordinates. After I drop the message we will take up our normal position looking for enemy fighters."

"Why risk it, Thénault?" de Laage asked. "And why you? I will drop the message."

"Non, mon ami. It is for me to do. I know that some of our pilots question whether their commander has any stomach for battle anymore," he said glancing around to the men present. "I must do this. It is the least I can do for Mac. Besides, if we are lucky the message will produce an immediate response."

"What's that mean?" Thaw said looking as confused as Keeler and de Laage together.

"You'll see when you get to read the message. I don't doubt we will have plenty of game on the morning patrol," Georges Thénault said with a slight wink.

"It's my patrol," Keeler observed. "Do I tell the pilots what you have said?"

"In due time, Keeler. Let it be my little surprise."

THE WAR HAD TURNED A CORNER THAT FEW OF THE WEARY participants could discern. Changes in the high command on both sides over the nearly three years of conflict reflected frustration at the failure to achieve any decisive success. Joffre's quiet removal and replacement by Robert Nivelle foreshadowed a move toward a more aggressive pursuit of *l'attaque à outrance*, the traditional Napoleonic all out offensive. To the poilu in the trenches this bluster was hardly the stuff of good tidings.

Nivelle's promised offensive aimed at penetrating the lines, achieving a major opening in the German defenses, and driving through to split their forces. His mastery of English helped earn him British Prime Minister David Lloyd George's support—so much so that George nearly placed the BEF under French command. An outraged military high command supported the vehement objections from his field commander, Marshal Haig. The average Tommy brewed his 'cuppa' in the dark corner of a dugout ignorant of such intrigues, which, in the end, would matter not a whit in how he or his mates would die.

On the German side, the Kaiser relieved von Moltke in late 1914 for his faulty execution of the Schiefflen Plan, the grand envelopment that was supposed to sweep through Belgium, encircle the French, and drive the British off the continent. Dreams of rapid conquest and resolution expired when it failed. Erich von Falkenhayn, who would later preside over the bloody debacle of Verdun, replaced von Moltke. Verdun proved his undoing. Ludendorf now headed the beleaguered German forces gathering strength behind the so-called Hindenburg Line. Typically, the hearty Hanoverian or Bavarian on the front lines was more interested in his black bread and ration of beer than in why the higher leadership was changing.

Aviation units on both sides could boast of rising above the muddy squalor. A measure of nobility survived in the group some journalists dubbed *Knights of the Air.* Higher education accounted for some of this distinction as did wealth, but other factors were at work. Men mastering the air, themselves, and their opponents, developed a bond and commitment to their fellows that even extended to some degree to their enemies. Like knights, airmen feigned indifference to politics. Yet, passions still ran very deep. Often the cause for which they fought became muddled in their minds, but the death of a friend could fan the smoldering coals of indifference into all-consuming flames of vengeance.

Bill Thaw showed little interest in grand strategy, but he actually followed the papers and listened carefully whenever Thénault invited him to group headquarters. In his mind the German pullback indicated neither a weakening of their will nor a lessening of their ability to continue the war. Bill Thaw reminded Charlie of what he'd so arrogantly said to Count von Bernstorff in New York over a year ago. *War is hell.*

Chapter 59
America Acts

Ravenel, April 6, 1917

"We're in it! Wilson's declared war!" Jack shouted having just gotten off the telephone with Paul Rockwell. Most of the pilots were in the popote finishing dinner. Buck's news brought cheers and calls for champagne. Even the French officers cheered. Most thought it was about time the United States entered the nearly three-year old conflict.

Speculation began in earnest. Most of them assumed they would be wearing their country's uniform in a matter of days. After all, the American Army would need their experience, they reasoned. Thénault expected commissions to arrive almost overnight. He and de Laage were as happy as the others, but also a little disappointed, realizing the escadrille would no longer be theirs. Thaw kidded them saying they could become the first French volunteers to serve in the American Army.

Genet cheered as loudly as the others. This was good news regardless of his personal situation. He thought about his brothers. Both of them had served in the militia, and Rivers had even been down on the border with the Punitive Expedition. Edmond both hoped for and dreaded the thought that they would come over with the first troops. He hadn't gone home like Jack and the others in more than two years. Always afraid he'd be arrested as a deserter, he turned down several chances, and he missed his family dearly.

"Boy, we'll fix those heinies now!" he shouted, voicing the thoughts many of them shared. Yet, none of them was prepared for the reality of their nation's woeful lack of preparedness.

When the drop mission approached the captain chose the two new lieutenants to be his escort. They, along with Lufbery, were his top aces. He wanted to demonstrate firsthand that their captain was no coward. He hadn't told the rest of the escadrille what was in the message. Just before they climbed into their waiting Spads Thénault showed them the carefully lettered note. It began:

> *To the commanding officer of Jasta 6:*
> *I regret to inform you that Fliegersergent Kleinschmidt perished from injuries after he crash-landed in French lines. He was buried near Ham with full military honors. Before he died he begged to convey a message to you. 'Watch Keller.'*
> *I too wish to convey a message to you. Send Keller. We'll watch him for you.*
> *Commanding officer French Escadrille*

"Wow! Now I see what you meant about stirring them up. Do we wait for a response?" Charlie asked, only half-joking. "I mean we might not get any takers by flying over their field at such an ungodly hour." Thénault hoped to dive on the German field, drop the note in its empty shell casing and make a beeline back to safety. He knew the Germans protected their fields more carefully than the French. It would take considerable *sang froid* to brave the defenses in order to drop the message.

"You know what I ordered, Lieutenant Keeler. No unnecessary action. We go in, and get the hell out as quickly as possible."

Charlie couldn't understand taking the risk, but he did like the thought of sowing dissention in the German ranks. Whoever this Keller was, he was going to catch hell. Charlie hoped to catch the Germans trying to get off the field. Regardless of Thénault's orders, if he saw anyone taking off Charlie was going to nail them, and Jack agreed to do the same.

Charlie thought that Kleinschmidt must have really hated this Keller guy or he would never have given the coordinates of his Jasta. Thénault crossed the lines at 5,000 meters and headed directly for the spot the German sergeant had indicated. Fearing some kind of trap, Thénault planned for the early hour and high altitude to achieve some surprise.

At the designated coordinates Thénault began to circle with Buck and Keeler trailing. There was just enough light to make out the ground, but no one could make out the signature of an airfield. The roads or trails that would show traffic to the field were indistinct. Evidence of hangars or other manmade features that would betray an airfield eluded their eyes. There was nothing for it but to descend to get a closer look. If Kleinschmidt had lured them over an anti-aircraft battery, they would know in minutes.

At five hundred meters features on the ground became more distinct. Thénault focused on the largest clearing as the most likely airfield. He didn't want to descend into easy machine gun range. Failing to discern an operational airfield, Thénault was about to give up the search, relieved in a way that the silly mission hadn't gotten them killed.

Just as he began to pull up, a flash caught his eye. He turned to circle back over the spot, only to see both Buck and Keeler dive on the flash with their weapons blazing. Startled and angry, Thénault couldn't see the men on the ground scattering from the machine gun pit.

Jack and Charlie could hardly believe what they saw as they strafed the pit from no more than two hundred feet. In the trees were dozens of vehicles, tents, hangars and airplanes under enormous nets. All of it had been completely invisible from altitude.

Georges saw no alternative but to join his lieutenants. Angry at what he thought was blatant disobedience; he quickly changed his mind when he saw what they had discovered. He released the canister. It had a long streamer of white cloth with 'message' printed in German. He hoped they wouldn't consider it a bomb and destroy it. Thénault zoomed skyward hoping the headstrong Americans would break off and follow. The jasta didn't have time to react. They didn't push even one plane out of the woodline.

Thénault glanced back to look for Buck and Keeler closing up on his tail. He expected the German aerial defenses near the front lines to be well alerted to look for the three Spads. He just hoped to get back in one piece. Féquant may not appreciate the gesture. Thénault chuckled to himself when he realized how much the Americans had rubbed off on him.

WALDREP COULDN'T UNDERSTAND HOW THE FRENCH HAD FOUND THEM. He'd personally overseen the camouflage effort and had flown over the field at different times of the day looking for telltale signs like tracks, unusual shadows, brown or wilted foliage, and shapes too regular to be natural. It had been virtually perfect.

One of his soldiers interrupted his thoughts. The man held up an apparently empty French 75-millimeter shell casing with a white tail. After explaining that one of the French planes had dropped it, he showed the captain the note. It was neatly lettered in both French and German.

"Who else has seen this?"

"No one, Herr Hauptmann."

"And you?"

"I did sir. That is why I brought it directly to you."

"You did well. Now I must insist that you say nothing about it."

Waldrep cursed Kleinschmidt for giving away their position. He wouldn't have expected that from an experienced senior non-commissioned officer. Confident the French would never have found their field without additional information, he consoled himself that at least it wasn't a failure of the careful camouflage.

Watch Keller. He'd been doing that very thing for several days without discovering anything untoward about the lieutenant's performance in the air or on the ground. The sergeant must have seen something. But the more he thought about it the more he discounted Kleinschmidt's treachery. Even under duress, the sergeant would never give anything to the enemy without a compelling reason.

Waldrep considered his next actions carefully. At worst they would have to move again. At best, the mystery of Keller was bound to be broken. Keller would surely cover his tracks if he confronted him directly, and dead men can't testify. The French may have fabricated the message without Kleinschmidt. Maybe the man was delirious when he let Keller's name drop. Maybe French intelligence got his location from one of the locals. He had to give his lieutenant some credit. It was time to pay the French airfield a visit.

Within minutes of the brief attack, Waldrep formed a patrol. He assigned the patrol to Keller. Unbeknownst to the lieutenant, Waldrep climbed into the trail triplane as the flight lined up. A startled corporal gave up his seat, thankful he wouldn't have to follow the lieutenant. Too many pilots got into trouble on flights with Keller.

Waldrep had ordered Keller's morning patrol to go to Ravenel to hit any French airfield in the area. Intelligence reports indicated that the famous Storks were somewhere around the small village. It was a great way to test Keller. If he disappeared this time, Waldrep would see it himself. The captain still held out hope that his suspicions were unfounded.

Keller climbed to ten thousand feet and tested his guns. He'd briefed the mission just as the captain ordered, but he had no intention of diving on any enemy airfield. He expected to see some enemy in the air well before they got near St. Just. It was nothing more than standard procedure to attack enemy machines.

Over their old field south of Ham Keller searched vainly for enemy patrols. He didn't like crossing the lines for any reason, but they were already over them at Ham. Ravenel was even farther behind the lines. White puffs dotted the sky below them. Thankfully, the French gunners hadn't found their range. Lacking a valid excuse to break away, Keller had no choice but to press on to the target. He thought about claiming motor trouble, but was troubled that the mechanics wouldn't find anything wrong.

Meanwhile, Waldrep kept his position in the trail aircraft still hoping Keller would prove him wrong. The man *was* vexing, but he was also a decorated ace. His connections on the German General Staff were also well known. Catching him in something off color would create a nightmare of inquiries. He didn't want to think about the paperwork and the ordeal of proving his suspicions to Keller's powerful uncle.

Waldrep could see Saint Just fairly clearly from some distance. The railroad tracks ran in from the south and came out north of the city. He searched for Ravenel, the little village on the map where they expected to find the *Stork's* field. With the sun behind them they would be difficult to detect.

The French made little attempt to hide their airfields. They were almost never attacked during the day since most German fighters stayed on their side of the lines. At night, bombers bombed blindly or went for lights. Camouflage was an inconvenience to the French.

Waldrep finally saw the line of canvas hangars. The large number suggested more than one escadrille. Sure that Keller saw the field, he began his descent. Keller gave no indication of seeing the field. Maybe he'd missed it. Waldrep decided to break formation and slide up into the lead wagging his wings and pointing down.

He got close enough to get Keller's attention, confident his helmet and goggles would mask his identity in the corporal's blue triplane. If the attack went as planned, Keller should be madder than hell at the 'corporal' in the trail aircraft. Waldrep hadn't thought out that possibility.

Keller nodded recognition of the signal and pointed at Waldrep and then the ground. This made sense. Since he was already in the lead and had been first to see the target, Waldrep should start the attack. He dove away in a tight descending spiral to keep from overstressing the upper wings. Banked hard over to the right he couldn't see behind very well. He always marveled at how quickly one could descend after laboring for long minutes to get to altitude. It reminded him of climbing mountains. It also increased his wariness.

At about a thousand feet he leveled off momentarily to allow the flight to form for the attack. Looking back he counted only two triplanes—neither of them yellow with red stripes. He checked again thinking somehow he had missed the lieutenant. Soon the frenetic activity on the ground made him forgot about Keller. He singled out one of the big canvas hangars and laced it with a long burst before beginning a rapid climb. He hoped he'd at least damaged a Spad or Nieuport. There didn't seem to be any parked outside. Probably off on missions.

The other two Fokkers, flown by experienced sergeants, completed their runs before climbing to join Waldrep. They'd left their calling card. It was time to head back. Waldrep would have to deal with Keller. Or would he? Maybe the Prussian had a good reason for not attacking. With the captain and two other witnesses, it would have to be damned good.

Waldrep hadn't seen any aircraft on the ground because nearly every machine from *Groupe de Combat 13* was on a regularly scheduled mission that morning. Additionally, French artillery had alerted Féquant of a flight of German triplanes headed their way. Féquant directed the field cleared and all nonflyable machines pushed into the hangars. The canvas hangars wouldn't protect anything, but they would at least disguise the presence of the new Spads.

With the excitement of America's declaration of war, Féquant had expected the Germans to pay the Lafayette Escadrille a visit soon, but he expected it to be another night bombing raid. He barely had time to order every available weapon on the ground manned before taking off to assist in protecting the field.

Thénault's flight was still out. Thaw and de Laage led the rest of the pilots to the lines to look for the errant Germans. It simply didn't seem possible for them to be going after the field at Ravenel. It had never happened before. Bombings yes, but never fighters. Thénault's flight of three patrolled the lines after attacking Jasta 6. They hadn't seen Keller's formation pass over them hidden by an intervening cloud layer.

As Thénault approached Ravenel on his return with Buck and Keeler he saw smoke rising from the field. It was coming from the hangar area! He saw tracers looping up, whipping the sky as if they were driving the attackers into the air. What in the devil? Seeing brightly colored triplanes gave him the answer. He realized they had been gone long enough for Jasta 6 to launch a counterattack. He hoped they still had enough ammunition to give the Germans something to remember them by.

Charlie wondered if there were any other French planes available. It wouldn't take much to overwhelm these three. Then he spotted a fourth triplane high and at some distance to the north. He broke off to chase this one lest it hamper the captain and Jack in their attack on the other three. He was happy to see a Spad bearing Féquant's markings join in pursuing the three Fokkers coming off their attack on the field.

As soon as Charlie came into view of the yellow triplane the pilot bolted for the safety of his own lines. He didn't have far to go and Charlie didn't have enough fuel to chase him. The Spad, however, was considerably more powerful and faster than the Fokker. Charlie cut off the fleeing Boche and closed on his tail. The German pilot began some very inept evasive maneuvers, all the time trying to regain a northeasterly heading back to relative safety. He made no attempt to turn and fight. Charlie decided the man had jammed weapons or he would have joined his mates in the strafing run.

To test his theory Charlie fired a short burst across the German's path. The plane's reaction made Charlie think the man had never been fired at before. It fell like a spinning leaf. Charlie knew he hadn't hit the triplane so he assumed the German was playing possum or trying to free his guns. Catching up easily just as the triplane came out of its spin, Charlie inched up parallel to the gaudy yellow machine and pointed down at the field. If the man couldn't fight he might want to take his chances as a prisoner rather than get shot down. Charlie couldn't stomach killing the German if he was in effect unarmed.

The DR 1 made no effort to return to the field but kept trying to head to the northeast. Charlie couldn't dally. If the son of a bitch was too stupid to save his life, Charlie would have to accommodate him. He decided to try one more time to convince his apparently toothless adversary that landing was the only way he would live.

Charlie whipped the Spad around and over the top of the yellow triplane. Then, rising sharply, he used his superior speed to dive right in front of the enemy. If the man cleared his guns at that moment Charlie was in for it. But there were no signs of fight so Charlie took up a position above and behind the Fokker and fired a short burst into the left bank of wings. When the German turned right, Charlie stitched the right bank. Finally the German gave it up. Charlie almost laughed when the man put both hands in the air.

He herded the hapless Hun like a stray calf until they landed at Ravenel. He rolled to a complete stop in front of the triplane. As Charlie excitedly climbed down, Paul Rockwell came up and patted him on the back.

"Damnedest thing I've ever seen! Good Lord, Charlie what a show! Wait until my paper gets this story."

"Hello, Paul. Sorry we couldn't meet you. Are Thénault and Jack back yet?"

"I don't think so. That must have been them then mixing it up with the other Fokkers."

"Yeah. I probably should get back up there to help them, but I am almost bone dry. Hey! Let's go over to see how our guest is doing before he tries to burn that pretty yellow machine." He shouted to the men running up to secure the Fokker to point it away from the hangers and safety the guns.

Keller's scarred face almost frightened the two mechanics that now held him. They were nearly as scared as Keller was. After all he was a German officer. They'd never seen one up close and alive. The man's face was twisted in a hideous expression made worse by the scar. His arrogance was palpable even though he hadn't uttered a word.

When his opponent walked up with the tall man in civilian clothes Keller's demeanor changed dramatically. First he gasped and then he began to shake like a leaf. His haughty manner dissolved instantly. Charlie thought the noble thing to do was shake the man's hand. His war was over.

Just then a short burst from the twin Spandau's on the Triplane startled them. A couple men dove for cover. Charlie steadied Paul Rockwell who hadn't been around guns for some time. He knew they were clearing the guns on the German machine. He looked at the prisoner curiously. If he had ammunition why hadn't he fought back? Maybe the guns were jammed, but both fired on the ground.

"*Parlez-vous français*?" Charlie asked as the realization of the man's likely cowardice sank in. The German Lieutenant looked Keeler in the eye for a fraction of a second almost as if he recognized him. He didn't respond to the question. Charlie didn't remember much of his father's German. "How about English?" he asked, not expecting a response.

"A little, lieutenant," Keller said in a trembling voice. Coming face to face with this man thoroughly unnerved him. He couldn't be sure, but one doesn't easily forget such an experience. Keller thought his mind might be playing games with him when he concluded that this man looked like the same madman who had wiped out his patrol that fateful night so long ago. Keller ventured a longer look at the man's face, a face burned into his nightmares. The face was that of his uncle, the hated one whose picture hung draped in black back home; the man who fled to America.

His mind raced back. Rejik had told him an *American* led the patrol that night. Hadn't Waldrep just mentioned an American escadrille in their sector? Deciding the man would never make the connection if indeed he had been the one in No Man's Land that night, Keller tried to turn the situation to his advantage.

"American?" he ventured.

"And proud of it, Mr. German. Where did you learn English?"

"In school," Keller lied. He'd spent most of June and July, 1914, touring the United States with his uncle Fritz. They were looking for the missing uncle in order to give him a chance to come back to Prussia. The other brothers were all officers on the vaunted German General Staff. With war clouds gathering, they wanted to find their youngest brother who had cut all ties with the family.

During their unsuccessful search Keller picked up a little of the language along with a venereal disease from one of the loose women he frequented with his uncle. Much of the English he'd learned had to do with the coarse vulgar language of the bordello. Some of the girls swore and cussed at him because of the way he liked to hurt them. The one who had infected him wouldn't infect anyone else. Keller had seen to that. She'd died painfully.

"What's your name, rank and unit?" Charlie asked somewhat coldly. He'd imagined being in this guy's shoes some day and hoped to be treated with respect.

"Keller, Johann, lieutenant. I don't have to give my unit." Keller said, regaining some of his composure while rapidly thinking.

"Charlie, it's Jasta 6! The ones you visited this morning." Lufbery announced waving a small booklet he'd taken from the triplane. "Why didn't you defend yourself, German?" Lufbery asked. "There is nothing wrong with your machine or your guns."

Keller looked at the short man who spoke English with a French accent. Seeing it was a sergeant, he decided he didn't have to answer. Lufbery walked away in disgust. He hated Germans generally, but he hated cowards even more.

Charlie was so excited about forcing a German to land at his own field that it took a while to dawn on him that this Keller might be the *Keller* of Kleinschmidt's message. Even after Luf announced the unit, Charlie discounted it as an impossible coincidence.

Thinking about the yellow plane so many had mentioned, he realized the connection. He gave Paul Rockwell a brief explanation. Paul just kept shaking his head, pointing out that the German lieutenant's failure to fight could well be the reason for Kleinschmidt's message.

"I can see that now, but it's almost as if Jasta 6 delivered him. Thénault's note said 'Send Keller. We'll take care of him,' or something like that."

"You still had to force him to land, Charlie," Paul noted.

"Who do we have here who speaks German?" Charlie asked the small group that had gathered around them. Haviland stepped out. He'd learned some German in college, but the captain also spoke German.

"Let's get this *kamerad* to tell us about himself before giving him to *Groupe*." Charlie said.

For the next half-hour while Nieuports and Spads arrived and departed, Keeler interrogated Keller. Buck finally showed up anxious to find out how they'd acquired the triplane. Thénault's German was even better than his English. He doubted they would get any useful intelligence from the man, but it wouldn't hurt to try. When he found out their man's name he was as dumbfounded as the others.

Keller seemed unable to speak directly to Haviland, a mere sergeant, but he relaxed when Thénault arrived. Jack thought the disfiguring scar interesting. Willis asked about it and Keller told them a partial truth about being wounded early in the war.

"So you were in the infantry?" Keeler asked in English after hearing the translation.

"Cavalry," Keller responded, continuing to develop a scheme to ingratiate himself with these fools. If he could convince them he wanted to aid their cause he might be able to avoid being sent off as a prisoner. Switching to English, he began to weave a tale of corruption in the German Army. He said that many believed that the war was lost now that the United States was in it. He said he was disgusted by the way his own people destroyed peaceful villages when they pulled out.

Thénault asked if he knew Sergeant Kleinschmidt. Keller, wondering if they held him as well, thought for several seconds. He saw no harm in admitting he knew the other pilot since they already knew his unit.

"Ah so! Perhaps you would be interested in the message Kleinschmidt gave us for your commander?" Thénault said with a sideways glance.

Keller stood stone-faced wondering what Kleinschmidt might have told them. Thénault reached in his breast pocket for his draft of the note, unfolded it, and held it up for Keller to read.

"The *schwein*! That is how you found us? He should be shot." Keller quickly pieced together the events of the last days. He had to discredit Kleinschmidt. It was perfect! He would depict the man as a vindictive subordinate dedicated to the lost cause.

Jack had only listened for a few minutes, but he'd heard enough to doubt Keller's claims that Kleinschmidt was a cheat at cards who owed Keller lots of money. It wasn't even a plausible story. Why would the dying sergeant care about money? But then again, Keller didn't realize the man was dead.

Charlie also sensed something off key in the manner and attitude Keller displayed. He remembered the man shaking when he first saw him. Why was that? Charlie hadn't menaced him nor done anything on the ground to cause him fear. Something set the German off. Clearly his arrogance and disdain for enlisted men was no act. He had to believe he was truly better than they were.

Willis asked Keller when he'd started flying. Keller gave the precise date he'd left the trenches near Pont à Mousson, March 8, 1915. Keeler froze in position.

"Ask him if he was in the front lines."

Keller nodded.

"Ask him if he remembers a Foreign Legion deserter." Charlie was fishing blindly. Keller darted a glance at Keeler and saw instantly where the man was going. He answered negatively.

"He's lying," Jack said. "Every time he answers truthfully he relaxes a little and taps his hand on his knee. When he lies his cheek twitches and he clenches his fist. What do you want to bet that this piece of shit was in the patrol that ambushed you, Charlie?"

Keller's obvious fear showed that he understood Buck better than he'd allowed.

"What was the traitor's name, Charlie? Retig?"

"Rejik. Ask him if he knows Rejik." At the mention of the word Keller tensed up and refused to answer any more questions. Things were just not going his way. He looked to the captain for support.

Charlie, remembering Hamed and the grenade they'd placed in his hand, began to relive some of the anger that had propelled him through the wire. He placed a hand on Keller's right shoulder and looked at him coldly. "You know Rejik?"

Keller shrank. Charlie squeezed the shoulder enough to make the lieutenant grimace. "I asked you a question. You were at Pont à Mousson in the front lines at the same time as my unit. Did you know a traitor named Rejik?"

Keller shook his head his cheek twitching like mad and his fists tightened until the knuckles were white. He was scared, so scared that he blurted out in nearly perfect English: "Would you hurt your own cousin American?"

"What are you talking about? Somebody tell me what he is talking about. Maybe you should get him out of here before I do something regrettable."

"He's a liar, Charlie and a proven coward. Don't let him goad you," Jack said easing Charlie's hand away from the German. Thénault couldn't let them badger the prisoner let alone hurt him. He stepped in and suggested they turn Keller over to Group right away.

Seeing that he was out of danger, Keller became emboldened. "It is true American. We have a picture of my uncle at home, an uncle that fled the fatherland to avoid his duty. He looks just like you." If Keller was trying to curry Keeler's favor he'd made a major mistake.

"Get him away from me!" Keeler shouted. "At least my father had the courage to leave." If this *was* a relative he wanted to pummel him for disgracing his own uniform and country and implying John Keeler was a shirker. In the end though all he could muster was disgust. This wasn't the noble enemy they faced in the air. This was a cowering phony.

"Capitaine, why don't we let this sorry excuse of a man fly back to his unit? We can take off his guns and let him take his chances getting back. I'm sure they will be pleased to get him back." Jack Buck said only half seriously.

"Good idea, Lieutenant. The Fokker is of no use to us. He may not make it back anyway. I'm sure Hauptmann Waldrep will know what to do with him if he does make it." Upon hearing Waldrep's name Keller nearly wet his pants.

"You cannot do this! I am a prisoner. I have offered to defect! You can't make me return."

"Isn't it amazing how much his English improves with time?" Haviland observed. "Wouldn't his commander like to know that he had offered to defect?"

"I like it," Charlie finally said, joining in the effort to further frazzle Herr Keller. Perhaps my father would be willing to post a letter to his estranged family. Better yet, let's get Paul to put it in his paper. The Germans still read the American papers even if we are now at war with them. How about it Paul? 'Decorated German Officer Defects to Lafayette Escadrille' has a nice ring to it."

"Easily done. We can get it on the international wire and it will be all over Berlin even before the *Chicago Daily News* goes to print."

Keller looked from one of his tormenters to another absorbing every word. He didn't know if they were playing with him or serious. On the verge of crying, he saw his carefully crafted life coming to an unpleasant end. If they didn't kill him, his own people would. If he had an ounce of courage he would kill himself. He felt like a trapped rat.

Thénault ordered him delivered to Féquant. The man was a pitiful excuse of a soldier in any army. He wanted him out of the Lafayette Escadrille before his illness could spread to the real heroes. Keller didn't stand much of a chance of surviving captivity. His fellow prisoners would do him in. It might have been more humane to let him try to fly back. He could auger in on purpose in a spectacular crash and still get an honorable burial ceremony.

Chapter 60
Ham

Ham, April 7, 1917

Seeing the devastation left by the retreating Germans sickened the first arriving members of the Lafayette Escadrille. All had witnessed combat's havoc. Scenes of Verdun remained fresh in their minds' eyes. Yet the scarred countryside, denuded of trees and all other vegetation by months of incessant bombardment and soldier's shovels, did little to prepare them for the deliberate sabotage in and around the village of Ham.

De Laage walked about bewildered, muttering obscenities. He told Thaw and Keeler he had visited Ham before the war,. He led them directly to the building he'd remembered and knocked at the door. No one answered.

"A woman and her daughter lived here," he said. He told them the girl had been a special friend. Since they'd known him he had never mentioned a woman friend. Charlie remembered seeing de Laage escorting different ladies in Paris, but never more than once. De Laage turned and knocked gently on the door. He reached up to knock again when the door swung loose from a broken upper hinge. Pulling it open he shouted to see if anyone answered. They heard a faint moaning and caught the unmistakable odor of decaying flesh. Everything in the home was torn up, broken or tossed haphazardly. Excrement deposited in various corners attracted swarms of flies. The stench caused Thaw to gag. Charlie plugged his nose.

In the back room the source of the powerful smell lay crumpled on the floor. Shreds of an old dress barely covered the body of an old woman. De Laage pushed past Keeler and ran up the stairs toward the sound of the moaning. Thaw followed de Laage into the bedroom where a horrifying scene wrenched his stomach again. On the slashed mattress lay a battered and bruised woman curled up in a fetal position surrounded by vomit and blood. She didn't recognize de Laage but jerked violently when she realized someone was in the room.

Charlie stepped over the debris and stood motionless in the doorway as de Laage leaned over the woman and gently said her name. "Eva? Eva," he murmured. "Who has done this to you?" He looked up at Bill Thaw pleadingly and Thaw raced from the room in search of assistance, happy to get away from the terrible sights and smells. Charlie, inured to carnage on the battlefield, still reeled at the pathetic figure on the bed. His heart hardened at the race that spawned such evil, his own father's nation.

Soon the woman was on her way to the hospital in Compiègne with de Laage in attendance. Thaw and Keeler joined the rest of their comrades at the field south of the city of Ham so recently used by Jasta 6.

"I don't get it, Bill. The field seems untouched while the town is unlivable. It doesn't make any sense," Charlie said as they wondered around the old buildings and new shacks left intact by the Germans. "It looks almost as if they thought they were coming right back. Why the hell tear up the town then?"

"I've got a hunch the crowd that lived and worked here had leadership while those passing through the town went wild. The Germans my family dealt with that I knew before the war were refined, intelligent people. The swine that did that to de Laage's little Eva are a different sort. There's still a lot of the barbarian warrior left in their blood."

"Noble of you to be so democratic in light of what we just saw, Bill, but I guess you're right. We have our share of bad apples, but can you imagine an American doing this? Talk about leaders? Someone had to have ordered that destruction if not the rapes. The one thing I do know about Germans is that they understand authority and discipline."

"War does strange things, doesn't it, Charlie? We almost have to hate the enemy to keep doing what we are doing, but I can't hate so indiscriminately. I have real friends probably fighting for the Germans or Austrians. At least Jasta 6 has some degree of honor. That sergeant didn't give away his unit's location without reason. He wanted Keller to get caught whether by his own people or by us. I'd even go so far as to say their leader, Waldrep, might be a decent sort."

"I don't know how you can make that assumption, Bill. All we know is that he keeps a clean field and knows how to hide his Jasta better than anyone else."

"We also know that he ordered the attack on our field, something the German fighters have never done before. I'll bet old Waldrep and his fellows aren't shedding any tears about losing Keller. If that slimy bastard is related to you in any way it doesn't show."

"I'd just as soon forget what he said, Bill. It's bad enough trying to understand how a civilized nation can do this let alone accept the thought that I have family fighting against us." Charlie snuffed out the half cigarette he'd been nursing. He had all but quit smoking until coming through Ham where he bummed cigarettes from others in the futile hope of covering up the stench.

Charlie thought Bill Thaw took life in easy stride. Whatever made the curtain fall over Bill's open countenance now had to be very powerful. Charlie knew Jack would have a theory about it. Probably the father fixation he always talked about.

Back at their aérodrome the move had gone smoothly. Though the last escadrille to move, there was still plenty of room for them. Finally they were getting out of the dirt and into some decent buildings. Charlie found himself enormously hungry after seeing the devastation in Ham and the starving orphans on the streets.

Willis tried to brighten up their evening with some music. The old upright piano they'd bought and brought to Ravenel occupied a corner of the building now christened their *popote* at Ham. Hal tapped out a lively tune called *Alexander's Ragtime Band.* The music provided an almost pleasant backdrop and a relief from Thénault's discordant pounding.

Jack sat with Charlie playing an absent-minded game of gin rummy. Charlie frowned when he heard someone mention Johann Keller. It didn't seem likely that people were going to forget. Paul's article, published in the *Herald,* carefully avoided any mention of the so-called family linkage between the captured German officer and Keeler.

"Jack, why do you suppose Chouteau doesn't have the father problem you keep harping about?"

"Humor." Jack said taking a sip of his brandy water press. "The Johnsons laughed a lot. They could laugh at each other too. I doubt if old man Chapman ever smiled in his adult life. Imagine thrusting your hand into a fire? Unbalanced. Obsessed. I don't know. I can't see even you that serious. Besides, Michelle cuts your corners off too well for you to become a domineering father."

Their conversation had no beginning, middle or end. It was sort of a continuous stream of thoughts passing between two young men who had attuned themselves to each other. Charlie didn't go for the deep analysis that Jack enjoyed so much. He liked things straightforward.

"Might have something to do with his being an Army officer and a West Pointer too, you know," Jack said, thinking about how nicely David Dick Johnson had treated him.

"Other than Major Parker I've never met a West Point graduate. Until I talked to him, I wasn't even sure where the place was, although I did remember it being important in the Revolution and having something to do with Benedict Arnold." At the moment he was aching for action, not history or psychological gymnastics.

He wished there was some way they could fight more successfully at night. It didn't seem natural to stop just because it was dark or rainy or too windy. Those things didn't stop the ground soldiers.

Charlie's mind was in considerable turmoil. Images of Ham and of Eva alternated in his mind's eye with the face of the man who claimed to be his cousin. Charlie's blood boiled when he felt outraged. The little children holding hands in Ham struck a sensitive chord in his heart. He imagined Michelle as Eva and Michael, just now starting to walk, holding hands with another orphan hoping for a hand out. Then a wave of guilt washed over him for having tried to get away from Michael's crying. Charlie arrived at a simplified, if passionate, conclusion that the world consisted of friends and enemies with little distinction in between.

Jack, on the other hand, became more circumspect. He saw their fight as a struggle for survival as well as an effort to defeat a morally bankrupt enemy. There was a religious aspect to his way of looking at things. He was slow to judge and reluctant to group even the perpetrators of the evil done to Ham into one malevolent opponent. Jack reacted with typical human fury to the loss of his friends, but he strove to control his gut reaction to that fury, especially after seeing so many 'go west' in hasty efforts to obtain vengeance.

Philippe Féquant showed up at the popote without warning. A few chairs scraped as the men tried to rise, but he quickly waved them to stay seated. He said he had an announcement they would all want to hear. With that a couple of men rushed out to find any of the others in the area. Féquant accepted a drink and agreed to wait a few minutes.

He began in the slow carefully articulated French he always used with the Americans: "It is wonderful news that America is now an ally. I know you have all been hoping for this. So, of course, have we. I am very happy with the news, but not so happy with having to lose Spa. 124." Murmurs and a great deal of shuffling greeted this statement.

"As of today, by order of Corps, Spa. 124, also known as the *Lafayette Escadrille*, is to be outfitted with American uniforms and come under American control. . ." Cheers interrupted him, but he only smiled and twisted his mustache.

"Since there are no American uniforms we will not strip you of your colorful collection of unauthorized French *tenues*." More cheers and laughter.

"Since there are no American Army headquarters, no airplanes, no ammunition, no money to pay you, we will continue to provide these things—for a while," he paused for dramatic effect. Everyone now listened raptly, especially at the mention of pay.

"In point of fact, messieurs, things are essentially the same as they were before—no need to applaud my American friends...." Absolute silence greeted Féquant's attempt at humor.

"You will have many questions, I'm sure, but, I am also sure that you will not expect straight answers from me. After all, as I already said, nothing has changed." Now the men laughed, the old hands harder than the others. Nothing pleased them more than a senior officer able to make fun of himself or of the ponderous French bureaucracy. Even poking fun at America was fine under the circumstances.

"I must warn you that the war is not yet over though I expect the Boches to be quaking in their hobnailed boots at the thought of having to fight your mighty nation." Again, the laughter was genuine.

"You were the last to leave Ravenel and the last to arrive here, but I'm afraid you will be the first to fight. We have a big day tomorrow. Capitaine Thénault will brief the missions after I leave. One more thing: You will be allowed some time in Paris in the coming days as we finish picking up our Spads...." Raucous cheering drowned him out as the men took up the familiar chant, *Vive la France! Vive l'Amérique. Vive Féquant!*

EASTER SUNDAY, APRIL 8, WAS A DAY OF GREAT ANTICIPATION FOR GENET. He'd gotten eighteen of the twenty hours he needed to become a *sous-officier*. Today, the Lord willing, he would get the remaining two. He took off in his Nieuport right behind Jack Buck's Spad. Jack had modified his original *J* with bumblebee insignia. Edmond thought it was clever enough in the first place. Now, in place of the big letter *J*, Buck had formed the overlapped bee's wings into the shape of a big heart. Inside each of the wings he'd painted smaller J's. *Jack and Jennifer Buck*. Not only clever, Genet thought, but terribly romantic.

Willis had to test fire his machine guns before he could take off. His Nieuport sat on the south edge of the field pointed into the woods with the motor turning at normal RPM. Hal pressed the trigger release and was rewarded with the steady rhythmic beat of two perfectly synchronized Vickers. Unfortunately, the two guns were well synchronized with each other and *not* with the motor and propeller. Hal sat in horror as his propeller disintegrated into matchsticks before he could release the trigger.

Hinkle, Lovell, and Marr left the ground behind Genet, and Lieutenant de Laage brought up the rear. Even without Willis, it was one of the largest combat patrols the escadrille had mounted. Keeler and Thaw would take up another that afternoon. The Nivelle Offensive was finally building momentum. Fifth Army ordered almost continuous flying patrols during daylight. Group 13 divided up the sector to their front to give each escadrille some maneuver room. Thénault drew the easternmost for Spa. 124. It would take them across the lines as far as Saint Quentin.

Within minutes of forming the flight east of Ham, Lovell's Nieuport dropped out with engine problems. He made it back to Ham only to lose all power on his approach, falling through short of the field by only a hundred yards. His landing gear plowed into the softening ground, caught and stopped, flipping the Nieuport over on its back like a turtle. Walter hung unhurt in the harness trying to decide how to avoid falling into the freshly spread manure under his head.

Buck crossed the lines at eight thousand feet with the remaining four aircraft, two Spads, his and de Laage's, and three Nieuports. He arrived over the railroad bridge on the Saint Quentin River east of Jussy and turned north. He planned to fly up to Saint Quentin in search of action and then back to the starting point at Jussy. If they didn't encounter any Boches in the first hour, he'd briefed the flight to break up and continue individually until they needed to return for fuel.

The first circuit of the long oval passed quickly and almost without event. German artillery burst along the path behind them at the right altitude. Jack knew better than to fly that track again. Pop Hinkle didn't. Instead of following in the loose line formation, Pop stayed over the railroad. Black puffs reached up to greet him. They were so close that they caused his Nieuport to jump and drop uncommanded. He panicked for a moment and overcompensated for one of the drops by pulling up the nose too far. Jack looked back in time to see Hinkle spinning uncontrolled down toward the river. Genet peeled off to follow. While they'd never practiced it, the men talked all the time about trying to land to recover a fellow behind enemy lines. Edmond was bold enough to give it a try if Pop made it down safely.

Now Jack's flight was a total shambles. Naturally, German fighters chose that moment to appear in force. It looked like the whole German Air Force had risen to cut them off. Actually, Jack counted ten black-crossed buses, about half Albatroses and the rest Fokker DR1's. He wished Genet hadn't left, but he still had Marr and de Laage. Nasty odds, but he'd seen worse.

Hinkle recovered after falling only two thousand feet. Nothing seemed to be damaged, but more puffs of black smoke seemed to have followed him down. He climbed more cautiously almost running into another Nieuport bearing the chevron and star insignia of Edmond Genet.

Genet wagged his wings to get Hinkle to follow him as they labored back up to where Jack and the others were tangling with a nest of hornets. As they mounted through seven thousand feet a Fokker passed them falling in pieces. The upper wings of the triplane were entirely gone making it look like a normal biplane for a second or two until the remaining wings folded up. Edmond felt a rush of adrenaline as he steeled himself for combat.

Buck traded shots with a pair of triplanes that had attempted to form a circle with their mates to fight off the French planes. One had already fallen to de Laage. He zeroed in on another, nailing the pilot whose head seemed to burst like a melon. Sickened by the sight, Jack forced himself to search the sky for the others.

Marr found himself the object of affection of a parcel of unfriendly Albatroses. He fired at one while the other four fired at him. This was not his idea of a fair fight. His target, agreeing with Marr's assessment, somehow managed to join his fellows to make it more even—five to one.

Siwash searched his memory for all the tricks he'd learned, but could only come up with the image of fighting off hoards of Alaskan mosquitoes. That had always been a losing proposition if one stayed to fight. He pushed the nose over and dove for all he could squeeze out of the Nieuport, heedless of the upper wing fabric that began to tear in the fury of the dive.

His pursuers followed him down firing continuously. The only thing going down faster than him was a wingless Fokker. Then he saw a pair of Nieuports scrambling for altitude. The Albatros gaggle stuck with Marr until first one and then another Nieuport screamed through their flight spouting fire. This caused the Boches to scatter, saving Marr from further chase. Ken, now alarmed by the flapping cloth of his upper wing, had no choice but to head home.

Genet continued his climb, shooting his way through the Albatroses. Another Fokker fluttered down obviously out of control. It was de Laage's first double victory.

Jack saw Genet and Hinkle rejoining the flight, but could see no sign of Marr. The Germans had disappeared as well. He debated trying to look for Marr, but decided they had to stay on station.

Back at Ham Marr babied his wounded machine to the ground. He was getting out and thinking about kissing the ground when another Nieuport came down almost on top of him, clipped the upper wing of his own plane and crash-landed. Pop Hinkle still hadn't mastered depth vision. He might have avoided Ken's Nieuport had Marr not landed short in his effort to get down safely.

The strip was wide enough to land three abreast. Now Genet came down on top of Hinkle's broken Nieuport due to a freak gust of wind. Thankfully, Pop was already out of the machine. Edmond's Nieuport, Chouteau Johnson's old one, skidded to the right, bounced thirty feet in the air and tipped to the left. Genet struggled to right the machine but was too low and too slow to have any impact on its gyrations. The wings smacked the grass as his left wheel gave way. Following Newton's precepts, the Nieuport sprang once more into the air twisting to the right. This time Genet's forward momentum forced the right wings to dig into the turf turning him into a sort of pinwheel, tumbling tail to nose for three rotations before stopping. Incredibly Genet emerged from the wreckage intact except for reopening his facial wound. Three destroyed Nieuports for the day and it wasn't even noon.

Buck and de Laage landed without incident, avoiding the three smashed up birds and the debris scattered during their collisions. Willis showed up embarrassed to confess that he'd shot off his own propeller. This prompted de Laage, the double victor, to quip "We are our own worse enemy. Three downed Germans to our four wrecked machines."

"Yes, but our four pilots will fight again. There will be at least three less Fritzes to eat soup tonight, lieutenant." Jack observed.

Charlie's flight that afternoon consisted of the remaining flyable Nieuport and four Spads. Thénault was the only pilot not to fly that day. He remained at the field anxiously awaiting Keeler's return. If he lost any more aircraft Féquant might change his mind about keeping the Lafayette Escadrille on French rolls.

THE NEXT DAY THÉNAULT, Lovell and Keeler boarded a train for Paris to pick up replacement machines—Spads they'd been promised even before the bloody Easter Nieuport massacre. Keeler joked on the way down about the irony of slicing things up on Easter at Ham rather than slicing ham for Easter. Everyone laughed but Thénault who simply didn't get it.

Chapter 61
Spring Interlude

Paris, April 9, 1917

Charlie's first thoughts upon seeing Michelle and Michael waiting for him at the Gare du Nord were of the children in Ham. He had tears in his eyes as he hugged the two of them. He hadn't seen little Michael walking by himself, but Michelle had made a point of standing the boy on the platform waving to Charlie as he approached.

Soubiran had driven in the escadrille sedan more than three hours from Ham with Genet and Parsons. Willis followed later with a tractor and three mechanics. They were to meet at Le Bourget to pick up the Spads. Charlie had permission to spend the night in the city in order to see his wife and child. As it turned out, the weather wouldn't permit flying on Monday anyway, so Thénault brought the whole group into the city for the night.

Genet naturally sought out the Parkers. He found out the major was out of town, but accepted Mrs. Parker's invitation to dine at the *Roosevelt.* Thénault, with uncharacteristic generosity produced tickets for all of them for the evening performance at the *Folies Bergères.* Charlie caught up with them there. As they awaited the beginning of the show, everyone commented on the way the whole city seemed to be decked out in American flags.

Michelle was in a very gay mood that night. Jennifer had dinner with them and then stayed to watch Michael. "You two need to do this. Jack and

I have had a few more chances to get together. Let me stay here with the baby. I'm pretty doggoned pooped anyway," Jennifer had insisted.

Charlie hadn't been to the *Folies* but once and that was with Michelle's father before the marriage. It wouldn't have made any difference anyway. He was just as surprised as the other Americans in the audience when the music started with a jazz rendition of the American national anthem. Charlie was the first to stand up saluting. Soon men and women at other tables stood. It amazed him how many Americans were there. The revue continued with the usual risqué jokes, acrobatic acts and incredibly beautiful women. Everything, down to the skimpy frilly underwear covering the girl's bottoms, was done in stars and stripes. They even had a comic man on stilts dressed as Uncle Sam. It was great fun and a wonderfully stimulating boost to his morale.

Tuesday the men reported as scheduled to Le Bourget at ten in the morning to pick up the Spads. For some reason the machines weren't ready. No one except the outraged Thénault objected to having to spend another night in Paris. Charlie raced back to the city to try to find Pierre Flandin.

The Ministry of Defense claimed that Flandin was at a meeting at Versailles. Charlie wasted an hour driving out there in one of Fleury's motors only to find out the meeting was at Les Invalides less than a stone's throw from Flandin's office where he had started his search. By the time he got there, the meeting was over. Flandin and the others had gone to lunch. Frustrated, Charlie walked the two blocks to the Ecole Militaire on the chance they were eating there. He joined the line of students, junior instructors and others in the cafeteria. Before he could pick up a tray he felt a tap on his shoulder.

"Would you care to join Monsieur Flandin and me for lunch Lieutenant?"

Charlie nearly dropped the tray in total shock. "Claude! I mean Capitaine, oh shit what are you called in the Navy? God, it's great to see you!

But what are you doing here?" Charlie blurted out in rapid French without thinking that the last time he'd seen his cousin was on the *Rochambeau* before he could properly speak anything but the most basic of phrases in French.

"Later, Charlie, later. My word, you have changed! And such language in the officer's mess," he clicked his tongue twice. "And where did you get that uniform, not to mention that accent? Come, come into the other room with me."

They crossed the hall to the room marked *Officiers Superieurs*, the dining room for colonels and generals. A waiter took them to the corner table reserved for the most senior authorities. It was separated from the others by an elaborately decorated screen with oriental designs in gold on a black lacquered background.

Seated at the table with his back to them was Pierre Flandin who rose when they entered. On his right was a woman who, even from behind, looked familiar to Charlie.

"Charlie, may I present my wife, Marie. I know you met some time ago."

"*Enchanté, madame*," Charlie said, taking Marie's hand and passing his face close without actually kissing the hand in the manner he'd seen the French men behave.

"Oh my, what a surprise! Just as handsome as ever! Speaking perfect French and, most remarkably, the subject of our current conversation," Marie said, fixing him with a critical look and a pleasant smile.

"Charlie, I had no idea you were in town," Flandin said, beckoning him to sit on his left. "How fortuitous that Claude should have seen you coming in. Whatever are you doing here anyway? Forget that! Don't answer. *Garçon! Champagne, si'l vous plaît.* We must celebrate."

Charlie's confusion was only topped by his delight at finding Flandin, let alone Claude and Marie. They had arrived only minutes before him. After toasting each other with the champagne they settled down for the meal—exquisite *côtelettes d'agneau*, lamb chops served with a tarragon flavored sauce Charlie recognized as the classic *béarnaise* he'd been introduced to at the Captain's table at sea on the *Rochambeau.*

After the main course the waiter offered a selection of cheeses. Charlie had learned to simply point to one of them rather than try to recognize one of France's three hundred and sixty-five varieties. He gestured at the blue veined one.

"*Papillon*, Charlie? Haven't you become the gourmet after all that fuss on the *Rochambeau.* It is the best Roquefort in the world you know," Claude said, asking for a small piece of a sharp smelling green-veined cheese.

They all stood when Flandin left. Claude got Charlie to sit down for coffee in order to fill him in on the intervening months and his time with Jack Buck in Fréjus. Charlie couldn't believe all that had been happening to Claude and Marie. "Eventually, I hoped to bring Marie to Paris so we could get together. No time like the present! Do you feel like telling this story over again? Is Jack in Paris, too? No? Too bad. Is your evening free? What do you say we meet for dinner at about eight at *La Tour d'Argent*?"

"I must talk to Michelle. Can we, I mean, can you meet us at the Crillon earlier? I can't be sure of Jennifer and we have the baby..."

"Claude and I would love to see the child. We'll come to your hotel at seven. If you need to leave a message or talk to us please call my mother," Marie said, handing him an engraved card with her mother's name, address and telephone number.

Charlie walked slowly by the riding area on the south quadrangle of the Ecole and passed through the gates where he'd heard Alfred Dreyfus had been defrocked and degraded. He decided to stop in the chapel just to reflect for a few minutes before going back to the Crillon. During his first visit with Michelle she'd explained some of the paintings hanging on the stone walls. Charlie stopped under the enormous painting of Saint Louis.

Life started for me in Saint Louis. It started for Michael at l'hopîtal Saint Louis. Now I am here, Lord under this portrait in this holy place. I don't have any idea why You have blessed me this way or why I am here for that matter. The centurion said, 'I am not worthy that You should come under my roof. Speak but the word and my daughter will be healed.' I am terribly confused, Lord. I only know how to fly and fight and kill the foe. I want this cup, this war, to pass. I just want this to pass. I want to live. I want to love You, my wife, my child, my sister and parents. I want this war to pass. But, as Jesus said, 'Your will and not mine be done.' Help me Lord. Forgive me for killing. Forgive me especially for enjoying what I do and celebrating my victories. I must do what I must in the air, but it is wrong to dance on my enemy's graves. . . .

"Excuse me, lieutenant. Is there anything I can do for you?" a voice said from behind him, the person having entered and approached without a sound.

Charlie almost jumped. He quickly turned around to see a very tall man in a very long black cassock. "No. I was just admiring this painting," he replied automatically.

"He was a good man and a good soldier. It is said that he cried for every man he killed."

Charlie's eyes widened. *This* was too much. He felt spooked. Excusing himself, he rushed from the chapel onto the street facing the Champs de Mars. He broke into a run reaching the base of the Eiffel Tower in no time. Turning to the right he continued to run until he came to the Pont de l'Alma. He ran across the bridge and turned up the river's right bank, breathing deeply and finally getting over the feeling of being spooked. He didn't slow down until reaching the Place de la Concorde. He was breathing heavier than he should be for such a short run. Not enough exercise and too many cigarettes, he thought. *But, by God, I'm alive! Thank God I'm alive!*

Chapter 62
Heeby Jeebies

Ham, April 11, 1917

Going back to Ham in a new Spad was harder for Charlie than he expected.

The thought had crossed his mind while he'd prayed in the chapel that he could leave French service without shame, return to the United States, and get a comfortable job teaching others to fly. He knew the idea would appeal to Michelle. She had lost a brother to this infernal war. In the end, though, he suspected she would have some of the same reservations that he did. He thought of Kiffin, Chapman and McConnell. He didn't want to end up dead, but he would rather die in glory than sneak away with his tail tucked between his legs. Besides, he actually looked forward to donning an American uniform.

Charlie was suddenly filled with an irrational sense of dread. He had never felt anything quite so viscerally. He tried to ignore the feeling of foreboding, but it kept creeping back into his conscious thoughts. He didn't say anything to Michelle, but he'd treated her and Michael like he didn't think he'd be seeing them again. When he climbed away from Le Bourget in the new Spad, he couldn't resist a look back at Paris and the Eiffel Tower. Almost involuntarily the words *I shall not see you soon if ever at all* played in his head.

After settling down in the room he shared with Jack, he unpacked his things and said: "Jack, how little the things of this world really matter. I mean, look at this watch. It's worth maybe fifty dollars, but this locket with Michelle's picture and a lock of Michael's hair is worth infinitely more to me."

"What's with all this drivel? You are always the first to stop me from waxing philosophical. Did three days in Paris unnerve you?"

"Listen, Jack. I know it goes without saying that we will look after each other's families if one of us buys the farm...No, let me finish. I don't know why—and I know it's hoodoo to talk about these things—but I've got a feeling that something terrible is going to happen."

"Jesus, Charlie! Don't even say it."

"I don't know where the feeling comes from. Maybe that priest coming up behind me in the chapel put the fear of God in me. Well, you know what I mean, don't you? I mean, if something happens to me or someone else we have to keep going, right?"

"Charlie, nothing's going to happen to you unless you let it happen. You have nine victories and you don't take crazy chances. I'd be more worried about some of our zealots like little Genet."

"That's the key, isn't it? Worry about others and don't dwell on yourself. It's worked for me before. I just wish I could shake this crazy premonition."

"Don't let it keep you up all night. We've got a big day ahead of us tomorrow. Get some sleep, Charlie. Good night."

"Good night, Jack."

ON THURSDAY, APRIL 12, THE REST OF THE SPADS WERE SUPPOSED to come up from Le Bourget. Something fishy was going on with aircraft distribution. Thénault was happy to get Keeler and Soubiran off with Spads the day before. Now they were telling him he was to pick up new Nieuports and fly them up for the 84th Escadrille. His pilots would raise hell, but he had no choice.

Up at Ham the weather closed in before the morning flight and didn't lift for the rest of the day. Charlie spent several hours affixing his insignia on the new Spad. He would just as soon have kept his old machine, but Thénault insisted on putting the officers in the newest and lowest time buses. "Rank has its privileges, you know," he would tell them when they protested.

Before Charlie had left Le Bourget Thénault told him he was going to ask to make all of the American pilots officers. It would mean promotions for Buck and Keeler to full lieutenant. He thought he might be able to get Thaw a captaincy but only if de Laage got promoted at the same time. Charlie remembered what Thaw had told them about being token officers. What would it be like to have a whole escadrille full of them?

On Friday, Lufbery got the morning mission. Jack tagged along as a back up. They flew up to the lines at Saint Quentin as a flight of five. Lufbery dove away almost as soon as they crossed the river and all the rest followed. He routinely saw things long before the others. Sure enough, he'd flushed a pair of new Rumplers. Jack remained at altitude letting the others have a go at the observation buses.

In full view of soldiers on both sides of the lines Lufbery peppered the first Rumpler until it burst into flames. Jack knew Luf hated for that to happen. He didn't mind sending Germans to their final reward, he would say, but he hated to see any man burn. Lufbery followed the flaming enemy down firing short bursts into the cockpit area in the hopes that the pilot and observer were already dead. It was his eighth kill. He was one behind Keeler now.

Charlie flew the afternoon mission with Thaw, Rockwell, and Hinkle. They went to the same spot where Luf had flamed the Rumpler expecting the Boches to put more up in its place. No such luck. Keeler took them up to twelve thousand feet, which took almost eight minutes even from their starting altitude of five thousand. Up in those freezing rarified regions, Keeler always felt exhilarated. One had to breathe deeper after staying up there for any length of time, but the air was crisp and somehow cleaner. He kept an eye peeled for enemy machines, but began to relax and actually laughed out loud at himself for his silly bout of depression and premonition. When they returned empty-handed Charlie rushed to the bar for a celebration potion. He felt renewed, invigorated, and full of optimism.

Saturday Thénault returned early in the morning with only two new planes and a couple of the Nieuport 23's some of the escadrilles were getting instead of Spads. "It's a bloody balls up down there," he bitched in the British style he'd learned in school. "The fools are holding Spads for the Americans! Can you believe that? Here I've got the only damned American escadrille and I can't get Spads because they are holding them for Americans!"

Jack and Charlie hadn't seen Thénault so angry or openly demonstrative. He told them that the French authorities had laughed at his request to get commissions for the Americans. He'd never been so mad. "Just keep this between us. I don't want the rest of the men to get wind of how stupid our bureaucracy is, if you know what I mean," he stopped and broke into a grin, "as if they don't already know."

Charlie tugged at Jack's arm. They walked away leaving the captain at his desk fuming. Charlie told Jack they could now consider themselves genuine officers. "When your superiors are confident enough in you to bellyache in your presence, you're accepted."

"Another Keelerism? I have to admit I didn't expect to see old Georges blow up like that. It almost makes him seem human, doesn't it? What do you supposed the movie crew he dragged up here will shoot?"

"Beats me, but unless you feel like some extra publicity, you might want to skedaddle with me."

"Come on Charlie. It's probably for a good cause. Let's go act like the officers you just said we are."

Someone turned up with a large American flag on a staff that hadn't been seen before in the escadrille. The movie people wanted shots of the men with the flag, with the lions, and with the Indianhead showing on the fuselages of the planes lined up ready to take off. It wasn't the first time they'd been filmed. They seemed to attract the motion picture and journalist types ever since arriving at Luxeuil nearly a year earlier. What was different was that this crew was American.

It brought out the ham in many of them. 'Hamming at Ham,' they called it, dancing little jigs, poking each other, pulling off hats, throwing hats in the air, holding dogs, lions—anything to demonstrate the gay light-hearted atmosphere of combat aviators in the field.

The big show was set for that afternoon when the light would be best. Five Spads were lined up for a takeoff to the east, and five others to depart to the west. The head camera operator wanted shots of the planes taking off and landing with the sun both behind and in front of them. He explained that he could later edit it to appear as if they took off early in the morning and didn't come back until late at night. Fortunately the winds were light enough to permit departures in both directions.

The show came off almost without a hitch until the sun had dipped behind the trees. Harold Willis came in too high and fast. When he corrected by driving the wheels into the ground, they caught. Once again an escadrille machine catapulted end over end, spewing parts and pieces as it went. Willis emerged severely shaken and bruised but alive and embarrassed. The movie crew got it all on film.

Sunday became a day of enforced rest due to clouds, high winds and heavy rain. The rain abated in the afternoon, but the winds remained too high for flight operations. Charlie went to Mass with Jack and Genet at noon. The priest offered prayers for the people of Ham who had suffered or died during the German occupation. Charlie prayed in much the same way he had at the chapel at the Ecole Militaire, except now he didn't ask for the cup to be removed so much as for the strength to be able to drink from it should the time come.

After leaving the church Genet asked them if they wanted to take a walk around the nearby cemetery. "I'll bet there are stones going back to before our country even existed," he suggested.

"No thanks, Smiler. I've had my fill of graveyards and graves," Charlie said. "You two go if you like. I'll walk back. It's not raining and I need the exercise."

Jack stayed with Genet. They found some very elaborate tombs along with a number of simple markers. The oldest they could find was only a hundred years old. Sure the church had been there longer than that; they wondered if an older cemetery existed somewhere else nearby.

"What's with the interest in history all of a sudden, Edmond?"

"Oh it's not all of a sudden, Jack. You know I've been over here for more than two years and I never once tried to find any of my relatives. Look at Charlie and your wife finding cousins and uncles without even trying."

"Didn't Citizen Genet leave France for good and settle in America?"

"He did, but mother says there are Genets galore in France except that most of them are monarchists. They didn't appreciate the 'citizen' title one bit. Genet may be famous in our history books, but he is considered a traitor to their class over here. I was always curious why we never had any contacts in France. Now I understand."

"I had a little run in with some local royals when I was in the ambulance."

"Local? You mean people around here?"

"No, just an expression. We were working over by Pont à Mousson. I fell in with a widow. Her in-laws didn't want her to get their son's property. It was—forgive the pun—a royal mess."

"Wow! A widow? That had to be before you met Jennifer."

"It was my first time with a woman, Edmond. I don't tell everybody about it."

"Thanks, Jack. I appreciate that. I suppose I should tell you my sordid tale."

"Not at all. I only wanted you to know why I was caught up in that royalty crap. The family wanted to take me to court and force me to marry her. My commander stood up to them and so did the mayor. The woman was mortified by the experience and would have married me willingly even though it would mean the loss of her husband's considerable estate. I couldn't let that happen. When flight training became an option, I volunteered as much to get away from her as to fly. She eventually married my old commanding officer, the one who stuck up for me. Beat that! And she got the estate, too."

"All's well that ends well, right? I almost lost my virginity in Vera Cruz. Well, to be truthful, I was *planning* on it once I got ashore, but I never went. Gertrude and I never got beyond some serious kissing. A twenty-year old former sailor and soldier, now a pilot who has never had a woman, biblically speaking, I mean."

"You know, Edmond, it sounds like a happy ending story just like mine. Girl gets guy, saves reputation and retains estate, defeating the evil in-laws. In your case, you stay pure as the driven snow as long as you can." Jack said wistfully as they linked arms and headed for the waiting car.

That night a new man reported in. Andrew Courtney Campbell became the first volunteer to join them after the United States' declaration of war. Knowing he'd been in the schools for months before arriving, no one asked Campbell why he didn't go home and join the American Army. They learned that he hailed from Illinois and was another of the silver spoon crowd. Little did they know how much this Scotsman would affect the morale of the escadrille with his antics. He asked to be called Courtney. Only Adonis-like Haviland could challenge him for sheer good looks, but no two men were ever more unalike.

"Charlie, I got a feeling about the new guy. I don't like to talk about people, but he gives me the creeps. I think you guys need to keep an eye on him," Genet whispered to Keeler after supper.

"Right, Smiler! That one bears watching," Charlie said. "I'm not sure if I'll be the one to do the watching," he mumbled under his breathe.

Genet took him to mean it should be one of the French officers, so he merely nodded. He couldn't imagine the great Keeler getting the heeby jeebies. Charlie hadn't meant anything by the comment either, though he still suffered from waves of overwhelming dread, of anticipation of something absolutely awful. In fighting these feelings, he prayed with all his heart that he wasn't foreseeing something happening to Michelle or their child. He remembered his frustration when they'd been attacked in the Métro. Was she again in some kind of danger?

Campbell aside, Genet retired to his room to make his diary entry and bring his flight log up to date. His promotion to *sergent* had been approved. He couldn't wait to write his mother and brothers. Lord knows that if he'd stayed in the Navy he wouldn't even be a petty officer yet. He was as proud of the rank as he was of his Croix de Guerre.

Before he could get to sleep his stomach started rumbling. He had to get up and rush to the toilet. Something hadn't agreed with him. His cheek hurt mightily as well. He finally got to sleep trying to get the picture of Gertrude out of his head by imagining young Helen Harper in her place.

Helen was certainly prettier, he concluded, but she was still a kid. What he'd had for Gertrude would take a long time to replace.

Monday came with all the glory of a beautiful spring day. It was pleasantly warm in the morning when they launched the first flight. Despite a lingering upset stomach, Genet went out with Lovell and Hewitt at 7 A.M. He was determined to keep up the effort to get a Boche for Mac. Shortly after their departure Jack led Lufbery, Dugan, Marr and Parsons up to the lines where they split up to look for prey on their own. They had had such poor luck after de Laage's double a week earlier, that they wondered if the Germans were holing up deep behind the lines to avoid further losses.

Genet started feeling even worse once his flight reached Saint Quentin. He was the designated leader, but he knew it didn't mean much in their outfit. Lovell would carry on if he had to leave. German shelling shook them up and caused Edmond to execute some violent maneuvers that aggravated his nausea. By eight, he couldn't stand the waves of nausea and worried that he might pass out. He hastened back to Ham and climbed unsteadily into his bed for a couple more hours of sleep.

Buck's flight came in at eleven. Jack was worried about Genet. He'd looked terribly pale that morning. He found Lovell and asked after Edmond.

"Sicker than a dog, Jack. He shouldn't have even gotten out of bed this morning let alone into a machine. I think he's sleeping now. Did you guys have any luck? We didn't see a damned thing."

"Lufbery says he saw some action way to our north in the British sector. Unbelievable, that guy's eyes, and I thought I could see perfectly. We didn't get any action either."

Charlie took another flight out just after 11 A.M. They were trying to keep somebody in the air continuously. The beautiful clear morning gave way to overcast skies shortly after noon. As the ceiling lowered, Keeler had to bring his flight down closer and closer to the intensifying German anti-aircraft fire. When he landed at a few minutes after two that afternoon he told Thénault that he thought the Germans were keeping the skies clear to give their gunners free rein. Georges nodded, but couldn't think of anything to do about it.

Jack learned that Lovell had gone out at noon without Genet. He was glad to hear that. They needed to keep Smiler on the ground. Comfortable in that belief, Jack had taken off to try to marry up with Lovell. They were just landing when the 2:30 P.M. patrol took off. Jack thought he saw Genet's markings on the Nieuport following Lufbery's Spad, but hoped it was Haviland or someone else. When he saw Havvy standing watching on the ground, Jack got a sinking feeling.

A little later he asked Haviland why he'd let Genet go if he was so sick.

"I didn't let him go, Jack," Willis said evenly. "He wouldn't let me take his plane and insisted on going himself. Luf just shrugged his shoulders and got in his own machine. You know Edmond, Jack. He seemed somewhat better than he had at noon."

"You mean he tried to go on that mission too?"

"Yes sir. Jeesh, Jack. I tried to stop him!"

Buck looked at his friend's face and felt immediately ashamed about browbeating him. "Willis, forget it. I'm just edgy," he said contritely. "Come drink some coffee with me. I have a feeling this is going to be a long afternoon."

They found Keeler sitting at the bar with de Laage having coffee. Jack held up two fingers for the young soldier serving in the popote that afternoon. "Edmond went out with Lufbery on the 2:30 mission," he said with a note of resignation in his voice.

"I tried to get him to let me take his plane since mine was down for maintenance, but Genet insisted he was fine," Haviland added.

"The kid's either crazy or he's got a death wish," de Laage said. "How do you Americans produce such zealots? Genet is just like Chapman and Rockwell, I'm sorry to say. No, I'm proud to say. *Merde*! My English fails me…."

"I told you I had a bad feeling about something, Jack. Then you guys go poking around the tombstones yesterday. Talk about asking for it!"

"Get off it, Charlie! What's with this superstitious horseshit lately? One of us should have ordered Genet grounded. De Laage, I don't think the captain will do it. It will have to be you. Charlie and I are too close to him and I don't think he'll take our orders seriously."

"I should have done it this morning. I'll get Georges to put it in writing. Threaten Genet with a court martial if he tries to fly."

"Good idea," Charlie agreed. "At least he's out with Lufbery. Luf won't let him get into anything he can't handle."

They looked back and forth at each other wanting to believe this last observation. Finishing two more of the strong coffees made all four of them head for the latrine at once. Because the pilots had so much clothing on that disrobing to urinate was impracticable, the French had erected a number of troughs with a canvas windbreak around them. While they finished relieving their bladders a single Spad landed bearing the fancy

RL of Raoul Lufbery. Searching vainly for Genet's Nieuport, the four of them rushed out to ask Lufbery about Genet.

"But he ees not here?" Lufbery said truly shocked. "I watch heem turn around and go home. The Archie came awful close, maybe a hundred meters. But Genet, he was all right."

"Oh my God! So much for my silly superstitions, Jack. I told you I thought something terrible was going to happen."

"Let's not jump to conclusions, gentlemen," de Laage said with more calm than he felt. "If, as Luf says, little Genet was headed back, maybe he landed at another field."

"Telephone message from Mountescourt, messieurs," one of the runners assigned to the escadrille said, handing the paper to de Laage.

"Mountescourt?" Jack asked. "Isn't that where Mac crashed?"

"It is not good news my friends," de Laage said mournfully.

"No! Goddamn it!" Charlie said grabbing the sheet. He read it quickly and ran off dropping it on his way. He signaled his mechanic and was about to jump into his Spad when Jack caught up with him.

"What are you going to do, Keeler? You don't have enough fuel and you know it." Charlie turned to his friend.

"You've been bugging me a lot, Jack. Leave me alone. I'm going out to the lines to shoot some Boches for little Genet even if I have to land in No Man's Land to find any of them."

"Charlie, this is crazy!" Jack said, putting his hand on Charlie's shoulder.

"Don't get in my way!" They were hidden from view from the mechanic who diplomatically tried to ignore the angry officers. Jack was trying to talk some sense into him when Keeler swung around and leveled Buck with a massive right hook. Jack went down in a heap. Keeler hopped into the cockpit, called out the starting commands and was taxiing to take off before the mechanic saw the other officer getting up slowly rubbing his chin.

Must have been knocked down by the Spad, he reasoned, incapable of being surprised by anything the Americans did. He had learned to love them, especially his personal favorite, Keeler. Just then he remembered that he hadn't refueled the Spad.

"Where is he going, sir?" he asked.

"Straight to hell for all I care!" Jack spouted out in English unintelligible to the mechanic. He looked at the confused man and answered more civilly in French, "Only to the lines and back. He has what? Forty-five minutes of fuel?"

"Maybe an hour. They were out just over that on the last mission."

Jack began slamming his fist into his hand in frustration. His jaw hurt and he was mad as hell at Charlie for hitting him, but he was even more upset imagining Keeler getting killed or captured. He ran down the line looking for a plane ready to fly. His own was empty. He'd institute a policy that every machine would be refueled immediately in the future. Cursing and still slamming his fist into his right hand until it hurt at least as much as his chin, Jack ran to the operations shack, suddenly feeling terribly lonely and terribly inadequate.

Genet had become a surrogate brother to Jack. They'd shared diary entries, personal problems, and some intimate secrets. Jack had tried everything he could to keep an eye on Edmond, especially after Mac was killed, and even more so since Genet learned of Gertrude's abandoning him.

Everything wasn't enough. Jack shivered. His total lack of control became abundantly clear to him. Why had he been so arrogant as to think he could control things?

He sank into the chair in the empty office and began to sob. All the dead seemed to march before him sneering at him for thinking he was better than them at controlling anything. He didn't know how close to exhaustion he was personally. Hallucinations paraded in rapid sequence while his shoulders shook. Gone were the pleasant lakeside scenes. No more the lusty abandon of the marriage bed. Everything tumbled. All his firmaments fractured. He was fragmenting himself!

At some point Jack fell out of the chair and lie curled up on the floor shaking violently. Emil Marshal found him there and helped him get up. Emil became alarmed at the lack of recognition in Jack's tear-reddened eyes and the way he couldn't hold his head up. He rang for help.

Chapter 63
Gone East?

Ham, April 16, 1917

Thénault arrived at operations in minutes. He'd been at Group with Féquant when he heard about Genet. Stricken with guilt for not grounding the ill American, he was even more unprepared to see Buck in a semi-catatonic state. This was the man he'd given a brevet for sheer *sang-froid* after bringing the crippled Farman down at Pau. Buck was the most stable and reliable man in the escadrille. Every other one, including himself if he was honest, had a discernable quirk or flaw that kept them from true greatness.

Buck wasn't perfect or he would have been intolerable. He was, however, more capable of perfection than just about any other man Thénault had met. SPA 124 had some stellar performers to be sure.

Lufbery had to be the most efficient killing machine. If the man had any aspirations to join the ace race, he would give the best a run for their money. Only he didn't care. He probably had double his official count. He never fought for credit for his many behind-the-lines victories. Lufbery was as good as they came if you only considered one or two dimensions. Thénault couldn't for the life of him imagine Lufbery in a civilian job.

His Saint Cyr classmate, de Laage, was another case. Potentially de Laage could run circles around Thénault in sheer leadership and charisma. If a commander could get by on those characteristics alone, de Laage could become a general officer. But, Alfred couldn't handle administration, maintenance or most other inanimate activities. Give him a horse, a group of men, or a purring airplane and the man could accomplish miracles.

Bill Thaw could do it all. He too possessed the charisma as well as an impressive array of practical skills acquired in business. At first Thénault thought Thaw walked on water. Then he began to see how Bill eschewed the role of officer in favor of being accepted by the men. Thaw's open friendship with Bert Hall gave Thénault his first indication that Bill wasn't discerning enough or tough enough to demand the best from his men.

Keeler ranked higher than the other three in all dimensions but one. Charlie was the strongest and bravest man in the escadrille. Even if Keeler believed that—which he didn't—he was too modest to lord it over anyone. He was as skilled and efficient in the air as Lufbery though he took fewer chances—probably because of his wife and kid. Keeler was as natural a leader as de Laage was, though Thénault had a tough time accurately assessing this from his own French military perspective. With an escadrille of Charlie Keelers nothing could stop them. Nothing anyway, until something triggered Keeler's temper. Georges marveled at how well Charlie kept himself in check for the most part. Yet, he could sense the tension of the tightly coiled spring inside Keeler. Someday it would come loose and heaven help anyone in his way.

Thénault thought Buck's only human fault was an excess of compassion and love. Jack was tough and not overly sentimental, but there was much of the poet in him.

Georges had formulated his assessments over many months. They flashed through his mind as he tried to cope with Buck's evident nervous collapse. A hesitant knock at the door interrupted his thoughts. Marshal had gone for the doctor. Thénault said *entrez*, hoping it was him.

"Forgive me, captain, but I thought the lieutenant wasn't looking so well," Keeler's mechanic, Fortant, said.

"Yes, he appears to be sick. What did you notice?" Fortant described the angry words between Buck and Keeler that he didn't understand because they were in rapid English. He told how the officers seemed to be arguing about Keeler going out again with a less than full tank.

"*Attendez*! Keeler took off again?"

"*Oui, mon capitaine*," Fortant said in a worried voice, thinking he should have topped off the tank like Keeler always insisted.

Thénault got up and paced rapidly back and forth. This day was his worse nightmare. Genet was dead, probably because of his failure to keep the sick man on the ground. Buck was suffering some kind of attack brought on first by Genet's loss and probably aggravated by Keeler leaving half-cocked. Now he finds out that Keeler was out somewhere with a partial fuel load and vengeance in his heart. All they needed now was to lose Charlie.

He grabbed the phone and shouted to his operator to start ringing every field within an hour's flight to try to find Keeler. Then he dismissed Fortant after asking if he knew anything about the bruise on Buck's face. Fortant didn't want to admit that he'd allowed his machine to move on the ground without clearing it. He also didn't want to suggest that Keeler had hit Buck, but it sure did look that way. He honestly said that he hadn't seen what had happened other than noticing Lieutenant Buck getting up slowly, rubbing his chin. Glad to escape, Fortant went back out to keep vigil for his pilot.

When night fell without word on Keeler no one wanted to admit that their Hercules could have brought the temple down on himself like the biblical Sampson. Buck lay heavily sedated in his own room. The doctor thought it was a temporary disorder brought on by fatigue or the knock Buck had obviously received on the chin. Jack didn't have a temperature. He had only been unresponsive for a couple of hours before the doctor medicated him. It was a glimmer of hope at the end of a day of three crippling blows.

The men returned from Genet's crash site stunned at the incredible force with which he'd hit the ground. Lovell said it was almost as if Genet had buried himself. De Laage pointed out that he'd gone down not three hundred meters from where McConnell had died. Everyone was keyed up enough to see the supernatural at work here. Genet's obvious closeness to Jim McConnell in life was now sealed in their proximate points of death. Parsons' description of Genet's featureless body as a bag of bloody bones left a graphic image in everyone's minds they wouldn't soon forget.

Thénault put off notifying Mrs. Keeler that Charlie was missing until the next day. He could see no value in alarming her or Mrs. Buck until they had more information. Parsons had already contacted Paul Rockwell and Dr. Gros about Genet. His passing would be in the morning papers. Rockwell, according to Parsons, observed that Edmond Genet was the first American killed since the United States entered the war. A lot of good that will do him, Ted had said, though it would make a good headline.

In the morning Thénault and de Laage asked to be notified as soon as Lieutenant Buck woke. The doctor placed an attendant in the room for the whole night as a precaution. At six the attendant knocked on the captain's door. Standing beside him was Jack Buck, a confused look on his face.

"You wanted to see me, sir? What the hell is going on? Charlie's not in the room and this fellow says he's been watching me all night long. They found Genet? I can't remember anything after hearing he had crashed. Tell me what's happening!"

"Easy, Jack. Let me get dressed. Come sit here on the chair. *Monsieur, merci.* Please go get some coffee for all three of us."

"That guy says I was delirious and unresponsive. Where's Charlie?"

"Missing, Jack. No reports as of last night. Maybe he'll turn up somewhere safe this morning. You were right to try to stop him."

"Do what? I tried to stop him? Good Lord, I can't remember!"

"Relax. You've had a shock to your system on top of exhaustion. I should be shot for letting things get so bad. I'm just happy to see you back to yourself this morning."

"Myself, captain? I lost what, fifteen hours of my memory? I don't even know what happened."

"Near as I can make out you were all together at the field when the message arrived about Genet. Lieutenant de Laage took a number of men with him in the car to try to find the body. Genet came down very close to Mac, you know.

"Charlie read the message about Genet and rushed to his plane. You two had words and maybe a scuffle. He departed. We found you semi-conscious in the operations building. *C'est tout.*"

"A scuffle?" Jack asked putting his hand to his chin tenderly. "Could that explain this?"

"I'm not sure. No one saw."

"Either I got kicked by one helluva mule, conked by a whirling prop or punched by our resident he-man. I haven't had such a bruise since I tried to lower the ice on our skating pond with my head. Damn! I'd let him hit me again if he'd just walk through that door right now."

"I'd like that too—him walking through the door, I mean, well opening it first, of course. You have such funny expressions in English."

"Well, sir, I wanted to speak French, but the words don't seem to be there."

The doctor examined Buck later that morning and pronounced him generally fit, slightly dehydrated and suffering from bruises and contusions. "He has a concussion, a jarring of the brain that may affect his speech and memory for a few days, but I think you can keep him here on light duty," the doctor reported to Thénault.

Thénault had gotten word that a Spad had been seen crossing the lines at low altitude at around 4:32 P.M. Monday. It had strafed the German trenches, zoomed to altitude and disappeared in the clouds. There were no reports of the aircraft crossing back from the German side.

Jack asked when they were going to bury Genet. Thénault said Wednesday. Jack asked if it would be all right for him to go back to Paris to tell his wife and then to go to Michelle to break the news to her. He also wondered if he could bring either or both of them back for Genet's funeral. Thénault readily agreed to all, shamelessly thankful that Buck, not himself, would have to break the news.

Jack's head throbbed on the train ride back to Paris. He tried to remember the people he ought to notify about Genet. He knew Paul Rockwell would take care of the main ones, but there were others Paul might not know. He was thinking of young Miss Harper. This reminded him of Genet's admission of his virginity. How much of life Jack would have missed had he died before discovering the joys of women?

Why he wasn't more upset about Charlie puzzled him and made him feel a little guilty. He decided that Charlie's recent trips into the mystical regions had to have some merit to them. How much both Genet and Keeler contributed to their own fates was for God to determine. If Jack were to follow his own intuition, he'd say he *knew* Charlie was alive. He sensed it. It was almost a palpable presence. He also thought it might be wishful thinking, but dismissed that. He had to prepare himself to tell Jennifer and Michelle in as positive a manner as possible. If later events proved him wrong so be it.

CHARLIE'S MOTOR KEPT GOING AS HE ENTERED THE CLOUD. He figured he had about fifteen or twenty minutes with the reserve, but now he was engulfed and totally disoriented. He tapped the compass to make sure the needle was free. The glass broke! His knuckles were still numb from hitting Jack. He would live to regret that—if he lived that is.

The fluid ran out of the compass. Charlie glanced at the altimeter and saw he was descending. Seeing no choice but to feel his way to the ground, he continued the descent as slowly as he could. He lost track of time. He'd kept upright simply by keeping the altitude descending steadily and by centering the stick. With no idea of his heading he knew he was in big trouble.

The Hispano-Suiza sputtered. He switched to the *nourrice,* but the motor stopped!

He opened his eyes in the back of an open touring car with a puppy in his lap and some kind of bandage over his nose. He could only breath through his mouth. Looking around he confirmed his worse fears. German uniforms, German voices.

"So, lieutenant. Welcome to Jasta 6. It is good to see you are awake. My name is Hauptmann Waldrep."

Epilogue

America's eventual foray onto the European battlefields would not come until months after the declaration of war. From Genet's death until Spa. 124 could be assimilated by the fledging US Army Air Service, the American volunteers continued to fight in French uniform under French officers and French Army orders. It wouldn't be until February of 1918 that Spa. 124 would become the 103rd Pursuit Squadron of the US Army under its first American commander, Captain William Thaw.

Caught between two nations, the Lafayette Escadrille still excelled but it almost foundered in a morass of poor discipline, indecision, and sluggish bureaucracy. Raoul Lufbery scored eight more victories before February. Thénault grounded Jack Buck when he learned that Jack was planning a rescue mission for Keeler. Only Féquant's intervention prevented the authorities from stripping the American of his commission and sending him back to the Ambulance Service.

Michelle Keeler, sustained by the knowledge that her husband was at least safe, busied herself with their son and with Fleury's business. She hated the separation and feared for Charlie's well being, but she no longer dreaded hearing that he had been shot down. They were able to exchange a few letters through the Red Cross. She prayed for the war's rapid end while making fantastic plans for what they would do once they were reunited—an event whose arrival she considered an absolute article of faith.

Jennifer Buck continued nursing at the American Hospital. While she found Michelle's unshakable faith reassuring, she didn't feel the same relief. Jack's obsession and the way he blamed himself for both Genet's death and Keeler's capture drove a wedge between them. He became distant and uncommunicative. Were it not for Michelle, the Fleurys and Flandins, and Mildred Wilson, Jennifer would have considered running home to her folks. She cursed the war. It was an ugly monster that destroyed everything. Nothing could dull the pain from all the suffering she saw around her. She started attending Mass every day in order to pray for her brother, for an end to the war, and for the wonderful young man she couldn't seem to reach.

For all their accomplishments, the men of the Lafayette Escadrille would not be embraced as the ones to lead the American aviation efforts. Some would be considered unfit for flight by the medical teams fielded to screen the Americans already in service to France. Some would be shunted off to meaningless administrative duties. Others would languish under a batch of more senior officers lacking not only combat aviation experience but also common sense.

In time, the American Air Service would grow so rapidly that it would eclipse the little escadrille of volunteers that had contributed the last American to die before and the first to die after the United States declared war. But like celestial eclipses, this overshadowing would pass quickly. Legends of the Lafayette Escadrille would be kept alive by men like Jack Buck, a young hero whose own courage and persistence in the next several months would add at least one more incredible episode to their valiant legacy.

Journal entry of then-Sous Lieutenant John T. Buck, American volunteer pilot, French Army Air Service, SPAD 124, *l'Escadrille Lafayette*:

Ham, Aisne Sector, Central Northern France, Wednesday, April 18, 1917.

Sharp reports pierced the chill air while swirling snowflakes swallowed the smoke billowing from the seven rifles of the French honor guard. At eleven this morning the Moroccan Division Band scraped out the unfamiliar notes of the *Star Spangled Banner* before swinging more confidently into the stirring strains of the *Marseillaise.*

The simple wooden coffin, draped with the Stars and Stripes and the French tricolor, sat on the frozen ground beside an open hole. The red, white, and blue contrasted starkly with the dark dismal day. Bunches of lilies did little to relieve the gray pallor hanging over our little group of mourners. I could no more smell the flowers or the freshly overturned dirt than the faint perfume in Jennifer's hair. Between the cold air and my nearly dislocated jaw I had an excuse for my sniffles, but the tears welling up flowed from my heart.

Edmond Charles Clinton Genet lay in the coffin. At his request his terribly mangled body was wrapped in a second American flag. American flags are in high demand now since our declaration of war twelve days ago. I had a devil of a time finding it.

Genet was our benjamin, the youngest pilot and the brightest light in the Lafayette Escadrille. We buried him this morning, but he'd already buried himself the first time two days ago. Even though he was sick that day, he went out with Lufbery. They were forced to stay low because of the clouds. Edmond turned around, apparently heading back, and Luf followed him until he lost him in the clouds. When they found the wreck Lovell said it was the most total smash up he'd ever seen. Poor Genet went in full throttle, tunneling five feet into the hardened ground only a couple hundred yards from where Jim McConnell went down a month ago.

Coincidence? I have my doubts. Some think artillery knocked him out. I think he passed out, though I can't shake the gnawing feeling that he did this to himself. He was terribly torn up about Mac. Blamed himself, though he'd done all he could. His girl had abandoned him for some preacher back home. To top it off he was worried sick about his desertion from the Navy and what was going to happen to him when we came under our own flag. *Under our own flag.* I can't believe I'm writing that.

I should have done something to keep him on the ground. Charlie wouldn't be a prisoner, and we wouldn't be so damned down in the dumps. It can't be suicide. Edmond was too devout a Christian to do that, but he did seem to have a fixation on death. I'm one to talk with all my musings on the subject. Genet acted like he saw this coming too. So did Charlie.

Keeler sure snapped when he heard about Genet. I paid for trying to stop him from taking off with this awfully sore jaw. He knew he was low on fuel too. Why did he do it? So much for being our best ace. Lufbery will pass him up for sure, and I might even catch up to his nine victories now.

At least we know he's alive. It was bad enough telling Michelle and Jennifer he was captured. Jennifer wants me to write their parents. She says she's too broken up. I ought to tell them about the triplane Charlie forced down at our field. Talk about irony. We capture a German lieutenant and then give up one of our own. Maybe we can work out another exchange. Charlie didn't want his father to find out about Johann Keller. There was too much shame and bad blood in that one. I'd better leave him out.

If I don't get to shoot him down first, I'd like to shake Hauptmann Waldrep's hand. It sure is strange trading messages with the enemy. Like

Bill Thaw says, Waldrep must be a decent sort to let us know that Charlie crashed, his motor bone dry, while trying to land at their field. They'll take care of him. We hear captured pilots are treated fairly well. I hope so.

I won't ever forget the service this morning. After Thénault finished reading the passage, he set Genet's little black prayer book down on the coffin on top of the big cross that held the flags down. A gust blew the book open. Suddenly the snow stopped. Then the leaden sky parted allowing a beam of light to play over Genet's coffin. As if being thumbed by an invisible hand, the pages fluttered. Then, as suddenly as it came, the light left and another gentle gust closed the book. Maybe it was my overworked imagination, but several mentioned the light being like a message from God. Jennifer thinks I'm turning Irish believing in banshees and leprechauns and the like.

I'll miss Charlie terribly even if the bum clouted me. If he escapes I'll be too happy to return the favor. Need to talk to Thénault about the idea of an exchange. It has merit. I'm sure the Germans would be happy to get Keller back, but it wouldn't be a fair trade, the vanquished for the victor.

As for Edmund, I hope he's happier now. How could his childhood sweetheart treat him so cruelly? I ought to send her his diary so she can see how she tormented him. Edmond's devotion was lost on Gertrude. His mother will appreciate the heroic record of his service in France though. I almost wish I could keep the two books and his flight log myself. It has been humbling to read them.

May the Lord be good to him. To think that he was only twenty. He gets the honor of being the first American killed after the United States declared war. Jim McConnell was the last American killed before the declaration. Will anyone remember that the Lafayette Escadrille donated the two valiant heroes astride this event? I doubt it, but they damn well will if I have anything to say about it.

The valiant and the vanquished. It has a ring to it.

Damn this war! Damn all wars!

An ending, but not the end...

Principal Characters

(In order of appearance by Part and Chapter)

I-1
Charles Keeler- Born, December 9, 1894, St. Louis, Missouri.
John Keeler- Charlie's father, German immigrant.
Angelique Keeler- Charlie's mother, French immigrant.
Jennifer Keeler- Charlie's younger sister, born May 1, 1896.

I-2
Jack Buck- Born, August 3, 1894, Minneapolis, Minnesota.
Sandy Noslen- Jack's high school classmate and sometimes girlfriend.
Dennis Burns- Jack's high school nemesis.
Mr. Rowan- City Editor of the Minneapolis Tribune.
Annette Brunnell- Jack's cousin from Chicago.
Willis Haviland**- Minnesota native, born, 1891, friend of Jack's.[1]

I-3
Alexandre Fleury*- French businessman and diplomat.
Michelle de Vincent- French-English nanny/au pair to Fleury children. Born in London, April 7, 1885.

---

[1] Havilland actually existed and is one of the Lafayette Escadrille members. His history and account here is accurate in part though his interactions with others are fictionalized. An asterisk indicates actual historical figure. Double asterisks represent real members of N. 124, the Lafayette Escadrille.

I-4
Amory Ferguson- American volunteer and fellow passenger on the HMS Reliant.
Cyrus Teeter- American volunteer and fellow passenger on the HMS Reliant.

I-5
Captain Richard- French captain of the Steamship Rochambeau.
Claude Toussaint- Lieutenant de Vaisseau aboard the Rochambeau.
Marie- French woman aligned with Toussaint.

I-6
Colonel Gervais de Lafourcade- French Attaché to United Kingdom.

II-7
Pierre Étienne Flandin*- French bureaucrat and member of government.
Berangère- Flandin's wife.
Isabelle- Flandin's daughter.
Joffre, Jean Jacques*- Also known as "Père," or father. Commander-in-Chief of French Army at the beginning of the war and subsequent Marshall and representative to the US.
Dr. Frederick Gros*- American medical doctor living and working in Paris at the beginning of the war.
Jacques-Antoine Flandin- Son of Pierre and Berangère.

II-8
Stephane- Chauffeur to the Fleury family, later airplane mechanic.
Béatrice Fleury- Alexandre's spouse.
Captain Frank Parker*- US Army Assistant Attaché in US Embassy, Paris at beginning of war.
Mr. Myron T. Herrick*- Outgoing American Ambassador to France at beginning of war.
William Sharp*- American Ambassador to France during war.
William "Bill" Thaw**- American volunteer in Foreign Legion, son of wealthy Pittsburgh family.
Weston "Bert" Hall**- American volunteer in Foreign Legion, vagabond of questionable character purportedly from Missouri.
Kiffin Rockwell**- Among the first American volunteers for the Foreign Legion, from Asheville, North Carolina.
Paul Rockwell*- American volunteer in Foreign Legion, Kiffin's older brother.

Charles "Chouteau" Johnson**- American volunteer for flight, descendant of founding family of Saint Louis.

II-9
William K. Vanderbilt*- Wealthy American businessman with close ties to France.
A. Piatt Andrew*- American expatriate founder of the American Ambulance Service, former assistant Secretary of State in Theodore Roosevelt's administration.
Commandant La Garde- Chief of the Foreign Legion recruiting office.
Didier de Lafourcade- French Lieutenant Colonel and brother of Gervais.

II-10
David Fleury- Youngest son of Béatrice and Alexandre Fleury.
Elliot Cowdin**- American volunteer for flight, New York family.
Honora Gros*- Spouse of Dr. Frederick Gros.
Mrs. Alice Weeks*- aka Maman Légionnaire, expatriate living in Paris and, mother of American volunteer.
Jarousse de Sillac*- French bureaucrat and businessman.
Mrs. Ovington*- American expatriate and mother of ambulance driver.

II-11
Félix Alejandro- Spanish ambulance volunteer.
David Abramowicz- New Yorker former shoe salesman and ambulance volunteer.
George Masters- Volunteer ambulance driver from New York of unknown origins.
James Rogers McConnell**- Ambulancier and later pilot, graduate of University of Virginia.

II-12
Havel Rejik- Slovakian revolutionary and Légion volunteer.

III-13
Lieutenant Dombasle- French officer of the ambulance and motor corps, commander of American Ambulance Section Sanitaire Une.
Cartier- French Maréchal de Logis or Sergeant of the ambulance corps.
Marcelle Guérin*- French woman and McConnell's friend and lover.

III-14
Pasqualli*- Cruel Legionnaire NCO.

Antonelli- Legionnaire NCO and later officer.
De Lattre de Tassigny*- Regular French Army Captain.

III-16
Gueulard*- French NCO in the Legion and former naval Ensign.
Victor Chapman**- American volunteer legionnaire and later pilot.
Joussef Hamed- Algerian legionnaire.
Johann Hedjil- Dutch legionnaire.
Andrè Martini- Corsican legionnaire.

III-17
Robert Bacon*- Former US Ambassador to France and volunteer ambulance driver.

III-19
Norman Prince**- Harvard graduate and scion of a wealthy Massachusetts family.

III-20
Didier*- Moor legionnaire squad leader.
Paul "Skipper" Pavelka**- American volunteer with the Legion and later aviation.
Russell Kelly*- American legionnaire volunteer.
Larry "Red" Scanlon*- American legionnaire volunteer.
Neanmoin*- Indian from Delhi and legionnaire.
Zannis*- Greek legionnaire.
Jury*- Belgian legionnaire.
Godin*- Belgian legionnaire.
Morlae*- American legionnaire and translator.
Réné Phélizot*- American legionnaire.

III-21
Harold Willis**- Bostonian Harvard grad and ambulance driver and later pilot.

IV-23
Raymond Poincaré*- President of France during WWI.

Clyde Balsey**- American volunteer.
Lawrence Rumsey**- American volunteer.
Dudley Hill**- American volunteer.

Louis Dumesnil*-French businessman who supported formation of an American unit.
General Hirschauer*- Director of Military Aeronautics.

IV-24
Marie-Louise de La Croix de Valois- Widow of French officer killed early in the war.

IV-26
Monsieur de la Croix de Vaubois- Father-in-law to Marie-Louis, landed gentry before the war.
Nurse Mildred Wilson- American nurse at the American Hospital in Neuilly, France.

IV-27
Frasier Curtis*- Onetime volunteer for British aviation who washed out and became a supporter of the American squadron idea.
Santos*- Bartender at Chatham's Bistro in Paris.

IV-28
Georges de Vincent- Father of Michelle, French representative of Renault company to various British and US companies.
Janet de Vincent- British born wife of Georges.
Vierau*- French NCO pilot instructor at Avord.
Rolland Garros*- Famous French tennis player and aviator who was the first to cross the Mediterranean in an aircraft. Garros' use of deflectors on the blades to permit firing through the propeller inspired the invention of the synchronized firing gear.
Jean Navarre*- Famed French aviator and ace.
Michon- French Adjudant flight instructor.
Thieu- Annamite (Vietnamese) orderly and aide to Lafayette Escadrille pilots.
Puteaux- Vintner in the Champagne region of France. Old non-combatant and owner of vineyards near French flight school.
Breguet- French officer and pilot.
Jacquot- French NCO at beginning of war, one of the most accomplished of aces.

IV-29
Arnoux de Maison Rouge**- French lieutenant and second to take the position of second in command of the American Squadron.

Mademoiselle Bougeassie*- Young French woman and sister of Antoine, a flight student.
Capitaine Georges Thénault**- French officer and only commander of the Lafayette Escadrille.
Carroll Winslow*- American volunteer that flew for units other than the Lafayette.
Colonel Lefebrve- Commanding Officer of Flight School in Pau.
Lieutenant Réné Simon*- Chief of acrobatics at Pau, married to an American.
Harold and Judith O'Hara- Boston couple in Pau on business.
Madame Poussière- American wife of French Diplomat.
James Walker- American businessman and expatriate living with wife Claudine, née Toussaint, near Pau.
Commandant LeFarge- French major, commanding the student body at Pau.
Max Immelman*- Famous German aviator.
Oswald Boelcke*- German ace and tutor of Manfred von Richofen.

V-31
Mr. Jackson- American member of the French-American Committee in New York City.
Count von Bernstorff*- German Ambassador to the United States early in WWI.
Larry Buck- Jack's younger brother.
Toby Franzak- One of Buck's fellow workers at the Minneapolis Cartage Company.
Jarvis Jenkins- Buck's high school classmate and fellow Cartage Company employee.
Jeannie Buck- Jack's sister, nine years his junior.
Frederick Prince*- Norman's older brother.

V-33
Madame Rodel*- Proprietress of L'Hôtel de la Bonne Rencontre, Le Plessis de Belleville.
Raoul Lufbery**- French born American citizen and volunteer for Aviation service.
Alexis de Raneville*- Beautiful Parisienne girlfriend of Kiffin Rockwell.
Capitaine Phillipe Féquant*- French aviation officer and eventual group commander.
V-34
Madame Cartier- Wife and widow of French Sergeant Cartier.

Lieutenant Granger- Commander of Voisin 97.

V-35
Lieutenant Gaston- Morane Saulnier pilot.
Capitaine Franck- Nieuport Section leader at Le Plessis de Belleville.

V-36
Paul Koniatev- Russian bodyguard for the Fleury Family in Paris.
Christine Wheeler*- Volunteer at American Hospital and wife of Dr. Wheeler, a Foreign Legion infantry volunteer early in the war.

V-37
Lieutenant Gonnet-Thomas*- Commander of N. 65.
James Bach*- Early Legion volunteer and enlistee in French Aviation. Captured by the Germans with a French Sergeant Mangeot after inserting saboteurs behind the lines. First American POW.
Millerand*- French Minister of War.
Colonel Henri Jacques Regnier*- Replaced General Hirschauer as head of French Aviation in early 1916.
Lieutenant Alfred de Laage de Meux**- Former cavalryman turned pilot and first officer to be second in command of Nieuport 124, the American Squadron.

V-38
Michel**- French airplane mechanic and personal mechanic to Norman Prince.

VI-39
Auguste Groscolas*- Owner and operator of the Pomme d'Or, in Luxeuil.
William Chanler*- Wealthy American who sent N. 124 a number of Browning shotguns.
Capitaine Happe*- The Red Corsair, commander of a French bombing squadron in Luxeuil.

VI-40
Jonchre*- French aviation mechanic who crewed for Captain Thènault, killed in bomb attack at Luxeuil.

VI-41
Louis Bley**- Chapman's French mechanic.

Marc Pourpe*- Prewar exhibition pilot who joined the French Army to fly but died in an accident when his motor quit. He was Raoul Lufbery's best friend.
Charles Guynemer*- Young French Ace of Aces.
Didier Masson**- French-born American citizen and volunteer pilot.
Capitaine Saint-Sauver*- French aviation commander of Nieuport 67 escadrille.

VI-42
Dr. Alfred Lascasse- Military physician and French Naval officer.
Ockie Buck- Jack's father.

VI-43
Aspirant Smith- French medical officer.
Edmond Genet**- American volunteer for aviation from Ossining, New York. A descendant of Citizen Genet, the French representative to the new United States after the revolution.

VI-44
Nguyen Gho- Laotian medical doctor living in France.
Emile Toussaint- Grandfather of Jack and Jennifer Buck.
Andrè Jean-Jacques de Beauvais- Great uncle to the Bucks.
Jean-Claude Beauvais- Deranged son of Andrè.
John Jay and Alce Chapman*- Victor's parents.

VI-45
Jean Dressy*- Enlisted French cavalryman and orderly to Lt. de Laage.
Lieutenant Charles Eugéne Jules Marie Nungesser**- French Ace and temporary member of the Lafayette Escadrille.

VII-46
Williams- American ambulance driver from Yale.
General Douglas Haig*- Commander of BEF in 1916.
Alan Seeger*- American Legionnaire and poet.

VII-47
Dr. Animant- French physician in Paris.
Michael Keeler- Infant son of Charlie and Michelle.
Robert Lockerbie Rockwell**- American medical doctor and pre-war aviator who joins French Aviation.

VII-48
Catherine Groscolas*- Eldest daughter of the Groscolas family in Luxeuil, proprietors of the Pomme d'Or.
General Davout- French commander of the zone including Luxeuil.

VII-50
Mrs. Lawrence (Sally) Slade*- Bill Thaw's sister, and Paris resident during part of the war.
Blair Thaw*- Bill and Sally's younger brother.
Frederick H. Prince, Jr.**- Norman's older brother.
Robert Soubiran**- American veteran of the Foreign Legion and volunteer pilot.
Sampson**- Former sauce cook from the Hotel Ritz in Paris; a French volunteer to cook for N. 124 at Cachy.
Suchet**- French aviation mechanic with N. 124.
General Hugh Trenchard*- Chief of the British Royal Flying Corps.
David Dick Johnson*- Charles Chouteau Johnson's father.
Anne Victoire Chouteau*- David's wife and Charles Johnson's mother.
Fabrice Johnson- Charles Johnson's uncle.
Emil Marshal**- Only non-flying American in N. 124.

VII-51
Brancard- Jack Buck's French mechanic.
Anthony de Vincent- Michelle Keeler's youngest brother.

VII-52
Alain de Vincent- Michelle's older brother and an officer in the British Army.
Ronald Hoskier**- American ambulance volunteer who later became a flyer.
Archbishop McGuire- British Roman Catholic bishop.
Madame la Comtesse de Vincent- Michelle's paternal grandmother.
James Norman Hall**- American who served first in the British artillery and then with French Aviation. (Later novelist and co-author of Mutiny on the Bounty.)

VII-53
Sergent de Castres- French Spad pilot in Spa. 3.
Capitaine Duellin*- French commander of Spa. 3.

VII-54

Edwin C. "Ted" Parsons**- Prewar aviator and veteran of the Mexican Excursion.

VIII-55
Sergent Lucien Capouillet**- Supply sergeant for N. 124.
Brigadier General Guiscard- Reserve officer commanding division near Ravenel.
Hauptmann Oskar Waldrep- German squadron commander in Jasta 6.
Lieutenant Johann Keller- Flight leader in Waldrep's squadron.

VIII-56
Steven Sohier Bigelow**- American volunteer pilot.
Walter Lovell**- American volunteer pilot.
Edward Hinkle**- Oldest American volunteer pilot in N. 124.
Thomas "Jerry" Hewitt**- Accident prone American volunteer pilot.

VIII-57
Colonel Passard*- Legion officer.
Flight Lieutenant Sheridan- British officer and guest of N. 124.
Kleinschmidt- German sergeant pilot.
Weiss- German corporal pilot.
Dr. Spitiesse- French eye doctor.

VIII-58
Kenneth "Siwash" Marr**- American aviation volunteer and member of SPA 124.
Bill Dugan**- Legion veteran and aviation volunteer, member of SPA 124.
Bishop Bhrent*- French prelate and Paris Pastor.
Helen Harper*- Young American expatriate living in Paris.
General Robert Nivelle*- Commander-in-Chief of French Army in early 1917.

VIII-59
Rivers Genet*- Edmond's brother.

VIII-60
Eva- French young woman victimized by the Germans in Ham.
VIII-62
Andrew Courtney Campbell**- First American volunteer to join the Lafayette Escadrille after the US joins the war.

VIII-63
Fortant- Charlie Keeler's French mechanic.

Acknowledgements

My parents instilled in me a love of reading that led me to sweep the shelves of my high school library where I first learned of the Lafayette Escadrille. But, my accidental discovery of the Lafayette Escadrille Memorial on an early morning run from our nearby residence in Garches, France, in 1994, convinced me of my calling to write this book. My research began in earnest in 1995 at the French Air Force Historical Section at the Chateau de Vincennes near Paris. When I asked the librarians for what they had on the Lafayette Escadrille, they said, "Please sit down Colonel. We will bring you something." They rolled in a cart stacked high with books, papers, and reports dating back to the birth of N. 124. I was able to put my hands on actual hand written morning reports.

The Langley Air Force Base Library provided invaluable assistance with inter-library loans. The staff at the Smithsonian Air and Space Museum opened their collection of original photographs from the Lafayette Escadrille. At the University of Virginia I went through the James R. McConnell collection of letters and articles, obtaining a very close appreciation for both him and his correspondents. Washington and Lee University holds the Rockwell collection. Both Paul and Kiffin Rockwell are alumni. Paul's papers cover the entire war and continue following the surviving members until his death in 1985. At the US Air Force Museum at Wright-Patterson Air Force Base in Ohio, I climbed all over a SPAD until the worried curator caught me. In New Orleans I found Madame Tugache's Restaurant, a place fitting to serve as the one I'd imagined long before going there. In Saint Louis I traced Charles Chouteau Johnson's family and gained an appreciation of Charles Keeler's fictional origins.

First of my many readers was my mother-in-law, Marie Devine Wenzel, whose sharp observations and encouragement proved very helpful. My son, Brendon, didn't hesitate to tell me what he found both good and bad. His fluency in French enhanced my sometimes flagging grammar and usage. Dr. Lee Mendez, a great personal friend and an avid student of literature, read my book in parts as I produced them. Lee taught me the meaning of not telling the reader everything and the value of rich dialogue. He also tempered my tendency to employ purple prose.

My close friends from France, Cathy and Daniel Robert, reviewed an early version of the book. Again, their French language and culture comments helped keep me straight. Daniel, a retired airline pilot who flew biplanes early in his career, made great suggestions for the flying scenes. He also observed that he thought the book might be a better movie than a novel. I hope it will be both.

Thanks as well to my first sponsor in France and dear friend, Colonel (French Army, Retired) Jean-Marc Mèrialdo. Our long friendship and long conversations have given me an insight into the French I could never achieve by myself.

A group of men I've been meeting with for years has taken close interest in my progress. At one meeting I mentioned the Lebel rifle and the marksmanship issue of a left-handed shooter. Kenn White and Jim Ritter, accomplished experts on guns, immediately recognized the Lebel and corrected my description. Such help and constructive comments from Kenn, Jim, Bob Kukich, John Falk, Lee Mendez (another member), and all the members of the group helped keep me going.

Colonel (US Army, Retired) Jim Mowery, West Point classmate and friend, made several suggestions that I've incorporated in the book. Jim's enthusiasm upon reading an earlier draft was just the shot in the arm that I needed.

Colonel (US Army, Retired) Dan Williamson, a former G3 (Operations) of V Corps, US Army, Europe, and longtime officemate, read the first edition with a sharp eye. Dan's corrections were insightful and critical to improving this second edition.

General T. Michael "Buzz" Moseley, Chief of Staff of the United States Air Force, read the first edition and liked it well enough to share with the Air Force leadership. To him I also owe the opportunity to make a spectacular flight in an F15 fighter. Thank you, sir, for your support.

All through this long process of researching and writing, my partner for life, Ginny, provided moral and material support to the family. My children Brendon, Hilary, Patrick, and Jeremy have been inspirational in their support. My deepest love to them and to all my family.

Afterward

Nieuport 124, later SPA. 124, continued to exist as a French escadrille until February 1918 when its personnel and equipment were officially assimilated by the United States Air Service and redesignated as Pursuit Squadron 103 under the command of Major William Thaw. Most of the pilots made the move, though a few remained with French escadrilles for the remainder of the war. The legendary Raoul Lufbery also became a major, but was shuffled off to an empty desk at Issoudun to supposedly write training manuals for new American fliers. That piece of foolishness didn't last long and Lufbery found himself flying with and advising the 94th Squadron where he took such future luminaries as Eddie Rickenbacker under his tutelage.

The transition of the Lafayette Escadrille into the 103rd Pursuit was not without problems. That story and the fate of Charlie Keeler, Jack Buck, and the rest of the Valiant Volunteers will unfold in the second in this series, covering the remainder of World War I.

About the Author

Terry L. Johnson is a retired Army Officer and a graduate of the United States Military Academy at West Point. He served twenty-five years as an artilleryman and aviator, with combat tours as a helicopter pilot in Vietnam and Desert Storm. His assignments include two tours in France, first flying at their Advanced Combat Helicopter Training Center, and then teaching at the French War College. During Desert Storm his brigade included a French Combat Helicopter Regiment. He also led the armed escort that flew General Schwarzkopf to the peace talks at Safwan, Iraq. He is a co-author of Certain Victory, The US Army in the Gulf War. He is an Assistant Vice President and Division Manager for Alion Science and Technology currently writing future concepts for the Army. He resides with his family in the Hampton Roads region of Virginia.

Printed in the United States
127208LV00001B/138/A

9 781420 855876